CW00546599

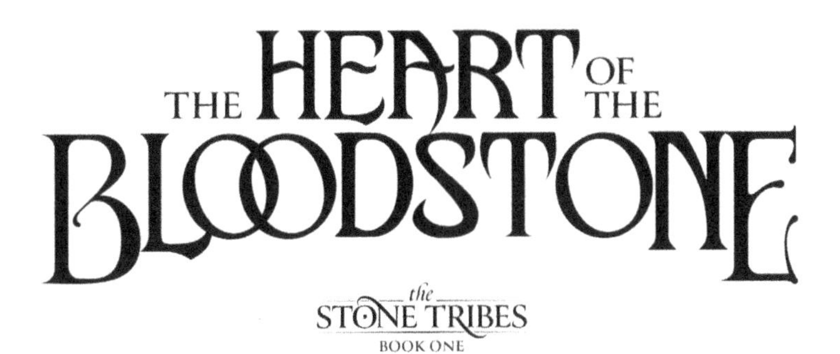

PHILINNA
WOOD

This book is a work of fiction. Names, characters, places, and incidents are the product of the author's imagination or are used fictitiously. Any resemblance to actual events, locales, or persons, living or dead, is coincidental.

Copyright © 2021 by Philinna Wood

All rights reserved. No part of this book may be reproduced in any form or by any electronic or mechanical means, including information storage and retrieval systems, without written permission from the author, except for the use of brief quotations in a book review.

Cover design by STK Kreations

Cover illustration by Felix Ortiz

Map by Philinna Wood

ISBN: 978-618-85766-0-5 (paperback)

ISBN: 978-618-85766-1-2 (hardcover)

ISBN: 978-618-00-3370-0 (ebook)

For my family

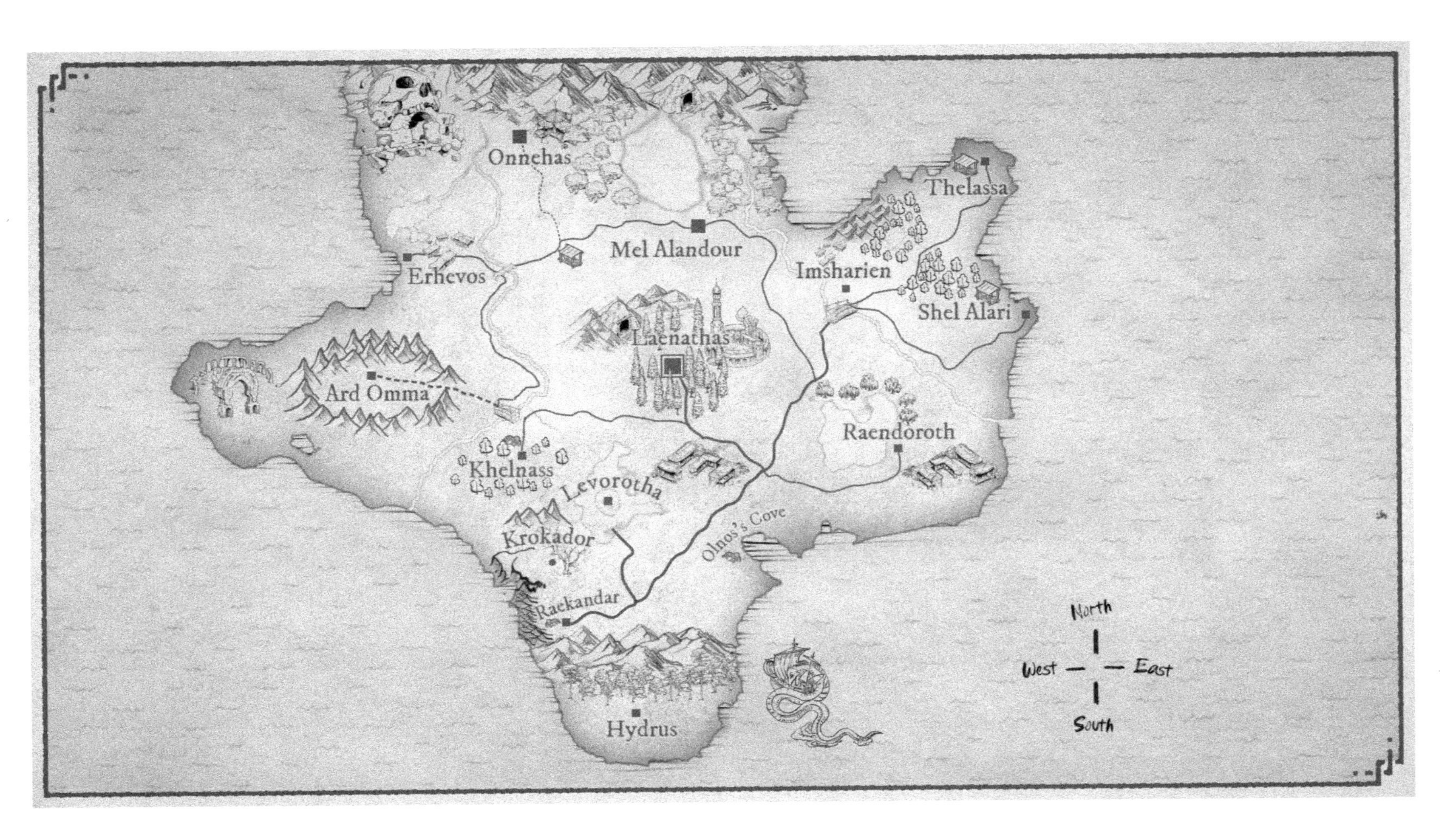
Onnehas
Thelassa
Mel Alandour
Erhevos
Imsharien
Shel Alari
Laenathas
Ard Omma
Raendoroth
Khelnass
Levorotha
Olnos's Cove
Krokador
Raekandar
Hydrus
North
West
East
South

When the stone speaks, the heart listens. It is the silence the stone bearer fears.

—Stonemaster Delion

CHAPTER ONE

AVALAN of the Bloodstone tasted the night. Ashen and wet, it shrouded the silent forest of Hydrus, obscuring the clearing from prying eyes.

The perfect night for a secret meeting, Avalan thought. A gnarled blackwood tree stood ten paces from him. He stared at it, his mind drawing the sneering face of the tribe's chief on its bark. With a quick flick of Avalan's wrist, his dagger spun through the night mist and lodged in the tree with a soft thump. The goat-leg hilt quivered and stopped, black hoof facing a blanket of fallen leaves.

"A good shot," Avalan said. "Right between the eyes. What do you say, Sigil?" He ruffled the fur of his companion, a tiger the size of a bear, with two long fangs, curved like war horns, and a coat that bore the colors of muddy snow. Sigil cocked her head and flicked her striped eyes to the wedged dagger. With a slight nod from Avalan, she leaped, scattering leaves behind her.

Not good enough, Avalan thought as he watched Sigil wrap her fangs around the goat leg. She pulled the dagger free. *Not nearly good enough to end Bassalt's life and free the village from a tyrant.*

He glanced around. Despite the cover of the mist and the shelter of the forest, Avalan had the unsettling feeling of being watched. It wasn't the first time. And yet there was no one there, Avalan knew. He'd taken every precaution to better hide himself. In the forest's darkness, Avalan became one with the shadows. His raven hair was tied high in a horsetail so long it flowed between his shoulder blades, and he wore only coal-black breeches. Even his eyes bore the colors of the forest, green shadowgrass speckled with red spots—the true colors of his Bloodstone.

Avalan rubbed the sweat from his thick brows as he retrieved the dagger from the tiger's mouth. The goat leg was slick with saliva, the hair on it so sparse Avalan could feel the smooth edge of the bone beneath. The blade he had lodged in it over six years past was now worn. Yet Avalan didn't care. It remained his most beloved piece. However, if he and the other tribesmen wished to win against the chief, they needed better weapons. Weapons that flew faster than thought and cut deeper than Sigil's claws.

Waiting for such provisions was why Avalan had been lurking in the woods for the past fortnight. Ronan had promised to return before Avalan's twentieth birthnight, yet that day had come and passed, and there was still no sign of the merchant. Avalan now worried. Twisted paths, teeming with death traps, were etched into the mountains in the north, and if the merchant had stepped on the wrong stone and slipped, his body would rot in a mountain fissure—unfound and unmourned.

The thought sickened him. Ronan had been the father Avalan had never had, and his only hope for freedom. The village was secluded, Ronan their only connection with the Stone Lands. Of course, Avalan could craft some makeshift arrows from tree branches, but they wouldn't be nearly as good as the metal Ronan had promised to bring back from the city blacksmiths. It would take more than a mere twig to scratch the chief's thick hide.

Sigil licked her whiskers and sniffed the air. Avalan smelled it too: the scent of roasting goat flesh and vegetable soup wended its way between the creases of the mighty wooden fence that surrounded the village of Hydrus.

"You go ahead now, girl," Avalan whispered. "I'll join you if he doesn't show. Save me some skin, will you?"

Sigil shook her massive head and pressed her body into him, a welcoming warmth against Avalan's naked waist. Despite his gentle urges, he knew the tiger wouldn't leave him. He only hoped Ronan would show before the feast was over—this wasn't a good night for a hunt.

The leaves behind them rustled. Soon the familiar silhouette of Ronan staggered through the bushes and stepped into the wan moonlight.

The tiger rushed to meet him. Avalan unslung the heavy sack from around Ronan's shoulder, and the merchant bent to the ground, pressing his forehead against Sigil's.

"It lifts my heart to see you, Sigil."

The tiger smacked a rough tongue over his cheek.

Relieved, Avalan helped him to his feet. "I thought you'd never show."

The green-blue eyes of the merchant—eyes blessed by his birthstone, the Larimar—glistened feverishly in their sockets, as if Ronan hadn't slept for days. A worn tunic of gray wool hung loosely over his haggard body. A short beard crowned his lips. The merchant took Avalan's hand in his. His skin was rough, bearing nicks imposed by rocks and thorns that lined the passage through the mountains.

"You're exhausted," Avalan told him, steering him to a fallen log.

The merchant flinched as he sat on the green moss. "I'm glad to see you."

"Are you hurt?"

"It's nothing," Ronan assured him. "I rushed this time, that is all. The path has always treated me well, but it demands respect and careful footing."

Avalan glanced over his shoulder at the clump of bushes. "You came from the shore. I was expecting you from the mountain path."

A shadow crossed Ronan's face. "I'm famished. I hoped to catch a quick bite before I came to meet you, being the goat game night and all ... but the beach is deserted. And the silence ..." He gave Avalan a questioning frown.

Truly, the air was filled only with the smell of food and no man's voice. But this was how it should be—all were to fall quiet during the goat game until the first blood was spilled. Afterward, the tribe's voices would rise in unison, welcoming a new summer.

"It was Bassalt." Avalan tried to hide his hatred. "The chief commanded the game take place inside the fence this summer."

"The goat game should be played on sand." Ronan rubbed a calloused thumb over his temple. "It is tradition."

Avalan shrugged. "Sand, soil, grass ... tradition makes no difference to him. As long as he can keep his watch on the tribe and his belly full."

"And you're not there."

It didn't sound like one, but Avalan knew it was a question. He fiddled with a stray lock on Sigil's tail. "You promised to meet me. I've been spending my last few nights here, waiting for you. I don't see why tonight should be any different."

Ronan scratched his short beard. "You used to love the goat games."

"I did. Before." Avalan felt his old wounds tighten. "This is the longest you've been away. You must tell me all about your travels. But first ... did you remember?"

A faint smile curved the hair over the merchant's lips. "Did you doubt me for even one moment?" Ronan rummaged through his satchel, then drew out a leather pouch. It jingled with the joyous sound of foreign metal. "Fifty of the best arrowheads, tempered and sharp as Onyx."

"Onyx?" Avalan frowned. If these weapons were made of the cursed birthstone, then he wanted nothing to do with them.

"Steel, in truth, but with the vicious cut and fearless spirit of the tribe that used to be." The merchant dropped the pouch on the ground. The thick blanket of leaves softened the landing.

Avalan reached for one arrowhead, studied it against the faint moonlight. Its surface was smooth and dull, but as Ronan had promised, its tip was sharp like a claw. His heart lifted—he'd waited for this day for too long. "Thank you."

"What will you do with them?"

Avalan flipped the arrowhead, testing its weight. "Hunt." When he curled his fingers around it, the steel bit into his flesh.

"Don't lie to me, son. You and Sigil are the best hunters the tribe can boast of. You need no arrows."

Embarrassed, Avalan lowered his head. The last thing he wanted was to mislead Ronan, but he wasn't sure what he should tell him. The men clearly weren't ready yet, judging by the last disaster during knife training. Colgar would have slashed poor Lhorin's head open had Avalan not raised his blade in time to meet Colgar's. In the end, Lhorin had suffered a cut to the ear, but a slashed ear was better than a sliced throat. Not that their blade skills mattered, anyhow. A knife attack wouldn't have time to even reach Bassalt and deal damage. An unexpected, lightning-fast arrow, however ...

"Fifty arrowheads," Ronan declared. "Five for each of your men, or have you convinced fewer to join you in this madness?"

Avalan stood, stretching his long legs. "Best if we don't talk about it."

"All these moonturns ... all these weapons. You won't stand a chance against him."

"You can't know." Avalan had heard these words of caution more times than he could count. And many more that spoke of Bassalt's great stone power, of his control of nature's force. An earthmage, the old tribeswomen called him, yet Avalan had always doubted it. In his mind, it was a mere fable started by Bassalt himself to scare them into further submission.

Ronan tugged at Avalan's breeches. "Sit, fighter, and hear me."

Avalan sat yet spoke before he listened. "I thank you for the steel, and I promise to help you in anything you desire, my old friend, but spare me another speech about Bassalt's power. Its enormity is constantly buzzing through my ears, as I hear it spoken in every corner. The truth is simple: he isn't fit to lead us. Not anymore."

"Will you kill him and take his place? Is this your scheme?"

"Kill him? No." Avalan recoiled. "I only wish him to forsake his position as chief."

"I see. Death it is, then, for Bassalt would sooner die than surrender."

Avalan knew this truth well, yet he still clung to hope. Perhaps there was a way. Perhaps if Bassalt saw he was surrounded, his life threatened, he might change his mind. "If it comes to that, it will be his stubbornness that brings it upon him."

"Yours and his alike."

Avalan clenched his fists. "Don't liken me to him. I only want to fight for our freedom. I won't stand living like a caged animal anymore."

Ronan gestured toward the village. "The fence is nothing to you. You climb in and out as you wish, and the guards never harass you."

"You've been gone long enough. More than a year now." Avalan threw the biting arrowhead into the pouch to join its brothers. "Bassalt becomes madder with every moonturn. First came the fence. Soon after, the inspection of comings and goings. We are not to swim in the sea, nor hunt in the forest without permission. One night the guards caught a couple swimming after sunset. Phet earned himself a nasty scar across the cheek, while Ayla was stripped naked and ridiculed before the tribe. What future do we have if young love is punished? I won't sit back and watch him. Not this time."

Ronan shook his head. His gaze went to the goat dagger that Avalan had secured in his leather belt. "Guilt isn't a wise companion, my son. It tears at your heart and eats at your soul. There was nothing you could have done to help Bhoran."

Avalan wrapped his fingers around the goat leg, his grip firm. Unbidden tears stung his eyes, and he dared not blink, lest they fall. He didn't want to think about Bhoran—not now. But the memory of their friendship kept Avalan going in these hard times. "What I didn't do back then, I plan to do now."

"You miss him," Ronan observed.

"He was my only friend, and Bassalt cast him out."

"It is as I feared. Well, if you intend to attack the most powerful man in this place, you will need a better weapon."

He swooped over to his satchel and buried his face inside it, searching for something at the bottom of the sack. When he emerged again, a dirk lay upon his open palms. Single-edged, it bore a glistening, flat surface marked by etchings that spoke a language Avalan didn't recognize. Avalan's gaze trickled to its hilt. Heavy it looked, and carved with waves of silver. In its middle, a gaping hollow marred its surface.

"This is for you, Avalan of the Bloodstone. For your twentieth birthnight."

"More gifts?" Avalan gripped the weapon. His palm closed effortlessly over the hilt, the meat below his thumb sliding into the hole. "I have no words for its beauty. Only ..." He eyed the hollow with great suspicion. "What is this for?"

"The birthstone's place."

Avalan shook his head. *The birthstone ... I should have expected it.* "It should find a better owner, for I don't trust the stones." He made to return it to the merchant, but Ronan pushed the blade back.

"A stone-enchanted weapon is much more powerful than a bare one," Ronan said with grave seriousness.

"I have no Bloodstone, anyhow. Bassalt made sure of it."

Ronan gave him a mischievous smirk. "That can be arranged."

Avalan shook his head. "Stones are *his* way. Not mine. They never were and they never will be. What good ever came from them? Where were the stones that cursed night?"

Ronan contemplated these words. "Son, if you wish to beat Bassalt, you must learn to trust the birthstones."

"There is no time to know them. The weapons training has begun. And I can trust the blades. I know them. I grew up with them. I can show the men how to wield them. But of birthstones, I know nothing."

"Keep it, despite that," Ronan said, resigned. "It should prove useful for notching shafts to receive the arrowheads." He gave Avalan a wink.

Clearly, Ronan was trying to lift his spirits. Avalan loved him for it. Yet he stood and placed the dirk on the fallen trunk, next to the merchant. Parting with it was harder than he'd expected, seeing as he'd only held it for some moments. "I refuse to disgrace a worthy weapon in such a manner. But I thank you for the thought. I owe you much already, my old friend. It would be many years before I repaid you such a gift. Forgive me, but I cannot accept it."

"Hydrus's freedom would be the most precious gift," Ronan said. "Tell me, what would be the first thing you'd do? Demolish the fence? Swim in the waters naked? What is your heart's deepest desire?"

Avalan searched the lines that marked the merchant's eyes. "I would go find Crystal."

A crooked tooth appeared beneath the hairy beard as Ronan bit his lip. "Avalan—" he warned.

"Assuming you'd let me know where she is, which I know you won't, no matter how much I beg."

"It isn't that." Ronan staggered to his feet. He slid the dirk back into his satchel, then slung the sack over his shoulder. "Some things are best let go."

"I still love her."

"You mustn't."

"And I won't stop." Avalan tried to capture his gaze. "Did you meet her during this long journey of yours?"

"It's better not to—"

"Is she faring well?"

Sea waves of wrath stirred Ronan's Larimar stones. "She is as happy as she can be. You should keep your heart empty of your desire for her. It belongs to the past, and much work awaits you in the future." His voice was firm, showing he'd reached the end of his willingness to speak about the matter.

Avalan was relieved. The merchant's answer left space for his hope. "We should return to the village. They will note my absence. Wait at least for one hundred breaths before you join, to lessen the suspicion we've seen each other. Once the commotion of your arrival dies, come join me and my mother. She will be glad."

Ronan shook his head. "I fear I've lost my appetite. My body is heavy with the need for sleep. I wish to keep my arrival secret for some time longer."

"Sigil," Avalan called. The tiger leaped to her feet. "She can take you to my place. It's far from prying eyes." He bent, brought his face to Sigil's eye level. "Home."

The tiger let out a small groan in response.

Ronan raised a curious brow. "You live alone now?"

"It would be hard to hide all these weapons from Mother," Avalan said with a broad smile, jiggling the arrowhead pouch. "And thanks to you, my collection is ever growing."

Gently the merchant touched Sigil's fur. "I shall unload my things at your place. Then I'm of a mind to pay tribute to the Great Warrior before I make my arrival known to the tribe."

Avalan watched them leave. He hid the arrowhead pouch in the log's hollow, then waited until the rustling of their feet was a distant whisper before he followed the path back to the village.

A hundred breaths and steps later, the spikes of the fence came into sight—the mighty palisade Bassalt had ordered built to encircle the village. A crude assembly of tightly woven beams with sharpened edges, the fence resembled the backbone of a spiny serpent. Around the village it twisted, to protect it.

From what, Avalan didn't know. The village of Hydrus was a fastness, nestled among the Craggy Mountains in the north and wetted by the warm, shallow waters of the Nameless Sea in the west, east, and south. And seeing as the only one who was allowed to tread the mountain paths and visit the Stone Lands was Ronan, and none ever traveled the sea for fear of the sea monster, it would be impossible for someone to penetrate the village.

Despite that, Bassalt had woken one day and ordered the building of the fence. The whole tribe—Avalan among them—had worked endlessly for two moonturns to complete this massive working. The fence was twenty feet tall and bore only two entrances—one in the north, overlooking the mountainfoot, and one in the south, facing the sea. Two crude watchtowers had been erected, and Bassalt manned them with men ordered to watch all the comings and goings of the tribe. No one was to linger outside after nightfall, and so Avalan would have to avoid using the gates tonight.

Instead, he slid through the small trench he had dug in a remote corner of the fence. The thorns in the shrubs that hid the entrance tugged at his breeches and scratched his bare chest. When he emerged, silence greeted him.

In the distance, the silver shine of a full moon mingled with the warm light of fire. Avalan took the path leading to the center of the village, thinking of Ronan's earlier words about tradition. *The goat game should be played on sand.* This custom's root went so far back in time that Avalan had never really known why it had to be so. Ronan had once told him the tale of the waterdragon—a monster that lurked in the waters of the Nameless Sea, watching over their village, sinking any vessel that dared to slice the surface. *It is for the waterdragon of*

Hydrus that the games are played by the sea, Ronan had claimed. *A tribute to its existence.*

Yet in his twenty years in Hydrus, Avalan had never once glimpsed any sea monsters. A mere fable this creature was, he was certain, and yet he'd always enjoyed the feel of sand beneath his feet when he had played the goat games. And if a waterdragon was watching, Avalan didn't terribly mind it.

This night, though, the game was taking place in the village's feasting ground, where the tribe gathered to sup. A small clearing had been created, surrounded by short tables laid with food and drinks waiting to be savored. Three young men, Eras, Phet, and Virko, stood in the middle. Their toes were buried in the sand Bassalt's men had carried from the shore last night to better represent the ground tradition demanded. They were all boys of not more than fifteen summers, standing three feet apart in a jagged trigon. Eras clutched at a goat skull with sharpened horns. His eyes darted right and left to his opponents, trying to decide which one he should try to score with the skull.

The horns had to be painted with blood for the game to be over, but having only three men playing made it a tedious task. Yet these were the only men of proper age. The village had seen little growth in numbers in the past ten years. Last Avalan had counted, the tribe amounted to three hundred and twenty. Bassalt's increasing madness and refusal to accept any new members from the Stone Lands was to blame. Avalan hoped that would change once Bassalt was removed from his position.

Thick smells of meat, spices, and boiling wine wafted through the night air. The cooking had long since ceased—heavy cauldrons still steamed over campfires, and crispy goat meat hung from the spits. All that remained was for the game to end so the feasting could begin.

Avalan's mother sat behind a low table, a space in the soil beside her, surely waiting for him. He nudged his way through the crowd, nodding silent greetings as he passed.

Farmera gifted him with a warm gaze. Avalan planted a kiss on her hair, taking in the familiar smell of lavender and fennel. Her long face was unusually pale tonight, but the green linen dress she'd donned brought out the Amethyst birthstone in her eyes. He sat beside her.

Much as he longed to tell her of Ronan's arrival, he'd have to wait until the game was through.

In silence, Avalan took in the feasting ground. Beyond the crowded tables stood a high wooden platform. Bassalt was sprawled over the chief's chair. A white panther's hide covered his torso, sparing the tribesfolk from witnessing his unsightly girth. Gray hair cascaded over his shoulders like waterfalls. His face was a grim mask, devoid of emotion. Thick fingers, adorned with silver rings, tapped the sides of his wooden seat.

Flanking him sat Theran, the chief's most trusted manservant and a mere shadow of Bassalt's presence, and Silver, commander of the tribesmen and defender of the village. Silver's name matched his hair, a gray shine cropped with a sharp razor around his temples. A short stub of a beard covered his square-jaw muscles, which quivered as he clenched his teeth. It was a common belief—one that was never spoken out in the open—that Silver was a better match for the position of chief of Hydrus. Avalan had heard how Silver's men always called him Chieftain in secret. Yet the commander's heart was just as cruel as Bassalt's, and Avalan wasn't keen on seeing him take the chief's chair.

The seat next to Silver remained empty. Avalan frowned. *Where is she?*

A stare weighed on his shoulders, and he twisted his neck to meet Colgar's gaze. Colgar twitched his lips in greeting—his notion of a smile. Once, Avalan would not have returned the gesture, but now things were different. Ever since Bhoran had been cast out, Colgar had changed. The boy who had once itched for a fight had transformed into a quiet man, hard of build and harder of mind. Avalan needed as many able men as he could gather for his cause, and so he gave Colgar a slight nod.

Gasping, Farmera squeezed Avalan's hand. He returned his attention to the game. Virko had tripped and fallen, arms sprawled to the sides. *An easy target.* Eras, his fiery hair catching the firelight, hurled the skull, easily scraping the fallen boy's back and ending the game.

Roars of laughter and cheers of celebration fractured the air—this victory marked the dawn of summer. The tribesfolk swarmed the sands and lifted the young champion in their arms, chanting his name.

"Eras! Eras! Eras!" Drums echoed all around, joining the joyous cries of the tribe.

"Were you on the other side of the fence again?" Farmera had a frown on her face and two cups in her hands. She offered him one.

"You know me." Avalan gulped the thick wine. He would have much preferred a cool ale in this heat, but he welcomed anything to quench his thirst.

Farmera squinted. "Where is Sigil?"

"She will be here soon. A seabird caught her eye, and you know how she gets when something's stuck in her mind."

Farmera laughed and rubbed his shoulder. "She got that from you, her father," she said over the celebrating yells of the men.

Avalan smacked his lips with satisfaction. "That she did."

He reached for a plate filled with succulent goat ribs and served some to his mother before digging his teeth into one. Soft meat melted in his mouth; juice dripped down his chin.

He motioned in the platform's direction. "Where is Lusha?"

Farmera frowned. Clearly, she had been thinking of the same. On the chief's platform, Silver had an empty seat to his left, where his daughter belonged.

"I thought she might be with you," Farmera said, taking a sip. "I don't want her to be alone during a goat game night."

Avalan nodded quietly. He didn't want that either. He dropped the rib onto his plate. "I should go look for her."

"I think someone has done that already." Farmera flicked her head toward the platform, where one of Silver's men was whispering in his ear. The news had clearly upset the commander, for he clenched his fist and barked orders to his men. It was hard to hear what he said over the noise, though Avalan guessed the orders were to search for Lusha again.

"They're looking in the wrong place," Avalan said. On a night like this, there was only one spot Lusha would choose to visit.

Yelps of surprise spread through the crowd, and the tribe parted to let Sigil pass. She trotted leisurely to Avalan's side, ignoring the fear on the tribe's faces. In the forest's wilderness, among the thick trunks of the lofty blackwood trees, Avalan sometimes forgot how big Sigil was.

Watching her tower over the tables now, he realized she'd grown much bigger than he'd expected.

"Here, girl." Avalan threw her a rib.

She gulped it down without chewing.

"I see no seabird," Farmera said.

Avalan shrugged. "Better luck next time."

"Or worse. These long hunting trips of yours—"

"Fear not, Mother. From now on, our luck will only get better."

Sudden gasps broke out from the center. Yells followed. The drumming ceased.

Confused, Avalan faced the feasting ground. The men had dropped Eras from their arms and had retreated, forming a circle around the young champion. Avalan leaped to his feet and strained to see the cause of the commotion. *Has Ronan made his arrival known after all?*

When Bassalt raised a palm, silence fell. Theran sprang from his seat and descended the wooden steps. Men parted, and the servant's brown hair disappeared from Avalan's sight as he bent to the ground to retrieve an object. Soon he returned to Bassalt, dropping whatever he had plucked from the ground into the chief's fat palm.

Bassalt's face grew dangerously dark. Avalan knew this face well. It bore no good omens.

"What was it?" he whispered to his mother.

Pale as the sand on the shores of the Nameless Sea, Farmera shook her head.

They didn't have to wait for long. Bassalt stood, his chair creaking ominously. He raised his hand for all to behold. A silver sphere glinted between his fingers.

A birthstone.

Horrified whispers spread.

"To whom does this belong?" Bassalt's voice boomed, ceasing all noise.

Men and women lowered their heads, none of them willing to be associated with treason.

"I will ask only one more time before I decide all of you are guilty."

Eras, the red-haired champion of the game, stepped forth. "It's mine."

"Tell me, Eras," Bassalt said. "Do you not know that birthstones are forbidden?"

Avalan clenched his teeth and pressed the corner of his table. Knowing Bassalt's hatred for the stones, this couldn't end well.

"I'm sorry, my chief," Eras said. "This Moonstone was my late father's. I only wished for some luck for the game."

"Luck?" Bassalt thundered. "You think stones bring luck? Stones started the war that savaged the lands. Tribes reached near extinction. Families were torn apart. The earth shook and burned and ripped. The Onyx tribe swallowed villages whole. Our village among them. Half of our tribe died here by the hands of the Onyx. And you still dare to carry a birthstone?"

The boy squirmed now, his head so low it almost touched his chest. The men who had celebrated him as their champion moments ago now withdrew, leaving him alone amid a sandy clearing.

Avalan made to move, but Farmera's hand on his stopped him. *Don't,* her gaze was saying. *Don't stoke his anger.*

With a sickening crunch, Bassalt smashed the Moonstone between his fingers, silver powder dusting his head. Eras's body shook, but he didn't make a sound.

"This is what stones deserve. Destruction. And this is what you deserve." Bassalt raised both arms in a calling. The earth trembled, and Avalan heard ripping sounds that spoke of uprooting.

Thick tree vines slithered over the fence like never-ending snakes. They struck all at once, coiling around the wrists and ankles of a dumbfounded Eras, tethering him. With a quick pull, they forced him to the ground as another one appeared. Like a whip, it hovered over the boy's back. Avalan's stomach churned. *What sorcery is this?*

An earthmage. The women's warning echoed in Avalan's mind.

Bassalt sneered, the same grimace Avalan had imagined on the blackwood trees of the forest. *Right between the eyes,* Avalan thought, clenching the goat leg. *I could end this all now.*

"*This* is your victory, our champion." Bassalt flicked his wrist, and the loose vine flogged the boy's back with such menace that his skin tore open. Droplets of blood showered the sand.

"No!" Avalan yelled.

Sigil leaped over the men and charged. Bare fangs glistened in the firelight. Claws shot out. When she reached the base of the platform, she faltered as if she'd hit an obstacle that stemmed her speed. The tiger whimpered.

Avalan pushed his way through the men. He watched as Sigil, his fierce companion, bent in a silent bow before Bassalt. An earthmage, the women had threatened.

"Bassalt!" Avalan yelled. "What have you done to her?" Cold grasps enshrouded his shoulders as the men held him back. Avalan fought them. "Don't you dare touch her!"

Bassalt shot him a heartless stare. The striped eyes in his face, eyes that looked so much like Sigil's, gleamed. For a moment, Avalan imagined the chief's strike on his tiger would be fierce, but Bassalt merely cocked his head and drove Sigil away with a wave, as if ridding himself of a small rodent.

Avalan struggled against his captors, wanting to go to her. A firm hand covered his mouth. He twisted his neck to regard Marebore, a sturdy tribesman of more than forty summers who overlooked the fairness of the goat games.

"The time hasn't come," Marebore whispered in Avalan's ear. Avalan stared into the liquid lava of Marebore's Ruby birthstone. There was caution there, a silent plea to not protest against the unfairness.

Muzzle lowered to the ground, Sigil crossed the sand. Eras's punishment resumed. The vines slashed, cut, whipped. Every stroke imposed Bassalt's will on the boy's back again and again, with greater force this time. More blood sprayed the ground, yet not a word left Eras's mouth.

Bassalt watched in silent satisfaction. When he'd had enough, he made the vines release the youth and slide back over the fence. "Let this remind you of what awaits those who defy my orders," he warned the tribe. "Now, let us feast."

As soon as the voices of the tribesfolk returned to their lips, Farmera ran to the fallen Eras. She helped him to his feet and took him away toward her house to tend to his wounds.

The sound of hundreds of voices filtered through the gathering. Some cursed. Some warned for calmness. And some begged for no more violence. Caught between rage and despair, Avalan watched Eras hang on to Farmera, the men's hold still strong around him. He twisted out of their grip. Guilt throbbed in his chest for heeding Marebore's warning not to interfere. He was of a mind to meet with Eras later to offer him a place in their group. Despite his age, the boy had stood his ground. Perhaps it would be easier to convince more of the men now—a goat game champion flogged like a beast before the whole tribe would not soon be forgotten.

Sigil's rough tongue licked his hand, and Avalan realized his palm was bleeding, the wound from the arrowhead reopened. As he wiped the blood on his breeches, the commotion quieted, and the feast began. Despite their shock, the tribe's bellies had been empty since dawn, and Avalan knew hunger always won in the end. Cups clattered, fingers dipped into platters, and bones crunched between hungry teeth.

He led Sigil back to their table and sat beside her. "What did he do to you?" he asked her, but the tiger's eyes were wandering, as if she hadn't heard him.

Avalan buried his fingers in her thick fur and pulled her into a close embrace. He'd lost his appetite, but he would wait for his mother's return. He'd promised her he would stay for the feasting, and Avalan hated to break a promise.

Yet this wasn't the only reason he stayed.

The celebrations gave him a rare chance to observe the chief without seeming suspicious. Scouting your enemy's weaknesses, Avalan knew, was paramount to winning a fight. *Yet what should I look for?* Bassalt seemed not to have a single stone on him, apart from the jewel on the snake ring that was half-buried beneath his thick flesh. To Avalan, it looked like a mere crystal, transparent and empty of life and power.

And yet as Avalan's eyes were rooted to Bassalt, the chief lost the sneer from his mouth. Instead, Bassalt had resumed his seat, a distant, haunted look on his face, his stubby thumb nervously rubbing the stone that adorned the snake ring around his finger.

CHAPTER TWO

THE FULL MOON limned Lusha's skin with pale blue light.

She hastened through the blackwoods, straying far away from the village. Her father's men were searching for her, she knew. Her absence would have been noted by now, an empty chair where she should sit, her father seething next to it.

Sliding through the fence unnoticed wasn't a hard thing on a goat game night. The tribe's attention was on the preparations and on the boys who tossed the skull between them, hoping to hit some flesh and win the game. The silence behind her betrayed that the game was still going. Perhaps if she hastened, she'd still have time to return with proper grounds for her absence, and fill her father's cup with wine to soften his anger.

As she picked up her pace, Lusha wished with all her might her colors were darker, like Avalan's. For her, blending with the blackwood trees was a hard task. Lusha's flaxen hair, opal eyes, and white dress shone brightly in the night, but it was her skin that most betrayed her presence in the darkness. When a full moon touched it, her skin sparkled—a blessing of her Moonstone, and yet a curse when being hunted in the forest.

Soft silk danced around her bare feet. The earth was warm tonight; it was indeed the beginning of the summer. When she glimpsed the marble head of Olnos the Great Warrior rising above the treetops, she slowed, allowing her chest to fall and rise evenly with her footfalls. The soil gave way to smooth grass. It would be hard for them to find her now. None would think she'd venture this far, and especially not close to the place where she had gained the unsightly scar that marred her face and took away part of her eyesight. But that was only the way the tribe saw it.

Lusha's truth was different. Soon she would see the base of the giant, the great flat stone on which Bhoran had sat her on that goat game night they'd exchanged their first kiss.

Her heart raced now, loud like the pounding of skin drums on a feasting night. *So close. Just one more step,* she convinced herself, gulping moist fear. The trees grew sparser. The clearing lay a few steps away.

A faint humming swam in the air, betraying the presence of another.

Catching her breath, Lusha ducked behind some spiky shrubs. She had been so certain all would be in the village; she hadn't imagined for a mere moment someone would be here.

With a trembling hand, she clutched her mother's pendant, a reminder of the promise she'd made to herself. *No matter what, I won't look back.* She had come here tonight to bid her farewells—to Bhoran's ghost, to the past, and to the pain that tore at her heart. The merchant would be back from his long travels soon, and then there would be no more time for her to return to the statue.

The humming went on, oblivious to her agony.

Of all the nights, she thought, *someone had to be here tonight.* She could have chosen another night, she knew. But deep inside her, the truth of her choice cut like a sharp knife: all she really wanted was to meet Bhoran. To be in his arms one last time. And so she had chosen a goat game night, like the one when she'd last seen him, hoping, like a fool, he might show after all these years.

She bit her lips until they bled. Best not to hope for such things. Her father had made sure seeing Bhoran again would never happen. And Bhoran had never hummed. Lusha knew then whoever was there tonight surely wasn't him.

She peeked over the thorny edge, weighing the distant figure of the man. His movements felt strangely familiar, the way he sat atop the flat stone at the feet of Olnos and caressed his short stub of a gray beard, humming his thoughts away over something lying before him on the stone.

Her heart fluttered. *Could it be?*

Abandoning her hiding place, she crossed the tree line. Once she stepped into the clearing, the looming moonlight touched her, filling the air with a blue haze.

The man shaded his eyes. "Lusha?"

It was Ronan, the traveling trader of Hydrus, their only connection with the Stone Lands, and Lusha's only hope to escape. His face looked slimmer than she remembered, a gray sheen patching his cheeks. His fingers were stained black from ink and coal; on the stone slab before him lay a stretched parchment with strange drawings.

Lusha embraced him tightly. His tunic smelled of the mountain—dust and freedom. Under the shade of the statue's knee, her moon glowing had dimmed. "When did you return? What brings you to Olnos?"

Ronan scratched his beard absentmindedly, tracing a gray smudge on his cheek. "I have a working to complete," he explained. "This place has the best light after dark. I can't risk fire next to my parchments."

Lusha studied the drawing. "Is it ...?"

"A map." A hint of pride painted Ronan's voice. "Shady drew it for me. Isn't it beautiful?"

Lusha thought so. Shady, a fellow tribesman, had been born of the Amethyst, and he had inherited all the artistic nature the stone had to offer. She didn't recognize any of the places Shady had drawn, save for one. At the bottom of the map, a settlement rested by the sea, a place protected by water and mountains, nestled among a great forest—Hydrus. In the old days, when they had still been allowed to swim the sea, Avalan had drawn the shape of Hydrus many a time for her on the white sand, and so she had learned to recognize it. She hovered a gentle finger over the parchment. "Our home."

"It is." Ronan waved a palm. "And these are the Stone Lands. At least, the part that has been mapped till now. There's word of plains of abundance on the other side of the northernmost mountains, though none of those who have ventured into them have returned, and so no one truly knows." His fingers found his beard again, tugged at it as if a heavy burden weighed on his mind.

"Something troubles you?" Lusha asked.

Every time Ronan returned, he strode his way straight to the feasting ground to fill his belly with meat and ale and rest his bones while the tribe pestered him for tidings from the lands. Yet now, here he stood alone in the darkness, looking famished.

"There is a whisper in the wind." Ronan's voice was thick with wonder. He tapped the map with a calloused finger. "Talk of a hidden treasure in the east. Eyedir and I have had our ears open for some time."

Lusha had heard the merchant talk about his dear companion Eyedir many a time. It wasn't common for merchants to keep friends, Ronan had always told her, but he and Eyedir always begged to differ. "Do you think the rumors hold true?"

Ronan shrugged. "Perhaps. Tribes always wish there were some better place, over the mountain, beyond the sea, below the earth … They're just never happy. One should be content with one's surroundings. Hydrus is all we have, and we should love it for being our birthplace. There are plenty of good tribesfolk to stay here for."

He's scolding me. Lusha tried to meet his gaze. *Has he changed his mind on taking me with him on his journey?* When she regarded the waves in his Larimar eyes, she knew it was so. Deep regret and fear were etched on the merchant's soul. "Ronan, you promised me …"

He placed an arm around her shoulders. "I know I did. But, Lusha, I beg of you. Think again. The village needs women like you. I've just met with Avalan."

"Have you told him?" Hot blood rushed to her cheeks. She had been meaning to tell Avalan of her plans to escape Hydrus with Ronan, only every time she looked into his eyes, she lost her courage. Avalan loved Hydrus so much.

Ronan shook his head. "It will break his heart to watch you go. You're the only friend he has left."

His words cut deep. "Avalan has you as well."

The merchant sighed. "I'm away most of the year, and every time I cross the Craggy Mountains, it takes part of my strength. I cannot throw a dart to save my life from a fly, and I hate hunting. Swimming … I loathe it, and the mere thought of a blade in my hands makes me shake in terror of nicking them *and* my ability to peddle. I cannot share with him the things he loves. The goat games were the only thing that made him smile, and these … these are long gone for him, I see."

Lusha nodded quietly. Avalan, Shady, and the rest of the boys Bhoran had called his friends had never played a single goat game ever since that cursed night when Bassalt had cast Bhoran out. Many a time Lusha had tried to tell her father and Bassalt the snake attack had been an accident, but they wouldn't listen. Despite having raised Bhoran as a stepbrother, Bassalt had been quick to banish him from Hydrus forever.

"I can't do much of what you've just said, save for swimming," she told Ronan with a sad smile. "I cannot see how my running away with you will shatter Avalan's heart." It was a lie, and she knew it.

"Avalan sees Bhoran in you, moon child. He believes Bhoran's love for you will one day lead him back to the tribe."

Lusha leaned against the cool marble of the statue. For many years, she had believed that herself, only now she wasn't sure. Year after year, she had returned to the statue of Olnos in secret, hoping each time Bhoran would be there, waiting for her with open arms. Yet every time, all she'd found was silence and her dried blood on the stone's surface. "He's only six years late. I came here to bid him farewell before I leave with you. He isn't coming back. I know it now."

Ronan brushed back the golden locks Lusha always let flow over her scar.

Lusha flinched. She didn't want anyone's eyes on the right side of her face. Before the scab of her wound had fallen, she'd grown sick of the pity in the tribe's faces. *Silver's pretty daughter,* they used to whisper, *butchered like hunted game.* Losing her beauty had never mattered much to Lusha; all she had cared about was Bhoran. And yet one day she had dared look into the mirror Farmera had kept in her belongings. Strange little thing that mirror had been. A piece of round glass brought back by Ronan from one of his trips. Lusha had brought it close to her face. One heartbeat later, the mirror had lain shattered on the ground, and Lusha had never again drawn her hair back from the right side of her face.

Ronan's fingers smelled faintly of smoke as he caressed the silver line of her scar.

"It was here," Lusha said. A sudden desire to finally confess what had happened overwhelmed her. "Bhoran brought me to Olnos after the goat game. He was happy despite Colgar's victory. He placed me on this rock"—she touched the stone that now held Shady's map—"and gifted me my birthstone. A real Moonstone. Tiny and blue, like a pearlescent moon it shone. He was so proud to have secured for me such a forbidden treasure. And I took it." She gulped the clean air to draw some courage. "Then he asked me to close my eyes, for he had one more thing to show me—a surprise, he said—and I did. The rattling came … an awful sound. I didn't even see the snake before it slashed me. All I remember is warm blood between my lips and Bhoran's cries. Those terrible cries … I savor them in my mind, for they were the last thing I heard from him."

Silence fell as the merchant contemplated her words. The whole time, he hadn't ceased stroking his beard.

"Bhoran told me it was you who gave him the Moonstone," Lusha said.

Ronan looked at her with wide eyes as if he'd only just remembered. "Of course. I took it straight from Levorotha, the city of the Moonstone." Then his Larimar stones darkened, turned to troubled waters of a deep sea. "He asked me if I could get him an Onyx stone as well. He longed to see if anything would happen if he held it. I told him I couldn't risk bringing a cursed stone into the village. I was wrong."

A sadness bathed Lusha. It wasn't as if Bhoran wasn't used to harsh words about his birthstone. Ever since she could remember, the whole tribe had glanced sidelong at him, afraid of the darkness adorning the stones in Bhoran's eyes—the gloom of the Onyx, the tribe that had waged a war that had savaged the Stone Lands.

Eager to cast the shadow of the Onyx away, Lusha leaned closer. "Show me where we are going. Show me Levorotha."

Ronan's finger traced a piece of land floating atop a lake. "The city of moonhealers."

It was but a small smudge on a parchment, but to Lusha, it seemed the most beautiful thing she had regarded of late. This small ink stroke held her freedom. "The city of my mother."

"Silver won't like it," Ronan warned her, not for the first time. "Neither will Bassalt."

"You got away with smuggling Crystal out of the village before," she reminded him.

"True. I took Crystal away," Ronan said, raising a blackened finger, "but Crystal and you are hardly the same. One the daughter of a fisher, the other of the commander. Back then, I managed to convince Bassalt not to release a hunt after her, but for you ..."

Lusha swallowed hard. She had everything ready: a change of clothes, some salted meat and hard bread for the road, and the steel heart to say farewell. But now Ronan seemed to have changed his mind. A shadow of doubt darkened his face, his gaze, his words.

Am I so desperate as to risk the poor merchant's life for my gain?

"Ronan, I don't *want* to be the commander's daughter anymore. I wish Crystal had told me of her plans to leave." Crystal had been her heart friend, the one always ready to listen and love. Yet Lusha always lost those who loved her. "I would have gladly escaped with her. I would. After Bhoran was exiled, there was nothing for me here, and she knew it. You must take me with you before my father's anger—"

The faint roaring of distant voices broke the silence. Soon afterward, drumming echoed through the trees. They turned their heads toward the village.

"The goat game is over." Lusha's heart pounded against her chest. She'd been gone longer than she'd imagined. "I must return."

Ronan grabbed her arm as she made to leave. "Promise me you'll think it over."

"I have made up my mind. I'm coming with you once you leave."

"I see." Ronan let her go. "I can't imagine Hydrus without you, but I feel your pain. I hope you find what you seek in Levorotha. Now go, and, Lusha ... do not say that you've seen me. I have some matters to resolve before I show myself to the tribe." Ronan rubbed his eyes, smudging them with black. He rolled the map and tucked it into the side of his breeches.

Lusha released the locks from behind her ear and left the giant's knee. As she crossed the sward, the statue's gaze pierced her back. She turned and took in the calm face of the warrior. As the giant overlooked the stone where Ronan sat, Lusha had a warm feeling Olnos was watching over him. The same way he had watched over Bhoran and Lusha that night. *To you, Olnos,* she thought, *I say my farewell words to Bhoran. Should he return, tell him I will love him until I die.*

The way back proved harder than she'd imagined. As she drew closer to the village, fear joined the sadness in her heart—the dry realization that soon she'd have to face her father. *Not for much longer,* she consoled herself. *Soon Ronan and I will leave, and I'll be free.*

It was Gremian who found her first—her father's most trusted, a lean man of forty summers whose hands always trembled. She let him lead her toward the village, ignoring his pressing questions. Silver was the only one she owed an answer to, and she had to devise one soon.

The smell of crispy goat flesh wafted through the northern gate as they entered the village. Roars of laughter and the incessant clanking of plates and cups lifted her heart—the feasting was at its peak. Perhaps her father had enjoyed a drink or two by now, his anger somewhat faded.

Pale smoke rose from the tongues of a great fire at the center of the feasting. Women, men, and children danced around it, joyous cries leaving their mouths. Lusha wiped the cold sweat from her face as Gremian led her to the platform. A breeze had risen from the sea, and Lusha reached inside the fold of her dress for her bone brooch. As she climbed the small steps, she slid it over the ends of her golden locks, to better hold them in place and hide her face. Being displayed in front of the whole tribe made her worry about her scar.

She bowed her head at Bassalt, then swiftly glided to the empty seat next to her father. In her blind spot, she felt Silver's burning inspection. Lusha didn't like this. Theran slinked closer and poured some wine into her cup. She liked Theran. Despite his being Bassalt's most loyal servant, he'd always been good to her. With half a smile, she picked the cup up as Theran rushed back to his seat.

"Look at me when you drink," her father told her. The wine had mellowed his usually gruff voice. It only made him scarier.

Lusha twisted her neck to regard him. Anger wrapped Silver's face. His lips were a tight line, the Heliodor stones in his eyes reflecting the bright fire. It helped not to stare at them. "Who won the game, Father?"

"Eras. Where were you?"

Lusha swallowed a mouthful of spiced wine before she braved an answer. "In the woods." There was no salvation in lying. Gremian had seen her on the path that led to the statue. "I went to Olnos. Once the drumming broke the silence, I returned."

Her father swung his head, his gaze sweeping the crowd over the fire. The commander was staring at Avalan, she realized. Her friend sat on the ground, wine cup in hand. Sweet Sigil curled before his legs.

"Did he help you?"

Lusha squeezed her cup. "I was alone."

"Your place is here, by my side." Silver banged a fist on the table, the blow thankfully muffled by the crowd's enjoyment. "You should have been here to behold the game and see our celebrated winner. Soon enough, you'll hear about his fate."

Lusha's heart throbbed faster. Farmera wasn't by Avalan's side, she realized. Death wasn't a common mishap during the goat games, for the men were always careful. Yet Lusha still remembered that one time the skull had pierced the inner thigh of Bren, a young boy of fourteen summers. Lusha had rushed to help Farmera, only no matter how hard they had pressed, the bleeding from the boy's thigh hadn't eased. Lusha had never forgotten how the sparkle of the stones in his eyes had faded to a dim light and then surrendered to darkness as his soul had passed. "Did something happen?"

Her father studied her with a critical eye. "He was insolent. And thus he was punished. Now stop gaping at the Bloodstone and focus your attention on worthier men." Silver cupped her chin and forced her head to the left.

Over the dancing flames, she noticed Colgar. When he met her gaze, he raised a wine cup in greeting. Lusha brought a trembling palm to her father's arm. "You're hurting me."

Silver jerked her free. "For how long will you refuse him? The village needs a marriage, and you've long passed the able age."

"I do not wish to marry him, Father." Colgar's words still echoed in her memory. *You should feel lucky. Your beauty is not what it used to be.* Lusha hadn't felt lucky that night, or any of the other nights Colgar had asked for her hand in marriage.

"You embarrass me," Silver accused her. "Spending your time consorting with the ill and the weak, soiling your hands with foul-smelling potions. I had greater dreams for you."

"The village needs a healer. I am of better use aiding Farmera than being a tribeswife."

Silver clutched at his tankard so hard the metal bent. "I won't accept my daughter growing into a spinster."

"Then you should have let me take the one I love." Lusha gasped. The words had slipped out without her thinking. It was too late to retrieve them now.

"You dare mention to me this talon? After all he's done to you, you still declare you love him?" The veins in her father's neck popped, and he clenched his jaw so hard Lusha could have sworn she heard a tooth crack. "Was this the reason you sneaked away to the statue tonight? Were you with him? Has he returned? Look at me when I talk to you!"

Lusha brushed her father's spittle from her cheek. It wasn't the first time Silver had called Bhoran a talon—the sharp claw of the Onyx. It was a word used in spite, an abomination. She dared face Silver now. "No, Father. I haven't seen him since that night. He's gone."

Silver's Heliodors flushed with anger, and Lusha knew the only thing that kept him from swinging the back of his palm across her face was the presence of the tribe. His pride always rose higher than his narrow-minded principles.

"I hope he's dead. Filthy Onyx," he spat. "You're not to visit Olnos's statue. And if I find you've disobeyed my order—"

"I won't, Father. I promise." She wouldn't be returning to the statue, Lusha knew. Olnos had heard her farewell words, and though statues hadn't mouths to relay any biddings, in her heart she was relieved. Six years had passed since last she'd seen Bhoran; now she would leave with the merchant, knowing for certain Bhoran was gone.

"See that you change your bearing toward Colgar," Silver warned. "The tribe will see you married before the end of summer. I need someone strong and with an even head to succeed me." He turned from her, waving his damaged tankard at Theran, who was quick to oblige him with a swift refilling of thick ale.

Of all the things her father had said to her tonight, the curse for Bhoran's death tugged at Lusha the most, for it heightened her greatest fear. *Is Bhoran dead? Is this the reason he hasn't come back for me?* Hot tears demanded release. She let them fall. Shutting her eyes, she moved to the dull rhythm of the skin drums, smelled the sizzling goat meat burning, heard the tribe's cries of celebration, and tasted the saltiness of her own mourning.

Soft fur caressed her arm.

When she opened her eyes, Sigil was there on the platform, gazing up at her through heartwarming, striped eyes.

Lusha stroked Sigil softly and looked at Avalan. From afar, she saw him smile. He couldn't come to her, she knew, but he had sent Sigil in his place. She would need to meet with him alone soon, ask what fate had befallen Eras … and tell him about her intention to run away with Ronan. Avalan would never betray her secret, and he and Farmera deserved much better than just to learn of her disappearance.

Be brave, Avalan's eyes told her from the other side of the bonfire. She knew he would stay there watching her all night if needed, until the flames had been reduced to smoking cinders. Until his smile had etched hope into her heart that spoke of better days. Avalan always promised her better days.

She brought sure fingers to the bone brooch that weighed down her hair, and plucked it free. She pushed the long locks away from her face, fastened them atop her head.

The warm breeze caressed her scar for all the tribe to see.

CHAPTER THREE

Bassalt couldn't call to mind the last time he had bathed himself alone. On a day like any other, manservants would fill his bath chamber, making sure the water was warm and the salts to his liking.

Yet tonight an unnerving silence floated through the village, making Bassalt's footfalls echo across the stone walls. Flickering flames of tallow candles cast dancing shadows as Bassalt parted the humid air with his voluminous presence.

His household was fast asleep, the celebrations of a long goat game night having exhausted them. Yet Bassalt, belly still full from the feasting, could not wait till the first light to get rid of tonight's filth. The squalid forest mist and the sea breeze had turned his skin into a clammy hide.

He plucked the candles from the floor, laid them around the central bathtub. He undressed; the white panther hide thumped against the stone floor. Bassalt kicked it aside and climbed into the tub. Cool water sloshed around him, sending a shiver up his spine. Against the stone brim, he rested his nape and closed his eyes.

His thoughts went back to the fence that surrounded the village, and the ease with which he'd slipped through the seaward gate without being noticed by the idle guards. He was wrong to have let Silver convince him to open a gate toward the sea. *Should a fire break out in the village, we need access to the water,* Silver had advised, and Bassalt

—like a fool—had listened. But if Bassalt, with his enormous presence, had stridden through the gate undetected, it meant the village wasn't as safe as he had believed it to be. The guards were not taking their task to heart.

As various ways of punishment passed through his mind, he twisted the golden snake ring around his finger. Bassalt's calloused thumbs had polished the once-scaly surface of the snake to a smooth shine, but the stone on the ring had kept its edge.

Between the open mouth of the snake and its split tail rested a colorless gemstone. Candle flames danced on its transparent surface. Bassalt twisted his lips. He grabbed a block of fatty soap and lathered his fingers. Submerging his hand, he tried to pry his finger free from the cursed ring—but in vain. The piece of jewelry was stuck beneath his swollen flesh. Even if Bassalt loosened the snake's body, he knew his bony knuckle would make removing it hopeless.

When he had first put the ring on, his young fingers had been strong and lean. Twenty years later, the sedentary life of a chief had taken its toll on him—his whole body was a bloated mass, and he could barely stand without his knees creaking. His sight hovered over the ring. "Bloody thing," he murmured.

The diaphanous stone sparkled in response, as if to mock him. He eyed it with great hatred and submerged his hand, this time keeping his eyes rooted to the stone. As he'd expected, the change happened. With a loud curse, he twisted his hand out of the water and reached for a rough sponge.

Bassalt scrubbed his leathery skin until it hurt. When the sponge turned red with blood, he hurled it to the floor. He stood as fast as his heavy legs would allow, water splashing out. Cursing under his breath, he reached for a towel and set to get dressed. He donned a light, russet-colored tunic that hung over a spike in the wall, the garment he preferred for sleeping.

The door behind him creaked open to reveal the worried face of Theran. "Why, Chief, it's you!" he shrieked.

"Hush," Bassalt ordered. "Your voice can stir the dead."

Theran pushed the door shut. He rushed to his chief's side, eyeing suspiciously the spilled water. "You were having a bath at this hour?"

"I should be able to have a bath whenever I want." Bassalt moved to the oiling bench. He chose a narrow vial filled with lavender and dabbed its tip against his wrists and neck.

"Why, if only I had known, my chief, I would have sent someone for hot water."

"The night is hot enough as it is."

Theran stood by the bathtub, bloodied sponge in his hand. Concern spread over his face. "Are you hurt, my chief? So much blood ..."

"This filthy sponge is rough. Get me a new one once the merchant is back." He snatched the sponge from Theran's grasp and tossed it back into the water. "Now go make arrangements for Silver to see me."

"Why ... you mean now, my chief?"

"Yes, Theran, now."

"But—but it's the middle of the night ... Surely we could wait until dawn to bother our commander."

Bassalt glared at him so hard that Theran lowered his bewildered eyes. "Get on with it."

Theran withdrew, clutching his robes high above his ankles to cross the wet floor.

Satisfied with his cleanliness, Bassalt followed the short passage that led to his bedchamber. No sign of last night clung to his body anymore. A cool breeze slipped through the crevices of the walls, creeping below the edging of his tunic and making the hair on his freshly washed skin stand.

He pushed a heavy oaken door. At his behest, the walls of his bedchamber had been made of basalt. The constant mist of the forest air had turned the stones an earthy brown, and dark-leafed ivy crawled along the wooden planks of the roof. Two wall lamps illuminated the dark chamber with a faint brown glow, filling the room with the smoke of burnt oil.

Bassalt gave a rueful glance at his bed, then turned to his working table. Standing upon two wide logs, a wide board stretched in front of a window that held no glass. Instead, iron rods barred it to keep unwanted visitors out. He shuffled his feet to the table and collapsed onto his chair. Pressing two meaty elbows on the wood, he rubbed his temples to ease the throbbing of his head.

The moon had already begun its glorious descent when a firm knock shook his door. Bassalt grunted, and Silver strode in. Though it was the middle of the night, Silver had gone to great lengths to dress himself. Over his reed-brown breeches, green leather scales vested his broad chest, and sharp spikes adorned his square shoulders.

Seeing how well his commander maintained his appearance always gave Bassalt a pang of envy. Though they had shared the same years in the lands, Bassalt was heavy with flesh and the burdens of leading an insolent tribe, whereas Silver was lean and thrived in his leadership of his loyal fighters.

The commander rubbed his swollen eyes—the only sign he had been torn away from the arms of a deep night's sleep. "What has happened?"

Bassalt offered him the seat across the table. "You've become soft, Silver. When did you last inspect the men at the fencing?"

"Yorin reports to me every day."

"Then Yorin is a clot. The men are sleeping on duty. *Sleeping*. Do you know what that means?"

Silver huffed. "It's hard to stay awake when there's no real danger to force your eyes open."

"No danger, you say?" Bassalt threw his chair back and stood so fast his leg gave in under his weight and he collapsed.

Silver hauled him to his feet.

"Keep your hands off me!" Bassalt yelled. "Anybody can stroll in and out the village without your guards so much as blinking an eye. Damn you all! My orders were clear."

Silver's face remained calm as still water. "Your orders were as clear as an oracle of a witless child."

"How dare you—"

"Bassalt, listen to me." Silver raised his palm along with his voice. "The men are getting restless. You made them work for many moon-turns to raise this fence. And now you're asking them to sacrifice their needful sleep to guard the village … against what? There's nothing out there. There never has been."

Bassalt stared at him, his jaw hanging. Had it been someone else who had spoken to him in this way, he would have taken his head. But

Silver was an able commander, one Bassalt needed by his side at this time. He unclenched his fists. "What are you saying?"

Silver leaned closer, the thin lines on his face hardening with spite. "I don't believe you plucked me from the comfort of my bed to scold me for my men's lack of attention."

Bassalt stabbed Silver's chest with a meaty finger. "You feign indifference, yet even your own daughter slipped under their noses and strolled the forest during the goat game."

"I have taken care of this matter. She won't be going anywhere soon. Now, tell me the real reason for your worries. You're ready for it, or you wouldn't have sent Theran to fetch me at this hour. The weather's warmer, and the young ones will soon climb the fence or dig beneath it to reach the sea. I cannot keep them safe if I don't know what I'm protecting them from."

Bassalt rubbed his neck. It took him only a few moments to decide, but he saw no way out of it. He strode to the back of the room, beckoning the commander to follow.

A crock full of clean water rested on his bedside table. Bassalt submerged his ring-bearing hand in the water. Silver stepped closer, and they both watched the snake ring on Bassalt's finger. A dark cloud appeared in the stone's heart and kept growing until darkness consumed the gem. Bassalt twisted his hand out of the water, and the stone returned once more to its lifeless, transparent self.

Silver's face lost its shine. He dug his fingers into Bassalt's meaty forearm. "When did this start?"

"One day before I ordered the building of the fence."

"Filthy Onyx," Silver muttered.

CHAPTER FOUR

AVALAN CHISELED a groove into yet another arrow shaft. The dirk's sharp blade had proved useful, as Ronan had suggested, if a bit long for the task at hand.

He shaded his face against the dawning sun. Bright light licked the hill's grass and reflected over the blade's edges. Under the clean air, Avalan appreciated the weapon's beauty even more: a balanced blade of steel enchanted with etchings, and a sturdy hilt that proved a perfect match for Avalan's grip. Now he held it with the stone hollow facing the other side. *If I can't see it, perhaps it won't bother me.*

Avalan hadn't thought he'd ever hold this beauty again. Yet when the goat game night had ended, he had returned to his tree house to find the blade atop his bed. Of the merchant, there had been no sign. Sigil had stayed with Lusha, and Avalan's room had been too heavy with night mist for Avalan to sleep. Securing the dirk on his belt, he had leaped out into the night. After he had retrieved the hidden arrowheads from the forest, he'd climbed up the hill where he'd stashed the shafts. It was a blessing the goat game nights were held on a full moon. All night he had worked, and he hadn't halted even when the morning dew had wetted his brows.

Avalan dropped the dirk on the grass and threw the shaft onto the rising pile beside him. This was the last one. Sweet-smelling smoke wafted out from the shimmering coals to his side. He dipped a stick into the pot atop them and watched with satisfaction as it came away sticky—the pine sap was almost ready.

With the help of a blunt rock, he crushed some coal and added its powder to the mixture. Never before had he been so happy to watch the black glue thicken. He left it to simmer and stood to stretch his legs and take in the sight over the hill.

The Eagle's Eye was more than worth the name Avalan had given it. From its top, one could admire the whole village of Hydrus below: the serpent fence surrounding houses made of wood and thatched roofs, the feasting ground, where low tables were interspersed for the gatherings and common meals of the tribe, and of course, Bassalt's house—a monstrous boulder of basalt rock that looked more of a cave lair than a proper dwelling.

Over the horizon, the Nameless Sea glistened, so calm and inviting that Avalan felt a familiar ache in his heart. It was the same ache that had been tugging at him for the past six years, ever since Bhoran had been cast out. A longing for freedom, for swimming in the warm waters of the shore once more after an exhausting game of tossing the goat skull between them, for tasting the saltiness of the sea and digging his toes into the white sand.

Soon, Avalan promised as he returned to his workings.

Later on, the shuffling of fallen leaves and cracking twigs told Avalan someone was approaching. He spat out the sinew he had been chewing and stuck his head over the edge. Colgar trod the forest path with careless footings, paying no heed to Avalan's warnings to cover his tracks.

"Up here," Avalan called.

After a short climb, Colgar stood over him, shading him from the sun. He wore only light breeches, his copper-skinned chest glistening with sweat. "Have you been here long?"

Avalan nodded. "Didn't sleep. Care to give a hand?"

As Colgar sat, Avalan pointed at the pile of arrows beside him. The dark steel arrowheads Ronan had brought him were lodged in the notches, some of them already secured on their shafts with tightly tied sinew. Avalan pointed at the pot over the shimmering coals. "Use the stick to slather the glue over the fastening. Be quick and sure of hand.

It dries fast. And here"—Avalan threw him some white goat sinew —"chew this in the meantime, and spit it out when it softens."

Colgar began his task. Between mouthfuls of sinew, he spoke. "What do you make of Eras's punishment?"

Avalan tightened the goat's tendon around a shaft, imagining Bassalt's neck. "It gives our cause advantage. I spoke to Eras after my mother bound his wounds. I hope he'll join today's training."

"Do you trust him?"

"He stood his ground."

Colgar spat some sinew out and dipped the stick into the pot. "Those vines dripped with Bassalt's hatred. The way they whipped the boy ... He must have used stone magic."

"They were mere vines," Avalan said. "Vines can be severed. Bassalt wants us to think him all-powerful and undefeated. He's not."

Colgar smacked his lips and pressed on with gluing the arrows. He said nothing, but Avalan felt a tearing doubt in his silent resolve and in the way his fingers fiddled with the blackened stick. No matter how hard Avalan tried to deny it, he felt it too: the creeping despair that no matter how many weapons they crafted, Bassalt would smash them all into splinters.

When the sun peaked, the men arrived. Their whispering voices traveled up as they gathered at the foothill. Avalan crept over the edge and counted twenty of the tribe's young men, Eras among them with new recruits. Weapons of all kinds hung from their belts, and some clutched arrows—the hunting excuse was one that always allowed the men to cross the fence.

"Come," Avalan told Colgar. "They're all here."

They threw the piles of arrows over their shoulders, and Avalan secured the dirk in his leather belt.

Colgar whistled as his gaze caught the weapon. "Fine blade you've got there."

Avalan nodded and skidded down the slope. He greeted the men with a broad smile, then beckoned them to follow.

Tangles of long-stemmed, woody vines hid the entrance in the stone boulder. The footfalls of the men echoed through the passage. One after the other, they emerged into a cavernous chamber whose air was heavy with dust and smelled of dry earth. Warm sunlight caressed the tawny walls through an opening in the high ceiling. Avalan had placed a wooden crate over it to prevent animals from falling to their deaths.

Against the north wall stood a rough-hewn plank. A tunic stretched over its surface, nailed in place. Hands, feet, and a bulbous head were drawn on the wood with coal—an eerie mimicry of a man.

Once inside, the men sat on the soft soil.

Regarding the assembled, Avalan's heart lifted. Their numbers had doubled overnight, just because of Eras's punishment. The youth seemed to be faring better after his unjust whipping. When Avalan had spoken to him last night, Eras had promised to join and bring some of his trusted friends. As it turned out, this had been an easy task, as no one was willing to forget the abasement of a champion. Some of the men had donned their tunics, while others had their chests bare. Yet all of them bore a solemn expression on their faces, and they had tied their hair over their scalps with bones and brooches.

They are ready for training, Avalan thought, pleased. "I see new faces among us." Avalan greeted each of the new men, gazing firmly into the stones of their eyes. "Our cause is simple, yet one that shouldn't be taken lightly. We fight for our freedom. For justice. For a better Hydrus."

He stood and took the blackwood bow he kept in the cave. From the north wall of the cavern, the imitation of Bassalt's body mocked him. Nocking an arrow, he spoke. "Aim for the arms or shoulders." With a soft twang of his string, the arrow went hissing through the air. It pierced the left hand of the makeshift target. Avalan spun. "I noticed Bassalt lifted his arms to call the vines to his aid."

The men nodded, and Avalan gratefully noted he had their full attention. "And now, let us practice."

One after the other, the men joined him, twenty paces away from the target. Avalan showed them how to embrace the bow, steady their aim and breathing, brush their cheeks gently with their arrow-holding fingers, and … release.

Arrows ripped the cave's air, some finding their target and others smashing against the stone walls. All the while, Avalan paced the cave, passing equal measures of criticism and praise. His fellow tribesmen had proved much better than he'd expected. Hatred, Avalan knew, transformed the greatest amateur into an able archer.

When the sun painted the walls of the chamber crimson, the men sat, exhausted.

Avalan nocked one last arrow, aimed at the center this time, and let it fly. It lodged itself in Bassalt's head, splintering the wood. *Right between the eyes.*

"A good but useless shot." A man's voice came from the entrance of the cave.

Avalan spun, squinted against the dimming light.

A tall man strode in with the sure footing of a leader. Long white hair, braided to the side of his brawny neck with colorful beads, rattled as he moved. His build was strong and proud, untouched by the many years he carried on his shoulders. On his bare chest and just above his heart, a sanguine Ruby rested without the aid of any neck chain or leather string. It was as if the birthstone was affixed there.

"Marebore," Avalan greeted him. "How did you find us?" He was certain he'd covered his trail well, but he couldn't swear for the caution of the others. "Are you here to halt us?"

"I held you back once," Marebore said. "Not anymore." He looked at Colgar. "You haven't told him?"

Colgar rubbed his nape.

Avalan tightened the grip on his bow, glanced sideways at the fallen arrows.

"Lower your weapon," Marebore said. "We have come in peace."

We? Avalan tore his gaze from the floor. In Marebore's face, he read the truth of his words. The tribesman's blood-red eyes burned with a low simmer, like incandescent coals. Marebore had indeed come in peace. Otherwise, he wouldn't be flaunting a birthstone on his chest.

"Are you here to train with us?" Avalan said. Marebore was a sturdy man, but Avalan had never seen him wield a blade with grace.

Marebore shook his head. "I'm here to talk about the birthstones. And if you wish to win this fight against Bassalt, you'd better pay heed to my words."

Avalan threw the bow to the ground and faced Colgar. "I thought I could trust you. I guess the old ways die hard."

"I knew you would refuse to listen," Colgar said in his defense. "You don't trust in the stones. Perhaps now you'll change your mind."

Avalan's chest tightened. "What are you getting at? I crafted the best weapons for all of you—"

"'Scouting your enemy's ways.'" Colgar repeated his own words back to him. "Isn't that what you always say to me? Bassalt uses the stones. The same ones he denies us."

"These arrows bear the finest steel of the Stone Lands—"

"Weapons are useless against Bassalt." Marebore raised two hands in a reconciling gesture. "Stones, on the other hand ..."

Eras moved to Avalan's side. "I thought the stones powerful, yet Bassalt crushed my late father's Moonstone with a snap of his fingers, and my wounds force me to sleep on my face."

Marebore edged closer, one careful, jingling step at a time. The Ruby caught the setting sun and came alive with a fiery glow. "Bassalt was able to crush it with such ease only because its owner was dead. Your father's stone, Eras, has returned to where it belongs," he said, not unkindly. "It should have followed your father a long time ago. An overstaying guest is never welcome."

A heavy silence descended. Avalan sensed the curiosity that swept over the young men's hearts. Their ears were more open than he'd ever seen them, their hearts clinging to Marebore's lips, ready to devour any word about the birthstones. Bassalt's menace against them had created a shroud of mystery over their existence. Even Avalan felt his own heart stir.

"How so?" he asked.

Marebore cleared his throat. "In the old times, when the customs still held, your birthstone was also your deathstone; when your time came, it followed you back to the ground. A birthstone is a powerful gift, bestowed by the stonemasters on each of us, but it also bids returning so the balance remains unchanged."

"My father told me how he had to hide his Moonstone from Bassalt," Eras said, his voice solemn. "When the chief ordered the birthstones thrown into the Nameless Sea, he buried his in the forest."

Avalan raised a curious brow. He'd asked his mother once where her Amethyst birthstone was, but silent tears and a shake of her head had been all he'd gotten for answer. *Did she sacrifice her stone at Bassalt's behest, or did she conceal it as well, waiting for a chance to use it again?* Judging by Marebore's Ruby, it seemed more tribesmen had defied the chief's order. Now Avalan understood why all these years the older tribesman had never removed his tunic before the tribe.

"How do you keep your stone on your chest?" Avalan asked.

Marebore ran a tender finger over his Ruby. "This is a story better told by a stonemaster—should you be ready to listen."

"There is a stonemaster in Hydrus?"

When Marebore nodded, awed whispers rose. Avalan knew no outlander was allowed to enter Hydrus, but Bassalt held a special spot of hatred in his heart for stonemasters. Without stones, the chief had claimed, there was no need for any teaching of their magic. *And without any teaching,* Avalan thought, *soon all customs will be forgotten.*

Thirsty stares burdened Avalan's shoulders. He couldn't refuse to listen to this master, he knew. The sun had almost set. The men were tired. There was nothing more Avalan could teach them tonight about weapons. He nodded.

A satisfied smirk appeared on Marebore's proud face. "Come," he called over his shoulder. Something stirred at the entrance of the cave. Avalan took in the whisper of a long cloak and light footfalls as they caressed the sand.

Through the fast-descending darkness, the frail silhouette of a man stepped into the chamber. He was older than any tribesman Avalan had laid eyes on before, his skin ashen gray and body scrawny and as short as a child's. Old bones creaked with his every step. This man, Avalan was convinced, much like the stone that belonged to Eras's father, had cheated death and overstayed his welcome in the lands.

A gnarled finger peeked out from beneath the sleeve of the man's silver cloak. When it shot into the air, a swarm of fireflies flew in. They hovered above the tribesmen's heads, bathing the chamber in warm sunlight.

The men gasped at the wonder.

Avalan took in the man's face. Stonemaster, Marebore had called him. Avalan had heard this title from his mother. *A stonemaster gifts the birthstones to newborns and teaches the tribes of their magic,* his mother had said in a sad voice. *But Bassalt doesn't allow them to come to our village.*

Avalan had asked her why she couldn't be the one to teach him, but his mother had reminded him he'd inherited his father's stone, the Bloodstone, and Farmera didn't know its ways. That was enough to convince Avalan he never wanted to learn a thing about his Bloodstone —why should he care about the stone of a man who had left behind his pregnant mother?

"All greet Stonemaster Delion!" Marebore shouted.

The men gave timid bows, uncertain of the proper way to welcome a stonemaster.

"You have the honor of standing in the same room as the man who has proved himself worthy of teaching the stones," Marebore declared. "This man is your chance of removing Bassalt from the village once and for all, and restoring the balance, for it was this man who taught Bassalt the ways of his birthstone."

Stonemaster Delion looked at them through clouded eyes. Then, unexpectedly, he bent his old back and sat on the floor. "Form a circle," he said, his voice the rasping of crumpled paper.

The men sat, while Marebore stood guard beside the cave's entrance. Avalan was the last to join the circle, after the gentle nudging of Eras.

"How much do you know about the past of Hydrus?" Delion asked of them.

Avalan's mind burned with unanswered questions, the history of the village not among them. *How did the stonemaster cross the mountain paths when no one knows the way but Ronan?*

"I thought we were here to train," Calos said. He was a heavy youth with cropped black hair and the liquid blue blessing of the Azurite stone in his eyes. "Why should we care about the past?"

The master traced a circle in the air. "The past can be a great teacher. Round and round it goes." He paused one moment, as if to pick his next words. "Tell me, what are you fighting for?"

"Freedom." They answered in unison.

"Hydrus was the greatest place of freedom—the epitome of it." The stonemaster shook frail arms to quiet the doubting whispers. "You cannot see it now because Bassalt has clouded your judgment. But if you knew … The village was founded more than a thousand years ago, and for a good number of these years, it was the only place where the tribes lived as one. People of all stones, together. Surely your parents have spoken to you about this."

Several heads nodded, and Avalan recalled a warm night when he had found Farmera whistling a sad tune. When she had lifted her eyes to regard him, she'd said Avalan reminded her of his father when he was young and they had first eloped to the village. *We thought we'd be safe here,* she had told Avalan, *he of the Bloodstone, I of the Amethyst.*

"All the stones were welcome here," the master said when none of the men answered.

"Even the Onyx?" Eras asked, earning glares and superstitious spitting.

The master raised a hand to cease the commotion. His eyes were so cloudy when he regarded Eras that Avalan wondered if the man was blind. "Even the Onyx. And if an Onyx has never set foot in Hydrus, it is of his own accord, for Hydrus welcomes all who want to be here. Now, tell me, how much do you know about your birthstones?"

The men shook their heads. They were all born after the war, after Bassalt had forbidden the stones' existence in the village and denied entrance to all stonemasters.

"Very fortunate," the master said, with a hint of mirth. "One can learn better when his head is empty." He faced Eras, patted the sand before him in invitation. "Let us start with you."

Eras hesitated. Avalan wiped sweat from his brows; the fire insects above their heads had raised the heat in the chamber. He leaned closer to Eras's ear to whisper. "How much of a threat is an old man who brings fireflies with him?" Eras grinned at that and took his place before the master.

"Tell us your stone," the stonemaster ordered.

"The Moonstone."

"The proud Moonstone indeed, but not any kind." He took Eras's hands in his, forming a small nest between their joined palms. A faint whisper left the stonemaster's mouth, and when he withdrew his hands, a glowing silver stone hovered in midair between Eras's palms.

It was a flawless sphere—a pearly full moon, mesmerizing and inviting.

Avalan admired it, forgetting for a moment the torment of the heat.

"The moon is shy," Delion taught them with passion. "Ofttimes it hides its face behind the night clouds, revealing but a part of its true self. But sometimes it forgoes all its inhibitions and shows itself in its full splendor, shining so bright it makes a watcher blind."

"Is it real?" Eras's gaze transfixed the floating stone.

"It is as real as your soul," the master told him. "Essentially, it is you. Know it, and you'll become it. Ignore it, and you'll never know who you truly are."

Avalan's heart clenched at the words. Ronan had oft recited the same words to him, only Avalan had always refused to listen to talk of birthstones.

"How do I know it?" Eras murmured.

The master waved his skeleton hand. "The Moonstone shines brighter when it's surrounded by darkness." And with that, he flicked his fingers and the silver sphere vanished.

Eras looked as though he'd just woken from a deep sleep. Dumbfounded, he stared at his empty palms. After he resumed his place by Avalan's side, the men were invited by the stonemaster in succession. Through the master's soft whispers, the stones sprang forth. Birthstones of all shapes and colors hovered over open palms, some glowing like stars in a midnight sky, others dark like shadows, and some so transparent they were barely visible.

Avalan studied the faces of the men. Their souls came alight with the realization of a power that lived inside them. The stones gave all kinds of emotions to their owners—anger, happiness, tears of joy, and sometimes a glint in the eyes that made Avalan wonder if the men were still in their right minds. He looked over at Eras, who sat quietly beside him with his head low, lost in his own thoughts. *Has the stone changed him?*

All the while, Avalan knew his turn wouldn't be far off. The waiting was the worst part. Uneasiness tugged at Avalan's chest, suffocating him.

What do I really know about my stone? He had inherited it from his father, Azirrad, who belonged to the great tribe of the Bloodstone. Avalan had no memory of him. Before Avalan had been born, his father had disappeared, leaving Farmera behind, and he was never to be heard of again. Growing up, Avalan had listened to his mother weeping deep into the night, until one day her eyes had dried, and she spoke of him no more.

How can I trust a thing that caused so much pain? Why did I have to inherit Azirrad's Bloodstone instead of Farmera's Amethyst? Once revealed, what will my father's Bloodstone do to me?

At long last, the stonemaster called him forth. Unsure he was ready, Avalan sat before him. He closed his eyes and surrendered his palms. The master's bony touch was warm, quieting the voices inside Avalan's mind.

"Whatever happens, don't move your hands." The master's grip became tighter, and he whispered, "I wish to see."

Liquid warmth spread from the master's touch, crawled up Avalan's body. When it reached his face, Avalan's forehead burned with fever. Gasps filled the chamber. He opened his eyes to find his stone within the nest of his palms: a dark green, earthy gem, splattered with blood spots, just like his own eyes. Shaped like a teardrop, the stone reminded Avalan of his mother's weeping. His chest tightened, his breathing became faster, shallower.

"Behold the Bloodstone," the master said with a glint in his eyes. "A stone of leaders and blood magic. Liquid crimson, it flows in your veins, from the heart to the soul."

Unsure of what to do, Avalan remained silent. Sweat broke through his skin, his whole body alert to danger. *I do not trust it.* It was then he heard it—a voice, colorless and demanding, calling out his name.

Avalan.

He looked around him, but salty sweat trickled down his forehead, stinging his eyes. "Who are you?"

Come to me, the voice whispered inside his head.

Avalan shivered with fever. He blinked wildly now, resisting the urge to wipe his brow, for fear of losing the stone. "Where are you?"

Find me.

His vision cleared in time to see the blood spots widen, consuming the stone's surface, until it became a sanguine teardrop. A rain of blood dripped from the stone onto Avalan's open palms. The drops touched his skin, burning their way through it. Avalan screamed, parted his hands, and the stone vanished.

"Avalan!" Eras gripped his shoulders. "Your hands!"

Avalan stared at his palms. Swollen blisters covered his skin. Confused, he flexed his fingers, only to be rewarded with a fresh bout of pain.

Stonemaster Delion studied the wounds. "Look at your hands," he said, peering into Avalan's eyes. "I'm afraid it will leave a mark."

Avalan twisted away from the old man's grip. "What did you do?"

In the dim firefly light, the stonemaster looked fragile, a twig ready to snap under a heel.

"It spoke to me!" Avalan yelled at him, his chest drenched with sweat. "Why did you let it hurt me?"

"It wasn't him. It was the stone." Eras wrapped his arms around Avalan's shoulders. "You were talking to yourself!"

The master stared at him, the cloudy veil that obscured the true nature of his birthstone vibrating as if assaulted by a great storm. In his eyes, Avalan perceived fear and a strange pleading. The shame of the old man was too much to bear. Avalan gritted his teeth and headed for the tunnel.

"Not so fast!" Marebore blocked the entrance.

"Let me pass. I don't care about the stones." Avalan thrust his scorched palms into Marebore's face. "And it's clear they don't care about me either. My work here is done."

"You were the one who brought these men together. Will you abandon the cause because of a small wound? The stones can be great allies."

Avalan clenched his fists. "The clang of steel in my hands overpowers the whispers of the birthstones. Look for me when you've decided you want to fight Bassalt with weapons and not rely on whimsical rocks that change their ways as they see fit and hurt their own."

Marebore brushed his fingers over his Ruby. "You insult things you know nothing of. I insist you stay, for you will want to hear what we have to say." Marebore stepped toward the dazed crowd. "The stones hold great power, as you have witnessed. But none of you was raised under their teachings. We don't expect you to understand them yet, only to accept them, for a stone-enchanted weapon is much more powerful than a bare one."

The repetition of Ronan's words from their meeting in the forest stopped Avalan in his tracks. He turned. Ronan had something to do with this, Avalan now knew. It would explain how the frail stone-master had crossed the mountains, and why Ronan's journey had been much longer than any other. As powerful as the stonemaster may be with the birthstones, he was a frail man who crawled with the pace of a turtle.

Marebore wore a triumphant smirk on his lips. "Care to stay, then?"

"Speak," Avalan said, the pain in his hands forgotten. "What is your plan?"

"We train with birthstones on weapons. Then we shall attack Bassalt during the Night of the Spirits."

Gasps swept the air.

Avalan bit his lip. Marebore's choice was more than fitting. The Night of the Spirits was a revered tradition, an ode to the late chief and a celebration of the present one. During the great feast, the chief's chair was placed in the middle of the feasting ground, surrounded by offerings of food and drink. If the former chief's spirit was pleased with the ruling of the current leader, the seat remained empty, and the chief could sit on it for one more year. Should the spirit of the late chief prove to be dissatisfied, tales told, it would occupy the seat until a more suitable chief was chosen.

Each Night of the Spirits, Avalan had hoped it would be Bassalt's last. He waited for the spirit of Volkan, Hydrus's late chief, to come and challenge Bassalt's reign. Yet the seat always remained empty, and Bassalt would smirk and sit on it and call for a sumptuous feast. He would laugh, drink, and pick his ugly teeth with starling bones until they were stained red with blood and wine. After seeing Bassalt sit on the chief's seat time and time again, Avalan had lost his faith in the spirits. And judging by the number of men gathered here tonight, he was not the only one. If the spirits would not remove Bassalt from his place, someone else had to.

"Marebore is right," Colgar said. "Bassalt will be drunk. He won't stay awake past the rising of the stars. This is when we should attack. When his belly is full and his eyelids heavy."

"Don't forget his servants will be there," Eras said. "They won't be drunk. Bassalt never allows them to lower their guard. There's also Silver and his men."

Marebore brushed his Ruby. "Leave them to me. Silver never managed to attach his stone to his body. He carries it on his sword. Should he lose it, then …" He bared his teeth.

Avalan frowned. "How will we get our birthstones?"

"Ronan," Marebore said. "He's returning to the village with birthstones hidden among his wares." He pointed at the stonemaster, who remained on the floor, silent and unmoving. "Stonemaster Delion will teach you how to harvest the power of your stones and transfer them to your weapons."

Avalan touched the dirk on his belt, thinking of the stone hollow that lacked a Bloodstone. *That can be arranged,* the merchant had said to him. Was Ronan's sack heavy with the weight of birthstones? Was that the reason he had wished to keep his arrival a secret? Yet Ronan had told him nothing of Marebore's plan.

"The Night of the Spirits is only a few nights away," Avalan said. "We know nothing of the stones."

"You are children no more," Marebore told him. "Men can learn the teachings of the stones faster. Return here on the morrow, and we shall begin your training."

Avalan had his doubts. But then, one after another, the men nodded.

"We're ready," Calos said, bringing a fist to his chest. "We might not be able archers such as you, Avalan, but I can wield a spear."

Five more fishermen grunted.

Avalan stared at the stonemaster, but Delion seemed to be deep in thought or even sleeping—his chest barely rose. Heart heavy, Avalan stared at his blistered hands. *What choice remains to me?* Even with the mending touch of his mother, it could take a long time for his wounds to heal. If a stone could strengthen his arrows, then … "Let it be so."

Silently he crossed the stony passage. This time, Marebore didn't obstruct him.

Once out, Avalan gulped the crisp air. A cool breeze chased away the cavern's cursed heat. He took the path back to the fence, his anger ebbing with every step. He would think about Marebore's words tomorrow. Now he longed for a good sleep.

At the easternmost corner of the village, the white poplar that housed his home peeked over the long palisade. Avalan had chosen this part of the fence because of the curve that forced the beams to be placed shorter. Avalan grabbed a sturdy vine to hoist himself up. He cursed out loud when a blister on his hand burst, but kept going despite the pain. By the time he'd climbed through the opening that served as both window and door to his small house, his palms dripped with fresh blood.

Silence greeted him; the corner where Sigil slept stood empty.

His bed creaked as he collapsed onto it. The swollen blisters on his hands gaped at him, a painful reminder of what an encounter with the stone produced.

Avalan clenched his fists. He'd never cared about magic, and he wasn't sure he should care even now, after all that had been said tonight. Of course, he had witnessed the power of the birthstones, but how could Marebore ask him to trust a thing that had burned his hands?

The raging storm in the stonemaster's eyes still haunted him. If Eras was right, and it was the stone's doing and not the master's, Avalan hated to think what that meant. *Perhaps the Bloodstone doesn't like me as much as I don't trust it.*

Being an able hunter, Avalan knew fear was a man's worst enemy when he faced an unfamiliar beast. The body of a fearful man reeked with a mistrust that invited animosity. *Did my Bloodstone punish me for this mistrust?*

Avalan watched the shadows on the ceiling change as the sun set. Soothing silence entered his head and his room. When he felt his eyelids become heavy with the need for sleep, he rose and went to the trunk at the foot of his bed. After pushing the lid open, he let the dirk fall inside.

He stared at it for some moments before he slammed the lid shut.

CHAPTER FIVE

The girl's fever eased at dusk, as the last of the daylight painted the walls of Farmera's house a warm crimson. Relief washed over Lusha. She wiped her palms on her apron, the smell of the healing paste so strong she tasted its sweetness in her mouth.

"You did well," Farmera said. "By the first light of tomorrow, she will be well again."

Lusha hoped it would be so. She brushed Ivory's auburn hair off her clammy face. The child lay on the sickbed, her eyelids leaden. Through her pale lips escaped the whispers of an exhausted sleep.

Lusha looked up at Farmera. "The last concoction proved effective. Pulp of sweet-smelling nightflowers, a drop of the lake's water, and cinnamon."

Farmera smiled. "Thank the stones. I feared for her." She padded her way to the cooking bench. "Come. I'll warm us some spiced wine. We deserve it."

Lusha nodded but didn't leave the bedside. As Farmera prepared their celebratory drink, she watched the child's chest closely, making sure it rose and fell with shallow breaths. In her mind, Lusha could still hear Ivory's mother cry for help when her daughter had collapsed from a bout of fever that wouldn't abate. Lusha had carried the child to Farmera's home herself, and she had stayed by her side all day. Together they had sluiced Ivory's hair with cool water from the Crystal

Lake, dabbed her nose with shadowgrass essence, and poured through her parted lips all kinds of potions to ease her suffering. Thankfully, the last one they'd given her had caused her tiny body to sweat.

Farmera placed two earthen cups on the table. "Come."

Lusha staggered to feet numb from hours of kneeling. As she took her place on the bench, Farmera lit short candles of brown tallow and carried one over to their table. Lusha waited for her to sit before she gulped a mouthful of wine. Warmth spread through her empty belly; fresh sweetness stung her lips.

"What did you use this time?" Lusha asked.

"Pepper, cinnamon, and cloves," Farmera sang.

Lusha smiled and drained her cup. Farmera's wine was always the tastiest; her house was filled with cupboards teeming with spices, herbs, and flowers—some plucked from the forest of Hydrus, others brought to her by Ronan from his various trips. The pale flames that licked the cauldron's bottom caught her eye. Lusha wondered how wine tasted north of the mountains. *Soon I will know.*

"What's on your mind, sweet child?"

Lusha lowered her cup. Despite their hard day, Farmera's face shone with love, the Amethyst stones in her eyes glinting with true interest. "You're always so good to me. Like a real mother."

"You can talk to me, my love. Tell me what torments you."

Lusha's gaze flickered to the bloodied linens soaking in the trough. "Is this Eras's blood?"

Farmera nodded, a shadow crossing her face.

"I meant to ask Avalan about him." Lusha was suddenly embarrassed for having remembered much too late. What with the sick child and Ronan's return, she had forgotten to look for Avalan. "Silver told me Eras was punished for insolence."

Farmera tapped her fingers on the table. "He carried a birthstone—his father's Moonstone—for luck in the game. When the crowd hoisted him, it fell. Bassalt whipped him before the tribe to remind them all that birthstones are forbidden."

Lusha's chest tightened. Six years ago, Bhoran had gifted her a Moonstone, but after the snake's attack, she hadn't found it, no matter how hard she'd searched. "Why did Bassalt spare me?"

"How do you mean, child?"

"When Bhoran took me to the statue of Olnos that goat game night, he gave me a Moonstone. After the snake attacked me, they brought me here. To you." She paused, searched Farmera's eyes. "When I woke up … it was gone. Did you perchance …?"

"Did I perchance find it and withhold it from your father and Bassalt?"

Hot blood rushed to Lusha's cheeks. "I beg your forgiveness, Farmera. I know I shouldn't talk about these things."

Without a word, Farmera stood and fastened the hut's door, making the light in the room dimmer. She returned to the bench. "I shall say this only once, and I want you to believe me. If I had found the Moonstone on you, I would have saved it until you had gotten better, and returned it to you. A birthstone belongs with its owner, and cursed are those who try to meddle." She rubbed her eyes. Dark circles sat beneath her lower lids. "Though what good is a birthstone if you don't know how to use it? Perhaps if your mother were still alive … You got her eyes, her stone, her kindness for life."

"My mother," Lusha whispered longingly. Of late, she had been thinking about her with renewed fervor. She'd never met her, as her mother had died shortly after giving birth to Lusha, of an illness none were willing to talk about. "Tell me about her. Tell me what took her."

Farmera's eyes flicked to the sleeping Ivory. "There is no use in dwelling on the past. Your mother loved you. Know this, and do not think about that cursed sickness."

"You must tell me. Silver never talks to me about her. But I know he loved her … He never took another to his bed. And there are times I catch him staring at me not with his usual disapproval but with love … I know he doesn't see *me.* It is her he's seeing."

"You resemble her closely. She was as beautiful and fair."

Lusha leaned closer. "Farmera, you're the greatest healer I've ever known. You must know what sickness took her."

The Amethysts in Farmera's eyes darkened. "There are healers much greater than I will ever be. I'm a mere herbalist, child. Your mother, though … she was one of the most gifted moonhealers." She peered into Lusha's eyes. "Those born under the Moonstone are blessed with powers beyond potions and ointments. No wonder you're stepping onto your mother's path."

Her words gave Lusha comfort. She was glad she'd inherited Amara's Moonstone and not her father's Heliodor.

Farmera went on. "When your father brought her to Hydrus, she had already mastered the ways of her Moonstone. We were both girls then. Younger even than you are now. Your mother had this spark in her. You'd have thought she'd never die. Yet one day ... she fell gravely ill, right after the Onyx attacked our village. The sickness was so swift, so vile ... It spread through her like a storm."

Lusha gulped. Silver had once told her of how the Onyx had penetrated Hydrus shortly after Lusha had been born. Though the battle had been short, many lives had been lost. The village had once boasted the number of a thousand souls. "What did this sickness do to her?"

"It started with fever. Your mother's head burned for three days and three nights. She spoke words unknown, and her eyes were unseeing. When the end came and we undressed her, her body was covered with curious blotches of purple and blue. It was as if her blood had spilled beneath her skin."

Lusha shuddered. "Did she suffer much?"

"No, my love. The end came swiftly, and it was dully welcomed."

A leaden silence fell in the room and Lusha's heart. Farmera took both their cups and stood, breaking the spell. Lusha watched as she dipped a ladle into the cauldron and refilled their cups with warm, sweet-smelling wine. Despite the warmth of the first days of summer, a coldness spread to her core.

"I don't remember her. I can't remember her face."

"How could you? You were but a baby, only a moonturn old. They kept you away from her, lest she give you the sickness."

Lusha's heart sank. She would have liked to hear that her mother had held her, kissed her forehead, whispered to her words of farewell and strength to deal with a world without the loving touch of a mother.

"In her last moments, she sent for me," Farmera said, words of comfort. "She asked me to take care of you. To love you like my own daughter."

Farmera had done more than that, Lusha knew. "Thank you."

"I would have done it whether she had asked or not."

Lusha swirled the wine in her cup for some moments. "Do you think Bassalt knows what that sickness was? He seems to hold more knowledge than us."

"Knowing the magic of the stones is one thing, but using it to heal, another. Bassalt showed no interest in using his powers to comfort an ailing body." Farmera shifted closer. "Lusha, you need not fear this sickness. Though Silver ordered us to keep you away from your mother, I did not think she could have given it to you. Not then, not now. You're as healthy as a woman can be."

Lusha bit her lip, ashamed to mislead Farmera in this way. If only for all those years of motherly love she had given her, she deserved the truth. Slipping two slender fingers under the collar of her dress, Lusha found her mother's pendant nestled against her warm bosom. She placed it between them. Against the wooden surface, the carved silver pendant seemed to her so small, yet when Lusha wore it, she felt as if she carried a great burden.

Farmera studied it under the light of the candles. "I remember this," she whispered with amusement. "It belonged to Amara. Your mother."

"This is the only thing I have of her," Lusha said.

Farmera turned it over.

"It doesn't open," Lusha told her. "I have asked Ronan many a time. There is a small slot at the bottom. Ronan says that's where the key goes, but I've never found one in our house."

Farmera laid it on the table. "It's beautiful."

"It's not enough." Lusha searched for the right words. "I want—I *need* more. And Ronan is going to help me get it."

Farmera set her ebony locks behind her ears. "Whatever do you mean?"

"Ronan will help me leave the village, as he did with Crystal. He'll take me to my mother's city—"

"Lusha."

"No, please hear me. I know how it sounds, but I can't stay here any longer. My father ..." Tears ran down her cheeks.

Farmera rounded the table and closed her arms around her in a tight embrace that smelled of lavender and fennel. "Now, now. Your father is rough, but he holds a great love for you."

"It's not only that ..."

Tracing the silver scar over Lusha's face, Farmera said, "No, it's not. It's your love for Bhoran. I should have known the moment you tied your hair back to reveal your scar."

"I've let you down."

Farmera gave her a sad smile. "That could never happen. It's only ... I thought time would heal your wounds. Yours and Avalan's. I thought perhaps you two ... I know he loves you greatly."

"It's Crystal he loves," Lusha reminded her. "And I can't forget Bhoran. I keep seeing him all around me. At times, I hear his voice in my head, calling my name." Fresh tears dribbled down her cheeks. "There will be no other man for me."

"Oh, sweet child, stark words for a solemn moment." Farmera sighed. "It won't be easy. Your father will come after you tooth and nail."

"Then I will run to the corners of the lands."

Farmera cupped her chin. "You are determined. I can see it in the stones of your eyes. If it will be so, then you should know your mother had a sister—Shelanna was her name. Last I heard, she lived in Levorotha. Go to her. At least this way, you'll be among family, and I won't have broken my promise to your mother."

Shelanna. Lusha had never heard that name before. Silver had always refused to talk about Amara's family. Her heart now lifted. There was someone who knew her mother, had grown up beside her, and could tell her all the things Lusha had wished to know ever since she'd been a little girl. "Silver never told me."

Farmera's lips twitched, as if with shame. She passed the pendant over Lusha's hair and let it fall over her chest. "Now you know." She kissed her eyelids. "Rest now, my child, and we shall talk again when Ronan returns."

He already has, Lusha thought, but she didn't want to break her promise to the merchant. She hugged Farmera one last time and stroked Ivory's clammy cheeks before she left.

Dusk had settled over the village. Carefully Lusha trotted over the sown mounds of soil in the garden and threw a black fur-lined cloak over her body, tucking her hair beneath its hood. Despite the heat, she had to endure its embrace. During the full moon, she and the tribe both preferred her night strolls to be under the cover of fur. Better a shadow in the night than a glowing ghost.

Eras had also been born under the Moonstone, as had his late father. Yet neither of them had ever glowed under the full moon. It seemed this strange gift the Moonstone had reserved just for Lusha—a thing to taunt her, to make her feel even more like she did not belong.

Yet Lusha didn't much mind it anymore. She knew the full moon wouldn't last long—perhaps a fortnight more before it waned and her skin would no longer shine blue under its light, scaring the tribe.

As she passed the bushes that concealed the trench Avalan had dug, she glanced at it, half-expecting to see his smiling face peeking through the thorns. The shrubs didn't move, but a small stone crunched beneath her sole, making her trip and almost lose her footing.

Her mouth dried. It was but a small pebble, yet it was enough to make her father's words echo in her head. *A chieftain's daughter never stoops. She fixes her gaze ahead. This way, she knows where she's going before she gets there.*

She rubbed the top of her shoulder. Though it had been years since her father had last strapped a sack full of stones over her back to shift her posture, she still felt it from time to time. As if the burden would always follow her every step.

Lusha frowned at the dread in her heart. *I'm only worried because I know I'll run away. Silver doesn't know; he can't know.* She was almost home now.

Resting atop fourteen wooden beams, her father's house was ten feet above the ground. A blanket of sun-dried coconut leaves covered the roof, casting a deep, cooling shadow. The house had no walls. In their place, a line of waist-high wooden rails surrounded the top story. *These rotten beams can't even stop a sleepwalker from falling to his death,* Avalan had always jested since they were children.

Lusha sensed something was amiss as soon as she drew closer.

Urgent, gruff whispers tore the air. Crouching, she hid among the wooden beams and peered up from beneath her hood.

The silhouettes of three men—one of them belonging to her father—paced the upper floor. Lusha frowned. Her father's men would never dare come to his house unless they bore news of the utmost importance. She slid through the shadows and climbed the wooden staircase, avoiding all its creaking spots. The voices became clearer.

"Where is he now?" her father demanded.

"Where we found him, Chieftain." Lusha recognized Gremian's steady voice. She had always wondered how a man whose hands always trembled carried such sureness in his speech.

Silver grunted, and Gremian was quick to add, "I've left two of our men to watch over him."

"Does Bassalt know?"

"No," Gremian assured him. "We came straight to you."

"See that it remains this way. I need to see it for myself first."

Lusha climbed a couple more steps and craned her neck forward to take a closer look. The three men seemed to be in great distress. Silver paced the room, wearing only dark gray breeches. Blue veins throbbed under the pale skin of his chest, like rivers rushing to the sea. The wrinkles on his face seemed deeper than ever. Gremian stood awkwardly in the middle, his trembling hands stretched out to his sides. Leaning against the beam, head low, chest heaving, was Fyridion. Both of her father's most trusted men wore breeches soaked in sweat, as if they had made their way here running.

At last her father ceased his pacing and faced Gremian. "You're certain it's *him*?" he asked, dragging his words out, daring his man to think twice about his answer.

"Well, I daresay, Chieftain, he looks different, but ... but his eyes ..."

Lusha raised a brow at Gremian's falter. *Whose eyes have scared him so much?*

"I see." Her father pointed to the bucket of clean water beside the table. "Clean yourself up as I'm getting ready. You'll take me to him."

Gremian bent to the floor. He dipped his trembling hands in and out of the water, scrubbing them thoroughly, while Silver disappeared behind the reed parapet of his room.

A few moments later, her father returned, wearing his green-scaled vest, his sword sheathed and secured against his belt. "Fyridion," he commanded. "Find Lusha and bring her home. She mustn't hear about this. Tell her she is to stay here until I've returned."

Lusha leaped down the stairs just as the men descended. She threw herself into the bushes. There she lurked until they took the path that led to the south entrance. Then she raced upstairs. She headed for the bucket Gremian had used to clean his hands. A metallic smell filled her nose. The water in the bucket was still and dark. Lusha's stomach churned. *Is it blood?*

Something terrible must have happened, or her father wouldn't have left in such haste, barking orders for her incarceration and for concealing their find from Bassalt.

She threw the cloak over her head once more and rushed down. *They must have passed through the southern gate by now, heading for the forest.*

Lusha crawled through Avalan's secret trench. Thorns tugged at her cloak and scratched her face, but she ignored the pain—if she was to follow them, she had to be quick.

The other side of the fence was quiet. She shimmied behind the thick trunk of a blackwood tree and stilled for a few moments, unsure of whether she should wait or march forth. Then the low, serious voice of her father echoed in the silence.

"Has he said anything?"

"Not a word, Chieftain," Gremian said solemnly as they hastened through the woods.

"Make sure the men don't spread words about this before I've had the chance to talk with Bassalt."

"As you wish."

The two men remained quiet for the rest of the way. Lusha followed right behind them, leaping over fallen branches, making sure she didn't land in any sinks. Shafts of silver moonlight shone through thick branches, forcing Lusha to keep pulling the cloak around her. One flash of her skin would be enough to betray her.

Beads of sweat crowned her lips when the two men finally halted. Lusha's foot caught a rising root. Grabbing the bark of the rude tree, she held her balance.

"Who goes there?" demanded Silver, his hand ready on the hilt of his sword.

Lusha threw herself into a patch of nearby nettles, biting her lip at the stinging pain. She prayed hard her father wouldn't notice her; she wasn't ready to face his fury or, worse, to be held in the house against her will without first finding out what had happened in the forest.

Silver swung his sword around like a walking stick, poking through the dense undergrowth here and there. Lusha bit her lip as her father approached her hiding place. She would be forced to jump out, she knew, or risk facing his well-polished blade.

"Perhaps an animal," Gremian suggested.

Silver grunted, lifted his blade ...

"Chieftain?" A voice came through the woods. A young man with fiery hair and a grin of relief upon his freckled face limped toward them, holding a loaded bow. He lowered his weapon and placed the arrow he had been preparing to unleash back into the leather quiver around his shoulder. "You scared the life out of me. It's good you're here, though. You'd think we wouldn't be scared, but even the glowing moon can't chase away the shadows of this place. What with the body and—"

"Quit gabbling, Lhorin," Silver barked. "Lead me straight to him."

Lhorin didn't quail at her father's rough words. "Over here, Chieftain, at the bottom of this cliff." He led the way, putting most of his weight on his right leg, dragging the left one along.

Lusha was relieved to see Lhorin. Most of her father's men wouldn't even meet her eye, as if doing so would offend her precious maidenhood. But Lhorin was different. Despite his efforts, he couldn't conceal that he was besotted with her. Whenever he saw Lusha, he'd put on his toothiest grin and show off his archery skills. One time, he had pinned Gremian's breeches to the trunk of a tree, trying to impress her. Lhorin had laughed heartily about it; Gremian had not.

Slowly Lusha emerged from her hiding place. Men's voices rose from below. When she broke free from the clutches of the ruthless bush, her dress was shredded, and her pale limbs were covered with small grazes, bloody rivulets trickling from them. Over the edge of the cliff, she peeked down.

Silver and his men were standing above the body of a man. Torches illuminated his head. It rested in a dark pool of blood, which mingled with the clear water of a running brook. His throat had been sliced open, leaving behind a gaping wound. Lusha met his lifeless stare. Her blood froze.

Ronan. No …

She bit her fist, trying to suppress a scream. Could her eyes have betrayed her? She looked again. Stones forbid, it was the ashen face of Ronan.

Stomach churning, she swallowed back the spiced wine that rose to her throat. With a clammy palm, she wiped her mouth and looked behind her. Could she find her way back to the village? She'd have to tell Avalan about it. *Oh, how it will break his heart.* Ronan had been the father Avalan had never had. *And my only hope for freedom.*

But that was now gone. Perhaps it had been bold of her to hope. Hot tears streaked her face, yet she didn't rise. She crawled to the edge once more, wishing to regard the poor merchant.

"What was he doing out here?" Silver demanded of Gremian, as if the man had all the answers.

"Returning from his trading trip, most like."

"Did any of you know of his arrival?" When his men shook their heads, he frowned. "He is far from the mountain path. Where is his sack?"

Gremian exchanged quick glances with the rest of the men. "We found nothing of his belongings."

Silver knelt to examine the body. He took the merchant's limp hand in his, studied the fingers. "He didn't fight back." Then, tracing the morbid gash in Ronan's throat, he added, "Clean, swift cut. Whoever killed him was no stranger to knives. Where is the weapon?"

The men shuffled their feet and mumbled among themselves.

"Well?" Silver rose. "Did you not find it?"

"We've found it all right, Chieftain." Gremian's voice shivered. "It's only that none of us has dared to touch it …"

"Have you gone all weak in the knees? Let me see it."

Gremian pointed at a place on the ground. "Over there."

Lusha watched her father bend down a few paces away from Ronan's body. She waited for him to pick the weapon up, curious to see what blade had caused her father's men to cower, but whatever lay on the ground was left there, as her father didn't dare lift it.

Silver frowned and rose. "Has anybody touched it?"

"Only *him*, Chieftain," Gremian said gravely. "We found him over the body. He threw the weapon to the side when we caught him, and nobody has touched it since."

"Where is he?" Silver barked. "Take me to him. Now!"

Lhorin pointed at some thick ferns on the other side of the running brook. "We thought it best to keep him away from the body before he did any more damage."

Lusha's heartbeat quickened; she knew she couldn't leave without glimpsing the man who had taken away Ronan's life. When Silver leaped over the brook, his men were quick to follow. Ronan's body was left lying there, unprotected.

Knowing this might be her only chance to closely regard the merchant, Lusha clambered down the cliff.

The sweet smell of death clung to the merchant's body, making her wince. She knelt beside him. His once-azure eyes had lost their shine, as the light of his stone had left them. It was hard to see him so unmoving. Ronan had been born under the Larimar, the most beautiful waterstone Lusha had ever seen, and he, just like the water, had never been able to stay still. Lusha had always enjoyed his tales of cities that never slept, filled with laughter and celebrations. *My beautiful Lusha,* he used to tell her, *one day I'll take you with me to show you the lands. A gem like you should never be kept in the shadows.*

But now, here he lay, dead beyond doubt, and Lusha would never have the chance to experience that beautiful world with him. Or go to Levorotha and meet her aunt. "My poor little merchant. Who could have done this to you?" she whispered, her fingertips sliding gently over the swollen eyelids. She pulled them down.

Then she remembered ... *The map.*

A strange longing to have it overtook her, as though she could still find her way out of Hydrus. It was a foolish notion, she realized, for she knew not how to read. And yet … she brushed the sides of Ronan's breeches, where she had last seen him tuck away the map. Her fingertips met with the rolled parchment. Trembling, she fished it out and concealed it against her bosom.

Through eyes that stung with fresh tears, she searched the ground for the weapon. Avalan would want to know. Gremian had pointed somewhere around here, but she couldn't see anything. There wasn't much time, she knew; she needed to cross the brook, conceal herself, and glimpse at the killer …

As she stood, she met Lhorin's freckled face. He stared at her, lips apart, as if ready to shout. Lusha brought a finger to her lips, pleading with him to not betray her. When she made to cross the brook, Lhorin grabbed her arm and pulled her behind a thicket of low shrubs.

"What are you doing here?" he whispered in her face. His breath smelled of sweet plums. It made her sick all over.

"Ronan's dead," she told him, as if this cold truth would distract his attention from her unexpected presence.

"I know." Lhorin's distressed face was a rare sight. Lusha had never seen him so much as frown before. "You can't be here, Lusha." He flicked his eyes to the other side of the brook. "Are you alone?"

"Whom did you catch out there? Who killed Ronan?"

Lhorin's gaze lingered on her face. For a mere moment, Lusha was certain she discerned pity in his eyes, mixed with something else—jealousy … perhaps even anger. It seemed Lhorin was fighting something inside him while trying to decide what to do with her.

"You can't give me up, Lhorin. Ronan was my friend." Her voice cracked. "I deserve to know who killed him."

"You need to leave. Now."

"I'll leave after I've seen whom you—"

"Shh," he hissed. "You leave *now*."

"My father's set Fyridion on me," she said, expecting some kind of explanation.

At that, Lhorin tightened his grip on her arm.

"You're hurting me."

"I'm only trying to protect you."

"I'm doing fine on my own. Either you give me up or let me see whom you've got there."

At last Lhorin gave in and let her go. Lusha rubbed her arm and crept through the bushes until she heard the whispering voices of her father's men.

Across the brook lay a small clearing. Silver and his men encircled a man who sat on the ground. Lusha crept closer to catch a better glimpse of the killer's face. At first she thought she didn't recognize this strange-looking young man, yet a second glance was enough to rekindle the fire of hope that had been smoldering in her heart all these years. It was *him*—he looked different, but she *knew* it was him.

Bhoran.

His once-slim body was now full of swollen muscles. Across his chest, etched with black ink, ran a chain of intertwined trigons. Like a wide necklace, it stretched from one shoulder to the other. Then down his right arm it spiraled, ending on his wrist. His head was shaved at the sides, the pale blond hair on top elaborately braided in the pattern of a turtle shell. Sharp fangs pierced his ears, and several more transfixed the corners of his brows and chin. A nasty scar ran over his right eye, the stone inside it dark and empty, like the Onyx.

Silver held the tip of his sword against the soft notch in Bhoran's neck.

Lusha's heart pounded faster. Her mouth dried. *No. It cannot be …*

Lhorin grabbed her just as she made to launch forth. In her ear, he whispered again and again, "I'm sorry."

CHAPTER SIX

THE NIGHTMARE ALWAYS RETURNED.

In the heart of the feasting ground, Bassalt stood alone beneath a deathly silence. The absence of sound made his chest pound, his knees go weak, his eyes dart to every corner of the fence, searching, scouring, trying to pierce the veil that clouded his judgment. Then came the Onyx ring—this cursed gem held by the snake. It grew and grew, like a dark cloud over his head, looming, watching, waiting ... Darkness descended, a pitch-black whirling mist. Black sand whipped his skin, stung his eyes. His long cloak billowed and twisted around his body, tighter and tighter, until he could no longer breathe.

"My chief?"

Bassalt gasped, fighting the strangling cloak, only to realize it was his bedsheet.

From above, Theran peered at him, the light of a tallow candle casting dour shadows across his bony face. "My chief, I regret having to wake you, but you have guests."

"Guests?" Bassalt choked on his own spit. He coughed hard. The room was drenched in darkness. "At this hour? Have you lost your mind?"

"No, no ..." Theran stole a stealthy glance at the closed door. "Silver is insisting on being the one who tells you, but I think I should give you warning."

Bassalt threw the bedsheets off and tightened his robe around his girth. "Silver is here? The bloody man is paying me with my own coin because I plucked him out of his bed that time. Is that it?"

"I'm afraid the news is dire, my chief."

"Speak, then, before I lose my patience!"

Theran gulped. "It is Ronan … They found him dead in the forest. Slit throat."

Bassalt rubbed the sleep from his eyes. *Cursed, cursed,* he thought. *Keep your calm.* "Dead, you say? Is this a jest?"

"I'm afraid not, my chief." Theran's lips trembled. He brought the candle nearer his face, the flame dancing dangerously close to his brown locks. "And there is more. Something worse—"

"Worse?" Bassalt thundered, staggering to his feet. "You tell me our only connection with the Stone Lands is dead! What worse fate have the stones in store for us? Speak, damn you!" Bassalt raised a fat palm before Theran's face, as if he'd changed his mind. "Or don't. We're wasting time. Show Silver in. Why are you gaping at me in this way? We must find whoever did this!"

Theran's eyes bulged. "Your brother, my chief."

Bassalt cast him a curious glance. "What do you mean, my *brother*?"

"Why, I only meant the boy … although he looks a boy no more, if I might say—"

Bassalt grabbed his manservant's collar. "What is it you're saying?"

"Bhoran … It's Bhoran, my chief. Your stepbrother. Silver's men found him over Ronan's body."

Bassalt released Theran with such force the poor man stumbled. *Can it be true? Can the stones be in our favor after all?* The tightness in his chest eased. He suppressed a bout of laughter that rose to his chest. Then, he drew his lips back in a grotesque smile. "Show them in."

Theran studied him as if he thought him ill. "Will … will you require my presence, my chief?"

"No."

At his dismissal, Theran used the candle to light the oil lamps in the room. Fickle flames bathed the chamber in golden-brown light. He cast Bassalt a worried glance before he crept to the door. "I shall be without, should you need me."

Mere moments after Theran had left, the oaken door burst open. Silver and his men dragged a man in. Under the dim light, Theran's earlier words proved true; Bhoran indeed was a boy no more, Bassalt saw. Instead, he was a man—one whose appearance would have scared Bassalt had they not been in his basalt chamber, where his power was at its greatest.

Silver forced Bhoran to a chair. "One move, and I'll let them have at you," he warned.

Bhoran shot him an angry glare but didn't deign to answer.

Silver skipped the greetings when he faced Bassalt. "Theran has told you?"

"Indeed he has." Bassalt clucked his tongue, edged closer to his stepbrother. "I never thought to see you again, *brother*. But then again, the stones have plans of their own. Our merchant. A slit throat, I hear. Why?"

Bhoran raised his eyes to him, the cold, blank stare of the Onyx stone. He spat at Bassalt's bare feet.

Silver slapped him hard. "You filthy—"

"There is no need as yet for violence." Bassalt spoke over him. Then, turning to Silver's men, he said, "Leave us."

The men waited for Silver's gesture of approval before they took their leave, a thing Bassalt noted with great displeasure. He didn't much like their allegiance lying with the commander. That was why ofttimes he displayed his stone power before the tribe. Bhoran's fortunate capture now offered him another chance to remind the tribe of who held the ultimate might.

Once the door closed, Bassalt faced Silver. "Where is the weapon?"

"This was found at the spot." Silver presented him with a wrapped-up item. "It bears his stone."

Bassalt unfolded the old rag. Inside he found the golden dagger, the blunt blade dark with dried blood, a pitch-black stone embedded into its hilt. *Filthy Onyx,* he thought, trying to keep a straight face. *Cursed, cursed.* "A fine weapon," he mused aloud. "Whence did you steal it, brother?"

Bhoran clenched his jaw and dropped his gaze.

"Look at me when I talk to you. Did you use this to kill the merchant?"

"Speak!" Silver ordered, raising a threatening arm. When Bhoran didn't answer, he turned to Bassalt. "My men found him standing over the merchant's body, dagger in hand. He tossed it away before they got closer, but they *know* what they saw."

Bassalt studied Bhoran curiously. Fangs and claws pierced his face. His skin was paler than Bassalt remembered, as if his stepbrother rarely saw the light of day anymore. "Will your men say before the tribe they saw him holding the weapon?" he asked Silver.

"They will."

"That settles it, then. Take him. We'll hold an open trial tomorrow."

"A trial? We should punish him at once—"

Bassalt raised his hand. The snake ring caught the oily light and glistened. "Ask Theran to show you the way to the cellar. Keep him there. Tomorrow his punishment will be decided before the tribe."

"If this is another scheme of yours to have him land in feathers," Silver warned, "I swear, this time I won't let it pass. It is enough to scar my daughter for life, but *killing* Ronan ... Murder shall be repaid with murder."

From the corner of his eye, Bassalt saw Bhoran's head rise at the mention of Silver's daughter. *Old loves die hard, or perhaps they never do,* Bassalt thought. "Do not presume to threaten me, Silver." Bassalt folded the cloth over the dagger. "Murder shall be repaid with murder. Now leave me. I must think."

Silver shot him a cold stare, the golden stones in his eyes glimmering with anger. He spun on his heel, barked orders at his men waiting outside, and let them haul Bhoran out of the room.

Once alone, Bassalt dragged his feet to the bed and sat heavily on the sheets. He placed the cloth beside him and unwrapped the edges, taking in the dried blood on the golden blade. Now that he had time to study the dagger closely, it seemed to him more of a decorative piece than a killing weapon, the blade too blunt to slice the throat of the merchant. *But one would know that only if one looked very closely ... and luckily, no one is brave enough.*

None except Bassalt. His time with the Onyx tribe rushed back. The city of Onnehas seemed so far away now, at the other corner of the world. The world he knew, for Bassalt was convinced there was more behind the cursed mountain spine that slashed the north of the Stone Lands. *What are you?* he thought, hefting the knife. Too blunt to cut flesh, too heavy to carry around … it must be one of those display items that spoke of the splurging instincts of the Onyx. *If it is a true Onyx …*

The door creaked open once more. Theran slipped inside like a quiet shadow, balancing a tray full of food. "I've brought you some breakfast, my chief." He left it on Bassalt's table. "I surmised you won't get much more sleep tonight."

Bassalt eyed him suspiciously. Theran's curiosity leaked from every pore of his body, yet Bassalt couldn't blame him. A murder in Hydrus was a rare thing, an Onyx weapon even rarer. "Thank you, Theran. That will do."

The servant eyed the bloodied dagger disapprovingly. He reached for the cloth that held it. "Let me clean this one for you, my chief—"

"Theran." Bassalt rested a heavy hand over his servant's before Theran touched the weapon. "I need you to fetch something for me from the cellar."

"Oh, why, yes. Anything you need, my chief."

"Inside my late father's cupboard, you will find a tiny glass bottle shaped like a teardrop. Bring it to me."

Theran nodded and withdrew.

"And, Theran," Bassalt said before his servant had crossed the threshold. "Not a word to a living soul."

It wasn't long before the servant returned, holding a minute bottle. Bassalt gave him his gratitude and dismissed him. He cupped the teardrop-shaped glass. *So much power held in such a tiny space.* Dagger and vial in hand, he went to his table. Bread, honey, and a cup full of strong mead rested on it—a rich breakfast. Yet Bassalt had lost his appetite. He pushed the tray aside and sat.

Much as he dreaded the task ahead, he knew it had to be done. Now he was alone, he had ample time to put the dagger to the test.

He held the weapon with great trepidation. Yet the bloodstained blade, Bassalt knew, was not the source of his debilitating fear. It was the brooding jewel embedded in the hilt—a gem so dark and soulless it scared him to his very core. Bhoran's studded face swam before his eyes. The soulless glare behind two Onyx stones. *What would you think, Father, seeing him like this? Did your potion prove wrong that night?*

Shaman had never confessed to Bassalt the origins of the vial. And at the time, Bassalt's soul had longed for different things: glory in the ways of his stone, the love of a woman who loved another ... Bassalt hadn't had the time to care about trying dark stones.

Trembling, he knocked off the cork that sealed the vial. The foul smell of rotting eggs made his stomach churn. *One drop will be enough.* His father's voice echoed in his mind. *This way, you will know for certain.*

One drop was all Shaman had used that cursed night, and Bassalt remembered it well. The potion's smell awoke the memories in his mind, throwing him back to the times of war.

The night was dark, the time when nature and all its creatures were in their deepest sleep. Howling winds whipped the shutters; heavy rain poured from the charcoal sky. Bassalt was lying in bed, awakened by the anxious voices of his parents coming through the wall.

"He cannot be more than a month old," his mother said in a trembling voice. "Poor little thing. Who would do something like that, Shaman? And with that terrible storm ..."

"Keep yourself calm, my love," his father said. "This is no time for impatience. Come, let us have a closer look."

Bassalt heard his parents move. Claps of thunder shook the house to its core. He jumped to his feet and threw a light garment on to hide his nakedness. He approached his parents' chamber cautiously. The door was ajar. Peering inside, he watched his parents bending over a moving bundle on the bed—a swaddled baby.

"Shaman, his eyes ..." his mother whispered.

His father's face grew dark. Bassalt felt the sour taste of danger in the air.

His father rushed to the cupboard under the window. After rummaging through it, he drew out a glass bottle, so small Bassalt could barely discern its contents.

"No!" Bassalt's mother screamed as she threw herself on his father. "You can't do this! He's just a baby!"

"He might be one of them!" Shaman retorted, removing the lid from the bottle. "There is only one way to find out. Step back."

The foul smell of rotting eggs reached Bassalt's nostrils, but he made no move to cover his mouth. He watched in terror as his father pushed his mother aside, held the head of the baby still, and tipped the bottle over its face until one drop dribbled over its eye. An agonizing scream pierced the air, and Bassalt had but a moment to cover his ears before he sank into darkness.

Bassalt opened his eyes now and inhaled sharply, a sudden pain shooting through his palm. His fingers, clenched around the dagger's blade, were bleeding on his lap. He let the blade fall with great surprise. "The cursed thing!" he exclaimed. "It hurt me!" Blood licked the stone on the snake ring.

Could it be?

As Bassalt's fresh blood mingled with the dried blood of the merchant, he decided he could wait no longer. The sooner he knew, the sooner he could decide Bhoran's fate.

He tipped the bottle over the gem in the dagger's hilt, one drop dribbling onto its polished surface. Bassalt widened his eyes, watching closely. Yet nothing happened. The gem remained as dark and heartless as it had ever been.

"A true Onyx stone," Bassalt murmured to himself, confirming his greatest fear.

CHAPTER SEVEN

AVALAN WAS loath to part with his deep sleep, but warm sunlight burned his face, and a woman's soft voice whispered—pleaded—in his ear.

Through bleary eyes, he saw the pale face of Lusha. She knelt by his bedside, her flaxen hair a tangled mess, her eyes swollen. Fresh tears wetted thin scratches on her face. A cloak laden with thorns and brambles hugged her shoulders, and the dress she wore beneath was shredded in places. He propped himself up on his elbows, his mouth dry. "Lusha ... something attacked you?"

"Brambles. I ran through the forest," she answered. "I do not like the sight of your wounds. How do you feel?" She pressed a palm to his forehead. Her cool touch soothed his burning skin.

"What wounds?" Avalan looked around the room. *What is that smell?* The air was heavy with the foul stench of rotting flesh.

"Your hands ..." Lusha said.

He followed her gaze to his palms. The crimson blisters of last night had given way to scorched skin. Charred and raw it was, as if Avalan had held a burning stick for longer than he should have. *Many burning sticks,* Avalan thought as he gazed at the patterned marks on his palms. He flexed his fingers, expecting the pain of last night, only it never came. "I don't feel a thing."

"What did this to you?"

Avalan stared at his blackened skin, the stonemaster's words echoing in his mind. *I'm afraid it will leave a mark.* It had done more than that, Avalan realized. It had destroyed his palms. He rolled out of bed and joined Lusha on the floor. "Worry not about me. I'm used to cuts," he said.

"Did Bassalt do this? Did he punish you as he punished Eras? Silver told me Bassalt flogged him after the goat game ..." Her voice broke. Her face, her lips paled.

"Nothing as such," he was quick to assure her. "I gathered the men for weapons training. We wish to remove Bassalt from his place, Lusha." When he saw her eyes flood with fresh tears, he felt a strange kind of shame. "I thought I could fight him with weapons, but now I see I was mistaken. It is stones that we must use."

"Stones?"

"Ronan has brought them with him from the lands." He made to run his fingers over the scrapes on her face, but the foul smell of his hands made him burn with shame to touch her. "Tell me the truth. Did Silver do this to you?" Fresh anger flooded him. "This will stop once Bassalt is removed. Your father won't touch you again. The village will be free."

"Bhoran ..." Lusha whispered.

"For Bhoran," Avalan agreed. "A free Hydrus where he can return and not be feared anymore for his stone."

She shook her head, her features twisting with sorrow. "It's ... Ronan ..." she managed through sobs. "He's dead."

Avalan pushed thick strands of hair behind his ears. Perhaps he had misheard. But how could he have? Lusha's body shook with grief. "Ronan is ... *dead*?" The words sounded foul, wrong.

"I saw him. In the forest. He was lying there ... so lonely. His neck sliced from ear to ear. The light from his stones gone. I had to close his eyelids. Couldn't stand to see him so ... lifeless. I don't think I can ever forget his face like that."

Avalan's chest tightened with grief and anger. "Who did this?"

Lusha hesitated. With a trembling hand, she wiped away her tears. "My father's men caught Bhoran over his body."

Avalan squeezed his jaw so hard he bit his tongue. He swallowed the metal taste of blood. "Bhoran?" His voice came thick with disbelief. His heart raced. He eyed Lusha. She truly had been in the forest, Avalan knew. She carried on her the smell of soil and blackwood. Yet her words made no sense to him. *It can't be. Perhaps the grief has struck her hard.* Even Avalan had a heavy heart whenever the goat game nights came. "Lusha, Bhoran isn't here."

"I saw him." She had stopped crying now. Her Moonstones shimmered with flecks of silver.

The Moonstone always speaks the truth. Farmera's words echoed in Avalan's mind. Yet how could it be? Bhoran had been gone from Hydrus for six long years. And now here Lusha was, bringing him news that hurt Avalan twofold. *Ronan dead by the hands of my friend?* "Bhoran would never do that," he declared, his stomach a knot from the ill omens and the foul smell of his churned hands. "Take me to Ronan. I must see him. If I look at his body …" His words trailed off, and he pressed his eyes shut. *It was just yesterday I saw him. Just yesterday …*

"It is too late," Lusha said. "After they dragged Bhoran away, I stayed by Ronan's side, as much as I could. My father's men returned soon after to bury the body. The soil has Ronan now."

That angered Avalan beyond measure. "How could they do such a thing? We give the dead to the sea!" Something foul was stirring, Avalan knew. "Bassalt wants to keep his death a secret." He pressed his face close to hers. "You must take me to the spot."

Her face pale, Lusha shook her head. "I … I can't … I'm not so good as you around the forest. All trees look the same to me. All night I tried to retrace my steps back to the village. It was at dawn that I managed to come find you. I'm sorry, Avalan … I'm so sorry."

Filled with guilt, Avalan let her go. It wasn't her fault, he knew. The blackwood forest was a true maze to the untrained. Only two paths were etched into its ground, one that led to the statue of Olnos and another to the mountain. Both often turned to mud or filled with brambles, as few feet trod them. Avalan had no need for either of them, yet Lusha … she always seemed to lose her way. "It matters not," he said to comfort her. "Bhoran didn't kill Ronan."

Lusha made for his hands, then winced and grabbed his wrists instead. "We must move fast to aid him. My father took Bhoran to Bassalt. And the way he looks ... they'll never believe his innocence."

"What do you mean?"

"His body's covered with strange etchings, symbols, and his face is pierced with bones and fangs and claws. He looks ... *wild.*"

Avalan tried to paint an image in his mind and failed. Bhoran's ghost smirked at him instead, through tight lips. Never a broad smile. The Bhoran he remembered was too alive in his mind and had clear skin and no claws in his face. "What was he doing there? Did he see you?"

"I can't know for certain. I followed my father and his men to the spot. They had circled Bhoran like a dangerous beast. My father dragged him to Bassalt after examining Ronan's body. They took the weapon too. Some kind of knife. I saw them wrap it with a dirt cloth, for no one was willing to touch it, out of sheer fear."

Avalan frowned. "Why would they be fearful of a knife?"

"They whispered of the Onyx. We must help him, Avalan, I beg of you. I don't know what Bassalt will do this time."

"He will kill him, for certain."

Lusha gasped, her face twisted with terror.

His mind working hard, Avalan gazed out the window. The first light bathed the room, warm and bright, oblivious to their dark predicament.

He turned to Lusha. "There's only one who can sway Bassalt from a harsh punishment."

"Farmera?" Lusha asked. The notion seemed to lift her heart. "She can also tend to your wounds. Your forehead's burning with fever. We made a new paste last night. I think it will help." She caressed a lock of his hair with pity. "I'm sorry for Ronan."

Avalan clenched his fists. *Who could have done this?* "I met with him in secret the night of the goat game. He'd promised me steel arrowheads from the Stone Lands. He wished to keep his presence a secret. Who could have seen him? All were at the game."

"I met him," Lusha admitted, biting her lip. "I went to Olnos. He was there, studying a map. He asked me to keep his arrival a secret."

Avalan frowned. "We must go to my mother at once." He stood, body burning with fever, mouth dry with revulsion at Ronan's death. Despite Lusha's presence and the heavy stench from his hands, the room felt strangely empty. It took him but a mere moment to realize Sigil hadn't returned. *Has Bassalt gotten to her for charging at him when he punished Eras?* "Have you seen Sigil?"

Lusha shook her head and looked around. "Where is she?"

"She's been gone since the goat game night. Curious." When he saw the despair in Lusha's face, he was quick to add, "Sigil can take care of herself. Caught up in a hunting game in the forest, most like." Or so he hoped. "We must go to Farmera. Stay close to me."

"My father's set Fyridion on me. What if they see me?"

"Silver's men most likely won't be searching in the village. They'll think you've run off to the statue or the woods again."

"The tribe ..."

"Most will be out in the sea at this time, fishing. And if perchance someone glimpses you, we'll still have time to get to my mother before your father's men arrive. You can't evade them forever. It's best, I think, for them to find you in the end. Silver's anger will be all the greater if he thinks Bhoran holds the blame for your disappearance."

Lusha nodded and threw the cloak over her head.

Avalan's words proved true—the village was just waking; the tables at the feasting ground glistened with morning dew; children jumped from one table to the other. They laughed merrily when they saw them, increasing their efforts but paying them no further heed.

Once they had entered through Farmera's door, Avalan fastened it. Thankfully, they were alone. The sickbed below the window was empty, a colorful quilt now covering the sheets. His mother was crushing some seeds in a mortar. A brown tunic fell over her slender figure, and her raven locks were loose. She gifted them with a warm smile that quickly turned into fearful concern once she noticed their wounds. "What befell you?"

Lusha threw back her hood. "Avalan's hands need urgent tending," she told Farmera before rushing to the cupboard and pulling out a vial full of thick brown paste. She poured some into a pot and placed it over the slow-burning coals, stirring it with a long spoon.

Farmera winced as she took Avalan's hands in hers. The stench was getting worse. When she regarded the damaged skin, her Amethyst stones burned with something Avalan hadn't seen in his mother's eyes before. *Fear.*

"Wounds of magic." Her voice was grave. "What did this?"

Avalan knew it was no good to lie. Ronan's death could scarcely remain hidden, nor Bhoran's capture. What more harm could the presence of the stones in the village cause? "The Bloodstone."

Lusha stopped stirring and looked at them.

Yet Farmera seemed less surprised. "Sit. I must scour my things. It's been a lifetime since I've seen the marks of a birthstone."

Avalan closed his eyes, taking in the soft clinking of Lusha's spoon against tin, and the twinkling of Farmera's bottles at his back. *Ronan is dead; Bhoran is not.* His heart sought comfort. His temples throbbed.

"Give me your hands," Farmera told him. She'd brought clean linen and a paste that smelled like the flowers that grew atop the Eagle's Eye.

When his mother smeared the paste over his wounds, he felt nothing. Lusha returned, offering him a cup full of a tawny concoction. "For the fever," she said.

He gulped it down, its taste a spice.

"Now, tell me all," his mother ordered as she wrapped the linen over his hands.

Avalan exchanged a sad glance with Lusha before he spoke. He knew his mother wouldn't take the news kindly, but a swift blow was always better than a slow burning. "We have little time, Mother. Ronan is dead."

Farmera halted her wrapping. "Ronan isn't here …"

"My father's men found him in the forest," Lusha said, her voice low. "Someone cut his throat."

"Who?" Farmera yelled. "Who in the Stones' name would do such a vile thing?"

"We don't know," Avalan said. "But at an ill moment, Silver's men caught Bhoran over Ronan's body."

Farmera clutched a fist to her chest. "Bhoran has returned?"

"My father says Bhoran killed him," Lusha said "but I don't believe it. I beg you, Farmera, you must talk to Bassalt like last time.

My father took Bhoran to the chief's house last night. I fear for his life."

Farmera looked bewildered. "Does this have to do with your scheme?"

"What scheme?" Avalan asked.

"You haven't told him?" Farmera looked at them both. At last she dropped Avalan's hands—her work half-finished—and said to him, "Ronan promised to take Lusha with him, away from Hydrus."

The shame on Lusha's face told Avalan it was true. *Why hasn't Lusha told me she planned to leave?* Perhaps he was to blame. Of late he had spent much of his time with weapons and angry men rather than by her side. "Could Silver have found out your plans and ordered Ronan killed to stop him?"

Lusha shook her head, her eyes wide with fear. "No. I saw my father standing over Ronan's dead body. He was sick with disgust. He couldn't have known. And if he did, he wouldn't have taken his fury out upon Ronan, but me."

Avalan knew it to be true. If Silver suspected Lusha had plans to run away, she'd scarcely see the light of day. He wrapped the linen over his wounds himself. His heart ached terribly. Ronan was dead. *Mourn for your dead later,* his heart told him. *Protect the living.* "Mother, you must go to Bassalt. Convince him to stay his hand. I have a plan, but first, I need to speak to Bhoran."

Farmera paced the room. "What good would it do? It's not a matter of an injury this time. The boy killed a man—our Ronan. Bassalt will want his head. I know it."

"Lusha said the men whispered of the Onyx. Bassalt will use the tribe's fear of the cursed stone to convince them Bhoran did it."

"How can you be so sure he didn't?" his mother demanded. "What else could he have been doing in the forest? After all these years, he appears, and he brings death with him." She lowered her gaze as if in shame at the harshness of her words.

"Bhoran had no reason to kill Ronan," Avalan said kindly, remembering the times of old. "Ronan brought him a Moonstone for Lusha. I still remember his face when he showed me. Bhoran said he'd be forever grateful to him."

Farmera had no answer to that. Only tight lips on a worried face. "What is your plan?"

Avalan told them about last night: the gathering of men who sought freedom and revenge, the plan to overthrow Bassalt, and the stones that had danced before their eyes. "If I can bring Stonemaster Delion before the tribesfolk to reveal Bhoran's true birthstone, perhaps he can show them he is no Onyx. That would create enough doubt in the tribe's mind until we find the true killer."

Lusha's face shone with hope, yet Farmera's was dark with shadows when she spoke.

"Bassalt won't like this one bit. His old teacher in the village. Stones, a murder ..." Farmera shook her head. "This can't be good."

"It is the only way," Avalan insisted. "Bassalt will be forced to listen to a stonemaster."

Farmera huffed. "What if Bhoran *is* an Onyx, Avalan? Have you considered that? What if the stone that springs from the master's palms is an Onyx? You will condemn Bhoran to a swifter death."

Avalan looked at his hands. Their stench had lessened now they were swathed. "It is a risk we must be prepared to take. I see no other way out of this." In truth, he could be condemning Bhoran, but a hastened attack on the chief's household would cause much bloodshed.

The door shook with a loud banging. "Open up!" a gruff voice called.

Farmera looked at both of them through eyes filled with pain. When a second bang shook the door, she removed the plank that fastened it.

Gremian burst inside and strode to Lusha. "Come with me," he told her, clawing her arm. "Orders from your father."

Lusha gave them both a pleading stare before she followed Gremian out.

"I shall go speak to Bassalt, son," Farmera told him once they were alone, "if only for the love I know you bear for your old friend. Now go and see that you return with the stonemaster. We can only hope Bassalt will listen to his old teacher."

. . .

Brown paste had seeped through the linens when Avalan reached the Eagle's Eye. The sun burned now, his forehead sodden with salty sweat. Whatever Lusha had given him had eased his fever. He strode through the stone tunnel, hoping he'd find Stonemaster Delion there. After all, he couldn't imagine where else Marebore would hide the master. Marebore's house stood near the center of the village, a terrible spot for concealing an intruder.

In the cavern, he found Marebore and the rest of the men standing in a crude circle. They all fell silent when they saw him, their eyes darting to his hands. Avalan searched their faces for signs of knowledge.

"Do you know?" he asked Marebore.

Marebore gave a sullen nod. "Lhorin sent word of Ronan's death."

Eras stepped closer. "We've heard whom Silver caught for the murder."

"No." Avalan shook his head. He had no time for such a talk. "Where is the stonemaster?"

Marebore tossed his hair back, the rattling of his beads echoing in the tall chamber. "Back there."

The men stood aside. Avalan glimpsed the hunched silhouette of the stonemaster sitting atop the makeshift target of Bassalt. Avalan strode to him and knelt before the hem of his cloak. Unsure of how to begin, he brushed his brows; the sweet smell of rotting flesh seeped through the wrappings and into his mouth. It made him sick. Everything had fallen apart faster than he could handle. Ronan lay dead; his own hands were rotting; Bhoran was captured, accused of murder; and the only man who could absolve him now stood so silent and broken. "You must help us," Avalan said.

The stonemaster looked at him, the veil in his eyes rippling.

The air around Avalan grew denser as the men closed in around them. He would have much preferred to have these words far from prying ears, yet these men had stood by him. They deserved to know the truth.

"What of our stones now Ronan's dead?" Colgar said.

"A man has died." Eras knelt next to Avalan. "The stones can wait."

"We must go out and find them," Colgar urged.

From above, Marebore silenced them all. "If Ronan's dead, the stones have already fallen into Bassalt's hands. And, I'm afraid, this misfortune will only serve as the beginning of a dire season."

Ignoring them, Avalan cupped the bony edge of the master's knee. "Bassalt has caught the wrong man. I need you to talk to him. Convince him Bhoran isn't an Onyx."

Uncomfortable shuffles followed the mention of the cursed tribe. "I heard the talk," Colgar said. "They found a dagger with an Onyx stone. They say it was with this that the talon killed the merchant."

Avalan leaped to his feet, grasping Colgar's sturdy neck. "Call him 'talon' again, and you will taste my goat dagger."

Marebore shoved them apart. He shot a warning glance at Colgar, whose hand had slipped onto his own dagger. "A fight will weaken us. Whether the boy is guilty remains to be decided." He turned to Avalan. "You cannot ask the master to speak to Bassalt. His presence must remain hidden."

"He's Bhoran's only hope," Avalan retorted. Forgetting his anger for Colgar, he faced the old man. Delion hadn't spoken a word, his face as still as the Crystal Lake's surface. "If you can reveal before the tribe Bhoran's stone, perhaps Bassalt will spare him. Only you can prove he's not an Onyx. You brought our stones forth. You can do the same with Bhoran's. I grew alongside him as a brother. I know he didn't kill Ronan. And once you show them, the tribe will know it too."

The master remained silent.

Marebore placed a steady palm on Avalan's shoulder. "Son, I never much liked the boy, but I can feel your pain. Ronan brought the stone-master to Hydrus, risking his life, promising to protect him. I shall not allow Delion to surrender himself to Bassalt. For Bhoran or any other. One death is enough."

Avalan twisted out of his grip. All the anger he had suppressed since hearing of Ronan's demise burst out of him now. "This was all your doing!" he yelled at Marebore. "Why did you have to bring Ronan into this? The stones are bad luck. They only bring death and destruction." His voice caught in his throat. "He was like my father."

"We need the stones, son," Marebore said, not unkindly. "We cannot hope to win without them."

"Look at my hands!" Avalan brandished his sodden linens. "*This* is the doing of the stones. Ronan's death was their doing as well. Of that I am convinced. Much as you hate Bhoran, he isn't guilty. I know him. He'd never kill Ronan. He'd never kill the man who stood for me like a father."

The men lowered their faces, ashamed to meet his eyes. They didn't believe his words, he knew. Blaming the Onyx for every ill always came more easily. He spun to leave, his heart heavy with failure.

"Your father"—the voice of the stonemaster came low, as if from the depths of his chest—"was of the Bloodstone."

Avalan halted. With a hesitant heart, he turned.

"Your father would fight with steel and birthstone, knowing." Spindly fingers waved in the air. "A leader bows before the power, humble. Accepts. Listens. Does not reject what he fears more than three times."

The master's words cut Avalan deep. "I never knew my father."

"A father always goes looking for his missing children. Otherwise, he isn't a father." The stonemaster smiled, a faint curving of his wrinkled lips. The veil in the eyes of the master thinned now, faint striped stones peering through, eyes that reminded Avalan of his tiger's.

"I have no children ..." Avalan began, yet even as he said it, Sigil came to his mind. Avalan stared at the stonemaster, his mind racing faster than the arrows that sprang from his bow. *Missing children ...* His tiger hadn't returned to their tree house. *You're telling me to find Sigil,* he thought. He did not need to speak it. Even though the veil in the master's gaze had thickened once more, the proud lift of the old man's chin told Avalan his assumption had grounds.

He backtracked, sprinting through the stony tunnel.

Once out, Avalan crouched, sniffed the ground, read all its markings. Dozens of footprints disturbed the soil, their toes distinct and human. Yet what caught Avalan's eye wasn't human at all: a spoor was etched into the soil, a few paces away from the cave's entrance. Avalan traced the outline of a print. It was Sigil's; he held no doubt. *What was she doing here?*

He sprang to his feet.

Sigil's prints continued through the forest. Avalan raced over familiar paths paved with stones and twisted woody vines. He ducked to avoid catching his hair in overhanging branches and leaped over logs and muddy brooks, never losing the trail from his sight. Sweat trickled down his forehead, stinging his eyes; his soaked breeches clung to his thighs.

The smell of sea wafted through the air.

Blissful voices came from the shore. Fisherfolk were returning from the sea, carrying between them baskets teeming with fish—a good catch that would have made Avalan eager to rush and help them. His knives were the best at gutting and scraping, they always told him. Their unwary faces told Avalan they still hadn't heard of Ronan's death. *How could they have? Most of them left the village before sunrise.*

He crouched in the underbrush until they were gone. Then he picked Sigil's trail up once more. It crossed the lengthy shore, the sand making it easier to follow. She had been racing here, her tracks spaced out as if she had been chasing something. *Or was being chased.*

He hated this notion.

The hunt led him to the easternmost side of the shore, where soft sand gave way to rocky pebbles. He cursed. Loose rocks always proved harder to read than soil.

Where could she have gone?

To his left, a rocky hill rose, offering little purchase. The waves had smoothed the surface over the years. He hunted for scratch marks left behind by Sigil's claws and found none. *She hasn't climbed up the hill.*

He followed the pebbled path; the shore became narrower and narrower with every step. Warm sea licked the soles of his feet as he splashed in the shallow waters. And then he saw it: an opening in the otherwise smooth rock some paces ahead, a dark hole that reminded Avalan of the burrows in the forest, only this one was much larger. *Sigil could easily have slipped inside.* He raced to it, stuck his head in.

"Sigil?" His voice resounded in the tunnel but didn't return to him. The burrow had more depth than he'd imagined. It looked a passage, big enough for a man to crawl through should he be willing to bend the knee.

It was a strange feeling to find a tunnel he didn't know of. Since he'd been a boy, exploring Hydrus had been Avalan's most beloved task. After all, there was only so much one could do in a small fishing village. Yet Avalan had never come across this passage, and he didn't much like it.

Uneasy thoughts of Sigil following prey here and getting trapped made his heart clench. *A father always goes looking for his missing children.* The stonemaster's voice echoed in his mind.

Avalan crawled through the wet darkness.

CHAPTER EIGHT

GREMIAN'S TREMBLING hand offered Lusha scant stillness to think what she would say to her father. As he escorted her through the village, childish whispers surrounded them. To Lusha, they sounded like whimpering apologies. The younglings eyed her with shame. They had betrayed her, Lusha knew.

As she passed them, she gifted them with a wan smile.

It mattered not. As Avalan had said, there was no way she could evade her father forever. And with Ronan dead, she'd have to tolerate his presence until Avalan and the rest of the men made their move.

The Night of the Spirits, Avalan had said, and Lusha saw how fitting this choice was. If the spirit of the late chief, Volkan, wasn't willing to end their suffering and rid them of Bassalt, they had to see the task through themselves. The former chief's indifference was something Lusha had never understood, nor forgiven. The tales spoke of Volkan as a great and compassionate leader, yet perhaps that was all they were, after all—mere tales.

As much as she longed for freedom, the notion of a rebellion terrified her. She knew Bassalt would retaliate with great stone magic, as he was wont to do when challenged. And her father ... Silver would surely slash whoever came his way.

Despite the warmth of the day, she shuddered.

Once on the upper story of Silver's house, Gremian took his leave.

Silver sat on the floor. On the short plank before him that served as a table rested a wine flagon and two cups. Lusha had never seen her father drink or eat in their home. All his meals were taken at the feasting ground, alongside the tribe.

With a quiet nod, he bade her sit.

The calmness in his demeanor upset Lusha more than the infuriated burst she had expected. Silver tipped the earthen flagon over her cup. Red wine dribbled out, reminding Lusha of Ronan's crusted blood.

"Drink," Silver ordered.

Lusha's stomach lurched. "Isn't it too early to drink? It's not even midday."

Looking like he'd hardly slept, Silver watched her. His eyes sank deep into wrinkled sockets. His tunic was ruffled and sodden with sweat. Even his hair had lost its shine. "Drink."

Lusha brought the cup to her lips but didn't swallow.

"Not like that!" her father stormed. "*Drink!* Drain your cup. Like the real daughter of a commander." He drained his cup and banged it on the plank. The clay bottom cracked, but Silver didn't seem to care. He chuckled. A pitiful sound. "Look at you. Dress shredded and soiled, cloak rich with the forest's odors, and your fingers ... they reek of Farmera's potions. Did she send you foraging through the forest? Why does *my* daughter look a mess?"

Lusha held her tongue, her mother's pendant cool against the rising warmth inside her.

"Where were you?" he demanded.

Tired of bowing in terror, Lusha lifted her chin. Ronan was gone, and Bhoran was treading on the edge of death; there was nothing left for her to lose. "I followed you. I saw Ronan dead in the forest."

The Heliodors in Silver's eyes sparkled. He poured himself yet another cup. Red wine trickled through the fracture, and he cursed at the spillage. He tore Lusha's cup from her grip. "If you won't drink, then I'll have it." He gulped the wine. "You saw who killed the merchant?"

"I saw you captured Bhoran, but I won't believe he killed Ronan."

"What you believe matters not. The merchant's throat was slit. From one ear to the other."

Lusha closed her eyes, the crimson neck wound returning in her mind's eye.

Silver grabbed her wrist. "Open your eyes, sweet daughter, and see the truth for once."

"And what is your truth, Father?" Her throat tightened. "That Bhoran killed him because he's a *filthy Onyx*? Can a stone compel you to kill?"

His grip tightened. "You speak of things you know nothing of. What do you know about the Onyx, Lusha? Nothing! So let me tell you, then, and let this be my last warning to you about this boy you so much love. The weapon used to slaughter the merchant held an Onyx stone. The blade was blunt, unlikely to have caused such damage. Yet the dagger's power can be increased *only* by an Onyx bearer. You hear me?" He shook her now. "There is no Onyx alive except for him. Of that I'm certain. The War of the Stones was an ugly thing. Yet we won it. And rest assured, a dark stone like the Onyx toys with your mind. If you had seen the things of old, you would have understood."

He unleashed her, his words a stinging slap across her face. *If what he says is true,* she thought with horror, *and Avalan brings this stone-master before the tribe, what will happen to Bhoran if he is indeed an Onyx?* "Father, even if he is an Onyx, it doesn't make him a murderer."

"You speak like your mother," Silver said. "Naive and innocent. Always believing in the good side of things. The Onyx has no good. It is pure evil."

"You said it yourself. The blade wasn't strong enough to cause the trauma. Perhaps if you let Farmera examine the wound, we could—"

"The merchant is already buried. There's nothing of beauty in a deathly cut. This is the last time my men will find you engaging in this dirty work. Do not mistake my tolerance of Farmera for acceptance of this trade."

"Strange you'd say that, when you married a healer." Her father slapped her so hard she tasted blood.

Silver's stones sparkled with relentless force. "I brought your mother to Hydrus in hopes she'd soon forget about the ways of her

Moonstone. Her blind faith in the stones got her killed and left me alone to tend to a child. One who took so much after her, in presence and in spirit, it made my heart bleed. I swear I'll die before I lose one more to the Moonstone."

This rare moment of Silver's confession could be used to her advantage, Lusha knew. Her father rarely talked about Amara, much less her illness. "The Moonstone killed my mother?"

Silver smashed his cup on the floor. "We will not talk about it. And drop your hair over your scar. I won't have you ridiculing yourself by taking pride in something a talon did to you."

Lusha sprang to her feet. "For the hundredth time, it was a *snake* that slashed my eye! Not Bhoran." She threw her cloak on the floor, her dress beneath a mass of shredded linen. "I won't cover my scar, Father. As you refuse to talk to me, I refuse to take your counsel. I'm tired of living in the dark. You didn't even tell me I had an aunt. I had the right to know!"

Silver staggered to his feet, disgust etched on his face. "I should have expected Farmera would give in sooner or later to your probing questions." A piece of clay crunched under his naked sole, but he paid it no heed. "I want nothing to do with the Moonstone, you hear? And you will forget it too. Bassalt is right for forbidding the birthstones. You young ones think there's greatness in them? There's only destruction and death; the tribe will see it now with the punishment of the talon. And pray this is the last execution you'll witness, for I have noticed how the men disappear for hours on end under the pretense of hunting."

Lusha swallowed hard. "Execution? Bassalt will kill Bhoran?"

"The trial will take place tonight. After that, he'll join his tribe in the ground."

"No!" She made for the stairs, but Silver coiled a strong arm around her waist. She buried her fists in his chest, the sweet smell of wine on his breath sickening her. "You can't kill him, you hear? Bhoran didn't do it. I don't believe it. Let me talk to him. I will die with him!"

"You will do no such thing. *Gremian!*"

The wooden ladder creaked with heavy footsteps. Gremian stormed up and seized Lusha. Using a rough vine rope, he tied her wrists into a tight knot. Despite her twisting and turning, they forced her to the floor, her screams piercing the roof. Silver tied her ankles in like manner. "You will remain here until tomorrow, when all is done."

"No, Father," Lusha pleaded as Silver rose. Fear drenched her anger now. "Let me come to the trial. Let me see him for one last time. I swear I will forget him after. I swear!"

Silver exchanged a brief glance with Gremian, then strode toward the stairs. He took one step, then halted, his head low.

Lusha dared hope. She squirmed against her restraints. "I beg of you, Father."

His hand on the rail, Silver turned. "As you wish. Perhaps after you've seen him for what he truly is, you will forget him. One can only hope."

CHAPTER NINE

Bassalt bit into a blood orange. Its crimson juice trickled down his fleshy jowl.

Lazy sunlight sneaked through the open window of the cooking chamber, bathing the room in colors of flax. This morning, Bassalt's household was quiet, his servants having been sent away to prepare for the first trial he would lead as the chief of Hydrus. And as stone luck would have it, the charged one was his *brother*.

Bassalt couldn't have wished for a better sign.

He kicked a heavy heel into the rock. The cellar rested right below it, with Bhoran chained to its cool walls. His stepbrother hadn't said a word since they had caught him—a thing that unsettled the rest but gave Bassalt great satisfaction. One who didn't defend himself left no room for doubt of his guilt.

Soft footfalls echoed from the entrance. "Bassalt?" came the smooth calling of a voice he knew and loved well. Before he had the time to stand, Farmera crossed the room's threshold, a violet linen dress wrapping the curves of her mature body. A bone brooch fastened the fabric across her bosom. "You're here," she said, her voice carrying great surprise, as if she hadn't expected to find him.

Or perhaps she didn't expect my calmness in the face of the recent occurrence.

Her puffy eyes told him she had been crying, a sign she knew about the unfortunate demise of their merchant. He glanced at the hollow stone windows overlooking the village. *The whole tribe should know by now.* "If you have come seeking mercy, know there will be none this time." He wiped his fingers on the table, sketching crimson rivulets on the wood.

Farmera straddled the bench beside him, her dress slipping away from the white flesh of her knees. She stole a quick glance at the wooden shelves on the walls behind him. Laden they were, with goods of all kinds from Hydrus and the cities of the Stone Lands beyond the Craggy Mountains: aromatic herbs plucked from shady forests and tied together with string; jars filled with dried venison meat, a delicacy Bassalt much enjoyed; and lots of pots containing ground spices of colors beyond any birthstone they had ever seen.

Bassalt knew Farmera longed to use them, and he would gladly have given her all, had she asked—except she never had.

"Tell me all," she said, her gaze finding his face.

"Not much to tell. The boy went too far this time. Finding a new merchant will be a hassle. I'll have to pester Ethelnar to spare me one of his. Although I don't hold out much hope of that. The journey to Hydrus isn't easy, and we won't find lots willing to risk their lives. Fresh fish and goat bones make for poor trading."

Farmera cringed. "Is that all you care for?"

Bassalt knew Ethelnar's name would unsettle her. *Good. Whatever might stir the talk away from Bhoran.* "You still haven't told Avalan about the chief, have you?"

"My son is miserable enough as it is. I won't twist a knife in his gut."

"And so you let him hope—dream, even, of taking my place." Her widened eyes gave him great pleasure. "How does that differ from a knife in the gut?"

"Where is Bhoran now?" she dared.

Bassalt pointed a stubby finger at the floor. "Right below us. Keeping the company of fresh produce."

She edged closer. "You must let me speak with him."

"Not much good it will do you." Bassalt savored the scent of lavender in her hair. "The boy hasn't said a word. He isn't what you remember. All those years spent in the wild have turned him into a beast."

Farmera's lips fell apart. "How so?"

"I guess you'll know once you have seen him. Fangs, teeth, bones, strange etchings ... a curious way to decorate oneself. But then again, Bhoran has always been a curious child."

"He is your brother."

"Not by blood. My father forced him upon me." Bassalt shrugged. "He is an Onyx. If I had a doubt before, the weapon he used has confirmed my suspicions."

"Where is it?"

Bassalt slid his palm into a fur-lined pocket of his tunic. He laid the dagger on the bench between them, Ronan's dried blood still on it. Despite Theran's persistent requests to clean the weapon, Bassalt had kept the bloodstains to better scare the tribe.

Farmera's hand hovered over the black gemstone in the hilt. She didn't dare to touch it. "Is it an Onyx?"

Bassalt nodded. "I used Shaman's solution. The gem didn't so much as spark. Soulless it is, and as such it will remain."

"It cannot be." Farmera shook her head in solemn denial. "Perchance somebody else wielded the weapon, and Bhoran stumbled over Ronan as he lay already dead. Did Silver's men even consider the notion? Did they properly search?"

Bassalt felt the pain in her words but couldn't allow her disillusionment. "Bhoran killed him. If he hadn't done it, why the silence? Besides, who else now lives that carries the soulless stone?"

"Your father didn't believe Bhoran was of the Onyx," Farmera reminded him. "And we both know Shaman held great wisdom. How can you be so fast to condemn him? If Shaman were here, he would show mercy. Listen to what Bhoran has to say before sentencing him."

"For all his great wisdom, my father never became a chief." Bassalt concealed the weapon again in the warmth of his tunic. "He wouldn't even touch an Onyx stone with his bare hands. Yet I am not afraid to do that, and Hydrus has enjoyed the longest period of peace under my rule."

"It has enjoyed suppression as much as peace," Farmera retorted.

"Bassalt, the tides are changing. The youths are growing restless. Fewer and fewer of them want to take part in the goat games, and you whip one of their champions before the tribe. You build high fences around them and deny them the playfulness of the sea. You force them to retire before sunset, as if to liken them to craven animals that hide from night predators."

"Such predators proved me right. The poor merchant paid with his life. What would you have me do, Farmera? Leave Hydrus unprotected? This trial will prove to all they have nothing to fear—even the Onyx will kneel before my power."

"What will you do to him?"

"Only what I should have done six years ago on that cursed goat game night when he scarred that poor girl. A swift death will be a great mercy."

Farmera gasped. "Bassalt, no. You mustn't. Lusha's heart won't take it."

He knew, of course. In his whole lifetime, Bassalt had never seen a love so fierce that stood the test of time. Over the years, he'd listened to Silver's endless complaints about his daughter and how the spindly fingers of her misery for Bhoran squeezed every ounce of happiness from Lusha's body, leaving her but an empty carcass. He knew that feeling well himself, only his carcass wasn't empty. It was filled with rage and a stony heart. "These two cannot be together."

"You cannot choose whom you love, Bassalt."

I know that well. "Again I ask you, what would you have me do?"

"Remember what this place stands for—Hydrus."

Bassalt remembered well. Back in the days when the tribesfolk hadn't been allowed to marry another stone, Hydrus had been founded, a place where true love between two different stones could thrive. Once the war was over, Hydrus had ceased being the only place where lovers eloped. With the Onyx gone, the tribes married however they pleased. "We cannot let Silver's daughter be with a talon."

"We cannot keep them apart. In the day, the sun rises, and the night welcomes the moon. Yet there comes a day when sun and moon meet and spread a darkness over the lands with their union. If you kill him, then kill them both, for throughout all these years, it was for this rare moment that Lusha's heart waited."

Bassalt rubbed his beard with ringed fingers. "Lusha is of the Moonstone, but what is Bhoran? Pure darkness."

"She will shed light into his corners."

"And what of their offspring?" Bassalt retorted, pleased to see the seed of doubt in Farmera's Amethyst. "Have you forgotten what comes from Onyx?"

"We can't be certain ..."

"We cannot risk it either. For the future of the lands. The ones we fought so hard to preserve."

Farmera bowed her head. "I came seeking the mercy in your heart. I know now it lies empty." She lifted the corners of her dress and slid off the bench, swift as a suckling goat. "Where did you bury Ronan? I wish to see him."

"His Larimar needs to return to the soil. We mustn't disturb it."

"Curse you, Bassalt." Tears glistened on her cheeks. "You could have let Avalan say farewell."

With that, she turned on her heels.

Bassalt watched her as she left, taking with her the smell of lavender and fennel and whatever little filled his chest. He fished out the Onyx dagger, laid it before him on the table. Pressing fat palms against his forehead, he stared at the stone, the merchant's caked blood, the sheen of gold ... *Cursed, cursed, cursed. Why has it come to this, Ronan? You were the greatest merchant.*

He stood, hobbled down the cellar stairs.

Dust sprinkled the underground chamber as he descended. Stopping midway, he searched the darkness. The cellar was kept dark and cool, to better preserve the meat and fruits of his larder. In the far corner, he glimpsed Bhoran. Ivory fangs transfixed his stepbrother's face. Iron shackles chained him to the wall. Bhoran saw him, his eyes one with the darkness.

"Who are you really, *brother*?" Bassalt asked into the silence.

And silence was returned.

CHAPTER TEN

THE SUNKEN PASSAGE was lined with slimy moss, its carious aroma too sharp for Avalan to bear. He quickened his pace, gratefully noting that the tunnel grew taller and drier with every step.

Farther down into the darkness, Avalan glimpsed a feeble light. Its trembling told him this was no sunlight pouring through a ceiling hole. Rather, it resembled the dancing flame of a candle. As he drew closer, the passage became brighter, the wide opening of a cave bidding him welcome.

At the threshold, Avalan halted. Long shadows of flickering candle flames swayed across the stone walls. He knew fire needed the clean air from above to thrive, and so he guessed the cavern couldn't lie deep inside the rock hill. The thought comforted him—being underground made his skin crawl. A faint clinking, glass on glass, came from the other side.

Someone is here.

"Come in now. I was waiting for you," the voice of a man came, silky as the slimy moss covering the passage.

Avalan hesitated. His gut bade him run, yet the thought of Sigil kept him rooted. He had to make certain she hadn't slinked in here; her trail had left him no other choice.

"Do not force me to repeat myself," the voice demanded.

This time, Avalan peered around the corner, grasping the goat dagger in his belt. The cavern was small yet spacious, with glistening white moss lining the walls and a tall ceiling. Pots of burning tallow bathed the chamber in mystical light, revealing the cave's dark corners. Stony protrusions, carved and smoothed into benches, jutted out of the walls. On them lay mixing bowls, colorful mists rising from them as though whatever they held was boiling. Trinkets hung on the east side of the cave, adorned with birthstones of all shapes and forms.

A Larimar necklace caught the candlelight and Avalan's eye. Even in the dim-lit cavern, the blue stone shone with pride, probing a memory in Avalan's mind. *Look at this beautiful stone,* Ronan had told him, a Larimar bracelet in his palms. *By giving this jewel to Crystal, you aren't giving her just a stone, Avalan; you're giving her the sky!* But Avalan had never gotten the chance to give it to her, as Ronan had smuggled her out of Hydrus.

"Now that you have feasted your eyes on my possessions, do come in. Time is of the essence."

Avalan shook his head, removing Ronan's eager smile from his mind and his grasp from the dagger. His searching gaze landed on the tall, hooded figure of a man. He wore a cloak of raven velvet with long black feathers around its collar. Bent over a slab, the stranger held a bottle. Inside it, an orange liquid sloshed as the man shook it with a sickly-pale hand. *A sorcerer?* "Who are you?" Avalan demanded.

The strange man let the bottle down with a soft clink. When he raised his head, Avalan glimpsed a gaunt face the color of wax framed by long strips of snowy-white hair. His lips were thin and red, the color of crushed berries. *He has the colors of an old man,* Avalan thought, *but his eyes haven't seen more than forty summers. His eyes …*

The stranger suddenly laughed, a heart-chilling cackle, deep and penetrating the soul. "Do I frighten you?"

"Who are you?" Avalan asked again. The man's laughter died as fast as it had come. Avalan felt the dampness of the place crawl under his skin.

"I am who I am, and that does not matter much. There is not much time." Then, as an afterthought, he added, "I wonder, do you have the opulence of time, Avalan of the Bloodstone?"

"How do you know my name?"

The stranger reached for a pile of crimson cloth on the slab. "We shall talk. But first take this." He threw the fabric to Avalan. "To cast away the chill."

The crimson cloak flew toward him like a twisting blanket, yet Avalan made no move to catch it. It landed before his feet, sprawled like a hide. It looked soft and warm, but Avalan let it lie there, too careful to admit weakness before the stranger. "Where is my tiger?"

"Sigil isn't here ... anymore. When the time is right, you will find her."

"What have you done to her?"

"I'd never harm her. She has returned to Hydrus."

"Then I shall go find her." Avalan turned on his heel, made for the tunnel. The stonemaster wanted him to find Sigil. Perhaps in some way she could help him save Bhoran.

Behind him, the stranger sighed. "That would be a shame. A shame indeed. For there's a lot we ought to talk about."

Avalan turned, his patience ebbing. "I don't speak with strangers. Much less those who withhold their names."

"A name? Is this all you're asking in return?" The hooded man shook his head as if disappointed. He sauntered to the back of the cave and sat atop a polished slab. "Very well. I will give you my name, Avalan of the Bloodstone, if you so much wish to have it." He threw his cowl back, baring his wan face. "My name is Dizredek."

His last words were a fierce whisper. To Avalan, it felt like a dart trying to pierce his tightened chest. Now that the man had lowered his covering, Avalan had a better view of the stones in his eyes. Flakes of gold whirled in the gray darkness of his left eye. A crescent birthmark encircled the blackness in his right eye, which remained unmoving. Avalan had never seen stones like these. *How much do I not know?*

Dizredek cocked his head to the side. "You're wondering about my birthstone now. But that was not what we agreed. I was only to give you my name, and then you would listen to what I have to say."

"I made no such promise."

"I've been watching you for a while." Dizredek waved an elegant hand, ignoring Avalan's refusal. "Hunting, slashing, crafting ... training the men for a fight they cannot hope to win. Seems like you never slow. Perhaps it's time you did, Avalan of the Bloodstone. Perhaps it's time to listen."

A familiar prickling in Avalan's back told him what he had suspected—he had been no fool when he had felt someone's eyes on him all this time. When he'd hunted in the blackwood forest, when he'd bathed in the Crystal Lake, even when he'd been inside the close walls of his room, he had felt a burning gaze on him. Now he held his proof. "What do you seek of me?"

"To guide you to your heart's deepest desire. Tell me what is it that you want the most."

To bring Ronan back from the dead was the first thing Avalan thought. *I wish to save Bhoran and learn the truth. Then I wish to leave and find Crystal and bring her back to a Hydrus that is no longer ruled by a man cold of heart and harsh of spirit.* And yet there was only one way his wishes could come true, Avalan knew. "Bassalt," he said. "I want to overthrow the chief and free Hydrus."

"Freedom." A slender finger raised, Dizredek nodded approvingly. "Then I shall offer you a way to end Bassalt and save your tribe."

Avalan clenched his teeth. "Other men have offered their help, but I've found my workings slow when many muddle. I now see the stonemaster wanted me to find you. You lured me here using my tiger. Where is she? What did you do to Sigil?"

Dizredek chuckled. "Fear not for Sigil. The stonemaster ordered her here. I couldn't risk meeting you out in the open. I'm nothing like this mummer Delion. My stones have flesh and bones—not pitiful ghost forms. And yet it is the same cause we all share, so we must work together."

"Why would you help me?"

Dizredek looked at him through narrowed eyes, looking like Sigil when stalking prey. "You don't know much about the times of war, now, do you?"

Avalan shook his head.

"Of course. Bassalt does not speak of things that besmirch his honor. Let us say I have open tradings with him. He has a thing of mine I very much desire to retrieve."

What could that be? Avalan thought. Smoke from a bottle rose in the cavern, swirling and filling the air with the sweet smell of burning amber. Avalan gazed at the various trinkets: birthstones, gems, colorful liquids, metals. He did not know what Bassalt was doing behind the monstrous basalt walls of his lair. Yet he'd never seen the chief much care for things as these. There was only one thing Bassalt possessed that looked as if it didn't belong; even Bassalt himself seemed to fear it ... "The snake ring," Avalan finally said.

Dizredek's eyes sparkled. "Indeed, indeed. Your mind is sharp as Onyx."

"What stops you from getting it yourself?"

"That would make for an ugly sight." Dizredek wrinkled his nose. "My birthstone is elegant. Cunning, yes, yet peaceful. Ours is not the way of war or fighting. Besides"—he waved an airy hand—"the village needs a leader. What would it look like if a stranger were to attack the chief and strip him of his position? Do you expect the tribesfolk to look up to me when I have no interest in leading them? You, however ... young, ambitious, righteous—a fitting chief. If you bring freedom to the tribe, they will accept you. After all, they've known you; they've seen you be born, grow, and rise. Of me they know nothing. And like this I wish it to remain. All I ask of you is the ring once you have freed the village."

Avalan cringed at the superfluous compliments of the stranger. "Do not presume to flatter me. I don't know you, nor trust you. Why would I help you get this ring?"

"You need my aid to defeat Bassalt," Dizredek declared.

"I can make do on my own. I always have."

Dizredek arched a silver brow. "Your tiger is two days gone. The merchant keeps the company of earthworms, the birthstones he carried all gone. The stonemaster brought forth a stone that maimed your hands, and your beloved friend Bhoran ... well, tell me, do you know what fate awaits an Onyx? How do you hope to save him?"

Avalan clenched his jaw. Loath as he was to admit it, the past events were spiraling out of his control.

"I see I have your interest now."

"Speak."

Dizredek pointed at the cave floor. "The cloak first. Then approach."

Avalan draped the cloak over his shoulders, the fabric warm and soft around his cold body. He'd never donned a cloak before. A garment for the idle, he'd always thought it. "Why did you make me wear this?"

"The blood. It must run warm."

Avalan sat beside him on the polished slab. "My blood?"

Dizredek nodded. "The blood of the Bloodstone," he said solemnly. "When you were born in Hydrus, you were refused what's rightfully yours: a true piece taken right from the Heart of the Bloodstone. The birthstone is given by a stonemaster, yet since Bassalt has let none near the village for the past twenty years, all the youths of Hydrus remain unblessed by their birthstones. If you wish to hold true power—power that will help you defeat Bassalt—you must find the Heart of the Bloodstone and seek what was denied to you. Your true stone."

Avalan stared at him, his mind working hard to make sense of his words. "Why can't the stonemaster give me my stone now? Why do I have to seek it?"

Dizredek sighed. "I forget how little you know. Stonemaster Delion isn't of the Bloodstone, and hence, he holds no such power."

"Where is this heart you speak of? How can I find the stonemaster of the Bloodstone?"

Dizredek's lips curved like a gutting blade. "There is no time to go through the proper ritual. Your true stone is hidden and protected, awaiting your arrival. Fear not, though, for I will help you. You won't have to look for it alone. I told you when you arrived that I seek to guide you."

"Will you take me there?"

"No. I'm not of the Bloodstone either. Besides, my presence can hardly go unnoticed." Dizredek flaunted his long ashen hair behind his back. He stood and retrieved an earthen bowl, a pricker, and two small vials.

When he returned, Avalan watched a flaxen liquid bubble in one vial; in the other one, an azure rested. "How do you know all these things?"

"I watch … I listen. Hydrus is a small place, but teeming with secrets."

Avalan watched him fiddle with the pricker. Uneasiness filled him. He glimpsed at the cavern's corners. Aside from the entrance he'd crawled through, the cave held no more escape routes apart from a small skylight above, riddled with root vines. The light fought to get through, a dim orange glow. The cloak had warmed Avalan's body, yet his mind was still stiff and on guard. This stranger knew far too much. Of him, his loved ones, the stones … "Who killed Ronan?"

Dizredek shot him a curious glance as he uncorked a vial. The smell of rotten eggs spilled into the chamber. "An Onyx dagger, they seem to believe, only who the wielder was remains unknown."

Sensing the lie in his words, Avalan watched him closely. "Did you kill Ronan?"

Irritated, Dizredek clucked his tongue. "Were you not listening to me when I told you my stone's ways aren't vicious? Why would I kill a man who aided my entrance into the village?"

Avalan closed his eyes. He had feared as much. There was no other way to enter Hydrus except by following someone who knew well how to tread the mountain. He wished with all his heart he could see Ronan again. From his lips, he'd gladly listen to all. The truth, the plans these strange men had, the stones … "Bassalt says the village is impenetrable, yet I have witnessed otherwise. You, the stonemaster …"

Dizredek huffed. "Only a scared man builds fences around his house, and only a foolish one believes them potent. Bassalt is both." With a bony finger, he pushed the cork off the vial with the azure contents. "You and the merchant were close. What has he taught you about the stones?"

Nothing I was willing to listen to, Avalan thought, the sour taste of guilt in his mouth. "The teaching of the stones is forbidden in Hydrus."

Dizredek sniggered. "It is funny, you see. Bassalt's rules hold no sense. You cannot deny the tribesfolk their true nature."

He tipped the second vial over the bowl. When the two liquids touched, there was a spark, and then a gurgling sound, as if each one was fighting to swallow the other, retain its identity, and not get lost in the blending. The unison of the two liquids left behind a green, clotted mass. Dizredek took the pricker. "Give me your hand."

"What for?"

"Just a small prick of the finger. One drop will do. The blood should be warm by now."

Eager to be done with this, Avalan stretched his palm out to him. He felt no pain when the needle pierced his skin. And when his blood dripped, crimson and alive, Dizredek placed Avalan's finger over the bowl and let it weep over the mixture. As soon as the fresh blood touched the liquid mass, it stirred, whirling and bubbling, shrinking and rounding its edges until all that was left behind was a small rock—earthy green with bloody spots.

"You see," Dizredek said. "It doesn't matter who I am"—he plucked the stone—"but who *you* are."

"The Bloodstone." Avalan's voice was hard with remembrance of what the stone had done to him. He eyed its size, for the first time wondering if it could fit the hollow of the dirk Ronan had given him. *Perhaps with a small trimming.*

"Here." Dizredek urged him to take it. "Have you ever held your birthstone? A real stone, that is, and not some ethereal existence the stonemasters produce."

Avalan faltered. The caustic pain as the Bloodstone had scorched his palms was still held in his mind.

"You're afraid of who you are," Dizredek exclaimed.

"I'm not afraid of anything," Avalan retorted, but then his breath caught in his chest. The voice of Delion boomed in his ears: *A leader does not reject what he fears more than three times.* Avalan rubbed his temples. *Was this the third time?* Ronan had asked him to use the stones in the woods, the stonemaster in the Eagle's Eye, and now this odd man who made his skin crawl was asking him once more to believe in his birthstone. "You don't know me."

"Perhaps." Dizredek ruffled the feathers on his collar with an elegant finger. "Yet the grievance is you don't know yourself."

Avalan eyed the Bloodstone in the bowl with great suspicion. The wrappings around his hands were soaked. The smell of rotting flesh still lingered.

"It won't hurt you," Dizredek promised.

"You speak behind a veil of lies. Why should I trust you?"

Gold sparkled in Dizredek's left eye. "You shouldn't, really. But you will because you have no choice. You long to free the village, to save Bhoran and the tribe. Now take the Bloodstone."

Avalan reached for it. Yet no sooner had he touched the gem than it melted on his palm, a liquid mass slipping through his fingers and dyeing the wrappings of his palms sage. This time, though, he felt nothing. "What ...?"

Dizredek chuckled. "As I thought."

Avalan watched the mass cower in the bowl's bottom, taking with it whatever little patience he had left. "Are you jesting with me?"

Dizredek's smile faded. "Tell me about the voice of the stone."

"What voice?" Avalan made to stand, but Dizredek grabbed his arm. For a spindly man, his grip was firm.

"The night Delion brought your stone forth, the Bloodstone spoke to you. What did it say?"

Struggling to disentangle himself from Dizredek's grip, Avalan frowned. "It asked me to find it."

"A calling of the true stone." The grip tightened. "How did you answer?"

"I didn't," Avalan shouted. *Why do the stones taunt me so?* "The pain was overbearing."

"You refused your destiny."

Avalan twisted away. "I make my own destiny."

"It breaks my heart to hear a descendant of the Bloodstone speak these words. Nothing great ever comes to those who don't believe in the powers of their stone."

Avalan bowed closer to Dizredek. "I don't think you even have a heart. I'm sick of your preaching." He tore the cloak off his shoulders and hurled it to the floor. "You toy with me like I'm a mindless boy. I may not hold your great knowledge, but my heart beats fiercely in my chest. And right now, it thirsts for freedom and justice. Not for blasted birthstones."

Dizredek stood, straightening his velvet cloak. "You writhe in anger and curse the stones, yet you forget they're not your enemy.

Bassalt is. And he's accepted the fate of the stones, while you are running from it with all your might."

"Speak, damn you! What do you wish of me? Twice I've tried to hold a Bloodstone, and what good has that done me? Fire and water, it slips through my grip."

"Mere shadows," Dizredek returned. "The stones Ronan brought back were mere carcasses of dead souls; the stones Delion brings forth, spirits of air; the stones born of alchemy are blood and soil, as you have witnessed. None of them are the *true* Heart of the Bloodstone. Many might try to sell you a gem that isn't yours. You must refuse them. It is the Heart you must find if you wish to free the village."

The words made Avalan's skin prickle, the way it always did when he sensed danger in the forest. "Where is this Heart?"

Tallow flames limned Dizredek's left eye, the golden flakes in it glinting brighter than ever. "Hidden, as I have told you. Away from here. Away from Hydrus."

Avalan's temples throbbed. "I can't leave Hydrus behind. Not when the tribe needs me."

"What use are you to them when you cannot wield the stones? When you cannot free Bhoran? Even if you do, where will you hide him? Bassalt will unearth you as long as you stay here. And that poor girl, Lusha. What of her heart's desire for freedom? Will you not aid her to cross the mountains? Will you condemn their love because you are afraid to claim what's rightfully yours?"

Broken in half, Avalan stood. *The sorcerer is right,* he thought, much as he loathed to admit it. *Bhoran and Lusha cannot stay in Hydrus, and as for Bassalt ... weapons aren't enough.* He clenched the goat leg of his dagger. "How will I find it?"

Dizredek gave him a sly look, as if what he was about to say was of the utmost cunning. "I'll give you the greatest guide of them all. One others won't discern, even if they look hard. He will be with you at all times and guide you to the Heart of the Bloodstone—your heart's deepest desire. Armed with its power, you will face Bassalt as an equal and free Hydrus."

CHAPTER ELEVEN

In the easternmost part of the forest of Hydrus, the statue of Olnos stood gallant. As soon as dusk fell, a fire was lit in the clearing, casting golden flames onto the faces of the tribe. All patiently awaited the trial.

On the silky shadowgrass, Bhoran sat, chest bare, breeches clinging to his thighs, carrying the smells of Bassalt's cellar. His back was to the crowd. Braided wood vines bound his wrists and ankles. A warm breeze had risen, brushing the sweat beads away from his forehead. This summer had proved warmer than any before it, with days and nights of sultry air and no rain.

Bhoran closed his eyes. Behind him curses flowed—superstitious orisons to the stones and solemn requests for punishment. Between these spiteful noises, Bhoran's heart searched for a familiar sound: the warm, wistful voice of a woman, clear and dreamful like the Crystal Lake in the forest.

Yet it didn't prove an easy task. Words of hatred surrounded him, booming in the night.

"He's proud of what he's done."

"He's not going to escape this time. Bassalt *hates* the boy."

"Rightfully so. He is *not* one of us. He looks a beast."

Bhoran smirked. He knew his new appearance would do nothing in his favor, yet he didn't mind. For every fang and claw and etching on his body, there was a story of pain and sadness only he knew. It wasn't as if the tribesfolk had loved him before, when his ivory skin had been smooth. They had hated him much the same then as now.

For Bhoran had the ill luck to have been born with dark stones in his eyes. The jewels of the Onyx, the tribe that had savaged the Stone Lands during the war. *Shortly after you were abandoned in the village as a baby, the Onyx invaded Hydrus,* Bassalt had always loved to remind Bhoran, as if it had been his presence that had caused it.

It was the mercy in the heart of Shaman, Bassalt's father, that had saved Bhoran from an untimely death. The man had adopted Bhoran and planted the seed of doubt in the tribe's mind, that though Bhoran's stones resembled the Onyx, in truth they weren't of the same nature. They hadn't believed him, Bhoran was certain. But couldn't find it in their hearts to murder a suckling.

And now they try me.

Steadying his breath, Bhoran turned his mind inward. The loud voices faded to whispers and at last to a relieving silence. *Why did they have to light a cursed fire?* he thought. *The air's already scalding. It has to be Bassalt—this old bear's eyesight must have worsened if he can no longer depend on the moonlight to see. But what is it you see, brother, when you look at me? An Onyx? Why can't you see what I see?*

When he was still a boy, Bhoran had spent unending mornings by the Crystal Lake, peering into its mirror surface, searching for the white flakes in his eyes. They were too small to be noticed by an unsuspecting eye, but Bhoran had spotted them from time to time in his dark stones. When they had come, whirling and dancing like the snow Ronan had told him fell in the north, Bhoran had always run to Bassalt, eager to show him—to convince his brother he wasn't an Onyx. *Look, Bassalt,* he would shout. *Look how my eyes are full of snow.* Yet the flakes had always gone before his stepbrother could see them, and before long, Bhoran had grown tired of the pity in Bassalt's eyes, and his visits to the lake had halted.

What difference would it have made? They all thought him an Onyx, and an Onyx he must be. A stone full of darkness, to be feared and hated.

He raised his face to the man who always gave him comfort. *Olnos.* At the base of his feet, Bhoran had spent his darkest times. Abandoned, feared, and alone he had been, a true outcast even though it had been much later that the chief had cast him out.

Being next to Olnos made him feel less alone—an Onyx in the company of an Onyx—for tales told this great warrior had turned against his own tribe by blood and helped the tribes win the war. If Olnos had rejected the nature of the Onyx, perhaps Bhoran could do the same. This thought had calmed him in dire times, and so he had returned to the statue every day until the accident that had scored Lusha's eye.

Olnos's head scraped the night sky, his marble gaze rooted to the Onyx stone he pushed with both his hands into the earth. It was on this stony slab that Bhoran had placed Lusha to gift her the Moonstone. The brown marks of her blood had long faded, washed away by forest rain. *Did I push my luck by placing Lusha on a stone that stands for the Onyx?* He knew it was a mere rock, yet somehow Bhoran had come to believe superstition proved to be the cause of ill luck.

The crowd behind him was growing restless, he could tell. Their loud accusations had turned to whispers that spoke of black spirits and places haunted by pain. Bhoran was sure they'd rather this trial was over sooner rather than later, so they could scurry back to the safety of the palisade. *This is what happens when you stay long inside a prison,* Bhoran thought. *Freedom makes your skin creep.*

He twisted his neck to glimpse the guards who loomed above him. Fyridion gave him a sly smile that spoke of great satisfaction for Bhoran's ill fate. *If I could turn a little more, perhaps …*

The guard buried the butt of his spear in Bhoran's nape. "Look to the front," he ordered.

Bhoran tightened the muscles in his belly. *Just one whistle is all it takes, and I'll be free.* Yet he wouldn't do it. Not before he proved Bassalt weak before the whole tribe. Not before he saw Lusha and learned if she still remembered, if she still loved him.

A sudden unrest behind him betrayed the chief's arrival. Bassalt waddled to the front, accompanied by the sure strides of Silver and the timid footsteps of Theran. All of them had donned plain brown tunics and breeches. *To better draw attention to their harmlessness before my figure,* Bhoran thought ruefully. Bassalt's cunning had no match. He watched as Theran spread a white quilt over the Onyx slab. Silver stood beside Olnos's knee, while Bassalt clambered onto the rock.

Bhoran peered into Bassalt's eyes. *How fitting to choose this place to punish me, brother. The only place you knew I found peace.*

Bassalt returned a baleful look. His thick brows were so pressed together they formed a uniform line from one corner of his fat face to the other. The snake ring around his finger caught the firelight and glistened. A leather glove hugged his other hand.

Bhoran was no fool. He knew full well why his stepbrother had chosen this place for the trial, and had for once allowed the whole tribe to leave the safety of the village. The way Bassalt sat there, beneath the hands of Olnos, he looked as though he were being blessed by the Great Warrior of the tribes. While Bhoran sat on the ground, all bound up, in the middle of the clearing, an enemy waiting to be crushed by the chief's judgment.

When Bassalt finally spoke, his voice poured out hoarsely. "We are gathered here tonight, under the unwearied eye of Olnos, to bring justice to Ronan, the victim of a brutal murder."

Gasps filtered through the gathering.

Bhoran tried the tightness of his fastenings. He didn't feel the least bit of sympathy for the tribe. Most of them had seen the merchant as a means to learn the tidings of the outer lands, or to get hold of goods and trades. The people who truly loved Ronan, he could count on the fingers of one hand. One of them was he, for Bhoran loved Ronan for being the father Avalan had never had.

The chief cleared his throat to ease the commotion. "Near twenty years I've stood as chief of Hydrus—years during which you have savored peace. Yet it is also during these years that many of you have spoken against me and doubted my judgment." A leaden silence descended, and Bassalt lifted a proud chin. "When I ordered the fence to be built, you moaned and spoke of a lack of freedom. When I ordered the strolling through the forest to cease, you mocked me and buried your axe blades in blackwood trees to spite me. When I forbade the birthstones, you retorted with pleas of power and tradition. *Tradition* …

"What good is tradition, I ask you, when it endangers the lives of our tribe? How much is a Larimar's life worth to the Onyx? Nothing. The Onyx shows no mercy. The Onyx finds the Larimar merchant returning from his trip, strolling through the forest, paying no heed to the protection of my fence, and what does the Onyx do? He kills. And he does so swiftly and without mercy." Bassalt slid his glove-bearing hand inside his robe and drew out a bloodied dagger.

Under the firelight, Bhoran glimpsed the golden blade sparkling in places that weren't caked with dried blood. In the hilt, the Onyx stone remained unchanged by the flames. Bhoran closed his eyes, the memory of dead Ronan coming to mind. That night, Bhoran had heard a scream. He'd charged at once in the direction of the plea, yet he had never been good at finding his way through the forest—the blackwood trees, huddled like siblings, offered him no opportunity for marking his way, and no matter how hard Avalan had tried to teach him growing up, reading the signs of the ground was a task Bhoran had never mastered.

When Bhoran had finally found Ronan, he was already dead, his unseeing eyes wide open, the azure light of the Larimar gone. Next to him had lain this cursed dagger. Bhoran had picked it up, and it was then Lhorin had found him. Bhoran had thrown the dagger aside when he'd heard the rustling of nearby bushes, but it had been too late. Silver's men had been on him faster than lightning. A cursed moment of weakness he had no one else but himself to blame for. He never should have gone so close to the village, yet his heart had been full of longing.

"The stone on this dagger is, as I feared, an Onyx," Bassalt declared.

The crowd gasped, disgusted.

"Only an Onyx can wield an Onyx-enchanted weapon and remove a life. Bhoran of the Unknown, rise." The guards hauled Bhoran to his feet. "You stand before the whole tribe, accused of the murder of Ronan."

Bhoran gave him a daring stare. *Just a whistle.*

"Speak, damn you!" Spittle frothed on Bassalt's lips. "What have you to say? A fair trial demands your side to be heard. Why did you kill our merchant?"

Nothing is fair about this, brother. Nothing ever was, Bhoran thought, but to Bassalt he said nothing.

"Very well." Bassalt stood. When he flicked his wrists, the crunching sound of uprooting rose behind the statue. The earth shook. Over Olnos's head, ropy vines slashed, their ends tethered to a wooden cage they hauled forth. "It seems the cellar did nothing to break your spirit. Let us see what happens when you spend the night caged and folded before the whole tribe. Perhaps tomorrow your tongue will have loosened."

When the guards dragged him forth, Bhoran finally spoke. "Prove it."

Bassalt raised an arm to halt the guards. "What did you say?"

"Prove it, *brother,*" Bhoran mocked. "Prove that I'm an Onyx."

The silence returned, heavier than ever. Bhoran knew he was toying with fire, yet he didn't care. *What more is left to me? Onyx or not, I have no love. Let Bassalt show them who I really am.*

Bassalt's ringed fingers flexed with anger; his temples turned beetroot red. Theran whispered something in his ear, yet the chief shoved him aside. He bared his teeth in a grotesque smile. "Very well. Leave him," he ordered the guards.

Bhoran felt their grips merely loosen.

"I said leave him!" Bassalt growled. He tore the dagger out of his robes. With a swift move, he hurled it toward Bhoran.

Screams resounded. For a moment, Bhoran thought the blade would pierce his heart, yet it landed before his feet, edge dipped into the soil, hilt quivering.

"Pick it up, *dear brother.*" Bassalt gifted him a fake smile. "Pick the Onyx weapon up."

With the murderous dagger now near, the guards cowered away. Bhoran scowled. *It's just a weapon, stone or not. Bassalt plays with your minds!* he wanted to scream. *He knows I've held an Onyx before, and this serves no proof of who I am.*

Now that the guards held him no more, Bhoran turned to the tribe. A sea of faces stared back at him, a tribe he hadn't seen for over six long years. To Bhoran, they all looked the same: faces of young and old, women and men and children, all scared of him, all hating him for something he hadn't done, for something he wasn't. Among them he had hoped to see the ones he loved. *Avalan. Lusha.* Yet the only familiar face he spotted was Farmera's. Tear-stricken and horrified she was, her head shaking in warning as if to tell him not to indulge Bassalt.

"Enough," Bassalt ordered. "Pick—it—up."

Bhoran stared at the murder weapon before his feet. *Why haven't they come?* Anger and sadness raged inside him, and he longed for the rush of venom. *Curse you, Dhylinea. You were right. I should never have returned. There's no one left for me here.* He tore the blade free from the ground. His fingers brushed the Onyx stone, yet he felt nothing but cold emptiness.

A soft whistle left Bassalt's lips.

He's calling an animal, Bhoran knew. Sure as the waves of a sea storm, a small bird chirped down from the night sky. A starling. It landed on Bassalt's palm, and with a quick whisper from him, the bird plunged toward Bhoran.

Bhoran backtracked too late. The starling impaled itself on the dagger in his hand. Warm blood trickled to his fingers. "No ..." He held the bird's tender body, his heart heavy.

Behind him, a deathly silence fell.

"Regard!" Bassalt roared, mad with excitement. "His eyes are dead as the Onyx. His soul is empty as the Onyx. His heart is dark as the Onyx."

The tribe took up the chanting. *"His eyes are dead as the Onyx. His soul is empty as the Onyx. His heart is dark as the Onyx."* Drums fractured the silence. The vines stirred with life, shaking the cage. *"His eyes are dead as the Onyx. His soul is empty as the Onyx. His heart is dark as the Onyx."* The fire's flames rose higher. The crackling of burning wood tore the air. The singing voices grew louder. *"His eyes are dead as the Onyx! His soul is empty as the Onyx! His heart is dark as the Onyx!"*

Bassalt shot an arm into the air, ceasing the cursed cries. "Bhoran of the Unknown, child of darkness and death and emptiness, I sentence you to death by hanging for the murder of Ronan. Before the eyes of Olnos, the night of tomorrow will witness your last breath. Take him!"

Fyridion knocked dagger and bird from Bhoran's hands. The guards dragged him forward. He didn't resist them. When they forced him to bend and threw him in the cage headfirst, Bhoran felt nothing. When they closed the cage door on his face, Bhoran felt nothing. When they spat and cursed at him through clenched teeth, Bhoran felt nothing.

Bhoran's heart, mind, and soul were empty as the cage rose into the air, hoisted by vines that pulled from opposite directions. From above, he stared at the crowd below. He clutched at the cage bars, the spark of hatred igniting in him.

But then his soul they had called empty stirred, and his heart they had called dark fluttered, for down there in the crowd was a face. A linen gag muffled her mouth. Her face shone with the colors of the full moon, and a silent tear stroked her silver scar.

Lusha.

CHAPTER TWELVE

The night had fallen, dark and silent, when Avalan crawled out of the passage. Warm seawater licked the soles of his feet. He gulped fresh air, trying to cast away the cavern's foul smells.

A full moon hung low above the village. It was the first time Avalan had seen it come so close, as if it stood witness to a solemn working. "Bhoran," he whispered. Over his shoulder, he watched the cave's entrance. *How long have I been down there?* When he had slid through the maw, the sun had still been shining in the sky. Dizredek's stories, and the binding ritual to the guide, had kept him underground for longer than he'd expected.

Now the village was drenched in an uneasy silence.

Avalan quickened his pace as Dizredek's workings swirled in his mind. The sorcerer had drawn more blood from him—a binding ritual, he had said. Then after Dizredek had chanted and mixed all kinds of liquids together, filling the chamber with a sickening haze, he'd finally set Avalan free. All Avalan had to do was follow Sigil's trail, and she would lead him to his guide.

Once on the beach, Avalan scoured the sand for footprints but found nothing. Even the trail he had followed to the cave was gone. Avalan cursed. He didn't much like how things were unfolding—he felt a mere doll in the hands of a child. Yet the guide could wait. He had to return to the village, learn of Bhoran's fate.

He hoped with all his might Farmera had convinced Bassalt to stay his hand.

The south gate came into sight. A lone guard stood atop the watchtower, his gaze rooted to the sea. When he noticed Avalan, he raised his spear for a moment, then lowered it with recognition.

Avalan ran to him. This time, there was no point in hiding, nor sneaking through the trench. He recognized Kar, a youth of only eleven summers. "What has happened?" he asked him, wondering why a boy stood in the usual place of the guards.

Kar's face was twisted with fear. "It's the Onyx. Bassalt gathered the tribe for his trial at the statue of Olnos."

A trial? Bassalt had moved much faster than Avalan had expected. He gazed through the gate at the deserted village. The silence drowned him. "When did they all leave?"

"Long ago. Silver told me not to abandon my place until someone returns to relieve me of my duty. I am to spear anyone who tries to escape." He leaned forward, clutching the rail. "Avalan, I'm scared. Would you stay with me? The talon was your friend. He won't harm me if you tell him not to."

Avalan clenched his fists. "His name's Bhoran, and he's no Onyx. You have nothing to fear."

At that, he darted forward, the statue of Olnos in his mind. He cursed Dizredek and his magic for luring him into the cave. A free Hydrus would hold no meaning if Bhoran was dead.

He leaped over the tables in the feasting ground, headed for the east side of the fence. Though the north path would lead him to the statue faster, he couldn't chance upon whoever guarded it, for fear they might not be as frightened or friendly as Kar.

Using thick vines, he hoisted himself up. Sharp spikes at the fence's peak tugged at his breeches. He groaned and swung down, rolled over soft shadowgrass. Bhoran's face floated in his mind as he ran; the cold clutches of fear clawed at his spine. *What if he already lies dead, like Ronan?*

He bit his tongue. Pain constrained his dark thoughts. The statue of Olnos rose over the treetops. He was closer now. He could hear the thousand whispers of the tribe's voices. Over them, Bassalt's voice boomed as if the chief was giving a solemn speech. *Is it over?* Their backs came into view—the whole tribe had gathered here. A tribe that rarely left the confinements of a fence had joined together in the face of punishment of an Onyx. *He didn't do it,* Avalan wanted to scream, yet all he did was elbow his way through sweaty backs and sodden tunics, slipping through the line of Silver's guards.

Chest out, he slid over the silky grass out into the open. Silence fell around him. Under Olnos's watch stood Bassalt and Silver. Of Bhoran there was no sign. A bloodied golden dagger lay on the ground, next to it a dead starling. Avalan watched the blade with hatred and horror. *This must be the murder weapon,* he thought, bile rising to his mouth. *Ronan's blood.* He made to pick the dagger up.

"Don't touch it," Bassalt warned, his voice thunder in the silence.

Forgetting he was surrounded, Avalan strode forth. "Where is Bhoran? What have you done to him?"

"Take your hand away from your weapon," Silver commanded.

Surprised, Avalan looked down. His grip on his goat dagger was firm, an instinct gained from all his years hunting. "You beasts!" Avalan called out. "What proof do you hold, Bassalt? Where is Ronan? What did you want to hide by burying him?"

Bassalt stood, tore off his glove, and threw it to the ground. On his other hand, the stone on the snake ring caught the moonlight and glistened.

Thief, Avalan thought, but then the chief twisted his wrists.

"Avalan!" a familiar voice warned from a distance.

Bhoran? Before he had time to see where his friend was, thick vines coiled around him. Like writhing snakes, they curled around his knees, his arms, his torso, one of them slinking upward around his throat, twining and twisting … suffocating him.

His eyes watering, Avalan fought against his creeping captors to reach his dagger. Yet their grip was firm. He felt his head lighten, his consciousness leaving him …

Bassalt strode toward him and retrieved the golden dagger. "The Onyx has returned to our village!" he roared. Avalan saw him brandish the weapon before the whole tribe. "Those of you who survived the battle of Hydrus know well what that means. I am the only one who can protect you. The only one whom the Onyx fears." He dropped the dagger to the ground.

Avalan felt the chief's stubby hands poke around his belt. Then came a tearing sensation, and Avalan's eyes widened when he saw his goat dagger in Bassalt's hands. *No!* With a sickening crunch, the chief broke the dagger, blade and bone parting. He hurled them to the ground.

"I do this only for Farmera," Bassalt whispered in Avalan's face. His spittle reeked of hatred. "Challenge me again, and I shall not spare you."

As soon as the chief turned his back, the vines around Avalan loosened. As he caught his breath, a surge of anger boiled inside him, blinding him. He swooped up his broken dagger from the ground, clutched at the blade, ready to send it spinning into Bassalt's back. Spear tips pinched his body, Silver's men at the ready to protect the chief.

Cursing, Avalan spun and made for the forest. "SIGIL!" he roared. *Curse you, Dizredek,* he thought, thrusting the goat leg and blade into his breeches. *Where is this guide of yours? Where is the Heart?* Bassalt shouldn't remain chief any longer.

Despair clawed at his chest. He'd heard Bhoran's voice, yet he hadn't seen him. He needed to find Sigil and return to the statue. *Follow the footprints,* Dizredek had said as Avalan had left the cave. And yet there were none. Avalan scoured the forest floor, kicked branches out of his way, sliced dangling vines with his arms. He wished to sever them all. Burn the whole forest down, and Bassalt with it. For a small moment, his heart told him to go to his secret lair in the Eagle's Eye, snatch his blackwood bow, and plant an arrow between Bassalt's hateful eyes.

It is no good, he realized, kicking loose stones. The chief's vines would smash his arrows before they'd even had a chance to near him.

On the soil, a familiar paw print caught his eye. His surprise was so great he stumbled and fell, the taste of summer soil filling his mouth. He spat the dirt out and crawled to the track. *Sigil!* A fresh trail. It led in the direction of his tree house. *Has she returned home?*

He stormed after her footprints.

As he'd suspected, the trail ended at the roots of the white poplar that held his house. He hoisted himself off the ground. The wraps on his hands ripped open. Warm blood painted the vines, yet he didn't mind. He felt nothing.

When he jumped inside, he found the room empty. "Sigil!" he roared. "Where are you, girl?" Sweat dribbling down his sides, he looked around. Silver shafts of moonlight shone through the opening behind him, but every corner of his room was painfully empty. He sniffed the air. *Forest. Rot. Sigil.* Then he spun to face the entrance, the sense of being watched heavy upon his shoulders.

He drew out the blade of his goat dagger, held it between his teeth, tied his loose hair up in a horsetail—

Feral like a wild beast, Sigil leaped through the opening. Her fangs were bared. Her spittle glistened. The jump was so sudden Avalan fell backward, his head biting into the edge of his bed. The blade cut his tongue; warm blood filled his mouth. Sigil stepped on his chest and growled, a cry of agony. As Avalan raised a hand to calm her, she spun and leaped down into the quiet village.

"No!"

Avalan sprang to his feet and grabbed a vine. He lurched forward and landed badly, rolling on the soil. When he stood, Sigil was racing through the village. He cursed, tearing the blade from his mouth. Her frenzied run led them to the fence. Avalan watched in terror as Sigil's claws found purchase in the wooden beams. The tiger climbed over them with ease, leaping above the spiky ends and disappearing on the other side.

Avalan charged at the fence, his fingers desperately grabbing for a hold, yet he fell again and again, his nails breaking. Lodging his blade in the fence, he pulled himself up. He expected a sharp pain to come, yet his wounded hands remained numb.

Once on the other side, he scoured the ground again for Sigil's footprints.

As if she knew he'd fallen behind, the tiger roared from the far distance. *The lake.* Avalan spun.

After some quick strides, he found her pacing the Crystal Lake's shore. Sigil didn't quiet when she saw him. Instead, she growled at the calm water and shook her massive head.

"Easy now, girl." Avalan knew how much Sigil hated the water. Ever since he'd rescued her from drowning when she was a mere cub, Sigil had never again dipped a paw into the lake. "What is it, Sigil? What is there?"

She snorted.

Carefully Avalan approached the shore. He knelt, his worried reflection staring back at him. The strange sensation of being watched returned, and this time, he finally saw the origin of the tiger's uneasiness. A shadow, black as a starless night, had formed on the moonlit lake next to his own reflection. He twisted his neck, ready to face the caster, but there was no one there.

Confused, he turned again to the lake's water. The shadow remained. It was the dark silhouette of a tall man, bearing a close resemblance to Avalan himself. He took an uncertain step backward. Sigil's fur brushed against his thigh. She stood by his side, calmer now, peering at the strange reflection. Avalan moved, and the shadow followed, leaving the lake's surface to form again on the ground.

A shiver ran down his spine as the words of Dizredek's binding ritual echoed in his head. *Two shadows standing side by side: one cast by a man in the realm of the living, and the other by the ghost of an aching past.*

Avalan rested a firm hand on Sigil's head to steady himself. Dizredek had kept his promise—he had given him a guide no one would easily discern. A second shadow.

Avalan raised a hand in greeting. The shadow returned it. Sigil growled, her back tensing beneath Avalan's grip. "Shh, girl. Easy now." He turned to the shadow. "Can you hear what I say?"

The shadow nodded, an eerie wave of its head.

"Before we leave for the Heart, I must save my friend. Bhoran."

To that, the shadow remained unmoving.

"I will run now," he said, dragging his words. "You won't stop me." He took some steps back, testing the shadow's reaction, yet it did nothing to hinder him.

Avalan knelt before Sigil, pressed his forehead to hers. "They have Bhoran. We must go to him. Olnos."

Sigil closed her eyes, and Avalan leaped to his feet. He ran for the statue without so much as a backward glance to see if the shadow followed. Yet all the while as he ran, he didn't feel the lightness his rushing through the forest used to give him. Instead, his every step felt heavy, as if a terrible weight was pulling against his will.

When he glimpsed Olnos's head peeking through the treetops, he slowed. Sigil trotted beside him. Through the musty air, the tribe's voices swam. The ground vibrated to the footsteps of men, women, and children. *The trial is over if they're returning. But what is the fate of Bhoran?*

He needed to get closer, hide in the trees that surrounded the clearing. There was no turning back now. After Avalan's attack on Bassalt, Silver was sure to place guards on him, watching his every move.

Swift as a darting arrow, he climbed the nearest trunk, Sigil on his heels. Perched on a thick branch, he watched as the tribe returned to the village. Some hung their heads low, while others chattered with excitement. Avalan bent down to listen.

"Did you see how he *touched* it?" Gremian's son told his brother.

"Did you see the bones in the talon's head?" the other boy retorted, ignoring the question. "That must have *hurt*, putting them there."

"Stop talking. Keep moving," Garlea scolded them. "Rain is coming."

Avalan frowned as the children skidded off. Now Garlea had mentioned it, he could smell a distant storm in the air. He didn't gain much more insight from the other tribesfolk. Most of them seemed too lost in their thoughts to speak, and those who spoke did so in hushed whispers. Avalan breathed more easily. As long as no talk of death reached his ears, he still dared hope.

As the procession thinned, he glimpsed his mother. She walked beside Silver's men, who had a hooded figure in their grip. He recognized the cloak of Lusha, her white feet peeking beneath the hem as they dragged her. Avalan clenched his teeth yet thought better of interfering. It would serve best if he remained hidden for now, until he'd seen with his own eyes what fate had befallen Bhoran.

Bassalt and Silver came sauntering by last, Theran a thin shadow behind them.

"Why didn't you do it right then and there?" Silver demanded.

Bassalt shook his head. "It serves us better to wait for the light of the sun. His execution will make for a better spectacle."

Silver stopped so abruptly poor Theran almost bumped into the scales adorning his back. "With whom are you jesting, Bassalt? If you're of a mind to let the boy escape again, know that this time you'll find me across you!"

Bassalt looked around. "Hush. I wouldn't think of—"

"You would." Silver cut him off. "Avalan called us *beasts*, you hear? Beasts! And yet you let him leave without a scrape. If your heart has grown weak before the sight of your stepbrother, then might I remind you he murdered an innocent man and our only means of connection to the lands."

"Stones curse you, Silver. Didn't I condemn him to death before the whole tribe? You think me so weak as not to keep my promise? Brother or not, I know what he is."

"Then why?"

Bassalt shifted his weight. "I have a matter to discuss with him before I send him to meet his tribe. After stewing in the juices of thoughts of his own death, I believe his tongue will finally loosen. And then I shall know."

"What is the nature of this matter?" Silver demanded.

Theran dared teeter closer. "My chief? Might I suggest you have this talk beneath the dry roof of our house? Rain is coming." He raised his palms against the light drizzle that fell from the sky.

Silver looked up and grunted, then stormed ahead. Bassalt and Theran followed.

Once Avalan heard their footsteps no longer, he climbed down and crawled closer to the clearing. Sigil whimpered, shaking her head, and Avalan knew well why. Alongside them slid the second shadow, dark against the moonlit shadowgrass.

The crackling of firewood and smell of burning bark wafted from the clearing. Avalan spied Gale, Fernar, and Jordel standing guard, all three Silver's men, armed with spears and knives, sitting around a fire. Judging by the size of the burnt logs, the fire must have been greater, only Avalan was too angered before to have noticed.

He searched the clearing for Bhoran. He circled the tree line, not daring to lose the cover of the forest.

"What do you see, girl?" he whispered to Sigil. "Where is he?"

Sigil scratched the ground with a thick paw. Avalan glimpsed the second shadow beneath his tiger's leg. The shadow didn't seem to mind the disturbance. Instead, it raised a pointing finger. Avalan followed its direction, and it was then that he saw him.

Perched twenty feet above the clearing, Bhoran was trapped in a wooden cage too small for his figure. Ropy vines held it in place—Bassalt's work, no doubt. Avalan's heart beat faster. It had been six long years since he had last seen his friend's face. And now he found it hard to recognize it. Lusha was right—Bhoran resembled little his old self. In the place of the boy Avalan remembered now was a man with sturdy muscles and etchings and fangs for adornment.

I have to free him.

Squeezing Sigil's paw, Avalan prayed for the rain to grow greater. Perhaps then the men would seek shelter beneath the statue of Olnos, and he could make his move.

To his dismay, the night went on with only a light drizzle. The men didn't enjoy it but thought better of abandoning their position. The fire soon fizzled, the smoke engulfed by the hazy air. From time to time, Avalan watched the guards glimpse up and then swiftly avert their gaze as if a look from Bhoran's eyes would be enough for them to suffer the fate of the merchant.

Avalan was chewing the soft lining of his cheek when the bushes behind him shook. He turned, pulling out the bare blade of the goat dagger. Yet he did not need to use it, for it was Lusha. Her pale skin was wet with tears, and dried rivers of blood crowned her lips.

CHAPTER THIRTEEN

Rain tapped on the ivy leaves of the roof, filling Bassalt's bedchamber with an endless rustle. Bassalt swirled the wine in his cup, watching Silver. The commander sat across from him, nervously rubbing his temples.

"What's taking him so long?" Silver grumbled after a while.

As if Theran had sensed their growing impatience, he pushed the door open with the heel of his foot. He carried a tray with a rich supper. Theran served them, then took his leave.

The smell of roasted quail and glazed spuds made Bassalt's mouth water. He forked a thigh and buried his teeth in it with great pleasure. Silver gulped the tankard of ale Theran had left to go with their supper. "Stop munching; start talking. What is this matter you wish to discuss with the talon before his execution?"

Bassalt wiped grease from his chin. "He didn't do it." He pinched a spud and tossed it into his mouth, savoring the look of dismay on his commander's face. "Bhoran didn't kill the merchant," he said, chomping.

Silver banged his tankard on the table. "I *knew* it. I knew you would find any excuse for not killing him—"

"Let me finish." Bassalt raised a fat palm. "He didn't do it, yet I *will* kill him."

At that, Silver seemed surprised. Through narrowed eyes, he

searched Bassalt's face, as if trying to discern the snare in his words. "Have the years messed with your mind?" the commander said at last. "The talon killed the merchant, and there's no doubt about it. My men caught him in the act. The whole tribe saw him touch the dagger."

Bassalt wagged a greased finger. "Your men caught him *after* the act," he corrected. "And as far as his holding the dagger, I had to see it for myself. And what I saw convinced me of the truth of the matter. He didn't kill the merchant, but he might sing a zestful song of what else happened in the forest that night."

Blue veins pulsated in Silver's neck. "What truth do you speak of? Your words better begin making some sense, or I swear, I shall stride down there myself and end the talon's life." He brushed the hilt of his sword.

Bassalt eyed the commander for a while, considering how much he could share with him without further arousing his anger. If they were to succeed in this, he and Silver needed to remain a tight fist. "Take your sword out."

Silver's eyes widened. "You mean to fight me for this filthy—"

"Do as I tell you."

Slowly Silver unsheathed his sword. It was a respectable piece of steel, forged in the city of Laenathas. The blade had seen its fair share of battle during the tribal war, its jagged edges the proof. In its hilt, the stone of Heliodor—Silver's birthstone—shone with power. When Silver's palm wrapped around it, the weapon came alive, sparkling, as if it drew strength from its owner's soul.

"Now give it to me," Bassalt ordered, wiping the grease from his hands with a napkin.

Silver did so reluctantly.

When the chief took it, the blade lost its shine at once. Bassalt cocked his head and smirked. "A curious thing, these stones, aren't they? In your hands, the weapon comes alive with power, yet in mine ..." He shrugged. "Though I do not approve of your failure to master your birthstone, its place on your weapon now helps me prove my point."

Silver took the blade off Bassalt's hands, then sheathed it. "The

Onyx dagger," he began slowly, his every word a realization of Bassalt's small show. "It didn't change once Bhoran held it."

Bassalt dipped his fingers into the food again. "A solid observation." His teeth crunched a leftover bone in the quail.

"What does that go to say? The Onyx remains ever dark."

Spitting the spiky bone out, Bassalt shrugged. "I do not claim to hold mastery over the ways of the Onyx. But to me, this incident raises serious doubts. Ones I am of a mind to probe further before the day of his execution dawns."

"To what end? If the boy is innocent, why didn't he speak up for himself? Why stand there and brood over a thing he hadn't done?"

Why indeed, brother? "Did you look at him? He looks more a beast than a tribesman. Perhaps these past years in the wilderness have loosened his mind. Despite that, I might extract whatever his memory holds of the night the merchant was murdered."

Silver clenched his fists. "Only a true Onyx can kill with this weapon. We all saw the starling die."

"I sent it to its death, and you well know it." Bassalt waved a dismissive hand without a shred of guilt.

"If not the talon, then who? My men and I searched for the Onyx, as you commanded. There's no one out there."

Bassalt looked at the beads of sweat crowning his commander's brows. He knew they weren't from the heat. Bassalt could conceal his thoughts no longer. Silver had always been a brave man. It was ripe time he learned the truth. "You remember the darkness?" he asked him, rubbing the stone on his snake ring. "I've had a strong feeling of the presence of the Onyx in our village. For many moonturns now. The feeling hasn't eased, I'm afraid, even after capturing my stepbrother. And now this cursed dagger has confirmed my darkest fear."

"It cannot be, Bassalt. We killed them all."

Bassalt kept rubbing the ring. "Magic makes no mistakes."

Silver banged his fist on the table. "It has to be him. Bhoran—the talon. It has to be, Bassalt. You wish me to believe that after twenty years an Onyx dwells among us? Then why can we not see him?"

Bassalt furrowed his brows. Stonemaster Delion's words after the War of the Stones had been won still echoed clearly in his mind: *All the true children of the Onyx are dead.* "Killing Bhoran will aid us." He looked at the snake ring. "If the stone no longer turns dark after his death, then we shall have our answer."

"No. There must be a way to know before we kill him."

"I'm afraid it is the only way."

"You'd kill an innocent man to prove a point?" Silver's words dripped with disgust. "What if we're wrong?"

Bassalt raised a curious brow. "I thought you wanted him dead. As I recall, it was you who pestered me through the woods for not ending his life right there and then."

"That was before you told me he might be innocent. Curse you, Bassalt. What games do you play?"

"The ones that keep a tribe together. Imagine what chaos would ensue should we release the boy now. The merchant was murdered with an Onyx dagger. The sooner we give them a death in retaliation, the faster their fear will recede."

"And killing him is better? What will we tell them then if your suspicions of his innocence prove true? How will we ever look them in the eye?"

"I don't recall you having a problem facing the tribe after what we did to Volkan."

That halted Silver's retorts. His jaw, though, remained clenched; the veins in his neck popped so blue and throbbing that Bassalt was certain they would burst open.

"That was different," Silver said. "Another time, another motive."

"Love, hatred, brotherhood ... does the motive change things?" Bassalt peered through the shame that shadowed Silver's face. "We must remain one if we're to surpass this. The Night of the Spirits is fast approaching, and the stench of rebellion is in the air. Ronan was carrying birthstones with him. If they fall into the wrong hands ..."

Silver slitted his eyes. "How do you hold this knowledge? Where are the stones now?"

"One of my servants found Ronan's sack stashed in a log in the forest, not far away from where he was murdered," Bassalt explained. "I held my tongue until I was certain of what I was seeing. There is only one reason Ronan would have smuggled stones into the village. The tribe will move against us."

Silver rubbed his temples, his lips a tight line. Before he had time to grant an answer, an urgent knock at the door broke the silence.

"Not now, Theran," Bassalt barked. Yet the door burst open despite his orders.

Gremian walked in, a palm pressed over his ear, blood running between his fingers. "Chieftain," he mumbled. "Your daughter … she ran away. She … she *bit* me."

Silver sprang up with such force his chair fell backward. He glared at Bassalt. "Let us go have this talk of yours with the talon. Once and for all."

CHAPTER FOURTEEN

BHORAN HAD NEVER MINDED the rain. Getting soaked in a cage twenty feet above the ground made to him no difference.

The bird's-eye position had given him the best view he'd had for six long years. Perched upon a thick branch were Lusha and Avalan. Huddled together for warmth, they waited in the stormy night, Sigil's thick tail wrapped around them both.

Bhoran kept wiping the droplets from his eyes, hungering for more sight of the woman who held his heart. In his mind, he kept calling her name. So much that he was afraid he might slip and say it aloud. He glanced at the guards below. Fernar, Gale, and Jordel. Growing up, Bhoran had learned to avoid them, as they had him. Gale had been kind to Bhoran just that once, showing him the way through the woods when he had been but five summers old and lost. But now even Gale dared not meet his gaze.

Three men against two they would be should Bhoran attempt to escape. They still had Sigil, Avalan's greatest weapon, her claws as sharp as he remembered.

A whistle could change everything, Bhoran thought. *Then why am I not doing it?* Even as he wondered, he knew the answer. He was afraid to lose Lusha. As long as he stayed in this cage, he had all night ahead to watch her. If he whistled, though, that would change in a heartbeat. He would once more be the hunted, the outcast, the one hated for his eyes …

Angry voices sounded over the patter of rainfall. Bhoran looked at the guards, but they seemed as confused as he was. They all stood now, abreast and pointing their spears in the direction of the tree line.

"Lower your weapons!" Silver ordered, striding into the clearing, swaying his sword. With a quick slash, he severed one of the four vines holding Bhoran's cage.

Cursing, Bhoran grabbed at the bars as the cage trembled and tilted.

Bassalt came waddling behind Silver. "Halt!" he ordered.

"Then get him down now!" Silver barked into his face.

With a flick of Bassalt's wrists, the outstretched vines loosened, and Bhoran's cage plummeted. Before it crashed, the vines tightened again, making the cage hover barely a foot above the ground.

Silver strode to him, his voice thunder over the pouring rain. "Where is my daughter?"

The man had aged well, Bhoran saw, his figure still strong and sturdy, his eyes still bearing the same special hatred for the talon who had dared to love his daughter.

"Speak, damn you! Where?" He shook Bhoran's cage.

Gale placed a hand on Silver's shoulder. "She isn't here, Chieftain. We would have seen her."

Silver shoved him back and gave Bhoran a lethal look. Through the anger, Bhoran discerned a sense of pity and wonder. *He fears me.*

"It is clear Lusha isn't here," Bassalt said, approaching with caution and soothing words. "Perhaps it's best you go to find her before any harm comes to her. Let me deal with him."

After spitting at Bhoran's cage, Silver turned on his heel, barking orders to Gremian. Together they disappeared through the blackwood trees.

"Give us some space, but stay alert," Bassalt ordered the guards. Then to Bhoran he said, "I'll lower your cage now, brother, so I can sit and have a talk with you."

Once the cage touched the wet shadowgrass, Bhoran braced

himself for more questions about Lusha's disappearance. He pressed his lips into a tight line.

With a sigh, Bassalt sat on the mud. His long white hair fell, a tangled mess, around his cloak. "It was a stormy night like this one when we first found you."

The thumping of Bhoran's heart quickened. He raised his eyes. Bassalt had never before wished to talk about that night.

The striped stones in Bassalt's eyes glowed with a dim light. "I won't lie to you, brother, I hated that night and all the nights that followed with you in our house. You stole my mother's love and shone a light on all my dark corners. *You* had the black eyes, yet my black heart was all my parents saw. And then your tribe came and took both of them away."

Bhoran could hold himself no longer. "Spare me the sad talk, *brother*. You had a family, and I had nothing."

Bassalt waved a ringed hand. "Talk of the past bears no matter. Our parents are gone, but we still have each other. And right now, it seems you are in great need of me."

"Need of *you*?" Bhoran clutched at the wooden bars. "You condemned me to death!"

"Indeed. And only I can be the one to save you. Much like I did last time the tribe cried for your head. I could have ordered your death then, but I spared you. Yet you had to return, forcing my hand, standing over the dead body of the merchant. What is a chief to do, I ask you?" Without waiting for an answer, he slipped the dagger out of the depths of his robes. "The stone is a true Onyx—I've tested this myself with Father's potion. Why doesn't the dagger come alive in your hands, brother? What is it you are?"

Bhoran clenched his teeth. *I've told you time and again about the snowflakes in my eyes, but you refuse to listen*, he thought, but to Bassalt he said, "Does this prove I'm not an Onyx?" He winced at the hope in his voice—hope was a dangerous thing for an outcast.

"No." Bassalt's denial carried a grave tone. "Perhaps some kind of a bizarre oddity in your eyes, or perhaps the stones see fit to mock us. Be that as it may, the shadow of the Onyx covers the village. I can feel it. I have proof of it, and yet … the cursed stone doesn't reveal itself to me. Tell me, what did you see the night Ronan died?"

Bhoran gave him a cold stare. Bassalt's words had crushed whatever little hope had emerged in his chest. "I saw only death, and this bloodied dagger."

"No sign of the killer?"

When Bhoran shook his head, Bassalt edged closer. "Where have you been hiding all these years?"

To that Bhoran gave no answer. There was more to protect than a mere hiding place. Dhylinea had made him promise to keep her secret.

Bassalt twisted the dagger in his hands. "You couldn't have been alone all this time," he pressed. "All these etchings on your body … such great precision. They seem to me the workings of a woman. I can feel great power rising from them. Tell me, brother, perchance in your years in hiding, did you sire any children?"

Bhoran ground his teeth. There was only one woman he wished to be the mother of his children, and he could not have her. He forced himself not to look up at Lusha, lest he betray her hiding place. "Do you mock me, *brother*?"

Bassalt shook his head disappointedly, as if he had exhausted all possible explanations of the misfortune that had hit their village. "You give me no other choice but to kill you. If only to gain some time."

"Time?"

"I know you didn't kill the merchant." Bassalt's expression now turned from disappointment to sheer contempt. "How could you have? It takes a man of strong will, not only muscle, to inflict such a blow. And you, *brother*, are neither of those. Not a man, neither strong. You are but a mere malfunction, a jest of the stones played on my family. To punish me for my arrogance, they sent you. Of that I am sure. And on the morrow, I shall repay their gift with your blood." He staggered to his feet.

"You beast," Bhoran cursed, grabbing for him a moment too late. The cage lurched upward, and it seemed to him much higher this time. When the vines tightened, Bhoran watched Bassalt go, his long hair billowing behind him. *Just a whistle,* he thought, yet he waited.

Once the guards had returned to their place, Bhoran stared at

Avalan and Lusha. All this time, they hadn't dared to move. Bhoran took in Lusha's alabaster skin, which he knew would have shone brightly on a full-moon night, had the dark clouds above allowed it. The rain poured harder now, or so it seemed to him, every droplet a whip on his skin. Avalan stirred as if he'd sensed the shift in Bhoran's heart. *I cannot take you with me*, Bhoran thought. *You cannot live the life I've tasted.* Yet in his heart, he hoped Avalan would follow.

Bhoran pressed two fingers into his lips and whistled.

It was an ear-piercing sound, a shrill harbinger of trouble, a call for aid. He buried a finger into his tightly braided hair, ripped out a fang. Having been entangled atop his head for all these years, it took a piece of his scalp with it as it went. He wedged it beneath the vine rope that held the door of his confinement, and ripped the fastening. As he kicked his way out of the cage, yelling and cursing broke the musty air below.

The guards raised their spears. Bhoran grabbed one of the vines. He hung himself upside down, hands grappling the ropy vine, ankles balancing his way. A spear tore the air, whooshing beneath his back. Despite the guard's efforts, Bhoran was still high and out of reach. *That will change soon*, he thought as he twisted his neck, taking in the rope's length. He moved fast, the vine swinging angrily beneath his grip as if it wanted nothing of him.

As he got closer to the ground, a spear got him, scratching his back. He winced, and his legs lost their grip. For a moment, he dangled from the rope, gazing at the ground below. Fernar and Jordel held their spears high above their heads, at the ready, while Gale scampered beneath him to retrieve the spear that had bitten into Bhoran's flesh. Bhoran cursed and hoisted himself back onto the rope.

With a blood-freezing roar, Sigil charged. At the sight of her sharp claws, the men sprawled to the ground, spears falling from their grips.

Avalan rushed forth, grabbed one. "Sigil, to me!" he called.

The tiger growled over the pale faces of the guards and leaped off them, retreating to Avalan's side.

"I wish you no harm, Avalan," Gale called, crawling to retrieve his spear. "But if you don't get out of the way ..."

Once closer to the ground, Bhoran swooped down onto the wet soil. He whistled again. *Where are you, Yekana?*

"Don't be a fool now, boy," Jordel yelled.

Unafraid, Bhoran strode to him. "Go on. Hit me." Bhoran banged his chest. "What does a dead man have to fear?"

For a small moment, the guard hesitated, but then he sent his spear flying straight at Bhoran's heart.

"No!" Avalan yelled.

Through the rainfall, the spear flew. Its steel point glistened. Bhoran glimpsed a blue figure dart in, wrap its scaly body around the shaft, and tear the spear asunder. Snake and wood fell to the ground before Bhoran's legs.

"Took your sweet time," Bhoran said to the snake, smirking.

Yekana flicked out a lazy tongue and rose, cocking a head as big as a newborn child's to regard the guards. Silver's men cursed, whatever little color remaining in their faces draining. Though much smaller than Sigil, Bhoran knew the men would hold no love for Yekana. Snakes, he found, were always hated—especially ones with bodies strong enough to smash weapons, and scales that glistened blue like a clear sky and cut like razors when flared out.

The rain pounded harder now as they all stood across from each other. Yekana slithered up to Bhoran's shoulders.

Raising his chin, Bhoran said, "Tell Bassalt my children will come for him. And the shadow of the Onyx will drown the village and take away everything he holds dear." He gave Avalan a swift look, not daring to linger, lest his heart break any further.

With Yekana's sturdy body coiled around his shoulders, he raced for the forest.

The angry voices and confusion he left behind him were soon drowned out by the splattering of heavy rain on broad leaves and muddy soil. From time to time, he halted to see if he'd been followed, yet the forest remained unmoving. *Have you forgotten your ways, my friend?*

He forged ahead until he crested a small hill. Thick trees covered with spikes blocked the entrance to his hideout. Bhoran pressed his finger to one pricker, savoring the sudden rush of poison. Yet the satisfaction proved too small for his liking, especially after having dodged death. He crouched and parted the vines that concealed a hollow. Bhoran let Yekana slide through it first, then crawled behind her, feeling safe once more as he emerged on the other side.

They slithered down a slope of rotten leaves. A shallow pond with a pebbled bottom, its usually still surface now stirred by the dribbling rain, welcomed him. Thin shafts of moonlight shone through the thick canopy, casting silver shadows across the water's surface.

Bhoran splashed through them to the stony room in the pond's middle. It was a small space, surrounded by walls that reached up to his waist. In place of a roof, two broad, overhanging boards balanced upon a wooden beam. Bhoran sat on the cold stone floor, his back against the wall. Yekana hovered above him, waiting. The time for relief had come. Bhoran extended his arm, and the snake bared her fangs, hungrily dipping them into Bhoran's pale skin.

As the snake sucked at his blood, Bhoran closed his eyes. Through the sharp fangs, the soothing rush of venom coursed through his veins.

When she was done, Yekana cocked her head, a glint in her slitted eyes.

"Thank you," Bhoran told her, stroking her azure scales. Tucked in, they were harmless and smooth to the touch, like wet velvet.

Yekana slid into the pond, coiling over the pebbles.

Bhoran knew he hadn't much time. Soon Silver and Bassalt would come after him, and the chief wouldn't rely on mere spears that could be smashed. He even feared for Yekana's life after what Bassalt had done to the starling. He stood and searched through the slimy moss on the boards above his head.

His fingers brushed a tiny leathery pouch. He pulled it out, unlaced the drawstring, and let a beady stone roll into his palm. It was even smaller than he remembered. It shone under the moonlight, a speck of watery, iridescent light—the Moonstone he had given Lusha that cursed night.

He closed his eyes, bringing her to his mind. Frightened, she had watched him at first from atop the tree branch. But then, as time had slid by, her gaze had softened … or so he dared to hope. The rain had been hard on his face up in the cage, and he wasn't certain it hadn't blended with his own tears.

The air carried soft whispers, and Bhoran knew then they were here. He slid the Moonstone into its pouch, secured it inside his breeches. The rustling of vines told him Avalan had found the entrance. His heart bursting with excitement, Bhoran raised his gaze.

Through the hole in the tree, Avalan and Lusha slid. Bhoran's heart beat faster. He watched as Lusha waded through the waters of the lake, flaxen hair bound proudly atop her head with a bone brooch, water lapping around her ankles. Strips of a shredded dress danced around her body. She quickened her pace, then stopped a few paces before him, her lips parting. "Bhoran?" she whispered, as if not daring to believe it true.

Bhoran stretched out a hand but quickly withdrew it when he saw Lusha's gaze travel to the puncture marks Yekana's fangs had left behind. The holes were still raw, red rivulets running around his elbow. He rubbed his nape and took a step back.

"Talk to me," she said, a soft demand. "All these years, I've heard your voice inside my head. And now you're here … you're silent."

"It is a good day when I see you," he said.

She ran to him then, wrapped her arms around him, pressed her head to his chest. He hugged her back, stroking her soft hair. Avalan stood back, all the while glancing over his shoulder at the tree hollow. *Sigil.*

Bhoran kissed the top of Lusha's head and broke their embrace. "Did you leave Sigil outside?" he asked Avalan.

Avalan nodded. "She's too large to crawl through."

Bhoran crushed him in a manly hug. When they parted, Avalan laughed, showing a row of straight white teeth. Bhoran smirked back.

"That's not how I imagined meeting you again." Avalan's face grew serious now.

"I didn't kill Ronan."

Avalan shook his head. "We never believed you did. We must get going. Silver's men must have alerted Bassalt by now. The whole village will be on our tracks."

Bhoran glanced at Yekana. She had no eyelids, yet Bhoran knew she was in deep sleep after a good night's meal. "You and Lusha should go. I shouldn't have returned."

"No." Lusha's face hardened. "I'm not leaving without you. Tell him, Avalan. Tell him about the stonemaster."

"There's a man in the village who knows the ways of the stones," Avalan explained. "I thought I could get him to reveal before the whole tribe your true stone and convince Bassalt to spare your life."

Bhoran huffed. "Bassalt knows I'm innocent. He promised to kill me despite that."

They looked at him through widened eyes.

"Why?" Lusha said.

Before Bhoran spoke, Avalan said, "Because Bassalt would rather die than admit his fault. He'd gladly sacrifice Bhoran to convince the tribe the village is safe against the Onyx and to keep his place as the chief."

Bhoran nodded. "Which is why you should go."

"But if the stonemaster can summon your true stone," Lusha insisted, "Bassalt will have no other choice but to accept it. We won't let him harm you. We shall—"

"And what if my stone *is* the Onyx?"

"It can't be ... I don't believe it."

"I hold no value in my stone." Bhoran peered into her eyes. "But Bassalt does. The tribe does." He wanted her to remember.

Avalan stroked his brows in thought. "Bhoran is right. Bassalt won't bend the knee to the commandments of a stonemaster. He banned them a long time ago, and he preaches against their power. Even the stonemaster refuses to reveal himself in front of the tribe. I now see the fault in our approach."

"I can't lose you," Lusha told Bhoran. "Not again. If they kill you, I will gladly die by your side."

"I am not willing to part with you either," Avalan admitted. "These past six years without you were ... tasteless, to say the least. You cannot stay in Hydrus. They will hunt you. We shall all leave together."

"The life of an outcast holds no better flavor," Bhoran retorted. "I can't let you."

Avalan shook his head. "It isn't exile if we leave willingly. Besides, it won't be forever. I will not rest until I've seen Bassalt on his knees and our village free."

"Where will we go?" Bhoran pressed. "The mountains are a dangerous place, and food is scarce. We'll only grow weaker, or worse, if lost ..."

"We shan't get lost," Avalan said, a strange conviction in his words. "We'll have a guide." With that, he took a step back and looked down at his reflection in the pond. He waved at the water.

Something stirred, and Bhoran pulled Lusha close.

"Fear not," Avalan said. "It is harmless."

Bhoran squinted. On the water's surface, cast by Avalan, were two shadows. One remained unmoving as he, yet the other ... the other kept glancing back at the spiked sentinel trees, as if with great agitation. "What is this?" Bhoran asked, his voice thick.

"A guide." Hesitation lingered in Avalan's voice. "It will lead us to what we need to defeat Bassalt. I can explain, but not before we get to a safer place."

"You're risking your life by staying around me."

"I should have done it sooner," Avalan said ruefully. "You would have done the same for me. For us."

Bhoran knew it to be true. Now he had found them, he was loath to part from them again. He looked at Lusha, at her scar, at her body. The rain had washed the blood from her wounds away, but he could sense her pain. If he left her again, he knew she wouldn't forgive him.

Bhoran nodded and took Lusha's hand. Carefully he guided her toward Yekana. As they got closer to the sleeping snake, he felt Lusha's grip tense. "This is Yekana," he told her. "She has been good to me. I can't leave her behind."

A small twitch crossed Lusha's face as she regarded the snake. She gazed up at him. "Then I shall learn to love her."

Bhoran caressed the thin silver line of her scar, then turned to Avalan and said, "Tell your shadow to lead the way."

CHAPTER FIFTEEN

BASSALT STARED at the roof of his bedchamber, the soothing patter of rain on ivy leaves making his eyelids leaden. He struggled to stay awake.

Curse you, little brother. Curse you and your stone and all the stones of the lands.

In his heart, Bassalt still dared to hope Bhoran's death would lift the shadow of the Onyx. Although he doubted it would. Yet someone had to pay the price for the murder of the merchant. Having a killer on the loose wouldn't serve the peace in the village, and if Bassalt wanted to find the source of the Onyx, he needed to move in the shadows, undisturbed.

The door burst open as sweet sleep was taking him.

Silver's angry voice boomed in the chamber, his hand fast on the hilt of his sword. "Curse you, Bassalt! I warned you, this time I won't tolerate it."

Bassalt propped himself up on his elbows, brushing a stray lock of hair away. "What is the meaning of this?"

"The talon!" Silver roared. "He escaped! And he's got my daughter!"

Cursed, cursed. Bassalt rubbed sleep from his face. "What do you mean, escaped? He was in a cage in the air."

Silver strode to him, casting an eerie shadow over Bassalt's face.

Behind the commander stood Gremian and Fyridion, solemn expressions on their faces.

Before Silver spoke, Theran burst into the room, his eyes bleary. "Chief!" he shrieked. "I heard loud voices!"

"Leave us!" Silver barked.

When Theran and the men retreated, Bassalt pushed himself up, coming face-to-face with Silver. "You presume to come into my chamber like this, your spittle wetting my face?"

"You should be grateful it isn't the edge of my sword. Speak! How did you aid him this time?"

"I did no such thing." Bassalt jabbed a thick finger into Silver's chest. "And you had best remember to whom you're talking!"

"I remember your empty promises of punishment. What did the talon tell you to convince you to let him go? What did he tell you to let him have my *daughter*?"

Bassalt gave him a look of contempt as he straightened his robes. "Perhaps it was you who let him go. After all, your guards were standing watch beneath him. Perhaps your heart couldn't handle his innocence, and you let him go to soothe your guilt for what you did to Volkan."

Silver made to grab him by the neck but seemed to think better of it, his fingers tightening into a fist in midair. "I swear, if you talk to me once more about him …"

"Go on, then. What will you do? Kill me? I'd like to see you try."

"If I lose my daughter to this filthy talon, I swear to the Heliodor, I might try to kill you. And die happily for it."

Bassalt turned his back to him and reached for his crock. He splashed clean water on his face. "Tell me what happened. How did he slide through your men?"

Silver ground his teeth. "He opened the cage and climbed down. A snake came to his aid after he whistled, the men said. Avalan was there with that beast of his. He sprang after him."

A snake? Curious … Bassalt had raised the boy, but Bhoran had shown no signs of stone power. Besides, it was only those blessed with Bassalt's own stone, the Tiger's Eye, who could command the animal kingdom, and he was certain the stone that lived inside

Bhoran's eyes had nothing to do with his. "How can you be so sure he has Lusha?"

"My men examined the tree Avalan sprang from. During the commotion, they missed her, but a piece of her dress was wrapped around a branch." Blue veins throbbed in Silver's neck. "She was there, you hear me? The more I think she's with him ..."

Bassalt paced the room, thinking how awry his plans had gone in a mere moment. He halted. "Why are you here, then? Go! Go find him. Do you understand what we stand to lose once the tribe glimpses an empty cage?"

"I will once you have told me where he went, for you can't shake it off my mind that the little talk you shared before he slid away—"

"You accuse *me*, you fool? I merely wanted to ask the boy if he had sired any children!"

At that, Silver froze as if the mere notion of this had only now crossed his mind.

"You see now why *I'm* the chief of Hydrus?" Bassalt said, venom in his voice. "Your mind is slow, yet your tongue is fast, and it slashes without thinking. It's not because of me that Lusha ran after him. And if your daughter cannot keep her thighs tight when she's around him, sooner or later you might hold another stone like his in your hands."

Silver roared, a cry of anger and desperation. With a swift move, he unsheathed his sword, his hands trembling on the hilt. "I will ... kill you," he muttered.

Bassalt dodged to the side as Silver came at him. He rolled on the floor, a familiar anger rousing in his chest. He pressed his palms against the floor, drawing upon the power of the basalt walls around him. When he closed his eyes, the power was unleashed. An earth-shuddering quake that made the ground tremble hard and fast. Long fissures cracked the walls of his chamber. Silver fell to the floor, clutching at his ears, screaming. Soon Bassalt's chest pulsated with such power that he thought it would burst open. He forced himself to tear his hands from the floor, the shaking ceasing at once.

When Theran burst inside, chief and commander were sprawled on the floor. Terror streaked the servant's face. He rushed to Bassalt's side. "My chief ..."

Bassalt shoved him aside and crawled to Silver, who still held on to his ears. He tore one hand free and pressed his mouth to the commander's ear. "Challenge me again, and it will be the end of you. Now go find the boy."

Throwing Bassalt off him, Silver strode out as fast as he had entered.

Theran struggled to help Bassalt to his feet. "Are you hurt, my chief? How can I—"

"Silence!" Bassalt limped to his bedside table and grabbed the earthen crock. Pouring the sweet water on the floor, he brandished the empty crock in Theran's face. "Bring me salt water from the Nameless Sea."

Theran was gaping at him as if he thought Bassalt's mind lost.

"Now, Theran!"

Trembling, the servant took the pot and left without so much as a glance behind him.

Bassalt cursed and collapsed on his bed, exhausted. *Cursed stones! If you will not help, perhaps it's time to ask for different aid.*

CHAPTER SIXTEEN

RAIN LASHED Avalan's face as he led the way through the thick underbrush. Behind him, Bhoran and Lusha followed, their hands so tightly entangled Avalan knew it would take more than a death sentence to force them apart now. Yekana hugged Bhoran's shoulders, and Sigil trotted to their rear, ears perked up, nose sniffing the mildewy air.

Avalan had decided it was unwise to cross the mountains in such weather. Instead, he was of a mind to lead Bhoran and Lusha to Dizredek's cave. He dared hope that if he didn't know about its existence, no one else from the village would.

Grateful for the storm that drowned out the sounds of their crossing, Avalan searched the ground for the shadow. The canopy was thick here; whatever little moonlight shone through was filtered by the pouring rain. He could not see it, and yet he felt the shadow's presence in his every step. A great heaviness pulled at him as if it were elsewhere the shadow longed to guide him.

It does not matter, Avalan thought. He needed no help from the shadow to lead the way. Every stone and dirt path through the forest of blackwood trees had felt the treading of his heels. *Yet I missed Bhoran's hideout.* The thought crept up on him. Ever since he'd devoted his time to making more weapons and training the men to rise against Bassalt, exploring the forest had fallen into a shady corner of his heart.

What else do I not see?

He glanced back. It was the first time he'd ever seen Bhoran and Lusha together like this. Their previous encounters, when they were younger, had always been held in secret. Avalan had only heard about them afterward, when he and Bhoran had spent their nights at the beach, heads filled with sand and dreams of a better future. He squeezed his fists and pressed forward, remembering the stonemaster's words that night in the cavern of the Eagle's Eye. The master had spoken about how Hydrus had been founded as a place of tolerance, where tribes of all stones lived as one. *Not all stones, as it turned out,* Avalan thought, for the tribe had never welcomed Bhoran. Bassalt had made sure of it.

I have to change that for them.

As they crested a small hill, Sigil trotted to Avalan, caution in her striped eyes. Avalan took the sign and stopped. Slowly he crawled to the edge. The air carried faint voices from beneath, and the sounds of parting bushes. *So close,* Avalan thought. "We need a different path," he mouthed to Bhoran and Lusha. "Can you swim?"

Silently they nodded.

Avalan waited until the voices from below had faded before he skidded down the hill and to the east part of Hydrus. The path he'd chosen would be rough, but it would lead them to a craggy edge with plenty of footholds to scale down the slope and reach the sea. After a short swim, they should find themselves in the safety of Dizredek's cavern.

When they reached the edge, Avalan halted. *I cannot take Sigil with me,* he thought gravely. The tiger would refuse to dive, but that was the least of Avalan's concerns. If he was to leave Hydrus behind, someone had to stay, care for Farmera. He knelt before Sigil, pressed his forehead against the tiger's. "You must go, girl. Hide. The forest."

The tiger growled as if to disagree.

"Protect my mother. I will return to you. I promise." She looked at him then, sorrow and fear in her striped eyes.

Avalan rose, his heart so burdened he feared he'd go straight to the bottom should he jump now. Behind him Sigil growled, but it was fainter this time, a grave acceptance.

The rocky climb down the slope was rougher than he'd anticipated;

the storm still held strong. Avalan cursed as he slipped on the wet bluff time and again. Bhoran had coiled the snake's tail around his arm and taken Lusha over his back, struggling as well to keep his balance. Thin trickles of blood ran from both their wrists and elbows, and their knees were covered in scrapes.

Avalan took in the angry sea. White frothy waves whipped the cliff. It was too late to retreat. Atop the hill, Sigil paced the crest. Her brown hide was sodden, and she shook the rain off it. "Go, girl!" he shouted at her as he slid lower, his belly scratching against the slope. "Hide!"

Sigil's striped eyes glistened. A low growl left her maw before she twisted out of sight. Avalan hated to watch her go.

He pressed his cheek against the crag and caught a breath. "We must jump!" he yelled at Bhoran. "I'll go first!"

Despite the beginning of the summer, the water was cold; the impact flogged his skin. He swam up, pushing to the surface. Head out of the water, he waved at Bhoran while struggling to keep himself from getting swept away by the strong current. Avalan saw him glimpse down, then speak into Lusha's ear before abandoning his grip.

They splashed into the water. Avalan swam swiftly to where they'd landed. He grabbed Lusha's wrist, pulling her up. Bhoran emerged beside her.

"Get on my back," Bhoran shouted at her. Yekana's tail whipped the waves.

Avalan waited until he was certain Lusha had wrapped her arms around Bhoran's sturdy neck, then swam across the craggy shoreline. Mouth pressed into a tight line to keep the water out, Avalan propelled himself through the angry waves that crashed into his face and threatened to swallow him. Underneath, the tentacles of the current fought like Bassalt's vines, reaching, pulling, seeking to punish him for escaping, for aiding Bhoran, for wanting to take the chief's place.

As they got closer to shallow waters, the sea calmed, the waves spreading more thinly. Soon his toes brushed the comforting slippery pebbles of the shore. He waded his way out, gripping at the slimy algae on the rocks. Now that he knew where the cave was, finding its entrance was easy. A thin light pierced the dark clouds.

"There's a cavern on the other side," he told them.

Bhoran's chest heaved. Yekana's tongue flicked impatiently next to his cheek. Lusha's shredded dress clung to her body like tangled seaweed. Her lips had turned a shade of blue, and her eyes were wild with fear.

"We must get to drier ground. Follow me."

Once in the passage, Avalan's heart raced. He'd pressed himself to think of a different place to hide, yet he'd thought of none better than Dizredek's lair. *What will the sorcerer think when I return with company?* Avalan shivered when he recalled the golden flakes in Dizredek's eyes, whose perception was too great for Avalan's comfort, though the closer they got to the cavern, the more he thought the sorcerer might not be there. There was no light like before. *No light, no warmth.* They emerged into an empty cave.

A musty smell clung to the dark walls; the slabs stood empty, with no oil lamps to chase away the dampness of the place. Bhoran and Lusha waded through the entrance.

"What is this place?" Lusha's voice echoed in the high ceiling.

"We should be safe here," Avalan assured them. "This is where I met the man who bound me to the shadow. He's gone."

Lusha found a wide stone and sat. "Who is he?"

Rain dribbled from the skylight, splashing softly on the floor. "He called himself Dizredek." Avalan shivered against a cold draft wafting from the stone passage. "Sit. It's time I told you all."

When Avalan finished the tale of his encounter with the sorcerer, he watched Bhoran's face closely. His friend had flinched when he had heard about the darkness in one of the sorcerer's eyes.

"A second shadow," Lusha mused. "Clever. No one would ever look twice. And where will the shadow lead you?"

"The Heart of the Bloodstone, Dizredek called it. The true stone that should have been given to me at birth."

"I don't like this," Bhoran said. All the while, he had been rubbing a thumb against Yekana's scales.

"Neither do I," Avalan admitted. "Yet I see no other way to face Bassalt. Before he passed, Ronan spoke to me of stones on weapons. Perhaps I can use the stone to enchant my bow or my dagger. Then I can use what I know to fight."

"We know nothing about stones on weapons," Bhoran said.

"Silver keeps his Heliodor in his sword," Lusha said. "It shines when he touches it. It must be precious to him. He even sleeps with it next to him—in the place of my mother."

Avalan nodded. He'd seen the stone on the commander's sword, yet Silver had never used it before Avalan's eyes. He faced the entrance, his sight now fully adjusted to the darkness. "We should spend the night here," he said. "Let them exhaust themselves searching for us. I shall go to my mother. Say my farewells." He glanced at Lusha. "And I'll return with warmer clothes. When the storm passes, we can brave the Craggy Mountains."

Lusha stood, the Moonstones in her eyes the only light that shone down here. "What if they catch you?"

"They won't," he promised. He turned to Bhoran. His eyes were one with the cave's darkness, yet Avalan sensed the struggle in his friend's mind. Bhoran wanted to come with him, yet he did not wish to leave Lusha alone. "I will be fine," Avalan told him. "The forest is my home. I know it better than all of them."

Bhoran squeezed Avalan's shoulder, a familiar greeting from their younger days.

"Besides," Avalan said, reciprocating the gesture, "I wouldn't dare to miss your story. When I return, you must tell me all about where you've been. And I shall make your ears bleed with talk of all the weapons I've crafted all these years. This isn't the last time we see each other." He crawled through the tunnel, not daring to glance back.

To his relief, the rain hadn't eased. He chose to swim his way to the west side of the forest. Though the seaward gate looked unmanned to him, he couldn't risk sauntering through it. The whole village must be after Bhoran and Lusha now, he knew. Mud splashed and stuck to his shanks as he crawled along his secret trench and then raced the wind to Farmera's hut.

The Amethysts in his mother's eyes sparkled once she saw him at her door. She ushered him in, bringing a soft cloth to wipe the rain from his body. "Thank the stones," she began. "Silver's men were at my door, telling me you helped Bhoran escape."

Avalan dropped the cloth on the table. The house was cold and dark; the thatched roof whispered and shook with the assault of rainfall. "I couldn't sit back and let Bassalt kill him."

"I tried to talk to the chief," Farmera said bitterly. "Yet he wouldn't listen. I'm afraid this time he truly means to kill Bhoran."

"I won't let him."

"Is Bhoran safe?"

Avalan nodded.

"And Lusha?" There was hope in her voice as she spoke, hope mixed with fear.

Avalan watched her closely, wondering how his mother would take the tidings. "She's with him."

To his satisfaction, Farmera smiled. She fetched the candle that burned on the windowsill above the sickbed. Deep lines were etched on her forehead, and dark circles had settled around her eyes. They sat across from each other.

"Where were you during the trial?" Farmera asked.

Avalan warmed his palms over the flame. His bandages had ripped, the blackened skin over his palms nicked by stones on his climb. He still felt nothing. Even the deep cut of his goat dagger when he'd climbed the fence hadn't caused him any pain. "I was searching for Sigil," he said at last. "Instead, I found a strange man."

Farmera wrapped her robe tighter around her shoulders and leaned closer. "What man?"

"He calls himself Dizredek. Have you ever heard his name, Mother?"

She shook her head. "Who is he?"

Avalan wished he knew. "He promised to help me defeat Bassalt."

"Oh, Avalan." His mother's voice was on the verge of breaking. "I know how much you're hurting. But with Bhoran and Lusha gone and Silver at their heels, it won't much do attacking Bassalt now." She reached for his hand. "Promise me, son. Promise me you won't do anything yet. Let the storm pass. Bassalt's anger is great, and when roused ..."

"I don't fear him. I only fear what I don't know."

Farmera squeezed his hand. "You don't know Bassalt the way I do." Then, as if she had just remembered, she added, "How are your hands faring? Let me see them."

"They don't hurt me anymore." He glanced at the door behind him. "Mother, soon they'll come again for me. I have to know some things before I go."

Farmera's voice broke. "Where will you go? I won't let them hurt you. I'll speak to Bassalt. Surely, he'll understand. It isn't you he wants ..."

"I have decided, Mother. I will aid Bhoran and Lusha out of Hydrus. Then I will go where this man leads me."

"This Dizredek? Why would you follow a man you do not know? Who is he? Where does he want to take you?"

Avalan scratched his chin. "He looks odd. He had these eyes ... They didn't match each other. One was dark like Bhoran's, the other gray with golden flakes."

"Gray with gold. A Nuummite," his mother mused.

Avalan furrowed his brows. "One of the twelve birthstones?"

Farmera nodded. "I do not like this, Avalan. A Nuummite is a dangerous stone—knows a lot yet reveals little. What did he say to you? How did he convince you to follow him?"

"He showed me the only way to defeat Bassalt was through my Bloodstone. The one I wasn't given at birth."

"He isn't wrong," Farmera admitted, flinching. "A birthstone is a great blessing. Bassalt draws his power from his, as do Silver, I, and all the other tribesfolk who still remember what it means to have a birthstone."

"You never told me."

"I tried many a time to tell you. You wouldn't listen."

Avalan knew it to be true. He hated the stones, for they were Bassalt's source of power, and the reason the tribe had sent Bhoran away. Yet now he needed to know. And he needed to go back to the root of his fear, the real reason he'd resisted his own stone so much. "My blades. I can trust them. *I* wield their handles as *I* wish. The stones ..."

"It takes mastery to control them," Farmera said, as if she sensed her son's discomfort. "The stones are part of who we are, son. They change. They can do many things. Much like us."

"Tell me about Father."

The Amethysts in Farmera's eyes caught the candle's flame and glimmered with sadness. "What do you wish to know?"

"I took the Bloodstone from him ..." Avalan hesitated. "Does this mean his stone is now mine? Was I supposed to have it when he died, like Eras ... or even before?"

"It doesn't work that way. But you're trembling." She stood and padded to the hearth. With a long stick, she rekindled the slow-burning coals. Over them, she threw dried twigs and poured oil to feed the flames.

Avalan was glad his mother was a healer. A low fire always burned in Farmera's house, for there was no knowing when a sick person would need a hot bath to chase away the cold, or a hot potion to battle illness. The sweet smell of wine filled the room as she placed a pot over the fire. Avalan watched her rub some herbs above the steam, flavoring the wine.

At last she returned with earthen cups filled to the brim. "If we are to have this talk about your father, it's best we drink. I need courage to remember."

Avalan sipped the warm wine with gratefulness, remembering Lusha's pale blue lips. "I fear I have little time, Mother. Lusha is cold and needs a dry dress. And I shall need some pine sap and string."

Farmera disappeared into her bedchamber. When she returned, a brown woolen dress hung around her arm, along with a fur headband. In her cupboards, she found some amber sap and untied the draw-string of a heavy sack before she handed everything to her son. "I trust these will do?"

Avalan nodded and drained his cup. He took the small piece of sap to a tin over the coal fire and stirred it. "How does it work? How does one get one's birthstone?"

Farmera watched him from the table, cup in hand. "When a baby is born into the tribe, a stonemaster goes to the Heart of its birthstone, asks for a piece of it to bless the newborn. The piece is given to the master, and he in turn gifts it to the baby."

"And where are the Hearts of the birthstones?"

A faint smile. "I'm not a stonemaster, and thus not privy to their locations. But I have never seen one, so I would guess they're underground."

Avalan shivered despite the warmth of the fire. He didn't much like to feel the ground above his head, pressing, suffocating …

"You see now, my dear boy, why this man can't lead you to your stone. Only a stonemaster of the Bloodstone would know the way. And Mel Alandour, the city of the Bloodstone, rests so far to the north it would take you many a moonturn to reach it."

Mel Alandour, Avalan thought. Ronan had spoken to him once about the city when Avalan was younger. The second-biggest city in the Stone Lands, Ronan had called it. Proud and well guarded. With rich soil and richer pockets. None of this was enough to make Avalan's heart stir. All he knew, all he longed for, was the familiar soil of Hydrus.

He dipped the stick into the sap, raised it into the air, satisfied with the glue's thickness. He took his broken dagger out and bound the string firmly around bone and blade, making them one again. This was a rough fix, he knew. One that didn't honor his crafting skill, yet it was all he could muster in such a short time.

"Dizredek created a Bloodstone out of my blood and some liquid," he told his mother as he slathered the warm glue around the ragged union of bone and blade.

"Nuummites are notorious for their sorcery." Farmera's tone didn't carry surprise. "Did he give it to you?"

Avalan took the tin pot off the fire and returned to the table. He placed his goat dagger on the bench to dry. "It dissolved the moment I touched it."

"Never trust a Nuummite, son."

"The stonemaster's Bloodstone served me no better." Avalan gazed at his scorched palms. "Why did my father leave us?"

Farmera sighed. "I don't believe he did, my love. The war was an ugly thing. Men, women, and children died in every corner. Stones changed hands as if their souls held no meaning. Great fires burned around us as we ran for shelter. Your father and I were fortunate to find a place in Hydrus. I was with child. You." She smiled. "Azirrad said he'd rather die than let me bring a child into a land torn apart. Before you came into the world, though, the war took an ugly turn. The tribes called for aid, and your father was too proud to stay behind."

"Did he tell you, then?" Avalan's mind twisted with memories of his mother crying and cursing his father for leaving her alone with a child. "Did he tell you he was going back to the lands to help fight the war?"

Farmera's lips twisted with sorrow.

She's lying. Avalan knew. It saddened him beyond measure. "Tell me the truth."

"Son ..."

"Why did he leave?"

"Your father was a good man," she declared, as if she feared her coming words would convince Avalan otherwise. "He loved me greatly. But there was one more thing your father loved before I came into his life. A son of the Onyx."

Avalan's heart quivered. "Azirrad had an Onyx son?"

"That was near forty years ago. A time of peace between the tribes. Do not judge your father. You cannot always choose whom you love, especially when it is your own child. When the war came, it raged ugly for both sides. The Onyx tribe is dead. Azirrad wouldn't have left me but for good reason. He would have stayed here with me if he could have." She squeezed his hands harder now, in silent begging.

She doesn't want me to leave. "What happened to his son?"

Farmera sighed. "The Onyx was wiped from the Stone Lands. The stonemasters claimed no true child remained."

Avalan glanced at his dagger, the glue on it now dry, the coupling steady. His heart was clenched—whether from fear, disgust, or pain, he couldn't discern. It was hard to know how he felt for the dead he'd never met. For him, the living always mattered the most. "I will find my stone, though what good that will serve me I know not now. I will fight Bassalt and free the village. This much I promise, Mother."

The shadow of a hand hovered over the candle. With a swift move of its fingers, the flame was gone, a wisp of smoke rising.

"What was that?" Farmera whispered.

Squelching footsteps outside made them both leap from their seats. Avalan grabbed the dagger and the garments and darted for the cellar. Before he disappeared under the trapdoor, he glimpsed his mother tossing his cup under the sickbed.

Avalan crouched on the top step of the ladder.

Silver's stride shook the floor. "Where are they?"

"They haven't come knocking at my door," Farmera said. "Though I share your pain. Do not forget my son is also missing." Her voice was cold now, like the cool breeze of night air slipping through the crevices.

A heavy hand banged the table. "Avalan's place is empty. Where does he go to hide? Where is the tiger?"

"I have seen none of them, but you have my word, if I do—"

"The filthy talon has my daughter! If any harm comes to her—"

"He loves her," Farmera retorted. "He wouldn't touch a hair on her head."

"Love? Did you see him? The beast has no heart."

"I know plenty of beasts with good hearts, Silver."

Above, Avalan heard swift strides and the door slamming shut. Silver had left, taking the stormy air with him.

Carefully Avalan emerged from his hiding place to find his mother preparing a waterskin and wrapping some salted meat in a cloth. Tears rolled from her eyes when she regarded him.

"Do you have to leave, son?"

Avalan hugged her, took in the faint smell of lavender from the top of her head.

"What of Sigil?" Farmera whispered.

"I asked her to hide in the forest. I won't take her with me."

Farmera's eyes widened with surprise. "But why? You and Sigil are inseparable. Oh, Avalan, I'd feel much better knowing she's with you."

I want her to be with you if I die, and also, she fears the shadow, Avalan thought, but for some reason he couldn't fathom, he refused to reveal its existence to his mother. *Best if I don't burden her heart with more fear.* "And I would feel much better knowing she's with you."

Determination grew on Farmera's pale face. "You must help them, son. Bhoran and Lusha. As long as they're here, they can never be together. Azirrad and I were chased until we found a shelter in Hydrus. It seems now our safe place is chasing away their love. Hydrus isn't a place for them."

This truth hurt Avalan beyond measure. "I promise to change that, Mother." He looked at the dress around his arm. "I must go now. The hiding place is dank."

She turned her back to him. "Go, then, if you must. My heart can't take watching you leave."

Avalan took the provisions. As he crossed the threshold, he glanced over his shoulder for one last time, taking in his mother's figure. "I love you," he whispered, before pounding forth into the pouring rain.

CHAPTER SEVENTEEN

IN THE MUSTY cave's darkness, Lusha and Bhoran sat apart. Now that the danger had passed, neither of them found the words or courage to approach the other.

Rainwater dripped through the skylight. The whispers of sea waves and howling wind crossed the pebbled tunnel, an eerie sound echoing in the naked cavern.

Lusha's gaze lingered on Yekana. The azure snake was larger than any other she had encountered in the forest. Yekana slithered across the stone ground, her tongue flicking about, tasting the air of the cold cave. Lusha's stomach churned, and not only out of hunger. Six long years had passed since the rattlesnake had slashed her face, taking away part of her eyesight. She'd never seen it. The warning rattle of its tail was all she'd heard before searing pain had torn through her head and warm blood had trickled into her mouth. Now, as Yekana slid about, a glinting shadow in the darkness, Lusha watched her every move, her body tensing.

"She's harmless," Bhoran said. He sat across from her on another slab, thighs spread out like butterfly wings.

Lusha turned to him, her heart beating faster. They had been apart for so long it was hard to believe they were in the same chamber, alone. She had dreamed of this day for many a sleepless night, yet the boy she had imagined holding and kissing looked nothing like the man who sat across from her now. His great muscles made her feel his embrace would crush her, and the fangs in his face ... *Would it hurt to kiss you? Are you still my Bhoran?* She gazed at the faint opening in the cavern's ceiling. "I wish there were more light," she told him at last. *To see you better.*

Bhoran fished out a small bead from his breeches. It glowed in the dark, a faint sphere of blue light.

"The Moonstone?" Lusha asked, her lips trembling with remembrance.

"Your Moonstone." His voice was warm.

"I thought it lost."

"I had to take it off you." Though Bhoran held it close to his face, his eyes remained dark, no light reflecting off the surface of his stones. "I was afraid of what they might do to you if they found it." He extended his hand now, much like he had done that goat game night, the Moonstone a perfect pearl and a gift of his heart inside his palm.

Lusha looked at it, longing and dread vying inside her.

"You won't have it?"

"I'm afraid," she admitted.

"What of?"

Lusha caressed the cool slab beneath her and stared at Yekana. "I'm sitting on a rock. You're offering me my stone. And there's a snake nearby."

Bhoran laughed, a rare and hearty sound like a warm fire. "Yekana. To me."

The snake slithered onto him, coiling around his broad shoulders. Even after she had wrapped herself twice around Bhoran's torso, Yekana's long tail still touched the ground. She sniffed his neck, tongue flicking.

"Hush," Bhoran hissed at her, a rough command. To Lusha he said, "Will you take it now?"

Leaning forward, she reached for it. When her fingertips brushed his palm and closed around the Moonstone, the faint blue light grew, and Lusha herself became their much-needed light in the darkness. It felt warm to the touch, a welcome change from the cave's dampness. "You kept it safe all these years?"

"I would have died before I lost it."

Now that the cave was brighter, Lusha could see him clearly for the first time—his etched skin, muscles, braids, fangs, bones … *You say one thing, yet your body says another,* she thought, her heart filling with sadness. In her mind's eye, she pictured a woman, her hands braiding Bhoran's hair, entangling each lock with great love and care; her delicate fingers running down his body, color on their tips, etching his skin, claiming it for her own; her lips on his lips, kissing him, whispering words of longing in his ears, pressing her cheek to the angles of his jaw, savoring the sweet sting of the fangs in his face …

"You don't approve of my appearance."

Lusha laid the stone beside her and tucked her palms beneath her thighs, desperate for some warmth; the wet dress clung to her body like an icy embrace, draining her defenses. "I was just looking at the scar on your face," she lied.

Bhoran's face bore a similar scar to hers, only much shallower and inflicted by his own hand as a harsh punishment for what the snake had done to Lusha. Farmera had nursed him back to life, but as soon as he had recovered, Bassalt had ordered his exile.

Bhoran raised his chin. "Does yours still hurt?"

"It was hard at first. When the air grew heavy with mist, I would feel its pulling. A storm like this one would have my head throb with pain. Not anymore."

"But you can't see." Bhoran's voice dripped with guilt.

She looked at him, surprised. She had told no one, for fear of his harsher punishment. "How do you know?"

"I've seen how you cock your head." There was sadness in his words.

"I don't mind it," she was quick to say. "A turn of my head, and I can take in all I want to see. It wasn't your fault. You shouldn't have hurt yourself for me. Farmera told me what you did with the snake fang … If you had died …"

Yekana hissed.

"It would have been for the best."

His words cut like a knife. She leaned closer, lips trembling. "What did you see in the forest? I was there when my father came to you. Followed him and his men. Did you see who killed Ronan?"

"No. He was dead when I found him. The dagger placed on his lap as if the killer wanted to make certain it was found."

"I don't understand. Who would want to kill Ronan? He was always such a ray of hope."

Bhoran frowned. "The stones got him killed."

Next to her, the Moonstone shone so bright and innocent it was hard to believe a small bead could be a source of death. She remembered Avalan's words when he had spoken of the stones Ronan had smuggled into the village. "Do you believe that? Why would the stones do this?"

"Ronan shouldn't have brought them to Hydrus, where they aren't welcome. It is bad luck."

He's talking about himself as well, Lusha realized. "The opinion of the chief shouldn't affect all the others."

"Bassalt's opinions are strong."

Lusha shifted uncomfortably on her stony seat, the dead starling haunting her mind. "Bassalt said only an Onyx could wield the dagger. Do you believe an Onyx killed Ronan? I thought they were all gone. That's what my father always told me when I was little and he was filled with wine's good spirits." *We killed them all, Lusha. All.* She had always felt queasy at the thought of women and children being killed, but her father had reminded her these had been the ways of the war. She was glad she hadn't seen them.

Bhoran fiddled with the fangs in his chin. "Bassalt impaled the bird on the dagger while I held it. It wasn't I who killed it; it was him. Onyx or not, whoever killed Ronan must know about the stones."

Lusha knew he was right. Ronan's sack was gone. Only the map had remained on him when she had found him. "What of this man Avalan spoke of? This Dizredek. Avalan said his eyes were dark and odd. What if it was he who murdered Ronan?"

Bhoran looked around as if he expected the man to emerge from beneath a stone slab. "I know not. But I don't trust this second shadow."

The water's trickling sound ebbed, and Lusha realized the storm was calming now. She didn't trust the shadow either. The way it resembled Avalan so closely, the way it moved with Avalan's every move as if it were part of his own soul …

She cupped her mother's pendant. "This belonged to my mother," she said, her voice crestfallen like the empty chamber around them. "Ronan was going to take me out of here." Then she slipped her hand to the fold of her dress above her bosom. The parchment felt distorted against her touch. When she made to unfold it, it resisted, sticky and wet. The salt water and the pouring rain had proved deadly for Ronan's map. She was loath to part with it, and so she replaced it against her bosom.

"Where would he have taken you?"

"The city of Levorotha, the city of healers. Away from my father." She swallowed hard, rubbing the embossed surface of the silver pendant. "My mother had a sister. I was hoping to start a new life with her. Learn the ways of moon healing. Farmera says the healers of the Moonstone know more than any other. I hope she's right."

"To know how to close wounds is good. Is this what you want?"

"It's more than that." Lusha looked at her pale skin, imagining her body overtaken by strange bruises. *As if her blood had spilled beneath her skin.* Farmera's words echoed in her mind. "I seek to find what took my mother. That strange illness my father refuses to talk about."

Gently Bhoran pushed Yekana's face away from his neck. "The Moonstone healers would know. Do you wish to be one of them?"

Lusha eyed her Moonstone. Before she could stop it, hope filled her heart. She imagined herself being in a place where her birthstone was celebrated, the ways of healing seen as a natural thing, the warm embrace of an aunt—a woman—who would love her, filling the place of her mother … *And what of Bhoran?* She'd never truly thought she'd see him again. Yet he was here now. "It does not matter anymore. Ronan is dead …"

Bhoran knelt before her, cupped her hand. "I will take you there."

Yekana's tongue flickered dangerously close to Lusha's face, but all she cared about was the warmth of Bhoran's touch. It was rougher than she remembered, his skin leathery from living in the wild for so long. "You've been there?"

"I never fully crossed the mountain. But I will this time, for you. I will help you reach your mother's city." He hesitated. "To start your new life."

As much as she took pleasure in his words, her heart trembled with fear. If before Bhoran had been an outcast, now he was accused of murder. "I can't ask this of you. They will hunt you. I can't bear to be the reason you lose your life."

"Silver will hunt you too," Bhoran reminded her.

"He will." She tightened her grip around the pendant. "If I can reach Levorotha before he finds me, perhaps I can convince him to let me stay with my aunt."

Bhoran traced her scar, his fingertips burning like fire on her face. "We will try."

Burning shame tugged at her. "What about your life? Was it hard?" She swallowed a knot in her throat. "Did you find any comfort in the mountain?" *A woman?*

Bhoran let her hands down gently. "I have found comfort now." He shook Yekana off his shoulders and sat on the floor beside Lusha's feet, his back against the stone.

Atop Bhoran's head, a scab marred his golden hair with copper. Before she could stop herself, Lusha slipped her fingers through his braids. Locks of soft hair were woven into the figure of a turtle shell, held in place on his scalp with bones and fangs. She caressed his sturdy shoulders and followed the inked necklace that spiraled down his upper arm, exploring, wanting to know. *Who are you?* Once she'd reached the soft inner corner of his elbow, Bhoran grabbed her wrist, pulling her down to him.

His chest felt warm against her sodden back as he wrapped his arms around her. "You're cold."

She rested the back of her head against his shoulder. When she spoke at last, her voice was barely audible over the trickling sounds of falling rain. "I could hear you. All these years, I couldn't get your voice out of my head, calling my name." She closed her eyes, letting warm tears wet her cheeks. "And then at the trial … you did it again. I thought I was going mad. But it was you. You were calling me, weren't you?"

Bhoran stroked the length of her arm. "It only works with people I love," he confessed.

"Then why did you leave me behind in Hydrus that day? Why didn't you take me with you?"

His whole body stiffened. "I saw you. With Colgar. Asking for your hand."

Your beauty is not what it used to be, Colgar's ghost whispered in her head. After the nasty accident, Colgar had asked her father for her hand. She had refused him, but before that, she had cried in his arms. *Was that what Bhoran saw?* "I would die before I became his tribeswife."

"He held you in his arms." Bhoran's words boomed in the barren chamber.

"Only because I was mourning. I was weeping for you, not him." She pressed her body against his. "My father has never held me for comfort. And you had left me."

He pressed his chin against her cheek, fangs digging sweetly into her face. "I'm holding you now. Silver would hate this."

Lusha smiled with pleasure as she settled better into his embrace. "With all his heart."

CHAPTER EIGHTEEN

BASSALT SQUELCHED across the muddy path, cursing the storm, the stones, the merchant. The only fortune the rain had brought was a quiet Hydrus with no stealthy eyes or eavesdropping ears. He passed the deserted southern gate and dragged his feet through the forest, his gaze rooted to the swaying water in the crock. Over his head, Bassalt had stretched his cloak to prevent the rainfall from besmirching the crock's seawater.

Too far, he thought, kicking a loose rock. The cloak's wool sucked up the rain, becoming heavier over his arms. Bassalt lengthened his stride, anxious to be done with the task ahead.

A pulse in his chest told him he was close now. The ivy vines over the grotto's entrance greeted him with a small waterfall as he shoved them aside. Once inside, he dumped his sodden cloak and trudged into the bowels of the cavern. A streak of water followed his path into the darkness. Bassalt wanted no peepholes in the walls of his shelter. That damned son of Azirrad had made it his life's purpose to know every tree, rock, and secret passage the forest of Hydrus had.

When the cool water licked his ankles, Bassalt stopped, satisfied. He knelt, fumbling in the dark for a dry place. The wooden crock clacked against the floor as he laid it down, its edges dancing dangerously. When he tried to steady it, he found himself trembling. *Cursed, cursed, cursed … Remember who you are.*

Bassalt stirred the seawater, brought a finger to his lips, and sucked at its saltiness. He had come here in a fury, a fiery blaze in his heart demanding quenching. Yet now he found himself in his cave, the words were stuck in his throat, a lump he could not swallow.

A filthy Onyx. Silver's words echoed in his mind so loudly Bassalt almost jumped out of his skin. He stuck his fingers into the crock. His skin crawling with fear, he managed the well-practiced words. "From the depths of the sea, rise again, Hydrus."

For a long moment, his heart fluttered in his chest; he was certain the summoning had failed. *Why would Hydrus obey me when …?* The water in the pot whirled around his wrist. He twisted his hand out of it, falling backward.

A splashing sound filled the chamber.

The waterdragon of Hydrus emerged from the crock's seawater and slithered across the wet floor. When it stood on its hind legs, the dragon's head scraped the ceiling. Tangled seaweed glistened over the silver scales of its body, dripping with salt water. The creature's torso, thick as the blackwood trees of the forest, held four short limbs. Bassalt spied ivory claws long like daggers, and fangs thin and sharp like rib bones. Tall and glinting, the waterdragon hovered over Bassalt, a pair of sparkling emeralds maliciously staring at him through tight leathery slits.

Bassalt had been Hydrus's chief for near twenty years, yet he had never seen the real protector of the village. *The waterdragon was raised from the guts of the sea, wet and strong, a mighty guardian of the waters,* Bassalt's father had told him when he was small. No matter how hard Bassalt had pressed him, his father had refused to tell him more. *The rite to summon the waterdragon is known only to the chief,* he used to say with a warm smile, *and with him it shall remain.*

But Bassalt had managed to trick the words out of Volkan as Krokador's Stronghold had burned.

Red steam rushed through the dragon's gaping nostrils as it snorted, an impatient sound, a harbinger of danger if Bassalt delayed confessing his reason for tearing the creature from the sea.

"Hydrus," Bassalt muttered, bowing so low his forehead touched the ground.

The waterdragon whipped its long tail, sending the crock into a frenzied spinning.

"The Onyx is back," Bassalt was quick to say, to soothe the dragon's anger. "The village needs your aid." He crawled toward the small pond and dipped his snake ring into the water to prove his words to the creature. To his relief, darkness engulfed the translucent stone—a clear sign of the presence of the Onyx.

The dragon leaned closer, its mustaches tickling Bassalt's forehead like slick tentacles. For a long moment, it just stood there, emerald eyes shining with an eerie glow. Then its silver snout opened to unleash a fast tongue. Bassalt screamed in pain as it coiled around his finger. With a sickening snap, the dragon's tongue severed the ring-bearing finger and tossed it aside. It rolled, the snake ring clinking against the rocks.

Bassalt wailed, cradling his hand, warm blood gushing from his wound. In his head, he heard the voice of the dragon, a low, guttural whisper like the stabbing of a thousand needles. "*You are not worthy.*"

Bassalt screamed, forcing his palms to the ground. Jaw clenched, lips a tight line, he *pushed*, demanding the basalt in the earth grant him all its power. The grotto shook; the ceiling rained small rocks about their heads. The waterdragon screeched and swayed a tail armored with sharp scales. It caught Bassalt in the shoulder, sending him sprawling to the wet floor. Through blinding pain, he watched as the waterdragon hovered above him, its cold smaragdine stare a talon in his heart. *This is my end*, he thought, his limbs loose with fear.

Breathing out a cloud of hot steam, the waterdragon swirled, then dived into the seawater and disappeared, sending the crock into another frenzied spin.

Without the dragon's silver glint, darkness drenched the chamber once more. Bassalt cursed and fumbled, the smell of seaweed mixed with iron blood thick in his nose. He retched, emptying his supper onto the ground. Groaning, he scoured the floor for his ring. It had been his these past twenty years, and only his it should remain. "Cursed, cursed, cursed!"

He thought of how many times he'd wished to be rid of the ring, the color-changing gem in the snake's head making his skin crawl.

Instead of aid for the village, the dragon had given him his wish, only the price Bassalt had paid was dire.

Before long, he realized he searched in vain—the ring too small to find in the dark, and his wound fast bleeding. He had to make it through the entrance for someone to find him, for only Theran knew how to enter this basalt cavern. Cursing, he staggered to his feet and followed the stream, a thought roaring in his mind.

I am the chief of Hydrus. Cursed, cursed, cursed …

CHAPTER NINETEEN

BHORAN WAS up at dawn as the fingers of first light slipped through the tangled roots of the skylight. On his cheek, Lusha's sleeping breath was a warm wisp. He savored the shape of her soft lips. *So close.*

Her forehead felt cool to the touch—a relieving sign. When Avalan had arrived last night with warmer clothes from Farmera, Lusha had been trembling, and her lips had turned the color of Yekana's scales. Now, garbed in a soft dress, she slept a much-needed sleep. Beside her, Avalan's chest rose and fell, his hand wrapped around the goat leg on his belt, his brows furrowed in a thick black line.

Thankfully, the rain had eased, leaving behind the damp smell of earth and mushrooms. Bhoran's breeches had dried over his body. The stones behind him whispered, and Yekana slithered her way to him, tongue out.

Careful not to awaken Lusha, Bhoran slid his arm out from beneath her head and stood, beckoning Yekana to follow. He sat in a small recess. When he closed his eyes, Yekana bit into his inner thigh. A warm thrill rushed through Bhoran's blood as venom spilled into him. Serpent's Spite, he liked to call it. It was his everything, a sweet salvation that numbed the pain of exile and mended his broken heart.

Six years past, the same venom had almost killed him when he had slashed his own face with the snake fang. Yet his survival had rendered him immune to the venom. *And Farmera's healing touch.* The first time. For there had been many more poisons he had tried up in the mountain when he had left Hydrus behind for good. Up there, it was no longer Farmera who had saved his life.

Dhylinea.

His jaw clenched at her memory. Being in a cave, it was hard not to think of her. He forced his eyes open before Yekana had ceased her feeding, and looked at Lusha. She hadn't stirred since he'd left her, but fear crawled up his throat like warm bile. *What would she think if she saw me like this?* Numbing away his pain, addicted to snake's venom to survive—the very thing that had almost cost Lusha her life. With a gentle nudge, he urged the snake to finish her sucking.

Reluctantly Yekana tore her fangs from his thigh and slid away. Bhoran wiped the trickling blood from the puncture marks. He pressed his head against the jagged stone, venom rushing through his veins, cold, gripping, rousing … He feared one day he'd lose this feeling, this tiny moment of happiness and clear mind. *I have her now,* he thought, his gaze falling on Lusha's flaxen hair. *But will she love me when she knows about Dhylinea?*

From the skylight above, sunny fingers found their way to Avalan's face. Bhoran watched him twitch and roll to the side. Then Avalan opened his eyes, slowly at first, as if unsure of his surroundings. He must have felt Bhoran's gaze on him, for he returned it. Relaxing the grip on his dagger, Avalan stood and shuffled over to Bhoran.

In the dim light of the cave, Avalan's bronze skin made him look a shadow himself. He raised a scorched palm to Bhoran. "We should leave," he said by way of a morning greeting.

Bhoran studied the blackened wounds on Avalan's hands. The escape had proved rough for the linen wrappings. Avalan had ripped them off last night, leaving the skin open, confessing he didn't feel much anyhow. "What is your plan?"

Sitting on the ground, Avalan brushed his brows. "We shall swim to the east side of the village, back to where we came from. From there we can scale the hill until the forest's edge. Ronan once told me there's an eastern mountain path. One less traveled." He searched the cave floor. "From there, the shadow should lead us through the crags."

Bhoran pressed his elbows to his knees and leaned closer. "Why not swim around the crags?"

"The currents are strong there. They'll drown us."

"The mountain path is not much friendlier."

Avalan looked up at him with great interest. "All these years you were gone, did you ever cross to the other side?"

"Nearly. I found shelter on the northern slope."

Avalan reached for Bhoran's wrist. "I want to hear all about it. But I would breathe much more easily if you told me once we've left this place. We must wake Lusha and go."

Bhoran stood. The venom had run its course, his vision now steadier, his heartbeat easier.

Lusha moaned softly before she opened her eyes. "My whole body hurts," she said, stretching. She patted the pocket of her dress in search of the Moonstone.

"I can keep it safe for you," Bhoran told her.

"No." She donned the fur-lined headband Avalan had brought for her. It pushed her locks back, baring her oval face. She looked him in the eye. "I won't part with it this time."

Avalan brushed his knife. "I should be able to find us some food once we're in the open. We must go now." He led them straight through the tunnel.

The sky was spotted with gray clouds, the morning air a cool breeze. Bhoran was grateful to be rid of the dark enclosure of the cavern. Yekana was slung around his neck, her belly content with his blood.

When they reached the shore, Avalan stopped, rubbing his neck while facing Lusha. "It is best if you ... I mean, the dress. It won't much help if this one gets sodden. I can hold it above water while swimming."

She frowned, shifting her gaze from Avalan to the sea. "You want me to undress?" She stole a glance at Bhoran. "Fine. You two turn your backs. I won't have you ogling my breasts."

The men did as she bade them. Bhoran closed his eyes, listening to the sound of the dress falling off her shoulders. A faint thump told him it had curled around her ankles. Her voice was low when she spoke to them, as if she was embarrassed. "Take it."

"Give me the stone," Bhoran told Avalan, his voice hoarse. Once in his hands, Bhoran pried Yekana's jaw open and pushed the Moonstone beneath her tongue. "Safe," he hissed.

He and Avalan entered the water first. Only after a gentle splash came behind them did he dare regard Lusha. She smiled, the ends of her flaxen hair wet and swimming around her.

Now the storm had eased, the swim was quiet and short. To Bhoran's dismay, once they found dry ground, Lusha ordered both of them to turn while she donned her dress.

Avalan led them to a spot where the hill was crowned with thick nettles and underbrush—easy handholds for a steep climb. By the time they found themselves atop the hill, Bhoran's palms were transfixed with minute thorns. *Poisonless and useless,* he thought as he brushed them off.

Avalan shaded his eyes against the sun that peeped out from behind the clouds. "The fastest route is past the statue."

"Won't there be guards there?" Lusha asked. A healthy color had returned to her lips.

"I don't think there will be," Avalan said thoughtfully. "They wouldn't think a free man would return to his prison. Regardless, we need not step into the clearing. The path behind Olnos's back is a swift and secure route."

Bhoran didn't much like the notion of seeing that nasty cage again, but bidding farewell to Olnos was to his liking. Not knowing if he would see the giant warrior again filled him with sorrow. "If we meet any men, stand down," he told both of them. "I am the one they want."

"No." Lusha took his hand. "I'll stay with you."

"As will I," Avalan promised.

As they approached the clearing, Bhoran glimpsed the second shadow. A dark projection of Avalan's figure it was, appearing in the shafts of light and disappearing under the canopy as they moved through the blackwood forest. *It moves so quietly I forget its presence,* Bhoran thought. He didn't much like that. He tried to keep his gaze on it, but the cursed thing was faster than he'd thought it.

A familiar sense filled his chest. He knew this ground, this soft shadowgrass, this path. He turned to his left, his gaze grazing the back of the statue. *Olnos.* Grabbing Avalan's arm, he whispered, "One moment."

Avalan returned a troubled gaze.

"I wish to say my farewells," Bhoran whispered. Ignoring Avalan's disagreeing stare, he crouched and got closer to Olnos, peering above a thorny bush.

He spied his former cage, smashed on the ground. The clearing was littered with loose vines, dead leaves, and nettles—leftovers of last night's storm. Bhoran unslung Yekana from his shoulders and stepped into the clearing.

Six long years had passed since last he'd sought the comfort of the Great Warrior's presence. *An Onyx in the company of an Onyx.* He knelt on the wet grass. *Olnos,* he cried in his mind.

Bhoran, a thought boomed inside his head in his own voice. It was a rush of relief, more potent than any poison. And now he had it, Bhoran stood, ready. The whoosh of an arrow was all he heard before Lusha screamed. It hit the giant's leg and splintered. At once Lusha rushed to his aid. Bhoran whirled around. He searched the clearing but found no one.

"From the trees!" Avalan yelled at him. "Get down!"

Bhoran forced Lusha to the ground, shielding her. He glimpsed a silver glint. The tip of an arrow. Heading straight for his head.

A ripping sound tore the air. Wood splinters exploded before his face. Confused, Bhoran looked at his feet. The arrow lay on the ground before him, steel head detached from a shaft torn asunder. But this time, it wasn't Yekana that had stopped it. The coolness of Avalan's second shadow fell across his face, and he looked at it with disbelief. The shock of magic must have stalled the archer too, for no other arrow came.

The shadow darted to Avalan, and Bhoran followed, lifting Lusha into his arms. A man cursed behind him. Over his shoulder, Bhoran watched Lhorin fall from a tree, his longbow still in hand. Yekana hovered above him, ready to strike. Bhoran's heart caught in his chest. Though Lhorin deserved it, Bhoran couldn't let the snake bite him.

Only a prick could prove deadly. He whistled, and Yekana obeyed at once. She hissed in displeasure and tore her head away from Lhorin. Bhoran felt her slither along his path.

As they ran, the blackwood trees gave way to tall pines with flaky bark and long limbs. *The mountain path is near.* Bhoran trudged through the soft blanket of needles, kicking pine cones as he went.

Avalan stopped at the foothill, catching his breath.

After setting Lusha on the ground, Bhoran pricked his fingers on the fangs in his face to calm his chest. "What now?"

Lusha's cheeks flushed red. "He shot you," she mumbled. Then louder, looking at Bhoran with wild eyes filled with anger, "He shot at your *face*!"

Bhoran grabbed her shoulders, trying to soothe her fury. "It matters not."

She twisted out of his grasp. "No! I *hate* them!" she shouted in the direction of the village. "I hate them all!"

"We must go," Avalan said, searching the ground. "Lhorin will set them on our tracks."

"The shadow ..." Bhoran began.

Avalan frowned, his thick brows uniting. "I know. I saw. Lhorin rarely misses."

"We mustn't trust it."

"It saved your life."

Despite that, Bhoran's mistrust still held.

"It will lead the way," Avalan said.

"I know the mountain path," Bhoran insisted. "It's been my home."

Avalan shook his head. "Yet you don't know the way to the Heart of the Bloodstone. My mother's still here. Sigil. The tribe. I can't just abandon them. I promised Dizredek I would believe. I'll follow the shadow and free Hydrus. But I'll understand if you two choose your own path. You have each other."

Bhoran's chest tightened with sorrow. "I didn't mean it that way."

The sun stood high above them, burning the tops of their heads. On the green blanket of needles, the shadow stirred, shifting impatiently from one leg to another. Bhoran shot it a look of disbelief.

At last he nodded. "We find the Heart of the Bloodstone. Then lose the shadow."

At that, the shadow darted away, and Avalan turned on his heel, chasing after it. Bhoran grabbed Lusha's hand.

The shadow slid silently over the steep mountain path that twisted and turned like the body of a never-ending serpent. Bhoran dared not look back, for fear of losing hope and heart. The journey would be harsh, he knew. After all, it had only been a few days since he'd descended the slope back to Hydrus. Even he didn't know how he had found his way. All the while, he had kept Olnos's statue in his mind, and it was the thought of the warrior that had guided him.

Once they left behind the merciful canopy of pines, the air carried the musty smell of wet rock and soil. The mountain showed its real face here, through barren plains swept by tugging winds.

For a good while, the sun burned their heads as they clambered up the slope. After long hours, their shadows lengthened, but not the second shadow, Bhoran noticed. Untouched by nature, it slid and slid, ever upward and never halting.

As soon as they came to even ground, Avalan stopped and looked back. "They can't follow us," he said, chest heaving with sharp breaths.

Thankful for this small respite, Bhoran squeezed Lusha's hand. He hadn't let go of it since they'd started climbing. At first her palm had been warm against his, but now it had become frozen and clammy. Despite Farmera's woolen dress, she shivered. Bhoran swallowed the taste of mist. "The air is thinner here."

"We haven't much time. The sun is descending." Avalan looked at the ground beside him where the second shadow stood, arms folded, waiting. "If darkness falls, we'll lose the shadow."

"Avalan's right," Lusha agreed. "I'll feel much safer once we've crossed the mountain."

Avalan shook his head. "I'm afraid it can't be done. Ronan knew these paths like the back of his hand, yet even for him, a day's travel wasn't enough. He often told me how he'd camp at the peak. Safer there. Perhaps we should follow his course."

Yekana's scales brushed against Bhoran's naked back. Her tongue flicked in his ear, longing for something he dared not give her before his companions. He disentangled Yekana's body from his shoulders and strode forth, his grip tight around Lusha's hand. "To the top."

The shadow led them through paths he'd never taken in all his years up in the mountain. Bhoran always thought it hard to brave a route whose endpoint was unknown. The path grew more whimsical every few breaths. Wide footpaths suddenly gave way to narrow passes with stones slippery from last night's stormy rain, only to open again into a barren plain that gave them neither hope nor hint of how far they had traveled or how much more was to come. From time to time, Bhoran lifted his eyes to the crags above them. Rough, heartless rocks. Never-ending.

Lusha's breath on his neck was a welcome warmth as the air grew colder and colder. They pushed on, desperate to get to the top before the sun set. *Should darkness fall, so will our end,* Bhoran thought.

Once, they had to leap over a gaping hole in the path, and many a time had to stick their backs to the coarse slope of the mountain as the path became a mere sliver of land above the abyss below them. Bhoran tried not to let his gaze wander and hoped with all his heart Avalan's shadow knew where it was taking them.

When the last rays of crimson light caressed their foreheads, the path felt surer beneath their feet, the mountain peak for the first time coming into sight. Bhoran turned to Lusha. "Almost there," he promised her. The Moonstones in her eyes shone, filling his heart with hope.

Bhoran was grateful to have the sky above his head for once instead of an outcrop of gray rock raining dirt over him. The air was clearer atop. A vast, barren granite land offered them safe footings and a place to rest. Lusha left his hold and staggered to a rock painted red with the light of the setting sun. She lifted the hem of her dress to reveal a pair of bleeding heels.

Bhoran knelt next to her, examining her wounds. His soles were accustomed to the cruelty of the forest and mountain ground, leathery skin covering them. But he still remembered the blistering pain after walking for two days on end to get away from the village.

"We need water," Avalan said, his voice croaky. "I will go over the other side. Perchance I'll find a descending brook, or if we're lucky, a lake."

Yekana slid to them, her head barely above the ground.

She's tired and cold, Bhoran thought. *And soon she'll need to feed.* He waved her closer. The snake could help them find some water. After all, she was the one who had led him to the small pond that had served as his hideout in the forest of Hydrus. "If there is water nearby, Yekana will find it," he told Avalan.

When both snake and man had disappeared on the other side, Bhoran spied tears on Lusha's cheeks. "What for?"

Lusha walked, leaving a trail of bloody footsteps in her wake. She crested the hill, outstretched her hands … then laughed. "I feel … free." Her voice was a blend of sorrow and joy. "Bhoran, look." She pointed at the far horizon.

Far below, beyond the treetops of a vast forest, Bhoran saw the village of Hydrus. The serpent fence's spikes caught the setting sunlight, encircling the place where he'd grown up, loved, and hated … Where the village ended, the white beach began, its sand now crimson as if burning. The water of the Nameless Sea was an endless blanket of blood. He pulled Lusha to his chest. In silence, they watched the sun dip into the sea and the sky turn violet.

When Avalan's footfalls echoed behind them, Lusha spoke. "I was so unhappy there, and yet … I will miss it. It is all I know."

Avalan laid a full waterskin down. "It won't be long before I free Hydrus," he promised them. "The day will come when we return, and it will be a better place."

Bhoran's heart clenched. From all the years he'd spent growing under Bassalt, he knew only one truth about his stepbrother: Bassalt would fight with stone and nail to keep his place as the chief, for there was nothing more he craved. *Power, little brother,* he used to tell Bhoran, *doesn't come only from stones, but from the heart itself. And what is your heart's worth without a tribe?*

As darkness settled, they took turns drinking from the waterskin and washing their wounds. They ate in silence, salty goat meat Farmera had given Avalan for the trip. All the while, they listened in the night for any sound from below. Bhoran doubted Silver's men would find their way through these mountain paths. At times, he had been certain the shadow had been leading them to their doom—such had been the brutality of their route. Yet every time, the shadow had seen them through, over steep cliffs, abyssal gaps, and craggy valleys Bhoran would sooner forget. He savored the meat in his mouth, chewing it slowly, wishing it never melted.

Later, dim stars rose above them in a sky so dark, like the stones in his eyes. He lay with Lusha's head on his naked chest, stroking her hair, his eyes closed, listening to the sweet murmurs of her songs.

"Bhoran," she whispered. "Why did you return?"

Bhoran continued brushing his fingers through her thick hair. Something soft and womanly in his cold life. "For you," he told her. *And for me*, he thought.

When he felt her steady, warm breathing on his neck after sleep had taken her, he let her down gently and slid over to Avalan. His friend had let his ebony hair loose. Beneath his shoulders it spread, a blanket. He joined him in gazing at the stars. "What burdens your mind?"

Some moments passed before Avalan replied. "Farmera confessed to me my father had sired another son."

That was the last thing Bhoran had expected to hear. "How so?"

"Forty years ago, she said. Twice my lifetime. He was of the Onyx."

"The Onyx?"

Avalan twisted his neck to face him. "It seems the cursed stone likes to gift me brothers. I only care about one, though."

Bhoran smirked. A short silence fell.

"Do you remember our nights at the shore?" Bhoran whispered at last.

"The sand offered much better bedding," Avalan jested.

"How many games did you win after I left?"

"None. I never played again. Never slept on the beach either."

Bhoran fell silent. Avalan had been to him the brother Bassalt had never been able to find it in himself to be. Like true brothers, Bhoran and Avalan had lived a life in Hydrus as it should be. Playing the goat games, swimming the shallow waters of the Nameless Sea, hunting with Sigil in the forest, singing, and feasting with the tribe under the starry night skies, and speaking of myths and legends of what lay beyond the Craggy Mountains. *What does one say after six years apart?* "And you let flapping Colgar win?"

Avalan sniggered. "He's not as bad as before. After you left … he changed. He even helped me with the weapons. Together we trained the men to fight. I hope he carries on while I'm gone. We shall need everyone who can aid us."

"Colgar will not change."

"Perhaps not," Avalan admitted. "He did call you a talon after all, though I now see it was in fear. The tribesfolk are horrified by Ronan's death. They need someone to blame, for if it weren't you, where would that leave them? The years after you left were tough. I looked for you."

It was an accusation, Bhoran knew. Six years ago, when he had been cast out of the tribe, Bhoran had stolen Avalan's goat dagger to take with him, a small token of remembrance for all the good years he'd had someone to call a friend. Bhoran still recalled how the blade had bitten the earth, sliding deep into the soil, as he'd tried to quench his anger. *Lusha in Colgar's arms.* A memory he'd tried to pry from his mind. He'd covered his tracks, then, traveling in circles before finally taking the stony path through the mountains, only Bhoran had never ventured that high up. Yekana had approached him the first night, becoming his foe and his salvation.

Avalan twisted his neck, a painful frown on his face. "Where were you?"

A chill caressed Bhoran's nape. "Hiding at the northern foot of the mountain."

"Why didn't you come to me? I would have helped you. I would have done anything for you."

"I didn't want help."

"You wanted to die?"

Bhoran closed his eyes.

Avalan rolled onto his belly. He reached for the fangs on Bhoran's brow, pricked his finger, and licked the blood. His lips twisted. "Snake venom. How does it not kill you?"

"I'm used to it by now," Bhoran admitted.

"The snake ... Yekana's fangs hovered over my calf once or twice while we scoured for water. As if she longed to bite me."

There was little Avalan missed, Bhoran knew. Lying to him was never a choice. "I let her taste my blood. It takes the pain away." When Avalan didn't speak, he added, "Lusha mustn't know."

"She won't from me," Avalan said. "But she should from you. She loves you. You'd be a fool to lose her again. Do you love her still?"

"Always."

"Why did you return?"

"I want a family."

Avalan smacked his shoulder. "Then stop stargazing and have one. She needs you."

Bhoran smirked as best he could. "I promised to take her to her mother's city. Start a new life."

"Good."

"And you? Crystal?"

Avalan's gaze darkened. The muscles on his jaw twitched. "She left me. Not long after you. Of course, Ronan was behind it. He said she'd begged him to take her with him away from Hydrus. He never told me where he took her or why she wanted to leave."

Bhoran rolled onto his belly as well. "Do you intend to find her?"

"I want to. But the only person who knew where she is lies dead and buried. It makes no difference. I don't expect she will have waited for me like Lusha did for you."

"We will find her," Bhoran said. "I will help you."

Avalan's eyes searched the cool rock surface. "You won't. Our paths are different. I have to follow the shadow to the Heart of the Bloodstone, and you have given Lusha your promise to find Levorotha." He gave Bhoran his famous smile, the one with straight teeth and a corner of his mouth that rose higher than the other. "But I will savor the time we spend together. And I shall send for you both once I've freed the village."

Before Bhoran had time to reply, Avalan stood and took his sleeping place beside Lusha.

Bhoran watched them for a while, dark skies above him, dark rock beneath. In the blackness, he felt Dhylinea's gaze on him, lingering, longing, calling for him to return. Tomorrow they would slide down the mountain, he knew. And he would be with Lusha. Once they'd crossed it, they'd be free, he dared to hope.

Beside him, the stone whispered; a forked tongue flicked. Thin fangs pierced his thigh. Then sleep took him.

CHAPTER TWENTY

THE DAY DAWNED misty and wet. The storm clouds of two nights past hung low over the mountain. Still lying on the cool stone, Avalan cracked a stiff neck. A cool breeze slid beneath the arc of his nape, sending prickles through his body. The safety of the mountain peak came with its own challenge—cruel wind. Like a never-ending wail, it had whistled through his ears all night, shuffling his hair, penetrating his bones.

Avalan patted the goat dagger over his breeches, assuring himself of its presence, then rolled to his side. To his surprise, the place where Lusha had slept last night between him and Bhoran was empty. He stood, relieved at once to see the back of her slender figure as she sat over at the cliff edge. He went to her, leaving a sleeping Bhoran behind. "Rough morning?"

She smiled up at him. In her grip, a parchment fluttered against the tugging air. "I thought I'd take a last look," she confessed. "It's foggy, though. Not much to see ... and cold."

Avalan sat beside her, brought a knee to his face. "It should get better once we reach lower ground." His voice came out rough, his throat sore. His gaze fell on the parchment. "What is this?"

"A map." Lusha handed it to him.

When he unfolded the thin goat skin, Avalan glimpsed the pattern of the Stone Lands. Black oak ink was smudged in places. Salt water and the heavy storm had partly distorted the map.

"It belonged to Ronan," Lusha told him. "I got it off his body when I found him dead in the forest."

Avalan clutched it tighter, as if this little thing could bring Ronan back. He knew well the merchant's fascination with maps and exploration. If it hadn't been for the goods Ronan had had to bring back to sustain the village, Avalan was certain the merchant's journeys would have been much longer. "What was he looking for?"

"A hidden treasure in the east. He mentioned this companion of his, Eyedir. The way he held the map ... I couldn't stand leaving it in the hands of my father and his men."

"You did well." *Eyedir,* Avalan thought. Ronan had oft spoken about this other merchant, who traveled more the middle parts of the Stone Lands. He traced a big smudge next to a line of mountains. "This must be Raekandar. The closest town to Hydrus. It lies at the foot of the mountain."

Lusha leaned closer. "You know how to read." Her voice came out a blend of wonder and envy.

Avalan regarded her over the edge of the parchment. "I know what little Ronan taught me as a child." Then, seeing her gaze roll down, he said, "Lusha, don't ever feel sad for the things you don't know, for they can be learned."

She pulled her fur band farther back. Her scar caught the morning glow. "What will my aunt say? How can I hope to be a Moonstone healer when I cannot even read?"

Avalan winked and handed her the parchment. "Mother doesn't know how to read either, yet she's the best healer the village has. And she has told me many times how able you are with the potions." He was glad to watch her smile return. "We'd better move."

Lusha offered Bhoran a sweet awakening: warm words in his ear, strokes over his cheek, fingers dancing around the fangs in his face. Next to Bhoran, Yekana slithered down the slope, disappearing to the other side.

When Bhoran's eyes cleared from sleep, Avalan helped him to his feet. "There's a town nearby, at the mountainfoot. I don't think we can cross without passing through it first. It might even be a good thing. Perchance we'll find some clean water and food. You two can ask about Levorotha."

Next to Avalan, the second shadow stirred, eager to lead the way. Avalan eyed it with equal parts gratitude and fear. He wished he didn't need it. Ever since Dizredek had taken some of Avalan's blood and bound him to the shadow, he had felt pulled, as if an invisible string was leading him into a world he neither knew nor trusted. *The shadow knows the way to the Heart,* he thought ruefully. As Bhoran and Lusha followed after it, Avalan gazed one more time over his shoulder at the village far below. The Nameless Sea glistened under the gold light.

As he turned, he glimpsed a swell in the water, an odd stirring in the depths.

"Avalan!" Bhoran called from down the slope.

He rushed to meet them.

The descent proved much easier than Avalan had expected. It seemed to him the mountain had two faces. The southern slope was rife with chasms and difficult paths, to deter unwanted travelers from reaching Hydrus, or perhaps even kill them. The northern part was very different. Smooth stone paths coated the uppermost part of the mountain, offering them swift and sure footings.

Along with the second shadow, Yekana led the way. Among the odors of damp earth and wildflowers, Avalan breathed in with satisfaction the distant smell of goat scat. Funny how an empty stomach welcomed any signs of life that betrayed the presence of a meal.

He glanced at Bhoran and Lusha, both their faces drawn. Avalan twisted his neck, regarded the slope above them. Some meat would be much welcomed. It wasn't an easy task to catch a mountain goat, Avalan knew. Even with Sigil by his side, ofttimes the perky animals proved much faster than Avalan's strides and Sigil's leaps. *Yet I have to try,* he thought, brushing the hilt of his dagger. Lusha's feet were bleeding afresh. Bhoran's face looked pale, no doubt because Yekana had feasted on his blood last night. And Avalan's own belly growled with hunger.

"It's best if I go hunting," Avalan told them. "Perhaps I'll catch us something to eat. We cannot know for certain if Raekandar will welcome us."

Bhoran's face hardened. "It isn't safe."

"The shadow's with me." For once, Avalan was glad to feel its cool presence beside him. "I promise to return if I've caught nothing by midday. We don't know how far away the foothill lies, nor what dangers crawl down there. It's best to fill our stomachs, regain our strength."

"You should go with him," Lusha urged Bhoran.

"No," Avalan said. "Your feet are bleeding." The smell of blood was a sure call for danger, Avalan knew. Ronan had told him white panthers dwelled among the crags. Avalan had never seen one, but judging by the size of the white panther hide Bassalt donned over his girth during the feasts, these beasts must be as large as Sigil. "Bhoran stays with you. I won't be long."

Before they had more time to object, Avalan sprang onto the rough stones. Eagerly the shadow followed, as if they belonged together. Avalan crouched, sniffed the rock for urine, made for higher ground. Goats loved barren cliffs exposed to wind and rain. The ground felt foreign under his feet. He'd never been over this side of the Craggy Mountains, knew nothing about its goat trails. Yet Ronan had taught him not to fear the unknown, for it could always be conquered. *These are the paths Ronan walked …* He should have asked Bhoran to take him to the murder site, but there had been no time. Besides, the storm must have erased any signs of the killer. He shook the merchant's face from his mind. *Mourn later.*

The shadow crouched, one with Avalan's heels. Like him, it stalked and looked for prey. As the sun journeyed over the mountain, they crawled over soft grass, rock outcrops, and basins, their ears perked up, their eyes watching. The hours went by, and yet there was no sign of mountain goats. Avalan's whole body dripped with sweat. *It could take a while,* Avalan thought, shading his eyes. He stood over a cliff, gazing down at valleys of wind-whipped rocks.

Beside him, the shadow sat. Was it Avalan's eyes, or did its legs dangle over the edge? Resigned, he joined it, hot rock scraping his shanks. "It's harder than I thought. The goats of Hydrus are more trusting. Yet this part seems empty."

The shadow shook its head, listening. Long strands of hair waved behind its back, the resemblance to Avalan so eerie he couldn't stop himself from asking, "Are you a part of me?"

As if surprised, the shadow turned. There were no eyes on its face, and yet Avalan was certain it was staring at him. Slowly it nodded.

"Is the Heart of the Bloodstone hidden far from here?"

Another nod.

"Will we be back before the Night of the Spirits?" he asked, as if the shadow's magic could allow it to glimpse into the future. If the men still planned to attack Bassalt during the night of the spirits, Avalan had to be there.

And yet the shadow shook its head.

The denial weighed Avalan down. He already missed Sigil, his mother, the embrace of the forest, and the warm shallow waters of the shore. Without warning, the shadow brought a silencing finger to its face. Avalan's ears perked up. He turned to the valley below.

There!

A glimpse of movement, the sound of a hoof on hard rock. Avalan pressed his belly onto the outcrop and crept up to the edge. Below stood a goat—milky-white fur, black horns, hunched shoulders. *A youngling,* Avalan thought with a pang of guilt.

He had no bow and arrow to shoot it from afar. All he could do was leap onto it, catch it unawares, slit its throat with a merciful swift cut. He'd never hesitated in a hunt before. Yet now Lusha's voice echoed in his head: *His neck sliced from ear to ear*. The notion made Avalan sick.

Beside him, the shadow stirred. Avalan glared at it. If the goatling sensed their presence, it would scurry to the safety of the higher hills, and it would be a long time before Avalan caught up.

He raised a finger to his mouth to calm the shadow, but it didn't seem to notice. Instead, it charged, quiet as death. Avalan watched the dark silhouette land over the white fur. Dark hands hugged the neck. The goat didn't stir until it was too late. With a sickening snap, the youngling collapsed on the ground, neck twisted.

Eyes wide, Avalan watched the shadow slip off the animal, hands around its waist, hugging itself in triumph. He slinked down the slope, gazed at the dead animal at his feet. The disgust in his chest bothered him. *It did admit it is a part of me, and I'm a hunter. Why, then, do I feel this way? The shadow killed that goat without a second thought. And beside me it sleeps every night.*

The sun glared down at them now, at its peak, reminding him of Bhoran and Lusha. Avalan hefted the goat around his shoulders and took the way back. In silence they walked. *What will I tell them?* Bhoran had already warned him he didn't trust the shadow, but it had saved Bhoran's life, and now it had aided Avalan with a dire task.

As he followed his own tracks down the slope, the tree line appeared. Avalan was thinking how they would cook the goat after he'd skinned it with his goat dagger when a terrible growl resounded from below. Its sound like Sigil's, it tugged at Avalan's heart. *But Sigil is back in Hydrus.* A sickening fear rose in his chest. He ran.

Kicking rocks and soil, he found a white panther circling Bhoran and Lusha. The animal was of the same build as Sigil: bulky head, curved fangs, claws at the ready. Bhoran stood, puffed out his chest, growled back at the beast, stomped his feet. Avalan threw the goat off his shoulders and charged. Its attention focused on Bhoran, the panther didn't spin until the last moment.

Avalan glimpsed saliva trickling down the panther's fangs as he thrust with the goat dagger, aiming right between the eyes, but the panther twisted. Cursing, Avalan sprang after the beast, grabbed at its fur. Bhoran was on them in an instant. He shoved the beast to the ground. Avalan grabbed his goat dagger, twisted it in and out. The beast roared in pain.

Through eyes dripping with hatred and hunger, it stared at Avalan, thrashing its long tail. It circled them now, twisting its snout. Crimson painted its fur where the dagger had kissed it.

"Take Lusha," Avalan told Bhoran, panting.

"I won't leave you." Bhoran charged at the beast with bare hands.

"No!"

Claws and arms met with fury. Beneath the beast's grasp, Bhoran fell to the ground, the panther's fangs a breath from his neck. Avalan thrust his hands into the beast's mouth, letting out a terrible howl as he pried the jaws apart. The panther yanked its head away, slashed at Avalan's face. Dirty claws missed Avalan's nose by an inch.

"Here!" A shriek tore the air behind them.

Panther and men turned.

Avalan watched in horror as Lusha stood behind the limp body of the goat. She waved her arms in the air, screaming, inviting. "Lusha, no!" he yelled, too late.

With a growl, the panther twisted and raced toward Lusha. A terrible cry resounded; the panther leaped. It closed its jaws around the goat and rushed for the slope. Lusha collapsed to her knees.

They were both on her at once, Avalan's hands painted crimson, Bhoran's face slick with saliva.

"Are you hurt?" Bhoran hugged her.

"I'm fine."

"Lusha, you could have …" Avalan's words caught in his chest.

"I had to. It was the blood of my feet that lured it here."

Avalan searched the ground. *Why did the shadow not help us?* At last he found it on the branch of a pine tree. There it had crouched like a scared squirrel. Avalan frowned. "We shall rest," he told Bhoran and Lusha. "Wash our wounds. Tomorrow we'll brave the forest and approach the town. Let us hope Raekandar holds no more beasts for us."

CHAPTER TWENTY-ONE

THE STUMP on his hand was the ugliest thing Bassalt had regarded of late—a gaping wound with crusted blood, white bone peeking out from beneath a mass of muscle and severed flesh, aching to find its missing piece. Theran was pouring crimson wine on it now, as if the blood needed more blood to be washed away. Apart from Bassalt's faint moans of pain, the cooking chamber was quiet. None dared to cross the threshold. The chief's wrath needed only lesser things to be roused, and losing a finger was a great thing.

Bassalt had to clench his jaw not to scream. "What takes her … so … long?" He banged his good fist on the table. He regretted it an instant too late as pain surged up to his bruised shoulder. The cursed dragon's tail had proved stronger than Bassalt's thick hide.

"Farmera's coming, my chief," Theran muttered. "She's coming … Let me …" He dabbed the wound with a soft cloth soaked in a foul-smelling paste, earning a roar of pain from Bassalt.

The chief shoved him away and tried to stand, but the floor swayed beneath his staggering legs. He collapsed on the bench. The bleeding had stripped Bassalt of his power. Whatever little blood remained in his body pounded like a hammer in his temples. He brought a clammy hand to his forehead. *I have to stay awake,* he thought, *or else I'm lost.*

Heavy footfalls echoed through the building, and Bassalt recognized with spite the sure stride of Silver. No one else walked through

Bassalt's door as if he were his better. Sure enough, Silver's tall figure filled the threshold. His face was pale with anger and exhaustion from what Bassalt guessed had been a fruitless search. When Silver saw Bassalt's wound, his mouth twisted in disgust. "Who did this?"

"Have you *found* him?" Bassalt roared, as Theran had slipped to his side again and was dabbing the wound. "Cease this!"

Silver sat across from him. The green scales of his vest caught the light of the oil lamps and glinted as if afire. "Lhorin said they returned to the statue."

"They?"

"Avalan, Bhoran, and my daughter."

"No tiger?" Bassalt asked through clenched teeth.

Silver shook his head. "No Sigil, but a snake. Lhorin swears he had the talon within shooting reach, even unleashed his arrow when this hulking serpent threw him off the tree."

"A snake?" Bassalt hissed. He snatched the cup of wine Theran had been using on the wound and drained it to the bottom. "Do snakes stop arrows?"

Silver's nostrils flared. His gaze was shadowed by a sneering doubt.

"Speak."

"Lhorin said the arrow splintered in the air, as if it'd hit a wall." Silver took his sword and placed it on the table, the steel clinking. A frown creased his forehead with deep lines.

"What is it, Silver? Speak."

Silver's chin twitched. "A shadow."

Bassalt caught Theran by the collar of his tunic, shook him as if the fault lay with him. "Get ... Farmera. Now!"

Theran scrambled out of the room, the sharp smell of crushed cloves a heavy trail behind him.

When he was gone, Bassalt turned to Silver. "What ... shadow?"

"The boy claimed his shot would have certainly pierced Bhoran's skull had not a *shadow* come in front of it, smashing the arrow to the ground right before it found purchase."

"Get him ... here. I shall question him."

"He's out there with the rest of the men, still looking."

"*Get* him."

Silver stood and poured himself a cup of wine. "No." He drained the clay cup, then smashed it on the floor. "This filthy talon has my daughter! I don't care about shadows and snakes. I won't call off the search until they've found them."

Bassalt stomped his foot, making the floor shake with a faint tremble. "Sit. My brother … Bhoran cannot conjure."

"I care not about stone magic now." Silver wiped his hands on his breeches. "I only care about my daughter. I daren't think they'll try to cross the mountain. The men have combed the forest, and they have found nothing. Nothing! This filthy talon snatched my daughter right from my grasp."

Bassalt fought back the blinding flashes of light. It had been an unwise move to use whatever little power he had to shake the ground. "Avalan is with them?"

"What of it?"

"If somehow they cross the mountain … Ethelnar …"

Silver bent his knee, his wine-soaked breath close to Bassalt's nose. "Why would Ethelnar help us? He holds no love for us."

"For us, no. But he does … for his wife."

Silver's eyes widened with realization.

"Call off the search," Bassalt said, groaning. He gulped hot wine with cloves, bracing himself. "Get me Lhorin. It is a bad omen when shadows … walk the lands."

"What if they don't go to Raekandar?" Silver insisted, ignoring the chief's urgency. "What if they fall in the sea or choose another path?"

"Empty stomach … won't get you far." Bassalt's breathing was getting harder now, his vision blurrier with every passing moment. "They will go … to Raekandar. I shall send word."

A flurry of footsteps and loud voices came from beyond the door, and soon Bassalt's cooking chamber was crowded with men and the smell of wet earth, sweat, and rotten leaves. Gremian strode to the front. In his grasp, he dragged what seemed to Bassalt a pile of bones dressed in a sack and framed by a waterfall of wispy gray hair.

"Chief," Gremian said. "We found this man nosing around in the forest where Ronan was killed."

When the skull of the skeleton man raised his cloudy gaze, Bassalt forgot all the pain that tore his body. His heart thumped in his chest. *Delion?*

Before he'd summoned the courage to speak, the mousy voice of Theran broke the silence from the back. "My chief, Farmera refuses to come. Says she won't see you after what you've done to the boy."

Bassalt flared his nostrils, taking a sharp breath. He stared at the stonemaster. "The stones are good," he rasped.

CHAPTER TWENTY-TWO

THEY HAD SLEPT BENEATH AN OUTCROP, taking turns. Avalan now held the last watch, a few hours before dawn. They hadn't dared light a fire, and so once darkness had settled, the second shadow had been lost to him. In truth, he was relieved—the goatling's death too fresh in his mind.

Even when asleep, Avalan had remained alert, uneasiness surging through him.

They had been too exhausted and hungry to exchange many words last night, but Avalan knew they all shared the same fear. *The unknown.* In Hydrus they had all grown and never hoped, nor cared, to visit the lands. *We once were happy.* Over his cuts, he lathered some of the paste Lusha had made for them, squeezing yellow wildflowers with drops of water.

He stared at the forest line below. For the first time in his life, Avalan glimpsed the Stone Lands. Torn he was between returning to the village to protect his tribe with his bare hands and forging ahead in search of his Bloodstone. As time went by, the pounding of his heart grew so much his teeth rattled. He could wait no longer.

Avalan nudged Bhoran and Lusha awake before the sun had risen, to get on their way.

As the forest invaded the stony slope, rocks gave way to dirt pathways brimming with underbrush. The trees were different here, slimmer and of smoother bark than the ones in the blackwood forest. They seemed much friendlier too. Yet Avalan believed a forest that couldn't hide you couldn't be trusted.

Dawn broke, warm and welcome.

From the edge of a high mound, Avalan glimpsed the town ahead. What he noticed first was a resplendent assembly of gray stones perching atop a hill—the keep. Its west end was one with the steep cliff rising above the sea. Waves that frothed and whispered licked the rocks there. Scattered windows broke the vast stone surface, making the keep look like a beast with ever-watching eyes. Spurting out through the cracks in the walls, lichen climbed up to reach lines of stone battlements, sparse like the gaps in Fyridion's teeth.

The serpent fence encircling the village of Hydrus seemed to Avalan meager before the thick stone walls that protected the town of Raekandar. From the western crags that lined the seashore, the walls sprouted on both sides, like the arms of a giant, rushing forward in a rugged circle to meet across an arched gate. It was too far for him to discern whether the gate was manned, yet Avalan wagered it would be. With men who might not be so eager to welcome them.

He halted, his eyes searching the forest floor for their guide. Under the burning sun, the second shadow slid over to him. It pointed toward the city with vigor.

"Is this the way to the Heart?" Avalan asked loudly, as if that would make his words better understood.

The shadow nodded, then rushed down the slope.

Bhoran and Lusha fell in beside him, Yekana now wrapped around Bhoran's shoulders.

"We know nothing about the tribesfolk or their ruler," Avalan said thoughtfully. "And they will be suspicious of us too. They have no word of our arrival."

Bhoran frowned, a sullen warning. "Or worse. They might already have word."

"How?" Lusha asked. "Bassalt?"

"Bassalt won't have had time to send someone to warn them of our presence," Avalan said, trying to suppress a feeling of doubt. "We moved fast and passed no one."

Yekana hissed, shook her head.

Lusha shuffled her bleeding heels. "We could say we seek healing for our wounds." She tapped the side of her dress. "Or that we have a map to give to this Eyedir. With Ronan's passing, the duty of deliverance had to fall on someone else."

Avalan knitted his brows. "A good scheme, though dangerous. No one else comes out of Hydrus but Ronan. And they might not have heard of his demise as yet."

Lusha's mouth tightened, her Moonstones dull against the daylight.

"The truth." Bhoran seized Yekana's head to stop her writhing. "It is the only way."

Avalan arched his brows. "How so?"

"We ran because of Bassalt," Bhoran explained. "A life beneath his heel is no life."

Lusha looked up at him. She stroked Yekana's head with trembling fingers. "A sad story is always a sure way to lessen a stranger's suspicion. And a story of love is one that tugs harder at the heart. We shall say Bhoran and I longed to be together. Ronan had promised to aid our escape, only now he lies dead." She fished the map out of her pocket, offered it to Avalan. "Before he died, Ronan entrusted you with this map. You helped us cross the mountain, for you are an able tracker."

Avalan pushed the map back to her. "We shall do as you say, though keep the map. No matter what happens, I have the shadow and my instincts to lead me. You need this parchment more than I do."

"We tell the truth, then. Apart from one thing," Bhoran said, pulling Lusha close to him. "She's not Silver's daughter."

Avalan nodded. It always served best to let a stranger assume you held no value. There was no telling how the tribesfolk of Raekandar would react should they know they held the daughter of a chieftain in their hands. No matter how much Avalan hated Silver, the commander remained a powerful force in Hydrus, second only to Bassalt.

The foothill ended in a slope of sharp scree that made Lusha's feet bleed all the more. Bhoran carried her the rest of the way until they reached soft grass and muddy soil. The storm had passed through here too.

As they crossed the plain stretching between the hill and the gates, voices of men wafted through the air. Faint at first and growing louder as they edged closer. Outside an iron-studded wooden door blocking the entrance, Avalan spied four guards. They wore tunics and breeches the color of earthy green. Bronze-scaled plates covered their shoulders, chests, and knees. They cradled wooden spears with iron heads more elaborate than any Avalan had mustered in the village.

When they saw them, they ceased their talking. One of them, slim of face and fiery of hair, strode to meet them, the point of his spear brandished before him. Avalan thought him to be no older than forty summers and didn't much like the glint of suspicion in his narrow eyes. A golden birthstone tied to a string around his neck swung as he moved. "Stop there." The man's voice came cold and demanding.

The guards surrounded them now. Avalan noticed with deep dissatisfaction their attention shift to Lusha. Despite her scar, he knew Lusha's beauty would scarcely go unnoticed. The guard with the golden birthstone raised an arm. "Search them."

At his command, the men surrounded Avalan first. They patted his breeches, quickly fondling the protruding shape of the goat dagger inside his belt.

"Surrender your weapon," a guard told him. The stones in his eyes were black and dotted with curious beads the colors of the rainbow, matching the stone that hung around his neck. Avalan had never glimpsed eyes like these before, but he had heard of the Black Opal. The man's breath stank of ale—a sweet tang that spoke of a different recipe than the one they used in Hydrus.

Gritting his teeth, Avalan plucked the patched dagger from his breeches and laid it on the guard's extended palm.

Securing the weapon under his armpit, the man motioned the others to search Bhoran. At the sight of Yekana, they hesitated. One of them, whose stone flared with red, yellow, and orange, dared raise the end of his spear to poke her. Yekana retorted with a swift whip of her tail, snapping the spear.

"Bloody beast!"

The guards raised their weapons in unison, all ends pointing at Bhoran.

"She's harmless," Bhoran assured them. He whispered close to Yekana's ear, and she uncoiled herself, sliding down onto the wet soil. Bhoran raised his arms, and they searched him.

"He's clear," one of them said. "But ..."

Avalan saw them staring at Bhoran's face. *Not them as well.* He had hoped the fear of the Onyx would be lesser here in the Stone Lands, but now he saw he had been mistaken.

"What?" the red-haired man said. "Will he attack the chief with his face? These bones are mere trinkets." He lowered his spear and moved to Lusha.

Avalan watched Bhoran tense, his entire body ready to spring forth should they dare touch her. Yet the guard proved wiser than that. He dipped the bottom of his spear into the ground and bowed to Lusha. "Daughter of Chieftain Silver," he told her. "Fear not, for we shall rid you of your captors. Take them to the chief."

Lusha shot Avalan and Bhoran a desperate glance, yet she dared not speak. The guards let her walk in the middle, while they flanked Avalan and Bhoran. When Yekana tried to follow, the man with the black eyes pointed his spear at her, and she hissed and slithered away toward the forest. Avalan feared Bhoran would lash out, yet his friend's face remained calm, his dark eyes betraying no emotion.

After some swift knocks on the hardwood, the studded door creaked open. Avalan's heart raced as the men dragged them through the archway. Many a time Ronan had described to him the beauty of different settlements in the Stone Lands, yet seeing it firsthand was a thing Avalan had never truly believed would come to pass.

The air carried a whiff of animal scent. The musky odor of goat skin and urine mingled with the warm aroma of wood. Avalan soon saw why. To the eastern side of the courtyard, a shed overflowed with mountain goats, much like the ones that skipped the slopes in Hydrus. Avalan watched a man garbed in a gray tunic girded with a drawstring guide the animals inside with a long stick. The clops of goat hooves were soon overwhelmed by the clinking sound of metal on metal. Avalan watched a man, his face dusted with soot, hammering a blade into submission over a stony slab. Inside a furnace of brick behind him, a great fire burned. Its heat made the man sweat all the more.

When they passed him, the man dropped his hammer and shot Avalan a glance through the violet eyes of the Amethyst. Avalan knew he'd like this man, and not only because he had been born under the same stone as his mother, but because he was a blacksmith. Ronan had told him about these men who forged weapons and wrought iron and steel with blood, sweat, and tears. Ofttimes also with magic. Perchance it was this man who had given Ronan the arrowheads ...

A guard shoved him forward, and Avalan lengthened his stride. The rankness of raw meat and fatty fish pushed aside the whiff of smoke from the smithy. Women and men with long, bloodied aprons and tied-back hair worked tirelessly over benches, tearing flesh from skin with sharp knives, gutting, peeling, scraping ... Earthen pots and tin jars overflowing with juices, spices, and herbs rested beside them, their savory smells making Avalan's stomach growl and his mouth water. He watched as several women kneaded the meat with thick pestles, slapped it over the bench, dipped their fingers into the earthen pots in succession and slathered the juicy flesh with affection. *They're preparing for a feast.* Avalan frowned. The Night of the Spirits was still two nights away—whatever great repast these people were preparing for was surely of another nature.

The stone path grew narrower here, like the neck of a tall flagon. As the guards led them through, Avalan heard curious whispers rise behind their backs. His ears caught the names of Hydrus and Ronan. Faint footfalls on the smooth stone told him the tribesfolk of Raekandar were edging closer, perhaps trying to get a better look at them—at the people of the fabled Hydrus, who always remained secluded from the world. *We're as much a strange sight to them as they to us,* Avalan reminded himself.

However, Avalan was certain they made for a much scarier sight than these quiet working people. Bhoran's etchings and fangs, Lusha's proudly flaunted face scar, and his long hair, bare chest, and bronze skin came into stark contrast with the plain robes, white skin, and tied-back hair of these people. *How savage we must seem in their eyes.*

Once they'd crossed the narrow passage, he was glad the piercing stares on his back eased. The yard grew wider here, as if a massive spill of endless grass had spurted out of the flagon's mouth. Over the verdant sward, trestle tables had been arranged in rows. Men carried long benches between them, while children straddled over them, kicking their heels and laughing. Women with colorful dresses and wooden shoes clacked down stone paths that led upward to the keep, carrying bouquets of flowers over their shoulders. Silky violet petals parted with their stems and rained down behind them as they walked, forming mauve rivulets.

At both sides of the town walls, pressed against the crude stones, stood small houses. Huddled together for protection and warmth, they were small spaces that offered little privacy to their owners. Avalan felt sorry for them. He much preferred the quiet of his tree house.

Despite their dire predicament, Avalan couldn't help but smile. It joyed him to taste the freedom in the air, hear the carefree laughter, and watch the people prepare for what seemed to be a long-awaited celebration. As they ascended the stony path, he looked at Lusha and Bhoran. Her face glowed with wonder, while Bhoran's remained stony with suspicion. Avalan couldn't blame him. He would have felt the same should the guards have attacked Sigil and forced them to separate ... *Only what is Yekana to him, a friend or a weakness?*

At the top of the slope, a green lawn stretched before the keep. On the smooth grass, Avalan looked for the shadow. *It hasn't followed,* he noted gladly. It would be easy to spot it on the exposed sward. Up ahead, he glimpsed heavy oaken doors leading into a great chamber. Yet the guards pushed them to the side, veering off the main pebble road and onto a dirt path leading to the side wall. They ushered them through a narrow passage, barely broad enough for two men to walk abreast. *The pathway of shame,* Avalan thought as they passed flaming torches bracketed to the walls. Smoke filled the stale air, making breathing hard. Thankfully, their journey wasn't long.

Soon they emerged into a small chamber that smelled of burning fat. Flickering flames of tallow candles illuminated the space. A faint breeze had extinguished some of them, wisps of dark smoke rising from blackened wicks. Avalan frowned. *Where's the breeze coming from?* There was no window he could see; the chamber was barren save for a chief's chair, much like the one they used in Hydrus during the Night of the Spirits. His gaze darted to a drape. It faintly shivered against the wall. He smirked. A covered entrance.

The guards forced them to the floor. One of them scurried into the tunnel they'd just passed through. Beneath them, the stone was cool to the touch. Lusha and Bhoran sat next to him.

"No touching," the guard with beady black eyes ordered, and Avalan watched Bhoran retract his hand from Lusha's.

In silence, they waited. Avalan's heart thudded with anticipation.

White fingers appeared behind the drape, pushing it aside. A rawboned man garbed in a black velvety robe embroidered with colorful threads stepped over the threshold. Long brown hair swayed on his back as he strode to take his place on the seat. He couldn't be much older than Bassalt, Avalan reckoned, yet his scrawny physique made him much more elegant and springy in his movements. His fingers were bare of the heavy rings Bassalt wore. *What a plain man to be a chief.*

When he looked at them, his stare was sharp and judging. He made a dismissive gesture at the guards.

"We know nothing about these men, my chief," the red-haired one objected. "They could be dangerous—"

The chief shot him a commanding glance. "I know enough. Leave us. And send word for my wife to join me." His voice was gravelly, a grinding of stone against stone.

The men obeyed.

Once their footsteps could be heard no more, the chief broke his silent regard and stood. "Which one of you is Bhoran?" He edged closer, the soft cloth wrapped around his feet muffling his footsteps.

Avalan frowned. *How has Bassalt sent word so fast?*

When none of them spoke, the chief approached Bhoran, grabbed his chin and tipped it up to face him. "Snake fangs, trails of ink, and eyes dark like the Onyx. Bassalt's description leaves no room for doubt."

Bhoran jerked his chin away.

The chief laughed, a startling sound like the flutter of the wings of scared crows. "First time I've met a killer who bears the proper look." His eyes glistened with excitement. Now he was closer, Avalan glimpsed colorful beads dancing inside them. "Usually they're modest, concealed among normal men. You wouldn't be able to tell their deeds even if they shouted them in your face."

"Bassalt is lying. I killed no one." Bhoran's voice was low with a hint of threat.

The chief seemed wise enough not to step foot into unknown territory. "Ronan held a dear place in my heart," he said, turning his back to them. He paced the room. "The lands will never be the same without him. The man was full of life, stories, and curiosity. Among his wares I always found the most unusual things—things of tradition and magic, filled with the pain and tears of the owners who had had to part with them."

"Ronan was our friend too," Lusha told the chief.

The man shot a curious look at her over his shoulder, then sauntered toward her.

"And we will not rest till we find his killer," Avalan said, trying to draw the chief's attention.

"An ambitious quest with an uncertain ending, Avalan of the Bloodstone," the chief said before returning to his seat. "Bassalt warned me of your insolence. And how you two stole Chieftain Silver's daughter away from her father."

"I came willingly," Lusha said.

The chief rapped his fingers on the wooden throne. It was a sound of doubt, a slight gesture of uncertainty.

Avalan studied the steep shadows the flames painted on the man's edgy face. *Doubt tears at his heart,* he thought. Avalan's spirit lifted. Perhaps this chief could be reasoned with.

"Tell me why I should not surrender you to Bassalt this instant."

"You would condemn innocent men," Avalan said. "You seem like a man who knows his affairs. Why would we get rid of the man who was our only bond with the Stone Lands? The man who filled our childhoods with stories of faraway chiefdoms that made us wonder and stay awake in our beds until dawn."

The chief raised a thoughtful brow. "What do you seek in Raekandar?"

"Food and drink. A place to rest before our journey. Then we shall leave in peace."

"Where is it you're headed?"

Avalan swallowed hard, his eyes flickering to the floor in search of the second shadow. He couldn't possibly give the chief an answer, for he didn't possess it himself. The shadow had left them the moment they'd reached the town's walls, yet it was the only one who knew where it was taking them.

The soft whisper of fabric on stone made them all turn their heads toward the entrance of the tunnel. Someone was swiftly approaching. The footsteps sounded light and close to one another. *The chiefess?* Avalan wondered.

Sure enough, a woman entered the room. Ebony locks dropped over her ashen robe as she approached the chief. "Ethelnar," she greeted him. "You sent for me?" When she spoke to her husband, her voice was but a low whisper, full of contrition.

Avalan stared at her womanly shape, his heart racing. For he *knew* this voice. It was a voice that had whispered his name in his ear many a time during the soft sweetness of lovemaking. A voice he'd dreamed many a time of hearing again, and that woke a longing in his heart. A voice he'd thought lost to him forever.

The chief motioned his wife to turn and look at them, and when she did, Avalan held her gaze gently, like treasure. Despite the darkness that concealed the true nature of her stones, Avalan knew them to be the azure color of the sea, a calm Larimar stone.

She lost her balance then, yet the chief was quick to catch her. He bent, his mouth close to her ear. "These men are from your *village*." She flinched. His words sounded like a harsh accusation, as if her origins should be a matter of great shame to her.

Fear and wonder crossed the woman's face as she stared at Bhoran, both of them quickly replaced by guilt as she noticed Lusha.

"Crystal?" Lusha whispered, hard disbelief in her voice.

Crystal's mouth twisted in sorrow. She swirled and threw herself at the feet of her husband. "I beg of you, my love. Lusha is my heart friend, and Avalan and Bhoran tribesmen I grew up alongside. Whatever they have done—"

From the corner of his eye, Avalan spied the second shadow slipping across the tunnel's threshold. Silently it slithered across the stone floor, a determined silhouette among the whimsical dancing shadows cast by the burning candles. Ice gripped Avalan's heart as the shadow stopped behind Crystal. It raised a tentative palm, as if to stroke her hair.

The chief cleared his throat. "If this is so, we should treat them as our guests." The gleam in his stones grew. He didn't seem to have noticed the ethereal presence. The skin around his eyes crinkled now as he helped Crystal to her feet. "After all, Bassalt is a deranged fool." He laughed at his own jest. "Tomorrow marks the wedding night of my youngest brother. You will be our honored guests. And let us not forget"—he straightened the soft fabric of his robe—"the Night of the Spirits is fast upon us."

CHAPTER TWENTY-THREE

SOFT BEDSHEETS COILED around Lusha's nakedness as she lay. Pale sunlight filtered through the window of her guest chamber. Lusha sighed, savoring the sweet tiredness. Beneath her head, the feather pillow smelled of soap. She rubbed her cheek against it, eyeing the heavy oaken door, willing for it to open and let Bhoran in.

She had waited for him last night, hoping foolishly he'd find the way to her room and spend the night with her. Yet she knew it wouldn't be an easy task. After the chief had welcomed them as guests, the guards had conducted them to a small chamber with a lone table and four chairs. Lusha had thought it to be close to the kitchens, for the smells that had slipped through the wall fissures had been tantalizing and had made her empty stomach cramp with pain. A mousy servant boy had brought them trays filled with food and drink. One glance at Bhoran had been enough to make him scamper off as soon as the tray had touched the table.

Famished by the journey, Lusha had forgotten all her table manners. Together with Avalan and Bhoran, she'd dipped her fingers in the succulent roasted game, tearing it apart, wolfing down the cooked flesh. Only once she'd had enough to appease her hunger had she drained the tankard filled with ale flavored with lemon and thyme.

When only stringy bones had remained on the tray between them, Lusha had dared glimpse at the shadow across Avalan's face. She had asked him then how he felt for seeing Crystal, but he had remained silent, licking the grease from his fingers, lost in his thoughts.

Before Lusha had found the right words to say, three women had entered the small room, each of them instructed to lead them to separate chambers for the night. Lusha's guide had been a young girl, swift of gait and tight of lip. The red ribbon tying back her hair at her nape had flowed in the breeze as she'd guided Lusha through a maze of rough stone. No windows lined the corridors, darkness broken only by the bronze light of low-burning torches secured in sconces. After the third or fourth turn, Lusha had lost count of the doors they had passed, the soft clacking of the servant's wooden shoes lulling her to sleep.

When they'd finally arrived at Lusha's chamber, the girl had bowed swiftly and left. Lusha had watched her go until the red ribbon had been swallowed by the darkness ahead. Then she'd entered the room, the door heavy under her pushing. A lone candle had lit the place. The sight of the tall bed with plump linens had been much welcomed, and she had eagerly stripped and burrowed under the covers.

The servants had provided buckets with clean water beside a small bathtub, yet Lusha had been exhausted. For some moments, she had lain awake, thinking of Crystal. Her once-beloved friend, free of spirit and body, had now become a chiefess. An unhappy one, by the looks of it. Avalan would never have allowed her to bend before his knees like that if she had stayed and been his wife instead.

Lusha stretched now, her body loath to part with the softness of the bed. Unwillingly she washed her face with the sweet water provided for her. Drops trickled down her neck and found her mother's pendant. Her eyes searched the room for the spot where she had dropped Farmera's battered dress last night. It was gone. A lump of shame rose to her throat. *How can I leave my room naked?*

In the far corner, atop a bench, the parchment caught her eye. She took it with relief. *Ronan's map.* A spot of grease marred the parchment where her thumb had touched it last night after the rich supper. She ought to find better protection for it than the pocket of her dress, though even that was now gone.

She eyed the closed door. *Has someone been in here?* Sleep had lain atop her like a leaden plank; she wouldn't have heard the door creak open. She followed the sunlight to the window. The glass felt warm against her palm. Timidly she peeked outside, conscious of being seen in her nakedness. Below, an inner courtyard was strewn with rows of stone tables over soft grass. Lusha spied two young men engaged in a game of dice and sticks. On the far side, across a table covered with a white cloth and a rich breakfast, Avalan sat with the chief.

Somehow it felt strange to watch Avalan garbed in a black tunic covering his bare chest. His hair now fell loosely over his shoulders. It seemed as though the simple garments attempted to tame his wild spirit. But perhaps what was even stranger was the calmness on his face as he conversed with the man who possessed the only woman Avalan had loved in his life.

A soft knock on her door made her dart for the safety of her bedsheets. Hot shame crawled to her cheeks. Crystal slipped inside. In her emerald dress and matching slippers, she looked a vision. Over her arm dangled a length of teal cotton. "This is for you. I took yours for washing and mending. There were some tears in the fabric." Her voice was soft, her tone imploring, as if a patched dress could grant her Lusha's forgiveness.

Lusha dropped the sheet, now unashamed of her nakedness. Though they hadn't seen each other for over six years, back in Hydrus she and Crystal used to bathe together in the waters of the Crystal Lake. Crystal had even taken her name from the lake, since her mother had given birth to her in its shallow waters. Lusha took the dress and slipped it over her head. It smelled like the old Crystal: coal smoke and forest fruits. "Thank you," she told the chiefess, straightening the fabric over her waist.

"Come." Crystal ambled toward the door. "You must be starving. Let us join the men."

Lusha much preferred private words with her. "There must be some other place where we can break our fast."

Crystal's surprise swiftly gave way to a familiar wry smile. "The kitchens. The preparations for the wedding keep them occupied, yet Paldma always keeps some treats for late risers. Follow me."

The golden ribbons tying back the chiefess's ebony locks glistened in the torchlight that danced across the keep's corridors. They descended a spiral staircase, and Lusha welcomed the light of day as they strode through a small, deserted yard filled with blooming flowers. Crude stone walls loomed above them, pressing closely together to form narrow, twisting passages. Much like the stone passageway they had led them through when they had first arrived, Lusha guessed this wasn't the usual route to the kitchens. She caught a whiff of freshly baked bread, and her mouth watered. Despite last night's rich supper, she was still famished.

At last they emerged into a wider enclosure, and Crystal pushed open a towering door. Lusha felt dizzied by the abundance of smells: the tanginess of cheese fought with the fruity aromas of wine and ale, only to surrender to the engulfing scent of roasting pork. The walls of the keep's kitchen echoed with the clanking sounds of plates and cups being stacked on the center table. A man, balancing over a stool, was pouring salt and lemon into a wooden colander. Cloudy liquid seeped through its bottom, carrying the smell of cheese. Barrels full of mead, honey, and spices lined the walls, servants lifting their heavy lids and scooping their contents out to fill the bowls they cradled.

As the kitchen folk noticed them, they bowed their heads in greeting. Crystal led Lusha to the back of the room, where the air grew warmer. Before a sizzling fireplace with revolving spits of skewered pork stood a lady with rosy cheeks and an apron tied around her heavy waist. Her eyes brightened when she saw them.

"Welcome, my chiefess," she said to Crystal, and then wrapped her stubby hands around Lusha's. "Hydrus must have the most beautiful tribeswomen." She gave Lusha a good look from head to toe. "But skinny as twigs. Come. I've just baked the most delicious bread. Raisins for sweetness and walnuts for a crunch."

"Thank you, Paldma." Crystal motioned to the back of the room. "We'll gladly take your offerings at the back. It's been many years since Lusha and I have seen each other."

Paldma frowned at the opening at the back of the room but then patted her apron, sending flour into the air. "As you wish. Make yourselves comfortable, and I'll send my finest treats." She left them, barking orders to serving girls.

"She doesn't much like the notion of our eating here?" Lusha asked Crystal as they stepped through the small archway.

"This is where the servants sup. The preparations are keeping them on their toes. We should enjoy some quiet."

Faint smoke trailed after them as they stepped onto the soft grass of the small courtyard. Tall walls rose around the area in a circle; crude, rough-hewn tables huddled among long benches. Lusha couldn't think of a better place to enjoy a quiet moment with her long-lost friend, away from the ears of men. Only … there *was* one man there now.

As they approached, he raised a head of brown locks and curious eyes, and let the chicken leg he was holding drop to his plate. He stood and bowed before Crystal, his gray cape jingling around him. When he raised his head, he gave Lusha a curious glance. His face was weathered, but his eyes held a gleam of adventure, reminding Lusha of Ronan. "Didn't mean to startle you," he said. His lips were painted red, and there was sweetness in his words.

Paldma's thick footsteps squelched on the grass. "Off with you now, Eyedir," she called, placing an empty tray on the table. She swept away the man's unfinished breakfast plates and wine cup. "The chiefess will have a quiet moment over food."

Lusha pinched the chain of her pendant. *Eyedir, the merchant.* She patted her side, where the pocket of her dress should have been, only she was wearing Crystal's dress now, and Ronan's map rested on the table in her chamber. She felt a fool for having left it there unattended. Eyedir's eyes were on her now, his gaze making the scar on her face feel as if afire.

"I'll be happy to make your acquaintance during the celebrations," Eyedir told Lusha. "My chiefess." His cape clinked as he strode away.

"Don't let the man frighten you, child," Paldma told Lusha. "I saw how he was ogling you. Our Eyedir is harmless. A peddler is all. I'll be back with food and will chase away anyone who thinks to bother your reunion." She waddled toward her kitchen.

"Is he a traveling merchant, like Ronan?" Lusha asked Crystal as she sat on the bench across from her.

Crystal nodded, her pale face glowing even whiter under the sun. "Word of Ronan's death reached us. Is it true, then? Is Ronan dead?"

"I saw him with my own eyes." Lusha caressed a knot on the crude table. "Throat slit from ear to ear."

The chiefess's lips fell apart, twisted. "Who would do such a vile thing?"

Lusha shook her head.

A look of shame marred Crystal's face. "We had word of Bhoran's trial. They say Bassalt condemned him for the murder."

Mugs rattled on a tray as the servant girl who had led Lusha to her chamber last night now approached with swift footsteps. She served them in silence: fresh bread, honey, sliced cheese, walnuts, and small bunches of loose herbs. Paldma had also sent for them earthen cups filled with spiced wine, despite the heat of the morning. As soon as the girl had unburdened her tray, she slipped away, brisk as a breeze.

Lusha ignored the pity in Crystal's gaze and reached for a slice of bread. "It isn't true," she told the chiefess, spreading the soft cheese on the white crumb. "Bhoran didn't kill Ronan. He had no reason to. My father's men found him standing over Ronan's dead body, that is all." After drizzling some honey and crushing some walnuts over the bread, she put it in her mouth, warm tears of gratitude filling her eyes. *This tastes so good.*

The chiefess hadn't touched her plate. "You two ... are you together now?"

Between gulps of wine, Lusha watched her. "You never approved of him. I still remember how many times you tried to convince me to forget him."

"I worried for you." Crystal's voice trembled. "He has the eyes of the Onyx. And all those fangs piercing his face ... does it not hurt to kiss him?"

Lusha felt her face boil. She banged her cup on the table. "I don't need your concern. Nor your pity. Bhoran *loves* me. He didn't leave me to start a life away from the village and take a seat of honor among the outer tribes. They chased him away with vile assumptions about his stone and his true nature." Her voice rose now. "And at least he came back for me. He *came back*."

Crystal's eyes watered.

Lusha bit her lip in shame. In anger, she found she wasn't so unlike her father. Smashing things, yelling … scolding Crystal for running away from Hydrus, when she herself ultimately had done the same, with or without the merchant's aid. She regarded her lost friend, now a chiefess. In Hydrus, Crystal had always been darker of skin. Yet now she appeared pale, as if she rarely enjoyed the company of the sun anymore. *Could she be sick?* She was prettier than Lusha had ever seen her—her black locks adorned with golden ribbons, her elegant neck with a pendant set with a stone as blue as a clear sky. Lusha reached for it. "Your true stone?" she asked to shift the matter.

Bewildered, Crystal brushed her chest. "A present," she said, her voice steadier now. "From my husband."

Lusha studied the waves of blue under the morning sun. Birthstones were forbidden in Hydrus, yet here it seemed the tribesfolk wore them with pride. Ever since they'd arrived at Raekandar, Lusha had glimpsed many of them in necklaces, chains, rings, brooches … She let the chiefess's pendant drop. "Are you really married to this man—this chief?"

"Ethelnar is kind to me." Crystal gave Lusha a wan smile. "It joys me to see you after all these years, but I have to ask … why are you here?"

"Ronan promised to take me to the city of my mother. But then he died." Lusha took a grape from the bowl and crushed it between her fingers. "Bassalt condemned Bhoran for the killing. Avalan and I helped him escape, and we left the village." She leaned closer. "Crystal, you've been in the Stone Lands for long enough. Surely you must have heard of my mother's city—Levorotha."

Crystal nodded. "The city of healers. It isn't far from here. If that's where you're headed, you should reach it in three days' ride."

"What's it like? Have you been there?"

The chiefess cupped her pale neck. "Stones forbid, no. That is where we send our gravely sick. Levorotha accepts all ailments Nexanthos, our medic, cannot heal. Some return and some don't." She lowered her voice. "You're wearing your mother's pendant, I can see. What are you looking for in Levorotha?"

Lusha fiddled with the cool chain. "I don't know. Love, acceptance, a womanly figure in my life. What did you seek when you left Hydrus behind? I want to be a moonhealer, I think. To take care of the sick. Find out what took my mother. Farmera knows little about that sickness, but I hope the healers of Levorotha will have more to tell me. Bhoran is coming with me. Far from my father, we might still hold a chance to start anew."

Wrinkles etched Crystal's pale forehead. "I don't know, Lusha … Though it's been twenty years since the war, the stigma of the Onyx lingers. The tribes haven't forgotten how the Onyx tried to conquer the Stone Lands, to enslave the tribes, absorb all their stone power. You must be prepared."

It will always come to that, Lusha thought with bitterness. *Bhoran's stone.*

"And Avalan?" Crystal's tone rose despite her feigned indifference. "Is he going with you as well?"

Lusha studied the chiefess's face—her lips had parted in anticipation, her breath caught in her chest. *She still loves him,* Lusha thought ruefully. "You broke his heart when you left. You broke my heart as well. I thought you loved us." She gulped the spiced wine to gain courage. The clove in it tingled the back of her throat. "Why did you leave?"

Like a scared animal caught in a snare, Crystal glanced at the small archway of the kitchen. Then she lifted her dress and straddled the bench next to Lusha. "I owe you an explanation, I know. I have told no one else but Ronan. I see he's kept my secret. He promised me on our stone, Larimar bless him."

"What secret?"

The chiefess fiddled with the end of her locks. "I shall tell you, because it pains me to watch this look of betrayal on your face. But know the truth might hurt you. It was that night—the night Bhoran was cast out from the village."

For a moment, Lusha gasped for breath. *What does my Bhoran have to do with it?* "Did you and Bhoran …?" She clutched the butter knife in her hand, surprising even herself.

"No! How could you even say that? I'd never betray you like that."

"I don't know anymore." Lusha stared at her, hot shame burning her cheeks. "Why are you speaking to me about that night?"

"You'll always remember it because you lost Bhoran." Crystal held her gaze. "I'll remember it as the night Colgar raped me."

The knife fell on the table, a clang resounding like thunder. All breath had left Lusha's chest. "What did you say?"

"Colgar … he came to me half-mad and stinking of wine. I was bathing at the lake. He kept rambling on about you being ungrateful when he had offered you marriage, and how nobody should ever refuse him. He said you had to be punished. Then he raped me." Crystal bit her lip so hard it bled. A tear fell on her pale cheeks. She stole stealthy glances toward the kitchen.

The bitter taste of bile rose in Lusha's mouth. In her mind's eye, she saw Colgar, sitting with her on a log outside her home, telling her how he'd arranged with her father to take her as his tribeswife now she had lost her beauty. She took Crystal's hands in hers. "I'm so sorry …" she muttered. "If I had known … I would have told him I could never love him … I didn't know what he … Why didn't you tell me?"

Crystal tightened her grip, desperate, hopeful. "I was ashamed. I had no family to turn to, and you … how could I break your heart like that? Ronan found me in the woods. He saved me. Later I begged him to take me away, and he did. And now he's dead."

An icy shiver crawled down Lusha's body. The thought someone would kill a man like Ronan filled her with dread. *Why is it the stones see fit to let mean men rule and allow the good ones to drop dead by sharp blades?* She had hated her father all her life for his misplaced cruelty from losing his wife. She had hated Bassalt for his oppressive nature and the torture he made of Bhoran's life raising him. She had hated Colgar for wanting to trap her into an unhappy marriage, when all she wanted was to be with Bhoran, and now Lusha hated Colgar even more.

Will I come to hate Bhoran too? Will his explanations of where he's been all these years, becoming someone else, make the hate grow and plant itself in my heart? And then, once it has lodged itself there, how can I uproot it?

"Promise me, Lusha," a teary Crystal said. "Promise me you will never tell Avalan."

Under the sunlight, Lusha watched Avalan's second shadow slip toward them. It crossed the soft grass and hovered behind Crystal, raising a hand as if to stroke the weeping chiefess's hair.

Sadness weighed on Lusha's chest as she said, "I promise."

CHAPTER TWENTY-FOUR

"ISN'T it too early for us to drink this much?" Avalan asked as a servant poured wine into their cups for the third time that morning. Dice of painted knuckles clacked on the stone tables around them, the men engaged in games Avalan didn't know.

Though his body ached from the journey, his sleep last night had been hollow and restless. Crystal's worried face had haunted him, and then there had been this whisper of rushing water through the walls, as if endless rivers ran through the keep's stones like veins. At last he'd risen and clambered to the stone seat of the window to find some peace.

A man had entered Avalan's chamber at dawn to let him know the chief would like his company. After Avalan had donned the black tunic and breeches, which felt much softer than the crude linen they had in Hydrus, he'd followed the man to the yard to find the chief half-drunk and dressed as if the wedding night had arrived—dark robes of velvet emblazoned with colorful beads, and gilded bracelets, chains, and rings that seemed too heavy for the chief's spindly fingers.

Ethelnar favored him with a hearty laugh and raised a brimming cup. "It's merely practice for tonight. It isn't every day a chief gets to see his younger brother marry." He gulped, licked his thin lips. "Do you have any brothers, Avalan of the Bloodstone?"

Avalan sipped his wine, his teeth sieving out the floating herbs and seeds. A bitter taste burst in his mouth as he bit a hard flake of nutmeg. "I am an only child."

The chief raised a thin brow. "A pity, that. There's much to be shared with a brother."

Bhoran is my brother, Avalan thought, dipping some barley bread into his cup. Wine crept up the white crumb, soaking the slice to the crust. He savored the soft melt against his tongue. "Not that I do not value your mercy, but why have you truly chosen not to surrender us to Bassalt?"

The chief studied him, the colors of the rainbow adorning his black stones. He drummed bejeweled fingers on the table, the tangled gold bracelets around his wrists jingling. "Let us say Bassalt and I haven't always seen eye to eye. What he calls a murderer, I call a man who's lost his way."

"Bhoran is no murderer."

"So you've told me time and time again." Ethelnar leaned closer, his sharp nose sniffing for lies. "Yet there's one thing I wish to know. What brings you to my humble town? It's curious how you crossed the mountain path so swiftly. Bassalt sent word but a night ago. Yet the morning after, here you were, strolling through my gates. Even Ronan, may the Stone receive his soul, wasn't that fast."

Avalan flicked his eyes to the ground, searching for the shadow. Yet once again it hadn't followed. It was as if it had led them there, into the hands of this mysterious chief, and left them to fend for themselves. He couldn't let the chief know the truth, much like the chief wasn't telling Avalan his. If there was one thing Bassalt had taught him, it was not to trust a man in power—especially one who carried a stone on his body. "Bhoran has been an outcast for half a decade. He knows the mountain well—its traps, its sure footings, the path that leads to the Stone Lands. Bassalt condemned him to death. Running for your life makes your gait swifter."

Ethelnar smirked. "So it would seem. What happened to your hands?"

Surprised, Avalan rubbed his palms. The lack of sensation in them made him forget his wounds. Under the morning light, the nasty burns appeared even worse. He curled his fingers into fists. "I toyed with things I do not know."

"Stone magic." Amused, the chief threw a grape into his mouth. "Bassalt is an old fool with hard views. Forbidding the birthstones is the dumbest thing a chief has ever done. How long did he presume to keep you from the truth? If you ask me, he fears you."

Avalan's stomach clenched. "Why would Bassalt fear me? He is the one with the stone powers."

The chief waved a dismissive hand. "Controlling the plants and ground, pfft. A mere ability of the Tiger's Eye. A Bloodstone, however, holds the power of blood magic. Nothing ever beats blood, the essence of life. It makes clear sense why Bassalt wouldn't have liked you to know your roots."

Through narrowed eyes, Avalan studied this chief. His words were provoking, reminding Avalan of the tricks Dizredek had used to lure him into a shadow binding. *What is it you want from me?* Dizredek, the stonemaster, and now this chief ... it seemed all of them tried to urge him down a path he knew nothing of, and wasn't sure he trusted. *How much do I not know? And whom can I trust to tell me the truth?*

As if reading his mind, the chief slipped a hand into his robes and produced Avalan's goat dagger. He placed it between them. "I am returning this to you. As a sign of goodwill."

Avalan was fast to grab it.

"This blade holds a great place in your heart," the chief noted.

"It does." Though it wasn't the strongest weapon Avalan had crafted, the goat dagger had always been his most beloved. With it he had hunted, sliced, played ... and the goat's leg in place of the hilt reminded him of Hydrus.

Behind the chief, a child with a bright smile and a dress that danced with her every step skipped to their table. She threw her arms around Ethelnar, planting a kiss on his cheek.

"Semara," the chief said, with the most genuine smile Avalan had seen him muster. "I want you to meet our honored guest, Avalan of the Bloodstone. Avalan, this is my daughter, Semara."

Semara, Avalan thought, pain piercing his heart like an arrow. *So Crystal had a daughter with this chief, and she named her after her mother.*

For a mere moment, he dared hope the child was only Ethelnar's, perhaps from an earlier marriage, since the chief was much older than Crystal, but the child couldn't be more than six summers old. And she had the unmistakable blue tint of the Larimar in her eyes. She had inherited Crystal's stone. "The honor is mine," Avalan said, gulping back hurt.

The girl backtracked, her smile fading. Her father reached for her arm. "No need to fear now, child."

"He's different," Semara said, her words a sharp reproof.

"He comes from the village of your mother, and he's our honored guest. We ought to treat him with respect."

Semara pouted. "Your eyes are funny."

"They're of the Bloodstone."

"Is it a good stone, Father?"

"A very good stone indeed, my child." The chief held Avalan's gaze. "A stone of evenhanded chiefs and desired soothsayers."

"It's just a stone," Avalan said. "Like all others."

Losing interest, Semara tugged at her father's sleeve. "Can I go look at Eyedir's wares? He's brought spices from the east that make your dreams come alive, and a lock of hair—"

Eyedir? Avalan frowned. If Ronan's companion was here, perhaps Avalan could talk to him, learn more of Ronan and his plans before he returned to Hydrus.

"You can, my child," the chief broke in. "In fact"—he reached into his pocket, fished out a golden coin—"take this and buy whatever your heart wishes."

Semara accepted the coin, squealing with joy, then skittered off toward the stony passage that led to the main courtyard.

"Children," the chief mused. "Their hearts fill with joy with so little. But tell me, Avalan of the Bloodstone, what fills *your* heart with joy?"

Avalan's eyes flickered to the goat dagger. Before he had time to answer, the chief said, "Weapons, is it? Then we shall pay a visit to our swordsmith. I think you will find it well worth your time." The chief drained his cup and stood. "He has talent with silver, steel, and stones. Among his things you will find more than mere bones and twigs."

Avalan rose, taking his goat dagger. "How about visiting this Eyedir instead? Perchance I can find something to cover my wounds."

"There will be ample time for talk with traders. It is a veritable master we need to visit now." Without waiting, the chief turned on his heel, his robes grazing the grass.

Avalan followed him through the small archway. To his relief, the chief didn't use the hidden passage to lead him outside. Instead, he crossed the keep's main hall, a look of curious pride on his face that Avalan couldn't decipher. He lifted his face to the ceiling. At least thirty feet above their heads, it was covered in a curious painting—a hoary woman, older than time itself. She wore silvery robes like the ones Delion had worn that night in the cavern of the Eagle's Eye. At the tips of her fingers, a black rock with colorful beads balanced. Instinctively Avalan ducked. So realistic was the painting that it was as if the rock would roll from the old woman's hands and fall on their heads to crush them.

Around them, the hall rang with the noise of wooden shoes. Up and down the workers clambered, busying themselves with preparations for the upcoming wedding. A long table had been set against the back wall, about twenty women stretching a crimson cloth over it now under the orders of a plump woman with rosy cheeks and a loud voice. Many more clumped past them, carrying trays burdened with plates, cups, flagons, jugs, flowers.

Avalan was glad to leave the commotion behind as they emerged into the courtyard. He lengthened his stride to match the chief's. The air was clear and crisp, a perfect day for an outdoor wedding, yet it seemed the chief had chosen for the ritual to take place under the watch of this strange woman that dominated the ceiling. *A stone-mistress, she must be,* Avalan thought, *much like Delion.*

The blacksmith flexed his shoulder blades as he saw them approach. He wiped away his sweat, smearing his forehead with a coal smudge. "Chief Ethelnar. I wasn't expecting you till later."

"Dagan." The chief pointed at a sword lying atop a stone slab. A long steel blade shone under the sun. A leather wrapping was still only half-swathed around the pommel. "Is this the one?"

Dagan nodded. "Just making the wrap. Would help to know what stone we're putting in." He turned to Avalan, his sharp gaze piercing his eyes. "The Bloodstone? I see. A rare one ... Will cost more."

"Worry not about the payment." The chief ran his fingers under the soft leather strips. He picked the sword up, presented it to Avalan. "A fine weapon, is it not? Much better than this goat leg."

Avalan shot a suspicious glance at the sword. The fine craftsmanship left no room to doubt the skill of the man who had forged it. The blade was sturdy yet thin and keenly edged, and it held the promise of a good fight. A fight Avalan had no intention of giving. "What is this for?" he asked, though he already suspected the answer.

"Why, for you." The chief chuckled icily. "I can't stand this meager goat blade. A Bloodstone bearer should wield a weapon worthy of his descent."

"If you hand me the stone now," the smith began, "the sword should be ready before evenfall."

"I hold no stone," Avalan said. If the chief thought to placate him with stones and swords, he had chosen the wrong man. And yet what if he took this blade the chief offered? Would that be enough to return to Hydrus and fight Bassalt? The sword looked long and sturdy, the edges sharp, and yet ... *It doesn't hold the true Heart of the Bloodstone.* Dizredek had warned him that many would try to offer him Bloodstones, but it was only the Heart that mattered. He flicked the goat dagger in his hand. "This meager blade has served me well over the years. I don't need any jewels."

The chief smirked. "Have you ever tried, Avalan of the Bloodstone? Have you ever held a bejeweled sword? Fought with one?"

"It's not a fight I seek. We shan't stay long. After this night, we should be leaving, and I couldn't indebt myself by accepting such a beautiful gift."

The colorful beads in the chief's eyes blazed. He let the weapon drop onto the slab, the metal ringing. "You cannot possibly leave before the Night of the Spirits. It isn't wise to brave the road at times like these. My weathermen have glimpsed terrible clouds on the horizon. Storms are brewing and will drench the main road, turning the soil to mud. Dagan will finish your sword. An opportunity to wield it might arise soon enough, and then we shall see what you think of weapons blessed with … jewels." He rubbed his temples, his bracelets clinking. "I've had too much to drink, I'm afraid. I trust you can return to the keep on your own."

With that, the chief swirled his dark robes and marched off.

Dagan gave Avalan a blank stare. "You shouldn't insult the chief so."

"He was the one to strike the first blow."

The smith knitted thick raven brows that rivaled Avalan's. "It isn't every day the chief asks me to forge a weapon of such power. I missed last night's sleep to finish it." His gaze drifted to the goat dagger. "I understand the sentiment an old weapon can hold, but things change. You either change with them … or perish."

"I'm sorry you lost your sleep for nothing," Avalan said before he strode away.

The smith's disapproval felt so hot on his back that Avalan was certain it would pierce a hole through him. He searched the ground for the shadow, suddenly eager to be on his way. All he saw was green grass and tribesfolk who went about their day. *They wear their stones with pride. Almost as if they are their talismans*. He gazed at his scorched hands. *What has my stone given me?*

He found Bhoran with some other men gathered around a table, a game of knuckle dice before them. He mouthed a greeting and sat next to Bhoran. After watching them play for a while, he nudged him. "What is this game?"

Bhoran shrugged. "Been watching them all morning. I'm damned if I understand a thing," he whispered, then raised his tankard. "The ale is different here."

Avalan studied the board resting in the middle of the table, brown and square, like a carpet of flat dirt. The men threw dice and moved around some sticks, gasping and cursing if their stick landed in the wrong place.

After a long while, one of them, with eyes that shone like Silver's Heliodors, sighed and leaned closer. "I guess we have to stop and unravel the secrets of the game for our guests," he told his companions.

"Count me out," the man with a thick mustache said. "I've no time for this." When he stood, the rest followed him, all except for the young man who had spoken first, now a wicked smile on his face.

"Good riddance. I was losing anyway." He winked at Avalan and Bhoran. "Dromer's the name. So, tribesmen from another father, here goes the game of death."

"Death?" Bhoran asked.

"Yes, yes, death." Dromer pointed at several squares on the cloth. "For these are places known to capture the soul. Mind you, some would say they're pure legends—but the bards sing of their existence, and there's always a sliver of truth behind a myth."

Avalan exchanged a curious look with Bhoran. He forced himself not to laugh in response to the pompous grimace on Dromer's face.

"What is this place?" Bhoran pointed at a square. It held the depiction of a ruined fort, an abandoned arrangement of blackened stones surrounded by wild bushes. Compared to the other squares, it looked freshly painted, as if the artist had added it much later as an afterthought.

"Krokador's Stronghold." Dromer shuddered. "One would be wise not to venture close."

"Why?" Avalan asked.

"Krokador was burned to the ground during the last battle of the War of the Stones. The fire was so high its flames licked the sky and touched the sun. Those of us who'd stayed behind to protect Raekandar saw the great fire from atop the battlements. A monster, it pulsed and swallowed. And no one made it out alive."

Avalan's attention stirred to the drawing of a cave. Mysterious symbols whose meaning eluded him were etched on its walls. "And what is this one?"

Dromer's solemn expression gave way to a queer frown. "This one's the Cave of Rath. Songs say it was used to trap evil spirits in the time before the twelve stones. Riddles adorned its walls, holding the key to freedom. No one has ever escaped. If you ask me, it's pure legend."

A chill ran down Avalan's spine despite the warmth of the midday sun on their skin.

"Let me tell you about this one." Dromer dropped his voice to a whisper and tapped a square with dark edges and waves. Through the turmoil of ink strokes, a beast rose, one whose form Avalan had never seen. Long it was, like a monstrous water snake, with heavy claws and a snout that sheltered a row of sharp prongs. "The Nameless Sea," Dromer recited solemnly. "And Hydrus, its waterdragon."

Bhoran huffed.

Dromer leaned closer, his breath stinking of sweet ale. "Have you seen it?"

"There's no such thing," Bhoran said.

"The men said you two grew up in Hydrus," Dromer said, crestfallen. "They must have been jesting with me."

Avalan frowned. "We've swum the Nameless Sea since we were younglings yet never chanced upon a monster. Nothing dwells there. It is a mere fable."

"This game is foul," Bhoran said.

Dromer shrugged and collected sticks and dice in a small pile. "Well, it might well be, but it rejuvenates the soul to think and talk of horrors. One feels much more alive in the face of danger." He folded the cloth. "Speaking of danger, there are whispers in town."

"What do the whisperers say?" Bhoran mocked. He was not enjoying this talk of ghosts and deathly traps, Avalan knew—Bhoran had never been one for adventures or the thrill of a hunt.

"You know, about the death of your merchant, Ronan, and"—he waved a hand at Bhoran—"your eyes."

Avalan flinched, certain Bhoran would grab the man's neck. Yet Bhoran merely smirked and said to Avalan, "Have you seen Lusha?"

"We should go find her," Avalan offered, as eager to get away from Dromer and his strange game of death as Bhoran seemed to be. They rose in unison.

As they sauntered uphill, Dromer shouted after them. "You won't enjoy the feast so much if your minds are closed to the mysteries of this world."

"What do you make of this mooncalf?" Bhoran said.

Avalan frowned. "Dromer and his fables are the least of our concerns."

"The chief?" Bhoran offered.

"He worries me. I was certain he'd offer us as hot prey to Bassalt. Yet in an instant, he names us his honored guests, grants us beds, rich meals to fill our bellies, invites us to his brother's wedding, and … even tries to gift me a sword of great value."

Bhoran raised a curious brow. "A sword?"

"One whose forging cost the blacksmith a good night's sleep."

"Why the haste?"

Avalan brushed the goat dagger absentmindedly. "I know not, but I have a feeling he means to press me into accepting it." He extended a halting arm against Bhoran's chest, then pointed to a lone table across the grassy yard. "Perhaps it's best if we talk outside the keep. I feel the presence of hungry ears between the walls."

They settled across from each other.

"Where is the shadow?"

"Last time I glimpsed it was in the chamber of shame, where the guards dragged us before Ethelnar." Avalan frowned. "It leaned over Crystal."

"Meaning harm?"

Avalan remembered the goatling. "I know not … It stroked her hair."

Bhoran fiddled with the fangs in his face. "Why would the shadow lead us here?"

Avalan shrugged. He had a queer feeling the Heart of the Bloodstone was hidden somewhere here. Perhaps in the keep's cellar. Or even deeper underground, as his mother had explained. "The chief didn't much like the notion of us leaving. He insisted we stayed for the Night of the Spirits. Some talk about a storm approaching."

"A storm?"

"Sounded like empty talk," Avalan admitted. "Yet I think it best to heed his insistence. We do not want to raise suspicion, nor force him to press us with Bassalt's threat."

Bhoran grimaced. "You don't want to leave Crystal."

Avalan's chest tightened, but he waved a dismissive hand. "After the Night of the Spirits, we shall leave. You and Lusha for Levorotha, and I with the shadow." *If I can force it to return to me. Can shadows be summoned?* "Ronan's merchant companion is in Raekandar. I'm of a mind to speak with him."

"How do you know?"

"The chief's daughter came to our table while Ethelnar and I were breaking our fast. She was excited to peruse a merchant's wares. Something about a spice from the east. She let the name of the merchant slip —Eyedir."

Bhoran studied him through eyes that betrayed no emotion. "Crystal has a daughter?"

Avalan swallowed hard and looked away. He wasn't ready to deal with this. Not under the warm sunlight, when his heart was dark with fear and longing. "It matters not."

"It does," Bhoran retorted. "You haven't said a word ever since you saw her."

"What would you have me do?" Avalan nervously brushed the goat's leg. "She left Hydrus without telling me. She left *me*. And Ronan ... I know now why he never wished to speak to me about her. He was protecting me. My heart."

"You should speak with her."

"What good would it do? She has a child. Semara. She has Crystal's Larimar stones. Blue like a clear sky."

"Despite that, you should learn why she left. It eats at your heart."

Avalan knew this to be true. Perhaps if he could finally learn the reason, he could move forth. "Crystal disappeared from the village not longer than a fortnight after you left. I thought it strange at the time, to lose you both in such a short time."

Bhoran pierced a finger on one fang, a crimson drop appearing on the finger's cushion. "I don't know why she left. I would have told you."

"All this time in the mountains, you weren't alone, were you?"

Bhoran stole a quick glance over his shoulder as if he wanted to ensure no one would hear them. "No."

"There was a woman?" Avalan pressed. Even in their days of youth, Bhoran had always been tight of lip and poor in words. As a man grown and an outcast, Bhoran had hardened even more.

"I'd rather not talk about her."

"She gave you these etchings?"

Bhoran ran his fingers across the length of his skin drawings. "She saved me," he said, but the pain in his face betrayed he would rather she hadn't.

"Lusha is bound to ask."

"I know." Bhoran rubbed his nape.

"Our love lives are a mess," Avalan jested.

They shared a hearty laugh. Avalan studied Bhoran's solemn face and the fresh puncture marks that lined the milky skin of his inner arm. Though they'd left Yekana outside the keep walls, Avalan was certain sliding over them would prove an effortless task for her.

A glint of gold caught his eye, and his heart lifted. Down the hillside, Crystal and Lusha were approaching, their arms entangled like in the old times in Hydrus. He nudged Bhoran.

When the women reached them, Lusha placed a gentle hand over Bhoran's shoulder. "Ronan's companion is in town for the night of the spirits," she said. "I want to show him Ronan's map."

Bhoran nodded. "I'll come with you."

Guilt filled Crystal's gaze when she finally found the courage to meet Avalan's eyes. She had been crying, Avalan saw. "Wait until I'm well away," she told him. "The east wing holds a tall tower. Follow the flowered sconces. I'll wait for you at the top."

With that, she padded over the grassy slope, two shadows trailing after her.

CHAPTER TWENTY-FIVE

BHORAN WAS USED to the stares whenever Lusha walked alongside him. At first the tribesfolk in Hydrus hadn't bothered their minds with indecent thoughts as the two of them had grown together. But when the years had shaped him into a man grown, and Lusha's figure had rounded, the stares had begun.

He tightened his grip on her hand now. *Hydrus or Raekandar, wherever I go, they will despise me.* As they passed under a small archway, Lusha looked up at him. The smile she gave him cast away his dark thoughts.

They found the merchant where Crystal had told Lusha he would be—down a narrow passage in the westernmost wing of the keep that led to a small courtyard within curved curtain walls. The place was deserted save for Eyedir's long bench, covered with curious trinkets. When he saw them approach, he straightened his cape, a jingle echoing against the rocks.

"It's a fortunate day when I get to lay my eyes on you twice, sweet Lusha," Eyedir said, bowing so low his forehead almost touched the rough-hewn bench. "And you ..." he began, wagging a thin finger at Bhoran, "I recognize you. Ronan told me all about the small boy who bears Onyx stones in his eyes but has a heart of gold. Bhoran, is it not? You are a small boy no more, if I may say."

Bhoran's lips tightened. It had been long since he'd let Yekana feed on him, and now he felt his anger rising. "I do not care about the stones," he said by way of greeting. He'd thought leaving Hydrus behind would rid him of the superstition of the birthstones, yet it seemed his reputation had reached far more people than he desired.

The merchant tittered, a curious glint in his red eyes. "It is refreshing to hear that for once. A rare thing to behold a man who doesn't value the stones. Most often it is the stones they seek us for, to sell or, worse, purchase. But we peddlers have many things to offer, as you will soon discover." He spread his hands over his goods in an inviting gesture.

"Why the secrecy?" Lusha asked, looking around at the deserted courtyard.

"Ah, most people prefer to carry out their affairs in the shade."

Bhoran frowned at Eyedir's words; the sun shone above them, bright and burning. "I see no shade."

"Now, now. Do not take me at my words' true meaning. 'Privacy' is what I meant to say."

"I only trust the true meaning of words," Bhoran said.

"Strange, that," the merchant began, a smirk twisting the edges of his mouth. "It's only just now that you said you hold no value in the stones, yet some six summers ago, Ronan trudged up the high steps of Levorotha to ask for a much-valued Moonstone. It was for you he wanted it, I believe, and now I understand why, if I may say."

Bhoran edged closer, his nose filling with the powdery smell of spices from the bench. Hot fire tore at his chest, but the look on the merchant's face made him restrain himself. Fear mixed with adoration. Fascination most certain for the dead stones in Bhoran's eyes. "Forgive me."

"Makes no matter. I shouldn't have touched on matters of the heart." His gaze darkened now. "If it doesn't pain you much, though, I'd like to learn about Ronan. His death, they say, was the result of a nasty cut delivered by an Onyx blade. How much truth is there in this tale?"

Ronan's dead, ashen face swam before Bhoran's eyes. For a moment, he thought of Eyedir's words. Bhoran still remembered the feel of the Onyx blade in his grip, both when he'd first found it next to the lifeless body of Ronan and when Bassalt had forced him to hold it to prove his true stone's nature. Both times it had felt to Bhoran a meager weapon, too light to the hold, with a blade blunt from usage. Yet the dagger was drenched in blood—the blood of Ronan. "Can the stones endow lesser weapons with power?" he asked the merchant. "If so, this killed Ronan."

Eyedir frowned. "It is the heart that gives power to the stone."

Bhoran pierced a finger with one of his face fangs to calm himself. He didn't much like men who spoke in riddles, and Eyedir certainly was one of those. Perhaps it would be best if they just showed him the map, learned about Levorotha, and went on their way. "We have something for you," he said.

Lusha fished out the map from the warm safety of her bosom. She offered it to the merchant. Eyedir's eyes glinted with joyous red fire.

"Even in death, Ronan has kept his promise," he mused, pinching the unfolded parchment from the sides so as not to smudge the paint. "But ..." With the back of his hand, he cleared a space on the bench. Jewels, shells, bowls, chains clanged as he pushed them aside. In their place, he stretched out the map. "What destroyed this fine work?"

"Water," Lusha admitted. "Things got rough after Ronan's death."

Eyedir eyed her with a glint in his red stones. "I can only imagine. Escaping Hydrus isn't a task for the fainthearted. And there was a terrible storm. I can smell another coming, worse even. Mark my words, a merchant is rarely wrong about these things. We live on the path."

"Ronan would want you to have it, I think," Lusha said, trying to stir the talk back to the map. "He said you two were looking for a treasure in the east."

The merchant fiddled with the ends of his brown locks. "East ... east," Eyedir mumbled, tracing a finger over the territory of the Stone Lands. A deep frown was etched in his forehead. "Curious ..."

"What are you searching for?" Bhoran asked.

The merchant raised his gaze to him. "The meaning of his words eludes me now. Perchance with a more careful study"—he tapped his finger on the sandy, undrawn part of the map—"I shall arrive at a conclusion."

Lusha cleared her throat. "Ronan promised to take me out of Hydrus, and to my mother's city. I cannot read maps, but perhaps you could show us where we can find the city of Levorotha."

"But of course!" Eyedir exclaimed. He dipped his head over the map once more and pointed a finger over a rough drawing of what seemed to be a crude assembly of rocks upon more rocks, tall and scraping the sky. "Levorotha lies right here. A Moonstone like you should find great comfort in this city. As for you, Bhoran, you might find the moonhealers much more accommodating than Bassalt and his lot. After all, all lives matter the same in sickness."

Lusha gave Bhoran a look full of hope. Then she threw her hand into her bosom once more. This time she fished out her mother's pendant. "This belonged to my late mother. Perchance you know how it opens."

Gently Eyedir twisted it around while his Ruby eyes searched for notches. At last he dropped the pendant on the counter and searched his robes. Metal jingled as he fished out a wooden shaft that carried small key rods. Of different lengths and shapes they were, and of different colors. The merchant tried some in succession through a small hole at the bottom of the pendant. "Too small … Too big … Too fat … Too *thin* …" He clucked his tongue in disapproval. "I'm afraid it won't yield." He handed the pendant back to Lusha. "Most crafters are cunning, making the key a perfect match so as no one else can open their pendants. Breaking it open would be our only option, but that would destroy this beauty. No … best not to. Have you not the key, then?"

Lusha shook her head as she passed the silver chain around her neck. "I thank you for trying, though."

"Do not lose hope, sweet lady. In this old merchant's experience, things turn up when you least expect them. Or when you've stopped looking. I should know. I carry more things than a man should be allowed to carry. For all that, your pendant is a valued possession, if I may say."

Soft footfalls echoed behind them. Over his shoulder, Bhoran glimpsed two young women in white dresses sauntering toward them.

Once they discerned their presence, though, they halted, one of them gasping in surprise.

Bhoran huffed. He took Lusha's hand in his, a move that earned him disapproving mutters from the women. "We should go," he whispered in Lusha's ear.

"Thank you," Lusha told Eyedir. "Keep the map. I think Ronan would like for you to have it." They sauntered away.

"I'm to remain in Raekandar until the Night of the Spirits," the merchant called after them. "If the stones will it, we shall meet again."

As they passed under the low archway back to the keep, Lusha didn't speak, but Bhoran felt the sadness seeping through her body. *She hoped Eyedir could open the pendant.* Suddenly he longed to comfort her. In a place where he could lift her in his arms, swirl her around, and kiss her, with none there to see them. He grabbed a passing servant girl. "How does one go up?"

"Just ... follow that staircase." She pointed at the back of the hall, then twisted out of his grip and hurried out.

"Come." Bhoran ushered Lusha up the stairs.

Their twisting pattern reminded him of Yekana's body as it coiled around his shoulders. They emerged into the sunlight. The air smelled of the sea. Bhoran licked the salt on his lips. "Walk with me." He hoped the fresh air would waft away her pain and his anger.

The walkway was a snaking path broad enough to hold both of them sauntering abreast. On their right, the battlements jutted high, the gaps gaping between them. A whiff of rich soil rose from the ground below. Bhoran peered through a crude embrasure, glimpsing a dense forest with thick brown trunks and green summer leaves. Above the sea, it hovered atop a crop of land.

Beside him, Lusha halted. Under the overhanging sun, her scar glistened. "Do you truly believe what you said earlier? You don't care about the stones?"

Bhoran pulled her down, and they sat together, their backs against the battlements. His heart was screaming the truth he'd always known growing up, the truth revealed to him over the still waters of the Crystal Lake. *My eyes aren't dead, for there are snowflakes drifting in them.* And yet his mind held him back. *I've only seen them in the village. What if the lake has some strange power I do not understand, showing you only what you wish to see?* "All I wanted was to be free."

Lusha caressed the length of his veiny arm. "You *are* free. We all are. We escaped Bassalt, my father …"

"You asked me about my stones. They hold me prisoner. I never wished for them."

"I used to think the stones were the source of a great evil," Lusha said, her voice lowered now, as if she didn't wish for the stones to hear the insult. "I had Bassalt to blame for that. But then you gave me my stone." She took the small Moonstone bead out of her pocket. The sunlight did nothing to change the birthstone as she pinched it between elegant fingers. "I know it is *my* stone, but when I look at it, I think of you. Our love. Our bond. It fills me with hope."

A faint smile crept up to his lips. It was a mere grimace that hid the pain. "You'll never feel at ease not knowing who I really am."

Swiftly Lusha secured the Moonstone back in her pocket. She slid in front of him, her knees touching his, her hands cupping his chin, fingers carefully spread to avoid the pointy fangs. "Avalan spoke of this stonemaster. There must be more in the Stone Lands. We could search for one. Then we shall ask about your stone. Once we know the truth, it will be easier. It will be better than to live in doubt for the rest of our lives."

The truth, Bhoran thought bitterly. *How does one find the truth and shield one's heart from it?* He stared at her now, wanting to taste her cherry lips. "And what if the truth is I am an Onyx?"

"You don't know that—"

"I do. I feel it, Lusha. Bassalt has made me see it too. I touched the dagger, and I felt … nothing. A terrible sense of emptiness. Isn't that what the Onyx is? Soulless?" He watched Lusha shiver, her eyes wide. In them, Bhoran saw the truth he feared most. *She is afraid of me. Afraid of who I might be.* "Couldn't you just live with me not knowing? What does it matter if you love me?"

She dropped her hands. "It isn't me I'm thinking of. Not even you. I'm sure after all this pain you've been through, nothing could really hurt you."

Losing you could, he thought, but he made no mention of this. "Then let us live without the stones. You heard Eyedir. We could start a new life in Levorotha, among the healers."

"And what of our children? Don't they deserve to know who they are should they inherit your stone?"

Bhoran's heart stuttered. The memories came back to him like a waterfall, cruel, caring not about him but only about the bitter truth of life. He'd been abandoned in the village by his parents, the only ones who knew the truth about who he really was, the nature of his true stone. No matter how hard he had searched, no matter the endless hours spent above the Crystal Lake, he remained with eyes dark and unmoving and no real answers. Ofttimes he just wished he knew for certain he was an Onyx, but even that merciless kindness had never been granted to him.

Even Bassalt, whose eyes missed little about the stones, couldn't hold certainty in his words. Though he oft called him an Onyx, Bhoran had felt the doubt painting the chief's words. Growing up, that brackish cloud of doubt always lingered above Bhoran. *Would I dare do this to my child?* "You wish to have children with me?"

Lusha laughed. It was a hearty sound, warm, soothing, freeing. "My father said he wouldn't have his daughter be a spinster. You'd better heed his warning."

Hands shaking, he took her in his arms, his lips finding hers. Their kiss was deep and warm. Like liquid gold, it mended all the cracks in his broken body. When he released her, her chin was red from the pressure of his fangs. Tears perched on her lower lids. He brushed them away. "Did I hurt you?"

She shook her head. "No. It's just that … it's been too long since I last saw you. I grew beside you in the village. You were my first and only love, and so I wish it will remain, but the boy I knew …"

Bhoran pressed a finger to her lips, knowing full well the meaning of her words. The face of the boy she had known wasn't transfixed with bones and fangs, and his skin was smooth and white like goat's milk and not etched by the hand of another woman. "She meant nothing to me, I swear. Just soothing my tearing pain. These"—he circled his hand over his chest—"are just the marks of healing. After I left the village, I tried many a time to end my life. She covered my wounds with an ink from the tip of a sharp stone and fed me the sweet taste of poison."

"Tell me no more." Tears now streaked Lusha's soft cheeks. "I cannot bear to hear of you being in the arms of another."

"I loved her not, I swear." Bhoran clasped her hand in his. "I swear to your stone and mine, whichever that may be. One day, I woke. My head was sober. And I remembered. I remembered what it feels to be alive. I remembered I only felt like this with you."

"And Yekana? Doesn't she still give you the same venom you claim you have left behind?"

Bhoran rubbed the puncture marks the snake fangs had left in the soft inner skin of his arm. "Yekana has been kind to me. We were each other's solace. But I see now it isn't healthy for either of us. She belongs to the forest. And I ..."

"You belong with me," Lusha said. "I will be your family."

"You heard me." He still recalled Avalan asking him the reason he'd returned.

She nodded, letting him know it was the truth.

"For you, I'll change," he promised, though inside he knew how difficult a task that was. His fear cut him deep. His body trembled, making him long for Yekana's sweet bite. He clenched his fists.

"You have changed enough," Lusha told him. "Perhaps it's time we just lived." A faint smile curved her lips. She straddled him. "There is a thirst in me to know the lands. I dream of Levorotha and my aunt, waiting for me with the mother's embrace I've never tasted. I dream of forests and lakes and rivers and plains where I can dance and sing the sweet songs that live in my heart without my father's shadow over me. I want to taste every food and drink all the wines the lands can offer." She cupped his face. "I want to make love to you and bear your children and have them live free, like I never did. And when I'm finally content with all life has to give, I want to return to a free Hydrus. A village where Avalan leads with love and justice. Where I can swim the sea and feel the powdery sand between my toes, and bury my head in Sigil's soft fur." She leaned closer, her lips a breath from his. "And then I shan't cry if I die, for I would have lived a happy life."

Bhoran locked his arms around her. He planted soft kisses on the golden peak of her forehead, whispered in her ear. "We shall have all that and more." Then he kissed her, deeply. His loins stirred as he held her. He wanted her, but … *Does she want me?* His answer came when she lifted her dress. He fumbled with his breeches, then became one with her. With his Lusha.

At last Lusha slid off him, looking content but also bewildered. "It was more painful than I'd imagined."

"It will get easier," he promised.

She laughed, then stood. Her gaze traveled beyond the battlements, down to the forest. "It's so beautiful up here."

Still on the walkway, Bhoran was trying to ease the frenzied beating of his heart when he saw Lusha's face change, her smile fading to a worried frown. She raised a shading palm to her eyes. "Bhoran …" Her voice trembled. "It's him. It's Olnos."

Bhoran's heart throbbed. He leaned closer to the parapet, trying to follow the direction of her pointing finger. When he saw it, his breath caught in his chest. In the heart of the forest that perched over the sea lay a small clearing—so small Bhoran had missed it the first time he'd gazed at the woods. But now, as a breeze blew over them, carrying the tears of the sea, Bhoran spied the distant figure of the marble giant he had learned to adore. Proud and imperial the statue stood, untouched by the years, calling to Bhoran's aching heart.

"Olnos," he whispered.

CHAPTER TWENTY-SIX

THE AIR in Bassalt's bath chamber was thick with the smell of rotting flesh, stale sweat, and burning fat. Warm flames flickered in the four corners, burning away oil and Bassalt's precious time. For two days and two nights, he'd kept the old body of the stonemaster submerged in the bathtub, yet the old man's mouth had remained stubbornly sealed.

Bassalt spat out the willow bark he'd been chewing, washing down its bitter taste with a gulp of thick wine. He shifted in his chair. "How did you get into Hydrus?" he asked for the hundredth time. Not expecting an answer, he rose on unsteady feet and made to leave. The smell of his stump made him nauseous. *Cursed, cursed, cursed stones. How long can a man last in water before he dies?*

"Stay," the stonemaster croaked.

Surprised, Bassalt turned. The master had raised his head now, the stones in his eyes a barely visible gleam beneath a veil of secrets. Bassalt wanted nothing more than to snatch that veil and tear it to pieces. It was hard to read the master's face, and after the misfortune with the waterdragon, Bassalt had to know the true intentions of his enemies. He rushed to the bathtub and grabbed the thick stone rim for support. "Speak," he said, his mouth frothing with pain and anger. "Why are you here? I told you to leave and never return. I *ordered* you!"

Water splashed around the stonemaster as he tried to sit up. "Age makes a man deaf to threats and brave to disobey the young."

"You should be dead by now," Bassalt spat. The stonemaster's face was a mask of gray flesh stretched over sharp bones. The man was clearly standing before death's door, only death refused to hear the knocking.

"Take your pitiful eyes off me, Bassalt." A bout of wet coughing shook Delion's chest.

"Why did you return?"

"A father will always love his children, no matter how far they've strayed from home."

"This is *my* home now," Bassalt said. "And your presence here threatens the peace I've worked so hard to keep."

The master stared at him, a disdainful look that spoke of knowing. "What have you done, Bassalt?"

The chief clenched his teeth. *What does he know?* "I had to punish the boy. The tribe needs peace, and only I can grant it."

"The whole village is ignorant of the power of the stones."

Ah, so it is the absence of stone knowledge that burdens your wizened heart, Bassalt thought. He should have expected that. After all, when Bassalt had forbidden entrance to all of the stonemistresses and stonemasters, Delion had wagged a bony finger in his face, warning him he'd be back one day. "The mastery of stone magic should be left only to those who know how to wield it," Bassalt claimed.

The master sighed. "Bassalt, we have spoken of this. You can't deny the stone knowledge to your people. One deserves to know of one's true nature—"

"Don't you remember what happened when last the tribes were given the chance to know of their true nature? Have your many years in the lands caused you to see the War of the Stones as a speck of turmoil in the tapestry of time? Did you not hear the cries of agony, the rattles of death?" Bassalt inhaled sharply as his wound grazed the hard stone. He had clenched the tub harshly, forgetting to take caution. "Stones only bring death."

"And what do you bring, Bassalt?"

"I bring what should have been there since the dawn of the Stone—

protection. I carry the burden of death and war on my shoulders so the rest can live unbound and carefree."

"I wonder, will a mockery of a serpent fence keep your tribe safe?"

Bassalt snarled. "You know full well it's just a pretense. My earthen spell is broken. There's only so much I can control with my stone's power. Your presence here is a dire reminder of that." He halted, trying to collect his breath. "Now speak openly, old teacher, for my patience is ebbing. Why are you really here?"

The stonemaster studied him for a moment. His naked body shivered, making the surface of the water ripple. "Where is your snake ring?"

Bassalt glared at his hand. The bloody stump gaped at him. He grasped the sponge next to him and flung it into the master's face. *I must control myself … not kill him before I have my answers …* "The cursed Onyx is back, isn't it? Speak! It is the truth. I know it. The snake ring's stone changing color … If I had still my finger, I would show you. Darkness. Death. But the cursed waterdragon ripped it from me. Hydrus! The one who swore to protect the village is maiming *me*—the only one who can protect the tribe. I ask you, what will become of them if I leave them? What will become of the tribe if I lose my powers? Cursed Onyx talons. Perhaps I should just open the earth and bury the village whole. An early grave awaits us anyhow."

When Bassalt's rambling was done, Delion granted him a faint smile. "From stone we all come, and to stone we return."

Bassalt's anger blazed inside him now, a monstrous fire sucking fuel from the stonemaster's feigned calmness. Unable to contain it further, Bassalt let his anger shake the chamber, sending the water in the tub spilling over the rim. "Spare me the old adages. I know them by heart. I shall ask you one last time, and then stones have mercy on you, I shall kill you, for it seems you have naught to offer me I don't already know myself. Why—are—you—here?"

"I came to aid my children during these dire times."

Bassalt roared with frustration. Dirt from above showered them both.

"Remember my teachings, Bassalt," the master prompted. "Let the

Tiger's Eye stretch open and watch over the pain, yet keep its gaze centered."

Old guidance coming from his former teacher softened Bassalt's rage. He felt the stone ease its pulsation, the anger ebbing faster, giving way to a horrible sense of dread. "You're here to spite me, are you not?" His voice was harsh, but its power diminished now, like the flames of the surrounding candles.

The stonemaster pushed his body upward. His withered torso rose from the water. "Your cruelty has rendered you heartless, Bassalt. Would you keep an old man a prisoner? Or perhaps you'll sentence another innocent to die."

There was little he could hide from Delion, Bassalt knew—the old crank's intuition was his greatest gift. A gift Bassalt had thought he'd taken from him, but the master's presence here proved him wrong. Bassalt hadn't felt the master's footsteps on the earth as Delion had approached Hydrus, nor had he seen the threat of Onyx over the village. All he smelled was the stench of a heartless shadow. All he saw was the cursed nightmare of dark mist that whipped through his peaceful sleep. All he thought of was Bhoran's dark eyes, which dripped with hatred, the same hatred he felt when the snake ring changed color underwater.

"There is an Onyx in the village," Bassalt said, repeating what had kept haunting his mind the past few moonturns. "I can feel him. I can't see him, though, so that I can squeeze a vine around his neck and take the breath out of him. Six years went by in peace, and my beloved stepbrother edges closer to the village just when the Onyx strikes. Isn't this a sign from the stones, I ask you? Bhoran has to die." Bassalt punched the stone again and again. "He *has* to. For the good of the tribe."

"Bhoran's death will solve nothing."

Bassalt stared at the stonemaster's ugly skin. "If not him, then who? What will I say to the tribe now? Why won't you help me?" He leaned over the stale water, sniffing the odor of the master's wet body. "You know who the Onyx is, don't you? You *must* know."

"You shall tell the tribe the truth, Bassalt. And pray for forgiveness."

"I will die before I do such a vile thing!"

"If you won't lead them to the truth, it falls on me to show them."

"You would dare lead the tribe *against* the rightful chief of Hydrus?" Bassalt's rage swelled again. The blood coursed through his veins like lava. He thrust his fists into the water, raising seething waves. One after the other they slashed at the stonemaster's face, invading his gaping mouth, drowning his frugal attempts to cry out. Bassalt pushed more; the water swirled like a vortex, pulling the master under. Delion flailed his bony arms around, helplessly searching for purchase on the stony rim.

The door burst open. Theran screeched like a wounded animal. When Bassalt ripped his hands out of the water, the storm ceased at once. The stonemaster grabbed for the rim, spitting water, engulfed by bouts of wet coughs.

"My chief!" Theran shrieked. "What are you—"

"Silence!" Bassalt ordered. His voice boomed in the small chamber, forcing Theran to cover his ears. "Make preparations for a tribe gathering. I want all of them to be there. You hear me? All of them!" He grasped Theran by the collar and shook him. "Women, men, and children. None shall disobey my orders."

Theran whimpered, a pathetic sound. "What … what for, my chief?"

Bassalt turned to the stonemaster, who was still coughing. "When the stones deprive us of an offering, they give something else in its stead."

CHAPTER TWENTY-SEVEN

When Avalan reached the top of the swirling staircase, his mind was rich with words. The thumping of his heart warned him that when the time came, he'd lose them all.

The door swung open with ease, revealing a room so bright Avalan had to shade his eyes against the sunlight. Five tall floor-to-ceiling glass windows illuminated the room. Scattered paintings littered the floor, some of them half-finished, others mere outlines. The ones completed rested on crude easels.

Behind one, he spied the raven locks of Crystal, the sunlight illuminating the ribbons in her hair. She'd donned robes the color of green seagrass. Avalan felt guilty to be there, alone with her, but he might not have another chance. Deep inside he knew Bhoran was right. The reason Crystal had left him ate away at his soul.

He closed the door firmly behind him. Crystal's pale face was streaked with dried tears. "You were crying," he said. He clasped her hand in his, only to let it go soon after. The horrified expression on her face swiftly reminded him of where they were and who she was. *She's my Crystal no longer, but a married woman, and a chiefess.*

"Seeing all of you after so long ..." Crystal began.

Avalan's gaze fell on a coal painting of a face that seemed unsettlingly familiar.

"Does he look much different now?" Crystal asked behind him. "I wouldn't know after all these years."

Avalan frowned, her words clearing up the likeness of the face in his mind. *Shady.* On the white paper, the coal strokes had shaped the face of a tribesman from the village, only it was a much younger face, one that spoke of earlier times of their youth in Hydrus. He picked it up. "Shady is always Shady. Did you draw this?"

Crystal nodded, her eyes flickering to the rest of the paintings.

It didn't take him long to understand. *The drawings.* In one, the white beach of Hydrus stretched as far as the eye could see, warm shallow waters frothing. The forest of blackwoods engulfed another, the bark of the trees so real he imagined Sigil dangling from their branches after a good hunt. He turned, his eyes taking in more pictures of the village: houses, thatched roofs, fishing poles, even Bassalt's ugly lair of a house ... it was all there, ghosts of Crystal's memory frozen in time.

"It was Shady who taught me," Crystal explained. "When you got lost in the forest for days on end, hunting."

Avalan nodded, noting the faint marks of coal beneath the chiefess's fingernails. The same marks always marred Shady's. He had once told Avalan that no matter how hard he tried to scrub his nails clean, he could never completely rid them of the blackness.

"Shady would have been proud to see all these," he said, cursing himself for not finding something more intimate to say. "Is this where you spend much of your time?"

Crystal smiled. "When I wedded Ethelnar, he was kind enough to grant me this place to use as my own. It has the best light and keeps me and my paintings protected from the whims of nature." She fiddled with her pendant as she spoke. She'd donned a different one now—a heavy golden chain that carried a chip of Black Opal. Inside it, colorful flakes swirled, as if they much enjoyed her touch.

She's wearing the chief's birthstone. Avalan's heart clenched, but he kept a straight face. *What did you expect? She's married, and your random appearance won't change the truth.* "It is a great keep," he managed. "Surely more interesting than our small village." He didn't mean his last words. Hydrus would always hold a special place in his heart, and no keep or stronghold of the Stone Lands would change that, no matter how impressive.

Crystal raised her Larimar eyes to him. "I am sorry for leaving without telling you."

Avalan studied her face. Her once-bronze skin had turned as pale as white honey, like the one Ronan had once brought back from one of his eastern trips. He imagined Crystal spending endless mornings in this tower, her fingers dipped in colors and coal, stroking feverishly as she rushed to depict her memories on the blank parchments. "It matters not now," he told her.

"Don't you want to know why I left?" she dared. "The reason I had to leave Hydrus and all of you behind?"

I do, Avalan thought, but he had a queer feeling the truth would serve no better than a knife in the heart. "I met your daughter. Whatever your reasons, they matter not now. You have a family. I have no right to pull you back into the past."

Her lips fell apart. "You met Semara?"

"She takes after you and not her father."

Crystal managed a faint smile. "She is a delicate child. What did she say to you?"

"Not much. I think my presence somehow upset her. She accused me of looking different, as if she had other expectations of a man from Hydrus."

The chiefess's smile quickly faded to a deep frown. "I knew she'd seen it."

"Seen what?"

Crystal bent over a stony chest. On it rested a wooden cover. Its hinges creaked as Crystal pushed it open. From the bottom of the stone chest, she pulled out a rolled parchment, then handed it to him.

Avalan unfurled the edges and regarded his own face. Just like Shady's, it was a face of the past. His hair was tied into a high horsetail, which made his thick eyebrows stand out more. Beneath them lay his Bloodstone eyes. There was no color in them, as the drawing was mere coal strokes. Yet his drawn eyes brimmed with affection and longing, as if his gaze held the sight of a beloved—a woman. Avalan raised these eyes now to Crystal.

"I knew Semara had noticed you," she explained. "A terrible storm raged that night, and the rumbling thunder made my hands shake. I took the painting down to my apartments to finish. Next day, I found a small smudge on it, made by a tiny finger." She ambled to the tall windows.

The drawing brought back all the memories that raged in Avalan's heart. Everything he'd kept hidden all these years. His love stood just a few footsteps across from him. If he stretched out his hand, he could have her—he could have all he had wanted all these years. *Yet what does she want? Why is she showing this to me now?*

His heart winning over his mind, he approached her, his arms closing around her body, drawing still in hand. The ribbons in her hair tickled his chin as he spoke. "I never gave up on you. I asked Ronan many a time where you were, but he wouldn't tell me. He made me think you didn't love me. That you were better off without me. I thought if you'd had to run off without a warning, he was right."

Crystal trembled. "I should have told you how I felt about the village. In Hydrus, I was suffocating ... I wanted to see the lands beyond, glimpse all the majestic sights Ronan had talked to us about. I couldn't imagine spending my entire life as Bassalt's prisoner. But you loved Hydrus so much I knew you'd never leave it ..." She took a deep breath, as if to find courage. "After it was done, Ronan told me I should let you go. I didn't have the right to let you hope, he said, when I had started a new life. Year after year I sent words to you, but Ronan held his tongue. To quench my grief, I drew you, then locked you in the chest."

Avalan tightened his grip around the drawing. His reflection on the window gazed back at him through earthy-green eyes speckled with blood. Beyond the windows, he glimpsed the sea splashing the crags covered by a thick emerald forest. *We won't be Bassalt's prisoners for much longer.* He wondered if it wasn't too late. If he could free the village, perhaps Crystal would consider returning with him. *Perhaps ...* He squinted his eyes against the sun, to make certain what he had seen was right. There, in a small clearing, the head of a giant statue peeked over the treetops—a giant that looked much like ... "Is that Olnos?" he asked.

"I was as surprised as you when I first saw him," Crystal admitted. "The stonemistress told me there is a statue of him in all settlements. To watch over the tribes. He must have been the greatest hero to ever walk the lands."

Avalan frowned. *How much do I not know?* "The painting on the ceiling of the great hall," he began, "shows an old woman holding your husband's stone."

"Stonemistress Luthea. She is the keeper of the Black Opal, Ethelnar's stone. She keeps much to herself these days. Admits only my husband when Ethelnar direly needs her counsel. Ethelnar told me last night Luthea will perform the union of the stones during the wedding. It will be a great honor for the ceremony to be held under her gaze. Grensis, Ethelnar's younger brother, is marrying a girl of the Ruby."

Listening to her talk of the birthstones with such ease made Avalan queasy. He had never trusted the stones. How could he when Bassalt only used their power to suppress the tribesfolk yet forbade them from even keeping them in their possession? Yet now Crystal spoke of them as if they were a natural part of her world. A thing that held no shame, or fear, or reproach. He liked that. "Everyone wears their stone around the keep," Avalan noted.

Crystal looked up at him. "Don't let Bassalt close your heart to the stones. They are part of who we are. I know that now. It takes time, but I promise you, eventually you will see it for yourself."

Avalan had hoped it would come to this, but a doubt still lingered in him. All he wanted was to find the Heart of the Bloodstone and return to free the village. If he could live a free life in Hydrus for the rest of his days, then he would gladly die a fortunate man, without need of the stones or their powers he didn't understand.

"Your husband insists we stay until the Night of the Spirits," he told her, inhaling the faint smell of lilacs from her hair. "Then we shall leave." He felt her stiffen in his embrace.

"Lusha has told me how she and Bhoran are planning to go to Levorotha. I think it is a great start. She failed to mention where you will go, though. I felt she didn't want to tell me. As if the secret wasn't hers to share."

Avalan fiddled with the goat dagger in his breeches. The sun was descending now, a golden disk. Suddenly he felt an imposing presence in the room. Glancing over his shoulder, he spied his and Crystal's shadows stretched long over the rough stone floor. Above them, as if to guard them both, the second shadow stood on watch, its silhouette darker against the dusty sunlight. *The Heart of the Bloodstone.* Dizredek's elegant voice echoed in his head. *Your heart's deepest desire.*

Avalan lowered his lips over Crystal's ear to whisper, "I'm looking for something. And now I think I know where to find it."

CHAPTER TWENTY-EIGHT

WHEN NIGHT FELL, Lusha descended the steps to the main hall, lifting the hem of the golden dress Crystal had granted her for the wedding. It had taken two maids to help her slide it over her head, and three more to tie all the ribbons and threads and cloth bands. The silken dress flowed over her like liquid gold, and she savored its embrace, wondering how Bhoran would like it when he saw her.

The neckline was low and square in cut, revealing Lusha's proud, milky neck. Her mother's pendant shone on her bosom. Long strips of fluid silver ran along the length of her arms, stopping just before the rings of silver the maids had pushed onto each of her fingers. Around her wrist, covered by the soft fabric, rested a bracelet set with her Moonstone, another present from Crystal.

"Silver and gold," the maids had told her, eyes sparkling. "The true colors of the Moonstone. A great honor for the daughter of Chieftain Silver."

Lusha had fought back a powerful urge to purse her lips at the sound of her father's name. Swallowing icy dread, she had forced herself to smile, a gesture the maids had taken as a sign of pleasure. The women had plucked the bone brooch from her head, loosening her golden hair over her scarred face. *They think I should cover my wound,* she'd thought with great displeasure, but had let them braid her locks and weigh them with beaded strings to keep them in place.

As a finishing touch, they had glided a pair of soft slippers over her naked feet. Lusha's footfalls were a soft whisper as the maids now led her down the winding staircase, their wooden shoes clacking loudly as if to announce her arrival.

A thousand voices traveled up, making her heart thump. At the end of the stairwell, the main hall opened before her, rich with the smells of food and wine. She smiled with pleasure as a servant with mellow eyes lifted his tray to her. Obliging him, she picked up a black cup and brought it to her nose, taking in the sweet scent of cinnamon and cloves. It reminded her of Farmera's warm embrace.

Across the walls, hundreds of flowered sconces held blazing torches. Their dancing flames bathed the chamber in amber light.

Lusha swirled the wine in her cup. It whirled like a liquid Ruby. To her, it seemed that night everything in the buzzing main hall of Raekandar's Keep bore the colors of the Ruby stone. A velvety crimson carpet, spreading from corner to corner, covered the stone floor, soft to the heel of her slippers and swallowing the clacking footfalls of the servants. Drapes the color of carmine covered the stone walls above the long table on the northern side. Over the table, a scarlet tablecloth hosted the rich feast Paldma and her kitchen servants had prepared for the wedding.

The same type of cloth covered the small table in the far corner where Avalan and Bhoran sat. Lusha sauntered over to them, feeling her cheeks redden as Bhoran's gaze found her. Though the chamber ceiling shielded her from the magic touch of the moon, she felt as if her skin were aglow.

Bhoran had donned a raven tunic with golden threads that complemented the pale flax of his hair. His face was calm, his gaze like the surface of a dark lake whose waters only Lusha dared to brave. To his side, clad in an earthy-green tunic, Avalan smiled. The same crooked smile that showed his white teeth and creased the corners of his eyes.

"This is splendid," she told them, slipping over the bench across from them.

"You are splendid." Bhoran brushed her fingers.

His touch was soft, his lips red from the wine. She wanted to kiss him, but that would have to wait. Her gaze drifted toward the master table, reserved for the honored ruler of the keep and the betrothed. The chairs around the table were empty, and only black clay plates and cups lay on the red cloth. Lusha searched the sea of faces that crowded the hall, but didn't spot the chief or Crystal. Of the soon-to-be-married couple there was no sign either.

She stole a glance at Avalan. With every sip of his wine, his eyes darted to the ceiling, as if he'd found something of interest there. She followed his gaze and almost sprang from her seat as she saw a huge Black Opal dangling over the fingertips of an old woman.

"That was my first reaction as well," Avalan told her, raising his voice to be heard over the thumps of serving cups.

"Who is that?"

"Stonemistress Luthea." Avalan arched a curious thick brow. "Keeper of the Black Opal. She trains those blessed by her stone. Crystal said she will perform the union tonight."

Lusha leaned closer. "Is she like the stonemaster you met in Hydrus?"

Avalan frowned, his previous amusement now gone. "I daresay she looks almost the same: old, with creaking bones, long ashen hair, and eyes so tired as if they have seen it all and more than they had wished for."

Despite the warmth of the hall, Lusha shivered. She felt the stare of the stonemistress judging her through beady eyes speckled with the colors of the rainbow. Though the Heliodor bore no resemblance to the Black Opal, Lusha felt as if those eyes belonged to Silver—his presence a dreadful cloud above her head, ready to unleash a storm when she least expected it. A mouthful of wine warmed her chest and gave her the courage to avert her eyes.

"Avalan," she said, lowering her voice. "Did you speak with Crystal?"

Avalan nodded. "She seems to be happy here alongside her husband and her daughter." Though he tried hard to hide it, a layer of sadness gilded his voice.

Lusha bit her lip as the gaunt face of Colgar swam before her eyes. She waved a hand to rid herself of it, earning Bhoran's curious stare. *I promised to keep her secret,* Lusha thought.

Then Avalan's face changed, his features twisting into a grave mask Lusha had last glimpsed during the goat game night back in the village. "I think I know why the shadow led me here," Avalan told them. "The Heart of the Bloodstone. The shadow keeps appearing whenever I'm around Crystal. I think it wanted me to find her."

Lusha swallowed back fear. The memory of Crystal crying in her arms after her terrible confession and the shadow standing above her, stroking the chiefess's hair, was a sight she couldn't forget. At the time, she had wondered what Avalan's guide had wanted, overlooking their reunion. *Could Avalan be right? Did the shadow really lead him to her?* Avalan was sharp of wit and quick of thought, Lusha knew. *Perhaps it is true, but ...*

Bhoran leaned closer. "What are you saying?"

"I think somehow *she* is the Heart of the Bloodstone." Avalan cringed at the sound of his own assumption.

"How can a woman be a stone?" Lusha asked. "Besides, Crystal was born under the Larimar."

"I know it doesn't sound right," Avalan admitted. "Yet it's the only thing I can think of. Dizredek told me the second shadow would be my guide. He said it would lead me to the Heart of the Bloodstone, and it has led me here. To her, and to my heart's deepest desire."

"Crystal can't help you free the village." Bhoran's voice was thick with caution.

Lusha chewed on her lip. "Avalan, she's married. I don't much like this Ethelnar, but he's the ruler of this keep. He has an army. Making more enemies can hardly aid you in facing Bassalt. These men are well trained with their stones."

Her words must have touched a raw spot in his heart, for Avalan's lips tightened, and he stared at the blackened marks on his palms.

"She left you," Bhoran reminded him. "She left you to marry another."

The blood spots in Avalan's eyes grew larger. "That doesn't mean she doesn't still love me."

"She had her reasons," Lusha blurted before she could hold herself. A gnawing realization chewed at her heart. She couldn't stand the pain in Avalan's eyes, but she had promised to keep the rape a secret. She turned to Bhoran, her cheeks afire. "Besides, you left me too. And you had *your* reasons. There's nothing more unfortunate than a mistake made by a loving heart. But now you're back, and so is Crystal."

Bhoran lowered his gaze in shame.

Avalan covered Bhoran's hand with his blackened palm. "I know you mean to protect me. But I saw the pain in her eyes. She still loves me as much as I do her."

"What will you do?" Bhoran asked.

"I know not," Avalan confessed. "But I'd better decide soon. As Ethelnar said, the Night of the Spirits is fast upon us. Marebore wanted to attack Bassalt then. I hope Ronan's death has stirred his mind, but I can't be certain."

The chamber echoed with the deafening clacks of forks hitting earthen pots. Lusha spun to watch the chief, his arm wrapped around Crystal's shoulders, descend the staircase. Clad in black robes and raven slippers encrusted with colorful beads, the chief wore pride on his face as he led his wife toward the master table. Crystal walked beside him, her eyes lowered. She had donned a resplendent dress the color of her stone, blue like a clear sky, emerald like a shallow sea. Her black locks were fastened up, exposing a long neck that looked to Lusha so white, so vulnerable ...

Once the rulers took their seats, the hall burst with music. Back in Hydrus, the melody of a bone flute and the rhythm of a skin drum accompanied their feast nights. Yet now the jingle of a thousand brass plates complemented the mellifluous vibrations of strings on wooden frames. Women clad in golden robes raised their voices in unison, picking up the pattern of the sweet and sharp sounds and enriching it with a high song, mellow like warm honey.

The crowd parted then to let the betrothed couple pass. The chief's brother came first, his hand entangled with his future wife's. Lusha found him a handsome lad, no more than twenty summers, with an earnest smile and the twinkle of the Black Opal in his eyes. The bride was radiant in a crimson gown that flowed like a river behind her back, her brown locks caressing naked shoulders. Onto the small platform before the master table they climbed, facing each other, their hands intertwined.

Then the music changed—the melody and clanging of metal gave way to a low, guttural sound. Seeing the solemn expressions on the tribe's faces made Lusha's hair stand across her nape. *Is something wrong?* The crowd parted once more, only this time it was the silhouette of a frail woman that staggered forth. Lusha recognized the wizened face and long ashen hair of Stonemistress Luthea. Though Avalan had warned her of her arrival, the sight still gave Lusha an ominous tightening in her chest. She couldn't tell if the mistress was barefoot—such was the length of the robe flowing behind her. Gray it was, and simple, threadbare even, as if it had a lot to tell about her past. A staff aided her gait as she clambered to the platform, taking her place before the couple.

A sudden pinch in her arm startled Lusha. She turned to find a little girl beside her, with curious Larimar eyes and a mischievous grin on her round face. "I'm Semara," the girl whispered. Lusha's face must have betrayed much bewilderment, for the girl sighed and explained, "Crystal's daughter. You must be Lusha. I can tell by the scar. My mother told me not to mention it. She also told me to keep you company. It's boring being with the boys."

Lusha glanced at Avalan and Bhoran. Their faces were both serious, their minds impossible to read. If she were to hazard a guess, it was hard for Avalan to meet the offspring of another man, the daughter of the woman he loved, and for Bhoran ... *What does Bhoran think about children?* She stroked a lock of Semara's brown hair. "It is a pleasure to meet you."

Their small talk earned them sharp glances and shushing.

Semara edged so close Lusha smelled summer fruits on her breath. The guttural sounds ceased, a solemn silence filling the chamber. "She will perform the ritual now," Semara whispered excitedly in Lusha's ear. "Have you ever seen a union of the stones? Mother says you haven't."

Lusha shook her head, wary of breaking the silence. The crowd might not be so lenient with an outlander as they were with the daughter of their chiefess.

The stonemistress threw two bony arms into the air. From her right and over the head of the bride shot out a blood-red Ruby stone, while from her left a midnight-black Opal, crowning the air over Ethelnar's brother. The stones hovered there, and Lusha exchanged a worried look with Avalan. She still remembered how he had described the stones that had sprung from Stonemaster Delion's hands, Avalan's blackened palms a dire reminder of their power.

When the excitement in the crowd settled, the stonemistress spoke. "When temptation and lust cause the Black Opal to suffer, the Ruby will soothe him, making the hard judgments. When the Ruby agonizes with dreams of death, the Black Opal will console it with manifestations of the afterlife. When the Black Opal follows a dark path without ending, the Ruby will persevere for them both. When the Ruby spreads bloody battles in its wake, the Black Opal will remind it of the suffering the wars cause. When the Ruby races to fight, the Black Opal will follow, for it and only it can trace the path back." The mistress paused for breath, her arms now trembling as she strained to keep them high.

Lusha sat on the edge of her seat, her eyes rooted to the back of the old woman.

"Stones shatter, spin, and spur; stones blend, flow, and blur," the mistress recited. "The great path always leads back to the One Stone, for from stone we all come, and to stone we return."

Loud cheering broke out from the crowd. Lusha gulped, her heart thrashing in her chest. Her fingers slid to her Moonstone, seeking protection. "It's coming," Semara shouted, her small hand gripping Lusha's wrist.

"What is?" Lusha asked, her fear growing.

Semara pointed upward. "The union!" Her voice trembled with excitement. "We will see what offspring the blending of the stones will give!"

Lusha watched as the stonemistress clapped her hands, forcing the stones to unite. At first they resisted, refusing to give in to the blending. Slowly, though, they surrendered, fusing, becoming one, the red Ruby crying crimson rivers over the Black Opal ... The two stones danced and fought and wrestled until a booming sound tore the air, and above the couple stood a scarlet stone—a proud Ruby.

The crowd cheered once more, and at last the stonemistress's arms collapsed to her sides, taking with them the existence of the stone.

Holding her breath, Lusha stood, eager to see the expression on the chief's face. *Is he disappointed the Ruby prevailed?* To her relief, she saw him stand. With a mellow smile across his lips, he applauded.

Semara leaned closer. "I knew it would be the Ruby!" she squealed. "I told my uncle so!"

Lusha studied the girl's flushed face. "How could you be so certain?"

"You can't, really." Semara shrugged. "Chances are always equal. Except …" Her voice drifted, and she turned ever so slightly to shoot a timid glance at Bhoran.

"Except what?" Lusha urged, sensing she wouldn't much like the answer.

"The Onyx." Semara's breath still smelled of summer and fruits. "From Onyx always comes Onyx." With that, the girl slid away to join the growing line of tribesfolk waiting to compliment the wedded couple.

Swallowing back the acid taste of wine that had risen to her throat, Lusha turned to Bhoran. His unreadable dark eyes were on her. *I fear him,* she realized, ashamed of herself, *but I also love him with all my heart.* As the sound of horns and strings returned to the chamber, she gave him a warm smile.

"Come here," he told her.

She circled the table, sat on Bhoran's thigh. She planted a gentle kiss on his fang-free forehead. Avalan's face beside her held a solemn expression. Empty wine cup in his hand, he was staring at Crystal. The chiefess had her eyes lowered, as if in shame.

"Do you wager Ethelnar fumed when Crystal's stone rose above his head?" Avalan said at last.

Lusha gave him a questioning look before the true meaning of his words sank in. *He's thinking of Crystal's union with the chief.* Of course, it had to have been the Larimar that had prevailed, seeing as the stones in Semara's eyes were crystal blue. *Only … is Semara …?* "Avalan …" she began.

"It is fine," he said.

A servant shouldered her way through the crowd and to their table. After unloading a tray filled with roasted fawn, figs, cheeses, grapes, and a flagon of red wine, she smiled at them and rushed away. The feasting had begun. Avalan was quick to refill his cup to the brim.

"There's a statue of Olnos in the woods around the keep," Bhoran told him, to lighten his spirits. "If you feel like gulping down some fresh air ..."

"I know." Avalan's eyes never left the chiefess. "I saw it from the drawing room with Crystal."

"Let us eat, then," Lusha offered. These past days at the keep, she had been stuffing her mouth at every chance, trying to erase the memory of the sheer hunger up in the mountains.

Avalan drained his cup and got to his feet. "I shall go find this Eyedir, see if he holds some knowledge about Ronan's death. Perchance his goods will also offer something to hide the ugliness of my ruined hands."

They watched him leave.

"You should go with him," Lusha urged.

"His heart needs time to settle. After, he will be ready for words."

Lusha looked at him, annoyed, but the honesty in his face told her what she needed to know. Growing up, Avalan and Bhoran had been like brothers, and she trusted now a brother knew well when to give the other the space he needed. She slipped from his thigh to Avalan's empty seat. She eyed the silver forks and knives neatly arranged beside the plates and gave Bhoran a smiling frown. He shrugged and dipped his fingers into the fawn's flesh, tearing it apart and dropping a thigh onto her plate before serving himself. She laughed.

Before long, their bellies were full of food and wine, their fingers slick with fat and oil. "I feel so free." Lusha sucked a finger clean and washed the food down with wine. She giggled. "Would that Silver could see us. Eating with fingers, drinking—"

Bhoran bent to kiss her on the lips. "Kissing," he added, his lips crimson and slick with oil.

The music had become louder now, faster and more inviting. The tribe swayed to the rhythm.

"Dancing?" she dared him, relishing the surprise on his face.

Before he could deny her, she stood, grabbing his arm and forcing him to his heels and into the crowd. Most of them paid them no heed. Wine flowed freely in the tribe's blood, clouding their minds, lightening their steps.

Bhoran glanced around, uncertain, as if to see what moves he should adopt. Yet Lusha didn't much care. Silver's absence had driven her soul mad with joy. Forgetting all her manners, she reached for his hands, clasping them tight, and led him round and round in circles, her feet skipping across the floor. On their tenth circle, he laughed. A joyous sound Lusha had never heard escape Bhoran's mouth. She twisted, coiling his arm around her, pressing her body close to his. She had to get close to that rare laugh, steal it, cherish it forever. With a gentle push, he forced her away, resuming their frenzied dance that fell in with the crashing of cymbals. Before long, their bodies met again.

"Let's go to Olnos," Bhoran whispered, breathless.

She pushed her beaded locks behind her ear. Her scar was out in the open now, but Lusha didn't care. From now on, no one would make her feel shame. "Yes," she gasped.

The grounds grew quieter as they skidded down the soft grass to the keep's gates. Lusha's skin shone under the moonlight. It seemed the whole tribe had gone to the keep to attend the wedding, except …

"Where did you say you're headed?" The guard's words were an awkward slur. Beside him, a short stool leaned dangerously to the side, burdened by the weight of half a dozen empty tankards.

"A quick stroll through the forest," Bhoran said. "Clean air to chase away the smoke."

The guard sniffed the night, as if to try the truth behind Bhoran's words. The air wafting down from the castle was indeed thick with the smell of charred meat. He leaned on the shaft of his spear and granted them a suspicious look through slitted eyes. "It will not do to wander in the forest. Nothing of interest there." He looked at Lusha, raising a hand to shade his eyes. "Are you of the Moonstone?"

She nodded, put sweetness in her voice. "But I've heard there is this marvelous statue of the warrior …"

"Olnos?" The guard perked up. "Only the chief's allowed to go there. Not a place for strangers, or talons." He flipped his spear, pointing the tip of the silver end at Bhoran's chest. "I killed hundreds of you during the war, boy."

Bhoran shoved the shaft down and landed a heavy heel on it, splintering the wood. The guard's eyes widened like an owl's.

"We're no strangers," Bhoran hissed into his face, "but honored guests of Chief Ethelnar and Chiefess Crystal, and honored guests shouldn't be threatened."

The guard stepped aside, muttering curses under his breath. Bhoran grabbed Lusha's hand and led her forth.

Soon, soothing silence drowned out the disgruntled guard's cussing. Bhoran led her through the engulfing forest, the soft glow of Lusha's body illuminating a snaking path. The trees here were no match for the blackwood trees of the forest of Hydrus—their bark was thin, with branches so light they bent beneath the weight of wide silvery-green leaves. In the air, she tasted the saltiness of the sea and heard the soft splashing of waves far below. She glanced at Bhoran, the image of the pointed spear before his chest a thorn in an otherwise perfect night.

"Bhoran ..."

"It matters not," he said, as if he'd read her mind. "Nothing I'm not used to."

Lusha felt her heart clench in anger. *It shouldn't be this way.* She remembered the wrestling stones, her head still heavy from wine and love. "How do we know this is the path to the statue?"

"He calls to me."

Fallen leaves whispered beneath the frill of her golden dress. "Olnos?"

As if in answer, Bhoran tightened his grip and rushed ahead. It wasn't long before Lusha felt it too—a familiar summoning, as if she were back in Hydrus, ready to step on the shadowgrass of the statue's clearing.

The stone slab that represented the Onyx was what she saw first. Smooth from the years of rain, it stood beneath the powerful push of the giant's hand. She raised her eyes to meet Olnos's gaze, her heart filling with gratitude. *You brought him back to me.*

Bhoran edged closer to the man who had served him as a great comfort. He caressed Olnos's fingers.

Lusha glanced around. The trees huddled closer there, obscuring her view. "Do you think we're safe here?"

"You heard the guard. Only the chief's allowed near." There was resentment in his words.

"Bhoran, what is wrong?"

"How soon do the tribes forget those who helped them? Olnos doesn't deserve to be alone. If not for him, they wouldn't have won the war."

Lusha eased her way close to him. "It was a long time ago, my love. People wish to forget the times of blood and pain." *I among them.*

He swept her off her feet, lifted her to the stone. He kissed her then, and in his lips she tasted all the things he hadn't dared to tell her. Despair and pain for being away from her for so long, shunned by the only tribe he'd ever known; anger and a promise of revenge for those who had hurt him and torn them apart; and guilt—a heart-wrenching guilt—for giving his flesh to someone else to worship, for letting another woman touch him and explore his body inch by inch, leaving her marks behind, scarring him for life.

Breathless, he pulled his lips from hers. "Remember that night at the statue when I first gave you your stone? I had more to show you. I only hope this Olnos is like the one we have back in Hydrus. It is time."

Bhoran led her to the back of the giant. His fingers brushed the rough stone that formed the statue's base. He searched until his fingers slipped into a recess. With a grunt, Bhoran pulled.

Lusha's mouth dropped as she watched a small, dark chamber appear before them at the base of Olnos. "The statue is hollow?"

Bhoran nodded with a tight smile. "I liked to hide there when I was small. It was my safe place. Come."

The air inside was stale, the chamber no wider than a stretch of both Lusha's arms.

"I didn't know," she said with awe. Her eyes fell on the small projection of a stony bench, a sphere above it. "What is this?" she muttered.

"It can wait."

Bhoran lifted her again, this time his kiss deeper, more demanding, the fangs in his face pressing over her chin. He caressed the softness of her inner thighs, his hands warm, exploring. Her breath caught in her chest, all other things around her fading, his face the only light in the shadows.

From Onyx always comes Onyx, she thought with dire shame. "Bhoran …"

"I'm sorry." Bhoran made to back away.

"No." Lusha pulled him close. She wouldn't be like them, hurt him because of his stone, no matter how much she feared it. "I want this … I want you."

Their union was warm and cold, soothing and painful, peaceful and yet warring, like the wrestling of the two stones in marriage. Together they fought and loved and surrendered, until only their heavy breathing remained.

Against her back, Lusha felt the smooth surface of stone grow warmer. She turned, bewildered, as golden etchings emerged on the sphere. "What is this?"

"I've seen these in the statue in Hydrus," Bhoran admitted. "Never knew what they meant."

Lusha's stare lingered on the strange markings. More of them appeared now, forming indecipherable lines. As her fingertips dug into Bhoran's skin, Lusha wished with all her heart she knew how to read.

CHAPTER TWENTY-NINE

"WHY WOULD a young man like yourself not dance?"

Over the brim of his cup, Avalan eyed the merchant. He had the same glint as Ronan in his eyes, that all-seeing spark of stones yearning to explore the world. Yet now the merchant's choice of table spoke of a man who desired no company. Big enough to only host a modest meal for one and cramped against the western corner, it wasn't the most companionable choice. *It offers a great view of the hall, though,* Avalan thought. Ronan would have approved. "I'm not much of a dancer."

Eyedir smirked, rubbing wine off his lip with a thick thumb. "No, a *fighter*, Ronan used to call you."

Brushing some plates aside to make space, Avalan placed his cup on the crude table and watched the merchant. Their sparse conversation had reached the matter in his heart faster than he'd expected. "It is for Ronan I have come. Perchance we might go somewhere quieter to have some words."

The merchant shook his head and held out his cup. A servant rushed to fill it. "We shall stay here," he said, eyeing the flowing wine.

Avalan's chest tightened. He didn't much like speaking of Ronan and Hydrus where everyone could hear, though most of the tribesfolk paid them no heed. Especially when he kept his scorched palms pressed against the clay of his cup.

"Don't you scowl, now. I'm doing this for you. You won't want to miss what's coming." A curious smirk curved Eyedir's lips.

The wedding celebrations held Avalan's interest no more. "Ronan was like a father to me."

"I know. The first and last thing on his mind was to find things to bring back that would make you smile." Eyedir fiddled with the pin that fastened the edges of his cloak. "Did he have the chance to give you his gift? Anxious he was to reach Hydrus before your twentieth birthnight. Said you were like to be sleeping in the woods until he showed."

Avalan rubbed the goat leg on his belt. "He did. And I was foolish enough not to see its value. Twice I refused it."

Eyedir's lips curled. "We had a bet, you know. Two silver pieces. I said none in their right mind would refuse a weapon of such beauty. Ronan laughed and said I didn't know you. A simple stone hollow would cause you much grievance. Ah." He shrugged and reached inside his cloak. "Here. It seems I've lost. Since you're his only family, you should take the burden. My debt is paid." Two coins landed on the table with a soft clink.

Avalan made no move to pick them up. "You haven't asked me about the manner of his death." He tried to keep suspicion out of his voice. Avalan had thought the merchant's curiosity would burst out of his chest, yet Eyedir seemed to have accepted the rumors of Ronan's death without objection.

"I know the stones got him killed. I told him many a time it was wrong, unearthly. To carry all that pain in your sack. No. A burden I wouldn't wish to bear."

"You knew he was carrying birthstones back to Hydrus?"

The merchant nodded.

"How can a stone kill you?" Remembering the grueling pain the Bloodstone had caused him made Avalan's stomach sick.

Eyedir drained his cup and motioned to Avalan's hands. "I thought you *held* the answer. Isn't this one of the reasons you've come to me? To seek a cover for your stone wounds?"

"How do you know?"

Eyedir hooted. "The mind cannot control the eyes better than the heart. And yours have been darting to your hands. Tighter and tighter you hug your mug, yet I have seen the blackened skin. Am I not right? People come to me when they need tidings or wares. Something tells me you seek both."

"I cannot deny it. Ronan was looking for something on the map of the Stone Lands," he said, deciding to be upfront. "What lies in the east that's so important?" The drums sounded louder, and voices rose in unison, singing a tribal song. The wine was getting to his head; Avalan's temples pounded.

"Would that I knew," Eyedir said.

The lie's foul smell made Avalan cringe. "Ronan was searching for years. He made Shady draw all these maps for him. The last one, he told Lusha, was one to be studied with you. What were you searching for?"

"Shh," Eyedir hissed, leaning closer. "Look, I shall give you a pair of the finest gloves for nothing. It will be a gift. The finest leather, soft and so supple, you'll never even know it isn't your own skin you're wearing. In return, you will speak of this map no more."

"I have no need for gifts." Avalan pushed the two silver pieces to the merchant. "Ronan's coins can buy me the gloves, and there will be no debt to seal my mouth." He only hoped these pieces were enough. Avalan had no notion of the value of things.

The annoyance in the merchant's face gave way to amusement. "You really are Ronan's trueborn son. I wouldn't be surprised if the old rascal had arranged for this exact exchange as an afterdeath jest." He pocketed the coins, fishing a fine pair of gloves from the abyss of his cloak. Supple brown leather, the color of Avalan's skin. "They're yours."

Avalan slid them on. Even in death, Ronan granted him gifts. Great sadness filled him. "I can help with whatever Ronan searched for. I owe him so much."

"Perhaps ..." Eyedir mused. "Though you hold no knowledge of the stones, nor have you had the blessing." He gazed at his empty cup with great displeasure. "Stone's luck. The time is approaching. What can a young man who has never before left Hydrus offer me when it comes to the lands?"

"I am an able hunter." *And soon I'll have my true Bloodstone,* he thought, although he dared not say this aloud.

"Hunting? What good will it do us? I know the pathways and the crossroad inns like the back of my hand."

"I also know how to fight."

Eyedir leaned closer, his breath heavy with the heady sweetness of wine. "Forgetting what you know would be best," he advised. "Out with the old knowledge, the head can flourish anew."

"You will not tell me what Ronan was looking for," Avalan said. He wasn't convinced the stones had killed Ronan. A dagger couldn't wield itself, and Ronan had no enemies Avalan knew of. Perchance his death had to do with what he had been searching for …

"Eh." Eyedir shrugged. "My debt is paid. If Ronan wished for you to know, he would have told you."

Anger warmed Avalan's chest. The constant begging made him feel a fool. It mattered not. He raised his gaze to Crystal. All the while, she had been supping, never once leaving her seat to join the dancing. *She* was all that mattered. She and the Heart of the Bloodstone. Armed with them, there would be nothing to prevent him from overthrowing Bassalt. True freedom was nigh. So close he could almost taste it.

The merchant laid his hand on Avalan's. "Son," he said, the fire in his Rubies mellowing now. "If Ronan were here, he would tell you not to meddle in things you do not understand. The union of the stones may have let the chiefess's Larimar win, but the Black Opal is the one to be feared. There is great cunning lying in the shadows. Either learn how to tread the darkness, or keep your footing on the paths of light." He looked up then, just as the music suddenly ceased and the last voice died. "I am truly sorry."

Avalan never got a chance to answer.

The chief rose, a greatsword in his hand. The blade was sharp, with no notches marring its length. Black Opals encrusted the hilt of the vast two-handed weapon. "It is a glorious night when a chief sees his brother wed," he began, his voice cutting through the respectful silence. "A humbling night as well, when we witness another stone win the fight against our Opal. It seems my wife's stone wasn't enough." Timid giggles rose at the chief's jest, only to die soon after.

Concerned, Avalan searched the hall for Bhoran. Yet he was nowhere to be seen. Wherever he and Lusha had gone, it would be a long while before they returned, he knew. A single night wouldn't do to make up for all the years they'd spent apart.

"To the Ruby," Chief Ethelnar declared, raising his cup with his free hand. The crowd raised theirs in greeting and drank. "To the Black Opal!" This time the chief thrust his sword in the air. He flipped it then, its tip pointing at the back of the hall, straight at Avalan. "And to our honored guest, Avalan of the Bloodstone."

Avalan felt the crowd's stares pierce him. He watched as the tribe parted to allow the swordsmith to cross. Dagan's face was no longer covered with soot. His ebony hair, slick with wax, was tucked behind his ears, revealing a face full of grave seriousness. He carried the longsword Avalan had watched him polish when he and Ethelnar had paid a visit to his smithy. Dagan offered Avalan the sword.

The hilt was set with a proud Bloodstone. Earthy green like the shadowgrass that grew in Hydrus's forest it was, and speckled with blood spots.

Avalan pressed his brows together, then turned to Eyedir. The merchant averted his eyes, his fingers fiddling with the silver coins. "You knew about this," Avalan muttered, liquid warmth rising in his chest.

The chief laughed then, a harsh sound that climbed Avalan's spine.

"Forgive me," Ethelnar said, giving him a small bow. "I keep forgetting where you come from. If you unburden Dagan of the sword and join me on this platform, we shall provide a sight more charming than mere dancing and singing. A sway of swords. Black Opal against Bloodstone."

Avalan stood on unsteady feet. *Bloody wine.* He made no move to take the weapon, only raised his chin proudly to address the chief. "What slight has caused you to challenge me?" He tried hard to keep his eyes off Crystal, but as the merchant had painfully reminded him, the mind stood powerless to the will of the heart. Her pale face was even paler now as she watched the encounter.

"Slight?" The chief laughed. "It is but a mere gesture to celebrate my brother's union and to honor our beloved Ronan. He used to speak to us about your skill with all kinds of weapons. A great fighter, he called you. I thought a chance like this shouldn't be wasted. Perhaps this is too big a sword for you, and I am thus mistaken."

Avalan clasped his goat dagger, his temples throbbing. It was too late to refuse now, he knew, for it would mar not only his pride but Ronan's memory. He circled the table, relieving Dagan of the longsword. The leather felt sure under his grip, his blackened skin protected by Eyedir's gloves. The sword was much heavier and longer than any other Avalan had held. Back in the village, the swords Ronan had brought for him were shorter, edgier—weapons meant to be swung and twirled. Yet this one ...

This one's made to chop, cleave, kill ...

The crowd parted before him, forming a human passage leading to the wooden platform. The stone floor whispered beneath his borrowed cloth slippers as he lumbered through.

Once up, Avalan threw the slippers off his feet—naked soles always gave him better purchase. He curled his toes over the rough wood, staring into Ethelnar's eyes. Though the chief had claimed a mere showcase of a sword fight, Avalan could read his thoughts between colorful beads that swirled furiously amid the blackness of his Opals. *He knows I love Crystal.*

Avalan's gaze trickled down to the greatsword in Ethelnar's grip. Its tip almost touched the floor. Great uncertainty tore at Avalan's mind. *I should attack him first,* he thought, knowing full well the first blow was of the greatest importance. *Yet how do I dare attack a chief in a chamber full of his soldiers?*

Ethelnar moved, his face distorted with rage. As he raised the greatsword in the air, Avalan glimpsed the Black Opals coming alive, their darkness stirring.

Cursing, Avalan raised his sword just in time to parry the blow. It was much fiercer than he'd expected, throwing him backward to the edge of the platform. Instead of pain, a voice exploded in his mind.

Avalan!

His heart thumped in his chest. *I know this voice.*

Ethelnar charged at him again, all his stone power behind the strike. Avalan rolled to the side. The Bloodstone in the hilt of his sword caught his attention. The green surface was now engulfed in crimson, the whole stone a teardrop of blood. It felt warm under his grip. Ethelnar's howl made him turn. Steel scraped against steel as Avalan raised his sword to block the deathly attack.

Avalan! the voice cried when the blades met.

Staggering to his feet, Avalan backtracked. He put as much space between himself and the chief as the platform would allow. His head throbbed. A familiar and unwelcome blaze soared through his body. *This was how I felt before the Bloodstone scorched my hands.*

"Fight me!" Ethelnar screamed. "Feel the power of the Bloodstone!"

Eager to be done with this grotesque demonstration, Avalan raged forth. He brought his sword down with a strong chop to meet Ethelnar's.

Avalan! The voice exploded in his mind like a thousand flaming needles.

The force shoved Ethelnar to the platform. Bitter wine mingled with bile rose to Avalan's mouth. He spat. *What is this?*

Untainted, the chief rose. "Do you feel it yet?" Ethelnar demanded, pointing his sword at Avalan as if to accuse him of great treason. "Do you *feel* the *power*?"

Avalan! the voice boomed in his mind, fraying his nerves.

"Stop this," Avalan muttered.

"I think not." The chief wiped an elegant hand across his forehead. "We've only just begun."

Ethelnar's blows came one after the other. Avalan parried and returned vicious chops of his own. Once, the tip of Avalan's blade bit into the chief's shoulder, shredding his tunic and spraying crimson blood over the crowd. Soldiers stirred below, but Ethelnar gestured them back.

The dance went on and on, only with every coupling of their swords, the voice boomed in Avalan's head. Louder and louder it grew, until he could no longer hear the gasps of the crowd, nor the cheering—all he heard was this otherworldly shriek in his mind, calling his name, accusing, begging, prompting …

His body blazed, as if with great fever. Twice he slipped on the sweat from his soles, almost losing the sword.

Avalan! the voice called. *Avalan!* Hit. *Avalan!* Chop. *Avalan!* Slice. *Avalan!* Kill ...

"Enough!" he yelled. Eyes stinging with sweat, he tore the goat dagger from his belt. He lodged the tip of its blade beneath the bloody Bloodstone and wriggled it. With a quick snap, he broke the sword free of the stone's cursed presence. At once the voice in his mind ceased. Yells rose as the Bloodstone arched in the air and landed before Ethelnar's feet.

With a vile cry, the chief stomped the wooden heel of his shoe over the stone, smashing it into a hundred pieces. The crowd gasped. It was a stirring sound, disgust mixed with shock.

Chest heaving with regret, Avalan eyed the cracked pieces of the Bloodstone.

It was too late.

The chief charged at him again and again, each blow stronger than the last. Now Avalan's sword was unblessed by the Bloodstone's power, it caved in beneath tremendous pressure. Tossing and turning, he rolled all over the platform, trying desperately to save his life from the chief's blinding rage. With a sudden move, Ethelnar knocked the longsword from Avalan's clasp. Then, shrieking with laughter, he brought his greatsword down over Avalan's head.

Two shadow hands cuffed the blade.

Its sharp end hovered over the tender skin of Avalan's neck.

"Shadow," Avalan muttered. His breathing was hard, the fear a cold blade in his heart. His stomach coiled, forcing him to roll to the side and empty it.

Over him, the chief laughed, oblivious to the ethereal presence. He raised his arms in the air in triumph. "Black Opal!" he roared, showcasing his greatsword.

At first the tribe remained silent. Then slowly the first cheering broke out, and soon the whole chamber boomed with chanting. *"Black Opal! Black Opal! Black Opal!"*

Avalan thrust his goat dagger into his belt and leaped off the platform. No one tried to stop him as he raced out of the hall, climbing the swirling staircase that led back to the guest apartments. He traced the rough stones with cold hands, scouting the way back to his chamber.

Around and around he circled, exhausted. He collapsed against a wooden door. Under his weight, it creaked open, the gaping mouth of a torch-lined corridor behind it. Without thinking, he slipped inside, the trembling flames guiding his footsteps until he reached a heavy drape.

Pushing it aside, he crossed over a raised threshold, finding himself in the small chamber of shame where the chief had first welcomed them. The chief's seat stood empty, inviting. He sprawled upon it, his entire body aching, his mind burning with anger.

A tongue flitted in the dark. Yekana's scales glistened. Over the stone floor, she slithered to him. When she coiled herself around his body, he made no move to stop her. Even when he glimpsed her fangs, he didn't stir. *Perhaps her venom will numb the shame,* he thought, hot sweat stinging his eyes.

"Down," a voice cracked like a twig.

The snake retreated, and Avalan watched Stonemistress Luthea emerge from the shadows. Yekana slipped by her feet, raising her head as if in spite, but not daring to harm the mistress.

When the snake had disappeared through the dark corridor, the stonemistress spoke again. "A good fight."

Avalan rubbed his eyes. "A mere humiliation."

"A lesson," the mistress returned, not unkindly.

Avalan made to stand. Though his body still ached with the exertion, he felt it wrong to sit in the presence of an old woman.

As if she'd read his mind, the stonemistress sat on the floor, dark robes flowing around her. "Join me," she urged.

"The last time I sat before a teacher of the stones, my hands were scorched." He collapsed back in the cold wooden chair.

"You are afraid."

Avalan eyed the mistress. A frail and kind woman she looked, only how much of her kindness was honest, Avalan wouldn't know. *After all,* he thought, *does age change a cunning spirit?* He still recalled the great ease with which the stones had sprung from Delion's hands. Yet it was great torture the stones imposed on Avalan whenever he touched them.

There is great cunning lying in the shadows, Eyedir's voice whispered.

"I'm losing my strength," Avalan said, looking at his gloves. "I thought myself skilled with the sword."

"To fight with stones, it isn't easy. You were never trained. I taught Ethelnar myself ever since he was a suckling."

Avalan pressed his eyes shut.

"A great burden weighs on you."

Her words unleashed all his fears at once. He had to free Hydrus, to free Crystal, to free his heart to trust his stone. But he knew not how.

"Never lose sight of your thoughts," the mistress advised.

With that booming voice inside his head, it had been hard not to. With every coupling of the blades, it had shrieked ...

"The stone calls you?"

He watched her. There was no use in asking her how she knew. Much like Delion, the stonemistress looked like she could read his mind. "Where can I find the Heart of the Bloodstone?" The words poured out of him before he could stop them.

Luthea raised a feeble hand to stroke her chest. Then she stretched out her arms to him. It was a gesture to join her on the floor, Avalan knew, much like the one Delion had made that night in the Eagle's Eye. Avalan didn't stir.

"You do not trust me," the mistress said, a glint of amusement in her voice.

Trust no one who tries to sell you gems, Dizredek whispered in his ear.

"I do not." Avalan regretted the words as soon as they had left his mouth.

"Very well." Stonemistress Luthea rose, straightening her robes. She teetered toward the corridor, faltering at the threshold. "The lesson is taking root."

CHAPTER THIRTY

BASSALT RAISED his right fist to knock, then thrust it down in disgust as the smell of his festering stump invaded his mouth. *Cursed, cursed.* He pushed the door of Farmera's hut open and staggered across the threshold.

The air was laden with the thick smell of slow-simmering potions and the cold sting of healing salves. It only made his pain worse. Despite his chewing willow bark, the cursed throbbing in his arm hadn't eased. Farmera was bent over a fire, the only light that shone in the darkness. She hadn't bothered lighting the candles. When she faced him, her irate stare made Bassalt realize the visit would only aggravate his suffering. There was no remorse in those proud violet eyes.

"You scorned my summoning," he accused her, kicking the door shut with his heel.

Farmera rose, wiping her forehead, her face bedewed with steam from the cauldron. Despite the heat inside, a heavy fur was draped over her shoulders, above a brown dress that reached her ankles. "What brings you here, Bassalt?"

"Won't you offer me a place at your table?"

"Why?" she dared, crossing her arms over her chest. "Last I heard, your larder had food aplenty. What could I offer our mighty chief that he doesn't already have?"

Bassalt threw the cowl of his cloak back. Trying hard to ignore the contempt in Farmera's eyes, he made his way to her table. "Your company," he said, his crippled hand gesturing at the bench. Even a simple movement such as this caused boiling pain to crawl through his arm. Yet Bassalt hoped Farmera's healing instincts would prove enough for her to put aside her anger.

Her eyes flickered over his wound. "You sentenced Bhoran to death."

"He isn't dead, though, is he?"

"Only because he escaped," Farmera retorted. She wrinkled her nose. "Whatever happened to you? Theran said you lost a finger."

The chief searched the fine lines of her face. *We've been through so much together, yet after all these years, you have come to hate me, have you not?* "I summoned Hydrus."

Glowing coals crackled, joining the low bubbling of potions. Across Farmera's pale face, flame light danced, illuminating her trembling lips. "Why would you do such a thing?"

"It is worse than I feared. I beg of you, Farmera. For the sake of times of old, sit with me. My heart is burdened."

Pulling the fur tighter around her shoulders, Farmera sat on the bench across from him. A great fight must have raged inside her, and as Bassalt had hoped, her compassion seemed to have won, for she reached for his injured hand, gently exploring his wounds. "Theran has managed the tending well. Did Hydrus do this to you?" she said.

"Cursed beast." Bassalt withdrew his hand, the embarrassment of his severed finger too much to bear. "I would have much preferred it to be you who tended to my wounds."

She shot him a disapproving glare. "You must have slighted it greatly. I wonder ..."

"I implored aid. Yet it doesn't deem me worthy as a chief. Much like your son." There was a fleeting sparkle among the violet of her eyes, enough to tell him what he had always suspected.

"Avalan would never—"

"He has been plotting my demise." Bassalt raised a fat palm. "There is no point in denying it any longer. For hours on end, the young men disappear into the forest, hunting as their pretense for the sharp weapons in their belts, only no game burdens their shoulders when they return. And I can feel the thrumming of steel on steel in the air. The birds sing to me of secret meetings … Avalan must think me a great fool."

"He's only a young man." Farmera was quick to justify her son's actions. "Trapped in the village, longing for a freer life."

"Freedom isn't the only thing he seeks. There is also revenge for Bhoran," Bassalt retorted.

"Can you blame him? Bhoran was his only friend, and you and Silver cast him out because he dared raise his eyes to Lusha."

Bassalt drummed his nine fingers on the rough table before the shooting pain rose to a peak. "You and I both know Avalan takes after his father. Much as it pains me to admit it, your husband was a fine leader—he understood the enemy well, had studied the sly ways of the Onyx, had mastered the fine powers of his Bloodstone … Yet even all that didn't prevent his untimely death. Now, Avalan is … different. Raised in ignorance, he's quick to reject the things he doesn't know, and aches to lead the tribe to a freedom that comes with a terrible price. Under my wing, the tribe is safe from the dangers lurking out there." He leaned closer. "I ask you, Farmera, is freedom worth more than one's life?"

Farmera edged back, her eyes wide. "Why are you telling me all this about my son? If he hasn't learned the ways of his stone, you are to blame, for keeping the entire tribe in the darkness."

"You know full well it had to be. You've seen firsthand what a war of stones does to the mind."

"Why, Bassalt? Why did you raise Hydrus? What danger can you not fight yourself?"

"The presence of the Onyx hovers heavy above our village. For twenty long years, I've kept their shadow fingers away. Yet now they have slipped through my defenses. The balance is shifting, much faster than I would like … than I can control." He staggered to his feet. "It is a dire time when the stone of my snake ring changes to darkness, when our merchant is struck dead by an Onyx-enchanted weapon, when my brother returns to a place that cast him away, and when a heedless young man tries to turn the tribe against its sole protector.

Such dire times indeed when a stonemaster returns to the village after I've banished the birthstones."

Under the dim light, Farmera's face twisted with worry. "You know ..."

"About Delion?" Bassalt scoffed. "The old fool took no great measures to conceal himself. Almost walked into my arms."

"How can you call your teacher a fool? He's the reason you're well versed in your stone's ways. Or has your long reign as a chief made you forget whence you started?"

Bassalt swallowed the metal taste of pride. "Stonemasters are cunning creatures, and the tribes would fare much better not knowing their vile teachings of the stones. I'm not alone in this notion; there were others, long before I was born, who founded this great place as a place of peace and freedom from the stone powers. Who has a need of stonemasters when they can live a content life not needing to know about the darkness that lives inside them?"

"And you?" Farmera stared at him now, the Amethyst in her eyes a velvet glowing in the darkness. "Have you known this darkness well? Is it this darkness that moves you to act so? Or have you just chosen the dark path because it's easier?"

"Nothing about my life has been easy," Bassalt said through clenched teeth. "But for this place, you wouldn't have found a safe piece of land to foster the seed of your love with Azirrad. But for the humble village of Hydrus, which remained neutral through the war that savaged the Stone Lands, you'd still be alone and loveless, and Avalan condemned to live in shame. If my path seems dark to all of you, it is because the shadows of the Onyx float above it. All Avalan sees in me is the violence of the Tiger's Eye, but he doesn't *know*. He hasn't seen the true vileness of the war."

Farmera tugged at the fur over her shoulders as if to warm her soul. "Why are you truly here, Bassalt? Enough fear crawls in my heart with Ronan's death and the departure of my only son. Your words are stiff hands around my throat. How much more do you think I can take before my breath leaves me?"

His stone heart raced. He'd gone too far, he knew, but this cursed pain was stirring his actions. He wanted to hurt her, to make her feel what he felt—all the betrayal, the mistrust, the hatred … *Cursed, cursed …* His lips quivered. "I didn't mean to cause you worry." Using the little power he had, he stood. "We may not always agree, but I need you to remember I never truly tried to harm your son. It wasn't I who tried to lead him to the ways of the stones, but I fear Delion has come to stir the waters I have tried so hard to keep undisturbed." He dragged his feet to the door. Placing a heavy hand upon the wood, he faced her. "Do not come to the gathering, I beg you. I won't be able to stand the hate in your eyes when I must do what is needed to protect this place."

With a small creak, the door opened.

"Bassalt," she called after him. Rivulets of tears streaked her cheeks. "How do you know …?" She gulped. "How do you know Azirrad is dead?"

The stone in Bassalt's chest he called a heart sank. "I can think of nothing that would hold a man from returning to you, but the light of the stone leaving his eyes."

With that, he left her, raising his cowl again as he entered the darkness.

Faint firelight danced in the distance as Bassalt teetered his way to the feasting ground. Soon he heard the worried whispers of his tribe. *Are they still my tribe, though?* A dire thought for dire times. *I am, still, the chief of Hydrus,* he reminded himself, trying not to let the brief incident with the waterdragon unsettle him. *You aren't the creature's master, though,* a little voice inside his head reminded him. The cursed thing was of another era. How could Bassalt hope to tame it when magic ran plentifully through its veins?

When he saw the tribe, he halted. They were all facing the platform. The sand was now gone from the ground, returned to the beach where it belonged. Here and there small mounds of it remained, sprinkled over soft grass and dirt. Atop the platform, Silver sat. Dressed for the occasion he was, as always, with glinting scales covering his chest, and his hair slickly combed back from his stern face.

For a small moment, Bassalt just stood there, peering at the imperious figure of Silver beneath the rim of his dark cowl, imagining him rising from his chair and taking the one that belonged to Bassalt. In his mind's ear, Bassalt heard the crowd cheer, rejoice, and celebrate. *You might look more of a chief than me,* Bassalt thought with resentment, *but I am the chief of Hydrus. And I am worthy of my place.*

He elbowed his way through the crowd, obtaining shocked stares and slight bows of heads. *They will* all *bow to me,* Bassalt promised himself. *Soon.*

His chair had never felt so fitting beneath his heavy weight. Silver shot him a curious glance, but Bassalt ignored him.

"Tribe of Hydrus," Bassalt began, his voice booming through the silent night. "As I am certain you all know, Bhoran of the Unknown has escaped."

Short, fearful gasps echoed around the feasting ground, filling Bassalt with satisfaction for what was afoot.

"I fear our guards have not been up to task as of late."

"Are you blaming me and my men for the talon's escape?" Silver had sprung from his seat.

Bassalt ignored him. "I see my words have caused offense to our dearest commander, yet it is I who should be angered. I put my trust in men who aren't worthy of safeguarding our village. I put my trust in all of you. Together we all built the fence. You by hand and wood, and I by the magic of the birthstones. You cursed me for caging you when all I tried to do was protect you.

"I now fear this protection is coming to an end. Ronan's murder stands as a dire reminder that the shield of our village has been breached. The fence stands no longer as a wall of protection but as a means for all of you to defy me. The guards are slack in their duties; a condemned murderer escapes with your aid, and some of you connive in secret meetings in the forest for my overthrow."

A grave silence followed Bassalt's words. The air carried the sultry smoke of fire and the odor of sweat. With a swift flick of his wrist, thick vines rose and went slithering behind him, as if in search of something. Bassalt ground his teeth against the pain the magic stirred in his wounds. He relished the shocked whispers of the crowd as the vines returned, thrusting forth the bound stonemaster.

Bassalt had ordered his servants to keep the master ready and stripped to the skin. He wanted the tribe to see Delion as he truly was —a frail man with one foot in the grave.

A sea of worried whispers rose, giving Bassalt great pleasure. He willed the vines to free the master, to unwrap their tentacles from his ankles and wrists.

"This man is a reminder of a past many of us wish to forget. War, pain, the struggle for victory ... all because of the birthstones. Great forces threaten the peace of Hydrus, an Onyx dagger killing our only merchant. Some of you still remember the day the Onyx invaded our village—those of you who lived, for we lost many that day. Instead of running to me for protection, you chose this man to lead you into the same pain that had caused the war that decimated the tribes." He spat out the piece of willow bark he had been chewing. The cursed thing was numbing his mind along with his pain.

"I could choose to punish you all," he stormed, forcing the ground to shake. Swiftly he let the quake subside, his powers too few and precious to waste. His temples throbbed and ached. "Yet I shall punish only *him*, for you knew no better." He pointed a stubby finger at the stonemaster.

Delion lay on the ground, his wrinkled body shivering from the cruel days spent in Bassalt's bath chamber. Long silver hair tangled around the master's shoulders, hiding his face from the crowd.

"I promised you a death for the murder of our merchant," Bassalt announced gravely, "and my promise remains. My bond with the Stone Lands stands strong. Bhoran will be returned to us. And when that happens, our tribe must come together as one fist. Whoever pries the fingers apart must be punished. The Night of the Spirits is fast upon us, and along with my new reign, it will also mark the punishment of the stonemaster."

Towering above the old man, he said, "Stonemaster Delion, keeper of the Tiger's Eye, I sentence you to death for bringing birthstones into Hydrus, for defiling the sacredness of our village, and for attempting to stoke a rebellion against the rightful chief."

A tumult of angry voices rose from the crowd as old and young protested. The tribe's youth may have been denied the nature of their stones in the past, but as Bassalt had feared, the stonemaster had already dispelled this veil of blissful ignorance.

Silver's arm was fast upon him. "Have you lost your mind?" the commander yelled. "You cannot kill a stonemaster, a keeper! The Stone will curse us, Bassalt. It will destroy us!"

Anger simmered within Bassalt's chest, and for a moment, he was tempted to lash out with his magic at his commander. Lucky for him, another creature won his attention, for behind the yelling crowd at his feet, atop the serpent fence, perched Avalan's tiger, her slitted eyes staring at him with malice. *Where is your master?* he thought at her, but before he could grab her with his power, Sigil spun and leaped off, disappearing behind the long palisade.

CHAPTER THIRTY-ONE

THE WATER WAS WARM. Lusha rubbed her inner thighs, washing away the stickiness of Bhoran's semen. At first she had thought it strange for a bedchamber to hold a bathtub, but when she had returned with her dress ruffled and her thighs dripping, she had been glad to find pails of warm water waiting for her.

When they'd returned to the keep, Bhoran and Lusha had parted ways—he eager to find Avalan, and she aching to wash away the juices of their lovemaking. She had begged a maid with hazel hair to lead her back to her bedchamber. Despite her efforts, Lusha had still not managed to find her own way through the stony corridors; the torch-light cast misleading shadows over the walls, making her see turns where there were none.

In her quiet bedchamber, the air was thick with the smell of long-extinguished tallow candles. The room was dark but for the shafts of moonlight sneaking through the threadbare curtains. Over the water's surface they slid now, like long fingers reaching for Lusha's body. Sweet tiredness engulfed her. The night had proved much better than she had hoped, her union with Bhoran inside the secret chamber of Olnos more intoxicating than any wine she had tasted. She closed her eyes and rested her nape against the stone rim. Just before sleep took her, Semara's words flowed into her mind, faint and distant like the flutter of wings through a foggy night.

From Onyx always comes Onyx.

When she woke, her body shivered. Water lapped around her, cold now. Pale sunlight filtered through the curtains. Lusha rubbed her aching neck. During the unexpectedly long sleep, the tub's rim had bitten into her flesh. She looked down at her nakedness. As she brushed a cold palm across her belly, fear clutched at her throat. The stale waters of the tub had doused the seed of doubt planted in her heart. And now it had grown, threatening to devour her.

She clambered out of her stony bath, her eyes falling on the dress Crystal had lent her. A pile of used gold, it lay on the floor. Even if it were in good enough shape to wear, it would be too lavish for the light of day. Slipping out of it had been easy, yet donning it would require the aid of servants, and now Lusha wanted none around her.

Luckily, a familiar dress lay folded on the bed. "Oh, thank the Moonstone." Though it had been washed, Lusha caught a whiff of Farmera's scent as she pulled the dress over her head. *It's only because of what I must do,* she told herself.

Around and around she went in the warren of corridors until she glimpsed the familiar swaying of a woman's hair disappearing around a corner. The girl was kind enough to take her straight to Crystal's chambers. When the door opened to admit them, Lusha saw the chiefess was garbed in a plain flaxen dress, relishing some warm herbal concoction.

As soon as she saw it was Lusha, Crystal's lips twisted in a tremor. "Leave us," she ordered the maids, and they all rushed out.

Lusha studied the pale face of her friend. Dark circles under Crystal's eyes betrayed she had hardly slept. "What's wrong?"

"You weren't there," Crystal observed. Her eyes flickered to the door. "Last night, during the wedding, you and Bhoran slipped out."

Lusha sat next to her. "I … I didn't think our absence would be noted. We needed some time … alone." Blood rose to her cheeks. "I didn't mean to cause offense. Did the chief—"

Crystal grabbed Lusha's wrist. "Lower your voice," she begged. "The chief is mad, I swear. He wanted to kill him, Lusha. I was so afraid he would kill Avalan."

Lusha gasped. "But why?"

The chiefess's eyes darted to the closed door as if she were expecting it to cave in at any moment and she to be dragged away with grave accusations. "Ethelnar challenged Avalan to a sword fight before the whole tribe."

"I don't understand. Is this a custom? Did Avalan get hurt?"

Crystal shook her head. "His pride got the hardest blow, I fear. It was a mere display of power from my husband. A punishment, I'm certain." A sea storm raged in the chiefess's eyes.

"Why would Ethelnar want to punish Avalan? You said he's kind to you. Did you and Avalan … come close?"

"Yes," Crystal confessed. "But I fail to see how Ethelnar would have known. I … I took all the precautions. I was so certain …"

Lusha suddenly felt like the air in the room was thin, the faint smell of lilacs that scented the chiefess's chambers impossible to bear. "Oh, Crystal, I would be the last one to judge you, but did you not think about Avalan? If the chief learns you lay with him …"

Crystal released her hand suddenly, as if burned. "But we didn't. It was a mere hug, I swear. Why would you think thus?"

Hot shame rose to Lusha's cheeks. *I am a woman grown,* she reminded herself. *And free to choose with whom I sleep.* Her pity grew for Crystal, for it was clear she still held love for Avalan in her heart. "Perhaps because Bhoran and I came close," she confessed.

The storm in Crystal's eyes eased. She smiled. "I knew nothing would keep you two apart. Seeing your glowing face next to his, I know how wrong I was not to support you."

Her old friend had never liked Bhoran, Lusha knew. But it was out of fear—Crystal didn't share the tribe's hatred for him.

"You can support me now." Lusha's palm slipped over her belly. "Semara sat next to me at the wedding. She told me about the union of the stones."

The chiefess's eyes grew wide with realization.

"I know it's just these few times Bhoran and I have made love, and there was lots of blood, but … what if …? I'm not ready, Crystal. What if the seed of Onyx is planted inside me? I need your aid … the herb …"

All the color drained from Crystal's face. "One time can be all that's needed," she agreed gravely. "Come with me."

Once out in the corridors, Crystal whispered, "We must see Paldma for this."

Lusha's stomach lurched—she would have much preferred a proper healer to a cook, but Crystal's choice made sense. Paldma seemed kind and loving, a woman who wouldn't scorn a choice made outside the bonds of marriage. When they finally emerged into an open-air stone alley, Lusha said in a low voice, "She knows how to take care of such things?"

Crystal turned, her eyes heeding caution. "No, and you mustn't tell her anything. Yet in her kitchens, we will find the herb we need."

The kitchens bustled with preparations much greater than the ones for the wedding of the chief's brother.

"Do they never stop?" Lusha asked Crystal.

"Tonight's the Night of the Spirits," Crystal said over her shoulder. She snaked her way through the servants, stepping over spilled food and drink.

Her words were a slap across Lusha's face. *How could I have forgotten?* Her mind traveled back to Hydrus and all those nights she had prayed to the full moon that lit the ceremony for salvation. Yet the chief's chair had always remained empty, as the spirit of Chief Volkan had never come.

Before she could reply, Crystal grabbed her wrist and dragged her to a small recess at the back of the kitchen. They descended a creaking staircase, its end lost in darkness.

"What is this place?"

"Storage for things that should remain out of reach."

Once at the bottom of the steps, Lusha glanced over her shoulder. Faint light illuminated the top of the staircase, calling her to return ... A loud creak sounded behind her as Crystal pushed open a heavy door. Spicy air escaped the small room. Small flames shone behind glass lamps mounted on the walls, shedding light onto short shelves burdened with jars and pots and jugs. Some of them, Lusha noticed curiously, had lids fixed with locks. Others brimmed with piles of spices and herbs, standing there unprotected.

A leafy plant spilled over the rim of a small pot. Crystal separated a few leaves from their stem.

Lusha gulped. "Why are there so many lamps here?"

"For the warmth. Herbs need it."

Much like us, Lusha thought. She stared at the chiefess's hands.

"It might work, or it might not. You must prepare yourself for pain."

Lusha's belly tightened. She knew. Once, she and Farmera had given it to Garlea when she had fallen with child. *I am too old for this,* Garlea had said, and Farmera had agreed. Last time Garlea had given birth, it had almost cost her life.

"Pain worse than when we have our moonturn blood." Crystal's voice echoed in the warm cellar. "It will be like a thousand claws, long and heartless, ripping your insides. They will leave you breathless and despairing, wishing you'd never dared to do this. In time, you will know if your sacrifice has borne fruit, or if you suffered for nothing."

Hot tears streaked the chiefess's face now, and Lusha knew. "You've had this." She took a step closer. "You took it after Colgar ..."

"Farmera was loath to give it to me, but she had no choice. I threatened to drown myself in the Crystal Lake. In the end, she succumbed." Crystal stared at the leaves in her hands. "She gave me the mourning."

Mourning, Lusha thought. *What a fitting name.* Anger and pain fought in her chest then. And a sense of shame for all Crystal had had to suffer because of her refusal to marry Colgar. "You suffered to remove a seed from a man you hated," she said carefully, "and I ... I want to do this to myself because I'm afraid of a stone."

Brushing her tears away, Crystal gave her a wan smile. "I suffered, yes. But the seed was much stronger than I thought. Though I won't ever forget the pain, I am glad the mourning didn't work on me. And now I have my daughter."

But of course, Lusha thought, her heart now racing. The way Semara's cheeks dimpled when she smiled, her oval face, the copper skin ... "Semara is Colgar's."

The chiefess glanced at the heavy door before pressing the leaves into Lusha's hands. "Remember your promise. You swore you wouldn't tell a soul about Colgar. And now I must burden you with the same promise about my daughter."

The leaves scathed Lusha's palms. "Does Ethelnar know?"

"There are days when I swear he knows it all, and others when I see him play with our daughter as if there's no seed of doubt in his heart. I thank my birthstone every day for blessing Semara with its azure hue. I was so scared her eyes would carry the gold of Colgar's Heliodor, and then there would be nothing to shield me from my husband's rage."

Lusha squeezed the leaves in her hands. Anger always reminded her of her father. "Tell me how you met him. How far along were you when you were married?"

"Not far. I knew early enough the herb had not worked. My breasts swelled, and my stomach lurched at the sight of food. I went to Ronan, begging. Stones bless his soul, he listened with a kind heart. Soon after, he took me with him on his journey and presented me to Ethelnar, told him the only way I could be free from Bassalt's clutches was to marry a chief. Then Bassalt couldn't order my return. Ethelnar was kind to me and tended to my every need, and soon he took me to his bed." Her gaze fell to the floor with her shame. "I didn't want to at first, but I had to cover for … my condition. Then I thought his touch might not be so bad, and so I accepted his proposal to marry. I never truly loved him, though. Not like I love Avalan. How much he must hate me for leaving him behind. I never thought to see him again, nor you …

"I beg of you, Lusha, do not take this accursed leaf. I've witnessed the power of the stones; they are not as evil as Bassalt makes them out to be. If nothing else, they give you comfort and strength. You are of the Moonstone. A woman like you is blessed with the powers of healing. Do not rip your soul apart. Even if Bhoran is of the Onyx, a mere stone doesn't make you evil."

Lusha's throat was dry, her chest tight from shallow breaths. "I am not ready … I have only now left the village. Bhoran and I are unmarried, and his eyes … More and more I look into them, and I'm convinced he truly is of the Onyx. There's this terrible fear in my heart. I know he will not hurt me. His love is great, as is mine. But love shouldn't be enough to condemn a child into living among tribes who will hate it."

Liquid leaked from the leaf as she squeezed it. It stung her skin. "There will be another time for us. Perhaps after we've found my aunt. She might help us find the true nature of Bhoran's stone, and then my mind will have the peace it needs to bring forth a child." She thought of the stonemistress then, the way she had brought the birthstones forth. "Do you think Stonemistress Luthea can help us? Do you think she will know Bhoran's true nature?"

Crystal shook her head. "I very much doubt it. She is the keeper of the Black Opal." She hesitated, as if a small war raged inside her. "Ethelnar talked to me about Bhoran last night as we lay. He said his eyes reminded him of the war. He said that he feels a great shadow in our bedchamber, the umbra of the Onyx. But that means nothing, Lusha. Nothing. We cannot know for certain."

I think I can, but I just refuse to see it, Lusha thought.

With a trembling hand, she brought the mourning to her mouth. As she chewed on it, its juices ran, bathing her tongue with bitterness and sorrow.

CHAPTER THIRTY-TWO

AVALAN COULDN'T TELL whether it was day or night—such was the darkness of the chamber. He had slept on the chief's chair, a shallow and tormented rest. Trickling water whispered through the walls, the same sound that had driven him mad the first night they'd spent at Raekandar. Yekana was coiled at his feet. He could feel the slick surface of her scales against his naked soles.

The Night of the Spirits, he thought ruefully. He was a fool to have ever believed he could return to Hydrus before it. Perhaps a greater fool, even, for thinking he could find the Heart of the Bloodstone and win against Bassalt when he had lost the fight with Ethelnar. He caressed his goat dagger.

What am I missing? How can I silence the voice in my head, make the Bloodstone work with me, not against me?

"Shadow," he whispered into the darkness. It wasn't with him, he knew. He would have felt its presence, the terrible burden that gave him hope and despair. It had saved him from Ethelnar's final blow. Thankfully, the chief hadn't seemed to notice its presence. But the shadow hadn't followed Avalan to the chamber. He wished it had. He longed to talk with it, confess his greatest fears, ask it about the Heart of the Bloodstone. *It must have stayed with Crystal.*

He knew not how to feel about it. She was his heart's deepest desire, and thinking of Hydrus now filled him with guilt. Crystal had escaped to live a better life, and all he wanted was to return. She had been right when she had told him he would never have wanted to leave the village. Hydrus was his life. Its forest, the beach, the friends he had grown up with …

He stroked Yekana's sturdy body. "Can you find Bhoran?"

The snake led him through the maze to an oaken door. Avalan placed a curious ear against it. By his knees, Yekana nodded an impatient head as if to say this surely was her master's door. No sound came from within, and Avalan pushed the door open, hoping the snake wasn't mistaken.

To his relief, Bhoran was sprawled on the bed, buried among the pillows. Yekana climbed onto the bedsheets, her head hovering over Bhoran's thigh with clear intentions.

"Down," Avalan ordered, hoping Stonemistress Luthea's command would prove effective on his lips.

The snake hissed and recoiled. Bhoran opened his eyes.

"Where have you been?" Avalan asked, much more harshly than he'd intended. After all, if Crystal had been his, he, too, would have wanted to be alone with her for hours on end.

Bhoran rubbed the sleep from his eyes. "I came to find you last night. You weren't in your bedchamber. I heard talk of a sword fight." Those cold, dark eyes of his searched Avalan's face.

Yekana lifted her head, coming between them. Her flicking tongue stroked the fangs on Bhoran's face. Bhoran placed a gentle palm atop her head, pushing her down. "Go, Yekana. Forest."

Unwillingly the snake obeyed. She slithered down the bed and over the stony rim of the bathtub in the room's middle. A soft splash followed as she swam through the water before she finally climbed out the open window.

"How long has it been since she last bit you?"

"Long enough," Bhoran said. "It's hard to control my anger even when I'm with Lusha. Tell me all."

Avalan looked down at his battered clothes. He still wore the tunic that bore the colors of his stone, but it was now ruffled and torn in places. "Ethelnar challenged me to a sword fight. It was ugly and painful. My whole body aches, and I now envy this bed of yours."

Bhoran moved over. "You don't look well."

"I know." Avalan climbed onto the bed, resting against a soft pillow. "The night was good?"

"It was," Bhoran said, though his lips looked pale, his eyes red. Not letting the snake feed on him was taking a heavy toll.

"You need to let her go," Avalan said.

Bhoran grunted in answer. "Tell me more about Ethelnar."

Avalan looked at the supple leather covering his wounds. The gloves he had bought from Eyedir had stood the test of a sword fight. His heart, however, hadn't. "I managed to score him, but he beat me, before all. Came at me again and again with his sword. A double-handed one, the finest work I've ever seen. And all the while, my ears rang with this *maddening* voice inside my head." When he saw Bhoran raise a brow, he was quick to explain. "Ethelnar gave me a longsword with a Bloodstone in its hilt. The stone talked to me the whole time, begging me, accusing me, tearing my mind apart. I had no choice but to pry it out with my dagger. The voice vanished then, but so did my sword's power."

Bhoran frowned. "He knows about Crystal."

"He must. For I made no other slight against him that would cause him to challenge me."

"You must take the shadow and leave. Find the Heart of the Bloodstone."

Avalan swallowed hard. "*She* is the Heart, of that I am convinced. The shadow only shows when I'm around her. And around her I wish to remain. I am of a mind to free her and take her with me."

Bhoran's face hardened. "She has a child."

The words were a knife in Avalan's gut. "In time, we shall return for Semara. But it is Crystal I need to free first. Ethelnar doesn't love her, Bhoran. I see it. It is a great fear that binds her to him. I mean to tear that bond, but I will need a blade strong enough to inflict the cut." He caressed the hoof of his goat dagger.

Bhoran raised a curious brow. "Fighting Bassalt isn't enough?"

"You think me a rebellious fool." Avalan made to leave, but Bhoran placed a heavy hand on his shoulder. Avalan met the unmoving darkness of his friend's stones. "You defied Silver and Bassalt to be with

Lusha. How, then, do you expect me to just leave Crystal behind when I can see her heart still longs for me?"

Bhoran held his friend's gaze for a moment. "I would have done the same," he said at last.

A wave of relief washed over Avalan. "I need a Bloodstone. I now see why Silver keeps his stone on his sword. A hundred times stronger the attacks were. I'm certain Ethelnar would have killed me but for the crowd watching."

"The merchant. Eyedir."

"I thought of the same. If Ronan could find birthstones, Eyedir should prove useful in the matter. Come with me. I fear these are our last days together. After the Night of the Spirits, our roads will part. For only a while, I hope."

To his relief, Bhoran nodded, and they both left the chamber.

Behind a sturdy bench filled with curious trinkets, Eyedir sat on a rough stool, scratching his chin. His gaze turned stern when he saw them, and he crossed his arms before his chest. "If you have come here to accuse me, let it be known it wasn't my place to warn you against the fight. A mere amusement the chief had promised, and I am not a man to spoil the celebrations of a wedding."

Avalan exchanged a glance with Bhoran before he banged his fists on Eyedir's bench. His wares jingled and rolled. "Learn how to tread the darkness, you told me. I am here for that."

"You are?" Eyedir raised a curious brow. "How are you faring after the fight?"

Avalan's entire body ached, except for his hands. Even after a fight like that, the scorched skin remained unfeeling. *Will my hands ever heal?* "The gloves gave me a fair grip. I thank you for that."

"But now you wish to have more reasons to thank me, I take it."

"A Bloodstone," Avalan offered. "So I may forget how you jested with me and failed to give me fair warning."

Eyedir stood, his long robes softly clinking. "You have come to the wrong place, son."

Bhoran edged closer, waving his hands over the bench. "You sell all these curious things. What's a stone to you?"

The merchant made a fist. "What is a soul worth to you?" he asked them both. "Nothing, I see. It is astonishing to behold how much Bassalt has kept you in the darkness."

"A stone is just a stone," Bhoran retorted.

Avalan placed a calming hand on his friend's wrist. "I am tired of hearing of how much I do not know. If you would, explain to us, and don't judge us for our ignorance, for it wasn't by choice."

"Not by choice, you say, yet Ronan many a time sang to me a different song. A song that tells how much you despised the birthstones and wished to fill your hands only with weapons. He tried to tell you again and again, and his words fell on deaf ears. Why would you listen to me now?"

The dirk Ronan had given Avalan before he died still rested in his clothes chest. The merchant's words made Avalan ache for it now, to hold it in his hands and listen. If he could just see Ronan one more time, he *would* listen. "I was wrong, and now I've changed my mind."

Eyedir's gaze softened. His hands relaxed. "You really have a gift with words, I'll give you that, son. Ronan taught you well. You weren't bad with the sword either, I suppose. Should you have known how to leverage the Bloodstone, perchance we might have witnessed a very different ending to that fight. But ... eh." He shrugged. "It does a man no good to think about things past."

"You will tell us about the Bloodstone, then?"

"There is nothing to tell, son. I told you in our short talk in the wedding hall. The stones were the ones who killed Ronan. Do you suppose I would make the same mistake of carrying them? Would you carry another man's soul? No matter how Ronan got his hands on those birthstones, it wouldn't have been a blessed deal."

"Someone once told me you get your stone when you're born, gifted by the stonemaster of your birthstone," Avalan prompted.

"Aye, and this birthstone belongs to you and no one else. Yet there are those who think otherwise. The War of the Stones brought desperate times. I've seen whole tribes with bellies so empty they sold their stones for a piece of bread. Birthstones changed hands to win allegiances, protection, a place to sleep without fear. Nothing good ever comes of using someone else's stone."

"You mean to say these birthstones Ronan brought to Hydrus weren't granted to him by stonemasters?"

The merchant laughed. "You're catching on now, son. Look, I shall be the last to judge him, seeing as I've had my fair share of shadowy trade in the past. But those days are long behind me, you hear? I shan't paint my hands with the sorrow of someone who lost his stone in a moment of desperation."

The stone of Eras's father, gleaming in the firelight, came to Avalan's mind. Just before Bassalt had crushed it, the Moonstone had appeared to Avalan whole and potent. "What of the stones of souls who have passed? Surely they mustn't miss them."

Eyedir's Ruby eyes flamed with passion. "This is the greatest disgrace. The stone of a soul who is no more must be buried along with its rightful owner. So it can return to the One Stone. The balance must be kept, you hear me? The tribes have forgotten this, and all the stonemasters and stonemistresses seem to do nowadays is unite stones that don't belong together. I miss the olden times. When one married within one's stone. But now ... eh ... everyone's eager to blend their blood with another stone."

Avalan frowned, a sense of foreboding rising in his chest. If the merchant's words were true, then he was being played for a great fool. "I refuse to believe Ronan would deceive me in such a way. He'd never give me the Bloodstone of another." He tried to keep his voice steady. "He was like a father to me."

"Now, son, understand. Someone else's Bloodstone will still grant power to your hands. Not the same as if it were your own, but close enough. You must have felt it when you held the sword. Look, why don't you knock on Stonemistress Luthea's door with these matters? I'm but a mere merchant."

"For a mere merchant, you talk much," Bhoran retorted, his anger rising.

Avalan bit his lip. After witnessing the great power the stones bestowed upon a weapon, he had dared to hope for a moment he could stand against Ethelnar as his equal. Yet the merchant refused to help him. *What a great fool I've been.* "We thank you," he told Eyedir. Then he turned to Bhoran. "Let us go."

As they crossed the small courtyard, Eyedir's voice sounded behind their backs. "Now you wait there." The merchant strode to them. "It pains me to see such great disappointment in your face. I may no longer deal with birthstones, but I know others who do. The Night of the Spirits has arrived, and glorious celebrations will take place in the keep of Raekandar. Tonight, keep your cups full and your eyes open. And once the chance arrives, I hope your hands are swift and your fingers agile, so you take what you desire."

"You mean *steal*?" Avalan asked, his pride wounded.

The merchant shrugged. "Can someone really steal something that is already stolen?"

CHAPTER THIRTY-THREE

UNDER THE MIDDAY SUN, the grass glistened before the keep's gate. Over it tramped servants arranging the tables for the Night of the Spirits. Where the wedding had taken place indoors, under the watch of the stonemistress, this night's celebration would take place under the blessing of the full moon.

Lusha won't much like that, Bhoran thought with amusement, picturing his beloved's skin glowing under the moonlight. He bit into the soft bread, the starchy taste filling him with pleasure. As he sat behind a small table balanced against the wall, none paid him much heed. A sweet girl had been kind enough to serve him a modest breakfast: soft bread and soft cheese and a generous cup of boiled barley flavored with thyme. The golden liquid reminded him of Lusha and the way her dress had flowed around her, cupping her figure.

If he closed his eyes, he could relive it all again. The smell of her sweet breath on his neck, her cries of pleasure and pain, and the pounding of his heart ... a heart that hadn't truly beaten in near six years. He smirked like a fool at everyone daring to flick their eyes in his direction.

Could I be happy?

The keep rose above him—cold stone, the twisting of a maze in its bowels. He suddenly wished Avalan hadn't retired for some rest. Bhoran didn't much like the scheme of plucking Crystal from Ethelnar's grasp. His heart was torn between escorting Lusha to Levorotha and aiding Avalan in his cause. He was of a mind to talk to Lusha about his fears. He knew she'd never agree to return to Hydrus while Bassalt remained in power, but perhaps she would agree to linger in Raekandar longer while he and Avalan came up with a better way to snatch the chiefess away.

Content with food and drink, Bhoran rose, falling into step beside a young girl who raced to the keep. "Lead me to the women's apartments?" Bhoran asked.

She blushed, gazing at him coyly. Even with fangs and etchings on his face and body, Bhoran knew his presence could still stir a woman's heart.

"Why?" she asked him.

"I wish to see my woman. Blond of hair, pale of skin."

The girl frowned, disappointed. "The village girl. I saw you with her. The way you looked at her … ah, I wish someone would look at me like that."

Bhoran rubbed his neck, proper words eluding him.

She sighed. "Follow me. One can get lost in the corridors."

Inside the keep, Bhoran's heart beat louder than the clacking of the girl's shoes on the stone floor. She gestured at a closed door and made her way back, giving him a final rueful look.

Without bothering to knock, Bhoran pushed the door open, his body numb with anticipation. A warm bed would serve as a much better place to dance with her again, caress her sweet skin …

He halted.

Flaxen hair spilled over the stone rim of the bathtub, a rushing waterfall from Lusha's head. But the angle … the angle of her neck was wrong, he knew at once.

"Lusha!" he cried, rushing to her side. Her face was pale but serene, as if she'd fallen into a dreamless sleep. No breath or words escaped her parted lips. Around her nakedness, clear water mingled with blood. Bhoran's knees gave in, the memory of her face slashed by the snake haunting his mind. He gulped back fear and bent over the rim, shaking her shoulders. "Lusha … Lusha … wake, my heart. Wake!" Her skin was clammy.

"Bhoran ..." she whispered, her voice a faint plea.

He hefted her from the bloodied bath. Next to his heart, her head rested, weak. He crossed the threshold, striding down the dark corridor, a sick feeling rising in his chest. Before him the maze stretched, heartless and eerie. *I won't find my way through in time,* he realized with terror, *and then it will be too late.*

Cursing, he rushed back to the room, put Lusha on her bed, and snatched the curtains open. He stuck his head out. The window overlooked a small courtyard filled with empty tables. In the corner, a man tended to the flowers that lined the walls.

"You," he shouted down to him. "Quick, call the healer. She's barely breathing."

The man shaded his face against the sun. "You need the medic?"

"Be quick."

Once Bhoran saw the man disappear, he rushed to Lusha's side. The sight of her naked body made his breath ragged with terror. He ripped a bedsheet free, gently wrapping it around her. He stroked her hair. "My heart ..." he whispered over and over until the room echoed with hurried footfalls.

A short man with stained sandy robes stormed across the room, two women at his heels. "What has happened?" His voice was stern, cutting through Bhoran's fear.

"I found her." Bhoran waved at the bathtub. On its stony rim rested the jewels Lusha had worn last night, her Moonstone shining among them, set in an elegant chain of gold. "I don't know what happened to her."

The man nodded solemnly. "I shall need to uncover her." He pulled the white sheets away from Lusha's body without waiting for permission.

It sickened Bhoran to watch the medic's fingers probe the soft skin of her belly. "Help her. I beg you."

Slapping her face, the medic tried to bring Lusha to her senses. "Speak to me, child of the Moonstone. What ails your body?"

Lusha's lips moved, and the medic bent closer, pressing his ear to her mouth. Then he rose, a deep wrinkle creasing his forehead. "We shall need to move her to my cavern," he told the women.

"I'll carry her." Bhoran took the naked Lusha in his arms.

"Has she mastered her Moonstone?" When Bhoran cocked his head in confusion, the medic said, "Where is her birthstone?"

Bhoran snatched the golden bracelet and handed it to him. His heart raced when he saw a fleeting shadow pass across the man's face. *He's disappointed.* "Tell me you can save her."

"Pray to your stone we're not too late. Follow me."

Bhoran tailed the medic through dark corridors and sunny alleys, across hard stone and soft grass, all the while uncertain if he should pray to his stone or curse it. It seemed to him whenever he came close to Lusha, it always ended with her wounded in his arms. The harrowing whispers that rose in their wake felt to him like the curse of the Onyx. *Cursed, cursed.* Bassalt's words echoed in his mind.

Small braziers warmed the medic's lodgings. It was a spacious cavern with a high ceiling and plenty of beds and benches. The air was sharp with the coolness of concoctions and pastes lathered over sick bodies. The ill twisted in their beds, thin moans leaving their mouths.

To the bowels of the cavern, the medic led them. On a shadowed bed, Bhoran let Lusha rest at the medic's instructions. Then the little man disappeared behind counters filled with pans and bottles, whose contents Bhoran didn't wish to know. He stroked Lusha's hair, his heart aching for an answer.

The medic returned, a cup of a steaming, cloudy concoction in his hands. "She needs to drink it all," he instructed Bhoran. "And place the bracelet with her Moonstone around her wrist. Keep it close to her heart."

Bhoran took the cup in one hand and with the other grabbed the medic's arm. "The stone … I am uncertain it is truly hers … a merchant gave it to me …"

A faint scowl rumpled the man's tired face. "I see. May the soul of this Moonstone have mercy on her, young man. And do not make to kiss her. These fangs of yours carry venom. Her body can't take any more poison."

"Poison?" Bhoran glanced at Lusha's weakened features. "Is that what runs through her?" He pried her lips open, dripped the thick liquid into her mouth.

"The mourning, they call it. A vile thing."

Confusion simmered in Bhoran's mind. "Lusha would never take poison."

"Her whisper was weak, but there was no mistaking the words in her mouth."

"But why?" Bhoran felt the medic's gaze. It spoke of pity and fear. He met the man's eyes, knowing full well whatever came out of the healer's mouth would serve him cold pain.

"In small amounts, the mourning is harmless," the medic explained, brushing sweat from his forehead. "Those who want to rid their belly of a child may take more."

To that, Bhoran bowed his head. "I thank you," he managed.

After the man left him, he continued pouring the potion through Lusha's lips. Soon her breathing eased. Color returned to her cheeks. Bhoran hoped his heart would unclench then, but he still found it stiff and ungiving—the thought of Lusha risking her life to not carry his child, a thorn that stung him much more harshly than the fangs on his face.

Perhaps if I could hear her side … He brushed away wet hair from her forehead. "Lusha?"

No answer came. Her soul had sunk into a deep sleep, and Bhoran didn't know if she would surface in time to soothe his pain.

He stood, his body numb. *She fears I am an Onyx.* He passed between the sickbeds, eager to be rid of the smell of ailments and potions.

Outside, the air didn't give him much comfort. The day's heat brought out the smells of earth and animals. *She fears to bear my child.* He followed the keep's outer walls until he reached a small recess.

She fears my stone.

Bhoran looked up and screamed inside his mind, *Yekana!*

Not long after, sure as the thunder that follows the lightning, the azure snake slid over the wall. Bhoran sat, his back against the rough stone. When he lifted the sleeve of his tunic, Yekana bared her fangs.

They punctured his skin like merciful pins. The familiar pleasure of venom raced through his veins, devouring his pain, smothering any feeling daring to rise in his chest. Bhoran let the snake feed on him.

I failed. It was an empty thought.

Bhoran knew then that despite Lusha's great love for him, the fear of the Onyx would always hang above them—a dark cloud shading the sun, freezing them both. The cloud had come for him now, swollen and dusty, choking him, making his head light. He was drifting, he knew.

He closed his eyes, the sucking sound of Yekana's feeding becoming distant, until Bassalt's voice boomed in his ears.

Who are you really, brother?

CHAPTER THIRTY-FOUR

DARKNESS HAD FALLEN in his room when Avalan awoke. He pushed himself onto a sore elbow, instinctively reaching beside him for Sigil. His touch met with nothing.

I'm not in Hydrus.

The walls behind him whispered again, a lazy rush of water.

The thin curtain was aglow with moonlight. He clambered out of bed, his bare chest prickling against the cool air. Whatever little warmth the day's sun had gifted, the night had chased it away from the stone halls of the keep. Avalan dreaded to think how winters went by in Raekandar.

He climbed onto the stony window seat. The room's position in the keep didn't much allow for a splendid view such as the one enjoyed from Crystal's high tower, but the window overlooked a small garden. It reminded Avalan of his mother. In his mind's eye, he pictured her there now, plucking roots from the ground, brushing the dirt away, and gifting him with a joyous smile as she raised her gaze up to show him her findings.

Moonlight scattered over azure scales. Yekana slithered lazily through the thorn bushes below. Avalan spied her coil amid mounds of freshly dug soil, her eyes glinting. He wished the snake would leave Bhoran alone. It was a foul addiction, Avalan knew, but he could understand it. After all, he'd also been tempted in the chief's room to let her dip her fangs into his skin, take away the hot pain of shame.

Does Bhoran love her as I love Sigil?

Thinking of his tiger now offered him more sorrow than comfort. He longed to run his fingers through her thick fur, just to cast away the murk that clouded his mind. *At least she is protecting Mother,* he reminded himself. That thought always made him breathe more easily.

He drew the goat dagger from his breeches. The makeshift coupling of bone and blade still held. It would take much more to break his dagger, he knew. In a way, he saw himself in it. He traced the smooth part of the bone where the goat hair had thinned. The blade Ronan had gifted him had a stone hollow in its hilt, and now Avalan tried to remember how big it had been and how he might go about carving one in the goat leg. If Eyedir kept his word, Avalan might soon get a Bloodstone to fight the chief. Yet now he knew how stones came to be, the thought of using someone else's soul sickened him.

It's not your true Bloodstone, Dizredek's voice whispered in his mind.

There is no other way, he tried to convince himself. *Once I have freed Hydrus, I shall allow the tribesfolk to return to their roots.* Those who wished to reclaim their birthstones would be free to do so, and those who wished to stay away from it all—like him—would be free to see them as weapons for dire times and nothing more.

He had a feeling Ronan would have disapproved of this resolution. Somehow Avalan had always felt the merchant had wished him to know more about the stones. If Avalan had shown even the slightest interest in them, Ronan would have swept him to the outer lands and taught him all their secrets. Yet, growing up, Avalan had only cared about metal and wood and bone and all the ways he could combine them to make weapons. He only cared about the village, his home, his tribe …

Who would do this to you, Ronan? he wondered, though he knew that dead men gave no answers. Eyedir had told him it was the stones, but could an Onyx dagger wield itself? Was not a hand needed to cast the blow? Avalan frowned, twisting the tip of his dagger against his finger. *How much do I not know?*

His door creaked open. Through the curtain, he glimpsed the

silhouette of a maidservant carrying a tray. Faint candlelight flickered next to the plates, driving away some darkness. The smell of roasted roots made his mouth water, but he made no move to leave the comfort of his corner. There was more thinking to be done, and it all came down to how to deal with this arrogant chief who had almost killed him and free Crystal.

"Avalan?"

The voice startled him. He peeked behind the curtain. She had donned a servant's brown tunic with matching wooden shoes. Her ebony locks were tied up in a horsetail with a red string. He smiled at the brilliance of her scheme. "Crystal?"

She put down the tray and threw the wooden shoes off her feet. Then she climbed onto the window seat with him, knees drawn beneath her chin. "I'm sorry my husband caused you pain."

"Pain is welcome. It reminds me I'm still alive."

Her Larimar eyes widened. "I don't believe he meant to kill you ..."

"I'm not so certain." The ferocity of Ethelnar's blows stung him once more. He had to get his hands on a Bloodstone. "It's just as well. You're here with me now." He reached for her hand, his palm big against hers.

She let him hold her for a while. Then she dipped her face behind her knees. "Tell me about your life in Hydrus."

He raised a curious brow. "What do you want to know?"

"All," she said, breathless. "How do you spend your days, and whose company do you keep? How long does the sun linger on the sand, and how bright does our beach glisten? Does the feasting ground still burst with songs and fires and dances? And who won the last goat game?"

Her words were a leaden weight on Avalan's chest. He tried to remember the good and forget the ugly things. "Sigil keeps me company and follows me on my hunting. I left her with Farmera, to watch over her until I return." His voice broke at the thought of them so far away. He was mistaken to think he could pretend all was fine. Those azure eyes of Crystal's always had a way of unlocking his deepest fears. "The feasting ground has seen its fair share of pain. Not long ago, Bassalt punished our young champion before the whole tribe. Do you still remember Eras?"

The chiefess nodded.

"He's a man grown now. But he made the mistake of fostering his father's birthstone."

Crystal inhaled sharply.

"Bassalt whipped him bloody, and then some more. No one sings around the fires anymore, Crystal. All that reaches my ears is Silver's yells and Bassalt's threats. I haven't danced since Bhoran and you left Hydrus, and the big fires are now only lit to shed light on violence and shame."

"Ethelnar said there was a trial at the statue of Olnos."

The leather of his gloves crinkled as Avalan clenched his fists. "Bassalt forced Bhoran to touch the Onyx dagger, thinking he could convince the tribe of his origins and sentence him to death with a light conscience."

She edged closer. "But you don't believe he did it?"

"No. I cannot imagine what Bhoran would gain from killing Ronan. Yet the time he chose to return to Hydrus proved a mischance. Bassalt didn't so much as conduct a proper search of the area once he got his hands on Bhoran." He frowned. "If only I'd had more time to trace the ground or even look at Ronan … but Bassalt buried him swiftly and without a proper ceremony."

Gently she held him. "Avalan, I am so sorry."

He swallowed his anger and sorrow. He knew he hadn't properly mourned the loss of Ronan, perchance because he hadn't been the one to see him lying dead in the forest's heart. *I cannot think about it now, lest I lose my courage.* There would be plenty of time for pain once the village was free.

Avalan glimpsed movement beyond the curtain. The second shadow slid beneath the closed door.

"What troubles you?" Crystal said.

The memory of the stone's voice was still raw in his mind. "The stones," he confessed. "No matter how hard I try, I cannot trust them. Every time I come near a Bloodstone, I walk away injured, defeated. Friend or foe, what do they stand for? The voices in my head blind me.

Bassalt, Ethelnar—all this hatred blinds me. I fear it's started to seep into my heart. My thoughts … they have darkened."

A determined frown was etched on Crystal's face. "Come with me. There's something I think you should see."

She led him through the corridor maze, their naked feet quiet on the stone, and yet the rush of water through the walls seemed to grow louder as they sneaked through the keep.

Is it only in my mind, or do the walls try to speak to me?

The weight of the second shadow burdened Avalan's shoulders, yet now wasn't the time to reveal its presence to Crystal. He had to tell her first of his intentions, reveal his heart to her slowly, lest he scare her away.

Crystal took a torch from the wall before squeezing through a narrow crevice. Steep steps led them into the bowels of the keep. Water burbled so loudly now it was hard to ignore. *It must be an underground river,* Avalan thought.

At last they halted before an iron-studded door. Crystal knocked. When no answer came, she pushed the door open. Thick, stuffy air wafted out. Avalan tasted dust, ash, leather, and iron.

When Crystal raised her torch, the flames illuminated a chamber full of parchments. Some lay scattered over the floor. Others were bound with thread and leather in heavy tomes. Stacked atop each other, they lined the walls. A lone plinth stood in the middle of the room. On it, a heavy tome lay open as if someone had been studying it.

"What is this place?" Avalan asked.

"Stonemistress Luthea's memories." Crystal strode to the open tome, licked her fingers, then turned its pages.

"Memories," Avalan mused as he joined her. Endless the logs seemed to him, a working no one less than one thousand years old could have accomplished. "How old do you think the stonemasters are?"

Crystal smiled. "Older than the stones, that is for certain." She let out a cry of joy as her finger landed on a page. The first letter was gilded. Crystal offered Avalan the torch. "Here, hold this for me while I read to you. It is a tale from the times of war. 'And when the Onyx demanded the surrender of the tribe's youth, Chief Othor came seeking my counsel. "The talons will spare our town, but for this small sacrifice," the chief confessed to me. A thousand able boys, the tribe held, and near two thousand gifted girls, all of them trained with their Black Opal birthstones. I begged the chief not to relent to the extortion of sharp claws, and yet he wouldn't listen. A fortnight his forehead burned with fever and fear, and swiftly his mind rotted. A thousand talons were sent forth, escorting our young blood away from Raekandar.

"'That night, Zilthana and Uldrev came to me, two of our master stonecarvers, their faces pale, their souls near departed. Through moans of pain, they avowed their deed to me. Both of their Black Opals they had broken into a thousand pieces each. These pieces of their birthstones they had hidden under the skin of our surrendered children before the talons took them away. "I shall find them," Zilthana said, and of her words I had no doubt, for only the Black Opal traces the path back to itself.

"'Once I had nursed them back from death, Uldrev felt the calling. The thousand pieces of his soul tugged at his heart, leading his footsteps. Despite the chief's refusals, our stonecarvers led the tribe into the lairs of Onyx. Slaves our children had become, and once freed and returned to Raekandar's walls, a black tear marked Zilthana's and Uldrev's faces. "We could only break our stones into a thousand pieces each," they had said, their words a dire reminder of those other Black Opal souls that were lost, and never found. I told them they had used their stones well.'"

Crystal's eyes were filled with tears when she raised her gaze to him. "I used to think my husband's stone was evil. But then I read the mistress's logs. They speak of brave deeds during the war and before it. The stones aren't evil. The ways you use them are. You must trust your heart, my love. Without trust, your Bloodstone cannot guide you. Ronan told me he wished you could see that."

The light from the torch licked Avalan's cheeks, his heart heavy. As if the black walls around them had heard the tale, they glistened with the colors of the rainbow. Beads of hope in the darkness. Hope that the stones weren't all evil. Avalan reached for Crystal's hand. "Thank you."

In the dim chamber, the shadow stirred.

Avalan's heart lifted. Never before had he been so eager to follow the shadow and reach his Bloodstone. Yet he had to wait for this night to be over. He peered into those Larimar eyes that gave him hope. "Come with me, Crystal. Along with Hydrus, I shall free you as well."

She recoiled. "You mustn't. Promise me you will forget me. Soon you will be gone, and all will return to how it was before."

"You're miserable beside him."

"I have my daughter ... She's worth staying for."

Avalan pulled her closer. "And we shall return for her. I promise you this. Ethelnar may be mad with anger because he sees my love for you, but the child has no blame in this. He wouldn't dare touch her. Once you're safe back in Hydrus, I promise you—"

She put two fingers on his lips. "You mustn't talk like this. You mustn't ..."

"I still love you."

Though her lips trembled, she managed a smile. "And I you, but you don't know Ethelnar. He'll never let me go. Never."

Her words couldn't suppress the hope that swelled in Avalan's heart. "Once Hydrus is ours, Bassalt will no longer hold the power to send you back to Raekandar. All the young men will fight alongside me. I have left Colgar in my place, and we even have the aid of a stonemaster."

Her eyes widened. "Colgar is helping you?"

"He's a changed man. We left our differences behind for the same cause—a free Hydrus."

Her touch suddenly felt colder, stiffer. "It will never work," she told him, her gaze defiant. "You always were a great dreamer, but what do you know about the power of the stones? Ethelnar and Bassalt are accomplished in their ways, and yet all you have to show is a mere dagger. Going against them will risk your life and all of those who follow you."

"You mean to hurt me," Avalan said, lowering his voice. "But it won't work. I have witnessed the power of the stones on weapons, and now I feel much surer of what I should do. Once I find the Heart of the

Bloodstone, it will be they who should fear the fire in my soul, for I will not live one more moment of my life in slavery."

"The Heart of the Bloodstone?" Crystal shook her head. "Is this the scheme you're preparing? Oh, Avalan, how can you be so arrogant to think you can go only where a stonemaster is allowed?"

"I do not fear the challenge. I shall take the birthstone that was denied me and use it to free my tribe."

"You'll never find the way … It is forbidden. No one ever goes—"

"I have a guide."

She halted, her eyes searching his for the truth. "What guide do you speak of?"

"I shall show you." Avalan bit his lip. Perhaps he risked too much by confessing this to Crystal, but he couldn't bear to see the hopelessness in her gaze any longer. He lowered the torch to the ground. "Make no move."

For a long while, they stood still, their breaths catching in their chests. Until the second shadow stirred. Crystal started, but Avalan held her in place.

"It's harmless," he told her as the shadow's dark hand fell over her face.

"A shadow guide?"

"It will lead me to the Heart. I'll take back what Bassalt tore from me. From all of us."

Before she could answer him, he pulled her close, pressing his lips to hers. Their kiss was filled with guilt and lust and was swiftly broken by the sound of drums. Muffled and distant they were, coming from above, but their meaning was clear to both of them.

"The ritual is starting," Crystal said, caressing Avalan's cheek. A faint guilt shadowed her eyes. "I wish so much to be with you. All of you. Bhoran will need you tonight after what has happened. Nexanthos, our medic, said he looked a broken man when he left Lusha's side, feared he might harm himself."

At her words, Avalan frowned, confused. "Has Lusha learned about the snake?"

Crystal's blank stare told him that wasn't the matter.

"I promised Lusha not to speak, but it appears the herb was too strong for her body. I never should have … She's fine now, resting. Nexanthos said she just needs sleep." She bit her lip.

"Whatever herb are you speaking of? Did something poison Lusha?"

"She feared she might catch Bhoran's child."

Though startled, Avalan nodded slowly. He was no stranger to the notion of women taking herbs to cleanse their bellies of seed. After all, his mother was the only one in Hydrus who would listen with a compassionate heart to the mistakes of a drunken night in the forest of blackwoods. "Are you certain she will recover?"

"I am. I gave her only little. I feel so ashamed … The union of the stones poisoned her mind with dark thoughts of the Onyx. No matter what I said, she wouldn't change her mind."

In truth, that part of the ritual had vexed Avalan too. The way the stones had fought reminded him of Dizredek. His liquids had wrestled the same way before they had formed a Bloodstone. "You did well," he told her. "If you hadn't given it to her, perchance she would have found another way herself, and then it might not have been a little she had taken."

She held his face with both hands. "I must go. My husband is already drunk. I beg of you, Avalan, stay far away from him tonight. I daren't think what else he'll do once more wine flows through him."

"Fear not." *The next time I see Ethelnar, I will be better equipped,* he thought. If only Eyedir kept his word, Avalan could possess a Bloodstone after this night. One that would be no match for the Heart, but it would do to fight the chief and free Crystal.

Unwillingly Avalan watched her slip through the door, taking his heart with her. As he'd expected, the shadow slithered after her. His chest tightened, and he knew it wasn't because the shadow trailed Crystal now instead of leading him to the Bloodstone. Rather, he knew the Night of the Spirits had arrived. A full moon would be shining bright now over Hydrus, and he hoped with all his heart Marebore wouldn't lead the men to a hopeless fight.

CHAPTER THIRTY-FIVE

DRUMS POUNDED IN THE NIGHT. Bhoran flinched. He reached for Yekana but found she was no longer by his side. Above him, the sky glowed with the silver light of a full moon. *The Night of the Spirits,* he thought, pushing himself onto unsteady feet. He teetered toward the sickhouse.

Bedsheets shrouded Lusha. Under the ample candlelight, Bhoran was glad to see some rosy color had returned to her lips. "How is she?" he asked the medic.

The small man gave Bhoran a good look, from shaved, fang-pierced head to naked feet. "She will sleep through the night. Do not expect her to wake before the sun rises."

"I'll wait." Bhoran made to sit, but the man whipped the air with a sweet-smelling cloth as if to rid the place of a fly.

"I think it best you leave. She'll be afraid when she wakes, disoriented and guilty. Best if she has a moment to realize the consequences of her actions before she has to explain herself to you. The Night of the Spirits calls for a great celebration. Go. And this time, choose to have only some drink. Our ale and wine are strong."

"I will go. You will care for her when she wakes?"

"I shan't leave her side," the medic promised.

Bhoran followed the clangor of tankards and clatter of wooden plates. As he came closer to the feasting ground, he saw a wooden platform had been raised in the middle of the sward. A long table hosted Chief Ethelnar and Chiefess Crystal. On it, platters and flagons overflowed with game, wine, and roasted roots. Bhoran caught their aromas on the wind, his stomach an aching grumble. Above the rulers, four high poles held two tapestries. In one, the Larimar flowed like a tamed sea, and in the other shone the Black Opal, colorful in the middle and black around the edges.

He stared at the two stones for a while, trying to picture a union of the Moonstone and an Onyx. *Which stone would prevail? Light or darkness?* His gaze went to the courtyard. There, a lonely chair stood, and Bhoran knew it at once to be the chief's seat. Plain and old it was, much like the one they used in Hydrus to celebrate the Night of the Spirits. Around it, a rope tethered to poles shielded it from approach.

Bhoran lifted his head to the full moon. He knew the courtyard's position hadn't been chosen at random. The light of the full moon would fall on the chair at its peak. Then, if the stones willed it, the seat would remain empty, and Ethelnar would still be the ruler of Raekandar. If not ...

"Bhoran." Avalan's hand fell heavily on his shoulder. His smile was broad but held a sadness that told Bhoran he already knew about Lusha.

"She's asleep," Bhoran told him. "Will be till dawn."

Avalan nodded. "Come," he said with a breath that already smelled of wine. "I've found us a nice place by the roasting pits."

They sat on soft grass by a fire. They feasted on roasted pork and honeyed spuds and clanged their full tankards with tribesmen they hadn't seen before and shared nothing with but for the mutual understanding of this night's significance—the honoring of the fallen in the War of the Stones, and the celebration of the chiefs left behind to lead the tribes to a better future.

The sound of drums grew louder and louder, and soon the mellow singing turned into a powerful clamor of rhythmic voices. Bhoran felt the spirits of the tribe rise, and soon enough he watched them leave their companies to join each other in a fervent dance, where legs and arms and fingers entangled in a circle of sweating human flesh.

Despite the joy of the night, his heart remained heavy.

Another arm landed on Bhoran's shoulder, and this time, Bhoran knew it wasn't Avalan's. It took him some moments to discern the face of the man looming above him. Backlit by the roasting fire, he looked sturdy, scarcely forty years of age, with hair shaved so short he would have passed for bald. Works of ink like the ones Bhoran had on his own body covered his scalp.

Bhoran brushed the stranger's hand off his shoulder. The man backed away, raising his arms. "Calm. I come in peace." A wide smile revealed golden caps on some of his teeth. It was too dark to see the color of his eyes, yet Bhoran thought it wouldn't matter. After all, no one had eyes darker than his.

"Who are you?" Avalan asked from beside him.

"Name's Elaforn of the Azurite. Why don't you join me and my company for a good game?"

Bhoran drained his ale and stood. "I've no interest in stupid death games. Avalan here loves a good legend."

The stranger brought a fist to his chest, as if offended. "The only legends we deal with are the *real* ones. It is the Night of the Spirits."

Bhoran leaned dangerously close to the man's face. "Why do you seek us? We know nothing of these games."

The stranger cracked his knuckles. "We play with true tribal heroes and stones—*real* stones. And they say you're of the Onyx, and you"—he looked at Avalan—"of the bloody stone. We've never played with a true Onyx among us before. Dead men play no games."

At the mention of the Onyx, Bhoran could hold his anger no longer. He grabbed the man by his tunic. "The stones matter no more than horse's shit to us. We are of Hydrus."

Avalan shoved them apart. "What has bitten you?" he yelled. Avalan's green eyes pierced Bhoran's, the way they always did when he wanted Bhoran to understand without words. Whatever Avalan wanted him to grasp, however, the sweet drunkenness of ale and wine and Yekana's venom made it hard to discern.

Despite the fervor of the music and the dancing, the tribe was noticing the commotion. Bhoran didn't care. He'd let them watch all they wanted. He had nothing more to lose.

Avalan grabbed Bhoran's arm and turned to the stranger. "Lead the way. Now."

The man slid through the crowd with a determined gait that betrayed no intoxication. Bhoran grabbed a cup from the tray of a passing wench and gulped it down before he even smelled its contents. It gave him an unpleasant jolt in the chest and a sting on his tongue. *What was that?* He glanced over his shoulder, but the girl was lost in the crowd, and Avalan kept pulling him along the trail of the Azurite.

Why does Avalan trust him? Bhoran didn't know which smelled worse—the stranger's breath or his intentions.

The man steered them through a door and up a spiral staircase with narrow steps.

In the darkness of the slim tower, Bhoran could barely see the stranger ahead. "How much farther?"

"Almost there."

Soon after, the man pushed a trapdoor over their heads, and the glowing light of the full moon touched their faces. They emerged atop the tower. Sparse battlements lined the edges. The feast's clamor sounded fainter from up here.

Three men rose to greet them.

"Tribesmen of Hydrus, welcome," the shortest of them said in a soft voice that didn't match his vicious appearance of a hunter. His skin was scarred with old wounds and fresh scores. A short axe hung from his belt, perfect for a swift, merciful kill. "My name is Aras, and these here are Jorgamur"—he gestured to a hooded man who cradled a flask—"and Erieth." A bare-chested, scrawny man raised his dagger-holding fist in greeting.

"Avalan," Avalan said, bringing a fist to his chest. "And this is Bhoran."

"Names bear no meaning," Bhoran said. He glared at the short table amid the men. "What are we here for? And where are the drinks?"

"We need our wits about us for this," Elaforn said. "Come, let us begin. I want to return to the feast to witness the calling of the spirit of the former chief."

Bhoran huffed. "This is all a jest." He motioned to the celebration below. "No spirit ever comes."

Jorgamur, his voice slow and slurred, told him, "The summer of nineteen years past speaks of a different story." He pulled his cowl back and looked at them, flecks of gold in his icy stare. "The spirit challenged Chief Othor, the ruler of Raekandar after the war. Ten good men fought him then, and it was Chief Ethelnar who landed the final blow and took the place on the chair."

Bhoran didn't blink an eye. *If that story is true,* he thought, *then cursed be the spirit of past chief Volkan for letting the old boar Bassalt rule our village in such a way.*

"Don't bore our guests with stories of succession," Elaforn said, sitting on the tower's stone. The men followed his lead.

Bhoran exchanged a glance with Avalan before sitting on the uneven surface.

The full moon bathed the table in opal light. Bhoran saw a pile of stones, the familiar colors of Avalan's Bloodstone on one of them. He knew then what Avalan was trying to tell him. *Eyedir promised Avalan a Bloodstone.* Next to the birthstones lay a deck of round tiles. Baked clay they seemed to be, and the one on top held the drawn figure of a man Bhoran had never seen before.

"What is this game?" Avalan asked.

"As I've already told you, this is a game of heroes and stones," Elaforn said, spreading his arms in a dramatic gesture.

Erieth, the bare-chested man, spoke for the first time. "Every year during the celebration of the Night of the Spirits, we gather away from prying eyes to reenact the final battle of the War of the Stones. To pay our tribute to the real heroes, the ones who helped us win the fight against the filthy Onyx." His eyes, sharp like a hawk's, searched Bhoran's face.

Clenching his fists, Bhoran waited. He didn't much like where all this was going, but Avalan's need to get his hands on a Bloodstone was enough to make him tolerate the insinuations.

Erieth spread the tiles faceup on the table before tapping a finger on one drawing. "I believe you'll have no difficulty recognizing this hero."

A chill crawled up Bhoran's spine. Beneath Erieth's finger, Olnos stared at him through eyes of dark Onyx. Without thinking, Bhoran took the tile. Until now, he had only seen Olnos as a marble statue. Yet here …

He drank in the features of the brave warrior who had kept him company and borne witness to the happiest and darkest moments of his life. Everything that had mattered in Bhoran's life—his lonely moments, his first kiss, his condemnation to death, and his lovemaking with Lusha—had happened beneath the eyes of this dead man, these dark Onyx eyes, black and soulless like Bhoran's. And yet there it was, a small speck of white, like a grain of dust, staining the warrior's eye. Bhoran rubbed a thumb over the stain.

"These tiles are rare," Erieth complained, snatching the tile back. "Don't go smudging the ink all over now." He restored the tile to its place.

Bhoran shot him an angry glance, but when he looked at his finger, it had a small dark stain on it.

"Whom else have you got there?" Avalan asked, leaning closer.

"Everyone who matters," Erieth said. He pointed to a slender figure shrouded by a dark cloud. Bhoran had never seen him, but it wasn't hard to deduce who this man was. "Velderith, the lord of the Onyx. He was the chief who started it all—greedy for domination."

Aras, the snippy hunter, placed a stubby finger over the figure of a man with a stern look on his bony face. "This was our chief, Abarat, the leader of the Tiger's Eye. Fought bravely, but soon after succumbed to wounds inflicted by the war." More names were spoken as Aras presented them with all the chiefs of the twelve stones.

Yet Bhoran's head was heavy from drink and dark thoughts about his future with Lusha for him to pay much attention.

"Enough explaining," Elaforn said, gathering the stones and tiles. "A tale is best told through actions, so we had best proceed. Aras, Jorgamur, Erieth … if memory serves me well, it is my turn to be the chronicler this year."

The rest shook their heads, and Elaforn gave Bhoran and Avalan a grin. "Let me tell you the story of the battle of Krokador's Stronghold."

"The one that burned to the ground?" Avalan asked, earning a disapproving glance from Elaforn, who ignored him and got back to his story.

"As I was saying"—he placed the tile of Velderith in the middle —"it was a night like tonight. A full moon burned with red fury, and mist danced around it. Later, that night would be celebrated as the Night of the Spirits, but for them, it was the night Velderith, the Onyx chief, and his cronies invaded Krokador's Stronghold and hid themselves away, desperate to regain their footings and replenish the power of their stones." He plucked an Onyx stone from the row and placed it over Velderith's tile.

Bhoran exchanged a surprised look with Avalan. *He can touch it, and he isn't of the Onyx,* Bhoran thought, his belly squirming. *Bassalt, you wretched ...*

Elaforn's voice rose higher. "But the noble warriors soon surrounded him, ready to wield their stones of justice and wipe the Onyx from the face of the Stone Lands." He laid out the tiles of the other leaders around Velderith one by one until he'd formed a perfect circle, and then he went on with his story. "The tales speak of Volkan of the Fire Agate, the mighty chief of Hydrus, who sacrificed himself for the good of the tribes." Elaforn pinched a stone of colorful fire and placed it atop the tile of Volkan. He was a tall man with long, raven hair streaked with red. Then his fingers reached for the Bloodstone. "Erharis," he said, offering the stone to Avalan. "The just chief of the Bloodstone, and the one who united them all."

Avalan studied the stone, cupping it in his gloved hand.

Elaforn waved a guiding hand over the tile of the Bloodstone ruler. "Go on. Pay your tribute to your former chief."

The Bloodstone cracked against clay as Avalan released it. Bhoran watched the men shoot him sharp glances, yet Elaforn picked the story up from where he had left it.

"Chief Othor of the Black Opal," he said, placing the birthstone atop him. "Eryhan of the Moonstone."

Bhoran eyed the Moonstone Elaforn placed over the tile. It was much larger than the one he'd given Lusha, and yet it didn't glisten under the moonlight as hers always did. *Curious.* For a small moment, he wondered where these men had found these stones he very much doubted were theirs to keep. He tried to recall what Eyedir had told them about the birthstones and their owners, yet his memory failed him. Though he'd slept through the middle hours of the day, a cloudy tiredness tugged at his mind and body.

He pierced a fingertip against one of the snake fangs in his face, hoping the venom would clear his thinking. From below, the clamor got louder. *Just a few moments more,* he thought. *Then the Night of the Spirits will be over, and Avalan will have his stone.*

His gaze still lingered on the large Moonstone. The way it stood there, dim and heartless, made the hair against his nape stand. *Could they be stones of the dead?* Suddenly he had a relentless urge to go to Lusha, hold her and feel the blood pulsing through her body. To *know* she was alive.

A thousand stares weighed Bhoran down; the attention of all the men was on him, making him realize he'd stopped listening.

"What will it be?" Elaforn said.

Confused, Bhoran glanced at the board before him. They had placed all the other stones over their chiefs ... all but one. The one that belonged to Olnos. An Onyx stone now rested in the open palm of Elaforn. He patiently waited for Bhoran to take it and do the honors.

Avalan nodded in encouragement, and Bhoran plucked the stone from Elaforn's hand. As in Hydrus during his trial, he felt nothing.

"Place it over Olnos," Elaforn whispered, as if not to disturb a higher power.

Bhoran was sick of these games. He made to do as he had been told, only the stone resisted. It was a faint push at first, but it grew stronger, as if the stone was loath to touch the tile beneath it. With a determined push, Bhoran forced the stubborn stone over Olnos's tile.

As soon as the Onyx touched Olnos, it spun and rolled to the side, falling off the Great Warrior. The men cheered and laughed. Bhoran glanced at Avalan, who had an equally confused look on his face.

"Why won't the Onyx settle on Olnos?" Avalan asked.

"Because, my fellow," Elaforn said with a victorious smile, "Olnos denied his birthstone. He conquered his true nature and fought against his brothers. An Onyx against Onyx. Without him, the fight would have been lost, and none of us would be here to sing of their sweet victory that night."

Much like the stone, Bhoran's head spun from all the talking. He wanted to roll out of here, down the narrow steps, and across the yard. He wanted to hold Lusha and tell her he could conquer his birthstone too. That they could do it together. Like Olnos, Bhoran could be a hero. "Finish the tale."

"The chiefs stormed the stronghold, killing the Onyx in their way, and when Velderith knew the fight was lost, he started a great fire. It burned so tall and fierce that the weeping tears of the moon fell like fiery rain. All the chiefs raced outside to save themselves. All but one.

"Your great chief Volkan, who wanted to see with his own eyes the end of Velderith. And so he hurled himself through the fire, brandishing his sword and the fire power of his birthstone, sacrificing his life for the good of others. And just like that, the Onyx was defeated, and the tribes came to be one and celebrate their dead during the night of the spirits."

A deathly silence descended below. The men rushed to the battlements. Bhoran went with them. Over the stony ridge, he glimpsed the chief's chair far below. Shafts of moonlight shone directly above it, and it remained empty. *The spirits approve of the chief.*

"Ethelnar! Ethelnar!" The chanting spread like wildfire. Elaforn and his companions picked up the song.

Crooked fingers cupped Bhoran's shoulder, and he turned. Jorgamur, the man who had worn a cowl despite the heat of the summer, had now thrown his hood back. In his eyes, Bhoran saw the glimmer of molten gold. On the tight line of his lips, Bhoran read unspoken words that made his heart freeze. He wanted to brush the man's hand off, but it was as if his arms and legs were frozen. *I shouldn't have had so much to drink,* he thought.

Without a word, the man released him.

Over his shoulder, Bhoran looked at the table. Avalan was staring at the Bloodstone in his hands, his brows low in concentration. *This is your chance,* Bhoran thought. The men still had their backs to the table, cheering and yelling. *Take it.* Avalan put the stone back on its tile.

When he raised his head to meet Bhoran's gaze, a haunted look was etched on his features.

Bhoran returned his attention to the hailing tribe below. As he stared at the empty chief's chair, all he could think of was Volkan. Elaforn had said the former chief of Hydrus had sacrificed his life for the good of the tribes, and yet his spirit had yet to come to overthrow Bassalt.

CHAPTER THIRTY-SIX

A COOL WIND whispered through the fissures of the basalt walls in the chief's bedchamber. It chilled Bassalt to the bone.

The night of the spirits had fallen, and Bassalt could have sworn he'd never seen a sky so purple before. Bruised it was, like a deep wound, like the spilling of bad blood beneath the skin of those stricken by the Red Weal. He shivered as two of his servants draped a white panther's hide over his shoulders. *Summer nights shouldn't be this cold,* he thought, disgruntled. *Or is it my own soul that's frozen?*

Behind the closed door of his bedchamber, muffled voices came. He glanced at the heavy iron barring the entrance. No one was to cross his threshold tonight, he'd warned Theran. Not even Silver. Yet it wasn't the voice of Silver that he heard. Rather, it was a voice he loved, but from the sound of it, she loved him not.

With a deep sigh, he turned to his manservants. "Leave me."

"Your hand, my chief," one of them protested, holding out a glove.

Bassalt followed his gaze to the purple wound of his maimed hand. *I ought to have returned to the cavern, retrieved my finger,* he thought bitterly, and yet whenever he made to think of this task, a harrowing tightness in his chest threatened to squeeze all life out of him. *Cursed, cursed ring.* "There is no shame in injury," he said. Farmera's voice outside grew hotter, her demands to see him overbearing Theran's protests. "I shall not need you further."

The men bowed, lifted the bar, and shuffled outside. As soon as Bassalt had seen the last of them, Farmera strode into the room, her eyes burning with rage. "What have you done, Bassalt?" Theran followed behind her, trying desperately to stop her. Yet she would have none of it. "You cannot execute a teacher of the stones!"

"Theran, leave us. I shall lock the door."

All color had left the poor man's face. "I ... I am so sorry, my chief. She slipped through the guards with the pretense of coming to tend to your wound ..."

Would that it were true. Bassalt raised his maimed hand to silence him. "Go to the feasting ground. See that the preparations are coming along as needed."

Theran nodded and skittered out like a scared mouse.

"Look at me, stones curse you!" Farmera yelled as soon as they were left alone. "What madness stirred you to this decision? Where is the stonemaster now?"

Bassalt hefted the heavy bar into place. "Lower your voice when you speak to me."

"If my begging and reasoning do nothing to move you, perhaps my anger will," Farmera retorted. "What have you become, Bassalt? What hatred in your heart moves you to act so? Have you no mercy for your soul? For the good of our village?"

"It is for the good of this cursed village I am acting so. Need I remind you Ronan rots under this very soil? Need I tell you his death is still unpunished and the shadow of the Onyx looms above us?"

"You'd have me believe Delion killed Ronan? On what account?"

Bassalt threw his arms in the air. "Delion, Bhoran, the stones ... what does it matter anymore? Someone needs to be punished. My men found Delion lurking in the spot of the merchant's murder."

"A stonemaster would never—"

"I know him much more than you ever will." Bassalt brandished an angry fist, losing his patience. "I know what he's capable of. He didn't come here to pay us a simple visit. Stonemasters are evil. In their wake, they leave destruction and pain."

"He's your teacher!"

"Was," Bassalt reminded her. "And this madness, this hatred you say I have inside me, was planted there by his teachings. He was the one who taught me mercy is for the weak and justice should always prevail. Am I not to practice his own teachings on him?"

Farmera's face fell. "If you realize your threats …"

"Then what? You will love me less? You come here to insult my judgment and demand mercy from me when it was you who gave me none. You made your choice for a man, so don't act as if your counsel should stir my heart."

Resigned, Farmera shook her head. "I thought you a better man. You're condemning us all. I pity you, Bassalt, and all you have become." She turned on her heel, shoved the bar out of place, and let it fall. The clang of iron on the stone floor drowned out the sound of her departing footsteps.

Cursed, cursed. Bassalt felt utterly helpless, a feeling he loathed as much as the love that still seared his heart when he saw her. He stormed out, shoving aside the guards that came into his way.

The air outside was heavy with fear. Bassalt could smell it, despite the odors of soups simmering in cauldrons. The preparations for the feast would not serve as a distraction from all that had been said the night before of punishments and death. The tribe was simmering as well; anger and fear mingled in a concoction that would soon boil. Bassalt needed to hurry.

He hobbled down the dirt path that led to the northern gate. As he drew farther from the burning fires, darkness deepened, and the soil beneath his feet became damp. Wind swayed the branches of the trees. In his mind's eye, he saw the dragon, whispering to him over a flitting tongue: *You are not worthy …*

He pressed fat palms over his ears and lengthened his stride. A moan escaped his mouth as he strove to drown out the taunting voices.

Soon Olnos's head surfaced over the treetops, and Bassalt dared to remove his hands—relieving silence.

He circled to the back of the statue. There the stone was ragged and unshaped, as if the maker had paid it little heed. Nobody was ever admired from behind. Yet Bassalt knew better. He stuck his thumb into a hollow spot, then shoved the heavy stone wall to the side, revealing the chamber within.

Darkness drenched the narrow room until Bassalt traced a smooth surface on the wall before him. A glimmer of green light illuminated his face. He averted his gaze until his eyes got used to the sudden breach of darkness. The light grew stronger, filling the room with eerie shadows. He studied its source—a glass sphere the size of a small boulder was embedded in the wall.

Bassalt squinted but found no etchings on its polished surface. *Cursed Ethelnar. He hasn't sent a word.* There would be no aid from Raekandar, Bassalt knew then. The wretched Black Opal ruler had dared to defy him and his orders, and Bassalt would have to make this arrogant chief pay. But now wasn't the time, for there were greater forces lurking in the shadows.

He gritted his teeth and touched the stone. His stubby fingers worked, leaving behind a white trace as he etched the message on its surface. Words appeared and disappeared as fast as they had come, absorbed into the thirsty sphere.

The message was simple, yet one that hadn't been spoken nor written over the stones that lived inside the statues of Olnos scattered over the Stone Lands for years. A message sure to make the chiefs unite under a great council in the city of Laenathas: *The Onyx has returned.*

Bassalt breathed more easily as he emerged from the statue of Olnos. He had done his sacred duty—he had warned them—and it was now up to them all to honor the agreement of union against the greater enemy. For now, his own duty was to deliver proper punishment to the tribe.

He retraced his steps back to Hydrus.

A cool sea breeze welcomed him to the feasting ground. Tables and benches had been drawn back. Bassalt had arrived in time to see the men carry the chief's seat to the middle. A simple wooden chair it was, with planks so fragile Bassalt was convinced its construction must have been symbolic, for surely a mockery of a chair like this could not hold the voluminous presence of a chief. Especially the chief of Hydrus.

His servants and Silver's men surrounded the wooden platform that hosted his table. They were all armed with sharpened spears and wary eyes. Atop the platform and around a pole, Stonemaster Delion's hands were tethered. His head lolled to the side, a waterfall of gray hair streaming over his face. Bassalt tightened his fists. All his efforts to make the stonemaster talk had come to nothing. Delion's lips were tightly sealed, and no threats could dissuade him from keeping his silence.

Bassalt climbed the steps and collapsed onto his chair. Through slitted eyes, he watched the tribe prepare for the Night of the Spirits. Yet the air stank of their betrayal. What used to be a night of celebration and great feasting had now become a grim preparation fit only for a burial, rather than a protraction of the chief's reign.

Of course, they did what they always did, but only half of their heart was in it. He watched the women sit around big boiling cauldrons, sharp knives in their hands, cutting the vegetables with such hatred, as if it were the necks of men that they were cutting. Carrots and turnips were hurled inside the pots with such force that boiling water splashed around, scorching the grass beneath. The men skinned the animals with slow, steady movements, keeping their gazes low, muttering curses under their breath, and when they looked up but for a mere moment, Bassalt saw hatred dripping from their eyes.

They like me not, but that makes no matter. For a ruler, fear is a better concession than love.

Silver appeared when the tall fires had been lit and the rhythm of drums and voices filled the air. His shaven hair caught the firelight. A golden sheen blazed in his eyes. As he climbed the staircase to take his place, Bassalt gazed thoughtfully at the sky. Dark clouds loomed above them like a thick blanket.

Silver glanced at the fallen stonemaster, then sat heavily on his chair. He leaned over. "Tell me you haven't lost your mind and this is all a jest."

Bassalt granted him a stern look. "Spare me the talk of sacrilege. I've had enough of this from Farmera."

"She's right. I will have no part in this, Bassalt, I warn you. I will not stain my hands with a stonemaster's blood."

Bassalt raised a curious brow. "I didn't realize you held the masters close to heart."

"Look at the man. He has one foot in his grave. What sympathy do you think you'll gain by punishing a wizened relic?"

The sound of drums tore the air, startling them both. Bassalt leaned over to Silver. "It isn't their sympathy I seek, you fool. It is their anger. Don't you see how they seethe and fume? Don't you feel the hatred oozing from the pores of their skin? Do you not see the scowls etched upon their faces?"

Such a scowl distorted Silver's face now as he cast his gaze like a fishing net over the feasting ground. Bassalt shouldn't have called him a fool, he knew, but he was certain his mighty commander could feel the tribe's anger for himself. The air carried a pungent whiff. And it wasn't the smell of onions flavoring the soups, neither the sour wine that filled their flagons and wetted the tribe's lips. It was the sheer hatred that emanated from their bodies.

The drums boomed like the thunder of doom; plates clattered like lightning, and though the clouds weren't those of a storm, it seemed to Bassalt a great rain would pour on his reign tonight. *It will be as it will be,* he thought. *I am the chief of Hydrus.*

"They will attack us," Silver observed.

Bassalt grunted and threw a chicken wing in his mouth. Bones crunched between his teeth.

Silver faced him with angered eyes. "You *wanted* this."

Bassalt shrugged. "Rejoice and enjoy the food. They will wait until the moon has reached its peak and the spirits accept me for their chief once more. Then their anger will spill. Until then, there isn't much to fear."

His face lined with worry, Silver reached for his sword, caressed the Heliodor that adorned its hilt. "Blood will be spilled."

"They chose this. For a long time now, I have smelled the stench of their betrayal in the air. At first I thought Farmera's son to be their leader, but now I see it was all Delion's doing." He shot a hateful glance at the stonemaster, who hadn't moved since Bassalt's servants had dragged him to the platform.

"What of my daughter?" Silver demanded.

"Ethelnar has sent word," Bassalt lied. *So many lies.* "He will deliver her to us after the Night of the Spirits."

"Is she faring well?"

"She is." Bassalt hoped it was true.

"And of the talon?"

The wine slid down Bassalt's throat like a sour rivulet. "Bhoran won't be an easy task, but you should not concern yourself with him."

Silver leaned closer, his spittle flying out with every word. "As long as he lives, he won't leave my daughter alone."

Bassalt dug his knife into a succulent piece of goat. Juice trickled down the flesh to form a small pool on his plate. "He won't return as long as I stand as chief. So make it your life's purpose to see this fight through for both of us."

With plates and cups emptied, the tribesfolk soon left their feasting tables to join hands around the fire. Bassalt closed his eyes and *listened* to the ground. The men's footsteps thumped against the soil; their breeches jingled with hidden metal. Louder and louder, the clangs of concealed weapons resounded in Bassalt's mind as more tribesmen fell into the dancing circle. *They mean to trick my eyes, but they don't know there's little my Tiger's Eye doesn't see.*

"My chief." Theran's mousy voice broke his concentration. "The sky's filled with clouds."

"What of it?" Bassalt barked.

"How ... how will we tell, my chief, when the moon is at its peak? We cannot see it."

Bassalt raised his eyes to the gray sky. Theran had the truth of it, but it didn't matter. For as long as he'd been chief of Hydrus, Volkan had never returned to claim the seat. "Pick any time, and make it soon," he said with a dismissive wave. "If *we* can't see it, the men won't either."

At the chief's behest, Theran slipped off the platform and marched his way to the drum men to pass the orders. Bassalt watched with increasing satisfaction as the fervent beating of the drums eased to a much slower thudding. It fell into rhythm with the pumping of his own heart—slow, dragging. Confusion spread over the tribe's faces, as the celebration was reaching its most anticipated moment faster than they'd expected. Heads turned to the sky, and Bassalt heard curious whispers that spoke of clouds and signs.

The dancing circle broke; all words ceased. The fires crackled and burned; the drums resounded, faster and faster now, until Bassalt could no longer discern the vibrations of his stone from those of his surroundings. His seat could no longer hold him. He rose and knelt beside the stonemaster. "Behold how much the spirits love me," he whispered over the matted hair that covered the old man's face. "Behold the chief's chair remaining empty for one more year, and see for yourself nothing can beat me. As *you* taught me, *master*."

The drumming reached its peak, the palms of the men red with blood as they pounded the skins over and over. Then, with a desperate yell, the drummers gave one final stroke and fell back, dipping the celebration into silence. Bassalt held his breath. His gaze was transfixed by the chief's seat.

Beneath the shadow of the clouded sky, the seat remained empty.

Theran was the first to clap his hands, breaking the silence.

A glorious laughter left Bassalt's mouth. He staggered to his feet, clutched at the stonemaster's hair, and hefted Delion's head. "Tribe of Hydrus! Once more the spirits of old have deemed me worthy to lead you into another year of peace and union. Evil has sneaked through our defenses." He shook the master's head. "Penetrated our peaceful, stoneless lives, and spread lies that have marred your minds with thoughts of mutiny. Yet this ailment shall now end." From the pocket of his robe, Bassalt brought forth the Onyx dagger. "The same weapon that took from us our beloved merchant will now end the life of this filthy stonemaster—"

An arrow flew. It tore the night air like the swooping of a hawk, its prey Bassalt's dagger-cradling hand. Bassalt thrust Delion down and caught the shaft in midair. Beneath his swollen fingers, the wood cracked, and the two pieces fell onto the platform.

Above them, the clouds parted, the silver light of the moon bathing the chief's seat in an eerie glow. Salty rain poured from the sky.

It was then Bassalt saw it: a misty shadow, a silver wisp of a being drifting through the night. By the time the tribe had noticed it, the entity was soaring down toward the empty chief's chair. Terrified screams tore the air, and for a moment, Bassalt was certain it was the spirit of Volkan, returning to challenge him. Until he noticed this thing was bigger than a mere man. In truth, it was enormous, and when it finally settled over the empty chief's seat and coiled its spiky tail around its body, water dripping from its opal scales, Bassalt knew exactly what it was.

The waterdragon of Hydrus.

The dragon threw its head back, a terrible shriek leaving its snout, a thin, high sound at the edge of hearing. As if the tribesmen had reclaimed their courage, more arrows flew toward the platform. Silver sprang to his feet, swinging his longsword, swatting the arrows out of the air like flies.

Cursed, cursed! Bassalt clambered down to the back of the platform, knelt, and dipped his fingers into the musty soil.

The earth shook and moaned. Trees were ripped out of the ground as Bassalt bade their vines and roots to come to his aid. Forth he sent them, to form a cage around the platform to protect his men. Arrows kept falling like rain. Bassalt heard Silver scream. He circled to the front to see the commander struck down, a wooden shaft piercing his shoulder.

Bassalt hobbled toward the steps. A fiery blow stung his back, as if an ember burned its way through the white panther's hide. This wasn't natural warmth, Bassalt knew. Through the pain, he recognized the fingers of stone magic. He turned, his gaze meeting the blazing fire that had lit Marebore's Ruby stones. Bassalt's fury was stoked, the memory of war returning so fresh, as if it had only been yesterday that stone had fought against stone. "You dare use stone magic on *me*?"

In answer, Marebore threw his arms forward, twisted his wrists, flexed his fingers upward.

Blood boiled inside Bassalt, liquid fire burning through his veins, threatening to tear him asunder. He breathed, centered the Tiger's Eye in his mind. The fire cooled, but that gave Marebore the chance to slither closer.

"I've waited too long to watch this terror on your face, Bassalt. How do you feel knowing your reign is over? Hydrus has deemed you unworthy."

The waterdragon. Behind Marebore's back, the chief's chair now stood empty. A wild battle raged around it, and Bassalt glimpsed

Silver's men pushing back the angry crowd who wished to reach the platform. Steel met with steel, piercing the air with the shrieks of metal. Men fell on both sides, their flesh pierced by arrows.

"I will *kill* you!" Bassalt yelled in Marebore's face.

The ugliness of death didn't seem to bother Marebore. He charged, this time using the power of his Ruby to sneak into Bassalt's mind and unearth his greatest fear. The nightmare returned stronger than ever, and Bassalt's mind plunged into darkness. Sand whipped his face, and a cloud of whirling black mist raced toward him. *It isn't real!* Bassalt's mind roared. *Cursed Ruby!*

"Whip!" Bassalt roared, regaining his mind. A vine slithered forth, slashed Marebore's shoulder. "Whip! Slash! Kill!" With every order, anger grew inside him.

Marebore screamed as a thorny vine ripped his tunic apart. Beneath the rags, the Ruby on his bare chest caught the firelight and glowed fiercely.

Bassalt bristled. "You still wear your birthstone!"

"Stones curse you, Bassalt! You thought I'd throw my stone to the sea because you ordered it?" From his snakeskin belt, he drew a dagger, slashed at the vines that had crawled around his ankles.

Caught between anger and despair, Bassalt willed the vines to reach for Marebore's chest. Up they went, tugging at the Ruby, scratching and clawing. Marebore screamed in pain, but the stone didn't budge.

"No one," Bassalt said, the words coming out between short pants, "curses me!" *Cursed, cursed.* He spun, made for a nearby table, his fingers grabbling for anything sharp he could use. A silver fork shone in the moonlight. Bassalt snatched it.

The vines curled around Marebore's ankles, threw him back. As he fell, Bassalt was swiftly on him, his rage blinding his mind.

Marebore's eyes were bloodied and wild. "Don't you dare, Bassalt!" he yelled. Against the firm hold of the vines, he writhed with all his strength, yet it was futile.

Bassalt thrust the fork's teeth into Marebore's chest, right underneath the fiery Ruby. He pushed and wriggled until the stone finally broke free. To the ground it rolled, carrying with it some of Marebore's flesh.

Howls tore the air. Marebore fell limp as his strength left him. "Curse you ..." he whispered, his eyes rolling backward.

Bassalt hurled the fork aside and searched the ground for the Ruby on his knees. His fingers fumbled through trampled soil and grass. Behind him, the fight still raged. "Where are you?" he yelled. *Cursed stone. No one should know my greatest fears.*

From his right, a roar came, and Bassalt had but a moment to see the sharp, glistening claws before Sigil tore at the white panther's hide. She fell back, paced the ground, encircling Bassalt.

"Mine!" Bassalt shrieked, his soul reaching for Sigil's. Yet his power crashed against an invisible wall. He tried again, more fiercely this time, only to be thrown back once more, a sharp pain tearing through his body. *It cannot be,* he thought wildly, *unless ...*

He spun. Through the tangled vines of the cage that covered the platform, he saw Delion. The stonemaster's glassy stare was fixed on Sigil.

"What will you do, old man?" Bassalt yelled at him. "Have your years made you such a coward that you will use a tiger to kill me?" He staggered to his feet. "Release her and face me yourself."

"Your tribe is dying," Delion said.

A rain of arrows flew by, one of them scraping the skin of Bassalt's naked arm.

"Argh!"

A fresh bout of arrows answered his cry of pain. Bassalt ducked, called the vines to release Marebore and instead make a net around himself.

"Cowards!" he yelled. "You fight your own chief!"

"Your tribe is dying," Delion reiterated.

Sigil growled, but this time, it wasn't a cry of anger but of pain.

Bassalt grabbed at the vine cage as more arrows flew. The Tiger's Eye opened in his mind, letting him see for the first time with clear vision. Bassalt heard every scream of agony, felt every reverberation of the ground as feet stomped and bodies fell, smelled the stench of sweat and blood that filled the air. "The traitors are dying," he said through gritted teeth.

Sigil growled.

"The chief of Hydrus should protect his tribe," Delion said, his words a knife in the heart.

Fear and a sense of betrayal mingled in Bassalt's chest. He knelt, pressed his fat palms to the soil. A mighty roar escaped his lips as he sent a terrible shake through the ground. The vines that formed the platform cage loosened. Bassalt bade them slither across the ground and wrap themselves around fighting hands and yank their weapons from their grasps. At his behest, the vines forced men and women to the ground, snapped arrows in two, made attackers lose their footing, and brought all this fighting madness to a merciful stop.

Cold thorns needled his body, and Bassalt scrambled for Sigil's soul in a final attempt to stay conscious. It was too late, he knew. As his head touched the cool soil, the last thing Bassalt saw was a curious smirk stretching the stonemaster's lips.

CHAPTER THIRTY-SEVEN

"WHY DIDN'T you take the Bloodstone?"

Avalan shook his head as they walked to the sickhouse. The feast was still going strong, but both Bhoran and Avalan had had enough after the game of the birthstones. Feigning tiredness, they had excused themselves. "I am no thief," Avalan said.

Bhoran nodded. He had an inkling Avalan's pride would prevent him from pocketing a Bloodstone that didn't belong to him. Especially after hearing what the merchant had to say about stealing birthstones.

"Besides ... did you see how dull the stones were? As if their owners ..."

"Were dead," Bhoran finished. They exchanged a glance of mutual understanding.

"I'd rather follow the shadow to my own Bloodstone."

"What of Crystal?"

There hadn't been one moment when the chiefess had left her husband's side. As soon as the spirits of old had blessed Ethelnar as an able ruler for one more year, the celebrations had become even wilder. The dancing had resumed with much greater fervor, yet the chief and chiefess had remained seated. Ethelnar's lips had been stuck to his cup, but over its brim his eyes had been fixed on his wife, her every glance, smile, or nod accounted for.

Avalan grabbed Bhoran's shoulder, forcing him to stop. "Sometimes I wonder if Dizredek bound *me* to the shadow or *her*. I've lost control of it. It now comes only when I'm around her and leaves with her as soon as she crosses the threshold."

Bhoran didn't much like that. Perhaps Avalan's belief that Crystal had something to do with the Heart of the Bloodstone wasn't as unlikely as he had thought. "That leaves you only one choice."

"I need to take her with me. I know that now. It's the only way the shadow will guide me again."

Bhoran tucked his hands into his breeches. "What will you do?"

Avalan's face hardened. "It's best if my actions don't involve you, or Lusha." The cavern's maw was dimly lit by candles flickering in the wind, a wind that carried the smells of sickness and herbs. "Take Lusha to Levorotha. See that both of you make a new beginning. And once I've freed the village from Bassalt, perhaps you can convince her to return to Hydrus."

There was pain in Avalan's eyes. A stark fear rose in Bhoran's chest when he thought of Avalan going against Bassalt armed with a single Bloodstone he hadn't yet mastered. "Perhaps it's best you come with us." Even as he said it, he knew Avalan would object.

"I know there's nothing holding you back, but I cannot leave my mother and Sigil behind. Hydrus is all I know. And I want to see Ronan again, even if it will be his bones that I say my farewells to."

"There must be a way to get them out of the village—"

"And live the rest of our lives as fugitives?" Avalan clenched a fist. "Where would I go?"

Bhoran's heart ached for Olnos then, for that was a question he'd asked himself many a time sitting at the giant's feet. "You want to create a place for us."

Avalan smiled sadly. "Hydrus is a place I can call mine. The blackwood forest holds my heart, the white beach my soul. Our goat games and feasts used to fill me with joy." He tightened his grip around Bhoran's wrist. "This joy is what I long for. Free in our village, we could create a different future. A better one. We could have children, and raise them properly, without the fear of punishment for being different."

Bhoran admired him for these words. Of the two of them, it had always been Avalan with the grand dreams. Bhoran had always been wary and resigned to a life of pain. Lusha had been the only beam of light in his otherwise dark soul. And now she lay here, and though the medic had assured him she would live, Bhoran wasn't sure what he would face once she'd opened her eyes. His soul grew anxious. "I want to go to her."

They found her still deep in sleep. Behind them, the medic rekindled the fire in the middle of the room, feeding it with crackling twigs. "Return in the morning," he told them, mopping sweat from his brow. "She will not wake earlier."

"One moment," Bhoran told Avalan, and he knelt by her side. Her ear felt warm against his lips. "I can change," he whispered. "I can deny the nature of the Onyx. If Olnos could, then so can I. I promise you, my love."

He could not wait to wash the day's dirt from his body and throw himself into bed and a merciful sleep.

"I'll stay with you," Avalan told him as they crossed the keep's great threshold.

Bhoran shook his head. "Take your rest."

"Do not summon Yekana," Avalan cautioned him. "You will not outgrow your fears if you drown them in venom."

Maidservants led them to their chambers. Bhoran pushed the oaken door. Hinges creaked. He froze, a queer presence making his skin prickle. For a slight moment he thought the girl had led him to the wrong room, but soon he found the source of his uneasiness.

Beside his bed, a tall mirror leaned against the wall. Its silver frame glistened in the moonlight. Bhoran was certain it hadn't been there before. He approached it warily. From the glass's surface, his reflection stared back. The clothes the household had given him seemed to him strange and foreign. He took them off and stared at his naked body, fascinated by the image that greeted him. For the first time, he could see his whole reflection as it truly was and not distorted by the ripples on the surface of a pond or the hazy texture of a tankard.

He took in the golden color of his hair, the black etchings inked all over his sand-colored skin, and let his eyes roam over his knotted muscles. The glass was cool to the touch, and so weirdly … foreign. He leaned closer, his nose now almost touching the mirror, and gazed deeply into his eyes. *The snowflakes,* he thought. *I should be able to see them now.* Yet no matter how hard he focused, he couldn't discern anything other than blackness. His head still ached from all the cursed drinks and talk of stones and heroes ...

Giving up, he climbed into the stone bathtub. Cool water soaked his skin, sending icy fingers up his spine. He gazed at the glowing curtain, drinking in the moonlight, longing for Lusha. *If she were here, the water would feel warmer ...* His loins stirred, but the tiredness of a long day took over.

He drifted into the sweet clutches of sleep.

A soft knock at his door awakened him. Water splashed around him as he clutched at the stony rim. The door creaked open, and Bhoran watched a girl slip into his room. Over her nut-brown skin, an ethereal white dress fell, so transparent it did little to cover the curves of her womanly body.

Bhoran's words caught in his throat.

Yet the girl waited for no welcome. Two pails filled with water, hot steam rising from them, hung heavy in her grasp. She laid one before the tall mirror, and holding the other one with both hands, she approached the stone bath. "I've brought you warm water," she said, smiling.

The sparkle in her eyes as she gazed at Bhoran's naked body made him uncomfortable. He made to stand but halted when she suddenly dipped her arm into the tub.

"Let me just take some of the cold water away," she said. Her fingers plucked a small stone from the bottom of the tub. As the old water drained with a soft whirling sound, the girl gazed deeply into Bhoran's eyes.

She can't be over sixteen years of age, Bhoran thought uneasily, *and yet she acts in the manner of a woman who's been many a time in the company of men.* Bhoran wasn't certain if she was here out of her own lust's bidding or because her master had forced her. "What is your name?" he asked as the girl poured the warm water into the bath.

"You can call me however you like." A smile parted her lips, revealing pearly white teeth. "I'd like to join you."

Before he had time to respond, she dropped her dress and presented her nakedness to him with pride. Her body was young and pleasing to the eye, full of curves and promises of carnal pleasures. Bhoran felt a stirring in his loins and a numbing pain in his head. He loathed himself for it. "Leave."

The girl ignored his order. She plucked the red string that held her hair high, then climbed into the water with him. She took a gray pumice stone from the tub's rim. "Tell me," she said, moving closer, "how did you get these etchings?"

Bhoran watched her rub the stone up and down his firm chest for a while. "I don't remember," he said. It was a lie, but not an utter one. After all, when Dhylinea had worked on him, his soul had been drifting under the sweet influence of Serpent's Spite. Later he would always wake with a heavy head and more burning etchings marking his body. His skin felt afire now wherever the stone touched it. *What does she want?*

"I think they're beautiful," she said. Her strokes slid lower, almost brushing his manhood. "I also think the stones in your eyes are beautiful. I've never met an Onyx before, and I see no reason tribes should fear you ..."

Bhoran clutched her wandering hand. "Who are you?"

"I told you, you can call me however you like. I've seen how you look at that girl. She's pretty, but for that fearful scar ... I know what she's in the sickhouse for ... Your heart must be aching. I can make the pain fade." With her free hand, she reached for the side of his face, leaning in to kiss him.

"No." Bhoran pushed her away. "Who sent you to tempt me?"

Aghast, the girl clambered out of the tub. "You fool!" She stormed out naked, not even bothering to pick her dress up from the floor or close the door behind her.

Bhoran clenched his fists, trying to clear his mind. Lusha's serene face as she rested in the sickbed floated into his mind, clearing his vision for the first time that night.

It wasn't as if Bhoran had been a stranger to women's lust. He knew his manly figure made them all warm inside. One had even dared to take his hand once and place it between thighs that dripped with love juices.

He shook his head and got out of the tub. On his bed, he found a linen towel, its hug a warm welcome around his waist.

The darkness of the corridor made his skin creep. As he moved to close the door, the mirror caught his eye. The looking glass seemed different from before. He went to it and looked down at the bucket the girl had left there earlier. The steam clung to the cool glass, revealing a curious drawing Bhoran knew well. *Olnos.* Someone had clearly traced the outline of the statue on the mirror.

Touching the moisture, Bhoran glanced at the open door, his chest heavy with the feeling of being watched. *Someone has been in my room. Someone who sent this girl to taunt me and leave me a message.* His gaze fell on the tangled dress on the floor. The girl must know who the sender was, only now she was gone, disgruntled by his refusal to bed her.

Bhoran sat on the edge of his bed, rubbing his temples. He raised his gaze to the mirror, taking in the statue's image. A powerful urge to sprint to Olnos overtook him. And yet he needed to be certain; he needed to hear it from somebody else, whose mind and thoughts he trusted more than his own. He stood.

Avalan. The calling boomed in his mind.

He peered down the dark corridor. Bhoran hoped his friend could find his way through this maze of stone passages. In the distance, a lone torch hung from the wall, its flame guttering and threatening to go out. Unnerving silence filled his mind with worry.

The whisper of naked feet reached his ears. The silhouette of Avalan appeared in the darkness, his chest bare, his breeches girded with a snakeskin belt that bore his goat dagger. Over his nape, ebony hair swung tightly, caught in a horsetail. His face was raw from sleep. "I felt this cry in my head, and …"

"An inexplicable draw to me?"

Avalan nodded.

"I don't know how it works myself," Bhoran confessed. "I've only used it on Yekana. I need your aid."

"Is it Lusha?"

Bhoran shook his head. "A strange message on the glass."

"Glass?"

Bhoran beckoned him into his room.

Avalan frowned as he studied the drawing. "The statue of Olnos," he mused. "The detail is admirable." He circled to the back of the mirror, examined the floor. Then his eyes fell on the dress. "A woman?" he said, raising a curious brow.

"A mere messenger." Bhoran showed him the bucket and told him all that had happened. "What does it mean?"

Avalan stood, rubbing his chin. "Someone went to great lengths to draw your attention. Someone who knows you would perk up at seeing Olnos. I think the only way we shall know is by going there."

"To the statue?"

Avalan nodded. "Though the time and nature of the passing makes me think they want you there alone."

"No," Bhoran said. "We go together." He was glad to see Avalan smile.

"Follow me." Avalan led them through the corridors with ease, choosing the right turns, taking the proper paths without thinking, all the while his fingers grazing the walls.

"How do you know where to turn?" Bhoran asked.

"It took me some time to guess, but it soon came to me when I saw the servants touch the walls. Here." He took Bhoran's hand and rubbed it against the junction of two walls. "Wherever the corner stone is smoothed, that's where you turn. The path goes on like this and leads to the main hall."

True to his word, Avalan soon led them down the staircase and into a dark and deserted hall. The torches stood lifeless. Bhoran caught a whiff of freshly baked bread, which soon faded as they slipped through the gate.

They scaled the outer wall to avoid the guards at the barred gates. Soft grass muffled their landing. The forest floor was damp with night dew.

Avalan had fully woken by now, resuming his usual alertness. He scraped the bark of trees with the backs of his hands, smelled the air, and occasionally stopped and grabbed Bhoran's arm, bringing a silencing finger to his mouth. Yet it was always a night scavenger breaking the silence of the dark, and soon Avalan lowered his defenses and became less responsive to the sounds of the forest.

"Who do you think is behind this?" Avalan asked, his voice barely louder than a whisper.

"I know not."

"Someone who knows your fascination with the statue," Avalan offered. "To whom have you talked?"

"No one. Lusha and I came here, the night of the wedding."

Avalan glanced over his shoulder. "Someone followed you, then?"

Bhoran shrugged. The only thing that had mattered to him then was Lusha's love.

"I don't have a good feeling about this," Avalan confessed as the trees pressed closer around them. "Why would someone want you so far from the keep at this hour of the night?" Avalan grabbed his arm. "Think, Bhoran. Who else apart from Lusha would know you've been there?"

Bhoran thought long and hard. "There was this guard at the gate when I was leaving with Lusha. I broke his spear."

"Why?"

"He pointed it at me."

Avalan grunted. "They don't trust us, even though we're guests of Ethelnar. I wonder what his scheme is. His hospitality cannot extend forever. He won't lean back and watch us sip his wine and eat his food with nothing in return. Eventually, he'll come to us with a request."

Bhoran eyed him. "What does he want?"

"To use us against Bassalt, no doubt."

That caught Bhoran off guard. "Why?"

"I have a hunch little love is shared between the two. Something foul stirs." A twig snapped underfoot. Avalan kicked it aside and pressed on. "The lack of Silver's men at the keep's gate confirmed my suspicions. They should have been here by now, reclaiming Lusha. Why haven't they come?"

The chamber inside Olnos's statue came to Bhoran's mind. The warmth and glow of the letters on the smooth stone as he had made love to Lusha, a sight he couldn't forget. "The statue of Olnos," he said.

Avalan eyed him. "It should be close enough."

"No." Bhoran halted. "There is one here and one in Hydrus."

"What of it? Olnos was a hero. It should come as no surprise they wanted to erect statues in his memory."

"The back of the statue is hollow," Bhoran said. "Both here and in Hydrus."

Lifting a curious brow, Avalan leaned closer. "Hollow?"

"A hidden chamber with a smooth stone inside. Etchings appear on it."

Under the moonlight, Avalan's face glowed. "That is how the chiefs communicate."

Bhoran nodded. "Must be. I never knew there was another statue of him until now."

"Come. Perchance I can read the words."

They lengthened their strides now, making their way through the forest in haste, forgetting to muffle their footfalls. Soon the statue of Olnos emerged, a white ghost in the darkness.

A crunching of dry leaves behind them made them stop dead in their tracks. They both crouched.

"An animal?" Bhoran mouthed.

Avalan sniffed the air and strained his ears. Then he shook his head and reached for his dagger. Silently he beckoned Bhoran to the statue. Once in the clearing, Bhoran felt vulnerable, an easy target.

A sudden scatter of fallen leaves made them leap. Bhoran searched between the trees for movement but saw nothing. Another stirring came, this time ruffling the leaves before their feet as something landed there.

Avalan bent, retrieved a small object from the ground. It was a thin wooden pricker. "Someone's shooting at us!" Avalan flung the dart aside and grabbed Bhoran's shoulder. "To the hollow," he told him, his breath raw with fear.

Swiftly they broke into a run.

Bhoran was about two strides from Olnos when his toes met with a rock, and he plunged face forward into the ground. He raised his arm to protect his face as another dart landed beside him.

"Bhoran!" Avalan threw himself over Bhoran's body.

With a sickening low thump, a pricker found its way into Avalan's shoulder. He looked at Bhoran with wide eyes filled with horror. Blood trickled from the wound. Avalan's body loosened. At first he sagged against Bhoran, his breathing ragged. Then he collapsed on the ground.

"No!" Bhoran sprang to his feet. Without thinking, he charged in the direction he thought the attack had come from. "Show yourself!" he roared.

A dart launched from somewhere behind him, scraped his arm. He cursed and spun, but saw no one. The sharp pain was brief, and then a familiar warmth filled his body, a warmth he always felt when Yekana bit into his arm. *Poison.*

He rushed to Avalan's side. The blood from his wound had clotted, forming a nasty yellow scab. Bhoran dragged his body to the back of the statue and scraped the wound with a sharp stone. Blood started flowing again, and Bhoran picked some up with the back of his finger. He tasted Avalan's blood. His heart thundered. *Serpent's Spite.* He had to act fast, Bhoran knew, for once the snake's venom had settled …

He hurled Avalan over his shoulder and ran, winding his way right and left. The prickers tore the air around him, some falling to the ground, others piercing his shanks. He cursed and yelled, but didn't dare to stop.

Before the keep's gate, he laid Avalan on the ground and pounded on the door.

Through a small opening, a guard's voice came. "Who goes there?"

Bhoran peered inside. He recognized the leering gaze of the one whose spear he had snapped. "Open the gate," Bhoran yelled. "My companion's injured."

"I see no one." A sly smile curved the guard's lips. "Only a filthy talon."

With a roar, Bhoran threw his arm through the opening, reaching for the guard's face, but the man took a step back. "Damn you! Open this gate! Call for the medic!" Bhoran thrust himself at the door, shoulder first. The wood didn't so much as budge, the iron bars holding strong. "Open!" he yelled once more, only he knew it was in vain. When he peered through the opening, the guard still stood there, his smile even wider, relishing his revenge. A terrible fear coiled in Bhoran's belly.

"Scum like you aren't welcome here." The guard spat. "Go back to where you came from."

Behind him, Avalan moaned. Bhoran knelt, brushing loose hair away from Avalan's face. His forehead was clammy, burning. "No ..." Bhoran shot a last, desperate glance at the sealed gate.

Then he threw Avalan over his shoulder once again.

CHAPTER THIRTY-EIGHT

BASSALT AWOKE with the bitter taste of an undeniable truth on his tongue: he had lived to see the day the tribe rebelled against him.

Merciful darkness drenched his bedchamber, but Bassalt could smell the light of day outside, caressing the thick walls of his house. *A new day has dawned,* he thought hopefully, *and I am still the chief of Hydrus.*

Trying to prop himself up on his elbows won him a fresh bout of pain. He cursed, reached for the cup on the bedside table, and ruefully found it filled with clear water. *Some wine would be much preferred now, flavored with willow bark.*

"Theran!"

A soft knock came on his door, sending pounding waves of pain to Bassalt's temples. Theran slid inside, a bowl of soaked oats and a steaming cup on a tray in his hands. "Welcome back, my chief," he muttered.

"What is this thing?" Bassalt grumbled as he took the scorching cup. It smelled like damp forest soil. *And tastes much like it.* He went for the oats, but even these, watered down as they were, did little to stave off the bitterness of the potion.

"How does your head fare, my chief?"

"Your voice sears through my scalp. Must you talk so loud?" He gulped down two mouthfuls of the potion, staring at the dregs of mashed leaves. Clamors and clangors echoed in his mind when he dared think of last night. "How many did we lose?"

Theran choked back a sob. "Some from our household. Enareous, the cook, took an arrow between the eyes. Young Ulivar, who rushed to avenge the death, was rewarded with a swift end from an arrow to the heart. Then there was Ganevar and Koldren … I'm afraid they got in the way of the vines. Their bodies were pierced by hundreds of thorns."

This makes clear the awful taste of the food, Bassalt thought ruefully. "What of the rest of the tribe?"

"Chieftain Silver and his men cut down a dozen … An awful sight they made, lying there, soulless, butchered. I would have liked to make arrangements for the burials, only the fisherfolk got in my way and chased me back to our house with curses and promises of revenge." There were dark circles around Theran's eyes, as if the servant hadn't slept at all.

Bassalt swallowed back dread and disgust. "Women and children?"

"All safe, my chief. I shielded them from the fight."

Nodding, Bassalt pushed himself up higher on the bed. "You did well. Help me get dressed. Then send for Silver."

Theran fiddled with the corner of Bassalt's bedsheet.

"Don't make me repeat myself, Theran. Every cursed word booms like thunder in my head."

"I … I'm afraid the commander …"

Silver's howl as he had taken an arrow to the shoulder the night past echoed in Bassalt's mind. He grabbed Theran and gave him a good shake. "Silver is dead?" Spit escaped his teeth, spattering the servant's face. "Speak, damn you!"

Theran shook his head in terror. "He still breathes but is unconscious. Farmera's tending to him."

"Where is he? At her house?"

Theran nodded, his entire body trembling beneath Bassalt's hold.

"Marebore?"

"Lies in your cellar. I placed his birthstone on your working table, my chief, to deal with it as you see fit."

Bassalt shuddered. The cursed Ruby had entered his mind, bringing forth everything he dreaded. "The stonemaster?"

A glint of guilt shone in Theran's eyes. "I took the liberty of securing him in your cavern, my chief. Thought it'd be safer. I cast the shielding spell as you have taught me. It was dark, but the light of my candle found this." The mousy servant fished out the snake ring from his pocket. Between two fingers he pinched it, careful not to touch the stone. The gem looked lifeless and dull, as if indifferent to the destruction it had caused.

Bassalt clutched at it and threw it into the remaining liquid in his cup. The cursed stone changed color, its darkness mingling with the black shade of the potion leaves. *Cursed, cursed. Where is this Onyx?* He threw the bedsheet off his legs.

"My chief, you shouldn't—"

"Don't tell me what I should do, Theran." He staggered on numb feet and grabbed the headboard to steady himself. "Help me throw on a decent robe."

Theran returned with a light cloak of soft wool and helped Bassalt slip into it.

"Where will you go, my chief?" Theran's face was pale with worry. "Should I arrange for an escort?"

"No. The rightful chief of Hydrus has nothing to fear."

Outside, Bassalt threw the cowl of his robe over his head to shade his eyes from the bright sunlight. The day had dawned crisp and clear, brighter than any other day Bassalt had seen, as if last night hadn't been the darkest the tribe of Hydrus had witnessed since the War of the Stones.

The village was deserted. Lone cauldrons filled with pungent-smelling food rested over fires reduced to smoking embers. Tables and benches were overturned, the soil beneath them ruffled and caked with crusted blood, broken arrow shafts, and ripped cloth. The vines, no longer under his command, lay lifeless on the ground, their bloodied thorns a dire reminder of the fight. Here and there, Bassalt shooed away seabirds that swooped down in search of an easy meal.

He made his way between the tribe's lodgings. Behind the shuttered windows, Bassalt felt the frightened stares and the hatred of the tribe. Only once he was crossing Farmera's croft did he dare lower his cowl.

He found her sitting on the floor by Silver's side. All color had drained from her face. A rumpled tunic flowed over her body, stopping just above her ankles. When she saw him, her chest shuddered, and tears stroked her cheeks.

"I've tried everything. He just ..." She inhaled sharply. "He just won't return."

A dreaded coldness crept through him. The same feeling as when he'd seen the lifeless bodies of his parents, killed in the war against the Onyx. At least they had died for a noble cause. *But Silver ... So young, and for what? The bloody whim of a usurper.* He helped her to her feet. "Rest now. I shall see to him."

Farmera withdrew into her bedchamber.

Sitting on a stool, Bassalt took in the figure of his commander. Silver's waxen face seemed peaceful, as if he'd fallen into a dreamless sleep. Bassalt brushed his hand. Not so cold as he'd expected. Perhaps the departure of his soul had been only recent. Even so, he had to make certain.

Bassalt pressed his ear against Silver's unmoving chest. *Is this the beating of a fighting heart?* He looked around. Silver's sword leaned against the table; his stone—the Heliodor—gleamed in the morning sunlight. Bassalt hefted the sword, eyeing the birthstone. Placing it on the table, he rummaged through Farmera's tools, looking for anything to pry the stone from the hilt. A small dirk brushed his hand. It would have to do. He lodged the blade beneath the stone and twisted. The stone flew free, and Bassalt caught it before it hit the floor.

He used the dirk to slice Silver's tunic open and placed the golden stone on his chest, atop his heart. A light flickered inside the gem. It was a small, fleeting movement, yet there was little Bassalt's Tiger's Eye missed.

He went to Farmera's bedchamber. "Farmera," he whispered.

"Is it over?"

"No." Bassalt took a brave step closer. "I need your aid. Two voices, united, carry more power."

"He still breathes?"

"The Stone is pulling him, yet I dare think we could sever the cord. It is time to chant."

Farmera rose. She looked so pale; Bassalt wasn't sure she had anything left to give. Yet at this crucial moment, he needed her voice. He offered her his hand and steered her back to the room where Silver lay.

Together they knelt before him, entangling their fingers. Farmera spoke without tearing her eyes from Silver. "The old ode to the Heliodor?"

Bassalt squeezed her hand in answer.

Tears fell down Farmera's cheeks. "I haven't sung it since the war ..."

They united their voices in a chant—a song that spoke of the gift of the sun, of life, and death. It was a plea to the Stone to heal the fallen chieftain's body, to nurture and salve his beaten soul, and return him to his tribe.

With every verse they uttered, the stone on Silver's chest shone brighter and brighter, until the whole chamber was bathed in light. It seeped from the stone into Silver's body, and for the first time since Bassalt had crossed the threshold of Farmera's house, the commander's chest rose and fell with breath.

Farmera burst into heart-wrenching sobs.

Bassalt patted her back. *I must not cry,* he thought, his chest leaden. Clearing his throat, he said, "Thank you for keeping him alive." Even in anger, Farmera remained a healer. "Send for Theran when he opens his eyes."

"Stay with me," she pleaded.

Her words stirred Bassalt's heart, chasing away the dreaded shadow of the Onyx. He couldn't bear to meet her eye, and so he let his gaze go to her naked feet. They were dusted with white sand. "You went to the beach?"

"We gifted the dead men to the Nameless Sea."

Hydrus will eat them all, Bassalt thought, shuddering. A grisly fate. He had exposed the rebellion and forced the tribe's hand, leading to death and destruction. And yet where did that leave him? Even more hated he would be now, he knew, and more vulnerable to defiance. And the Onyx still lingered.

"Where is my boy, Bassalt?"

"I do not know. Though reason would have it he's in Ethelnar's clutches. Raekandar is the last town standing between Hydrus and the Stone Lands. I have sent word, but Ethelnar refuses to answer me."

Farmera's face twisted with fear. "What will he do to him?"

"Nothing if Avalan leaves the chiefess alone. And certainly not before the Night of the Spirits. Though that has now come to pass. If Ethelnar still stands as a ruler, he will toy with him some before ..."

She drove her fists into his chest. "You did *nothing* to stop him!"

"Ethelnar ignores my pleas for aid. I'm afraid there isn't much I can do now. I told you many a time to tell your son of Crystal's fate. If he had known ..."

Farmera's gaze widened in fear. "I shall go to him, then." She pushed herself up by pressing on Bassalt's sturdy shoulders. "Give me a guide to cross the mountain."

Still kneeling, Bassalt shook his head. "You know I cannot let you leave. Not after all that has happened."

"The dead are dead," Farmera retorted, "and Silver's fate lies with his stone now. I cannot sit idle. I must find my son. I cannot bear the thought of ill fate. Azirrad never returned. I won't lose my son as well ..."

"If you leave, I cannot protect you."

"Protect me? Bassalt, it is you who brought this to our village. Your unbending will and fears of the Onyx brought down even the wrath of Hydrus. You cannot hope to remain in charge for long. They haven't beaten you yet, but they won't stop until they do. The first bite of freedom is always the sweetest."

Bassalt sighed, closing his eyes. In his mind, he pictured the tribe tearing at his flesh with nails and teeth, taking turns at smashing his Tiger's Eyes beneath their heels. "Avalan will return," he said. His knees creaked under his weight as he stood. "There's nothing more perilous than an unyielding spirit, I fear." He staggered to the door. "Keep Sigil close, and do not venture far from the village."

After closing the door behind him, he flexed his fingers. A tearing pain soared through his stump, but the woody vines came. Around and around he bade them, to circle the hut, tying the house so tight there would be no escape. He couldn't hold them in place for long, he knew. That would take too much of his power. *Only for a while,* he thought, *until her soul calms, and I find the true Onyx.*

CHAPTER THIRTY-NINE

BHORAN DIDN'T KNOW if it was the fear of losing Avalan or the instincts developed during his time living in the wild that kept him going despite the weight he carried on his shoulders.

As he'd left Raekandar behind, the second shadow had slipped to his side, leading the way through the foot of the mountain, as if it knew where Bhoran intended to run to. Forest, rough dirt, bluffs and shale, cliffs and scree ... With the shadow for a guide, Bhoran scaled them all, his mind clear of poison, his heart heavy for what was to come.

A golden streak of light appeared on the horizon, illuminating the mountain peaks. He had been running all night, chest heaving, shoulders burning. He swallowed the salty sweat that trickled into his mouth, and resumed his race against time. Over his shoulders, Avalan's body lay limp; his moans had long ceased, making Bhoran's heart sink. Yet there was no time to halt.

When he finally reached the cursed cave, the soles of his feet were crimson, and his chest threatened to burst with every new breath he took. Bhoran laid Avalan on the ground and leaned against the cave's maw.

"*Dhylinea?*" he shouted into the void. He waited, praying to the stones she would be there. And that her anger had ebbed.

From the depths of the cave, a womanly figure emerged.

Bhoran breathed a sigh of relief.

Dhylinea faltered at the entrance, diaphanous silk hugging her comely body. Her flaxen hair was drawn behind her ears, making the glowing orbs of blue Moonstones in her eyes shine brighter. Longing and disbelief dripped from them now when she regarded him. "Bhoran." Her voice was smooth, like flowing water.

All words left him, the memory of her still fresh in his mind and yet so distant. In his heart, Bhoran had truly hoped that he'd never see her again, that if the stones had even the slightest mercy saved for him, he would have forgotten her, her memory fading like night vapor chased away from Lusha's moonlight.

Avalan's soft moan of pain broke the spell, and Bhoran dared raise his arm and cup her shoulder. Her skin was cool like the cave's air. "Help him. He's dying."

Dhylinea circled Avalan's body, bending for a closer look. "Long ebony hair, muscles supple and slender, angular face that makes a woman's heart melt, and the rebellious heart of a seeker." She lifted her face to Bhoran's. "Avalan of the Bloodstone."

With an exhausted nod, Bhoran fell to his knees beside her. "I beg of you, Dhylinea."

Chains of gilded bones jingled around her ankles. "What runs in his blood?"

"Serpent's Spite."

She arched a smooth brow.

"It wasn't mine. Someone attacked us. A dart lodged in his shoulder."

Dhylinea's chin tightened. "Bring him inside."

With a groan, Bhoran draped Avalan's body over his shoulders. The cave's air was musty but grew clearer as they approached the depths, where fresh sunlight slipped through a skylight above. Beneath his torn heels, the rock felt smooth, merciful.

"Where should I put him?" Bhoran asked, though he very well knew the answer.

A slab sat in the chamber's middle, so smooth Bhoran almost felt its slick surface across his back again. *No!* his mind screamed at him. And yet he said nothing as he watched Dhylinea sweep an arm above it.

Bhoran let Avalan down slowly, then wiped the burning sweat from his friend's forehead. "Can you cure him?"

Instead of answering, Dhylinea disappeared into a dark corner. Bhoran stared after her. *Promise me you'll never go there.* Her voice echoed in his mind, playful and yet filled with the sharp edges of a threat. Bhoran averted his gaze, trying to suppress his memories.

Yet it was a task harder than he'd imagined.

Everything in the small cavern screamed of the past he so wished to forget. It tugged at his heart and his very soul. To his right, against the wall, water splashed softly from a spring, collecting in a natural basin. He knelt, inhaling sharply as the cool water washed over his nape. He dipped the soles of his feet into the water, cleaning the crusted blood off them. *Clean yourself, my proud Onyx.* Dhylinea's voice echoed in his mind. *And then return to my bed.*

No.

Dhylinea returned with a vial filled with a transparent liquid. She gently opened Avalan's lips and let the liquid flow through them in small sips. "When did this happen?"

"Before dawn. I ran as fast as I could."

"Why seek me? Isn't Farmera able to treat her own son?"

A keen breeze iced Bhoran's face. "We were in Raekandar. No time to reach Hydrus."

A sly smile danced on Dhylinea's lips. "What was a Hydrus tribesman doing so far from the village?"

Bhoran felt a weight crushing his chest. He couldn't possibly trust Dhylinea with their task, but lying to a healer whose power he needed wasn't a clever notion. "Strange times forced us to leave Hydrus." This was as close to the truth as he could muster.

"Bassalt has made his presence intolerable, I see." Dhylinea started undressing Avalan.

No. Bhoran's grip was fast on her wrist before he could stop himself.

She wriggled free from his grasp. "You want him to survive, yes? His body needs to become one with the stone."

When she had stripped Avalan down to bare skin, she pressed her lips into a thin line. "It's not only the poison. There's blood magic running through his body."

Bhoran rubbed the back of his neck. Dhylinea's perception had seemed wondrous to him once, yet now it fostered a sensation of dread. "He made a deal with a sorcerer. He's bound to a shadow."

Dhylinea dug her fingers into his wrist. "You brought a shadow to my lair?"

Bhoran searched the cave's floor, hoping the shadow had hidden. "It isn't here. It remains in Raekandar." He glanced at Avalan's pale face, his lips so white Bhoran wasn't certain the end hadn't already come. "No one knows I came to you."

She smiled, as if his agony was a thing to relish. "Who else was with you in your escape?"

"No one," he lied again. His heart raced. "We were alone."

A shudder of disgust twitched Dhylinea's lips. She released him and circled to the other side of the slab. With long, elegant fingers, she traced lines on Avalan's chest. His skin reddened wherever she touched him. She found the spot over his heart, jabbed it with an accusing finger. "I can smell her on you," she told Bhoran.

Bhoran could have sworn the bath he'd taken had extinguished Lusha's sweet scent on his body, much as he hated the notion. Bhoran longed for her embrace then, her pale face becoming one with Avalan's. He tried to shake his head in denial, but it was no good.

Dhylinea chuckled. "You look so guilty. I don't need your words to tell me the truth. You made love to her."

"He's dying. Why must you torture me? It matters not what Lusha—"

"It matters to me!" she stormed. She withdrew her touch from Avalan's body, and the crimson lines faded. "You promised to stay with me, and then you left. I wonder, will you leave Lusha too? After you've had her one too many times—"

"Don't speak her name so."

"She makes you angry. So much passion." Her voice oozed with sour mockery. "You once had it for me. I can still taste you on my body, your hands, your lips, your thighs closing around me. Tell me, does she do to you all the things I did, or is she shy like a sweet virgin?"

Bhoran clenched his fists and granted her a fake smile. "I'm sorry if I hurt you—"

"I saved your *life*." Dhylinea thrust her chest forth. "I sucked the poison out of your veins, tended to your wounds, gave you my body. You must remember all this. Surely the poison didn't cloud your mind so much, or you wouldn't be here begging me to do the same to your friend."

"And for all that, I thank you." Bhoran struggled to drown the simmering rage in his chest. He needed her, but he had a gut-wrenching feeling she wouldn't make it easy.

"You truly love her."

Bhoran touched the base of his neck. *With all my heart.* "It matters not. She fears me." That much was true.

Dhylinea searched his eyes. "The Onyx in your eyes confuses her. But not me. *I* never feared you. Tell me, have you told her about me?"

"She knows, Dhylinea."

"The whole truth?"

"What was needed."

Dhylinea chuckled in triumph. "You fool. You think honesty was what she needed? You broke her heart, and now you've lost her forever."

Bhoran felt his stomach churn. *She's lying …* "Dhylinea, I beg you, save him."

Her attention returned to Avalan. His chest rose ever so slightly, and his breathing was becoming less than a mere whisper. Dhylinea held Bhoran's thumping heart in her naked palm. With one squeeze, she could crush it. "I will—only I want something in return."

"What is it? Speak."

Her features softened now. "You." She sidled up to him, caressed his naked chest. Standing on the tips of her toes, her lips brushed his ear as she whispered, "I want you to be mine one more time."

Bhoran's muscles tightened. He grabbed her arm so fiercely, and then released her, afraid of what his anger would cost him.

"Good," she said with a sly smile. "Be angry with me. Give me all your passion like you once did. I missed your anger. Nobody wanted you, remember? I was the only one. He"—she motioned to Avalan—"never came looking for you. Lusha was in the arms of Colgar. You saw them with your own eyes. She betrayed you. Now it's time to pay her with her own coin."

"I will never."

Dhylinea lowered her dress, exposing the milky skin of her shoulder. "So Avalan will die. Such a pity. He has a tiger's heart. So much potential gone to waste because innocent Bhoran couldn't indulge in an embrace of pleasure."

He tore his eyes from her, his gaze desperate to cling onto anything that wouldn't remind him of his past. Yet every corner in the cavern held a lustful tale of poison, mindless lovemaking, and desperate feelings of guilt. "Why are you doing this?"

"I do it because you owe me." She slid her other shoulder free from the dress and let it fall. She went to him, naked. "Give yourself to me. Then I shall cure him, and you'll be free to return to her if you wish. I won't stop you."

Bhoran closed his eyes. He should have known better than to come back to her. *Cursed guard.* If only he could reach him now, he would crush his skull with his bare hands.

"Come now." She took his hand, dragged him to the back of the cave. A bear hide was sprawled across a flat stone. The sight of it clouded Bhoran's mind with memories of old. A surge of pain rushed through him as he remembered the writhing agony he'd suffered when Serpent's Spite had flowed through his veins.

Six years before, he had done this to himself—allowed Yekana to feast on his blood for the first time, desperate to end his life, and along with it his suffering. He had been near death when Dhylinea had shown. She had been a vision of light and hope, so like his Lusha, yet so different. She'd carried him here and laid him on this very bed, and she'd cured him, chasing the venom away from his heart with potions and her lovemaking, tracing his body with ink that became one with his skin and his very soul, forever reminding him of what he'd done.

Now she undressed him slowly, with longing hands. Once done, she ran her fingers over his body, caressed the bones in his face, the ink on the inside of his arms, the valley of his abdomen, and then his manhood. Bhoran felt his loins stir and loathed himself.

When she was satisfied with her task, she pushed him back and climbed atop, pushing him inside her. With fierce passion she swayed, whispering to him words he couldn't fathom, for his head was bursting with pain and agony, and his mouth was full of the bitter taste of betrayal.

Bhoran held his breath. She could have his body if that would save Avalan's life, but not his mind. He gritted his teeth as the pressure became more than he could bear, and then he let his body go, exploding into a mixture of pain, pleasure, and guilt.

It stained his soul.

Gently Dhylinea slid off him and traced his cheek with a wet finger. "Good. As always."

Without bothering to get dressed, she went to her working bench, picked through a basket of herbs. She fished out a long green leaf and chewed it. "I wouldn't want to catch your seed," she said, shrugging.

Bile rose to Bhoran's mouth. *I hope the leaf kills you,* he thought with resentment, *yet not before you've brought Avalan back to me.* He stood and put on his breeches. "Avalan," he said, glaring at her.

She had already gone to him, both of them naked as newborns. "Calm. I shall get on with my spell now."

She threw pieces of scarlet stone into a mortar and mixed them with water from the spring. Then she began pounding. When she lifted the pestle, it was dyed crimson, like fresh blood. She grabbed another stone, black as a midnight shadow. Its end had been trimmed to an edge, like the tip of a sharp knife.

I remember this one. Bhoran flinched as he recalled the tip of the stone piercing his body. Dhylinea dipped the stone's tip into the crimson ink and traced the skin of Avalan's shoulder. A faint chant danced on her lips.

Bhoran looked at his own etchings. As he watched Dhylinea work on Avalan's body, he realized this ritual had saved his own life six years ago. He imagined himself stripped and unconscious on her table, her hands drifting over his skin, marking him forever as her own.

Unable to stand there any longer, Bhoran spun. He staggered to the carved staircase leading to the ledge above the skylight. The open air didn't cast away his sense of dread. The sun had fully risen. It burned his skin now. Everything inside him felt like it had caught fire. He brought his hands to his chest. A broken roar left his mouth as his nails dug deep, wishing to rip his heart out.

CHAPTER FORTY

A MAN two beds across from hers screamed. His cry was so shrill it tore Lusha from sleep's embrace.

"Hold him still!" a man bellowed. Despite his small stature, his voice held the power of someone in charge.

Lusha watched in silence as a woman with a shaved head rushed to the ailing man's side. The woman pressed his shoulders down, trying to ease his writhing agony with soothing words. The air was heavy with the sweet smell of stale sweat and the strange odors of milky potions. After a quick glance around her, Lusha knew at once this was a sickhouse, much larger and airier than Farmera's hut.

The man in charge returned with a tiny bottle in hand. With a flick of his finger, he knocked the cork off and waved the bottle's neck beneath the man's nose. Letting out a final, soft moan, the screaming man quieted, his lids closing.

"Prepare some willow-bark porridge for him," the man told the woman, placing a kind hand on her shoulder.

Lusha didn't mean to stare, but it was too late. The man turned, held her gaze sternly, then strode to her. She tried to struggle out of her sheets, but they were tightly bound around her. Beneath them, her skin felt warm, clammy.

"Do not fight," the man told her. "A cool breeze blew last night, and

I asked the women to keep you warm." He knelt, started unfolding the tangled sheets. "I'm Nexanthos of the Moonstone."

Numbly Lusha nodded. It was comforting to meet a moonhealer. Perhaps this man knew more about the city of her mother. "Why am I here?"

Nexanthos arched a disbelieving gray brow. "You don't remember?"

Shame clenched her belly, and Lusha tried to resist the urge to brush her palm over it. "I took the mourning." It all came back to her now. The pain Crystal had warned her about had come much earlier than she'd expected. Stronger and stronger it had grown, until all Lusha could do was strip and climb into the relieving embrace of the water. Then her womb had writhed and spat blood between her thighs. After that, all had faded to a serene blackness.

"How are you feeling?"

Shamed, confused … Did Nexanthos sway the same bottle under my nose to make me rest? Does Bhoran know? "How long have I been sleeping?"

"Long enough."

"The Night of the Spirits …"

"Has come and passed. Chief Ethelnar remains. It was a wondrous celebration. A pity you missed it for … a rash mistake."

Lusha brushed a hand over her belly. She had been foolish. She could see that now. Tears welled in her eyes. Tightness grabbed hold of her throat. How could she hope to explain to Bhoran what she had done? How the fear of a stone had driven her to empty her belly of his seed, to risk her life, to kill whatever might have grown inside her. "Have I had any visitors?"

"Three so far. Your lover, your village fellow, and the chiefess herself."

"Do they know?"

Nexanthos hesitated, but the flicker in his eyes betrayed his shame. "A medic is sworn to tell the truth. You can't fight ailments with lies."

Lies. Lusha's heart sank.

The medic cupped her hand. "You did well, child of the Moonstone. I loathe the pain and loss the mourning brings, but there are some souls that had better remain buried. I saw his eyes when he visited you. An Onyx, is he? I had thought them all dead after the war." He frowned. "A handsome man he is, I must admit, but do not forget what lies in his soul. Mayhap now you have learned your lesson to not lie with him again."

His words cut her deep. Lusha had placed high hopes on the acceptance of Bhoran by the Moonstone healers of Levorotha ... only this man spoke with cruel words bearing no compassion for a man with darkness in his eyes. She *had* to know. *If I pretend to fall in with his beliefs, perhaps he'll tell me more.* "Thank you for your words of comfort. Are you of Levorotha?"

Nexanthos looked surprised. "I ... am. I was born and raised a medic there. Left it before the war, though, and settled in Raekandar under Chief Othor's reign. He promised me shelter and respect in exchange for tending to his sick folk and teaching the healers all I knew. Chief Ethelnar was kind enough to honor this agreement, for the most part, after he succeeded him ..."

Kind, Lusha thought. For reasons she could not fathom, this was the last word she'd use to depict the gaunt chief that circled Crystal like a vulture. Behind the seated Nexanthos, she glimpsed the fires that kept the sick warm and cast away the stiff fingers of death. "Ethelnar killed Chief Othor?"

Nexanthos nodded. "Our chief is full of hatred," he admitted. "Yet Othor's spirit doesn't return to oust him. Out of deep shame, I would guess, for all he did during the war. But it pains me to think of those times."

Lusha frowned, but she thought better of pressing him. "All my life, I've lived in Hydrus. I've never known the wonders of our moon city. Speak to me about it. Will they accept a woman like me?"

Nexanthos smiled. "A child of the Moonstone is always welcomed in Levorotha—of that there is no doubt."

Ah, then not all stones are welcomed.

"I haven't been back in what seems to me a lifetime." He rubbed his chin. "Though I suppose not much has changed since I left. The square will be the most magnificent sight you'll ever behold. The castle rises tall and proud, and the tribesfolk, so elegant, so bright. A peaceful place that will fit you well should you choose to stay."

Lusha admired the way his eyes shone when he spoke of Levorotha. She hoped with all her heart the words that followed would not rip the smile off his face. "I am not decided on whether I shall stay there or not. In truth, I seek to find my aunt and learn what took my mother. She was a Moonstone healer, much like you, only a strange illness struck her. I never met her, though those who were close to her in her final moments spoke to me of curious blotches under her skin, bruises as if the blood had spilled …" She trailed off when she saw the look of horror on the medic's face. "You know of what I speak?"

Nervously he glanced over his shoulder. "You mustn't speak of the Red Weal, child. Dangerous times. Grievous. I am sorry your mother … caught it."

Lusha's heart thumped in her chest. "I beg of you, tell me more."

A shadow of doubt crossed Nexanthos's face. "The Red Weal, like its masters, is long dead."

How can a sickness be dead? "I do not understand."

With a deep sigh, Nexanthos rose. "I don't blame you, child. You've lived all your life under this Bassalt. We all know ambition got to his head. His hatred of the stones has transformed Hydrus into a breeding ground of ignorance of the Stone Lands and their ways. The Red Weal was a cursed illness, cast by the Onyx on the highest Moonstone healers. The war was a wretched thing, you see. Wounds inflicted by stone magic ofttimes are resistant to plain herbal healings. The Onyx had to take out as many able healers of the Moonstone as possible to turn the tide of war in its favor. And so they cast the Red Weal. From its menace, there was no escape. Death always followed."

Lusha clutched at her mother's necklace. "The Onyx killed my mother?"

Nexanthos gave her a look of pity. "Think not of the past, child, but press forth. The ground is still raw from war and has claimed many of our loved ones." He pointed to the side of the bed. "The chiefess was kind enough to bring for you fresh clothing. Go. And I wish the moon will lead your path."

All the hope Lusha had placed in the Moonstone healers quavered. If they thought the Onyx responsible for the Red Weal, how, then, could she hope for them to accept Bhoran into their midst? *Even I betrayed him by taking the mourning.* Hot shame burned her.

Nexanthos returned to his tasks. *He's right,* Lusha thought, swallowing back tears for a mother she had never met. *I should press forth.*

She stood, threw off her soiled smallclothes, and slipped the clean dress over her head. She needed to find Bhoran, tell him how she regretted her actions, and share with him all she had learned. He would understand. After all, he loved her fiercely, much as she did him. The healers of Levorotha would have to respect that, and if they didn't, then she'd be ready to cross all the Stone Lands until she'd found a place where their love could blossom.

Wooden shoes clacked along the stone passage as Lusha followed a maidservant to Bhoran's room. At first the oaken door resisted her touch, as if its end had struck an obstruction on the floor. But when Lusha pushed harder, it gave in.

She walked into the room, preparing her words, only to find it empty. "Bhoran?" *Strange.* Her gaze fell on the bedsheets. They were tightly tucked under the corners, the covers undisturbed.

A stone bathtub stood in the middle, much like the one in her room. She dipped her fingers into the water. It was cool, sending shivers down her spine. It must have been for last night's washing, for a used towel hung over the rim.

Across the room, her own worried reflection stared back at her as she raised her face to a mirror. She went to it, caressed its smooth surface. Pulling her hair back, she gazed at her scar. It was a truly ugly thing, with jagged silver edges. The rattlesnake's fang had torn her, an unclean cut. Despite Farmera's efforts, the healing had been incomplete, leaving behind *this.*

But where is Bhoran now?

As if in answer, she glimpsed movement through the open door. She turned. *It must have been the wind.* A soft breeze blew through the window. She'd wait for him, she decided then, only she would feel safer once the door was closed and the flickering torchlight from the corridor didn't play games with her mind.

Her foot brushed against something soft. She knelt, pulling out a piece of fabric that had lodged under the door. *No wonder the door resisted my entrance.* A woman's scent reached her nose—sweet lilac and orange. She untangled the fabric.

A woman's garment in Bhoran's room.

Confused, she sat on the bed, gazing at the soft cloth in her grip. *Why is this here?* The dress was short and so transparent it barely made for a decent garment. The sweet smell sickened her, and she tossed it aside. Lusha scoured the bedcovers, smelling them, feeling them, as though she could trace the woman's scent, feel the warmth of her body in her Bhoran's bed. Yet she found nothing.

If not the bed, then where?

She rushed to the stone bathtub, this time tracing the rough rim. Sure enough, she found what she was looking for: a crimson string, like the ones the maids used to tie their hair. She pinched it, stared at it, as if it were the greatest enemy in the world. She flung it into the water. *Curse you, Bhoran! Curse you for having my heart!*

Hot tears streamed from her eyes as she dashed through the door. She knew not where she was going, taking whichever turn came first. It mattered not. *No place will ever comfort me.* In her mind's eye, she imagined Bhoran leaning by her sickbed, listening to the medic's tale about the mourning. She remembered well the guilt on Nexanthos's face, and the way he had adamantly defended his honest nature as a medic.

And what did Bhoran do? As she had lain in the sickhouse, he'd let a maid into his room, into his bathtub … Her knees scraped the rough floor as she fell. Lusha remained on the stone for some moments. Then her gaze caught the mild glow of her Moonstone around her wrist. It wasn't much, but she felt some strange relief. *I will get over this, like I always do,* she promised herself.

She got to her feet and wiped her mouth with a clammy palm. This time, she moved through the maze with determined strides, letting her instinct lead her. She had to get away, as far as possible from his room, his life, his touch. Seeing the etchings on his body made by another woman was something she had gulped down and almost forgiven, but this …

Footsteps echoed in the corridor. It wasn't the clacking of a servant's wooden shoes. Lusha halted. Her cheeks burned with rushing blood. *What if it is the chief himself? How will I justify my presence in the men's apartments?* She backtracked, pressing her body into a small alcove, and waited. The footsteps slowly faded. She let out a relieved breath and made to leave her hiding place.

A man's face startled her, making her scream. She toppled to the floor.

"Oh, pardon me, my sweeting," a familiar voice said. "I didn't mean to scare you."

Lusha looked up. The man wore black robes fastened by a golden pin. *Grace the stones. It's only Eyedir, the merchant.* She took his offered hand.

Eyedir grinned. "Are you lost?"

"I believe I am."

"Were you looking for someone?"

Lusha dared to meet his gaze. It wasn't as stern as she'd thought it would be. "Avalan. You remember my fellow tribesman from Hydrus?"

"Of the Bloodstone," he said, scratching his short beard. "Of course, of course. One can scarcely forget him. Stubborn fellow."

"He promised to break his fast with me, only he never showed. I was wondering if anything had happened to him."

The torches sent dancing shadows over the merchant's face. "Curious you'd say that. Last I saw him was the Night of the Spirits. He seemed to revel in the celebrations. Along with that other, sulky fellow, if I may say."

"Bhoran."

Eyedir looked at her for a moment before smiling. "But you look starving. Did you get a good night's sleep? Perhaps you'd like for me to escort you to breakfast while you wait for Avalan to join you."

Lusha nodded. "That would be nice. Thank you."

"My pleasure." He offered her his arm.

Eyedir seemed to know his way all too well; he barely felt the walls, like the maidservants did. His arrival had been a relief. At least for now, she wasn't alone.

"Have you been here much?" she asked him.

"Why, I was born here." He gave her an honest smile. His Rubies caught the torch flames. "This town raised me."

"You stay in the keep?"

"Usually not," he said, stiffening. "But I have some urgent business with the chief."

"I didn't mean to probe. I was just curious. I know not much about life in a town. I've never left Hydrus before."

At that, Eyedir loosened his guard. "Well, you can ask me anything. Ronan was right about you—such an innocent soul."

Naive and stupid was how she felt for trusting men, but she kept this to herself as the merchant led her down a narrow staircase. They passed beneath a short archway and emerged into the open air. The sun glared down on the chief's small yard, and though there were only two men, drinking and playing a game of dice and sticks, Lusha felt as though she shouldn't be here.

Tall black pine trees cast cooling shade over the tables, and for that Lusha was grateful. The moon made her uncomfortable and uncertain, yet the sun was never kind to her either. Her pale skin was no match for the sunlight's power, and if exposed for too long, it soon surrendered, turning a painful shade of pink.

"Where would you prefer to sit?" Eyedir said blithely, as if to ease her fears.

"It's all the same to me."

The merchant laughed. "Then you would be wise to follow me. I'll show you the best table in this yard." He led her all the way across the enclosure to a small table in a corner. "Have a seat."

"Why here?"

"It's all about observing." Eyedir sat across from her, his back to the wall. "There's nothing and no one you'd miss by sitting here. So long as you're not too drunk, if I may say." He winked.

Lusha frowned. "Why would you need to keep track of who is here?"

"It's rather important for us merchants. You see, it's not only goods we peddle."

"You're spying on the chief?"

Eyedir fiddled with his mustache. "I wouldn't call it spying. After all, if the chief wishes not to be seen with someone, he wouldn't bring them here, out in the open. I just observe what the chief allows me to see, like everybody else in his keep does, and nothing more."

A knot lingered in Lusha's stomach. Suddenly she felt exposed, as though everyone was watching her—the merchant, the chief's men, and who knew who else was spying from the overhead windows? "I … I don't feel …"

"Let us get you some refreshment." Eyedir waved to a serving maid.

Soon the girl returned with a tray bearing cool ale, sweet wine, a bowl full of fruits, and a plate of cheeses. Her hair was up in a tight tail, held in place by a red string. The sight of it sickened Lusha, but she bit her lip and fought back thoughts of Bhoran.

As soon as the girl had left, she felt Eyedir's warm hand on hers. "You are sad, my sweeting. Perhaps I can be of help, if you wish to tell me what burdens your heart."

Lusha shook her head. "Tell me about Ronan," she said. "The way *you* knew him."

Eyedir sighed. "Such a fine man, full of life. Adventure ran in his blood—never stopped moving. I had a hard time convincing him to take more than just a day's rest when he'd set his mind to go north or east or west. I never knew where that man would end up."

"Did you ever travel together?"

"Rarely," Eyedir said. "You see, we merchants care for each other at keeps, inns, strongholds, or wherever else it is we stop to rest our bones, but when the time comes to hit the road once again, it's every man for himself. A merchant's resources should remain unique to him. Otherwise, he loses his advantage. It is lonely and cutthroat work, our business."

Lusha swallowed hard. "Cutthroat …" She clenched the cup of sweet wine until her knuckles went white.

"Pardon me, my sweeting. I didn't mean for it to come out like that. Yes, the work of a merchant is harsh; one always has to look behind one's back."

Lusha tasted the mahogany wine. It stung her tongue and trickled straight to her heart. "Ronan was being reckless, then?"

Eyedir leaned closer. "There's been much talk about Ronan's death ... There's word of this dagger. One with an Onyx stone on it. Did you, by chance, see it?"

Lusha had seen more than she had wished to. The cold, staring eyes of Ronan still haunted her dreams. "Bassalt presented it to the tribe." He had also made Bhoran hold it, she knew, but despite the pain Bhoran had caused her, she wouldn't go about spreading rumors that would add to the tribes' hatred and fear of him.

"Would you care to describe the weapon?"

"It was a short golden dagger, only it had an Onyx stone in its hilt." *And Ronan's blood on the blade.*

Eyedir threw a piece of hard cheese into his mouth. "And did you see that stone? How do you know it was an Onyx?"

"Bassalt said so." *What if Bassalt was lying?*

Lusha helped herself to some cheese and melon, and for a while they sat in silence, eating. She hadn't realized how hungry she was. She knew well what grief and uncertainty meant—she had felt them all her life—but she needed to eat. She needed her strength for what she had now resolved to ask Eyedir. Putting her mug down, she cleared her throat. "Ronan promised to take me on one of his trips someday."

Eyedir fished out a cloth from his pocket and wiped his mouth clean. "He did, now, didn't he? Ronan was always very fond of you, if I may say."

Lusha sensed some hesitation in Eyedir's words. She needed to cut to the heart of the matter before it was too late. "He wanted me to see the lands."

"The lands," Eyedir said wistfully.

"Would you take me with you?"

The merchant sighed. "My sweeting, the Stone Lands, especially their roads, are no place for a noble presence like yours."

"I'm not noble." Lusha's heart beat faster. "Just a village girl."

"Chieftain Silver's daughter isn't 'just a village girl.' You need to understand, my sweeting, you may not know your worth, but others see in you something more valuable than you'd imagine."

Lusha flushed. "Why? What would they want with me?"

Eyedir's face darkened. "You're of Hydrus, a secluded place, out of reach. Bassalt took great measures in keeping your village protected. Yet all this did was make the stories darker, the assumptions wilder. Memories of the war are still fresh in tribe minds, and the daughter of Silver could be a great asset in seeking to strike a bargain. If someone got their hands on you …"

Lusha froze. She'd never thought of herself as having any value.

"Stay here. Chief Ethelnar will protect you, if only because you're his wife's heart friend. This is a safe place for you. Don't seek to leave unless you're ready to return to your father. And with a high price for the exchange."

Desperate, Lusha grabbed his hand. "I can't go back. You don't know my father. And I don't wish to stay here either." What did it matter that Raekandar was bigger than Hydrus when it remained a prison?

Eyedir smiled sadly. "A tough hand is better than a thieving one."

Lusha wanted no more hands on her. "If you don't take me with you, I'll go on my own. But there's no going back for me. I seek a better life in Levorotha, by my aunt's side."

"What of your Hydrus friends? Why would you leave with a man like me instead of sticking with them?"

"Much as I still love them, I don't wish to be around men from my village anymore. All I get is pain." She fiddled with the slender chain of her Moonstone bracelet. Avalan had no blame in this, but she was certain he would take Bhoran's side. She couldn't bear it. "I wish to know where I came from. I wish to know my mother's side."

For an agonizing moment, Eyedir fell into deep thought. He drummed his fingers on the table, then reached for another grape and crushed it between his teeth. "We're leaving tonight. But you need to make some sacrifices." He reached inside his robes and took out a thin blade. He pushed it toward her.

"What would you have me do with this?"

"Your hair. It'd be best to cut it. Make yourself less desirable, if that's even possible. Then we must come up with clothes more suited to a wanderer. Leave that to me. We leave at nightfall. Meet me at the stables once you're ready." He stood.

Lusha swallowed hard, staring at the sharp blade. "But my scar … if my hair cannot hide it …"

"It will be visible for all to see," Eyedir finished for her. "That's good. A scar is the mark of a survivor. Let them fear you rather than desire you. So long, my sweeting."

Lusha watched him go, the clinking of metal in his robes sounding like a thunderstorm in her ears. She pushed her hair back and stared at her reflection on the blade. *A survivor.* She liked that.

CHAPTER FORTY-ONE

"I WILL *NOT* ASK AGAIN!" Bassalt bellowed.

Marebore spat blood on the cellar floor. The beads in his hair rattled. A snarky smile curved his lips when he raised his face. "Good. You're getting tiresome."

Bassalt sat across from his prisoner. In the musty cellar of Bassalt's house, smoked meat, herbs, and aged liquor surrounded the two men. Shackles tethered Marebore to the wall. A wound gaped on the prisoner's chest where his Ruby used to be.

Bassalt fiddled with the stone's smooth edge now but kept it concealed in the safety of his cloak. At first he'd thought it would not do to use his greatest advantage over Marebore so early in this battle. But as time passed, Bassalt was becoming more convinced that the time would soon arrive.

For two hours now, under the flickering light of a tallow candle, Bassalt had been punishing Marebore for his insolence, demanding the truth of his scheme. Bassalt had cast ancient earthen spells around the mountain paths to warn him of the unwanted presence of the stonemasters. And yet he'd felt no tremor in the soil when Delion had arrived.

"How?" he thundered, smacking Marebore across the face.

Through bloodied lips, Marebore just smirked and took the pain as if it served his noble cause. There was only one thing left to do, Bassalt knew. A move that might finally convince Marebore of the seriousness of Bassalt's words. He fished out the Ruby from his pocket and twisted it between pudgy fingers.

"Such a beautiful stone," Bassalt mused. "A shame for it to go to waste."

Marebore sneered. "You wouldn't dare break the stone of a man living."

"Oh, but I would." Bassalt squeezed the Ruby. Red powder painted his fingers as the stone ground against them.

"Stop!"

"Give me what I want, and perhaps I will."

Marebore writhed and pulled at his chains. "Stones curse you, Bassalt! You won't stay chief for long."

Bassalt pressed the stone harder. There was a splintering sound, and Marebore gritted his teeth. "How did you smuggle the stonemaster into Hydrus?"

"Curse you!" Marebore's eyes were now red and swollen, trickles of blood hanging at their corners. "Hydrus should no longer be yours."

"And yet mine it remains. As it should be. I'm the only one who can protect it from men like you. Now, tell me how you did it." The Ruby was powerful, Bassalt knew, but not in matters of the earth. It couldn't have been the one to break the earthen spell. And if it had been Stonemaster Delion who had done it, Bassalt would have felt the gaze of the master's Tiger's Eye over the village.

Marebore burst into a fit of coughing and laughter. "You can no longer hide, Bassalt. The tide is turning."

Bassalt paused, regarding his prisoner curiously. *What can he know about change?* There was no way Marebore would know about the snake ring—of that Bassalt was certain. The only person he had trusted with the truth was Silver, and he now lay in Farmera's house, fighting for his life. Cold sweat broke out on Bassalt's forehead as he remembered he had left the snake ring in a cup in his room when he had stormed out to go to Silver's side.

"You feel it too," Marebore pressed. "I know you are no fool. Fools don't build walls around themselves—only cravens do." His insolence earned him another slap. He groaned in pain.

"What do you know?" Bassalt's voice echoed under the low ceiling, sending dust raining down from above.

"The darkness is back. You've seen it too."

Bassalt shook his head. "I've seen nothing."

"Darkness killed Ronan."

Ah, and so it comes back to this deserved murder. "It was the talon boy," Bassalt said, venom dripping from his voice.

"You say so," Marebore scoffed, "and yet here you are talking to me instead of hunting him down. Tell me, if Bhoran is the darkness, how did you let him slip through your grasp?"

Bassalt jabbed a fat finger into the raw chest wound, making Marebore scream. "How did you get Delion into the village?"

"You thought Ronan was the only one with a knowledge of the paths?"

Bassalt grabbed his throat. "Liar! The paths are protected from the stonemasters. I made certain of that myself. Speak now before I kill you. How?" He squeezed hard, and for a small moment, he thought of ending Marebore's life. What good did it do speaking to him, anyhow? The man's lips were sealed tighter than a sea clam's shell. Marebore's face turned fiery red, and Bassalt cursed and released him with a disgruntled shove.

Chains rattled as Marebore hit the wall. He threw his head back, breaking into a harrowing cackle. "I do not fear you, Bassalt. Your threats are crumbling husks. You will kill me, you say? Much like you killed Bhoran or Delion? You do not scare me."

Bassalt rose swiftly, his cloak swirling around him. *Keep the Tiger's Eye centered,* Delion's voice warned in his head, yet it was no good. Anger simmered in him like water in a cauldron. He pushed crates aside, sending dried apples, figs, plums rolling to the floor. From behind, he snatched at a sack. Metal and rock clanked as he carried it over his shoulder. "YOU DO NOT FEAR ME?" He swung the sack into Marebore's face.

A crunching sound tore the air as the impact fractured Marebore's jaw. Bassalt relished the cries of pain that filled the insolent man's eyes with tears.

"Wipe your face," Bassalt commanded. "So you can see the truth."

Do not! his instinct screamed at him, yet it was too late. A madness stirred him. No one should defy him so.

Marebore coughed, a broken tooth shooting out. His gaze fell to the floor. The impact had forced the sack open, and from it had fallen all kinds of birthstones, which glittered under the pale candle flame. "No," he mumbled, his eyes widening with realization.

"Tell me again I cannot kill!" Bassalt roared. "Show me you do not fear me, and I shall bury you to keep the company of Ronan. Maggots will fill your mouth after I'm done with you." Spittle wetted his every word.

"You ... it was you ..."

Bassalt stomped down, crushing spilled birthstones. "This—awaits—you—if—you—do—not—*speak*!" He panted now, froth spilling from his lips. "How did you smuggle Delion into Hydrus?"

Marebore trembled, the beads in his hair clinking. "Murderer ..."

It was the final stroke. Bassalt grabbed a candle and pressed the Ruby to the tip of its flame. Marebore screeched like wounded prey, his back arching.

"How? Speak, damn you!"

A faint whimper left Marebore's lungs, and he writhed in pain.

Bassalt leaned closer, tugging at the fallen man's hair. "Speak or burn."

"Dhy...linea."

The name came out as a tortured whisper, distorted by Marebore's broken jaw. But in Bassalt's mind, it echoed like a merciful thunder. Soothing rain quenched the storm in his chest, and he withdrew the Ruby from the fire. *That cursed woman.* Bassalt had thought her gone. "Where is she?"

"Never ... find ..."

Bassalt snapped his fingers, crushing the Ruby. Its dust rained over Marebore's matted hair. "We shall see about that," he said over Marebore's screams.

CHAPTER FORTY-TWO

AVALAN.

The voice came, kinder this time, yet no less demanding. In Avalan's mind, it whispered again and again, a faint truth behind a veil of lies. It was calling him, Avalan knew, but he felt as if he floated in a sea of dark mist. The harder he tried to escape its grip, the tighter it coiled around him.

He opened his mouth to speak, and the mist swirled inside. It tasted brackish. *Hydrus,* he thought. The air around him twisted into the shape of a tiger, which slowly dissipated and gathered again into the face of his mother.

Sigil. Mother. Where are you?

Cold engulfed him. It wasn't the touch of a cool winter wind. Rather, a suffocating sense of loneliness in a barren cave. *Dizredek?* He felt filthy, alone, so hungry … The shadow came to him. He reached for its hand. *Please don't leave me here,* he begged, only his fingers were skeletal, crooked.

A face swam before him—long raven hair streaked with white, eyes of the Bloodstone, crinkles of happiness around them. *My son.*

He loathed it, slashed at it. His mouth screamed, *I am of Onyx!*

A soft murmur quivered the veil, scattering the mist. A woman's voice, soothing, chanting. The song reminded him of the ones his mother sang for those unwell. *Could it be?* He tried to open his eyes; a light blinded him.

"There, there," the woman cautioned. "Slowly."

It couldn't be his mother. The woman sounded younger and of a teasing spirit. He felt her fingers caress his cheeks as she spoke to him softly. "Try again."

He did, more slowly this time, taking in the face that hovered above him. Soft and round it was, with golden hair, rosy lips, and eyes of the Moonstone. "Lusha?" he croaked. *It cannot be. This woman has two perfect eyes and no scar.* His throat was dry. "Who are you?"

The woman smiled, looking pleased. "I'll leave the illumination to your companion."

When she retreated, the sunlight viciously returned, burning his vision. Shading his eyes, Avalan propped himself up.

The woman returned with a jug of water. Avalan took it gratefully, taking in her figure as he drank. Pale she was, with a thin dress that swirled around her curves like the mist in Avalan's dream. *Who is she? Where am I?*

When he had drained the last drop, he looked at his surroundings. The cave was shallow and rather small, with a broad skylight that let in the morning's blinding light. He lay atop a flat rock. It reminded him of a working table. Avalan made to stand, but his chest felt heavy and his legs weak, as if he'd lost a lot of blood.

And then he remembered: the statue, the stranger, the darts. One of them had gotten him in the shoulder. *Right there …* In place of what should have been a wound now spread an etching much like the ones Bhoran had, only his was of crimson ink, where Bhoran's were black. "Where is Bhoran? What have you done to me?"

"She saved your life." From the back of the cavern, Bhoran emerged from the shadows. Worry gnawed at his features. On his bare chest, claw marks marred the skin over his heart. Yet he was alive, and that was all that mattered.

Avalan breathed more easily. "How long was I gone?"

"Two short nights and a day." Bhoran edged closer to examine the fresh etching. "It stings?"

"It's … raw."

Bhoran nodded. "It will be for a while. That fades."

"You should listen to Bhoran." The woman's voice echoed from the back of the cave. "He knows well."

"Do not speak," Bhoran told her.

Avalan traced the etching on his shoulder. "Was that needed to save me? I wouldn't have minded a scar."

"Oh, but etchings are so much prettier." The woman chuckled. She returned, a tray in hand. "Herbs and salty meat. I'm afraid it's the only thing I can offer. Food is scarce in the mountains, especially since my hunter left me." She winked at Bhoran.

Hunter? Avalan took the steaming mug in his hands. Leaves with jagged edges swirled on the surface. He took a sip. It burned as it trickled down, leaving a sweet taste on his tongue. Over the brim, he saw Bhoran's skulking, his lips a tight line, his shoulders hunched. *He likes her not, but I should be wise not to raise the matter.* "Thank you," he said to the woman. "For saving my life."

The woman's eyes twinkled. "I thank *you*, Avalan of the Bloodstone, for bringing Bhoran back to me." She withdrew, threw herself atop a bear's hide like a promiscuous seductress.

Despite his hunger, Avalan ignored the tray next to him and turned to Bhoran. "She's the one." It wasn't a question. Though Bhoran appeared to hate her and hadn't even deigned to introduce her, Avalan was certain she had been his secret lover during his time in exile. And now he could see why. The resemblance to Lusha was uncanny …

Bhoran let out a low growl of shame.

"The etchings on your body …"

"She *saved* me too." Bhoran's lips twitched with disgust. "More than once."

"Where are we?"

"The Craggy Mountains. Northern slopes."

Avalan frowned and looked up as if expecting to see the village through the skylight. It was a foolish notion, he knew. The mountain stretched high and wide, and from here there was no telling where this cavern lay. "How did I make it so far? The last thing I remember was this thump of pain in my shoulder, and then … nothing."

"I carried you."

"Why here? Why not the keep?"

Bhoran clenched his fists. "Finish your food. The air here is sickening. We're leaving." Without so much as a glance at the woman, he strode to the cave's entrance.

Avalan gazed at Bhoran's scathed shanks, where darts had found purchase. Something had gone terribly wrong, he knew, and he was certain it didn't solely have to do with the trap in the statue.

"He's right, you know," the woman said. "The ritual is draining. I wager your head's still spinning. If you want to reach Raekandar and not faint on the road, you should eat."

Avalan eyed the meat warily. It didn't look like much, but his stomach roiled. He brought a small piece to his mouth and chewed. It was as salty as the woman had promised.

She sat on the bench next to him. "I hope you like my marking," she said, motioning to his shoulder.

It was a mix of swirling red lines with the puncture wound at the center. "What is it?"

"A maze. A symbol of guidance."

Guidance. Avalan forced the dry meat down his throat, and his eyes searched the ground. *Where is the shadow?* It seemed foolish for him to hope it had followed him here when all it had been doing of late was tailing Crystal ... and yet he had dreamed of it, and something more ...

"Though it seems to me you have a guide already," the woman said, breaking his thoughts. The Moonstones in her eyes glowed in earnest, and yet her lips ... a small twitch quivered them, revealing mockery in her words.

Avalan didn't trust her. "I do not know what you mean."

She sighed. "This is the matter—your ignorance of things, Avalan of the Bloodstone. Your blind faith in the shadows is dangerous. It could *end* your life."

Avalan stared at her. The shadow had never tried to harm him. It had saved Bhoran and even Avalan himself from Ethelnar's blade. *It killed the goatling, though,* he remembered. And it had abandoned him before it had fulfilled Dizredek's promise to guide him to the Heart of the Bloodstone. Perchance this woman held some truth he needed. "Who are you?"

"Dhylinea."

"Your eyes are of the Moonstone."

She smiled. "Bhoran loves his women that way. Tell me, has she taken him back?"

There is only one woman Bhoran loves, Avalan thought, taking another bite of meat. "You mean Lusha?" At the sound of Lusha's name, Dhylinea's gaze darkened, and her lips opened in anticipation. Avalan knew then he could use that raw spot in her heart to pry loose the tidings he needed. "I shall tell you only if you answer some of my questions."

"What do you want to know?"

"Hydrus," Avalan said. "How far is it from here?"

Dhylinea raised an elegant hand to the skylight. "Far. One has to scale the slope and visit the place where you camped to see the village on the horizon. Though don't expect the clearest view."

"You watch often, yes?" From her words, Avalan now knew there was little this woman's gaze missed.

She nodded warily.

Avalan took her hand. A gentle touch could open a woman's heart, he knew. "What happened during the Night of the Spirits? Does Bassalt still stand as chief?"

She wriggled free. "Do not ask me things like this, Avalan of the Bloodstone. It was dark. Perhaps I mistook what I saw … what I heard …"

Avalan's heart raced. *Did the men attack as planned?* "You must tell me."

"Must I?"

"The mountain must be very lonely," Avalan said, his voice soft.

Dhylinea's forehead creased. "Do not pretend to care about me."

"Why are you here? Why does a beautiful woman like you shun the embrace of a tribe?"

Her nostrils flared, and she inhaled deeply. "Not everyone's made to eat and dance and hunt and sing." Indignation painted her voice. "Some of us hold more sacred duties, guarding the lands."

"You're a guardian, then?" Avalan wondered if it wasn't the village of Hydrus this woman was watching over.

"Enough. I much prefer to tell you what the Night of the Spirits brought. Though you must promise me to keep it to yourself. Can you do that, Avalan of the Bloodstone?"

Seeing the sheen of sadness in her eyes, Avalan nodded. It was the least he could do after she had saved his life.

"That night, I climbed aloft to get a better view of Hydrus. The air carried the smell of roasting game and the sound of drums. For a while, the tribe danced. I could feel their footsteps, swift and careless, and a terrible dread nestled in my heart. Heavy clouds darkened the sky that night, but … I saw him. *Hydrus.* From the sea he rose, his scales glistening as he charged toward the village. A terrible fight transpired. The earth shook, and vines rose from the ground. The cries of men mingled with the clang of metal, and the air carried the smell of blood and death. When the end came, an unsettling silence shrouded the village."

Avalan's heart swelled. "Perchance Bassalt is defeated."

"No. There was no cheering. No celebration of a victory. He still stands—of that I'm certain."

Dread clutched Avalan's chest. "What do you mean, Hydrus *rose*?"

"The waterdragon. It is an ill omen when the creatures return."

"Are the tales true, then? A sea monster lurks in the Nameless Sea?"

Dhylinea laughed, a joyous sound that broke the sense of foreboding. "I'd be wiser than to call Hydrus a monster."

Suddenly Avalan wished he could return to the village, make certain his mother and Sigil fared well. He made to stand, but Dhylinea forced him down.

"You owe me an answer," she said, no longer laughing.

Avalan gazed at her for a moment. "Lusha has taken Bhoran back."

"I see." Her voice was hard now.

"You still love him?"

"No."

Avalan didn't believe her. There was something strange about this woman. Her body spoke of danger and mystical powers beyond his understanding. She was a healer, but so unlike his mother. Where Farmera was gentle, healing the skin with pastes and concoctions,

Dhylinea sang and marked the flesh. As if she wanted to own those she cured. *Is this how she feels for Bhoran? That he is hers?* His fingers brushed the maze etching on his shoulder. *Am I now to share the same fate?*

Dhylinea eased herself off the rock. "You should go now, and do not forget your promise to me. The Stone Lands mustn't know Hydrus has risen."

Avalan watched her disappear into the shadows at the back of the cave.

He gulped the rest of the drink down and made his way to the entrance. There, Bhoran was leaning against a lean tree, his arms folded. When he saw Avalan, he turned and, without a word, rushed down the slope.

"Wait for me." After some long strides, Avalan caught up with him, grabbed his arm. "Talk to me."

"No!" Bhoran's bellow sent a flock of nearby birds to the sky. "We must return to Raekandar."

Avalan knew that to be true. Much as he ached to know what had happened in Hydrus, they needed to take Lusha and Crystal away from the clutches of Ethelnar. "Someone tried to kill us."

"And now they will know poison does nothing to me." Bhoran banged a furious fist on his chest. "Let them poke me with spears if they dare. I will snap them all."

Confused by Bhoran's sudden burst of anger, Avalan glanced back at the cave. "What did Dhylinea do to you?"

Bhoran shook his head. "Let us go before I kill her. I want to find Lusha."

"But—"

"No. Our bond is weak. I *must* see her." A look of deep concentration creased Bhoran's brows.

He's calling her, Avalan realized, *but she won't answer.* In the darkness of Bhoran's eyes, Avalan saw a faint stirring, a swirl of white specks ...

Without waiting for an answer, Bhoran resumed his frenzied run toward Raekandar. Avalan cursed and followed.

His legs were still numb from all the hours he'd spent on Dhylinea's slab, but he swallowed back the pain and pushed on. Bhoran needed him, and Avalan knew the rush of an aching heart should not be delayed. *Once he has feasted his eyes on Lusha, his pain will be soothed.*

They ran and ran, and then some more. The sun burned, and then it didn't as the day faded. Once only, Avalan stopped to quench his thirst in a creek. Then he raced after Bhoran again. Raekandar's Keep came into view in the distance.

The setting sun bathed the keep's gray walls in crimson when they finally reached it. The gates were unmanned, the studded door securely fastened. As they approached, Bhoran grabbed Avalan's shoulders. "You do the talking."

Avalan pressed his face through the small opening in the door, hailing a guard. He gave Avalan a meek smile, then disappeared. Not long after, the gate creaked open.

Bhoran strode through without so much as a word of gratitude.

"Shall we visit the sickhouse first?" Avalan asked him.

Bhoran nodded.

They were both relieved to hear the medic tell them Lusha had woken well and rested, and she had returned to the keep. Bhoran got hold of the first servant he found and ordered her to lead them to Lusha's room.

Scared, the girl nodded, and scurried off as soon as they reached Lusha's door. Bhoran pushed his way in without knocking, and Avalan followed. He would make certain they were both safe before he'd leave them to talk. It was unwise to stride like this through the keep when someone wanted them dead, but there was no stopping Bhoran now.

The room was empty, a faint smell of iron in the air.

He watched Bhoran walk to the bathtub and came up beside him. The iron smell was stronger there. *Like old blood.* "What happened here?"

"I found her here," Bhoran said solemnly. "The herb made her bleed."

Avalan groped for words of comfort. "I'm certain she's with Crystal. We can—"

The faint whispers of a long dress over stone reached the room. Crystal crossed the threshold, worry etched on her face. She still wore the Black Opal pendant, Avalan noted, disappointed. "Avalan … Bhoran …" She paused, looked them both up and down.

They made for a dreadful sight, Avalan was certain. Their hands and feet were covered with dust, their breeches drenched with sweat and torn as if from a fight with a mountain panther. He went to her. "Where is Lusha?"

Crystal shook her head. "She's … I hoped she was …" Her gaze went to the etching on Avalan's arm. "I thought you all left together."

Her words pained him. "I would never leave without you."

Bhoran sat on the edge of the bathtub, knuckling his thighs. "Where is she?"

Crystal frowned. "Nexanthos told me she left the sickhouse in good health, though sad spirits. I questioned the servants." She peered at Bhoran. "A girl claims she brought her to your room."

"I wasn't here." Bhoran clutched at the rim so hard his fingertips turned white.

"Another servant said she served her and Eyedir a swift meal in my husband's supping yard. Said she looked flustered, and Eyedir slipped her a knife."

"A knife?" Bhoran was up on his feet now.

"Why would Eyedir give her a knife?" Avalan said.

Crystal shook her head. "I don't know." Then she took a deep breath, as if to find the courage to say the words. "Bhoran, I know she took the mourning. I was the one who gave it to her, and for that I'm very sorry. But did you perhaps say something to her … something that would make her upset enough to …"

"No."

The chiefess shot Avalan a desperate look.

"Bhoran was with me," Avalan said in his defense, though there had been a moment when Bhoran had whispered in Lusha's ear, he remembered, after the curious game they'd played on the tower. Avalan hadn't heard what Bhoran had said. But he was certain they had been words of love. He stared at the open door. *Someone tried to kill us. We have to find Lusha and leave.* "Where is your husband?"

As if by instinct, Crystal reached for her Opal-set pendant. "Ethelnar's gone to replenish the blessing of his Black Opal. I don't expect him to return before the morning."

Avalan considered the circumstance. With Ethelnar away, it would prove the perfect chance for him to convince Crystal to escape with him. Together they could follow the shadow, find the Heart of the Bloodstone, and return to Hydrus. Perhaps he could ask this strange woman, Dhylinea, to keep Crystal safe until he'd freed the village … "Is this a thing he oft does?"

Crystal nodded. "The waiting is the worst part during the Night of the Spirits. It always wears Ethelnar down until Othor's soul has assented to his reign for one more year. Then Stonemistress Luthea takes him to the Black Opal to regain his strength."

Bhoran paced the room now, a caged beast whose patience was thinning. He halted, a feverish look in his eye as he addressed the chiefess. "I care more about where Eyedir is."

"Gone, I'm afraid. Eyedir always leaves after the Night of the Spirits. It is his custom. He won't return until ten moonturns have passed. But … whatever happened to you two?"

Avalan looked down at his tattered breeches. "Someone tried to kill us."

The chiefess paled. "Who? *Why?*"

Bhoran smashed his fist against the wall, then strode to the window. He stared at the dimming sky, shook his head. Then he turned, looked at Avalan, hard determination on his face. "I'll go look for Lusha."

"You summoned Yekana?"

A quick nod. Bhoran made for the door.

"Wait. I feel your pain, but you should not forget we aren't safe."

"*Lusha* isn't safe. The merchant gave her a knife."

There was no stopping him now, Avalan knew. He plucked the goat dagger from his belt and gave it to Bhoran. "Take this. I shall feel more at ease knowing you have it."

"Yekana's fangs are all the knives I need. Should anyone come close—"

Avalan forced the dagger into his hands. "Do not disturb this place by having a massive snake slither through the grounds. This doesn't serve our purpose of staying low."

"I cannot stand idle."

"Nor am I saying you should. Go. Look for her. The servant said she came to find you. Start with your room. That would be what I'd do. I—" He glanced at Crystal over his shoulder, then lowered his voice. "I'll try to convince Crystal to leave with me now. Her husband's absence couldn't have come at a better time. Meet us at Olnos. It's time we left this place behind us."

For a moment, Bhoran's gaze lingered past Avalan's shoulder, his Onyx eyes peering at the chiefess. "Not everything needs saving. I hope your shadow's right about her." With a swift move, Bhoran secured the goat dagger in his breeches. He squeezed Avalan's shoulder and left.

I hope he finds Lusha. There isn't much time. Once alone, Avalan took Crystal's hands in his and planted a gentle kiss on her lips. "We must go somewhere else to talk. It isn't safe to linger here."

"The tower," she said.

CHAPTER FORTY-THREE

LUSHA HAD NEVER RIDDEN a horse before. In truth, Alana, the black mare that now carried her and Eyedir, was the first horse Lusha had ever met. Through rheumy eyes, Alana had stared at her last night when Lusha had sneaked into the stables to follow the merchant on his journey. In those beautiful, watery eyes, Lusha had watched her own scared reflection.

Alana had snorted then, breaking the wall of ice around Lusha's heart. *I can learn to love again. Perchance an animal like you,* Lusha had thought, stroking the soft mane.

The merchant eased the horse now to a lazy trot, but even so, Lusha clasped Eyedir's waist tighter. It was too dark to see more than a few paces ahead. The path beneath them was a snaking trail lined with gravel. On each side, the forest loomed, gloomy and unsettling, Lusha's glowing skin the only light in the darkness.

"Don't fear, my sweeting," Eyedir told her over his shoulder. "Alana's the ablest horse in Raekandar."

That much Lusha could see was true. The mare had gracefully accepted the both of them and Eyedir's wares on her back without flinching. She was also quick to obey the merchant's orders, both those spoken out loud and those implied by a touch of his hand or a gentle pull of the reins.

The gravel made the horse's footing uneven. It reminded Lusha of that one time the ground had shaken in Hydrus when she was a child, and for some moments, she had thought the world was ending. Later, Silver had told her it was a mere quake of the earth—a warning that things were about to change.

Things have changed forever now. That she had known for certain when her freshly cut hair had fallen on the soft linen. After the deed, the only thing that had comforted her had been Eyedir's nod of approval at her changed appearance. He had handed her a set of garments—rough breeches and a short tunic the color of freshly wetted soil—clothes worn by the stable boys. Clothes that faintly smelled like the stable boys even, but Lusha thought that a small price to pay for freedom.

The breeze bit into her naked nape now, caressed her scar. Yet she felt free. Truly free, for the first time, as if all it had taken for her to taste freedom was to lose everything she loved. *Not everything,* she reminded herself. Her mother's pendant still adorned her neck.

In silence they trotted on. Lusha found her eyelids feeling heavy. She closed them for what she thought was a moment, only to be awakened after Eyedir brought Alana to a sudden stop.

Ashamed, Lusha lifted her head from the merchant's shoulder. She'd fallen asleep on him. "I'm sorry."

"It's time we rested," Eyedir said. "Mind yourself now. I will hop down and then get you." And so he did, but as soon as Lusha's feet touched the ground, her legs betrayed her, and she collapsed.

Eyedir laughed. "Your legs are numb." He set her straight. "It was a long ride. Come. Let us stretch them. Make the blood return."

Lusha rubbed her legs, and slowly the numb sensation faded. Eyedir had even been kind enough to give her shoes—brown leather that hugged her feet and was secured with a small strap around each ankle. It was the first time Lusha had worn shoes, but Eyedir had insisted it was common practice in the cities, and her lady feet would only give her away, so she had gladly put them on. But now she longed to be rid of them and feel the ground. The grass over the hill looked so soft and inviting.

Eyedir must have followed her gaze, for he laughed and said, "Hating the shoes already? Trust me, you'll be glad to have them on when we continue our journey on foot, or for the time we spend walking the streets of Levorotha. Stone and granite this place is, not kind on the naked soles of newcomers."

Lusha flushed at her ungratefulness. "I love them. Thank you."

"We should make camp for the rest of the night," Eyedir said, glancing at the hill. "Catch some sleep before dawn. The sun rises early in this place."

Once they'd reached the forest, he unslung the heavy sacks from Alana's saddle. They met the ground with a thump, lifting clouds of dust. Eyedir untied the string of one and fished out a coconut shell, filled it with water, and offered it to Alana. She drained it to the last drop. Eyedir tethered her to a tree and searched the surrounding area, a look of worry on his face.

"Is something wrong?" Lusha asked.

He frowned, waved a dismissive hand. "I don't make a habit of often stopping on the road." He looked around him. "Just being cautious is all."

Suddenly feeling vulnerable, Lusha looked around too. Her disguise proved little comfort for the uneasiness in her heart. She suddenly wished Avalan were here. He always knew where to step to not bother the forest and what to do to appease its mistrust of strangers. She shivered.

Eyedir handed her a woolen cloak and sat on the ground. "I hope you will forgive me, my sweeting, but it isn't wise to start a fire. Attracts too much attention."

The cloak felt soft and warm and smelled faintly of the spices Eyedir carried in his pots. She joined him on the ground. "Avalan says a fire keeps the forest's beasts at bay."

"Your friend is wise, but there are some beasts who see fire as an invitation. We shouldn't risk unbidden guests."

Lusha frowned. "Thieves?"

"You shouldn't trouble yourself with these things, my sweeting. We shall take but a few hours' rest and then be on our way."

He dipped his hands into his sack and offered her a waterskin and some salted meat. "It isn't much," he said ruefully. "But we shall have a better meal once we're at Undeena's. She will be glad to see us—

especially you. She always talks about Hydrus. You should fill her with wondrous stories of the place. Might earn us both a good day's feast." He chuckled.

Lusha frowned. Speaking about Hydrus was the last thing she desired.

"Don't be so serious now," Eyedir said. "Speak not of the village if it grieves you. Undeena will stuff us with food anyhow. That is her way of thanking."

"Why would she be thanking us?"

Eyedir unfastened the buckle on one of his pockets, then fished out a battered parchment. Brandishing it, he said, "Undeena will be glad to receive this."

The parchment's color reminded Lusha of the sand on the white beach of Hydrus, where the boys played the goat games. She took a sip from the rough waterskin. "Who is she?"

"A brilliant woman—the greatest hostess there's ever been—or so she likes to say herself. Come to think of it, though, it's probably true. Ronan made sure he always had two nights to spare at her place. 'The inn that never sleeps.' We merchants always learn new things from her guests." He stuffed the parchment inside his robe and tightened his belt.

Lusha eyed him curiously. She'd never been to an inn, but she recalled Ronan talking to her about them. She tried hard to remember if he'd ever mentioned Undeena. "It sounds like a very galling place to be."

"It is." Eyedir took a bite out of his bread. "It provides great opportunities for new tasks as well. We merchants accept all sorts of things to get by. We deliver goods necessary for a settlement's survival, and messages to loved ones who live in separate places, transfer tidings between rulers, and from time to time, we guide a lost traveler like yourself."

Shame rose to Lusha's cheeks. "I mean not to slow you in your journey. If you point the way for me—"

"It is all right, my sweeting. I didn't mean it like it sounded. I'm glad to aid you in your cause. You seemed determined to leave the keep, and if I'd let you travel these roads alone, I'd never have forgiven myself."

Chewing her food slowly, Lusha wondered if it was right to leave Avalan and Bhoran behind like this. She hadn't even told Crystal about her decision. What if the chief sent soldiers to find her and bring her back, or even worse, surrender her to her father? The meat fell through her fingers. "I'm not so tired that I need rest. Perhaps we should get moving."

Eyedir chuckled. "Calm, my sweeting. The inn isn't far now. We should catch some sleep, for I intend to put up a bench in the market, and a tired man makes poor bargains."

Lusha nodded.

"This aunt of yours," Eyedir said. "Does she expect your visit?" He frowned when he saw her shake her head. "Did she ever send word to you through Ronan after your mother's death?"

Lusha shook her head again. She suspected Silver had gone to great lengths to conceal her aunt from her, perhaps even warn Ronan to not fill Lusha's mind with hopes of another family.

"How will you convince your aunt to accept you, my sweeting?"

She rubbed the back of her neck. Her appearance was her strongest argument, seeing as everyone always told her she was the spitting image of her mother. But now all that was gone. She showed him the silver pendant. "I have this. It belonged to my mother."

Eyedir nodded quietly but didn't offer his thoughts.

Chafed by the constant rubbing of the ride, Lusha's inner thighs ached. Even so, her eyelids were growing heavy.

"Why don't you rest now, my sweeting?" Eyedir stood and went to the horse, fed her raw oats. "I'll wake you once it's time for us to hit the path again."

Lusha found herself a nearby flat patch of sparse grass between brambles. Pulling the wool tighter around her as she lay, she raised her eyes to the dark sky, daring the moon. It still stood round, yet not full anymore—its right side was ever so slightly incomplete, as if someone had taken a bite out of it. *Like my heart.* In those sweet moments she had spent in Bhoran's arms, her heart had been round, complete. But now a part of it was missing.

She hid beneath the cloak to dim her glowing skin and let her lids fall.

Leaves rustled behind her, thunder in the wood's silence. Lusha opened her eyes, her belly squirming. *Is it time to leave so soon?* It felt but a mere moment ago she'd fallen asleep. A muffled scream pierced the air. Heart pounding, she peeked out from beneath the cloak. It had come from the merchant's side. She wanted to crawl to him, scream Eyedir's name …

"Search him." The order was harsh, the voice of an older man. Pairs of feet moved all at once. Over the thorny edge, Lusha spied three men and a woman. Eyedir lay on the ground among them. They were probing his robes, sticking their hands roughly in his pockets, throwing his possessions on the ground with no concern. They upturned the sacks—spices, pots, herbs, all spilled to the ground.

A faint glint caught Lusha's attention. *The moon,* she thought with horror, gazing at the back of her hand. Under the moonlight, her skin glowed. She pulled the cloak over her head, and crawled to the nearest tree, pressing her back against it.

"Stinky old trinkets." The gruff man spoke again. "Where do you hide the birthstones, merchant?"

Lusha heard Eyedir gasp as they pulled the gag from his mouth. "No stones," he said between bouts of coughing.

"Liar." A slap echoed through the trees. "Give them over now, 'fore we kill you."

"I told you—" Eyedir began, but then there was a thumping sound, and he cried out in pain.

"Shut your trap. Search the horse. You better hope we find something there, merchant. My patience is running short."

Leaves rustled beneath Alana's hooves. The horse snorted impatiently. Hands brushed the leather of her saddle.

"Nothing here," the woman declared.

Lusha heard a slapping noise. This time, she dared to peer around the tree's thick trunk. Eyedir lay on the ground, the strangers looming over him. It was too dark to be certain, yet she felt they couldn't be

Ethelnar's soldiers. They looked nothing like the peaceful tribe she'd met at Raekandar.

The tallest of them grabbed Eyedir's matted hair, hefted his head, exposing the neck. "Listen here, you scum. Your friend Ronan stole the stones from us. A game of dice, he called it, stones strike him dead. More like a game of deception. I should have known better than to trust that thieving mug. Now you be a good merchant and tell us where we shall find him."

"He ... he's dead."

The others sniggered. "Is that so?" The man turned to face his company. "Dead, he says. It seems the stones beat us to it." He thrust Eyedir to the ground, a nasty snarl twisting his lips. Then he nodded to the woman.

She knelt to face Eyedir. "Are you alone?"

"Merchants always travel alone," Eyedir managed.

Lusha's stomach coiled at the lie. *He's trying to protect me. I need to—*

Swift as a stormy wind, the woman unsheathed a knife and ran it through Eyedir's neck. The blade slid through flesh with sickening ease, and Eyedir fell to the ground, face forward. "And so you die alone as well," the woman said.

"No!"

It was too late to take it back. The thieves were staring at her now. Lusha had thrown the cloak back to free her hands, though what good that would do her without weapons, she didn't know. In the darkness, her skin glowed so bright she could clearly see all of their faces. To her, they all looked the same—heartless, ruthless thieves ...

"A moonmage!" one of them screamed, scurrying away.

The rest raised their hands to shade their eyes.

The woman brandished her knife, Eyedir's blood dripping from it. "Who are you?" she called.

"Stones curse you!" Lusha screamed, grabbing some rocks. She hurled them with all her strength, her fear giving way to terrible anger.

Alana snorted, disgruntled. The thieves shielded their faces, yet soon they realized how feeble the attack was, for they lowered their guard.

They will kill me, Lusha thought as her fingers dipped into barren soil. She grabbed a stick just as the woman snarled and charged at her, knife at the ready. The blade grazed Lusha's upper arm, tearing fabric. As she fell to the ground, the woman clambered on top of her, raising her knife.

The moon suddenly shone so bright it blinded even Lusha. She saw the knife plunging toward her chest.

Lusha screamed, grabbed the woman's face to halt her. A cold burning bolted through Lusha's touch. And then it was the woman who screamed all the more. She rolled off Lusha, holding her face. Terrible silver blisters now marred it, as if Lusha's touch had burned the thief's skin.

The woman staggered to her feet, scuttled to her companions. "She's of the bloody Moonstone!"

Cursing, the thieves scattered.

Bewildered, Lusha stared at her own hand. It bore no blisters or wounds. *Eyedir,* she thought with horror. *I must go to him. I must …*

She staggered to his body, rolled it over. His unmoving stare reminded her of Ronan's empty eyes. Eyedir was gone. Lusha wanted to shout for help, but fear had grabbed hold of her belly, so all she did was retch, emptying onto the forest floor what little food she'd had for supper.

CHAPTER FORTY-FOUR

THE TALL WINDOW of the west tower was cool against Avalan's touch, the candle flames faint on its smooth surface. His own reflection stared back at him, brows thick with worry, eyes earthy green and speckled with blood spots. As he waited for Crystal, he tried to recall the visions that had come to him while he had lain on Dhylinea's slab. Sigil had appeared, and Farmera, and then an otherworldly skeleton of himself, and something else, which eluded him.

It mattered not. There was no time.

Crystal must come with me, he thought, heart thumping in his chest. He had to convince her, but what if she would once again refuse his offer? *Not everything needs saving,* Bhoran had told him. Yet Avalan couldn't bear to lose her again. Not now that he knew she still loved him.

Over the coast, gray storm clouds gathered. Like a flock of scared sheep, they huddled, rushing toward the keep. Soon a great storm would arrive, much like the chief's weathermen had predicted. He hoped Lusha was safe out there. His gut feeling told him she was gone. No matter how hard Bhoran searched for her, Avalan was certain he wouldn't find her.

Behind him, the door creaked open. Tensing, Avalan brushed his belt, only to find it empty. *I gave Bhoran my goat dagger.*

Crystal slipped inside, her hair tied at her nape, a loose robe around her body, as if she had readied herself for sleep. "They found Lusha's dress in the stables, hidden under a stack of hay," she told him, closing the door behind her.

This affirmed Avalan's fear. "Did the stablemen see her?"

"No. Though Jherman, the stable master, said one of his boys complained his clothes had gone missing. The boy thought it a jest played by his mates, but ..."

"It's Lusha," Avalan said. "She's gone with Eyedir."

Crystal frowned. "Why do you say that?"

Avalan sat next to her. "I've had time to think it over. Ronan promised Lusha he'd take her to Levorotha. Eyedir is Ronan's trusted friend—a merchant journeying the lands. Your servant said she saw the two of them talking. That was when Lusha must have asked Eyedir to take her with him. If Ronan trusted him, she trusts him too."

Crystal's eyes widened, the pale sea in them stirring. "I was afraid you'd say that. But why would she leave Bhoran behind without farewell? After all these years of being apart ..."

"I do not know." Avalan had turned this question over in his mind many a time while waiting for Crystal. Now that his body had healed from Dhylinea's potions, his mind had unclouded, and his wits had returned to him stronger than ever. And yet Lusha's sudden flight made little sense to him. *Except* ... "She might be thinking Bhoran is an Onyx. She even risked her life by taking that herb."

"This can't be her reason," Crystal argued. "She's lived with that doubt all her life. There must be something else, or she might have overflowed with shame, not wanting to face him after taking the mourning."

The crack of thunder shook the tower. Avalan spun to glimpse the storm clouds slithering dangerously close, a mass of darkness against the leaden sky. The storm was at their doorstep, and he still hadn't convinced Crystal to follow him.

He took her hand. In his grip, it felt cool and unsteady, much like his courage. "Crystal, come with me." The look she gave him tore his heart. It was a look of fear and not love, as he had hoped.

"Ethelnar—"

"You said he won't return until the morrow. Now's the perfect chance for you to slip away. I promise to keep you safe."

In the dim candlelight, her lips paled. "I can't. You don't know my husband. He will kill me. Kill you. Stones know, he has already tried."

Avalan still remembered the sharp edge of Ethelnar's blade as it had hovered over the soft skin of his neck, ready to take a bite. "I won't let him. Now that I know what powers the stones carry, I shall use them to free us all. No longer will you have to suffer under his heel."

Crystal frowned. "What of Semara?"

"We will return for her, as I promised you. He won't harm her. He's her father."

A sharp breath tightened Crystal's chest. "You and Bhoran, where were you? You said someone tried to kill you."

He told her then the truth of what had befallen them at the statue, and when he was done, he saw her fear had grown even deeper. "Crystal, I cannot stay much longer. You must decide. Bhoran and I need to leave. It isn't safe for us here. And Hydrus still suffers under Bassalt."

She paled. "I can't … I'm so sorry … You must forget me. Promise me you will. Promise me."

"But I can't. My second shadow is bound to you because it knows you have my heart. As long as it lingers around you, I can't move on. You *must* come with me. For Hydrus. For our tribe. For our love."

At his words, Crystal looked around, as if expecting to see the shadow appear. The room was quiet, the only movement the faint flickering of flames in silver sconces. Around them stood her paintings of an old Hydrus. The white beach, the blackwood forest, the endless sea, the feasting ground.

"We can restore our village," Avalan told her gently. "Free from Bassalt, it can become the place of love we both remember."

Crystal touched his shoulder. "You're bleeding."

At first her words made no sense to him, for he felt no pain. But when he followed her touch, he saw she had the truth of it: the wound from the dart had seeped a brown stain onto the thin cotton of his tunic.

Crystal rushed to the corner where she kept her paints. She

uncorked a small bottle; the smell of thin wine spilled out. When she returned to him, she held a dampened cloth. "Take your tunic off so I can better look at it."

"I'm sure it's nothing ..."

"Take it off."

Avalan obliged her, sliding the tunic over his head. He brought his fingertips to his wound, and they came away warm and bloody. The center of the maze Dhylinea had drawn was now oozing. Gently Crystal dabbed the wound.

"What is this?" he asked her.

"I use it to dilute my paints. Nexanthos says it's suited to cleaning wounds and not brushes, but what does he know?" She smiled up at him now, for a moment the dread of her husband forgotten. Blood painted the cloth, his wound cleaned. And yet Crystal wouldn't stop. Over and over she rubbed his shoulder until the cloth dropped from her grasp. From his shoulder, her fingers slipped to his bare chest, exploring, longing.

Avalan swallowed hard. He cupped her chin, raised her face to his.

"I've missed you," she said through lips that begged him for a kiss. "So much."

Avalan kissed her then. Crystal eased out of her robes. Around her ankles they fell, exposing her nakedness. It was different from what Avalan remembered. The flames cast small shadows upon her curves, her womanly body now fuller than the one he had known when they had first made love in Hydrus.

Over the supple skin of her bosom lay the Black Opal stone. He liked it not, but then Crystal tugged at his breeches. Soon all his dark thoughts vanished, and he lay with her on the rough stone.

Rain pattered against the windows when they stopped moving. Gently it fell at first, but swiftly it grew more demanding, as if it wished for a way into the tower. Crystal's eyes filled with tears. Down the mounds of her cheeks they fell; her chest shivered.

"Hush, now." Avalan brushed the tears away, cool saltiness on his fingertips.

Darkness had now settled, the only light in the chamber the flickering candle flames and the pendant on Crystal's chest. A swirl of colors danced in its darkness, as if it were alive.

Avalan lifted it. "What is this?"

"Ethelnar gave it to me when we wedded. A part of his stone, he told me. To protect me."

"Protect you?"

Outside, lightning cracked, slicing the darkness. Fleeting though it was, Avalan had time to glimpse the second shadow outlined against the door. *There you are.* He dropped the pendant and reached for Crystal's robes, covering her naked body.

"I never loved him," Crystal confessed. She gazed at the dark ceiling with unseeing eyes. "I never forgot about you."

Avalan caressed the softness of her hair. It felt so good to be with her again, even so far away from Hydrus. Even if she had left him. She wasn't ready to confess her reasons, he knew, yet Avalan hoped with time she might come to tell him the truth. Her tears fell again, rigorous like the rain that poured outside. "Come with me," he urged her.

"What of my daughter? I cannot leave her with him."

Avalan felt her pain. Leaving your loved ones behind, even for good reasons, hurt a great deal.

She flinched, her body twitching. *"It burns!"* Crystal propped herself up on her elbows, the robes falling from her chest. The colors in her pendant violently swirled in a maddening vortex. Over her milky skin, a shadowy hand appeared, reaching for the pendant as if to tear it from her neck. "What's happening?"

"The necklace," Avalan said. "It looks as if it's ... alive."

Crystal gazed at it with great disbelief. "It does that sometimes. The colors of the Opal become more vivid. Mostly when my husband is near." As soon as she had said it, her mouth fell open with the dreadful realization.

The second shadow waved its hands, drawing Avalan's attention. It pointed to the window. Avalan turned, half-expecting to see Ethelnar's stern face peering in from behind the drenched glass.

"Avalan, someone's here." Crystal snatched her robes. "I saw some movement."

"It's just the second shadow," he said, though he leaped to his feet, his hunter's instinct kicking in hard. *I do not have my dagger.* He felt empty then, *exposed*. He slipped into his breeches. Still on the floor, Crystal struggled to fasten the gird around her waist. Avalan searched for the second shadow. He found it on the stone wall in the light of the candles, its hand outstretched, pointing frantically from Crystal to the tall window.

"Your pendant," Avalan said. "We must get rid of it. Ethelnar's not protecting you. He's *tracking* you."

Determined, he strode to the glass, smashing his elbow against it. A crack appeared on the smooth surface. Like lightning, it bolted upward. The tall window shattered, scattering thousands of fragments into the air. Whipping wind burst in with such force Avalan had to grab the wall beside him to keep his balance.

Rain invaded the chamber. The storm wetted the parchments, snuffed out the flames of candles, tugged at their clothes as if it wanted to grab them both.

"My paintings!" Crystal screamed. She was on her feet now, dragging some of them away from the gaping window to shield them from the ruthless rain.

"Toss me your pendant!"

She halted, confused. "I ... I don't understand. Ethelnar said he won't—"

"He's tracking you!" Avalan insisted. "Remember the story you read to me? Luthea's memory of the lost children." It all made sense now. He shoved aside the hair that whipped his face. "Stonemistress Luthea said only the Black Opal can trace the path."

Her eyes grew wide now, finally understanding.

The door caved in, smashing against the wall. Avalan glimpsed the silhouette of a man filling the threshold. Tall, lean, and with a sharp stare.

Ethelnar.

The chief strode to Crystal. "You *whore*!" he shrieked over the pounding rain. "You dare betray *me*? After all I did for you and your bastard?" Ethelnar yanked at her robe, stripping her naked.

Avalan charged at him. The force of the impact toppled both of them to the floor. Ethelnar snarled, thrust Avalan off him. The shove was powerful, much more than the mere bony arms of the chief should impart. Avalan's skull cracked against the stones, sending a sharp pain through his brain. *He's using stone magic.*

Crystal's pleading cries mingled with the roar of the never-ending rainfall. Water swiftly pooled on the floor. "Ethelnar, please!" she begged, stumbling to retrieve her dress.

After two long strides, the chief loomed above her. "You dare sleep with him in my keep?" he screamed in her face, then shoved her back. Crystal tripped, landing dangerously close to the gaping window.

"Crystal!" Avalan grabbled for Ethelnar's billowing robe. His fingers found purchase, and he tugged at the black cotton, hurling the chief to the floor.

Ethelnar's eyes were a deadly pool of seething colors. "Stay back!" he screamed. He grabbed at a fallen easel and smashed it over Avalan's head.

Avalan cursed and writhed to free himself, ignoring the splintered wood biting into his arms.

The chief loomed above Crystal now. Her head dangled over the windowsill; her hair, like drenched weeds, clung to her face, invading her parted lips, muffling her screams. Grabbing the soles of her feet, Ethelnar pushed. Crystal's body was sucked out of the window, plummeting to the ground.

A booming thunder drowned out Avalan's scream. Rage and wet wind blinded him as he pounced at the chief. Ethelnar ducked, and Avalan skidded over the wet floor, grabbing the window's edge to prevent his fall. He glanced down, hoping to see her, but the stormy sky was so dark that no ground could be seen below—just a vile darkness.

"Murderer!" Avalan screamed.

Ethelnar's cackle filled the room. "It was *you* who killed her," he said, his lips curling into a leering smile. In the drenched darkness, Ethelnar's dark figure was barely visible. "Perhaps I should send you to meet her." He edged closer. "Seeing as you were so eager to unite with *my* wife!"

Avalan caught a glint of a golden bracelet as the chief twisted his wrists. *He fights like Bassalt.* Avalan braced for an impact he knew should come, half-expecting Crystal's paintings to fly and swoop at him. Instead, a terrible dread invaded his chest, a feeling of certain doom, as if he faced his own death.

Sharp pain tore through his shoulder. He stared down at it, confused. Dhylinea's labyrinth writhed, the paths coiling like snakes. The puncture wound swallowed his mind, and he found himself lost in the maze's dark paths. *Avalan.* The voice of his stone called him, sorrowful, begging. He thrashed against the maze's walls, the feeling so real he could taste his own scarred flesh where Dhylinea's tools had carved him.

Avalan!

It isn't real, Avalan managed to think. He shook his head, his mind escaping the clutches of Ethelnar's magic.

Back in the chamber, the chief stood before him now, his face twisted as if he struggled to keep control of Avalan's mind. Ethelnar snarled, thrusting his arms out. A cold whip of wind smacked Avalan's face, crushing him against an unbroken window. He pushed himself up as a fracture crept up the glass. *It will break!* his mind screamed. His reflection stared back at him, wild, with eyes that were no longer green but glowing red globes, two drops of blood like the Bloodstone that had scorched his hands.

The glass shattered. Avalan rolled to the side, grabbed at the tail of Ethelnar's robe, glided his leg between the chief's, tripping him. *Don't look him in the eye.* Avalan grabbed a splinter of wood. It didn't bear the edge of his goat dagger, but it would have to do.

Thunder joined Ethelnar's laugh. "Avalan of the Bloodstone," he croaked. "Fighting like a scared mouse. What will you do with this, rodent? Stake me?"

Avalan leaped, put all his weight behind the blow as he pointed the sharp edge at Ethelnar's neck. The chief rolled; the stake impaled his thigh. His cry was of a tortured animal. Avalan leaped back, grabbing for a fresh weapon.

"Blood!" the chief shrieked. "It is your blood I'll take now."

He jumped at Avalan, his teeth sinking into the soft flesh of his belly. Avalan yanked at the chief's hair. He saw with horror the chief sucking at him. He staggered, his grip on Ethelnar's hair getting weaker.

The blood must run warm, Dizredek's voice boomed in Avalan's mind. Avalan tangled his fingers deeper into the chief's locks yet couldn't find the strength to pluck him from his flesh. Everything around him felt like a slippery pit out of which he couldn't clamber.

Shadow, please ...

A painting rose from its easel and smashed onto Ethelnar's head. The chief howled, finally letting go. Fresh blood dripped down his chin, mingling with the pouring rain.

"What—" the chief began, but another painting smacked his face. Ethelnar roared, baring stained teeth. "Is this how you fight me? You hit me with my wife's creations? Show yourself, craven!" He flailed his arms around.

Dizzied from blood loss, Avalan slinked behind a painting. *He cannot see me,* he thought, seeing for the first time his advantage. All light was long gone from the room. The candle flames had fizzled out; no moon shone beneath the gray veil of the storm. And yet darkness had never scared Avalan. Under the cover of night, he did most of his hunting with Sigil. *Ethelnar is no more than prey to me,* he reassured himself.

But Avalan had never killed a man before.

Lightning tore the darkness, and Avalan glimpsed a movement he was certain hadn't belonged to the chief. His heart lurched. *The shadow!* It started hurling paintings at the chief again.

Ethelnar crawled, staying low to avoid the onslaught of flying canvases. "Show yourself!"

Avalan felt his own cover being torn away from behind his back, exposing him. Through stone and water, he searched the floor for anything sharp. It was no good, he knew. Nothing could slice at the chief with the force he needed, and Avalan couldn't risk crawling close to him, for fear of another draining bite or worse ... The way Ethelnar's gaze had forced Avalan to drop into his own flesh was a nasty feeling.

A glint of metal caught his eye. Avalan plunged back just in time before the chief's dagger bit into the rock. *He has a blade. If I can grab hold …*

"Speak, damn you!" the chief roared. "Cursed Bloodstone. I stained my tongue with your blood for nothing. Such *weak* magic."

Avalan kept his silence. Through the streaks of lightning that limned the walls, he searched for the shadow. He didn't wish it to be here. For the first time, he wanted it to linger around Crystal, save her … *She's dead,* his mind reminded him. *Dead. Dead.*

Avalan's neck snapped back as Ethelnar snatched his horsetail. The dagger's cold blade threatened the skin of his neck. Ethelnar whispered in Avalan's ear, "It's not the stone of leaders after all."

Avalan glided his foot between Ethelnar's legs, tripping him. The blade slid from the chief's grip. Avalan lunged at it, but his fingers were stilled as though he'd hit an invisible wall. Cold hands groped at him, hands that didn't belong to the chief. Toward the storm that raged outside, they pulled him, pushing, bidding him to leap … *The shadow wants to throw me out? Kill me?* Avalan's heel caught the sharp frame of the smashed window. He grasped at the window frame on both sides, desperate to prevent his fall.

Still on the floor, entangled in his own cowl, Ethelnar raised a sodden head. "A shadow? A filthy Onyx!"

Avalan's head was spinning. If he fell, he'd certainly die. *Why is the shadow trying to kill me?* His eyes searched the floor for the blade. He was certain he'd seen it over there … The shadow flung him back again.

Ethelnar cackled. "The Onyx is rising from the *dead*. Bassalt, you fool! You FOOL!"

He's mad. I need to end this, find Crystal …

There was another stroke of lightning, and Avalan watched the shadow point him to the window. He shook his head. *I won't jump …* A shove in his shoulder told him the shadow was of a different mind. Ignoring it, he fell to his knees, searching for the dagger.

"Looking for this?" Ethelnar snarled, lunging toward Avalan, bringing the blade down again and again.

Avalan tripped, his back crashing against the floor. Ethelnar was fast upon him, pressing his nose so close to Avalan's as if to kiss him.

Don't look at him. Yet it was too late. Ethelnar wriggled the tip of the dagger to the labyrinth's heart, forcing Avalan to open his eyes and scream. *Don't look ...*

Avalan.

He knew that voice. It was mellow and familiar. Twisting his neck, he saw her. Beyond the smashed window, Crystal's naked body hovered in midair. Her open robes billowed in the dance of the storm, her hair streaming behind her. She stretched out an arm, inviting ...

"CRYSTAL!" Avalan shouted. He shoved Ethelnar off him and hurled himself out of the window.

As soon as his feet left the stone, Crystal vanished.

Avalan fell now, plunging through the storm. The wind around him twirled, rain pounding at him so hard as if to claim his very soul. *I will die.* Of that he was certain. He had looked into Ethelnar's eyes, he knew. He had looked.

Cold hands grasped at him. They pulled him not downward into the mouth of the storm but sideways. His fall slowed. The ground approached. He closed his eyes and braced for impact. Rough stone scraped his skin, and he cried out in pain. Yet he was falling no more.

Sparse battlements rose before him. Wet, cold stone spread beneath him. He was alive. Avalan stumbled to his feet and went to the edge. The ground wasn't so far below. He reached for the outer wall and traced its stones. They were uneven—it would be a tough descent, he knew. *I am just scaling the Eagle's Eye,* he comforted himself. He turned and balanced his weight on the first rock, finding a footing.

Rain whipped his back as he descended. Countless times he lost his grip. Yet he clung to the rough wall with all his heart, for it was the only thing that prevented him from plunging to his death.

At last his feet met not with a protruding handhold but with the softness of the grass. He'd made it to the ground. He shaded his eyes against the rain, looking up to gauge the tower, half-expecting to see the chief looming out of the broken window. It gaped emptily.

He raced along the wall until he met with a rounder part. *The root of the tower.* The frantic beating of his heart exploded as he saw her, white, naked skin glowing in the darkness, her body motionless on the grass.

He pushed the wet hair off her face. Her eyes stood open, no light of the stone in them.

Avalan threw his head back and roared, his mouth filling with heartless rain. His chest shook. His tears mingled with the storm. Curling his fingers into fists, he planted a soft kiss on her cheek, then unclasped the Black Opal jewel from her neck.

The pendant was no longer glowing with the chief's colors, but soon it would, Avalan promised himself, closing his fist around it.

And then I will be ready.

CHAPTER FORTY-FIVE

ON THE TALL LOOKING GLASS, the reflection of a golden waterfall of hair greeted Bhoran. He strode into his room, heart in his mouth. "Lusha?"

The chamber was cold and empty. Rain pattered against the window, growing stronger.

This is wrong, he thought as he looked down. Atop his bedsheets lay Lusha's hair. Bhoran ran his fingers through it. Soft like silk it felt, yet jagged at the edges where she had cut it. *The knife,* he remembered. A soft glint caught his eye. He pinched a small bead that rested next to the severed hair. It glowed dimly, as if it had lost its shine now that its owner was gone. *Her Moonstone.*

Bhoran looked over his shoulder, half-expecting Lusha to walk in, give him an explanation. Yet only silence lay beyond the threshold. He searched the bed again, in dire need of more of her things. His fingers brushed the softness of a dress. Hungrily he brought it to his nose, longing to smell her, only to be greeted by a foreign scent he couldn't place. Sweet and sickening it was, not belonging to the woman he loved.

He remembered then. The servant girl climbing into the bathtub with him, provoking him, taunting …

Whatever little warmth his body held slowly drained. Lusha knew, he realized. She had been here to find him, as Avalan had told him she would, and instead she had found *this.* He crumpled the fabric in his fist. All these things on his bed, they were a message. The careful placement of the woman's dress next to Lusha's hair and stone was to tell him she *knew*. The dress shouted that she knew of his betrayal. The hair signified she was no longer the same, and the stone … the Moonstone was her way to bid their love farewell.

No matter how many times he'd given it to her, the Moonstone had always returned to him, as if to remind him to never hope to call Lusha his own, for no matter how close they came to be, she always slipped away from his grasp. This little bead of the moon only reminded him of a bitter truth: *Lusha will never stay with me, for I'm an Onyx.*

He imagined her now, hair short like a man's, journeying alongside Eyedir through the night to reach the city of her aunt. He sat on the edge of the bathtub, pricked his fingers on the fangs in his face. *Not good enough.* He needed something stronger.

He rushed to the window, ignoring the slashing rain. On the glooming horizon, lightning struck, thunder booming soon after as he called for Yekana in his mind. He needed something to numb the pain, or he was certain his heart wouldn't survive. Perhaps he should go back to Dhylinea. Fall on the ground before her feet and beg her to accept him. *She* could give him what he was missing—the sweet pleasure of venom running through his veins, sending him on a journey to a world where there was no pain, or return.

He retched, the thought sickening him. *No more.* Without waiting for Yekana, he stormed out of his room, getting lost in the endless maze of trembling torchlight. Around and around he went, until the floor slanted, leading him downward. Soon the air carried the smell of rain. Once out in the open, the storm pummeled him.

He stumbled upon a cobble path. Hunching his shoulders, he kept his head low against the wind and followed it. To where, he didn't know nor care. The path descended in a slippery slant. Soon the rocks that lined the west side of the keep came into sight. Gray boulders, they loomed above him like a dead end.

The creaking sound of a rusted chain tore the air. Bhoran found a swaying sign hanging above an iron-studded door. He knew not how to read the curious writing on it, but he easily recognized the outline of a tankard.

Warm wind brushed his face as he entered, leaving the storm behind him. Below him, a different storm raged—one of men and women engaged in gambling, drinking, and singing. The clangor of tin tankards and plates rose over their booming voices, drowning out all his dark thoughts.

Suspended from the ceiling, smoking iron lanterns lit the place. Rows of carved stone tables and benches littered the chamber below, hosting large companies who wallowed in drink and games. Bhoran licked his lips as he descended. The sea was near, he knew. He imagined its angry waves splashing the cavern's chamber, seeking a way in.

He found a seat at the back, where the cave descended into a small recess big enough to host a table for two. Bhoran sat and eyed the crowd.

Some leaned against the walls, sunk into a snoring stupor. Others held tiles before their faces, their eyes glinting above the decks with sly curiosity as they watched their opponent's movements, but most of them drank, jested, and sang, and teased the serving girls. They, in turn, were good at avoiding trouble. Around the place they glided, smiling here and there to prevent some men from feeling more ignored than others, swerving to avoid extended palms meaning to grope them or pull them closer.

Bhoran wondered how long it would take these graceful girls to notice him—the ache in his heart was getting bigger with every passing moment, his lips longing to feel the mellow touch of ale. *Drink isn't poison*, his heart told him, to ease the guilt.

A girl with caramel eyes and hair that reached her calves approached him. "What can I bring you?"

"The strongest."

"That'll be three coppers."

Bhoran cursed under his breath. He had no coin, and here it seemed he wasn't regarded as the chief's guest. Perhaps it would be better to return to the keep, seek the kitchens, and drown his sorrows there. He was making to stand when a familiar figure slid up to him, his hand pressing against Bhoran's shoulder, urging him to stay.

The man threw his cowl back, a smile beneath his sharp nose.

"We'll have two Snakemint Ales," he told the girl. "Tell Aras to charge me."

As the girl snaked her way through the tables, the man turned to Bhoran, his gray gaze flecked with gold. "I trust the drinks will prove to your liking."

"Who are you?" Bhoran knew the man, he was certain, but his mind groped for a name.

"Jorgamur of the Nuummite." The man bowed solemnly. "You had the pleasure of my company up in the tower."

"The Night of the Spirits." Bhoran remembered. The man had held his gaze after the witless game of heroes and stones, only at the time, Bhoran had been too drunk to care.

Jorgamur winked, then looked around. "You cared not to join the company of men?"

Bhoran shook his head. He truly wished to be alone at a time like this, but an empty pocket could buy no drinks. "Even yours is more than I can handle."

"I see."

"I have no coin to repay you."

Jorgamur waved a dismissive hand. "There will be no need for that. But tell me, Bhoran of the Unknown, why did you not come? I waited for you."

"I don't recall agreeing to meet with you in this drinking dwelling."

Jorgamur raised a faint brow. "I would have thought my drawing skills had no match. My teacher was one of the greatest artists of the Amethyst stone."

The girl returned with a loaded tray. A thick flaxen liquid trickled over the brim of the pitcher, and dew clung to the tin tankards. "Aras sends greetings," she said, pouring them ale.

When she left, Jorgamur raised his drink. "To our stones."

Sweet ale warmed Bhoran's tongue, but as he ran his tongue over his teeth, snake venom stung him. Faint and subtle, yet it was the familiar taste of ... *Serpent's Spite*. He banged his tankard on the table, a terrible realization filling his mouth. "It was you. The drawing on my mirror."

Jorgamur smiled faintly. "I hope you'll forgive my choice of messenger—"

"You tried to kill us!" Bhoran's voice boomed over the singing, earning him curious stares. He grasped Avalan's goat dagger, made to draw the blade.

Beside him, Jorgamur kept his calm. "The Nuummite never kills." His tone was mild yet indignant, as if the mere notion of murder were a stain on the smooth velvet of his cloak. He frowned. "Your words, though, now make sense of the blood and poisoned darts I found at the statue. Were you attacked?"

Bhoran snorted his disdain. "You take me for a fool?"

"I do not make a habit of drinking with fools. Poison darts aren't the way of my stone. If you calm down, then I have many a thing to tell you."

"My friend was almost killed." The ale was mellow on his lips, the venom calming.

"Tell me what happened."

"We never saw who it was. Darts fell on us like rain."

"Yet only your friend was injured?"

The girl returned with a grease lamp. She placed it on their table, then capped it with an iron stand that held a bowl of mutton-and-cabbage stew.

"Snake venom cannot harm me," Bhoran told Jorgamur when the girl left. "But you know that, or else you wouldn't have ordered these ales."

Jorgamur smiled, stirred the steaming stew with a spoon. "You see now how I couldn't have been the one who wished you harm? Why use poison on you when you are wearing it in your face?"

Bhoran nodded. It was true. Now that he had calmed, he could see more clearly. Grabbing a spoon, he helped himself to the stew. The taste was to his liking, the meat soft; the cabbage crunched as if it had been added toward the end.

"Did you tell anyone of your nightly venture into the forest?"

Crushing a cabbage leaf between his teeth, Bhoran shook his head.

"I see. Then one must assume the girl's tongue was bought."

Jorgamur looked around, his eyes following the movements of the serving girls. "A foolish thing, to trust a woman."

"Men can betray all the same." Bhoran drank, trying to pry Lusha's face from his mind. "If not you, then who attacked us?"

"I don't know, but there's little that remains hidden from Jorgamur." He chuckled. "Soon I shall find out. Come, let us finish our dinner before the oil runs out. Then we shall talk."

Their spoons took turns dipping into the greasy stew, every bite salving Bhoran's hunger. *I will surely miss the cooking in this place,* Bhoran thought, gulping down the venomous ale.

Shushing voices rose to give room to a bard's song. The young man sat on a tall stool, clad in a feathered robe, his hair snatched up in a tight tail. His voice was high and pure like a maiden's, and his song spoke of the valor and courage of the tribes who had fought in the War of the Stones. Soon serving girls flocked around him, swaying to the rhythm of his voice, their dresses swirling, their hands clapping the trays against their hips.

"You are a strange man," Jorgamur said. "Aren't you curious in the least why I sent for you?"

Bhoran tore his gaze from the dancers. "Tell me if you like. I don't beg for answers."

Fishing out a cloth, Jorgamur dabbed his mouth. "I see. This wasn't the place I wished for us to meet, but given the pressing circumstances, it must do. There isn't much time." From the depths of his cloak, he pulled out a deck of tiles.

Bhoran recognized them as the ones they had used to play the game at the tower's top. "I don't play games either."

"It's not a game I offer."

Beneath the table, Jorgamur slipped him Olnos's tile. The tallow flame on their table was dim by then, but Bhoran could still discern the kindness in the warrior's face. "What *do* you offer?"

"The truth."

"Which one?"

Jorgamur gave him a pale smile. "The one about yourself. The nature of your stone."

Bhoran stared at Olnos, rubbed his dark eyes. *Was it hard for him,* he wondered, *to deny his own nature?* Without raising his head, he spoke to Jorgamur. "You're one of them. Those who feel obliged to solve the mystery of my pathetic existence. I will tell you one thing, Jorgamur of the Nuummite, and let it take root in your mind. I don't care about the stones. They mean nothing to me. So save your words." Bhoran laid the tile on the table and slid it to Jorgamur.

The singer's voice rose to a high pitch, eliciting gasps of appreciation from the crowd.

"You say one thing, but your heart says another. There's great significance not in our words but in our actions. There isn't much a Nuummite doesn't notice. Up on that tower, you rubbed Olnos's eyes. You did the same now. Tell me, why?"

Bhoran stared at the tile. He wouldn't tell Jorgamur a thing. It was a fool's task to believe what he'd thought he'd seen was true. The light here was yellow and dim, and so the eyes of Olnos looked dark, like a proper Onyx. Nothing floated in them.

Jorgamur waited for some moments before he leaned closer. "You saw something in his eyes. Something you see in yours too. The flakes of snow."

His words hit close to Bhoran's heart. "How do you know?"

"It is the nature of the Nuummite to see things beyond the veil." Jorgamur gestured toward the men who sang and drank and danced and paid them no heed. "Most of them see the surface. Were you to ask them the color of the Onyx, they would say black, like the feathers of a malicious crow, like the shape of a lurking shadow, like the shawl of death. They're afraid of it, and so they cannot *see* its true nature.

"The stones are not a thing of stagnation. They're ever changing, adapting to our very beings and to the whims of our souls. Tell me, how many times have you noticed the color of the stone in someone's eye change to suit their feelings? How many times did you watch the stones sparkle, deepen in shade, or even fade away when the person is no more?"

The air felt thicker around Bhoran. A strange taste invaded his mouth. It wasn't the ale or stew or even the fat-laden smoke of sizzling meat. Rather, it was hope. The same sweetness he had tasted whenever he'd seen the snowflakes in his eyes, twirling as if by the hand of an invisible wind.

It was a dangerous hope, he knew. One that always ended in despair when the flakes melted away and weren't seen again for many moonturns to come. "The flakes mean nothing." He said it more to drown his hope and less because he knew it to be true.

"Tell me, Bhoran of the Unknown, have you ever seen a true Onyx?"

Bhoran shook his head. "Some say I'm the only one that remains." Back in the small place of Hydrus, Bhoran used to think it true. Yet now that he had seen the map of the lands, he thought it a mindless notion. Vast they were, and parts of them still unexplored. *How can I be the only one?*

Jorgamur nodded thoughtfully. "I've met quite a lot of them. Perhaps more than I wished for. And don't forget, I can *see*. And what I saw was darkness. The Onyx in their eyes never changes. The Onyx isn't like any other stone. It remains ever dark, like a bottomless maw. There was only one among them that ever showed signs of change."

Bhoran's gaze hovered over Olnos's tile. "Olnos?"

"Yes. And now you."

Bhoran leaned on the crude table, burying his face in his palms. Was that the reason that all his life he'd felt a strange attraction to Olnos? Did they both share a side of the Onyx no one else had? The warmth of hope rose again—it had to be quenched. "Why are you telling me this?"

"I want to offer you a way."

"A way to what?"

"A way to glory. Absolution. Acceptance. Olnos died before I could discover the origin of the snowflakes in his eyes. But now it seems he and you share the same magic. You can protect us from the Onyx. And I would be a fool not to recognize it."

"I could never be Olnos. And the Onyx tribe is dead."

Jorgamur's face grew stern. "Then who killed Ronan, your merchant?"

The golden dagger had felt light in Bhoran's hand, the Onyx stone in it heartless. *And yet …* "The blade was too blunt."

The Nuummite clasped Bhoran's hand. "A man dwells in the east, on the small beach of the Red Bay. His name's Mheleras. He was the one who foretold the coming of Olnos, the glorious hero who denied the true nature of his soul and fought the Onyx to save the Stone Lands. You need to find this farseer."

Bhoran tried to wriggle free from Jorgamur's grip, but it only made the man clasp him all the harder. "Why?"

"Because the Onyx is returning. I can feel it. The veil never lies."

He's lost his mind. And yet Ronan's death spoke of a truth that might not be far from Jorgamur's words. Even Bassalt had visited him when he had lain in that cursed cage up in the sky, to ask him if he had fathered any children. "Bassalt thinks the same. It's him you should talk to."

"Bassalt can't be trusted to see the truth. Unlike his father, he's blinded, like the rest."

This time, Bhoran jerked his hand free. "Even if I found this man, this ... Mheleras, what would I tell him? That Olnos and I share the same 'magic of the snowflakes'? I cannot will my eyes to reveal them. I have tried."

Jorgamur glanced over his shoulder as if he'd felt a presence behind him. The singing and dancing had now risen to blissful wallowing. Men yelled for more ale, while others slipped their hands into the pockets of those who slept facedown upon the tables. When Jorgamur faced him again, more golden flecks than ever studded his eyes. "You must find Mheleras. The Nuummite is never wrong."

Bhoran snorted, eager for this talk to end. Nothing good ever came out of talking about the stones in his eyes.

Above, the heavy doors burst open. A cold gust of wind swept over the flames of the burning torches. Men charged through the entrance, bringing with them the rage of the storm. The singing froze, as did everyone in the cavern. A man clasped at the railings, his hair and clothes sodden. He waited for the others to close the door behind him, shutting out the howling wind before he spoke. "The chiefess is dead."

Bhoran started. *Crystal?*

The man leaned over, like a hawk ready to swoop. "Chief Ethelnar has ordered the arrest of the newcomers." He drew his sword, as if to prove the direness of his words. "The one with bones in his face is among you. Find him."

The clear order and the silver gleam of the man's blade woke the men from their drunken stupor. In moments, they all stood, shoving and pushing and grabbing at whoever came near them, eager to be the first to catch the wanted.

With a shove, Jorgamur forced Bhoran beneath the table. Swiftly he unfastened his cloak, threw it over Bhoran's head. "Put it on," Bhoran heard him say through the cloth. His voice was thick with urgency. "Then follow me."

As best he could manage while crouching, Bhoran threw the cloak over his shoulders, adjusting the cowl over his head. It smelled faintly of the forest—pine and wet soil.

Jorgamur started for the back of the cavern. Beneath the cowl, Bhoran glimpsed the first brawls starting. Venomous ale and a confined space made for an ill blend. Jorgamur sliced through the crowd, shoving men right and left, and tripping some of them on purpose, stoking the turmoil. Bhoran lengthened his stride so as not to lose him, stepping over fallen men and stinking pools of ale.

The cavern's air cleared at the back. Bhoran glimpsed what must be the serving counter: three stony boards, chiseled and smoothed, surrounding wooden crates and barrels with ale and wine. Several men leaped over the counter now, attacking the storage, far more interested in capturing a free drink than obeying the orders of the chief.

A falling man caught Bhoran on the back, jerking him forward. His heart raced. The light was becoming dimmer now, and he feared losing Jorgamur in the melee. He wriggled his way through, shoving. When they reached a rough wall, Bhoran thought the scheme a failure. There was no way out. Jorgamur murmured with crazed urgency, his palms exploring the stone. Suddenly he turned to the side, half of his body disappearing behind the wall. He waved a beckoning hand at Bhoran before he let the wall swallow him whole.

A passage. It was a narrow opening. The wall's edges dug into Bhoran's back and belly as he tried to squeeze his way through. Once on the other side, he looked around him. *A tunnel.* The air was cooler here, breezing from somewhere farther down.

"Come now." Jorgamur plunged forward. "And watch your step."

Above them, water dripped down, and puddles splashed beneath their feet. Loose scree littered the tunnel, and Bhoran cursed as the sharp rock bit into his heels. The breeze became stronger now, a pelting of the wind. Bhoran tasted salt. *The sea.*

At last Jorgamur's figure was lit by a silver beam of light that grew wider the closer they edged toward it. Booming rain pummeled the walls of the tunnel, and when Jorgamur halted unexpectedly, Bhoran bumped into him.

"Cover your eyes," Jorgamur ordered, then stepped aside.

A sudden surge of light blinded Bhoran. Rain slashed at his face. He shaded his vision. *Has the sun risen already?* When his eyes adjusted, he saw it was the moon. Larger and closer than ever, it hung, a silvery sphere across the starless sky. And yet it wasn't perfect. Its right side was incomplete, shaded by a spreading shadow.

Rain drenched them both as they stood on a short outcrop. Bhoran leaned over the edge, staring at the ravaging waves below. "What is the meaning of this?"

"You heard them. The chiefess is dead. And Ethelnar's rage is now unleashed. You *must* go. Now."

Bhoran doffed the cloak. "I need to find Avalan!"

"No." Jorgamur grabbed his shoulders. "You must promise me, Bhoran of the Unknown. Promise me you'll find Mheleras."

I can't. As the wind threatened to sweep him off the cliff, Bhoran's thoughts twisted with the rain. He ached to know what had happened, though in his heart he knew. *The chief must have seen Avalan with Crystal, learned of Avalan's plans to take her away from Raekandar and put an end to them. I must meet him at Olnos.*

The Nuummite shook him. "Promise me."

"I won't leave Avalan behind."

"A shadow haunts your friend," Jorgamur yelled, desperate. "It's all he needs, and nothing more. Go back, and sentence both of you to a painful death. I have seen it. The veil never lies. Go forth and learn the truth. About yourself. Your stone!"

"How do you know about the shadow?"

Gold and gray Jorgamur's eyes were. "I can recognize my own stone's magic. Now promise me."

Dizredek, Bhoran thought. Avalan had spoken to him about the flecks of gold in the shadowbinder's eyes, though he'd also said that one of Dizredek's eyes was different … "I need to help him."

"You cannot help him, because you don't even know your stone."

Bhoran clenched his fists. "Stones aren't—"

"You know they are. If you love Lusha, you will do as I say." Jorgamur's face was drenched, his hair dripping. "She won't accept you until you've realized your true nature." He shook Bhoran. "She won't."

The words hit close to his heart. *She won't.* All the venom cleared from Bhoran's body. Suddenly the rain fell more harshly, whipping, pelting. He craned his neck to watch the tunnel's entrance behind Jorgamur. It wouldn't take long for the chief's men to find them, he knew. "I promise. But there's no way out."

"There's always a way," the Nuummite said, and he shoved Bhoran off the cliff.

CHAPTER FORTY-SIX

THE RAIN POURED on Lusha now with heartless force, mingling with her tears, forcing her to stagger to her feet. *Just don't look at his face,* Lusha told herself. She grabbed Eyedir's boots and dragged him beneath the merciful outcrop of a nearby rock.

Behind her, Alana snorted. The horse was still tethered to the pine tree, nostrils flaring, hooves stomping. *I cannot stay here,* Lusha realized. She had been lying next to the lifeless body of Eyedir for ages, it seemed, staring at her bare palms. How had she burned the woman's face? The moon had seemed to draw closer, she remembered, as if to protect her.

Dark clouds now shaded the moonlight, unleashing their rage for the uncalled-for murder of the merchant.

"Hush now, Alana." Lusha hoped her voice would soothe the horse. She pushed Eyedir's cloak open and searched through it, her fingers meeting with various trinkets: spindles, whetstones, bottles of perfume …

Had the circumstances been different, Lusha would have loved to peruse all the things Eyedir was carrying, the same way she'd listened to Ronan talk endlessly about the things he peddled in foreign cities. But now all she wanted was a piece of parchment—the message for Undeena. If the inn hostess was to believe her, Lusha would have to show her proof of what she'd witnessed. Eyedir had said Undeena would be glad to receive the precious message he was carrying, and Lusha hoped this gladness would be enough for the innkeeper to offer her shelter and much-needed guidance.

I cannot find it. Could the thieves have snatched it from him? Lusha felt a cold pang in her heart.

She decided it couldn't be. After all, it was the birthstones they were after, and judging by the contents of Eyedir's robes, the merchant had spoken the truth. He wasn't carrying any. Stones or not, both he and Ronan had been murdered before the moon had completed a full turn. *Two merchants dead.*

Swallowing back despair, she went for his breeches. She turned out each pocket, palpating his legs for secret folds. After a while, she gave up. The letter wasn't on him, even though she could have sworn she'd seen Eyedir place it in his vest just hours ago, when he had still been alive and smiling.

Lusha looked at Eyedir's face. "I cannot leave you here like this." Digging a grave or carrying the merchant's lifeless body would be too hefty a task for her. She resolved to cover him with stones and fallen leaves. *Then I can tell Undeena where to find him.* Eyedir deserved a proper burial.

When she had dropped the last stone, her cloak was sodden, her body drenched through and through, her chest heaving.

Alana whimpered now. Lusha untied her from the tree, grateful that the thieves had spared her. As she made for the saddle, a faint clink resounded. She glimpsed a metal canister dangling against Alana's haunches. Lusha grabbed it and ran for the shelter of the stony outcrop. Trembling, she propped the lid open, dipped wet fingers into the dryness of the hollow. Rough parchment grazed her palm, and she plucked it out.

Ronan's map. It was a comfort to see it, yet it wasn't what Lusha needed the most. She slid her hand into the tube once again, hoping … Her fingers brushed another piece of parchment. She fished it out, and when she unrolled it, her chest lightened. She couldn't hope to read it, but it certainly seemed to be a letter.

Swiftly she rolled the two parchments and stuffed them into the canister. She fastened it back to Alana's saddle, then mounted her.

With a soft pull of the reins, the horse started trotting, and Lusha led her gently out of the forest. Eyedir had said the inn was close. If she kept to the path, Lusha hoped it would lead her there, long before the rain had drenched her very soul.

Alana cantered against the whipping winds. Lusha clasped her mane for balance. She hoped with all her heart Alana knew the path, for there was no way Lusha could guide her through the storm. The ride felt endless. Lightning cracked above.

At times, the path narrowed, branches scraping Lusha's arms, threatening to throw her to the ground. Their leaves offered her fleeting protection from the pouring rain. Afterward, the path would widen again, and the thick trees would give way to desperate openness, leaving her at the mercy of the angry sky, and wishing for the ruthless embrace of the branches once again.

Alana's hooves sank deep, slowing her down as she struggled to break free from the sodden soil. Yet she didn't halt—even the horse could sense the direness of their predicament and wished to find shelter from this vengeful rain.

At last Lusha felt a shift in Alana's footings. Her hooves clinked against wet stones beneath. Lusha smiled. They were on a cobbled road, which meant one thing—an establishment must be near. Alana fell into a trot.

Lusha now heard a different sound of water—the hurried rushing of a river. A faint light sliced through the misty veil. At first Lusha thought her mind was fooling her, but then more dots of yellow light crowned the first one. *We must be near now.* Beneath her, she felt Alana grow restless. Lusha clambered off her, clasping the horse's reins. The horse was clearly tired. She seemed to be dragging her hooves.

The inn finally emerged from the gloom. There was the clamor of voices and the sound of clinking metal and glassware. Three stories tall, Undeena's Inn burst with light. Lanterns swung on heavy chains from a lean-to shelter, candle flames danced behind glass windows, and a glow of crimson orange shone through. Lusha hoped with all her heart it belonged to a glorious hearth fire where she could dry her bones.

Rain pelted the roof now, water cascading down in noisy waterfalls.

Lusha led Alana up to the shelter, then unfastened the message tube from her saddle. She shivered as she let it slip through her breeches, securing it against her waist. *Best to keep this hidden.* She stroked Alana's proud neck. "I will be back for you."

Passing through a waterfall, she leaped up the stony steps, then halted before the threshold. She brushed the cowl back from her face and pounded her fist on the wooden door. Soon after, it swung open.

It hit her all at once: the splendid smell of cooking onions and spiced ale, mixed with the warmth of bodies and fire, and the cacophony of voices as people huddled together over tables. Merrily they talked to each other, as though they had just risen and the hour hadn't progressed into the middle of the night. Animal hides were scattered over the earthen floor; food and drinks loaded the tables. Eyedir had spoken truly. Merchants of all kinds festooned the inn, exchanging goods, tidings, and jests.

As soon as she stepped forward, the buzzing halted; heads twisted. Their gazes dripped with great curiosity. Only the crackling of firewood and simmering of what Lusha hoped to be onion soup in the cauldron over the hearth broke the silence.

Soft whispers rose, scattered here and there. Lusha caught the talk of scars and strangers. Behind her, the storm wind tugged at her sodden clothes. *It's not too late,* she thought, an uncomfortable lump rising in her throat from all the staring. *I could rush outside and be gone.*

"Is this the way you welcome a newcomer?" a voice bellowed from the back, silencing all others. Lusha glimpsed a sturdy woman with a face rounder than the moon and friendly eyes above plump cheeks. She was leaning over a corner table, overseeing the exchange of goods between two merchants. She slapped one of them on the back now. "Your oil isn't worth half of his iron key." The key merchant cried in triumph, and the woman pushed her way through the crowd. The woman's scolding was enough to send the men back to minding their business and cease their curious staring.

She strode to Lusha. She wore a plain gray dress with an apron fastened around her waist, so big it reminded Lusha of the bedsheets in her sleeping chamber at Raekandar's Keep.

Lusha clasped her hands in hers. "Thank you."

The woman regarded her carefully, leaving no corner of her body unexplored. "You're a woman," she said, surprised.

Lusha looked around, suddenly realizing she and this woman were the only ones in the inn. Even the servants were young boys. One of them slid behind the door now, closing it with a loud thump. *Are women not welcome here?* Eyedir had said no such thing to her, but Lusha didn't know the customs of the lands.

"A scared one, I'd say," the woman said.

"I'm looking for Undeena," she blurted, gazing into the woman's eyes. They shimmered with the liquid gold of the Heliodor stone.

The woman raised a brow and cocked her head, regarding Lusha as if she were the slowest wit she'd ever met. "Oh, for the sake of the stones, child, you can't be serious. To whom do you think you're talking?"

Lusha smiled.

Undeena slapped her own sweating forehead. "And here I thought my reputation had reached the five corners of the Stone Lands. Come." She grabbed Lusha's hands. "Let's get you changed before we feed that scrawny belly of yours."

"I have a horse outside. She's tired from the journey. I fear she might not make it in the rain."

"Of course," Undeena said. "*Figor!*" she barked.

A small stable boy hurried to them.

"Take the mare outside to the stables. Feed her and give her dry straw to rest on."

The boy scuttled away. When he pushed the door open, a gust of wind glided in, making Lusha grateful for having found shelter.

"Come now." Undeena led Lusha to the back.

Up a creaking stairwell, they climbed to the second story. The ceiling was much lower here, the air thick with the rising steam of onion soup. Closed doors lined the corridor, leading, Lusha guessed, to the lodgings of the various traveling merchants. Undeena strode to the corridor's end, then pushed a door open.

Thickly knotted woolen rags covered the cold stones of the chamber. Rain pattered against its lone window. Flames danced in wrought-iron lanterns. To her right lay the biggest bed Lusha had ever seen. It was large enough to fit three together. Its linens looked clean and soft, and tight rope knots protruded from holes in the wooden planks that supported the mattress.

Undeena closed the door behind them and ushered Lusha to a closet. The massive hostess ducked inside it and emerged holding a woolen dress. "Here. Change before the cold seeps into your soul. I don't have time to tend the sick—the inn won't run itself." She turned her back to Lusha, crossing her fat arms over her girth.

Lusha chose a bare corner to slide out of Eyedir's cloak and the sodden stable clothes. They splatted over the stone floor. She placed the canister on a rug and then slid the dress over her head. It smelled of stale cooking. Lusha was grateful for its dryness. "Thank you," she told Undeena.

The innkeeper gave her a good look, then pressed her lips into a tight line. "We'll need to do something about your hair. Who cut it for you? A blind man?"

I don't want to remember. Along with her hair, she'd left her heart on Bhoran's bed.

Lusha retrieved the letter from the tube and gave it to Undeena. "This is for you."

With a curious scowl, Undeena unfurled the parchment and read. Lusha watched her closely, hoping the tidings were good and wouldn't cause the innkeeper any grievance.

At first Undeena's eyes bulged with surprise. Then a curious simper appeared on her face. She tucked the parchment into the abyss of her bosom. "But where is Eyedir?"

Lusha shook her head, droplets trickling down her neck. "He … he didn't make it."

"What do you mean?"

"Thieves …"

Undeena edged closer. "He's dead?"

"Yes."

A soft whistle escaped Undeena's lips, and her hands fell to her lap. "Another one …"

Lusha met her gaze. *Does she know about Ronan, then?* "Our merchant is dead too."

A shadow crossed Undeena's face, and her jowls quivered. "Who are you truly? Where are you coming from?"

Lusha bit her lip, unsure of how much she should reveal to this woman. Yet Undeena's eyes pierced her like a hawk's—if she dared lie, the woman would know in an instant, and then she might show her the door. "I'm Lusha of the Moonstone. I come from the village of Hydrus."

"Hydrus?" Undeena exclaimed. She snatched Lusha's shoulders and shook her. "You mean to say Ronan's dead?"

Before Lusha could answer, Undeena slapped her greasy forehead once again. "Of course, it must be. The Moonstone never lies. But you ..." Like a hot knife, Undeena's gaze slid over Lusha's scar. "Lusha," she mused. "Ronan always spoke of you. Yet he spoke of hair that streamed long beyond narrow shoulders and the elegance of a lady. And here you barge into my inn, dressed in stinky stable clothes and looking like a boy. How could I have known?"

Lusha knew not what to say.

Undeena cupped Lusha's cheek with a warm palm. "You're Silver's daughter, yet your face doesn't remind me of him."

"The tribe says I take after my mother."

"That you must do. Speak now, moon child. What happened? Tell me of Eyedir's death."

"We left the keep at night. That was my fault." Lusha's cheeks burned with shame. "I had to escape unseen, and Eyedir said it was the only way. If ... if I hadn't insisted he take me with him, perhaps he'd still be alive." Tears welled in her eyes.

"Now, now." Undeena steered her to the bed and made her sit upon the soft mattress. "Eyedir was well trained in the matters of the road. If he thought it safe to leave the keep unseen, it must have been so. You can't always predict your fate, child."

Lusha wiped her tears. "The thieves must be punished for what they've done."

"I very much doubt they will be. It is a risk that comes with the merchant's trade. I don't suppose you remember their faces?"

"There was this woman." When Lusha tried to remember her face, it came back as a silver blur of blisters. "I was too frightened to notice more than her blade. She sliced Eyedir's neck ... At first I crouched, hidden." The thought made her empty stomach twitch. *How craven.* "Perhaps if I had yelled ..."

"You'd be dead beside Eyedir. You did well to hide." Undeena was fast to reassure her. "What did they want?"

"Birthstones." Lusha didn't dare mention the whole truth of how they'd claimed Ronan had cheated them in a game. Though dead, Lusha wanted to savor Ronan's memory as pure in her mind. Besides, no one needed to know the affairs of Hydrus, lest they send word to Bassalt and ruin Avalan's plans.

"This isn't a good sign. Eyedir's death raises the tally to three in less than a full moonturn."

"*Three* merchants dead?" Lusha asked. "There's another one, then, other than Eyedir and Ronan?"

Undeena looked over her shoulder at the closed door and stood. "Hush now, moon child. I'll send Figor to you with some onion soup and a cup of cinnamon cider to warm your bones. Don't leave your room. The men will be trapped here until the early hours of dawn, until this cursed storm has passed. And I can't protect you from indecent questions."

Lusha would have liked to mingle with the merchants, learn more about Levorotha ... And yet she didn't wish to disobey Undeena. After all, the woman had gone to great lengths to give her shelter, without so much as asking for a single coin.

"Figor will knock three times, spaced a breath apart. Now, lock your door. Come morning, we shall talk again."

With that, Undeena left her.

Lusha curled her toes through the rug's knots, listening to the rain rapping on the window. The taste of fear still clung to her tongue. She hadn't dared mention the silver burning to Undeena. How could she when she didn't know what it was herself?

A knock startled her. She stared at the door. A second knock came, and after a heartbeat, another. *Figor.*

Lusha pulled the door back just enough for her to peer through. Outside, Figor beamed at her, a loaded tray in his hands. "Food."

"Thank you."

As soon as Lusha unburdened the boy's arms, he darted for the stairs.

"Wait," she called after him.

He halted, his foot ready on the first step.

"What of my horse?"

"Fed and resting." He gave her a crooked smile before scuttling down.

He smiles like Avalan, Lusha thought as she watched him leave. From below, the voices of men held well. She peered down the lonely corridor, then withdrew inside, fastening the door behind her.

The onion soup tasted greasy, and the cider like thin, spiced water, yet Lusha devoured both with gratitude. *Once I leave here, there's no knowing when I shall have another meal.* The thought made the fair hair on her arms rise.

She took Ronan's map out. Though she couldn't read the names of the cities, the ink strokes comforted her. It was the only thing she had left to remind her of Hydrus. She wished she knew what Ronan had been searching for, but the thought of his death filled her with sadness, and she rolled up the map and stowed it in its proper place.

The stable clothes lay on the floor in a small mound. Lusha shook the rain out of them, then looked for a place to let them dry. Undeena's dress was a pleasant comfort, but it wouldn't do for the road ahead. She went to the window's stony ledge, hoping the sun would rise and shine through the glass come morning. The world outside was darkness. Backlit by the lanterns, her own reflection stared back at her.

Undeena's words were true, Lusha realized. She *did* look like a boy, with hair so short it barely reached her ears, and a nasty scar tribesfolk wouldn't expect to find on a woman's face. After she stretched the wrinkled clothes over one side of the ledge, she climbed onto the other, pressing her forehead against the window.

Her fingertips traced a face on the cool glass, one that had bones and fangs and pain transfixed through it.

CHAPTER FORTY-SEVEN

BASSALT COULD SMELL the approaching storm. The wind tugged at his cowl like a harbinger of change. Dust twirled around the beaten path, whispering distant warnings.

Bassalt could cease it all, he knew. With a snap of his fingers, he could chase the flock of clouds away, exile the wind, quiet the voices in the air. Yet he would not attempt it. He needed all his strength for what he had to do.

The foothills of the Craggy Mountains were an innocent slant of land with sparse pine trees and easily trodden paths lined with needles. Nothing to warn the unsuspecting traveler of the deathly slopes above or the twisting and turning paths leading to one's potential demise with a slip of the foot. Even Bassalt, who knew every scree and tree and flower scattered over the mountain, would not venture to cross it now.

Time was of the essence, he knew. And scarce time remained to him now.

On fat knees, he knelt, pushed back his cowl. Long silver hair billowed behind him, and he closed his eyes, drawing in the mountain's heart. In his mind, the Tiger's Eye opened, centered, and *searched* ... Over rivulets of frozen water, it waded; through chasms, it leaped, threading its way between barren trees to find what it was looking for.

There.

The vibrations were weak, but unerring. This supple shake didn't belong to a hopping mountain goat, neither to a lurking panther. It was the palpable pulsation of a stone. *A Moonstone.* Bassalt smiled and withdrew the Tiger's Eye. *Now I know where you are.* He staggered to aching feet, then marched toward the coast side, where the carpet of needles turned into heartless rock.

He stopped and caressed the wall before him. Trying to control the frenzied beating of his heart, he steadied his touch, sweating palm pressed hard against the rock.

"*Bend and bow,*" he ordered.

A tremendous power surged through him—one that forced the wall to split open with a deafening crack. As the stone parted beneath his touch, Bassalt gritted his teeth and *pushed.*

The rock obeyed. A jagged crevice appeared at first, which slowly formed into a crude tunnel. It would allow him to cross through the heart of the mountain without scaling its slopes.

Bassalt collapsed at the entrance, chest heaving from the effort. The tremble of the earth and the fracturing sounds must have reached Hydrus, yet Bassalt did not care. *Let them hear the cries of nature. Let them know the end is near for those who defy me.* Swallowing dust, he staggered through the tunnel. He needed much strength to preserve this distortion of earth, and time was running short. Once the Tiger's Eye tired from the effort, it would close, and he would find himself crushed beneath tons of stone, buried in the mountain.

The road through was dark, but Bassalt didn't mind. He did not need light to guide his steps. The Moonstone's pulse was more than enough. He followed it.

At last a light breeze caressed his closed lids as he approached the end of the pathway. Glad to feel the fresh air on his face, he clambered out, stepping on stone slabs.

A faint chanting, as if uttered through only slightly parted lips, rose in the air. Bassalt crawled to the rim of a skylight.

Below, Dhylinea was circling a working bench in a dancing and chanting ritual. Drenched, her dress clung to her body. She clasped a sharp black stone dripping with blood. On the stone bench, the crimson silhouette of a man had been etched—a set of fluid lines that must have surrounded a body that was no longer there.

Bassalt strained his ears to discern the words of the chant, but they evaded his grasp, sounding more like a mourning than a ritual of magic.

He sighed and withdrew. Slinking down the slope, he found the cave's entrance.

Dhylinea was so engaged in this crazed dance of hers that she failed to notice his appearance until it was too late. When their eyes met, her endless circling stopped, but her lips kept moving to the sound of the song. The Moonstones in her eyes shone so brightly Bassalt had to raise a shading palm against the piercing light.

"Cease that," he demanded.

Silence fell. Dhylinea folded her body as if to appear smaller. The light of her Moonstones dimmed at once, allowing Bassalt to shuffle deeper into the cave. She made no move to stop him.

"What is the meaning of this?" He swiped his hand above the drawn figure.

Dhylinea cowered, backing deeper into the cave.

Bassalt brushed the cave's wall, his fingers imploring the power of basalt in the rocks to rush to him. She wouldn't confess easily, he knew. If he was to fight a healer, and retain the tunnel, he'd need all the strength he could muster.

As if she took the meaning of his movement, Dhylinea broke her silence. "The spell is too *strong,*" she moaned. "Cannot be broken. My strength is failing me ..."

Fresh power rushing through his veins, Bassalt edged closer. He knew not of what spell she spoke, but first he had to know what she had done to his own. "Unlike mine?"

Dhylinea shook her head, her lips trembling. From the side of the cave, rivulets of water ran over stone, splashing into a stony pool.

It was all the confession he needed. For that, she would be punished, but first ... "What spell do you speak of?"

Dhylinea motioned to the outline. "The one binding him to the shadow."

"Who?"

"Avalan of the Bloodstone."

Bassalt regarded her through narrowed eyes. She was still clutching the sharp stone in her hand as though it were a knife. "The outline is his?" he demanded. "You mean to say he was here?"

Dhylinea nodded slowly, unblinking.

"Why?" Bassalt demanded.

"Wounded by a poisoned pricker. An attempt to end his life."

"And you healed him?"

Dhylinea shook her head, her eyes growing wider. "I tried, but it was only the body I could salvage. His soul, his mind are … taken."

Bassalt didn't like the sound of this. "How so?" The look of terror in the healer's eyes angered him. He wanted answers, and he knew she had them. "What did you see?"

"A shadow … a terrifying determination to reach the heart … a yearning for freedom … he has been trapped for too long … too long …" She averted her gaze, pressing her cheek against the stone.

Bassalt punched the wall to force her to face him. "Freedom?"

"He will return for Hydrus." The healer's face twisted with sorrow. "He longs for revenge …"

"You should have let him die!" Bassalt punched the wall again and again until the cavern shook. He leered over her now, his face so close to hers that he smelled the fear in her short breaths. "Tell me, Dhylinea," he whispered. "What punishment suits those who leave Hydrus unguarded?"

Dhylinea stared at him, a silent scream in her eyes. "No … no … Bassalt, I beg of you—"

Bassalt seized her neck and squeezed ever so slightly. "Ronan invades my village with a stonemaster, sliding through the spell wall as if it were a veil of thin mist." He squeezed harder. "Tell me, did you betray me, Dhylinea? I want to hear it from your lips. Did you break my trust and fiddle with my spell? Were you the one who let Ronan smuggle the stones into the village, knowing very well how my tribe was planning to use them against me?"

Dhylinea trembled in his grasp. She placed a clammy hand on his cheek. "Bassalt … Ronan is dead … the stones … the second shadow … wrong magic …" Writhing against his grip, she gasped for breath.

For a slight moment, the tunnel's demand for preservation pulled at him, cold sweat breaking out on the nape of his neck. Bassalt crushed his free palm against the wall, drawing the power of basalt from the depths of the earth. He clenched his fingers harder around Dhylinea's neck. "Nothing is wrong with the magic, my benighted Dhylinea. You thought I'd let a man live once he'd smuggled stones into my village? Do you think I'll let you live after you broke my spell?"

Dhylinea's Moonstones raged wildly right and left. Her lips had paled now, barely open. Through them, she chanted again, that painful mourning on the edge of hearing.

She's using her strength to resolve Avalan's spell instead of fighting me, Bassalt thought with disgust. Bassalt's heart burned with rage, his mind weakened.

He couldn't let her finish her song. He had to end this.

He squeezed her neck harder and harder, and for the first time since Bassalt had entered the cavern, Dhylinea blinked.

CHAPTER FORTY-EIGHT

PUDDLES OF WATER covered the earth. Avalan splashed through them, racing after the shadow. The sky had now cleared, the rain eased. Silver moonlight bathed the surrounding land: boulders, pine trees, nettles, the path …

After finding Crystal dead on the grass, the shadow had spun. Away from Raekandar it bolted, never stopping, never looking back. Avalan felt their bond growing stronger, hotter, as if he were but a breath away now from the Heart of the Bloodstone. Guilt burned in him like a hot iron. *This is what you wanted,* he reminded himself. *The heart. Freedom. A Hydrus without Bassalt. She told you she couldn't come. She begged you to forget her. She begged.*

A cry left his mouth.

He lengthened his stride. Sodden breeches clung to his thighs, stealing away his warmth. Around his neck, Ethelnar's Opal-set pendant swung fiercely, the stone cool and unmoving.

He tripped over a wood vine. Cursing, Avalan fell face-first into a puddle. The shadow didn't halt. Over the ground it glided, appearing over the still surface of a puddle only to disappear and cast its reflection onto another. *I should get up lest I lose it.*

In the moonlit water, he caught his own reflection. His eyes were no longer red. The earthy-green color flecked by red spots had returned as if nothing had happened. He slapped the water and stood. *I will avenge you, Crystal. I promise.*

Springing forth, he leaped over rocks, stomped over sodden land, his breeches drying over his skin. *This place is dead,* he thought. Barren foothills that kept getting steeper and steeper. "Where are you taking me?" Avalan called after the shadow, knowing full well it couldn't answer.

But it *had* touched him. Avalan had felt its cold embrace around him when it had saved him from the clutches of death. For yet another time.

Stone magic.

As much as he hated Bassalt, that bastard of a chief was right. The magic of the stones was dangerous, murderous even. The vision of Crystal just before she plunged to her untimely death made him grit his teeth. For the first time, Avalan saw the raw truth as it was. *If I ever hope to kill Bassalt, it has to be with this murderous stone magic.*

But first he would kill Ethelnar.

Two trees rose on the horizon, tall as giants. Sharp branches covered their gnarled trunks, jutting out like countless spiky arms. Between them, a wooden plank balanced thirty feet above the ground.

A gate, Avalan thought. A gate to nothing, it seemed, as there was no settlement behind it, nor a wall around it. All that was left was the ruins of scorched stones. Clumps of grass climbed over weather-worn rubble. The whole place looked blackened, as though it had been consumed by a great fire.

What caused such a great destruction?

Avalan leaned against the wet roughness of a boulder. His chest heaved now, his mind wild with realization. *Krokador's Stronghold.* A great fire that had licked the sky and killed them all, Dromer had said. The tribe of Raekandar had witnessed its burning from the battlements. The place where the Onyx was defeated. It was a haunting thought, much like the place around him. All water and black stone. *How many lost their lives here?* He wiped his forehead and searched the puddles. "*Shadow!*"

A breath later it appeared on the water before him. Its foot tapped impatiently yet sent no water splashing. It wanted to get moving,

Avalan knew, but he needed to catch a breath, regain his strength for what was to come. "Is this Krokador's Stronghold?"

The shadow nodded. They were but a few strides from the gate now. The shadow turned once again and dashed through it. A cool breeze crawled over Avalan's wet skin, causing the hairs to rise on his neck. He watched as the shadow emerged on the other side. The gate looked harmless, but Avalan couldn't fathom why the great fire had spared it. *How could the stronghold be so ruined and yet its gate stand like this, unscathed and imposing?*

He knelt, wetted his lips with water, then ran through the gate. There was no time for fear. Nothing stirred, and Avalan kept running. Mud clung to his feet as he chased after the shadow, knocking loose stones aside and jumping over the keystones of collapsed arches. *A place of death.* Dromer's words echoed in his mind. *The perfect place.*

Avalan halted, cupped the Black Opal with a gloved hand. The stone remained dead; Avalan hoped he hadn't raced out of the chief's reach. He wanted Ethelnar to find him.

He sat, taking in the night air. It certainly didn't smell like death—Avalan would know. When hunting with Sigil, he oft stumbled upon the stench of rotting flesh of animals killed by the larger predators of the night. Sigil would carry them onto a tree and feast on them, delighted she wouldn't have to make the effort herself.

Nor did the air carry the smell of smoke anymore. The great fire Dromer had said had reached the sky had long been extinguished, and now the only scent filling the air was the clear smell of rain and soil and barren rock.

Avalan picked up a handful of wet soil and let it fall through his fingers. He would wait. Forever if need be.

The shadow returned to him as he sat, its icy hands embracing Avalan's chest, trying to force him to stand.

"No." Avalan wriggled free, wishing he had his dagger with him. *What will I fight Ethelnar with? Pebbles and water?* The shadow gestured, a dance of urgent arms pointing upward to the mountain that loomed above the ruins.

"I won't run from him," Avalan retorted. His stomach coiled. *What if the chief brings reinforcements? How can I stand to fight against them?*

Crystal's painful cries filled his mind, and suddenly he knew the chief would come alone. It had to be. Ethelnar couldn't risk his tribe hearing that he himself had ended the life of his wife.

Against his chest, the pendant flamed. Avalan jerked, grabbed it. Colorful beads emerged from the darkness, swirling stronger and stronger in the gem's heart. Avalan spun to face the gate. "He's coming." He strained his ears, expecting to hear the chief's footfalls through the silence of the land before he saw him. There it was—a faint squelching, approaching. Avalan slid behind a boulder, his back scraping the jagged stone.

In vain, the shadow pushed and pulled. Avalan closed his eyes, gathered his courage as the pendant's flaming touch grew more intense with his every breath. The shadow cupped his face, pressing its cool forehead against Avalan's.

"He must die," Avalan whispered. "For what he did to Crystal." The shadow hands left him then, and he knew he was alone.

The Black Opal throbbed, a second heart against Avalan's chest.

Behind the boulder, heavy footfalls splattered on the ground. Steel whispered against leather, the drawing of a sword. Avalan's heart lifted. Steel was a thing he knew and understood. Slice, chop, kill. Unlike the dark stone magic, it gave Avalan comfort that he stood a chance, if only he could get his hands on the weapon.

Peering over the rock, he witnessed a lone dark figure slice through the azure mist of the night. Sword in hand, the chief had rid himself of his cloak, a plain tunic and breeches clinging to his body. Between the gate trees he strode, his blade glinting in the moonlight.

"I can *feel* you," the chief yelled.

Avalan ducked behind the rock, tugged at the chain of the pendant, making certain the clasp still held strong. *I don't want him to lose me.* The chief carried a sword, but Avalan held the advantage of an agile hunter. Nature was his ally and his only weapon in this battle. The rocks, the water, all the slippery surfaces where the chief could lose his footing …

The deathly knell of steel on stone echoed in the silence. Avalan dodged. Ethelnar's mouth frothed. The missed hit had thrown him back as the ripple of the collision spread to his arm. When he saw

Avalan on the ground, his lips twitched into a wicked smile. "There you are."

As Ethelnar stretched his arms, Avalan rolled to the side, half-expecting the chief to smash him with his magic. Yet Ethelnar joined two hands on the hilt of his sword, swinging it at Avalan's chest. *He's not using his magic.*

The chief panted, spat on the ground. "Stay still and *die.*" When another swing of his sword didn't find purchase, Ethelnar dipped its point to the ground, leaning against it like a cane.

He's exhausted. Spent much of his power up in the tower and on the road. Avalan eyed the sword's hilt. *If I can tire him further ...*

Avalan sprang, jumping from one fallen boulder to another. His toes curled over moss and brambles. He held the chief's stare, daring him to join him in the rubble.

Ethelnar roared and charged, but his feet never left the ground, his sword not chopping but swinging, and always at Avalan's chest. "I—will—rip—your—heart—out!"

It was no good, Avalan knew. If he couldn't get the chief to climb and lose his balance, he'd never win the sword. Dodging another attempt at his heart, he eyed the trees. With a tall leap, he sprang over Ethelnar's head, rolled to the ground. He sprinted for the gate, eyeing the jutting branches. Avalan thrust himself upward, scaling the rough bark effortlessly, as he'd done many a time with the blackwoods of Hydrus.

"You think a tree will stop me?" Below, Ethelnar sheathed his sword and followed.

Stinging sweat blurred Avalan's vision as he thrust himself higher and higher. He cursed under his breath. It surely was the tallest tree he'd ever scaled. He only hoped it wasn't his last.

His hand met with the smooth surface of the wooden plank. He clambered onto it, testing its stability. Its sturdiness gave him assurance, and Avalan sprang forth. When he reached the middle of the bridge, a sharp pain exploded between his shoulder blades. Behind him, Ethelnar's cackle split the air. Avalan clawed at his own back, plucked out a pricker. The sight of it sickened him, the memory of poison as it had rushed through his veins an icy grip at his throat.

Across the plank, the chief glared at him, chest heaving, a blowpipe between his spindly fingers.

"It was you," Avalan muttered. "The statue of Olnos ..."

"You sound surprised." Ethelnar loaded another dart. "This time, you'll die."

Avalan stared at the poisoned pricker in his hands. Crimson with his blood it was, and smelling of sickly venom. It already ran through his veins, he knew. *Ethelnar is right—I will die this time.* His knees felt weak. In the space of three heartbeats, his body would collapse, and he would faint—only this time, there would be no healer here to save him.

Another sickening thump came. Avalan groaned as a fresh pricker pierced his skin. He crouched, touched the plank. The dizziness would come soon, and a fall from this height would be deadly. *Assuming the poison doesn't kill me first.* "Shadow!"

The chief strode to him now, a wild grin upon his face, his teeth bare. He slipped another pricker into the tube, eager to end this. "You croak in vain," he yelled. "Lie down and die."

Avalan still held some strength. He sprang forth, toppling Ethelnar to the wood. The chief's breath smelled of wine and hatred. "If I'm to die," Avalan muttered through the pain, "then I shall take you with me."

He rolled, tried to force Ethelnar off the plank, all the while careful not to gaze into his eyes, lest the chief grab hold of his mind again.

The chief clutched at Avalan's hair, his shoulders, his chest. Icy fingers curled beneath the golden chain, tugging at the Opal pendant. "Give it to me!"

Avalan stared at the stone around his neck, a realization settling in his mind. *He can't use magic against me, because I'm wearing his Black Opal.* "You can't fight your own stone." Avalan sank his teeth into the chief's bony fingers. Ethelnar cried out and released his grip, cradling his bleeding hand.

His mind now clear, Avalan sprang up. *If only my body were clear as well ... and yet ...* His heart throbbed against his chest. His head pounded with the effort of the fight, but no dizziness had come. Though two poisoned prickers had pierced him, he hadn't fainted. He stared at the etchings on his shoulder. *The maze. Dhylinea.* The venom could no longer harm him, he realized. Much like Bhoran, he was now resistant to it.

Ethelnar scrambled to his feet, unsheathed his sword. "You took my wife, but I *will* have my stone back!"

"Why?" Avalan roared. "Why did you have to kill her?" The colors in Ethelnar's eyes blazed fiercely, inflaming the stone on Avalan's chest.

"Your painting," the chief spat, disgusted. "She loved *you*. After all these years. After all I did for her." He charged, blade held high.

Avalan crouched and barreled between Ethelnar's outstretched legs. Then grabbed his tunic and pulled him backward. The blade bit into wood, hilt quivering. Avalan leaped over the fallen chief, clasped the sword, pulling it free. A familiar warmth rose in Avalan's chest now. With a blade in hand, he felt once again the hunter. He licked the beads of sweat from his lips, the saltiness grounding him in the moment, his mind emptying of all words and filling only with fury and revenge.

Avalan brought the sword down with a chop. The chief staggered to the side. The blade bit at his shoulder. Screaming in pain, Ethelnar lost his balance, his body blundering off the plank. "Semara," the chief whispered.

Without thinking, Avalan sprang forth, grabbed the chief's tunic to stop his fall. He gritted his teeth, a raging storm in his chest. *He deserves to die!* Avalan's mind screamed at him, but his heart whispered of another truth. *He is a father.* Semara's round face floated in his vision. Avalan had never known his father, and no child deserved to lose both of its parents in a single night.

He murdered her mother! his mind screamed at him.

I promised you we'd come back for her. I promised I would protect you. I failed you, Crystal.

Ethelnar's tunic was slick with rainwater and blood. With a sickening rip, the fabric slipped through Avalan's grasp.

Ethelnar plunged to the ground.

Avalan held on to the ledge, dipping his head between his arms.

When he rose again, a harrowing cry left the gutters of his soul, echoing in the mountains that surrounded the stronghold.

He jumped to his feet, sword in hand, and descended the gate tree with painful urgency, his feet missing branch steps, his chest scraping against the rough bark. A dark figure lay motionless on the ground.

The swirling colors in Ethelnar's eyes had turned to darkness, the light of his soul fading from his stone. Avalan thrust the sword tip into the earth, ripped the chain from his neck, and threw the Opal pendant onto the chief's chest. *He's dead,* Avalan realized, *yet my heart is still ripped open.*

The timid rays of a rising sun caressed Avalan's skin as he stood above the fallen chief. *And now, I'm a murderer too.* Avalan turned and walked away in search of the shadow, his feet squelching across the muddy earth.

CHAPTER FORTY-NINE

THE RAIN HAD LONG CEASED when Bhoran found a small shale bay where he could drag his bones out of the sea. A pale dawn had risen, gray and misty.

That cursed Nuummite had shoved him down the cliff. Bhoran coughed out salt water, his skin still stinging from the fall. He raised his eyes to the crags above him, half-expecting to still see Jorgamur there, lurking over the edge, relishing his achievement. Yet all Bhoran saw was cold, wet stone. A steep slope he'd have to scale if he wished to stay alive.

The waves licked his soles as he took his first step up the slope. He roared and pushed harder, using his whole body as leverage, pushing his chest against the stony surface. His knuckles cracked and snapped as he heaved himself up. He didn't dare look down. He didn't dare look up either. He did not need to know how steep the fall would be should his body betray him, nor how much longer he would have to suffer to reach the peak of this cruel crag.

Below him, the sea still raged, and Bhoran kept pushing.

When his touch met with gravel, he groaned and clambered over the merciful edge. Sprawled on the ground, Bhoran's chest burned from the effort, his skin numb from the ruthless climb. *Yekana, I need … Yekana.*

From somewhere across the mist, the air carried the shouts of men.

Guards. Bhoran forced himself off the ground and scrambled along the rocks that lined the scarp. He couldn't summon the snake now, he knew. Much as he longed for her venom, her presence might lead them to him.

I have to find Avalan. Jorgamur's words of death still swirled in his mind. *Words that were merely meant to frighten me into giving my promise,* Bhoran thought hopefully. Much as he now needed answers about his stone, he couldn't run off to find a mysterious farseer when Avalan's life hung on a thread.

The outer wall of Raekandar's Keep rose before him. Bhoran followed the crude stones. He crawled through a thicket, edging closer. The gate creaked open, a groan of metal from its hinges. Dozens of armed men stormed through the gates.

One man's voice boomed over the others. "The orders were clear! We keep our places and wait for Ethelnar's return."

"The chief's stone is dead," one yelled back at him.

"You don't know that."

"There are no colors anymore, just darkness."

At that, the rest fell silent. Bhoran's heart ached to know what had happened. He couldn't face them all in one go, he knew, but if he could grab one of them … threaten him with his life …

"You all know what must be done," a familiar voice said. Bhoran recognized the short hunter, Aras.

Another man banged his chest. "We may not love him, but we swore an oath to him. We must go forth and find him." He turned on his heel, pressed forth, then looked over his shoulder for his companions. None of them had made a move. All the excitement to charge had fizzled out.

"We must summon Stonemistress Luthea, ask her to trace the path for us," Aras said mournfully. "But do not expect to find anything more than a corpse."

"What of the newcomers?"

"Silver's daughter ran off with the merchant. The Onyx is dead. You all heard how Jorgamur sacrificed him to Hydrus. And the Bloodstone … he, sure as the wisdom of the stonemasters, isn't returning."

Hydrus? Bhoran thought. The demented Nuummite had merely shoved him down a cliff …

The men looked torn. "We must get revenge, Aras."

"Must we?" Aras said. "We all saw Ethelnar's hatred when he challenged the Bloodstone. It was his vengeance that killed him."

Ethelnar's dead? Bhoran's heart swelled.

"The Bloodstone killed our chiefess!" a man roared.

"Jorgamur said it was Ethelnar himself," Aras retorted. "The chiefess's body had the deathmark of the Black Opal."

"Jorgamur could be wrong."

The leaden silence that followed told Bhoran what the men really thought of these last words. *The Nuummite is never wrong.* Bhoran found himself repeating the words of Jorgamur in his head. *The Nuummite can see behind the veil.*

He'd heard enough.

He traced the path to the statue. There was no other soul there but Olnos. Bhoran looked around, hoping Avalan would emerge at any moment. But that moment never came.

Exhausted, he collapsed beneath Olnos's knee. Head pressed against the stone, he closed his eyes. *Yekana.* This time the summoning was urgent. Bhoran knew they all thought him dead—Jorgamur had made sure of that. The Nuummite might never be wrong, but that man certainly knew how to lie, and that was something Bhoran wouldn't forget.

He only hoped this wasn't a common ailment the Nuummites shared, for then it could mean only one thing: Dizredek was lying to Avalan too.

The grass whispered, and Bhoran opened his eyes. Yekana's azure body glowed under a dawning sky. Bhoran stretched open an elbow and let the snake feed. This time, though, he didn't close his eyes, nor did he wallow in the sweet oblivion the venom gave him. He let the snake suck until he felt his body grow stronger, his mind clearer. Then he pressed on her head.

Yekana slid off him, dissatisfied with the swift ending. She would find others, Bhoran tried to comfort himself, only he doubted they'd be strong enough to deal with her bite without Dhylinea's healing. *And what will I find?*

Nothing if you smother your fears in poison. Avalan's voice echoed in his head. Bhoran looked at the empty clearing. Avalan wouldn't come, he knew. If Crystal was dead by the hands of the chief, then Bhoran was certain Ethelnar had died by Avalan's blade. And now that the chiefess was dead, the shadow would be free to lead him to the Heart of the Bloodstone, to the freedom of Hydrus.

Bhoran longed to follow, to return with him. But he couldn't. Even if Bassalt fell, the stigma of Bhoran's stones would remain. He was tired of living in doubt. He wouldn't return until he knew for certain who he was. *Cursed Nuummite. Why did you plant this soul-tearing seed in my head?*

He clenched his fists.

"This is farewell," Bhoran told the snake, as though she could understand him. The snake shook her head, then slithered away.

Bhoran watched her go until her sturdy tail had disappeared through the forest. *I'm free,* he thought. The notion was liberating and terrifying. He didn't want to think how he would feel once Yekana's venom wore off. As he stood, he hoped this Mheleras had Snakemint Ale amid his possessions.

Bhoran soared along the forest path. Mud and rainwater squelched. The trees showered him with drops as he crossed under thick canopies, only to emerge again under the clear sky. Soon Raekandar's Keep was but a mere dot against the pale pink sky behind him.

How does one get to the Red Bay? Jorgamur had said it lay in the east, but that could be anywhere. Bhoran knew not his way around. He would have to approach someone for aid, he knew, though he liked it not.

After long hours, the faint snorting of a horse halted him in his tracks. It wouldn't do him much good to crouch—the path here was wide, and he would have to run to the woods for shelter. *No one is searching for you,* he reminded himself. *Jorgamur declared you dead.* Bhoran edged forth. An empty carriage behind a tethered horse stood lonely on the path. *Merchants?* For a small moment, he dared hope it might be Eyedir, but then unfamiliar voices rose between the trees.

Behind a bush, he spied two young boys wearing plain gray tunics, and a massive woman with a disapproving frown etched on her face. The woods carried heavy smells—spices, human odor, metal, wet death …

"Undeena, he's too heavy," one lad complained. "If I were to run back to the inn and get some help—"

"No one's running anywhere," the woman barked. "Think I want them to know? Raise their fear? My establishment will be ruined should word of this get out. Now get on your knees and carry him, or I swear to the stones, I shall return you to the streets where I found you."

The boys groaned but obeyed. Bhoran watched them kneel and fiddle with a dark bundle, long enough to be a shrouded dead man. He knew then where all this smell was coming from. He backtracked and stroked the horse's mane as he left the path, wondering who the shrouded figure was. Bhoran had no time for this. *An inn,* he thought as he raced on.

When the sun had fully risen, the mud beneath Bhoran's feet turned to small pebbles. He felt their roughness as they lodged themselves between his toes and bit the soles of his feet. And then the pebbles became denser, a cobbled road.

Soon the inn rose before him. Last night's rain had drenched its old stones; water still trickled down its slanted roof, forming large puddles. Behind it, a small river gurgled by. Bhoran made for the fresh water first, to quench his thirst. Bent down, he heard the soft clops of horse hooves behind him, and soon the familiar burning of a stare at his back.

Bhoran brought a palm to the goat dagger, then twisted his neck.

A boy, not much older than ten, gaped at him, clutching the reins of a brown mare.

Bhoran granted the child a small smirk, hoping he wouldn't run away screaming. When the boy didn't talk, Bhoran knew he had to speak the first words. "A proper storm last night. I almost drowned."

The boy looked at the bright skies, then turned his gaze to Bhoran once again. "Who … who are you?"

"A traveler. Just passing by."

The boy cocked his head and narrowed his eyes. "Are you spying?"

Bhoran raised his face to the inn. Three stories tall it stood, its windows hazy with morning dew and last night's raging storm. "Can't see a thing," he said, pointing up.

Following Bhoran's finger to the cloudy windows, the boy scowled. "I guess so."

"Nice horse you have there."

At that, the mare shook her head, snorted. The boy led her to the river, throwing Bhoran sidelong glances, as if to tell him he still thought him a threat. "She needs to drink."

Rising slowly, Bhoran ran wet fingers over his brows to freshen his face. He studied the boy. Short and timid he looked, with the light-mindedness of youth, and yet he also seemed to be a smart lad whose eyes missed nothing.

After a swift glance at the silent inn, Bhoran decided this untrusting boy might be a better chance to learn more about the Red Bay than any curious tribesman who still snored inside. After all, the boy hadn't so much as mentioned his dark eyes. Bhoran sighed. "I seem to be lost. If only there were someone knowledgeable of the lands to point me to the right way."

Leaving the horse's reins, the boy puffed out his chest. "I can help you! I know the lands. I have studied under the greatest merchants. One day I'll be one myself."

"Then a great apprentice like yourself could tell me how to get to the Red Bay?"

The boy beamed at him. "See, this is tricky. Many would make the mistake of following the main road to the east, thinking that if they reached the sea, the Red Bay would be there. But that isn't quite so." The boy paused, a cunning smile on his face betraying he held a secret shared only by the greatest merchants of the lands.

"Hmm." Bhoran feigned confusion. "That was my plan exactly. A grand master like you would know the proper way?"

The boy slid closer, looking pleased. "There is a secret path," he said, mischief now in his voice. All former fears seemed to have vanished from his face, replaced by a glow. "Follow the main road to the east, but once you reach the statue of Olnos, leave the path and follow the direction of Olnos's gaze. You'll reach a crag. If you climb down, there is a bay sheltered under those rocks, hidden from the eye. The merchants say it is the best place for buying black moonpearls!"

Bhoran frowned. Something in the boy's words made no sense to him. "Olnos's gaze is ever downward. Onto the Onyx stone."

"Not this one." The boy grinned. "It's a small detail only few care to notice."

A statue of Olnos different from the rest? Bhoran had only seen two of them so far, and they had looked the same to him. Seeing one that gazed anywhere else but down felt queer. A lump formed in his throat. It seemed Olnos kept sprouting up. Where in the past being in the warrior's presence would give him comfort, now it seemed to Bhoran the statues were dangerous places to linger—his trial, Avalan's being shot, his lovemaking with Lusha ...

"Are those real?" the boy asked, pointing at Bhoran's face.

Bhoran caressed the fangs on his chin and at the corners of his brows. "Snake fangs. Once filled with venom, now harmless."

The boy gaped in awe. "Can I touch them?"

"Sure. Just take care you do not bleed." Bhoran leaned closer and let the boy explore the bones on his face.

The boy giggled. "I've never touched a snake's fang before! What happened to your face?"

Bhoran's expression must have grown darker than he would have liked, for the boy now took a hesitant step back.

"You could come inside ..." the boy offered shyly. "Undeena's food's the best."

Bhoran placed a firm palm on the boy's shoulder. "What is your name?"

"Figor of the Black Opal."

"Well, Master Figor, I thank you, but I must be on my way. Best if you forget about me."

The boy nodded. Then, as Bhoran scaled the small hill, Figor shouted after him, "You forgot to give me your name!"

"Bhoran of the Unknown," Bhoran whispered to himself.

CHAPTER FIFTY

LUSHA AWOKE to the sound of rushing water. Brushing a palm over the wet window, she looked at the riverbank below. Last night's storm had left behind an overflowing river full of scattered leaves and twigs from the forest.

Figor was standing on the bank, his hand resting on Alana's belly while she quenched her thirst in the streaming waters. Lusha was glad to see her horse well and rested, though she could not say the same about herself.

Sleep had taken her on the stone windowsill. Now she thought about it, she'd never stood a chance. Last night had been exhausting and scary, and Undeena's greasy onion soup had weighed down not only her belly but her eyelids as well.

She stared at the pile of stable clothes beside her. Though the light had returned, no warm sunrays came through the glass, and so the clothes remained sodden, unfitting. She'd have to beg Undeena to let her keep the dress. Warmth rose to her cheeks. *As if I need to put myself in more debt.* She felt useless then, a lost mountain goat that had strayed from the comfort of Hydrus.

Though she dared not admit it to herself, Lusha knew well her father's position among the tribes had kept her alive and well so far. It seemed everyone she met dared not treat the daughter of Chieftain Silver with anything less than undeserved respect. *Wherever I go, my father's shadow hangs low above me, an unwanted protector.* She would change that, she decided. She would find her aunt in Levorotha, convince her to take her in, and work hard to get a place among the highly regarded moonhealers.

Pushing the curtain aside, Lusha climbed down from the stone ledge. She grabbed the message canister, her only belonging, and rushed out. Unnerving silence greeted her as she descended the staircase.

Last night's revelry had ceased, leaving behind piles of tankards, empty plates, and messy stains on tables. Lusha doubted those would come off without a decent amount of scrubbing. Undeena's work and life must be hard. But where was she? Could it be she was still abed?

The great hearth was now cold. Around her, the windows were sweating. The front door was latched, Lusha saw. *Is the inn closed to morning guests, then?* She stared now at the iron bar, half-expecting it to rattle under the persistent pushing of a disgruntled guest whose entry was being refused.

A bird pecked the glass. Glancing over her shoulder, Lusha backed away until the hard corner of a table bit into her thigh. She fumbled for a knife, her stomach churning as she wrapped her fingers around its greasy handle. "Undeena? Figor?"

"At the back." The hostess's voice came like thunder from somewhere behind the hearth.

Lusha let the disgusting knife fall with a clang. She circled the staircase to find a door open underneath it. There, Undeena and a small woman with raven braids were bent over the motionless body of a man, their hands stripping him of his clothes. It seemed a hefty task. He looked as heavy as a log.

The whiff of a sickening sweetness stopped Lusha at the threshold. "What is this?"

Undeena turned and moved just enough to grant Lusha a glimpse of what she wished she'd never seen. *Eyedir.* The lifeless body of the merchant lay on the table. Lusha emptied her stomach on the floor, making Undeena raise her hands in the air in exasperation. "Great! As if I didn't have enough to clean up."

Lusha wiped her mouth with a numb palm. "Forgive me ..."

Undeena shot her a look full of pity and restlessness. "You must come closer, child."

Gathering her courage, Lusha approached. The woman with the raven braids bent over the merchant's neck, examining the wound with agile fingers. Eyedir's skin had turned a sickly shade of gray. The stiffness of death pulled his skin tight around his bones. "How is he here?"

While turning out Eyedir's pockets, Undeena said, "I set out to find him at dawn. I couldn't leave him rotting in the land."

Undeena's urgency as she went through the merchant's pockets made Lusha think the hostess's interest was feigned. Yet she held her tongue. She needed Undeena's favor, and if that meant Lusha should turn a blind eye to the plundering of Eyedir's possessions, she'd have to endure it. After all, he was dead, and spices and old trinkets wouldn't change that.

"Clean wound, swift slice, no hesitation, and a sharp blade," the other woman observed, speaking for the first time since Lusha had arrived at this grotesque scene. "He didn't suffer."

Undeena ceased her searching. "Similar to the other one?"

The woman nodded solemnly. "Stroke and depth, and the angle … yes, the angle doesn't lie. Every man has his own way of ending another's life. But who are you, sweeting?"

It was a woman that killed him, Lusha thought.

When she opened her mouth to speak, Undeena threw Eyedir's clothes on the floor and declared, "Nothing here. Come, child. I don't want you emptying your stomach on my floor again." She steered Lusha to the back of the inn and out a small door that didn't fit the both of them. Undeena pushed her out and then followed. "Walk with me," she ordered, clasping Lusha's hand. "Should we chance upon anyone else, you're just a servant seeking work at the fair."

Lusha nodded and sauntered with the innkeeper down the cobbled road. It was a sunny day—one that warmed Lusha's bones and revealed some beauty in this vile world where merchants fell dead under the knives of thieves. Thankfully they chanced upon no one.

The cobbles gave way to a long dirt road that led to a wooden shed with stacked bales of hay and the smell of horses. Lusha saw Alana bent over a feeding trough, lazily swinging her tail behind her. Her soft lips scooped oats into her mouth.

Undeena untethered Alana and clasped the reins. "You must leave. Now. There will be questions, and that scar of yours makes it even harder to hide you."

"But ..."

"Now, child. Bassalt sent word of your escape days ago—shady men and women will be after you once yesterday's merchants talk. Your entrance caused a scene, and though drunkards, these are smart men. It won't take them long to put the pieces together and seek to secure you for themselves to receive a hefty reward from your father."

A cold sensation rose in Lusha's chest. "My father has put a price on my head?"

Undeena pressed her lips into a tight line and tugged at the horse's reins as the offering of an answer.

"You knew this."

"Of course I did," Undeena said, not sounding in the least remorseful. "Eyedir's letter explained it all. He offered to share the reward with me. Said it would cover the debt he owed me."

Lusha pulled back. Eyedir had betrayed her. The letter he'd said Undeena would be so glad to receive, a mere promise of a share in the ransom. "Are you selling me to my father?"

Undeena chuckled. "Silly child. I wouldn't be urging you on if I was of a mind to do that. Eyedir forgot that I hold no love for Silver. And I still have a heart. Filled with fat, the medic tells me it must be, but it still beats. You hold no grudge against me, I hope." Her laugh had been sincere, but there was a glint in her eyes. One that spoke of greed and impatience. "We found no stones on Eyedir, nor in that place in the woods ..."

The way Undeena stared at her made Lusha uneasy. *She holds my horse. My only escape.* "Eyedir carried no stones." Lusha hadn't known for certain, but she had hoped it was true. She felt Undeena's stare go to the message tube she was clutching.

"What does it hold?"

"A map."

"The metalwork is fine. Such a detailed vessel for a simple piece of parchment."

Fishing out Ronan's map, Lusha gave Undeena the canister. "Here. You can have it."

"You didn't expect me to take you in without payment, did you now?"

"I suppose it's only fair." Lusha was glad Undeena hadn't demanded to take the map as well, or even worse, her pendant.

"Good." Undeena surrendered Alana's reins. "Now go."

"Wait." Lusha gritted her teeth, loath to ask for more help from such a person, but she knew she needed guidance. "How do I reach Levorotha?"

"The city of the Moonstone? Follow the path northwest until you reach the Moon Lake."

Lusha looked at the reins, swallowing hard. Finding Undeena's Inn had proved easy, seeing as she'd had Eyedir's instruction before he had died. But now she was alone. "Could I take Figor with me? Perhaps he'll show me the way."

"I'm sorry, moon daughter. Figor is but a childling. How do you suppose to keep him from all the dangers? You saw firsthand what can befall you once on the road. However ..."

"Yes?"

"If you take the road south, the path leads straight to the Craggy Mountains—"

"I'm not going back to Hydrus and my father."

Undeena sighed. "No matter how far you run, he'll find you. For his daughter, you do not seem to know him that well."

"You don't know how it is to live with him." Lusha rubbed at the stiffness in her neck. Next time, she would stay away from window seats, she decided.

Unexpectedly, Undeena closed Lusha in a warm, plump embrace that smelled of onions, flour, and faintly of Eyedir's body. Life and death all mingled.

"What if I get lost?" Lusha whispered against Undeena's sturdy shoulder.

The hostess held her at arm's length, peered into her eyes. "You'll never get lost if you follow the moonpath, my child."

"But it's daytime, and it'll be a long time before the sun sets—"

Undeena raised a hand to the sky. "For some days now, the moon has been strolling in the sky night and day."

Lusha saw what the greedy woman meant. A faint moon hung low over the mountains to the west, its pale color a shadow of a diamond.

"May you find what you're looking for," Undeena said. "I have to warn you, though. The city of Levorotha is not a place where strangers are easily welcomed. Despite what others might tell you, being of the Moonstone may not be enough to grant you your stay."

For once Lusha felt unwanted, soiled, desperate ... This onion-infused dress she wore felt foreign to her, her nape eerily exposed to threats now that her long hair was no more, and her marred face a terrible sight to behold. *Is this how Bhoran has felt all his life?*

"Thank you," Lusha finally said, tearing her eyes from the moon and climbing onto Alana. "For all you've done for me."

"And I thank you, Lusha of the Moonstone, for reminding me I can still be kind. For that, I shall let you keep the dress."

Undeena ascended the path back to her inn.

Once on the road, the gentle swaying of Alana and the aroma of freshly blossoming forest flowers made Lusha drowsy. More than once, she had to grab Alana's thick mane to stay in the saddle. Its leather chafed her inner thighs, and Lusha knew it wouldn't be long before her soft skin burned.

They had been following the faint moon for hours. Now its light had become ever so slightly brighter. *Perhaps the night isn't so far away.*

She leaned close to Alana's ear. Her mouth was so dry the words came out like a rasp. "Find us water, girl." As Alana kept on trotting down the road, Lusha rested her cheek upon the horse's soft mane. It was a small comfort. *Perhaps if I close my eyes, I shall forget about my thirst ...*

When Lusha opened her eyes again, she was falling. She met the polished pebbles with a loud splash. Chilled water spattered her face, bringing her to her senses. Lusha yelped, taking in her surroundings.

A heavy night had fallen like a blue velvet veil, but there was no doubt about where she'd landed: a lakeshore.

Alana sucked the water down through eager lips. Lusha cupped her hands and joined her in the drinking. The cool water tasted divine with a hint of salt, like tears of joy. "Good work, girl."

In response, the horse snorted, flared her nostrils.

Still knee-deep in water, Lusha lifted her face to see the cause of Alana's frustration. "Oh." There in the middle of the lake stood a castle on an island, so still it seemed to float over the lake's whispering waters. The moon shone down on it, bright and blue, illuminating the mists that danced around it like whirling spirits. The castle's gray stones reflected on the lake's surface—tall, slim towers huddled together, connected by arching stone bridges so thin Lusha wondered how it had come to be that they hadn't snapped during the storm. Spiral staircases carved into stone encircled the castle walls, traveling higher and higher, as if they aspired to reach the very moon.

Levorotha.

Lusha took a step back. Undeena was right—the moon had led her here, and now that she had seen her city, she knew it in her heart what tribesfolk meant by saying the Moonstone never lied. The castle stood proud but also humble, not imposing its presence on the land, but only blending in and becoming one with its surroundings, every stone in its walls remaining true. *Honesty can be the only way something so grand and delicate as this can stand,* Lusha thought.

Alana let out a small snort.

"Now, how will we get there?" There were no signs of a crossing. No boats sliced the calmness of the lake's waters. *How, then, do the people reach the island?*

Perhaps the moon held the answer. Lusha waded back to the shore. She strode along, water licking her toes as she followed the moon's reflection. Then she saw it: a moonpath etched upon the water's surface. A glistening silver light stretching from the shore to the island.

Lusha placed a gentle foot on the water. A sudden rumbling tore the silence, and the earth beneath her shook. From the depths of the still lake, a stepping stone rose, sending water splashing around its polished edges.

Landing on it, Lusha watched as another one emerged before her, smooth and inviting. She shivered. Half of her dress was soaked in the lake's water, clinging cold against her calves. *What if the stones leave me and I drown?* She turned to look at Alana, who was watching her with great interest. Then the horse clopped forth, joining her on the stone.

The moon and its causeway wouldn't leave her, Lusha knew. *The Moonstone never lies,* she reminded herself. She had to trust it. Trust it would deliver her safely, one stepping stone at a time, to the place where she sought comfort in the arms of a relative she couldn't even remember. Lusha only hoped that her aunt remembered her.

CHAPTER FIFTY-ONE

BASSALT TURNED the somber stone over in his hand. His chamber was quiet but for the light drizzle that tapped on the fastened shutters of his windows.

The storm had finally arrived, most of its rage spent on the Craggy Mountains. Now it was but a mere summer rain that would turn the dirt roads of Hydrus into muddy paths and nothing more.

Under the flame of a tallow candle, Bassalt dipped a cloth inside a water crock and rubbed the stone clean. Its polished surface reflected the candle's light—a dancing flame in a dark cove. A small chip marred the corner of the stone from when it had slipped through Dhylinea's clasp and met the floor. Yet brittle as it may have proved to be, this stone had made Bassalt's heart race with wonder.

He unwrapped the golden dagger that had been stained by Ronan's blood. *I shouldn't have admitted my actions to Dhylinea and Marebore,* he thought, cursing himself for letting his tongue slip. One was dead now, the other his prisoner—his secret would be safe, but such a lapse in judgment should never be repeated. Not if he cared to keep his place as chief. The tribesfolk had rebelled against him once, their hearts and minds seduced by words of stone magic. If they found out Bassalt was the one who had ended the dear merchant's life, and then tried to punish his stepbrother for his own crime, he suspected their loyalty would be forever shattered. His reigning days would be over.

An Onyx, Bassalt thought, staring at the golden dagger. His gaze then flicked to the stone in his hands. *But what is this?*

The two stones looked of the same essence—black and unmoving, no life surging through their beings. Bassalt wasn't surprised. Most of the stones came alive only when touched by one that belonged to their tribe, and even more so when their true owner held them. But to whom did this stone belong?

He brought a fist to his chest. Bassalt believed only a fool would give up his birthstone. It was like giving up one's essence, true power, the center of one's being. Some men didn't care about it anymore. The war had left deep scars on tribe's souls—scars Bassalt himself had used to convince them to forgo their stones and live in harmony and peace in Hydrus under his guidance. They'd have to worry about the magic no more, as long as he was there to guide and protect them.

Dhylinea's widened eyes floated before him. He hadn't meant to kill the moonhealer, but her beliefs rivaled his. For Bassalt, betrayal meant consorting with the enemy to harm his rightful reign. For her, betrayal meant upsetting the stone balance, Bassalt knew. *I am holding Hydrus's balance.* But Dhylinea didn't care about the village; she didn't care about Bassalt. For that, he'd killed her. And he would kill anyone else who dared challenge his place and the safety of Hydrus.

He stared at the sharp stone. He took the tiny bottle—the one he'd sent Theran to fetch from his father's cupboard—and gave it a slight shake, the liquid in it slopping about.

He popped the cork off and allowed a drop to fall on the stone's surface. Bassalt waited, bidding his eyes not to blink, lest he miss the stone's reaction.

Even the subtlest of changes would do …

A flurry of snow broke out across the surface, a gale of white in the darkness. Bassalt frowned. The stone wasn't of Onyx, but this discovery offered him little relief, for Bassalt knew all the stones that existed in the lands. And this … this was something he'd never seen before.

He eyed the contents of his father's bottle. *What is your secret?* The void of ignorance wasn't a welcome feeling. His father had often warned him magic wasn't a rigid thing; much like the human soul, it could change its ways as it saw fit.

Bassalt snorted. *Magic and men could never change their ways.* This stone was different. Bassalt could feel it. Yet he would need more time to study it in proper ways. To go through his father's logs and search for any mention of a stone as dark and ominous as Onyx that didn't react the way it should when put on trial.

He clenched his fists. And then he smiled, remembering. Perhaps there was a way he could reach the knowledge he sought faster. After all, it had been a long time since Hydrus had fostered a stonemaster, and yet at that fortunate moment, one rested under Bassalt's bondage.

Bassalt shoved the queer stone into his robes and left his house behind.

For once, Theran had thought it best to secure Delion in Bassalt's grotto. The master was weak, and the cave walls oozed with Bassalt's magic. The guards at the north gate gave him a timid nod but didn't dare meet his eye. *Good. Let them fear me more than before. Let the entire tribe see what happens when someone challenges my rightful reign.*

None had dared ask him about the waterdragon yet, and Bassalt was in no hurry to quench the curiosity of the tribesfolk. There were rumors, of course. Whispered behind closed doors, traded at small gatherings in the feasting ground. But only while the sun soared in the sky. For none of them was brave enough to walk the village paths at night. They feared the beast, perhaps even more than they feared Bassalt.

The path surrounded by maiden grass curved to the east, and Bassalt followed, admiring the blooming flowers. The rain splashed over their leaves, bringing out sweet smells. Bassalt breathed it all in. *Smooth and calm,* he reminded himself. He had to center his Tiger's Eye before he faced the stonemaster. Elsewise, the old man wouldn't part with the knowledge Bassalt desperately needed.

The cavern was wet and silent. A faint blue light shone from its depths, and Bassalt followed his own shadow. A cold sweat broke out on the nape of his neck, and his stump ached with the remembrance of Hydrus's tongue snatching the finger off him. *The snake ring,* he thought, cursing. In his haste, he had forgotten to ask Theran where he had put it.

The stonemaster crouched in the cavern's corner, surrounded by bowls of untouched food. The stale smell told Bassalt they'd been there long.

A faint illusion of a Moonstone shone above the master's head. Delion had one short finger turned upward to sustain it. Once he saw Bassalt, he flicked his wrist and sent the stone to the ceiling. It hovered above them, a silent witness.

Bassalt swallowed back his annoyance at the master's display of power. As much as he could master his own stone, mastering others was a skill Bassalt hadn't quite picked up. Perhaps after the fights had quieted, he'd force the master to teach him. But that would mean accepting the man's superiority—something Bassalt wasn't willing to do anymore.

"I've been waiting for you." Delion's voice was a thirsty croak.

Bassalt grabbed a bowl of water from the ground and offered it to the master. "Put your pride aside, and give that frail body of yours some life."

After gulping the water down, Delion wiped his mouth with a tattered sleeve. "I saw how you defeated Marebore."

Bassalt huffed. "You thought it would turn out otherwise? I told you this was my village. And now I have proved myself to you."

"What are your plans for him?"

"That shouldn't be your concern."

"Oh, but as I've told you, Bassalt, I'm here for my children. I know about the vines ... What have you done?"

Bassalt pressed his lips into a thin line and looked away. If he wished the master to speak and help him with Dhylinea's mysterious stone, he should suppress his anger at the master's meddling. "I took away Marebore's Ruby," he whispered, trying to paint his voice with remorse.

"You know the wound won't heal. Not until the gem is returned."

Bassalt shrugged. "He tried to kill me, Silver, my tribe ... He had it coming. You didn't think I'd let him hold on to it? I need to protect *my* children as well."

"This wouldn't have happened if you had listened."

"I beg to disagree. Marebore wants my place, and he wouldn't have rested until he'd gotten it."

"Marebore—" the old man started.

"The question is, why?" Bassalt raised a fat palm in the air. "Why attack me now?" He peered at the stonemaster through narrowed eyes. "Perhaps now you've lost the fight, you could tell me."

Delion sighed. "You don't listen, Bassalt. This village is staring at its own demise—children raised ignorant of their stones, the Stone Lands, their history—"

"They know as much as needed. The stones are dangerous. Especially in hands that cannot use them."

"Ah, I see your arrogance has grown stronger. You can't deny someone the chance to choose their own path."

"But I can guide them." Bassalt shrugged. "No one needs to follow dangerous paths, for I have traveled them and seen all the destruction."

"And so you've turned free men into prisoners."

Bassalt punched the wall, immediately regretting losing his patience. He cleared his throat, rubbed his knuckles. "I can protect them. Indeed, I *was* protecting them, until you came to threaten the peace. And even then, it was because of me the village still held. And you would have me killed for it. For wanting to protect my people."

The master raised his glassy stare to him. "There is no way for us to see common truth. Your heart is hardened." He waved a dismissive hand.

Bassalt clucked his tongue and reached for the stone inside his robes. "See, there you are mistaken. There might be a way we can work together, unite our knowledge for the common good."

"What could this work be?"

Bassalt revealed the dark stone, sat on the ground, and placed it between him and the master. "What is the nature of this stone?" he said, trying to make his demand sound less imperative and more curious.

Delion reached out a knotty hand to grasp the gem. Under the blue light of the Moonstone, he studied it. His lips trembled as a soft, wondrous mutter slipped through them. "Curious," he whispered. "Is it an Onyx?"

Bassalt shook his head. "Do you think I'd ask you if it were?"

Turning the stone around and around in his spindly grasp, Delion pierced the black rock with his stare.

He's trying to catch an imperfection, Bassalt thought. *Anything in the stone's heart that might betray its true nature.* He hoped the old crock would come up with something he had overlooked, for now this stone was giving him some uneasiness he didn't much like. "And so?"

Delion let go of the stone. And yet it didn't fall to the ground. Instead, it hovered in midair, as if held by an invisible string as thin as the silk thread of a spider's web. "I say it is an Onyx." The master raised a skeletal hand to stop Bassalt's protest. "But one I've not seen before."

"An Onyx is an Onyx." Bassalt didn't bother to hide the irritation in his voice. The master's ignorance of the essence of this stone comforted and agitated him at the same time. His knowledge, Bassalt realized, didn't fall behind the skilled master's, but that only left him with more work to do to reveal the stone's true nature.

Delion nudged the stone with the tip of his finger, sending it whirling into the air. "It fights," he mused.

Bassalt discerned excitement in the master's voice. He leaned closer. The stone spiraled down and hovered in the air again.

"This stone carries blood," the master said.

Bassalt shivered as he remembered the dripping crimson in Dhylinea's cave. He had wiped the stone clean since then, but perhaps the old master could smell the iron on it.

"The blood of heroes, the blood of sufferers, the blood of those who will bring down a fiefdom—"

"Enough guessing," Bassalt barked, no longer able to ignore the wild curiosity that tore at his chest. "What is it? What is its nature?"

Delion flicked his wrist, and the stone flew higher. A faint crack sounded, and a thin fissure emerged on the stone's polished surface.

"Don't ..." Bassalt said, but didn't dare stop the ritual. "Don't destroy it."

"It's strong." Delion gritted his teeth. The skin over his face stretched as he pulled his lips back, and his hands trembled with effort. "Reveal yourself," he ordered.

The fracture noises got louder, echoing in the chamber. Bassalt sweated profusely. "Delion ..." he warned.

But it was too late. The stone rose into the air one last time before it broke into a thousand pieces, falling onto Bassalt and the old master as droplets of frozen rain.

Bassalt extended his palm, capturing some drops of the stone's remnants. As soon as they touched his skin, they turned to water. Cool water. *Ice.* "What have you done?"

Delion had fallen back, too drained from the effort to even move.

Forgetting the niceties, Bassalt grabbed him. "What was that?" he asked, giving the master a good shake to bring him to his senses. "What is this stone?"

Yet the old man's glassy stare was nailed to the ceiling. Through trembling lips, his voice came in a whisper. Bassalt leaned closer to Delion's chapped mouth. A faint wisp of air caressed Bassalt's ears, carrying a name.

"Olnos."

CHAPTER FIFTY-TWO

AVALAN WOKE CRAVING WATER. The ground beneath him was mere dirt, and for a moment, he struggled to remember where he was, how he got there ... He raised his head. Around him stood the ruins of Krokador, moonlight limning the stones. Avalan made to stand, a sharp pain in his back reminding him of yesterday's fight.

I killed Ethelnar.

Avalan hoped it had only been the day before and he hadn't slept for longer. Exhausted as he was, the pain and grief of Crystal's loss had forced him to lie against a scorched rock, promising himself he'd only close his eyes for a moment before he followed the shadow. The last thing he remembered before sleep had taken him was the sun caressing the remnants of Krokador. Under the sunlight, it had seemed to him less ominous.

But now the darkness had returned, and with it Avalan's dire mood. He stood, his footsteps a faint whisper on the soft soil. Resting his hand on a wind-worn pillar, Avalan tried to imagine the hold's former glory.

Where now stood cracked stone walls invaded by roots and vines, Avalan imagined a mighty fort with walls as tall as they were long, surpassing in height the gate trees that marked the entrance. Battlements must have lined its top, protecting the warrior tribes that fought the Onyx. Corridors must have been filled with fights of sword, magic, and stone spells bouncing off the rough walls. Cries must have reverberated in the fort's rooms once the great fire had started, finding their way upward to the blazing sky. A fire that had ended it all …

Ethelnar still lay on the ground, unmoving. The greatsword's blade reflected the faint moonlight, a gray gleam so perfect. Avalan wrapped his fingers around the hilt and lifted it.

His father's eyes greeted him on the sword's polished blade. *The eyes of the Bloodstone.* His mother rarely spoke to Avalan about his father, the same way she refused to talk about the war, only last time she had confessed Azirrad had left not to join the tribes in fighting but to find his son of Onyx.

Did my father die here in this last battle? Do these ruins hold his ashes?

Something stirred beside him, and Avalan saw the shadow. It slid over to him, much calmer than the night before, as if it could sense the inner war that raged in Avalan's chest. Avalan clenched his jaw, threw the sword down next to the fallen chief.

He couldn't leave him like this in death, much as the chief deserved to stay unburied for his despicable deeds.

I have killed a chief the spirits anointed. Does that make me chief in his stead or a usurper?

Bile rose to his mouth. He wanted none of that. All he cared for was Hydrus.

"I have to bury him," Avalan told the shadow, bracing for a protest that never came. *Good. Even the shadow knows I need time.*

Avalan peeled Eyedir's gloves off and sank his blackened hands into the ground. He dug, ignoring the twigs and root thorns that scraped his skin. The ground of Krokador's Stronghold felt alive to him, its musty smells so strong their tangy taste filled his mouth.

He rolled Ethelnar's corpse into the grave. The chief landed with a thud in the pit. Avalan held the Black Opal pendant for some moments, the stone now dead, no colors stirring inside it. Memories of his lovemaking with Crystal emerged to haunt him.

You told me to trust the stones, my love. Yet what good did that do?

He curled his fingers over the pendant, half-accusing it of the death of Crystal. *He gave you this stone to protect you, and it proved your prison. My insistence to free you ended your life …*

Saltiness crept down to his lips, tears of guilt and sorrow. Avalan wiped them away before they fell. He threw the necklace into the grave, covered the chief with light soil, then placed the sword atop the shallow grave.

Back in Hydrus, they gave their dead to the sea, for the tribe believed the stones craved salt and water, the very essence of survival. Avalan would shed no tears for the fallen chief. The only salt that watered the chief's grave was that of Avalan's sweat as he had dug it. It was all Ethelnar deserved and all Avalan could give him.

Remembering his thirst, Avalan drank the dusty water from a small puddle, then washed his face and the crusted blood off from where the chief's prickers had pierced his skin. When he was done, the shadow slid over to him, its hands around its waist, its head motioning him to follow.

This time Avalan didn't resist. The shadow led him through the rubble. The lack of life made Avalan feel uneasy. Not even lizards, spiders, or insects dared to come near the fire-scarred rocks, as if the blaze and the great battle had left this place cursed. *A place of death,* Dromer had called it. And as it turned out, he was right.

Once they'd reached the foot of the mountain, the shadow crawled up the stones before him. Avalan looked around, trying to find a path he could scale. There was none. He groaned and launched himself onto the wall.

The climb proved rough. Many a time Avalan had to stop, turn his back to the mountain to rest his arms. His muscles burned. His entire body ached from the effort. Loose stones gave way under his groping feet—a rain of rocks over Krokador's Stronghold. The ruins from up above seemed less depressing. A mere scatter of boulders that had rolled off the mountain to form a city. Avalan wondered if the gate trees had been there first or if the builders of the stronghold had planted and cared for them, to see them grow and form the portal to their mighty fort.

He turned and resumed what seemed to him an endless climb. With every breath, he wished the Heart of the Bloodstone awaited him at the top. He didn't wish for another distraction, another pointless death ... In his mind, the faces took turns—Crystal's sad smile gave way to Bhoran's smirk, and then to Lusha's Moonstones, which sparkled with hope. Farmera watched over him with the velvet love of a mother, and Sigil groaned and urged him on.

Rockhold after rockhold, he climbed. Soon, though, the tiredness took over his will, and he allowed the faces that scared him to creep into his mind. Bassalt's snarl mingled with Silver's look of contempt, and Delion's cloudy stare became one with Dizredek's queer eyes, one black, one gray. *How can a man have two different eyes?*

His hands met with flat ground. Avalan groaned, pushed himself over the blessed ledge. It was a mountain path, he noted with pleasure. One wide enough to hold a cart. It didn't look manmade. More like a kindness of the mountain to the travelers that braved its slopes.

The shadow stood there waiting for him, making it look easier than it really was.

Avalan collapsed into a small recess. "Wish I could float like you," he told the shadow, panting.

The shadow shrugged and waited.

Avalan crawled out and raised his eyes to the mountain peak. It looked much farther away than he'd imagined. "Are we only halfway up? If so, I'd like to sleep here."

Shaking its head, the shadow pointed at the path ahead. It disappeared behind a turn, and Avalan's heart lifted. His arms were aching from pulling himself up the slope, but his legs still held some power. He'd gladly trade the climbing for some rough walking.

"Twice you saved my life," he said, peering at the shadow.

The shadow nodded.

"I thank you." Avalan stood.

They resumed their racing. Avalan kept his eyes on the ground out of habit. He tried to remind himself the shadow left behind no signs. Its gliding didn't affect soil or water. It didn't even leave behind a breeze as it sliced the air. Yet Avalan could feel its presence as if they were one. Ever since Crystal had died, following the shadow had felt like following himself.

The path proved full of sharp turns and dangerous passages. At times, it was wide enough to fit four men walking abreast, and at other times, it turned helplessly narrow. So narrow Avalan could only cross it by placing one foot before the other, keeping his eyes firmly fixed on the path ahead, not daring even to flick his gaze toward the abyss that lay below.

Soon the path widened again, and then, as if this had been its whole purpose all along, it ended at the dark maw of a cave.

Avalan halted outside the entrance. To his right, the moon caught his eye. Low it hung above a tranquil silver lake on the far horizon. A castle rose into the sky. Mesmerized, Avalan reached the edge. *What is this place?*

A cold hand tugged him. He turned his head toward the cave, half-expecting to see the shadow. But it had disappeared.

If it had slipped into the cave, it would be impossible for him to see it anymore. His eyes were sharp, but not so much he could see through the blackness of a lightless cave. Yet the calling was unmistakable. A powerful urge in his chest bade him to enter.

The heart is hidden here. My stone. I will free Hydrus.

Avalan picked up a pebble and sent it skipping inside, straining his ears for any returning sound. A sharp ringing of stone upon stone reverberated. Then he waited.

When nothing came charging at him, Avalan stepped inside.

CHAPTER FIFTY-THREE

Lusha reached the last stepping stone. One more stride, and she would land on the shallow shore of the island. The moon hadn't betrayed her. One after the other, the rocks had emerged from the lake's depths with guttural sounds. Lusha had trodden their wet surfaces with caution, heart in her mouth, pendant and map close to her chest.

But as the island now lay before her, a numbing doubt crept up in Lusha's mind. *What if word of my escape has reached Levorotha?*

Despite that, Lusha knew there was no turning back. She trusted the moon wouldn't have led her here only to snatch her back to an enslaved Hydrus. The stepping stones behind her had sunk. Only two of them now remained—the one Lusha stood on and the one behind her, where Alana waited.

Lusha took a step. Water invaded her shoe, sending a prickly chill through her body. Alana quickly followed. Behind them, the last stepping stone sank with a low rumble.

For a moment, Lusha thought the disturbance might have caught someone's attention, perchance that of some patrolling guards or a late-night wanderer. Yet there was not a soul around. High castle walls rose to her left, an endless expanse of milky limestone, betraying no gate Lusha could pass through. She took Alana's reins and walked along the wall, wondering if it was usual for the moonpath to lead visitors to a dead end. *Perhaps only unwanted ones ...*

The shoreline gave way to a wide lakefront with rounded pebbles. Their footsteps crunched through the silence of the night. A sandy path emerged in the distance, a proper way that seemed to lead to the castle's gate. The sound of rippling water came behind them. Pressing her body against Alana's, Lusha squinted.

A wobbly boat approached the waterline, slicing through the lake in true haste. A man and a woman paddled swiftly. Lusha knew not whether to hide or run to them. The boat bit into the pebbled shore. Hurling her paddle aside, the woman shouted at Lusha. "You! Help us. We have another one."

Lusha rushed to the lake. She reached the boat just as the two strangers were pulling it out of the water, lodging its front end in the pebbles. A soft moan came from the boat's belly. Lusha spied the wrapped-up body of a man. Sweat crowned his forehead. "Is he hurt?"

The strangers exchanged a quick glance. Both wore short white cotton breeches and tunics. Long dark braids flowed over the woman's slender shoulders, and her Moonstone eyes glistened in the night. *She's one of us,* Lusha thought. But the man clearly wasn't. Though old enough to be her father, his body was still firm and of the same height as the long paddle he held. His skin had the tan of a man who spent his days laboring in the sun. A colorful fire burned in his eyes as he stared at her. *A Fire Agate?*

"He isn't hurt, but ailing," the woman said, peering at Lusha. "I am Calla, and he is Rian."

The man gave a curt nod.

"Will you help us carry him?"

Lusha bent to part the hair that fell over the sick man's face.

"Don't touch him!" Calla slapped Lusha's extended hand, then grabbed her shoulders. "Just the linen. *Not* his skin. Nod if you understand me."

When Lusha nodded, Calla waded to the other side of the boat. Rian was already knee-deep in the water, holding the wrapped feet of the sick man.

"On my order, you lift," Calla instructed.

Lusha shoved her palms underneath the man's back, careful not to brush the naked skin of his face. The wrapping felt warm against her touch. *Poor man. He must be burning with fever.*

"Ready … lift!"

All together they pulled him out of the boat and placed him gently on the shore. "I have a horse." Lusha motioned to Alana, who was swaying her tail lazily. "She's strong."

"It will do." Calla tossed her braids behind her back. "Hurry."

"Bend now, girl."

The horse obeyed, and the man with colorful fire in his eyes balanced the wrapped body over Alana's back. Lusha was glad to see Alana rise with ease—a single man wasn't a burden for a merchant's horse.

Wiping her flushed face on her sleeve, Calla took Alana's reins from Lusha's grasp and led the horse up the sandy path.

Lusha fell in behind them. The braids of the woman's hair left behind a sweet aroma of summer flowers. A faint blue halo surrounded her body, much like the one that embraced Lusha on nights like this, when the moon shone in the sky. Its power was swiftly diminishing, though. It wouldn't be long now before the moon became a fingernail, and then Lusha's skin would shine no longer.

Rian's silhouette remained dark. Long raven hair threaded with red strands flowed over his back. He hadn't spoken a word since they had met, but Lusha imagined his voice to be deep. His sturdiness reminded her of her father, only Rian carried himself with gentle power, unlike Silver's arrogance.

As they approached the gates, Lusha readied herself to face the guards and answer probing questions. She brushed her pendant, hoping it would prove enough to grant her entrance. Yet there was no one there to challenge her, for there was no opening to be guarded. The gate was nothing more than a block of rigid stone with a deep depression in its middle.

Calla shoved her hand into the hole. The gates rumbled and parted, a soft illumination coming through. As they crossed, Lusha glimpsed at a Moonstone lodged in the flesh of the wall. It was the largest she'd ever seen. Not that she'd seen a lot … The only other one she'd ever laid eyes on was the one Bhoran had gifted her. But that had now been returned to him, along with her hair and her heart.

Lusha shuddered as the gates closed behind them.

In the distance, the castle loomed above them. Slender archways stretched between high towers and spiral staircases rose from the ground, crawling their way upward and disappearing inside gaping openings in the walls. Despite the late hour, Lusha saw no fires or flames casting away the darkness. Only the silver sheen of a bright moon that hung low over the city, as if to rule it all.

They stopped outside a three-storied establishment with no door but an open arch. Over it there was an inscription she could not fathom —a crescent moon cradling a flower and some lettering beneath it that was beyond her understanding. Windows filled the walls. In one of them, the shutters were open. A man with a waxen face stood with his palms pressed firmly against the stony sill, his chest heaving as he struggled to catch a breath.

A sickhouse?

Rian smiled at her. The flames in his eyes had the colors of the rainbow. Ever changing, ever burning … *He looks at me as if he knows me.* Rian hefted the ailing man over his shoulder. His moaning had stopped, and Lusha feared he might be dead. Rian rushed through the archway, and Calla swiftly followed.

"Stay here, my girl." Lusha stroked Alana's neck. "I'll try to fetch some food for you later."

The air inside was laden with lavender and fennel, a painful reminder of Farmera's house—the house of a healer, of a mother. But the air here carried much more. The aroma of medicinal plants mingled with the sweet odor of sweat, an earthy feel of unwashed bodies.

Benches and cupboards lined the dark hall. A pair of plain-cut tunics like the ones Rian and Calla wore hung in an open closet. Lusha took one.

"Go on," Calla's voice came from behind her, strict and unyielding.

"Put it on. We've got little time. Once the bruises settle, we'll lose the fight." Calla gave Lusha a glaring look.

Lusha slid it over her head, then followed the woman up the stairs.

On the first story was a large room full of beds, on which were writhing men and women. Some of them recited prayers to their stones, wishing for a swift cure, while others whispered the names of others, tears streaking their faces. They were all covered with brown linen, much like what covered the man from the boat.

What cursed ailment has befallen these people? Lusha had lingered here, she realized, while Calla had raced up.

On the second story, the air was clearer, and fewer beds lined the floor. Pale candle flames danced in the breeze from open windows. Rian was undressing the sick man, his fingers clearly touching the skin.

Lusha gasped.

"He's fine." Calla arrived cradling a bowl of a foul-smelling paste. "Rian's not one of us."

Now that he'd done his part, Rian got out of Calla's way.

Lusha knelt by the bedside. "Tell me how I can help." When she stared at the man's naked chest, thousands of prickers pierced her skin. It was covered with bruises, much like the ones Farmera had told her had covered her mother's body—curious blotches of purple and blue ... *As if the man's blood has spilled beneath his skin.*

"Here." Calla threw her a towel. "Hold his head still."

Lusha pressed the cloth against his perspiring forehead. The skin burned with the highest fever she had ever felt. Rian pushed on the man's writhing legs, pinning them to the bed, while Calla used a thick-haired brush to apply the paste over the bruises. The foul smell stung Lusha's nose, yet she dared not move. The man struggled, and she feared she'd lose her grip on him or, worse, touch his skin.

Calla whispered a faint chant while she worked. *An ode?* Farmera had spoken to Lusha about them—magical chants and pleading songs to the power of the stones—yet Lusha had never used one. Calla covered every bruise with precision. As soon as she was done, she grabbed a clean linen and shrouded the man, tucking the sheet's corners under the mattress. She then threw a blanket over him. At last the man calmed, as if his pain had eased.

An eerie silence settled that made Lusha conscious of her shallow breathing. Palms still pressed tight on the man's head, she looked at Calla, who seemed exhausted from the effort. "Is it the Red Weal?"

Calla and Rian exchanged a brief look. "As it seems." The healer's lips were pressed into a tight line now, her fingers sticky with paste. "I made this. I hope it proves useful this time." She raised her face to Lusha, for the first time looking less threatening and more understanding. "Thank you."

When Rian helped Calla up, she cupped his face and kissed him fiercely.

Embarrassed, Lusha averted her intruding gaze. She started for the stairs, but the man broke the kiss and gripped her shoulder. "It's not safe," he told her, his voice deep and mellow, as Lusha had imagined.

Lusha stared into his fiery eyes. The flames were burning low now, shining a ruddy light onto the fine lines on his face. It was a handsome face—that of a man who had seen his fair share of the world and was weary of its fortunes.

"She can stay with me." Calla came between them and placed a light palm on his chest, as if to assert ownership of his heart.

"I shall return in the morning." Rian threw Lusha one last glance and took his leave.

Once they were alone, Lusha swallowed hard. She wasn't certain the woman's invitation had been heartfelt. "It was kind of you to offer," Lusha began. "But for certain, there must be an inn where I can—"

"Nonsense." Calla rubbed her hands clean on her apron. "I was hard on you. That's not a proper way to treat a guest. I'll clean myself up, and we shall talk. There's a kitchen beside the entrance with clean water and some food."

Lusha nodded, removing the soiled tunic. "I was hoping there might be something for my horse."

"You'll find some roots in the basket."

Raw vegetables were scattered on the kitchen bench, fresh soil still clinging to their skin. Lusha scrubbed some twisted carrots clean and went to Alana.

The horse accepted the offer with a small neigh of satisfaction. The streets around the castle stretched out, deserted. Cobbled passages threaded their ways between huddled establishments with shuttered windows, and not a single pale light sneaked through the boards. The night was getting deeper, and Lusha guessed dawn wasn't so far off.

She wondered where Rian had gone. She would have loved for him to stay. His fire gave her a strange sense of calmness. Yet Lusha had the feeling her presence around him wasn't offering much comfort to Calla, and the last thing Lusha wanted was a fight over a man she didn't desire.

Why does she worry about me, anyhow? Lusha's beauty wasn't what it used to be. Wasn't that what Colgar had told her when he had been trying to force her to become his tribeswife? He'd even gone as far as convincing Silver that after the nasty accident that had taken Lusha's right eye, none of the men would wish to wed her.

How would my life have been different if I'd accepted Colgar right then instead of proclaiming my love for Bhoran? Crystal wouldn't have left the village drenched in agony and shame to seek shelter in the arms of a chief who, even though he had treated them politely, gave Lusha disturbing feelings.

She hugged herself, pretending it was the hands of Bhoran, bringing to mind his sad smile and the promise of love in his kiss. She knew he loved her—there was no doubt in her mind. But they weren't ready for each other. If it wasn't her father, it was the ghost of painful memories that kept them apart. The things he'd done to survive in this cruel world, and the things she hadn't done to accept him for who he was without fear …

Whenever she left him, he sought comfort in the embrace of other women. For them, it must have been just a game, the fascination of sleeping with the enemy. But only for a moment, for none of them wanted to be an Onyx's wife.

But for him … what is it? What other pleasure does he find with other women he cannot find with me?

Light fingers brushed the ends of her hair, and Lusha turned to find Calla smiling at her. "You did this to yourself."

"It was getting hard to care for."

As if she sensed Lusha's pain, Calla took her hand and led her inside. She had set a small table for them with two steaming mugs and a plate of bread and cheese. Inside a lantern, a quiet flame stood, calm in its confinement.

Lusha hugged her mug. "Thank you for taking me in."

"We were really fortunate to come upon you. Your horse helped us arrive faster. Might have given him a chance." Calla gulped some cheese down. "Stones, I'm starving. I can see you're one of us, but I don't recall your pretty face. Tell me your name."

"Lusha." She slathered soft cheese on bread and took a small bite. "The man with the Red Weal ... will he live?"

"None of them ever do. I went through the old logs, found a recipe ... I don't expect it will do much, but last time, I kept a woman alive long enough for her to bid her children farewell."

Lusha shuddered, smelled the hot liquid in the mug. The steam tasted sweet and cool. She took a small sip. *Not bad.* "I lost my mother to it." The words came out unbidden. She was getting tired, her guard now lowered.

Calla cocked her head.

"I never saw her suffer," Lusha explained. "I was but a baby when she passed, but the healer at the time said bruises were scattered over my mother's body as if her blood had spilled beneath her skin. Seeing them on the man now made me think of her."

Calla brushed her hand. "I've lost all of them. When we bring them here, it is too late. I can prolong their stay with pastes and prayers, but in the end, the sickness always proves stronger."

All of them? How many have there been? A cold doubt trickled down Lusha's spine. "A moonhealer in Raekandar told me the Red Weal was gone, disappeared along with the defeat of the Onyx tribe, for it was a curse cast by them on our tribe. If he is right, then how ...?"

Calla's fingers went white, pressing the mug. "We haven't spread word yet." She squeezed Lusha's hand. "And neither should you. You must forget what you saw here. You mustn't speak of the Red Weal."

"But shouldn't the other healers know? Nexanthos was kind to me. I'd hate to see him fall. If the Red Weal has returned, you *must* tell the tribes. Our stonemaster—"

A raucous laughter left Calla's throat. "I thought you were pretending, but you really are as ignorant as you look."

Lusha's cheeks flushed. "I was never given the chance to learn. I come from Hydrus."

The name of the village ceased Calla's laughter, her features now twisting into a pitiful grimace. "How old are you?"

"Two moonturns past, I turned twenty. Why?"

"Twenty years," Calla mused, "lived in darkness. I suppose I'd have liked that. You witnessed nothing of the war, neither of this sickness. What do you seek here? Why not stay in this ignorant bliss of yours? Most say Bassalt's cruel. I say he's doing you a kind favor."

"Bassalt rules with fear and pain. The healer of our village was kind to take me in as an apprentice. Farmera taught me to fight sickness. There's nothing more heartwarming than seeing the eyes of the ill clear. The way the sparkle of life returns to their stones ... I promised myself I'd make something more of my life. I wish to know what took my mother away, and how to cure it. I want to be a moonhealer, like you."

At that, Calla fell silent. The air in the room was still. Even the moans of the sick above had quieted, and Lusha hoped it was because of a merciful sleep and not because the light of their stones had faded.

At last Calla spoke again. "Our stonemaster is dead. All our wise moonhealers know not to speak of the Red Weal, nor to go hunting for its root." She gestured at the ceiling. "But every so often, some rise who think themselves braver than others and go look for its source. I have saved none of those who return, stricken by the Red Weal. So forgive me if I don't share your passion. I do not mean to crush your dreams, but you'll be better off returning to Hydrus. There, at least, you will be safe."

Lusha stared at her empty mug as if it could hold her disappointment. Whichever path she took, it seemed to lead nowhere. *This is the city of healers,* she thought. *And yet they stand helpless in the face of the Red*

Weal. Their own stonemaster dead … She took a deep breath. "I have an aunt. I was told she lives here."

Calla edged closer. "What is her name?"

"Shelanna."

Calla gave her a haughty stare. "Who are you?" she demanded.

"I told you. I am Lusha …"

"Your name means nothing to me. But you're saying you're the niece of Shelanna? The daughter of her deceased sister?"

"You don't believe me?" Lusha's cheeks flushed. She felt Calla's eyes examine her, taking in her hair, the shape of her face, the truthfulness in her eyes, trying, perhaps, to find some semblance to her aunt. Lusha knew she looked like her mother. But how much alike the two sisters had been was something Lusha couldn't be certain of. Silver had never spoken to her of Shelanna.

Calla smirked. "You don't know how to lie. It's clear. You truly believe your own words."

"It is the truth."

"We shall see on the morrow."

"Will you help me find her, then?" Lusha's heart lifted.

"I'll do something more than that." Calla rose. "I'll take you straight to her. With the first light."

"Wait." Lusha stared down at her battered dress. "Is there something more suitable to wear for meeting my aunt? And perhaps something to cover …" She ran her palm over the maimed part of her face.

"I have a suitable dress," Calla said, lifting a curious brow. "Perhaps I'll let you borrow it as a thank-you for your help tonight. But I don't understand what you're asking for your face."

Lusha wondered if Calla was far too kind to mention her scar or just plain indifferent to it—after all, as a healer, she must have seen much worse. "I mean the scar."

"What scar?"

What is her game? Lusha thought. "The one over my right eye. An old snake accident."

A smile twitched Calla's lips. "Come." She cupped a candle and led Lusha to the window. "Look," she commanded.

On the dark glass, Lusha's reflection stared back at her. It was her face, only … different. Two Moonstone eyes reflected the candle's flame. And they were both pure, the skin around them smooth. No scar ran from the tip of her brow to her chin. It was her old face, before the snake had struck. A face she hadn't seen for so long she'd almost forgotten how it looked.

She traced her smooth skin, great surprise pulsing in her chest.

Beside her, Calla smirked, a sparkle of satisfaction in her eyes. "Welcome to Levorotha."

CHAPTER FIFTY-FOUR

The boy spoke truly, Bhoran thought, gazing up at Olnos. The statue didn't have its gaze turned to the Onyx stone. Instead, it stared at the eastern horizon.

A flaming sun bathed the crossroads in fervent light. Bhoran looked over his shoulder to make sure no one was around. On the open pathway, he felt exposed. He wasn't used to finding Olnos outside the shelter of a forest clearing. And yet this statue stood out in the open, amid a rocky plain, just off the main road that traveled from west to east.

An offering of purple flowers rested against the statue's base. Bhoran brushed the soft petals. Their stems were still wet, as if the one who had gifted them had only just gone. Bhoran collapsed at the feet of the giant. He had promised himself to rest only once he had reached the statue. Day had turned to night and then to day again, and Bhoran had despaired this time would never come. The path had seemed to go on forever. Reluctant to cross anyone in his way, Bhoran had kept to the merciful shade of the forest line. The soles of his feet were bleeding now, small thorns prickling his arches, where the skin was softer.

I must get going. Bhoran rose. If Figor was right, and there was indeed a bay hidden at the foot of the hill, Bhoran would need all the light to descend the rocky crags unscathed. At least the cursed storm had passed, and he hoped the rocks wouldn't slip from his grasp.

He left the path behind, as Figor had instructed, and followed the way of Olnos's gaze. Soon the air smelled of the sea. Bhoran tasted its saltiness on his lips. The soft splashing of waves reached his ears as they licked the rocks below.

Cresting the hill, Bhoran lay on his stomach, craning his neck to observe the place beneath. He had imagined a small sandy beach, away from prying eyes, where a man had made his shelter, spending his days taking in the sun and braving the waters for the black pearls Figor had told him the merchants loved to purchase. Yet such a place was nowhere to be seen.

Instead, barren, uneven rocks stretched below and into the sea, battered by low waves. There was no way a bay existed here—Figor had believed the words of drunken merchants and had made Bhoran believe in them too.

He made to leave, but his heart bade him to stop. Before, he hadn't cared about the stones. Yet after this cursed Jorgamur had planted the seed of doubt in his mind, all he could think of now was his stone. An Onyx that differed from the rest. An Onyx that could fight its true nature. An Onyx like the one that lived in Olnos's eyes and had made him a hero. If only Bhoran could conquer his own nature, he might stand a chance of redeeming himself of the sins that separated him from Lusha and the tribe.

Bhoran returned to the cliff. Some truth always lay behind a rumor, and Bhoran would now unearth it. He walked along the edge, never losing the waves from sight. Some crashed with force, splashing the seawater so high Bhoran could taste the salty drizzle. These waves told him there was no opening in the stony boulders, and so he kept walking.

Until he found it: a place below where the flow of the sea wasn't so fierce, as if the rocks there folded to form an opening into the wall. Bhoran lowered himself over the edge, securing his footing over a jutting rock.

At times, he halted his descent to gaze below and make sure the wind hadn't drifted him off his path. The sight of a small sand beach made his heart leap in his chest. Figor was right after all. The bay was small, sheltered under the lee of solid rocks. Bhoran would never have found it had he not known of its existence.

With this new knowledge at heart, he aimed to land in a far corner of the beach. Even though it looked deserted, if there were people there, his sudden appearance might not be welcome.

He was but a few breaths away from land when an arrow clanged on the rock beside his head. Bhoran twisted his neck. A man stood below, feet planted apart in the sand, head cocked to the side. He held a bow, its string now stretched and ready to unleash another arrow.

Bhoran freed one hand. "I come as a friend," he shouted, waving. The second arrow whooshed by him, scraping the skin of his wrist. *Cursed man. Why doesn't he listen?* "Jorgamur sends me," Bhoran shouted, hoping this would convince the man to cease his shooting.

At the sound of Jorgamur's name, the man lowered his bow.

Bhoran grabbed at the rocks again, ignoring the stinging pain on his wrist and the blood trickling down his arm. This might be his only chance to get to ground. There, if the man insisted on his unwelcoming ways, perhaps he'd have a better chance to face him. Avalan's goat dagger was well hidden, tethered in the inner lining of his breeches.

The sand felt warm under his heels as he landed. He wiped the sweat off his forehead—a small gesture he hoped would make him look less threatening. Bhoran knew his appearance did little in his favor. It rather worked as a warning to the tribes not to venture close. But when he'd constructed it, one painful piercing at a time, it hadn't ever crossed his mind he'd find himself in the company of men once again.

"Who are you?" The man's voice was gruff, as if rarely used. Black, scaly skin hugged his legs, making them look like the dark serpents Bhoran had befriended on the mountain. His naked torso had badly healed grazes and scars. One of them stretched from his lower ribs to the base of his hips like a crescent, as if someone had torn him open. The man's eyes were dark, like Bhoran's, and his long black hair was slick and wet, pushed away from his high forehead and tied tightly against his nape.

A fierce look, Bhoran thought, *perhaps even scarier than mine.* He brought a fist to his heart, a greeting the tribesfolk of Hydrus had taught him. He hoped the stranger would return it. "I'm Bhoran."

"Of?" Though now lowered, the man's bow was still in his grasp.

Bhoran hadn't bothered to add the attribute of his stone after his name, as most tribesfolk did. "Of the Unknown." He shrugged. *Better that than the Onyx.* At least until he'd gained the man's trust or he knew for certain.

Unamused, the man raised his bow again, this time aiming straight at Bhoran's heart.

Bhoran backed away, the white sand beneath his feet bringing to mind painful memories of the goat games. He watched the tension in the man's wrists, trying to figure out when he'd let his arrow fly. *He has only one.* If Bhoran dodged it, they would stand as equals.

"I don't take kindly to liars. Why don't you tell me who you *really* are? And know this: I never miss."

Bhoran cursed under his breath. "Some say I'm an Onyx. Am I? I don't know. My bloody eyes seem to think so. Who am I to judge the ways of the stones?"

At last the man lowered his weapon. "Jorgamur sends me an Onyx?" His voice was dripping with curiosity. "Welcome to Olnos's Cove," he said, chuckling and throwing the bow and arrow onto the sand.

Olnos's Cove? Bhoran froze. "Am I not in the Red Bay?"

The man chuckled harder. "Bloody merchants always come up with names of their own."

Bhoran looked around. There was nothing the shade of red as far as he could tell. The rocks were a dull gray, the sand a bright white carpet. "Why?"

"They always whine about how much I make them pay for the black pearls. Say I bleed them dry. A thankless lot, those merchants. Always complaining about the hardships of their work as if the whole world should freely provide them its treasures just because they travel from place to place, peddling." He chuckled again with great amusement. "Ah, are you here to whine as well, Bhoran of the Onyx?"

With a smirk, Bhoran shook his head.

"I didn't think so. Then come with me."

His tension now easing, Bhoran followed the man to a small recess in the rocks—a shady cavern. Two short wooden tables held tools scattered on them, and the empty shells of oysters bigger than Bhoran's palms. Thick ropes coiled around sharp rocks by the seashore, their ends disappearing into the water.

Bhoran welcomed the cool shade on his back as the man motioned him to sit. Wet sand clung to his shanks. The man walked past him to the back of the cavern, where he picked up two mugs and dipped them into a barrel. When he pulled them out, Bhoran gratefully noticed golden trickles running down their sides. *Ale.* He had to control himself to avoid gulping it all down at once.

"To Olnos, our savior," the man said, raising his cup.

The ale was cool and quenched Bhoran's thirst, easing its way down his burning throat.

"Did Jorgamur send you to harvest pearls, Onyx bearer?"

Bhoran eyed him, trying to decide whether the man was jesting or being honest in his request. "No," he said at last. "He sent me because of Olnos."

The man's eyes remained dark. "I see. I'm Mheleras."

"Of?" Bhoran asked, following the ways of the man.

A smirk was all Mheleras gave him. "That is a story for another time. You hungry?"

"I could eat." More than that, Bhoran knew, but he didn't want to raise his expectations. There was no firepit, no stove, nor chests that could hold savory treats.

Mheleras started for the sea.

Is he going to fish now? The tide was high. Many tribesfolk had drowned in the waves of Hydrus after braving an angry sea, and Bhoran could never forget the emptiness in their eyes as the light of their stones had faded to gray. Bhoran leaped to his feet. "Wait," he called. "I'm not so hungry to have you risk your life."

Mheleras laughed. Ignoring Bhoran's protest, he pulled at the thickly braided ropes. Bhoran joined him in the effort. Whatever they were hoisting felt heavier as it approached the surface. With a last pull, the thing that was tied to the other end surfaced, rattling and clacking.

Bhoran let the rope fall and rushed to see what it was: a wooden crate with strings holding oysters that swung lazily back and forth. The man took out a short knife and cut loose two strings, each of them holding about a dozen shells. He handed one to Bhoran, along with the short knife. Mheleras shoved the crate back into the sea.

At the table, Bhoran lodged the tip of the knife between the oyster's lips and twisted his wrist, prying it open. Plump white flesh glistened in a small pool of seawater. Bhoran brought it to his lips and sipped the liquid before slurping the oyster and chewing its flesh, savoring its sweetness. He drained the rest of the seawater from the shell and pushed the knife toward Mheleras, who was watching him all the while through curious eyes.

"I see you know how to appreciate a mollusk." Mheleras pried another oyster open. "Raised by the sea?"

Bhoran reached for the ale to gain a moment. *Should I tell this man of Hydrus?* The arrow that had hit his wrist and Mheleras's threat of little tolerance for lies pointed him toward the obvious answer. "Raised in Hydrus," Bhoran said at last.

Mheleras nodded.

In silence, the knife changed hands as they ate, until Bhoran's teeth crunched on something hard. A sharp pain shot down his jaw. He spat his food into his palm.

"Aha!" Mheleras cried. He poked around in the slime, then picked something up, wiped it against his thigh, and raised it in the air. It was a small black pearl, misshapen and with a dark luster. "Now, that is what I call good luck." He patted Bhoran's back. "Lucky you didn't swallow it, or I would have kept you here until it came out of your rear."

Bhoran laughed. "These things are rare?"

"Very much so. This one's stubborn, but with some filing and singing, it will succumb to my shaping efforts."

Bhoran studied the adoration in Mheleras's eyes as he held the pearl. *Could it be?* "Is the black pearl your stone?"

A wrinkle grew on Mheleras's forehead. He hooted. "Look at your face," he said between bouts of laughter. "You truly believe that. Pearls aren't stones. Even these empty shells that give birth to them know that."

Blood rose to Bhoran's cheeks, and he stabbed the knife into the table as he stood. He'd had enough of mockery and evasion to last him a lifetime. "I never cared for the stones. It was a mistake to come here."

"Easy now." Mheleras sent the pearl twirling into the air and snatched it as it spiraled down. "Dealing with crude merchants who bargain for a steal and talking to oysters most of the time has made me forget my good manners. I meant no insult." He pressed Bhoran's shoulder. "Sit. Let us talk more of things that matter."

Reluctantly Bhoran resumed his seat behind the table. He drained his mug but didn't touch another oyster, his appetite for them now gone.

Mheleras placed the black pearl on the table. It rolled to the side and stopped.

"Do the merchants really climb down here to get them?" Bhoran asked him. Much as he admired the vigor of the men who traveled the lands, he couldn't imagine them scaling these slopes.

"No. Most of them can barely move. Old, creaking bones dragged about by loose flesh. No match for yours."

Bhoran took the flattery. His body was firm, his muscles tight and meaty, and now that he was clean from the snake venom, he felt its strength returning even fiercer. He scraped the dried blood off his arm. "How, then?"

Mheleras pointed a finger at a bucket. Its handle was tied to a rope that climbed the rocky hills and disappeared over the edge. "They lower their offerings, and I return the proper reward."

"Are black pearls all you've got?"

"*All* I've got? Do you know how rare it is to find one of these?"

Bhoran shook his head.

"This is my second one in ten moonturns. You were fortunate not to swallow it."

"And if I had? Would you have gutted me to retrieve it?"

Mheleras's lips twisted into a canny smile. "Without a second thought."

Bhoran laughed. He would have loved to see the man try. And then he realized he couldn't remember the last time he had laughed. He hadn't believed he would hear the sound of his laughter after Lusha had left him.

"Why the sulking face?" Mheleras raised his mug. "Life is a wondrous thing."

Bhoran stared at his own mug, now empty. "I think I've wasted mine."

"It's never too late to start again, Bhoran of the Unknown."

Bhoran swallowed hard. There was something about the way this name-calling sounded that made the hairs on his nape stand on end. It felt *wrong*. It felt as if those who used it knew more about him and mocked him.

"Why did Jorgamur send you here?"

Bhoran reached for the black pearl and twisted it between his fingers. Its surface was finely polished, like a mirror. After that night at the statue, Bhoran had resolved to never trust mirrors again. He let the black pearl down. "To learn the truth."

"Has something changed in the lands?"

Everything, Bhoran thought. *Ronan, Crystal ... dead.* Lusha had left him, following the merchant, and Avalan ... where was he right now? Would the shadow really lead him to the Heart of the Bloodstone? And would it be enough to defeat Bassalt? Yet Bhoran suspected none of these things mattered to Mheleras. "How do you mean?"

"Jorgamur sees beyond the surface. Why has he sent you to me, if not for the fact the balance has been disturbed?"

"What balance?"

"This village of yours, Hydrus. Ronan was here some moons ago. I saw the fear in his eyes."

"Ronan came to see you?" Bhoran frowned. "How could you see something like that from afar?"

"Ronan always braves the slippery rocks. He's a merchant true to his workings. We sat in this same spot some moons ago, musing on life and its meaning. As much as he tried to hide it from me, unspoken words haunted his eyes. That night, as he slept, I went through his sack. Filled with birthstones of all kinds it was. But I know that stones in your village are forbidden."

Bhoran listened, trying to suppress the fear that crept up his chest and threatened to seize his heart. Ronan had been here with the stones, and he had been afraid. *Of what?*

"Something has happened, has it not?" Mheleras said.

"Ronan is dead." Bhoran watched the stones in the man's eyes. Yet they were dark, and dark they remained, betraying no feeling. This man reminded him of himself. Perhaps he also was an Onyx, and that was why he lived alone in this unfriendly bay, surrounded by rocks and hunting for pearls.

Mheleras leaned back. "I see," he said calmly, though his face had grown dark. "And who was it that killed him?"

"Many will tell you it was me. I was the first to find his body and the weapon. A dagger bearing the Onyx in its hilt."

"Was the blade sharp?"

The man had spoken the aching thought that had been circling Bhoran's mind. "No. The blade was too dull. It wouldn't hold the strength to inflict this terrible gash—"

"Did you touch it?" Mheleras demanded.

"I did."

"And?"

Bhoran frowned. *Why did Jorgamur really send me here?* His patience was thinning now. This man pestered him with questions but offered no answers. "I don't know what you want me to say."

"I see."

Bhoran's heat rose. He'd had enough of Mheleras's vagueness, but before he could lash out, Mheleras stood and motioned him to follow.

At the back of the cavern, the air was cooler and dripping with salt water. Bhoran saw Mheleras rummage through the contents of a chest until he found what he was looking for—a small leather pouch, much like the one Ronan had given him to hold the Moonstone he had once gifted to Lusha, and that now nestled in his pocket.

Mheleras dipped two fingers into the pouch and took out a black stone. A proper stone this time. Shaped like a crude pebble, its outline was sharp, making the small black pearl look a mere fleck before it.

"What is this?" Bhoran asked.

Mheleras smiled with the assurance that came from possessing great knowledge. "This … is the truth."

CHAPTER FIFTY-FIVE

THE FIRST LIGHT broke over the horizon, beaten bronze threaded with hammered gold. Atop the south watchtower, Bassalt stared into the calmness of the Nameless Sea, a fresh breeze ruffling his gray locks.

He leaned against the wooden rail. The watchtower offered the most magnificent views at dawn. It wasn't often he came to relish the beauty of the shallow waters as they whispered over the sandy beach. But this morning, his chest was bursting with an uneasiness the basalt walls of his chamber couldn't soothe.

The nightmare still plagued his sleep—a wall of dark mist, threatening to swallow him whole. Then it was the failure. Despite his efforts, Bassalt hadn't succeeded in finding the Onyx. Ronan had suffered an ungraceful death; his adopted brother had escaped; the tribe had turned against him; Avalan walked with the shadows, seeking revenge; Dhylinea's healing magic had breached his spells of protection; and Delion kept his lips stubbornly pressed together about the presence of an Onyx.

Behind him, the village remained silent. Slowly the doors of the fisherfolk creaked open. They swarmed the gate, presenting to the guards baskets and spears as proof of their intentions. Bassalt watched the tops of their heads, heard their mumbling words of annoyance, and smelled the anger in their steps as they crossed the white sand to go fishing.

Only some days ago, they gave their loved ones to the sea, Bassalt thought. *And now they come claiming their share of the sacrifice.*

The sea would bless them with fish, he knew. It always did. Hydrus's waters had sustained generations of stone tribes throughout the ages. As he watched women and men dive into the sea, Bassalt remembered the nights when his father used to bring him to the shore.

To practice your control over the Tiger's Eye, Shaman would always say. Then it had always fallen to Bassalt to bend the seawater into tall waterfalls or make it part to form a pathway of wet sand and writhing fish and shells that glistened under the moonlight. Bassalt smiled as he remembered his father's laugh. Glorious and guttural it had been, as if it had come from the depths of his soul.

A great earthmage his father had been, with a keen eye and an eager ear. Yet Bassalt had inherited none of his patience to listen to the woes of others. *What good would it be when I know the cause to all the pains that plague the lands? The birthstones.* These little pieces of rock encompassed souls, passions, hearts. These were the bearers of hatred, the binders of fates, the bringers of wars. Banishing them from his village, along with their hateful masters, was the wisest decision Bassalt had made in this long reign of his.

He thought of Delion now, the way he mumbled the Great Warrior's name over and over in the cave. *Olnos. Olnos.* The old stonemaster's cries were calls for aid, but what good was it to call upon the dead? Bassalt had made a frightful mistake to take that stone to his teacher. It held a great meaning, Bassalt knew, but now that was lost—a frozen rain across his face that had long dried.

The ladder behind him creaked. Bassalt took a breath. It didn't reach the depths of his chest. There was no use fighting the dread, he knew. Sooner or later, he would have to face the tidings of the outer world, and his gut told him they wouldn't prove what he'd imagined.

He twisted his head to regard Theran. Swiftly his most trusted manservant climbed up, clad in robes the color of shadowgrass. Theran pushed back his cowl. Beads of sweat crowned his forehead and lips. "My chief—"

"What did you learn?"

"Nothing good, I'm afraid. Chieftain Silver's daughter escaped

Raekandar with a merchant, leaving behind her hair as a token. She was last seen at Undeena's Inn but was swiftly gone after."

Bassalt nodded. It was fortunate Silver remained in the clutches of a long sleep. He wouldn't have liked to hear of his daughter's escape. Ethelnar had promised Bassalt allegiance, but as it had turned out, he had dishonored his word. "What of Avalan?"

Theran wiped his eyes, cleared his throat. "Chiefess Crystal is dead ... A Nuummite discerned the Black Opal's deathmark on her body." He wiped his sleeve across his mouth to ease his trembling lips. "Rumors say the chief killed his own wife out of spite for raising her eyes to Avalan of the Bloodstone."

And so it has come to this. Bassalt had suspected Ethelnar's hatred for Avalan. After all, one rarely forgot old loves. Especially those whose flowers had been plucked too soon, before they had even had the time to blossom. Yet what Bassalt hadn't expected was this hatred to lead to Crystal's death. Surely, Ethelnar was cunning and able enough to rid Bassalt of Avalan's presence, and yet the wretched chief had punished his wife instead. "Chief Ethelnar holds Avalan to ransom? We must send word for ..." Bassalt trailed off, watching his servant's face paling.

"Chief Ethelnar is dead, my chief."

The knot in Bassalt's stomach tightened. The first sunrays caressed his nape yet did nothing to ease the cold dread that had grown in his soul since sunrise. "Tell me all."

Theran laid a quivering hand on the rail. "After the chiefess's death, Avalan lured Ethelnar away from the keep and *killed* him."

Bassalt's gaze traveled over Theran's shaking figure and beyond the thatched roofs of the huts, over the path that led to Farmera's house. *How would she feel to know her son is a murderer?* Killing the mountain beasts for food, skin, and bones was one matter, but killing a man quite another. *This must be Avalan's first kill,* Bassalt thought. And no matter the reason, Bassalt knew well the elation and disgust that followed a murder. Justice and death, all mingling to haunt you for the rest of your days. "Where is Avalan now?"

"Gone, my chief." Theran coughed as if he'd swallowed wrongly.

"Only the chief's body lay among Krokador's ruins, buried in a shallow grave, along with his greatsword and a pendant—"

"Krokador?"

"Yes. The men believe the fight took place on the Warden Trees."

Bassalt frowned. He knew Avalan to be a skilled tracker, but even a skill such as that couldn't have led him to Krokador's Stronghold. "How did Avalan reach the hold?"

"They say a second shadow haunts him, my chief. Leads his every step."

A second shadow? If that was true, then Dhylinea had seen in Avalan's soul a secret far greater than Bassalt could imagine. *A determination to reach the heart, an ache for freedom …* His mouth went dry, all warmth leaving his body. He tried to speak calmly, but his voice came out a parched croak. "What of my snake ring?"

Theran's eyes darted to the ladder, the guards, the sea … anywhere else but Bassalt's pleading gaze. "I am so sorry, my chief. I searched every corner … The snake ring is missing."

Bassalt rolled his hands into balls of anger. *Cursed, cursed.* Theran's body trembled more fiercely now, and that only stoked Bassalt's anger. "Calm down. I shan't hold it against you."

Theran gasped, a short cry of pain. Tears filled his eyes. "It isn't that, my chief."

"Speak, then. Is there more I should know?"

"Your stepbrother …"

"What of him?" Bassalt barked. Bhoran was the least of his concerns now, and so Bassalt hoped it would remain. His time hadn't come yet.

"Bhoran is dead. Given to Hydrus." Thick tears streamed from Theran's eyes, and this time, he made no effort to restrain his sobs.

Bassalt searched his soul for pain at Theran's dire words and found nothing. He'd always thought Bhoran's death would ease his mind, and now that it had happened … He turned, gazed at the Nameless Sea in disbelief. In his mind's eye, he pictured Hydrus, its massive jaws piercing his stepbrother's body with countless jagged fangs …

The snowflakes, he remembered. *The snowflakes.*

It is below the surface that monsters live, Bassalt wanted to tell Theran. *And I am the worst of all.*

CHAPTER FIFTY-SIX

The sullen silence bothered Avalan the most. It made him feel he'd followed the shadow into his own grave. Back in Hydrus, he'd always relied on his sharp ears to warn him of surrounding danger: the keen of a seabird fluttering away, the whisper of footfalls over shadowgrass, the distant warning of thunder …

Silence.

Avalan's fingers grazed the walls; his toes curled over the stone floor. In the darkness, they became his eyes, telling him how tall, narrow, or wide the passage became as he trod through it. *Rough stone, smooth stone, a puddle of water, the smell of mushrooms*—all would prove useful to finding his way out.

The air was thick. Avalan wasn't certain if he should blame his own fear or the dewy mist of trickling water that licked the walls. Behind him, the breeze had long ceased to cool the sweat across his nape. *Turn around!* Avalan's instincts screamed to him. Yet he didn't dare twist his body. Pitch black the tunnel was, and once he lost his course, there would be no telling if he could pick the path up again.

He tripped over a jutting rock. Biting his tongue, he suppressed a cry. Mountain lairs held other dangers, Avalan knew, and those might not need eyes to see through darkness. He inhaled musty air, the pain in his toes easing. *Turn and run,* his mind told him. A couple of swift strides, and he could find himself out in the open. He knelt, looked back.

Murky darkness greeted him, so thick Avalan could cut it with his goat dagger. Yet he no longer had it. *What good would it do to run back now?* Much as Avalan hated being underground, he knew this had to be the only way. A stone's Heart wouldn't lie out in the open. Only a fool would think that. It must remain hidden, in a place far from prying eyes.

At last the shadow had shown him the way.

Isn't that what I've been longing for? Yet not like this, he knew. Not with the deaths that had come with it. Not with a heart filled with sorrow and a head infested with vile thoughts. In a short time, he'd witnessed the power of the stones: adorning weapons and necklaces, merging in marriage, embellishing tales of bravery, blending in alchemy, leaping out of the palms of a stonemaster, bursting like thoughts into his own mind, killing those he loved … He'd seen it all, and more than he had wished for.

Will the Heart of the Bloodstone finally set me free?

He turned his head back to the path before him. He could not see it, yet he knew it must lead to the heart. His blood was throbbing with this truth. A truth that could lead to Hydrus's freedom.

He stood.

This time, he closed his eyes as he plunged forth. Keeping them open served as nothing but a dire reminder he was blind. Tracing the path, Avalan walked. He tried to fill his mind with memories he would cherish: Crystal's trembling lips when she had first seen him kneeling in that small chamber, her palm against his cheek, her body beneath his in their last union … The death of Ethelnar wasn't punishment enough for her murder, he decided. In fact, it stood only as a beginning.

No longer would he suffer under the heel of any ruler. And Bassalt would be next.

He quickened his pace.

Though the path now took a downward turn, the air remained cool and fresh. It filled his lungs with hope as he descended deeper into the mountain. The shiver of fear soon gave way to shivers of cold. His linen breeches, now clinging to his skin, did little to keep him warm. The ground suddenly leveled. His eyes were open now, grown so accustomed to the cavernous dark that Avalan had little hope he'd see again.

A wall came smashing into him.

It threw him off balance and onto his back. Sprawled on the ground, Avalan rubbed his face. He'd been so intent on tracing his sides that he'd forgotten to brace for his front. He staggered to his feet. Liquid fear rose to his mouth. *Have I taken a wrong turn?*

He fumbled around him. Ceiling, cave walls, wet ground, all seemed to be in their right place. *What is that, then?* He reached out a palm to consider the wall before him. *Perhaps it's only a rock I can scramble over,* he thought as he felt the heartless surface. After a while, he knew the truth.

I've reached a dead end.

Avalan ground his fist against the unmoving wall. *It cannot be.* He was certain he had followed the path to the last stone. But now doubt crept into his mind, numbing his senses. *Perhaps I missed a turn … or the shadow plain fooled me.* "Shadow," he called into the darkness. His voice echoed like thunder, bouncing off the cavern walls, booming in his ears.

The shadow wouldn't speak to him, Avalan knew. And yet if it was there with him in this soulless darkness, it could make itself known by touching him. He had felt its embrace before falling from the high tower, icy cold. He shivered. "Shadow," he called again, trying to keep his voice calm.

Avalan waited for a touch that never came. *Cursed shadow. What is its game? I should never have trusted it.* Eyedir had warned him, to be fair. The merchant had said the dark paths weren't a thing anyone could tread. *Keep your footing on the paths of light. Wasn't that what he cautioned me with?* Avalan twisted his neck, trying to imagine light penetrating this dense dark. Had the morning arrived outside?

If there was no way forward, then the only steps he could take were the ones that would lead him back into the open, onto a barren mountain that held no answers for him.

A soft rustle resounded.

It was a subtle whisper, but in the cave's stillness, it was clear. Closer and closer it crept. Something was moving toward him. *The shadow?* Even as he thought it, he knew it wasn't true. The shadow was silent, deadly …

As the rustling sounds neared, a cold realization crept into Avalan's mind—he was unarmed and blind. And whatever was moving toward him must have been alerted to his presence when he had spoken.

He backed away until he felt the wall jabbing the skin of his back. He raised his fists.

The rustling drew nearer. Avalan closed his eyes, trying to quench the fear in his heart, calm his mind. He focused on the sound. It was crisp with a strange rhythm that didn't match the movement of an animal—no sound of claws clinking against the stone, no snorting, sniffing sounds of a searching predator. *What is it, then?*

He listened harder: rustle, rustle, rustle, and light footfalls. The whisper of a dress scraping the floor. *A human? Who else would dare to reach the depths of the mountain?*

Then the sound ceased. Avalan dared open his eyes. Three paces away, a faint light appeared. Bright like the reflection of gold under the sun, it grew larger and larger as it floated toward him. A searing ache in his head forced Avalan to shut his eyes once again. After all this darkness, the mere wisp of light was enough to make him even blinder.

"Don't stare at it," a voice warned.

Avalan jerked, bumping the back of his head against the wall. "Who are you?"

"You don't recognize my voice?"

Avalan felt the words crawl over his chest, trying to penetrate it. That feeling was one he remembered. "You?" he said, half-opening his eyes. In the presence of all this sudden light, they watered. Through streaming tears, Avalan saw the truth of it.

Under a hovering sphere of golden light, Dizredek stood clad in feathered robes. He slinked closer. Though the tunnel now felt warmer, a cold tightness gripped Avalan's heart. "Where is the shadow?"

"You won't be needing it anymore." Dizredek waved an elegant hand. "Its task is complete. Now, I will ask you to stay still."

Avalan blocked his way as Dizredek slinked closer. "What do you mean, its task is complete? I *must* return to Hydrus with my Bloodstone. There's no time for games."

A vile twitch twisted Dizredek's elegant features. "Now, now. You speak of games, but it was you who took your time. Getting yourself drunk in celebrations and making love to women who aren't yours. Although, I must confess, killing the chief was quite impressive."

Grabbing Dizredek by the feathered collar of his tunic, he shook him. "Ethelnar *killed* her! You promised to bind the shadow to me, not her. It is all your doing."

A shadow of pity lingered in the sorcerer's eyes. "Ronan hoped you had forgotten her. He said the freedom of Hydrus burned your heart. He was certain it would overpower love. He was wrong, wasn't he? I warned him. It was your heart that bound the shadow to her. Your longing—"

"Speak not a word more, lest I kill you. Who are you truly? What do you want from me?"

Faster than thought, Dizredek grabbed hold of Avalan's shoulder. His touch felt like a hot iron. Avalan screamed. Dizredek pressed, forced him to the ground. A crawling numbness spread through Avalan's body, a spell that made his limbs freeze, ignoring his desperate commands for action. "What have you done?"

Dizredek's face hardened. "Are you scared of me, Avalan of the Bloodstone? Though I have told you my stone is peaceful, you still resist. Stay still."

Tethered to the floor by invisible shackles, Avalan watched Dizredek trace the wall with urgent movements. A glint caught Avalan's eye. Bile rose to his mouth when he saw what it was. Around Dizredek's slender finger rested Bassalt's snake ring. The very one he had demanded Avalan give him after he freed Hydrus. "The ring. You fooled me."

"I did no such thing." Dizredek's voice was indignant. "You were so ready to sell your soul for the freedom of others. I only gave you the push that was needed." With a flick of his wrist, he sent the flaming sphere close to Avalan.

Its heat was such that Avalan felt his forehead burning. He tried to writhe against his invisible bonds, but the stone magic was stronger. It crushed him down as if a boulder rested on his chest. "Why?" Sweat stung his eyes now. "Why did you lead me here?"

Dizredek faced him. The flare of arrogance had now faded to a pitiful look of worry. "Are you warm yet?" He touched Avalan's cheek. "I just … cannot wait …"

The blood must run warm, Avalan remembered. *He'll take my blood.* "No!" Avalan's mind struggled against the spell. "Release me. No—" A blade glinted, slashed Avalan's skin. He screamed, warm blood gushing out near his collarbone.

Dizredek thrust the blade into his robes and bent. He dipped his fingers into the crimson rivers that ran down Avalan's chest. Then he wrote upon the wall with wet fingers. His lips trembled with a chant in a tongue Avalan had never heard.

Though he wanted to scream, Avalan bit his lips, trying to listen, to understand. Yet it was no good, he knew. His body was no longer his, and the trickling blood had now reached the rim of his breeches, a warm waste of his life. "Stop that!" he yelled, confused. "All along it was *you*! You made me believe in the Heart. Tricked me into leaving Hydrus and my family behind. Why? What is this place? Answer me!"

A low rumble sent dust raining over both of them. With a loud groan, the wall twisted, more darkness stretching behind it.

Dizredek fell to his knees, as if in prayer. For a moment, his head hung low, his hoarfrost hair a waterfall hiding his face. Then he jerked his head back, a harrowing laugh leaving his mouth. It was the cry of a tortured animal finally escaping its trap.

He's lost his mind.

The snake ring caught Avalan's eye. The gemstone in it swirled with darkness, a wild whirlpool. Avalan knew it couldn't be a good sign—he still remembered the haunted look on Bassalt's face as his fingers had rubbed the ring during the goat game.

"Dizredek," Avalan called over the sorcerer's cackle. "How did you get the ring? What happened in Hydrus?"

The sorcerer's frenzied laugh died. When he turned his face to Avalan, tears streamed from his eyes. Of joy or pain, it was hard to know, but the dark mage crawled closer. "You deserve to have the truth, Avalan of the Bloodstone. For helping me get here. You deserve it, but you will not like it." He flicked his eyes to the ring and smiled, a sad twitch of his thin lips. "Pay no heed to the ring. Bassalt still stands as chief. But you should end his reign. Kill him, like you killed Ethelnar, and free your tribe of the man who murdered Ronan."

The words were a stab to Avalan's heart. His throat tightened. *Bassalt? No, it cannot be.* "But Bassalt … he sentenced Bhoran to die …" Even as he said it, Avalan knew that made no difference. Bassalt was cruel, and he would have done anything to keep his place in the chief's chair. Even sentence an innocent to die with the pretense of the Onyx. He swallowed hard. *It is all my fault. If I hadn't wanted to fight Bassalt, Ronan would still be alive.* "He killed Ronan because of the stones," Avalan said bitterly. "The birthstones he smuggled into the village for my cause."

"It is so." Dizredek wiped his tears against the feathers of his robe and stood.

"No! You cannot leave me here. You must free me. Give me my Bloodstone. How else can I return to fight him? How else can I free the tribe from him? You gave me your word!"

Dizredek shot him a pitiful glance. "The word of the Nuummite is worth nothing. Cunning and deceiving it is, to suit our purpose. I never meant to use you, Avalan of the Bloodstone. Your warm blood was all I needed. Remember this, and try to forgive me." He stepped toward the darkness behind the twisted wall, taking the golden sphere with him.

Avalan pushed against the spell with all his will. The numbness didn't abate. *If I am left here in the darkness, I will bleed out. Die.* "Wait," he called. "Where does this passage lead to?"

Dizredek's head hung low. "Do not follow me. What is life for me, for you is death."

With that, he disappeared behind the wall, his robe rustling against his heels.

CHAPTER FIFTY-SEVEN

CALLA'S DRESS whispered around Lusha's ankles as they crossed the cobbled streets of Levorotha. Thankfully, the two women were of a similar build, and so the dress had proved a good fit. But its colors were meant to heighten Calla's dark features—the long white lace did little to complement Lusha's milky skin.

Yet Lusha didn't mind. She had clean clothes, a friend to guide her through the city straight to her aunt, and her scar … it was no longer there. This was a thing she couldn't quite believe. She couldn't stop tracing the skin over her eye—it was no longer jagged, but smooth. And it felt *real*.

Such was the power of the Moonstone over the city of Levorotha, Calla had told her last night, that it could heal almost all afflictions. *Almost.* Lusha's eyesight remained jarred, and Calla had lost every man and woman who had fallen sick with the Red Weal. This sickness was a shadow the city couldn't fathom, a gray blotch that marred the otherwise perfect silver face of the moon.

Last night's deserted streets had now fully awoken. All shades of white garments spun around them, tunics that fell loose around the bodies of men and hugged tighter the waists of women with the aid of beaded belts that clicked with their every move. The crowds streamed through the narrow streets, their chatter bouncing off the walls of huddled buildings. Their footsteps made no sound as they glided over the stones on bare feet—no man or woman or child wore shoes. Lusha had also left hers behind in Calla's sickhouse, grateful for the warmth of the stones beneath her soles.

Most of the women kept their hair long, she noticed. Lusha combed her fingers through the ragged ends of hers. Now she was safe, she resolved to let it grow back.

A woman gave her an earnest smile as their shoulders brushed. The streets were narrow stone paths made even tighter by the various benches that had been placed there with the first light. Merchants displayed all kinds of goods; the tangy smells of fruits and spices made Lusha's nose itch with the need for a good sneeze. She gifted the woman with a smile of her own and rushed after Calla, who was now a few steps from the opening that led into Levorotha's square.

As they passed through the low archway, Lusha felt a sense of wonder. Under the clear sky, the sandstone of the square glistened in the morning light like the white beach of Hydrus. In the center of the square stood a majestic structure. A thick sandstone pillar rose to the skies, supporting a massive disk with thousands of tiny holes. Water trickled through them like rain, pooling into a round basin.

Unlike on the crowded stone paths, there were only a few people in the sunny square, and they seemed in a hurry to cross it and find shelter in the shade of the labyrinth. In haste, some of them stooped to wash their faces in the waters of the pool, and others drank from it.

"What is this?" Lusha asked, stepping alongside Calla.

The moonhealer halted her pace and pointed upward. "The fountain of Levorotha. Each night, it collects the tears of the moon and lets them rain over our heads. The water is healing."

"The moon cries?"

Calla huffed. "It's the dew. That disk on top is a bronze mirror. When the night falls, the moonlight shines upon it, and it turns the rays into dew."

Lusha smiled. It was the most beautiful thing she'd seen in a long time.

"Do you want to taste it?" Calla asked.

"I do."

They strolled to the fountain, the sound of raindrops getting stronger as they approached. Lusha dipped her hands in the water, scrubbed her face clean. The coolness refreshed her skin and her thoughts. "Thank you," she whispered to the tears of the moon. "For healing me."

Calla loomed above her, her silhouette backlit by the sun. "This scar of yours, how bad was it?"

"Half of my face was torn. My eye ..." She bit her lip.

"What about it?"

"After the accident, I saw from it clearly no longer."

"And now?" Calla leaned closer, her face alight with curiosity. "Can you see now?"

Lusha shook her head. "The scar seems gone, but my bad sight remains. Perhaps it's just an illusion."

"We must go now," Calla offered. "The chiefess allows audiences only until midday."

"The chiefess?"

Calla gave her a wicked smile. "But of course. So pure, so innocent, and so ignorant at the same time. Where have you been living? Under a rock?"

Confusion overwhelmed Lusha.

"Your aunt," Calla told her. "Shelanna is the chiefess of Levorotha. Now, we shall see if your words ring true when you face her."

Before Lusha could speak, Calla turned on her heel and rushed on.

My aunt, a chiefess?

Dread perching upon her shoulder, Lusha kept pace with Calla's swift strides. The castle loomed closer with their every step. Up close, it seemed ever more enchanting than when Lusha had gazed at it from the shore of the moonlake. Stone stood upon stone, forming slim towers that dared to scrape the sky. To Lusha, they looked like blocks stacked by the fingertips of a giant.

Calla led her to the foot of a spiral staircase. When Lusha dared to look up, she could not see its peak. Higher and higher it rose, and as they climbed it, Lusha felt dizzy. *I shouldn't look down,* she told herself, and yet she couldn't resist. From above, the moon fountain seemed all the more impressive, with its bronze disk and pouring rain. *I wonder if it can heal my heart along with my scarring.*

The air grew cooler the higher they went. Lusha had just counted the hundredth step when Calla halted their ascent and marched ahead onto sturdy ground. Lusha followed her, relieved. They had reached an opening in the tower, a stony passage wide enough to fit the both of them walking abreast.

Outside a high door stood two guards. They both wore tunics and breeches of milky thread and cradled spears. Calla bade her to stay and went to them, tossing her long braids behind her before she spoke. Lusha couldn't hear what she was saying, but only hoped Calla also had a beating heart, like Undeena, and wasn't leading her into a snare.

She wiped two clammy hands against the dress, pretending to straighten wrinkles that weren't there. Though the fabric flowed well over her body, to Lusha, it felt foreign. Ever since she'd left Hydrus, she'd donned dresses and breeches that weren't hers, and most of them had ended up in a pile of cloth on the floor.

The guards pushed the doors open.

Calla came to her and took her hands in her own. "I've secured you passage."

"Me? Not us?"

"I have to return to the ill." She gave Lusha a challenging look. "If you truly are who you say, you won't have difficulty facing your aunt, now, will you?"

Lusha sighed. Calla still didn't believe her, but it was just as well. She was so close to escaping her father's shadow and meeting a family member from her mother's side. Amara's own sister. *My aunt.* "Thank you. I'll come find you once I'm done. I'll help you with the sick."

"Not much you can do." Calla shrugged and took off, disappearing under the curl of the swirling staircase.

Lusha approached the guards, trying to look less frightened and more regal. In Hydrus everyone treated her with respect, for she was the daughter of Silver. Yet Lusha had never acted superior to them. That only served as a wall of thorns that rose between her and her father, separating them—his need to be above the men, and her need to live among them. Yet now she raised her head high as Silver had taught her, and entered the castle after the guards.

Inside, bare stone and wind awaited her. The great chamber was barren, with a high ceiling and windows tall and glassless. Though warm sunlight bathed the place, Lusha could feel the moon's power coursing through her very soul.

Behind her, the guard urged her on with a subtle nudge of his spear.

Lusha turned to face him. "What is this place?" she found the courage to ask him, peering into his eyes. They held Moonstones, of course, as did most of the tribesfolk's in this city. The only other stone Lusha had seen in someone's eyes was the Fire Agate in Rian's. Lusha didn't know why a man like him lingered in the city of healers. *To be with Calla, of course,* she thought, remembering their passionate kiss. She shivered. Lusha didn't know why that bothered her so much. Perhaps it was the difference in their years—Rian, though still in good shape, could easily have been Calla's father.

"Wait here," the guard told her, not unkindly. "The chiefess will see you shortly."

They left her alone in the middle of the room with nothing to rest upon. It was a magnificent chamber of nothing, built as though to give the visitors a sense of awe and powerlessness, to remind them of their place under the moon.

Behind her, the high door closed firmly. Lusha's heart raced with anticipation. A high room in a tower wasn't the place she had imagined meeting her aunt. Perhaps a sickhouse where they could both dip their hands in ointments and discuss things Lusha knew—things Farmera had taught her about life, the tribes, the ailments of the lands ...

Her chest tightened. A touch of remorse for leaving Farmera behind tugged at her heart. *She was my mother.*

Faint footsteps resounded in the chamber. A woman—the chiefess, Lusha was certain—drew closer to meet her. *Where did she come from?* Lusha had seen no other entrance than the one the guards had led her through. Yet these thoughts left her once her aunt drew nearer.

The chiefess was the most majestic woman Lusha had ever seen. Tall as a man, slender and agile, with locks of golden hair framing a pure oval face, and a silvery dress that floated around her body, hugging and setting it free at the same time.

Her aunt stopped a few paces before Lusha and peered at her through two imperious Moonstones. Her lips pressed tightly together. A faint scar on her lower lip was the only thing that marred her beauty. Lusha wondered how her own nasty scar had disappeared, but this faint one remained on the chiefess's lips.

"Close your mouth and stand straighter," the chiefess commanded.

Her words felt like a slap. It was a command much like the ones her father used to give her. Instinctively Lusha obeyed, lowering her shoulders and thrusting her chest out.

"That's better," Chiefess Shelanna said, but the twist of her lips revealed otherwise. "You wished to see me?"

At last Lusha found the courage to speak. "I am Lusha, Amara's daughter."

Shelanna's eyes sparkled. "So you say, but what proof do you hold?"

Lusha reached a trembling hand into her bosom and pulled out her mother's pendant. The metal felt warm in her grasp. "This belonged to my mother. Do you recognize it?"

"No."

Lusha's heart sank. "The tribesfolk say I look like her." She searched the chiefess's face for any signs of similarities between them. In Hydrus, Lusha had always been among the fairest, admired for her glowing skin and flaxen hair. Yet as she stood now before this chiefess, who looked as if she had been untouched by time, she felt ugly and insignificant. *Why did I have to cut my hair? I surely don't look like my mother anymore.*

Shelanna sighed. "You do look like Amara."

The words rekindled the hope in Lusha's heart. The chiefess believed her.

"Does your father know you're here?"

Lusha swallowed hard. "No."

"He's looking for you. Word has been sent to escort you back to him. Back to Hydrus." It sounded like a threat.

Lusha backed away, suddenly wary. *Have I come all this way for my own blood to betray me? Is there no escape from Silver?*

Shelanna laughed. "You look so scared, like a jumpy rabbit ready to dart. Tell me, dear, did you expect your father not to look for you? His only, beloved daughter?"

Flaming anger rose in Lusha's chest, and she spoke before she could hold her tongue. "Silver is the worst father I could have."

The chiefess clapped her hands. "At last, a spark! Some passion. Pity it is for hatred."

Lusha clutched at her mother's pendant. *What offense have I caused for her to talk to me so?*

"Your father said you ran away with some boys." Disgust dripped from her aunt's voice. "I guess you are, indeed, a true daughter of Amara. Promiscuous and careless."

"How dare you?" Lusha's voice echoed in the high ceiling. "How dare you speak of my mother like this? Your own sister—"

"How dare *I*?" The chiefess raised a hand between them. "You were the one to disobey your father's orders, running away, causing a riot in the village that has always known peace. And now you show your face in my city. For what? Why did you seek me?"

I hoped you could be the mother I never had, Lusha thought. She had been a fool, she knew. "I should never have come."

"Indecisive, and so weak," Shelanna said, poison dripping from her words. "I don't know why your father wishes you back. I certainly wouldn't."

Lusha stood so still she could hear the wind whisper through her hair. She held the chiefess's disdainful stare. "Perhaps, in his own troubled way, he loves me."

"And that will be his demise. Always loving the wrong woman and not seeing the one who *deserves* his love the most."

The hair on Lusha's arms stood on end. *Does she despise me and my mother so much because she wanted Silver for herself?* "You were in love with my father."

"Love?" Shelanna scoffed. "What do you know of love, childling? They raised you in that wretched village in pure blindness. You do not even hold your birthstone about you. How long do you think you can survive in the lands without its blessing?"

"I'm not afraid."

The chiefess laughed, a throaty sound. "Careless of danger. Much like your mother. In the end, the very thing she chased killed her. What are you chasing, *niece*? Being an Onyx bride away from Hydrus? I must admit, I was terribly curious to see that man of yours, but it seems even he has grown tired of your presence."

All words left Lusha then, the cruelty of the chiefess a sharp knife through the heart. She bit her lip, bidding her face not to betray her, her eyes not to cry.

"Go now." Shelanna waved a dismissive hand. "I'm finished with you. You can remain in Levorotha as long as you like. That small kindness I am prepared to give you. Perhaps if Silver's away from you, the effects of your poisonous presence will fade. It won't be easy, but it's a start."

With that, the chiefess turned on her heel, her long dress trailing behind her as she walked to the back of the chamber.

Lusha watched her disappear into a crevice she hadn't noticed before—a secret entrance.

Once again she stood alone in this bleak room so high above the ground. A heedless wind blew down on her, freezing her very soul, numbing her mind. Even her mother's pendant felt cold now in her hands, offering her no comfort.

Hot tears fell from her eyes, and the breeze carried them away. She opened her mouth, but the air choked her sob. She knelt. Lusha knew well the feeling of rejection. She had known it more than once: when her father had never accepted her for who she was, when Bhoran had left her behind in Hydrus, and when she'd found that wretched dress in his room …

The cold despair that none would ever truly love her squeezed her chest. Lusha had come to Levorotha to find a loving aunt. Instead, she'd found someone who perhaps hated her even more than Silver.

CHAPTER FIFTY-EIGHT

BHORAN GAZED at the dark stone, mesmerized by the frozen rain that twirled inside its black flesh. In his palm, it wasn't much larger than a pebble.

The sun had risen now, yet Bhoran had gotten no sleep. All night he'd sat on the wet sand beneath the stars, watching the small stone Mheleras had called "truth." Bhoran had begged the man to reveal its nature to him, but Mheleras had insisted Bhoran spent some time with the stone before he heard it. All night Bhoran had searched inside the stone for the self he had lost.

Cold sweat dripped down his forehead. He clenched his jaw. Yekana's venom had now cleared from his veins, and pure blood made Bhoran sick to his stomach. The only thing that kept his despairing thoughts away, he knew, was the anticipation of the truth this small stone held.

Light footfalls came behind him as Mheleras emerged from the cave. "Is this the first time you've seen them?" Mheleras asked him, breaking the spell.

Bhoran tried to recall the last time he had seen the flakes in his eyes. It had been so long ago, and so much had happened since then, that bringing the moment back to memory proved a hefty task. It must have been in the Crystal Lake of the forest of Hydrus, Bhoran judged, where he had spent countless mornings gazing at his reflection on the lake's still waters. However, the flakes in his eyes weren't so clear and pure as the ones that swam in the stone he held now.

"Ah, so you've seen them before." Mheleras filled the silence. "A thing of wild beauty they are."

Reluctantly Bhoran tore his gaze from the stone. "You see them too?"

Mheleras smiled and sat next to him.

"I thought I was the only one."

"We rarely are the only ones."

"How can this be? Jorgamur said the Onyx doesn't change. It always remains dark and unmoving."

Mheleras shrugged. "Jorgamur is right. The Onyx doesn't change."

It took Bhoran a few moments to understand the meaning of these words, but once he did, he wrapped his fingers around the stone, brought it close to his heart. "This isn't an Onyx." He peered at Mheleras's eyes. "I am not an Onyx?"

Mheleras smiled. "No."

Bhoran felt something inside him crack—a small fracture in a wall he'd built around his heart to protect it from the insults that came from being a talon. "You aren't an Onyx."

Mheleras shook his head. "I am not."

"You and I," Bhoran said, opening his palm to uncover the stone. "Are we the same?"

"We are."

If I am not an Onyx, then what am I?

Bhoran knew then Mheleras held the answer, but he couldn't bring himself to ask him. Instead, he thought of the last twenty-two years of misery the darkness in his eyes had caused him. All the pain and agony, losing his family, his ostracism from the tribe who had raised him, losing Lusha ... *Was that all for nothing?* Were the stones so cruel as to have punished him in such a way by refusing to reveal their true nature?

His anger rose, and he let the stone fall from his grasp. "No," he said, holding his head. He paced the wet sand. "It cannot be. Bassalt knows all the stones. I've seen his magic. He would have known. You hear me?" With two swift strides, he reached Mheleras, grabbed his shoulders, and shook him. "Bassalt would have known. But he didn't tell me? Why would someone punish me like this?"

Now Bhoran knew the truth, he didn't want it. He wished it would go away. He wished all this were a dream. He wished he were back in the mountain with Yekana, her sharp fangs sucking every drop of blood out of him. And this time, he might let her take it all.

Mheleras drew him into a close embrace and didn't let him go until all the emotion had gone and Bhoran's back no longer rose and fell with pain.

"Come," Mheleras told him. "Let me refill our cups."

Bhoran watched him go, making no move to follow. The sun no longer burned his skin, its golden light now making the sea sparkle. He could just stay here, staring at the calm waters until a different night fell. A night when Bhoran would go to sleep knowing the truth about his stone.

"Come," Mheleras called.

Sighing, Bhoran joined Mheleras at the table. Their mugs were filled afresh with cool ale.

"If it is of any comfort to you, Bassalt wouldn't have known. We have kept our stone secret even from the stonemasters."

Bhoran shivered despite the warmth of the day. He nodded, knowing this to be true. Bassalt couldn't have known. Otherwise, he would have tried to poke Bhoran and put him through countless trials to unveil the nature of his stone. Stones were Bassalt's enemy and love. "What is it?" he said, picking the stone up again.

"It's an Obsidian. A glass-stone, in truth."

Obsidian. Bhoran felt the word in his very bones. His stone. The one he had never known. He now held it in his hands for the first time. And then he wondered ... "To whom does it belong?"

"This one's mine," Mheleras said. He closed his eyes and sent the snowflakes in the stone whirling. When he opened his eyes again, he had a grin on his face. Mheleras's teeth were white, like iridescent pearls, so different from the black ones he was fishing out of the sea.

Bhoran let the stone fall gently onto the table.

"Do you wish to know more?"

Bhoran was uncertain. A thousand questions went through his

mind, but he didn't know where to start. "Olnos said he was an Onyx. He lied?"

Mheleras nodded quietly.

"Why?"

"To protect our tribe. Our stonemistress forbids us from making our existence known to the Stone Lands. This is how it has always been, and this is how it should remain."

Bhoran eyed Mheleras. There was something in the way the man had spoken, an unsaid pride in the way he explained how things should remain secret, as if he had a part in this. "You're a guardian?"

"I am. I offer the merchants a valuable thing." He motioned to the mollusks that lay on the table. "And they, in turn, offer me news of the Stone Lands."

A spy, then, Bhoran thought. "Why did Olnos come to the Stone Lands? Why risk exposing your tribe?"

"*Our* tribe," Mheleras corrected.

I have a tribe. Bhoran would need time to get used to that notion.

"It was for the War of the Stones." Mheleras's eyes filled with dancing snowflakes. "Olnos couldn't stand back and watch the tribes being slaughtered by the Onyx."

"And so he came here, and he became a hero?"

Mheleras shrugged. "A hero for you, a traitor for the Obsidian. Yet no one can deny his bravery. Without him, the talons would have torn apart these lands. The stones favored Olnos and his decision."

"How did he keep the nature of his stone hidden?"

Mheleras threw his Obsidian into the air and caught it with one swift movement. "That was easy. Tribesmen see only what they know, and our stone is very similar to the Onyx. Olnos convinced them he was one of them, one of the Onyx. And they believed him. I warned him about them, but he wouldn't listen. Said the only way to fight and keep our stone hidden was to be one with the most hated. No one really wants to know the true nature of evil."

"I understand." The tribesfolk's hatred of the Onyx was so great that they'd never pondered if Bhoran's eyes held a different truth. When he'd told Bassalt about the flakes in his eyes, Bassalt had asked Bhoran to show him. Yet when Bhoran had failed to summon the flakes, Bassalt had been quick to dismiss Bhoran's words and go back to hating him for being a talon. "The stories say that without Olnos, the Onyx would have won. Is our stone more powerful than the Onyx?"

"Our stone has power, yes. Similar to the Onyx's."

"Not greater?"

Mheleras shook his head.

"How was it, then, that one man defeated thousands of them?"

A shadow passed over Mheleras's face. There was a subtle tremor in his hands as he stared at the horizon. "Olnos proved braver than us all, but he took this truth to his grave."

"But he risked exposing you?" Bhoran pressed, feeling the battle of disapproval and admiration in Mheleras's words.

"He did."

"Is our tribe big?"

Mheleras smiled. "Big enough now. The war savaged the Stone Lands and left the tribes in them decimated. We lost only one man to the war, and so our numbers swelled."

Bhoran wondered how a big tribe could hide from sight all these years. *How is it that none know of them or their stone?* The merchants traveled the lands and visited all places known. *Is the Obsidian tribe hiding in a place far off the known map?*

He turned his gaze to the sea. Waves pounded the rocks. Suddenly he knew. "Olnos came from the sea," he whispered. "That's why you're standing guard here. That's why you never leave."

Even as he let the words escape his mouth, he knew of their absurdity. There was nothing beyond the Nameless Sea. None had ever sung songs of the waters. None had ever told tales of the sea, except for that crazy man in Ethelnar's yard. Dromer was his name, but he had mentioned Hydrus had a waterdragon, and so his words couldn't be trusted.

Mheleras clucked his tongue. "Dangerous words to utter. If they were to fall on the wrong ears ..."

Bhoran felt Mheleras's eyes slicing him like a knife. It was a naked threat, he knew. This man didn't need to disguise the meaning of his words. Yet Bhoran was now so keen to learn more he brushed the threat aside. "How did Olnos come from the lands of the Obsidian?"

For some moments, Mheleras studied him. At last he stood, motioning Bhoran to follow.

They swam along the shore. After a few long strokes, Bhoran glimpsed a small cove. It had no beach, only a small pebbly shore. Beneath his toes, Bhoran felt the slimy touch of seaweed.

Mheleras pushed himself out of the sea, clambering over low rocks. He led Bhoran along a slippery path inside a cave.

The air was thick with the smell of wet moss. Many a time, Bhoran lost his footing while treading the clammy rock path, but he stayed behind Mheleras. After a while, he heard it. The soft splashing of water from the opening of a cavern ahead.

Mheleras halted. "This is how."

On the shallow waters of the cave was a vessel made of wood. It floated and swayed to the soft waves that licked its belly. Bhoran's chest tightened.

Once, after an exhausting goat game, Avalan and he had lain on the shore of Hydrus, watching some night fishers searching for glowing sea glass. When Garlea had waded through the shallow waters, Avalan had wondered aloud why the fisherfolk had never braved the deeper sea.

Garlea had stopped then, salty water dripping from her hair, a stern look on her face. "No ships ever make it across the Nameless Sea," she had told them. "The waterdragon smashes them all asunder."

"A ship?" Bhoran now asked.

Mheleras smiled. "The ship of Ravenar."

CHAPTER FIFTY-NINE

In the small croft of Farmera's hut, Bassalt stood under the midday sun. The wooden door still bore marks left behind by the vines he had ordered to imprison Farmera in her own house.

She had refused food and drink when Bassalt had sent Theran to her. Every time, she'd send Bassalt's servant away, yelling and cursing, and swearing upon the stones she would not stand for this humiliation. On the fourth day, Bassalt had released the vines. Still, Farmera had continued to refuse to leave the comfort of her house. She wouldn't honor him with her presence, he knew. Not even if he stood before the claws of Hydrus.

Beads of sweat trickled down Bassalt's forehead. He wiped them away with a clammy hand. *I shouldn't have worn all this hide,* he thought desperately, but it was too late now to return to his house to change. After the cursed attack, Bassalt had made certain he always wore his white panther when he strolled the village paths. *As if a corpse's skin will make me a greater chief in their eyes,* he thought, the hide now heavy and irksome over his shoulders.

He pushed the door open, noting gratefully it wasn't barred. The last thing he wanted was to break his way in. A queer sweet smell hit him, the scent of old flesh on the brink of death. The door behind him closed with a soft moan. Despite the day's sunlight, the room was dark, a drape drawn over the window above the sickbed where Silver still lay asleep.

Farmera sat at the table, face buried in her palms. Her long hair streamed through her fingers; soft sobs shook her shoulders. When she sensed Bassalt's presence, she shot him a desperate look through wet eyes. The Amethysts in them shimmered like velvet embers in the room's shadows.

Bassalt's throat went dry at the sight. "Is he gone?"

"This is no life." Farmera pressed her forehead against her fists. "I wash him and feed him and sing to him, and yet his soul isn't returning ..."

The buckets of murky water by Silver's bedside spoke of this truth. In the bleakness of the hut, Silver lay still. His face had lost its silvery sheen, a thing Bassalt had always envied. On his bare chest lay his stone, the Heliodor, but even that sunny stone had now lost its light, a somber piece of rock the color of ashes.

"We need a Moonstone healer," Farmera said.

Bassalt swallowed hard. He understood the urgency of her concern, and yet ... "I cannot let anyone enter Hydrus."

Farmera shot him a vile glance. "You'd let your own commander *die* rather than open up our village to the Stone Lands."

"You do not understand—"

"Oh, but I do!" Farmera stood with such haste that the edge of her dress got caught on the bench's corner. She ripped it free with a strong yank. "You'd rather die than admit defeat. Our mighty chief never lifts a finger to help those in need if the purpose doesn't suit his needs. I wish Hydrus had ripped away more of your fingers."

Her heart was aching. If only she would listen. "Farmera—"

"Speak not my name." She buried her fists in his chest, the supple fur of the white mountain panther muffling the strength of her shove. "Leave! Leave me ... I cannot stand your presence."

Bassalt placed a heavy palm at the base of her neck, pulled her close to him. The sweet smell of lavender invaded his nostrils. Her body shook. Her sobs tore at his heart.

"I cannot do this," Bassalt heard her say. "I cannot be a healer. The stones haven't blessed me in this."

"You have always been the pride of our tribe," Bassalt assured her. "The earth has much to give, and in your hands, its herbs sing and heal. Silver is strong. In time, he will recover." *By then it will be too late,* he thought. He sat her down on the bench. "The Onyx has returned."

Farmera's eyes widened. Her mouth searched for words that never came.

"Listen to me, for I have not told a soul the whole truth. The snake ring"—he shot a pitiful look at the stump on his hand—"warned me of their dark presence in the village many moons ago. At first I thought it a mistake, a jest … but then the changing of the stone kept coming. At once I ordered the building of the serpent fence so I could better overlook the comings and goings of the village. It was fruitless, however. My men and I found no one. Fear led me to suspect my own folk. 'What if they're fostering an Onyx in our midst?' I thought day and night. Everyone looked to me a threat."

"And so you became crueler, stricter …"

Bassalt nodded. "That only served to raise Avalan's hatred. Soon more men joined your son in training, and I could smell the stench of rebellion in the air. 'They'd never dare to challenge me,' I always thought, yet the seed of doubt had already been planted. I wanted them to see what my stone could do, to warn them to not rise, and yet … despite all my punishments and threats, the soul that longs for freedom will always fight."

That's when I killed Ronan, Bassalt thought, but he didn't dare confess it. He could not hope to ever have Farmera's love, but her eternal hatred was something he feared.

Farmera glanced over at Silver with a worried look. The commander remained in deep sleep, oblivious to this dire exchange of words. "Did he know?"

"I showed him the ring and how it changed. When Ronan died, I had to present the tribe with a killer. A murderer on the loose would only stoke their fear. That was when Bhoran returned."

"And you sentenced an innocent boy to die."

Bhoran is dead. Yet Bassalt couldn't bring himself to say it. "My stepbrother is far from innocent. He carries the darkness in his eyes."

"Bhoran has shown none of the signs of the Onyx," Farmera retorted.

"And who's to thank for that? Under my guidance, the village has remained free from the birthstones. Could you have said the same if Bhoran had been taught by a stonemaster?"

To that, Farmera had no answer.

"When Bhoran escaped, I blamed the stonemaster. Delion was to die as punishment for them all."

Farmera shook her head in wild disbelief. "Only you would do such a vile thing. To kill a stonemaster is the greatest slight. A sin. An abomination—"

"I never truly meant to kill him. I did it to protect Avalan. I vilified Delion so your son could remain unscathed for stoking a rebellion. Stonemasters have exceeded their stay in this world. Better an old relic dead than a youth with fresh blood. I *had* to punish someone."

Farmera gazed at him, a mixture of disgust and confusion on her face. "And where is this Onyx now, Bassalt?"

The words tugged at his greater fear. *Would that I knew.* "My Tiger's Eye has betrayed me," he said ruefully. "No matter how hard I look, the Onyx eludes my stare."

"Perhaps because there's nothing to see."

"You don't believe me?"

Farmera stared at him, lips pressed into a tight line of disapproval. "Why, Bassalt? Why are you telling me all this? Do you expect me to thank you for—"

"I bear news of your son."

Farmera grabbed the corner of the table. "Where is Avalan? Where is my son? Tell me he is well. Why don't you speak? Just tell me."

"I do not know how he fares, but I got word of his deeds. Avalan killed Chief Ethelnar."

"You do not speak the truth." Farmera's anger flared again, all her despair turning to flaming disapproval.

"It might comfort you to know it was for love. Ethelnar killed Crystal, and Avalan avenged her death."

The flame of her Amethysts now shimmered low as she tried to grasp the meaning of his words. "But … why would the chief kill his own wife?"

"Jealousy," Bassalt guessed, though he knew it must have been true. "You've said it yourself that all these years, your son still loved Crystal. Did you think Avalan would not try to take her from Ethelnar? Did you think he would go on with his life knowing his one love was so close to him, just the reach of an arm away? Avalan always reaches for what isn't his—"

"This is all your doing!" Farmera screamed. Her voice broke. "If Avalan hadn't left Hydrus—"

"It wasn't I who stirred these notions in his mind. Rather, it is Delion you should yell at, for he awoke in Avalan the desire for the Bloodstone. I *tried*, Farmera. I tried long and hard to keep this tribe safe, away from the curse of the birthstones. And what have I gained for my efforts? Hatred and disdain. The men won't even share my table. The women cringe and spit whenever I dare walk past their doors. Children whisper behind my back and mock me …"

"How could you speak about yourself when my son's life is in danger? Where is my boy now? Where has he gone? Will Raekandar seek revenge for its chief?"

Alas, she couldn't feel his pain. Bassalt knew what would follow would be an ever more bitter truth for her to swallow, but once the medicine was given, it had to reach the core. "Raekandar isn't the one seeking revenge. Avalan will return craving my blood and Hydrus's freedom."

"Avalan is no murderer!" Yet even as she said it, her features twisted, the cold truth of it already sinking in. "He's not …"

"He was the leader of this uprising. My men have found his cave. Full of arrows, swords, knives, and all meant for my thick flesh. Should he have been here, the fight would have been much uglier than it turned out."

A shadow has overtaken him, Dhylinea had told Bassalt. *A shadow and a mighty thirst for freedom.*

"Avalan will return for Hydrus. But you must understand, I cannot let him take it."

"Step aside, Bassalt," Farmera begged. "Avalan will accept it. Let him lead, and stay by his side."

I am the rightful chief of Hydrus! Bassalt's mind boomed. "I've never touched a hair of his. I've always kept my promise to you. But you must know, there's more at stake here. The village, the balance of the stones. Avalan's magic is no match for mine. He cannot protect Hydrus. Once word spreads of my defeat, the tribes will rush to our borders. If I'm gone, no spell will hinder their descent. And with the Onyx—"

A loud thump came from Farmera's bedchamber that made the both of them turn. Sigil loped into the room, her fur ruffled and standing. In her striped eyes and bared fangs, Bassalt saw the pure hatred. He centered his Tiger's Eye … and took hold of the creature. *Where is your master?* he asked of her, yet all he got in response was the sheer hunger and pain the tiger felt in her guts. *She's starving. She won't live without him.* Bassalt released her soul, and Sigil slid over to Farmera, pressing her fur against her thigh.

Exhausted, Farmera ran her fingers through Sigil's fur, seeking comfort. "Avalan left her to look after me. She has been bringing me small game all this time for food, yet I can't convince her to gulp some down. If she dies … if my son dies …" She raised her face to meet his gaze. "You promised never to harm my son."

Bassalt closed his eyes. How could he ever forget that day? All this time, he had been thinking that he'd come here to unburden his soul to Farmera, but now he understood better. He had come here to break that old promise. "I also promised to keep the balance," he whispered to himself.

As he crossed the threshold, he felt Sigil's stare burning a hole in his back. *Live for him*, he thought at the beast. *Live, only to die.*

CHAPTER SIXTY

THE GOLDEN SPHERE disappeared along with Dizredek behind the skewed wall. Yet light wasn't the only thing that faded.

As soon as the sorcerer left the stony passage, Avalan's numbness receded as if the spell could no longer hold now that its caster had gone. A sickening pain exploded in his chest, a deep stinging where Dizredek had slashed him. When Avalan touched his wound, his fingers came away sticky and smelling of iron. *Cursed Nuummite.* Whenever they'd crossed paths, Dizredek had cut Avalan and stolen his blood as if he were an animal for slaughter.

Grabbing the wall, Avalan staggered to his feet.

The deep darkness had returned to taunt him. For a moment, he stood torn before the twisted wall that had been smeared with his blood. If he headed back, it wouldn't be long before he found himself out and on the rough slope. Now he had traced the tunnel, Avalan was certain he could follow it to freedom much faster and without the guidance of the shadow. *But what good would that do?* He'd followed the shadow here, searching for answers, for the Heart of the Bloodstone. Instead, he'd found a trap, and the bitter truth of Ronan's death.

Bassalt had murdered him for the stones.

Avalan pushed his fists against the wall, recalling the vileness of Bassalt's vines as they had flogged Eras during the goat game night, and as they had coiled around Avalan, threatening to crush the breath out of him. *If I am to defeat Bassalt, I can't return without the Bloodstone.*

He reached beyond the wall to touch the darkness. *What is life for me, for you is death,* the sorcerer had warned him. Yet if Dizredek really wished to kill him, he'd wasted many a chance. Avalan knew then he had to follow. Death may lie ahead, but death also lurked behind him in a Hydrus still ruled by Bassalt. The murderer of Ronan.

The tunnel behind the wall wasn't much different from the one Avalan had followed before. Low ceiling, rough walls with jutting stones, inviting emptiness, leading to the unknown. Avalan listened for any sound that might betray Dizredek's position, his footsteps cautious and light.

At long last, a dim golden halo broke the darkness. It seemed to emanate from a lower level, as if there was a chamber below. Avalan crawled the rest of the way, weary not to fall into a recess.

The light grew brighter. Suddenly his hands met with nothing, and he almost fell over a ledge. His instinct had proved right. A cavern lay at the end of the passage below. Soft whispers emerged from the gaping hole. Avalan peered down.

Tiny crystals lined the walls, sparkling in the amber light. Beneath the golden sphere, Dizredek held someone in a tight embrace. Skeletal hands grabbed at the sorcerer's back fiercely, the skin on them so drawn, so taut … They reminded Avalan of the hands of a stonemaster —parched and fragile. The feathers on Dizredek's robe obscured the face of the other.

As if he'd sensed Avalan's keen stare, the sorcerer broke the embrace and spun. Tears streaked his face, and he raised a twisted hand. *Begone,* Dizredek's motion seemed to say, but Avalan had no intention of leaving now.

For he had glimpsed the other.

His heartbeat pounded in his ears. Behind Dizredek stood the naked skeleton of a man, a cloth bound around his eyes. The man raised a hand now, forcing Avalan to tumble into the cave below.

"No!" Dizredek screamed too late.

Avalan crashed onto the cave floor, cold stone slapping his face. The fall made Avalan bite his tongue, blood filling his mouth. He crouched back, trying to get away from the glow of the light. The cave was large. *Perchance if I could crawl to a dark corner ...*

Dizredek's stare found him. His lips were twisted in disgust, yet his eyes held a command that seemed to Avalan a dire pleading: *Do not move.*

"Who is it, Diz?" the other man said. His voice was piercing, like claws scratching a grainy wall.

Avalan stayed still, taking in the man's revolting figure. Standing a head taller than the sorcerer, the man had long, matted hair; its ends reached far below his waist and covered his manhood. The skin over his bones was stretched so taut Avalan doubted the man's body held space for a heart. Yet there, right beneath the parched skin of his chest, an irregular bulge jutted. Dark and pulsing. A blindfold covered the man's eyes, and Avalan was convinced Dizredek had placed it there to protect this man's sight from the light.

"Dizredek," the man demanded. "Why won't you speak? I can feel a great presence ..." The words came out slowly, as if with great struggle from an unused voice.

Despair ran through Avalan as he realized this man must have been trapped here much longer than he could imagine.

"Take your eyes off me!" the man suddenly screeched. Bony fingers reaching blindly, he staggered toward Avalan. "I can feel you *staring ...*"

Avalan crouched in disgust. He lowered his gaze to the floor, and to his great relief, he saw the familiar silhouette of the second shadow. He reached to caress its outline on the rough cave floor. *I'm not alone.*

Upon Avalan's touch, the shadow stirred and caught Dizredek's attention. The sorcerer's face darkened. Hastily he raised a finger, etched a circle in the air. "You can return now," he commanded.

At his order, the shadow slipped away from Avalan. Toward the naked man it flowed, and Avalan watched it unite with him, forming a perfect fit with his rawboned figure. Hot anger mingled with the icy dread of betrayal in Avalan's chest. *All this time, I thought the shadow my friend, and yet it only served to lead me here, back to its true caster.*

"Your punishment has ended," Dizredek told the man. "We must leave at once. There's no one here."

Ignoring the sorcerer's plea to stay hidden, Avalan leaped to his feet. "No one? You lied to me! There was no Bloodstone all along."

"Is this man of the Bloodstone?" the naked man said, fumbling with the knot of his blindfold. "Let me look at him."

The sorcerer glared at Avalan, brought a silencing finger to his lips. "He's no one, my beloved. It's only the cave. It's disarranging your mind. You must listen to me."

"You lie," the man whispered, taking an uncertain step toward Avalan. "I am drawn to him. He and I, we share something."

"Only a shadow, Vildrith," Dizredek said, his voice now pleading. "The shadow that led me to you, and nothing more."

"My shadow." Great sorrow lingered in his words. "Was it you who took it from me? I felt it the day it departed. I thought even it couldn't stand to live like this anymore. It was so ... lonely ..."

Avalan's guts twisted. He tried to imagine how it would be to stay in this cave alone, without even your own shadow to keep you company. "Who are you?"

Dizredek clasped the man's hand. "Do not let the cave win. I'm with you now. Let us leave. The world awaits."

The man's lips twisted. "You're lying to me, Diz. You promised never to lie to me again."

"Please, Vildrith. Let us leave—"

"No!" Vildrith's voice echoed around the cave like thunder. Without warning, he leaped, his hands flailing as he tried to grasp Avalan. "Where are you? I can sense you. I can feel your presence. Why can I feel you? Why do I know your voice? Who are you?"

Avalan backed away as the man's fingers almost brushed him. Around and around they turned, in a peculiar circle, each of them clearly wanting to know the other, but neither daring to offer the truth about their existence. Every time Vildrith came closer, his stench made Avalan's stomach sick. He wanted to touch him, grab his matted hair, ask him what he had done to the Heart of the Bloodstone, or if there had ever been one to begin with. Yet every time Vildrith's fingertips almost found his skin, Avalan felt a hopeless dread.

And not only that; a queer bond between them, a sickening tie that served only to raise Avalan's revulsion. *Is what I feel the shadow binding?*

Avalan thought as he crouched back when Vildrith's hands almost had him.

At last Dizredek came between them. "Enough! I beg of you, Vildrith. Do not listen to the voices. You know the voices lie. It is no one. The cave has stolen your mind. It's showing you things that aren't there. Come with me, and we'll live again. We'll be together."

"Extinguish that sun of yours," Vildrith ordered, untying the cloth's knot. His voice had changed now, become the cold demand of a ruler. "I have no need of it. It only hurts my eyes. Darkness is my everything now."

"Don't," Dizredek warned. "You aren't ready …"

Despite Dizredek's pleas, the man tore the blindfold from his eyes.

Avalan didn't want to stare, but he felt drawn to this man. Strangely enough, the man's eyes reminded him of Bhoran's—dark like a midnight shadow. Perhaps the cavern in the belly of a mountain had made Avalan's ability to discern color harder. He knew nothing for certain anymore.

It wasn't long before the dark eyes found him, and Vildrith drank Avalan's figure in like a thirsty man. Then his features twisted. His jaw gaped open. *"Father?"* he said, his voice a mingling of surprise and longing.

Backing away once again, Avalan looked over at Dizredek, who just stood there, a look of resignation in his eyes as if to tell him he had brought all this on himself. *How can this man mistake me for his father?* Avalan was too young, and this man, filthy though he was, looked much older than him.

The same realization must have finally seeped through the man's mind, for his gaze grew harder, as if he'd been deceived. "No," he said, blinking. "Diz, the cave is playing a dangerous game on me …" A predator, he moved toward Avalan, hands extended like claws. "Stay still. Let me feel your stones …"

Avalan flinched and leaped back. The man halted, peered so intensely at Avalan's eyes that Avalan felt his sockets burning.

"The Bloodstone," the man mused.

"Vildrith, you have to stop," Dizredek pleaded. "Don't let the cave …"

"How can he not be Father? What is the cave trying to tell me?" For a moment, his features twisted as if he was in deep thought, but then the man suddenly thrust his head back and let out a harrowing chuckle.

Avalan retreated until he felt the cold jab of the wall against his back. *This man is mad. All his wit has been chased away by his entrapment in this lonesome place.*

"Vildrith, listen to me. It's only the cave—" Dizredek said.

At his words, the man's laugh turned to a whimper. "The cave," he muttered to himself. "It wants to keep me here forever."

"It won't. I've come for you, as I promised. Follow me to your freedom."

The man now trembled. "Can I trust you, Diz? You left me here. I feel … so old. Are you certain I am not dead? It was so dark …" He staggered toward the sorcerer, looking resigned.

Avalan couldn't just let them leave. He searched the cave floor for anything to defend himself with, knowing full well a fresh attack would be coming. He wanted it, needed it, even. He needed to know the truth. "Who are you?" he yelled at the man. "Why are your eyes dark? Dizredek is a liar. He tricked the both of us."

The man howled, violently lurching forward. Avalan lured him into the darkness, away from Dizredek's burning sun. *There must be something I can use,* he thought, and yet the floor was barren rock—nothing to hold, not even loose scree Avalan could throw.

Vildrith panted, his breathing coming out in short heaves. Yet he didn't cease his pursuit. Deeper and deeper they went. As Avalan leaped over an outcrop, the light of Dizredek's sphere returned, larger and blinding. Both he and Vildrith fell to the floor, shaded their eyes from its hot menace.

"Cease this madness!" Dizredek yelled. With a quick stride, he fell next to Vildrith, held his body while dimming the light of the sphere. "We must leave now before the cave changes its mind!"

The man raised teary eyes to Avalan. "I can't, Diz. I can feel a connection to him."

Panting on the floor, Avalan knew what the stranger meant. Every time he edged closer to him, he sensed it: an invisible thread stretching dangerously between them. *It must be Dizredek's doing.* Avalan was certain. *But why?*

"No more lies, Diz," the man implored him. "What magic is this that brought back my father from the dead? Why does he look so young ... so different?"

Dizredek sighed, parted the matted hair from the fallen man's face. "If I tell you the truth, do you promise to follow me out of this prison?"

Vildrith nodded but didn't turn to face Dizredek. Instead, he kept his empty gaze on Avalan, as if afraid that if he blinked, he'd lose him.

"I came for you as I had promised. Yet no matter how hard I tried, I couldn't enter. The cave remained sealed to me. For years and years ... until I found *him*." Dizredek pointed a trembling finger at Avalan. "This man is Avalan of the Bloodstone. Your father's second son. I used his blood to bind your shadow to him and bade it to lead me to you. Only the blood of the Bloodstone could have freed you. You feel attracted to him because I bonded you. I'm so sorry, Vildrith. Give me some time, and I shall see the bond safely severed."

Bile rose to Avalan's mouth upon hearing these words. "No!" He clenched his fists, his mind working faster than lightning. *This man can't be my brother,* he thought, disgust filling his gut.

There was one more thing your father loved. Farmera's voice echoed in his mind. *A son of the Onyx.*

His heart throbbed. "You lie."

Vildrith's lips twitched, and Avalan felt the thread between them strain. "I have no brother." His voice had changed now, deepened with bottomless hatred. "Father is dead."

Avalan swallowed hard. *Dead? His father isn't my father,* his mind screamed at him. *The mage is lying.*

"Let us go now, my love," Dizredek urged, sensing the boiling anger. "Let us go, and I shall explain more to you once we are far from this wretched place."

Vildrith shoved him aside. "Not before I kill him." He pressed one palm against the bulge on his chest, then twisted his free wrist.

Avalan fell to his knees, gasping for breath. His heart ached as if caught in a rabbit snare.

"You must not!" Dizredek yelled. Desperately he crawled to Vildrith's side, grabbed hold of his knee. "Not until your bond is broken. If you kill him, you will die!"

The grip around his heart eased, and Avalan gulped down the wet air of the cavern.

Vildrith's expression had now darkened. Confusion twisted his lips. "He doesn't fight me, Diz. Why? Why does my brother not fight me?"

"He doesn't know the ways of the stones."

When Vildrith lowered his hand, the pain left Avalan's chest. And yet a burning lingered, as if to warn him not to forget.

Vildrith cocked his head. "Everyone knows the ways of the stones."

"A lot has changed in the Stone Lands." Dizredek brushed off the feathers of his robes as he stood. "Come with me, and I will show you the world anew. Forget about him. You survived for twenty years in this place. He isn't worth your life."

Chest still burning, Avalan searched the ground. Soulless, barren rock stretched everywhere. His anger blinded him now. Anger and disgust, for he didn't know for certain if Dizredek's words held any truth in them. Avalan stared at the gloves that covered his blackened hands. *My wrists,* he thought. *Perchance if I twist them …* He did so, thinking with all his might mean thoughts about this wretched man, yet nothing happened. *I hold no magic of the stones.*

A blast of power rushed through Avalan's body as Vildrith stretched out his hands. The man's bony chest heaved now, and he let out a pathetic whimper. "But, Diz, I so much want to kill him." He raised his hands again, flexed his fingers. "Is he the reason my father left?"

"He wasn't even born. Save your strength."

Vildrith's eyes opened wide. "Then his *mother*. Father left me for her." When Dizredek didn't answer, Vildrith turned to look at him, finally breaking his gaze from Avalan. "Say it is so."

Avalan grasped his wound, panting heavily. He searched Dizredek's gaze. Vildrith was thirsting for blood and revenge, blaming the sins of a father Avalan had never known on him and Farmera. His stomach twisted when he saw the sorcerer shake his head as if defeated.

"It is so," Dizredek said quietly.

"No!" Avalan leaped to his feet, ignoring the shooting pain in his ribs. He charged at Vildrith, toppling him to the ground. Avalan gazed into the despairing emptiness of Vildrith's dark stones. *Don't look at the eyes,* his mind desperately told him, but it was no good. "Not my mother …"

Vildrith spun, freeing his skeletal figure from Avalan's weight. Then Vildrith flicked his wrists.

Writhing pain came fast, forcing Avalan to coil up on the ground. His breath left him. His mind screamed. *How does a haggard man fight with such force?* He gritted his teeth, trying hard to drown the screams that begged to leave his mouth. *I cannot let him win. I cannot. Shadow, I beg you. Shadow …* Cold hands embraced him, but whether it was to save him or to better aid Vildrith's hold, Avalan could not tell. *Whose are you now, shadow?*

The faint sound of Dizredek's voice reached Avalan's ears. "Vildrith … remember the bond …"

"Do you know where she is?" Vildrith's voice exploded in Avalan's head, drowning out all his thoughts, all his hopes. "Speak, Diz. Do you know?"

"Don't …" Avalan muttered.

"Shadow," Vildrith commanded. An icy wind crossed Avalan's face. For a moment, the cave fell silent. Then Vildrith whispered, "I remember now. I was there. A table, a low-burning candle, your farewell visit. She's in Hydrus."

Despair coiled in Avalan's stomach. He remembered that moment as well. The shadow had been there when he'd paid a last visit to his mother. It had extinguished a candle to warn them both of Silver's arrival … and now it had given Vildrith the knowledge he needed to find Farmera. Writhing, Avalan stretched out a hand, trying to grab at anything … to stop this vile Onyx …

Vildrith released his grip.

Avalan groped for words, but everything felt numb. His body, his mind, his will … *Mother …* He felt a toe jabbing his chest wound where

Dizredek had cut him. Through half-opened eyes, he watched the form of a monster, matted long hair, dark eyes like a hawk's, looming above him.

"You will take me to her, Diz. And after you've broken my bond with him, I will return to this cursed place to kill him."

CHAPTER SIXTY-ONE

By the time Lusha had reached the bottom of the spiral staircase, her tears had dried. The white square of Levorotha spread before her. Mist rose from the moon fountain. The sound of its raindrops had grown louder now, or so it seemed to Lusha, perhaps because she wished for it to drown out her thoughts.

Her aunt hated her mother even more than Lusha could ever have imagined. And yet … *What was I expecting from an aunt who'd never sent word to me?* Shame burned inside her for being so naive.

She walked. Beneath her feet, white stone blended with white stone, an endless sea of sand. Before she knew it, she'd reached the fountain. Droplets wetted her face as she sat on the rim. Going back to her father wasn't an option—as long as he and Bassalt held the leadership of Hydrus, she'd never truly be free. The threat of marrying Colgar still hovered over her, and this time, she was certain, her father would insist even more fiercely. She had Bhoran's return to thank for that.

A dagger of guilt pierced her heart for thinking of him in this way. *And Avalan … I left him behind without a word.* She had been thinking only about herself, she knew. Her happiness, her being with Bhoran, her freedom … She hadn't paused even for a moment to think about the tribe of Hydrus—their happiness, their freedom …

It is just as well I left, she thought, shaking her head. To Avalan, she would have been only a burden, slowing him down in his quest for the Heart of the Bloodstone. Besides, Lusha had no way with weapons and fighting. In a stand against Bassalt, her presence there would only compromise Avalan's cause. She still remembered the agony on Avalan's face as he thought of ways to protect Crystal, to free her, to free Hydrus ... *I can't have him worry about me too.*

What of returning to Raekandar? She wondered if Crystal had felt betrayed by her abrupt disappearance. A small part of her felt she deserved it. After all, it wasn't much different from what Crystal had done to her when she had escaped Hydrus with Ronan. Lusha bit her lip for even thinking this way. The meeting with her aunt had blackened her heart. *Crystal left the village without a warning because she had been raped*, she reminded herself. *I left Raekandar because Bhoran betrayed me.*

She closed her eyes, tried to chase the thought of him away, but it was hopeless. Every night, the crumpled dress wedged under Bhoran's door flooded her mind's eye. Its feel, its smell—the sweet, seductive luring of a young woman. Something that Bhoran hadn't resisted, judging by the signs in his room. *No.* She forced her eyes open and gasped for air. She wouldn't go back to Raekandar. Not if there was the slightest chance he still lingered there, waiting for her return.

I could stay here, in Levorotha. For a long moment, Lusha gazed at the tribesfolk who strolled through the square. *They seem happy*, she thought, *but how can I know for certain?*

She raised her face to the moon rain that flowed freely through the bronze disk, then placed a tentative foot into the basin. The water felt cool, and so inviting. Before she knew it, she found herself knee-deep in the water, letting the falling rain wash over her.

The dress clung to her wet skin. Raindrops brushed her face, her lips, her soul. And she welcomed its joyous feeling into her life. In that moment, she knew: *I am of the Moonstone.* She could stay here, become a moonhealer. She could help Calla fight the Red Weal and finally put to rest her mother's ghost.

When she opened her eyes again, a man stood at the edge of the fountain. The moon rain blurred her vision, making it hard to discern who it was. She took a small step back, almost losing her balance, but the man reached out a hand to steady her.

"I didn't mean to scare you," he said, his voice familiar. *Rian?*

He helped her out of the fountain, and she just stood there, ashamed of the wet dress that hugged her body and revealed her form. "Am I not allowed to go in? The water looked so inviting ..."

The man let out a hearty laugh. "It does, does it not? It's been a while since I've done the same." With that, he stepped into the water and slid his fingers through his raven hair. The rain wetted him through and through, as it had done Lusha. When he emerged, he was just as sodden.

Lusha smiled when she saw the fire in his eyes still burning—water wasn't enough to dim it. "You didn't have to do that for me. But it makes me feel less silly. Thank you."

"Thank me?" He scrubbed his face clean. "No. I thank you, for reminding me to have some fun in this place."

Fun wasn't the thing Lusha had in mind, but this man's presence was soothing to her, in ways she could not explain. Perhaps this was how fathers were meant to be. "I should go," she said. "Calla needs my help."

"Wait. It isn't often we get visitors in this city. At least not ones that enter walking and in good health. Why don't I give you a small tour before you dirty your hands with the city's ill?"

Lusha hesitated. It would indeed be a nice distraction, and it might be the last invitation she'd receive—Calla seemed too worrisome and focused on her task. And Lusha couldn't blame her, for her task was one of the hardest. But Lusha knew that once she went back to her, she wouldn't be able to enjoy this man's company freely. It might be the only time she got to get to know him, without Calla sulking over her head, thinking Lusha was trying to seduce him.

She looked down at her soaked garments. "I shouldn't go around like this."

Rian motioned her to follow. He led her down the nearest alley and cleared their way through strangers huddling in the market, idly chatting and perusing the goods scattered over the merchants' benches.

Surrounded by warm bodies, Lusha felt less exposed. Rian led her down a narrow path.

At last he stopped outside a small door with no markings on it. "Wait here." He slipped inside.

Lusha glanced nervously around her. The air was thick here; the walls cast cooling shadows. A dim light shone from each end of the path that led back into the crowded streets.

A warm hand on her shoulder made her jump. She turned to find Rian looming over her and smiling. "Come in."

Lusha eyed him for a while. *What is he hiding?*

The man seemed to have read her thoughts. "Just letting Zorul know he'll see a sodden girl. Warned him not to stare too much." He winked at her. "I promise he's harmless."

"I don't even know you."

"Rian of the Fire Agate." The light of the stones in his eyes flickered.

Lusha shivered. In this shade, the wet dress sucked out her warmth. The cool air in the dark alley wasn't much help either, and so she followed him inside.

A soft chime came from above their heads, and Lusha turned to see some metal rods hanging by threads. *More warnings?*

They climbed the stairs and emerged into a dimly lit room. The smell of ash, drinks, and sweet sweat hung in the air, reminding Lusha of Undeena's Inn, only the inn had been brighter, filled with the light of a thousand candles burning on windowsills and a hearth fire that simmered Undeena's onion soup. This room had only a few candles inside tall glasses, sparsely placed small tables, no windows, and instead of the smiling face of Undeena, there was a bald, stout man behind a serving bench, staring at Lusha through narrowed eyes.

Lusha raised a timid hand in greeting and let Rian lead her to the far corner. The bald man's stare burned on Lusha's back, and he didn't avert it even when she turned and sat herself on a creaking chair. *So much for warning him not to stare,* Lusha thought.

Rian laughed. "Our friend Zorul here is always suspicious of women."

Zorul glared at him but then smirked and finally left the bench and disappeared behind a door.

"My presence here offends him?"

Rian waved a nonchalant hand. "Not in the least. Zorul is ever dramatic. But he has a good heart."

A good heart and an evil stare. Before she spoke her thoughts, Zorul reappeared, carrying a garment much like the linens Calla had given her at the infirmary.

"Better change." Zorul handed her the clothes.

The cloth was rough, but dry. "Thank you," Lusha said.

Zorul nodded and cocked his head in the direction of the door he'd just come through.

Behind it, Lusha gladly gave up Calla's sodden dress for the dry tunic of the infirmary. It felt like a warm, familiar hug. *I was truly made to be a healer.*

She slid out, gave Zorul, who had moved behind his bench again, a soft smile. "It's perfect. Thank you, Zorul. I needed that."

"What we need is a fiery drink to warm our insides." Rian tapped his palm on the bench.

Raising a proud chin, Zorul gave him a narrow stare. "I'm saving my fiery drinks for people with actual coin."

For a moment, the room fell silent. And then both Zorul and Rian burst into a heartwarming chuckle. "Now, you two go make yourselves comfortable," Zorul said. "I want neither of your sneaky faces over my shoulder as I prepare."

As Lusha sat, she noticed Rian's clothes looked far drier than they should be. She frowned.

"Is something troubling you?" Rian asked.

"I'm just curious," Lusha said over the clinking noises from Zorul's bench. "Aren't you cold?"

Rian raised his brows and then took her hand in his. It was burning. Almost like fire. "One of the great attributes of my stone."

Lusha felt the warmth grow, and she twisted her hand away. "That explains the dryness of your clothes."

Zorul returned, placing a heavy tray on the table. It thumped down, making the thick amber liquid in the earthen cups sway. If

Zorul had seen them holding hands, he didn't mention it. He only took the cups off the tray and gave one to each of them before returning to his bench.

"Does he get a lot of guests?" Lusha cupped the short cup. It was as warm to the touch as she'd expected. After all, Rian *had* called them fiery drinks.

"This is more of a private place." Rian gulped down half of his drink. The flame in his eyes rekindled for a moment before returning to its slow burning.

Lusha stared at hers. The smell of honey reached her nose.

"Go on, then. It will help with the cold."

She took a tentative sip, swishing the liquid around in her mouth before finding the courage to gulp it down. Liquid warmth spread through her body, from mouth to chest, then lower. The effect was quick, but it lingered like slow-burning coals in her belly. "So, what is it you do here?" she asked Rian.

"How do you mean?"

"Calla is helping the ill." She took another sip. *This drink is really good.* "What do you do in Levorotha?"

"You're asking because my eyes are of the Fire Agate? So clearly I mustn't belong here?"

The warmth of the drink crept up her cheeks. "That's not how I meant it … Where I come from, tribesfolk of all stones live in peace."

"Hydrus," Rian said, a strange sadness in his voice.

"How do you know?"

"Tidings travel fast. Word came from Hydrus several days ago of Silver's daughter gone missing. Fair, with the eyes of the Moonstone and the long hair of a flaxen sun. It really isn't hard to make the connection."

"You know my father?"

Rian's flame flickered for a short while. "A long time ago." He lifted his glass toward Zorul, gesturing for more. "There's a hefty reward for your return."

Blood drained from Lusha's cheeks. She eyed the stairs across the room. To get to them, she'd have to jump over Rian before she could rush down the stairs and out to the dark alley.

"I won't harm you," Rian said.

Zorul approached with a jug, refilling Rian's cup before motioning to hers. "Care for some more, or is it too strong for you?"

Lusha nodded. As Zorul filled it with the fiery liquid, she kept her eyes on Rian, who watched her over the rim of his cup.

When Zorul returned to his bench, Lusha whispered, "Why won't you turn me in?"

"Because I hate your father."

Despite herself, Lusha smiled.

"Ah, the sentiment is shared, I see." Rian raised his cup. "To hateful fathers and to the healing of the Moonstone!"

Zorul hooted. "I'll drink to that!"

"Now, tell me." Rian leaned closer. "Was Silver the real reason you left the village?"

"No."

"I thought as much. You didn't leave alone, now, did you?"

What does he know? "I wasn't alone." She would not give him more, she decided.

"I see."

"Why do you wish to know?"

Rian pursed his lips. "The rest of us always hear that Hydrus is a dreamy place. Away from all the commotion of the cities. No illnesses, no fear of an uprising, no one getting into your face for choosing a partner of another stone ... just a quiet little place run by Bassalt, the mage of ancient soil, and his chieftain, Silver."

Lusha swallowed hard, thinking how wrong all these notions about their village were. It was true Hydrus represented a place of tolerance and freedom, only this freedom was of a false kind, one that was given under the strict orders of Bassalt to never use the magic of the stones. Inside, she was dying to know if the uprising had really happened. "Since word reaches your ears, what is the recent one from Hydrus?"

Rian shrugged. "There's been nothing of late. It is in Bassalt's power to share, and he is not one to talk openly about the matters of his village. Your escape stirred him to reach out to the Stone Lands."

Lusha frowned. How could Rian know about her disappearance

from the village, and what else was he not telling her? "How do the tidings travel? I mean, Bassalt never leaves Hydrus. And Ronan ..."

At the mention of Ronan's name, Rian's lips quivered. "Ronan is dead."

Lusha's eyes widened. "How do you know?"

"Chieftain Silver's daughter ran away with the murderer of Ronan, the rumors say, and a man of the Bloodstone. Avalan. Farmera's son."

Lusha shook her head, sickened to hear the same story once again. "Bhoran's not a murderer. Bassalt and my father got it wrong. You hear me? Who are you? How do you know so much about us—about our village?"

Before Rian could answer, the familiar chime of the metal rods came from below. Rushed footfalls echoed up the stairs, and a young tribesman emerged. He wore white cotton garments, like the rest of the men in Levorotha. His flaxen hair was cropped short to his skull, a silver loop with a Moonstone adorning his ear. His shoulders had stood broad and proud when he had entered, but now he hunched them as he saw Lusha.

Lusha's breath caught in her chest, thinking for a mere moment it was Bhoran. It couldn't be, she knew. Despite the sharp angles of his face, this man's white skin was smooth and bore no fangs or etchings.

How could I even think it was him? His assured posture and his age, she realized. He had the same air of fearlessness.

As soon as the man looked toward them, Lusha saw the sparkle of Moonstones. She'd never seen so many people from her tribe all in one place before. The young man looked from her to Rian and back again. His tense body screamed that he had urgent things to share, and Lusha guessed her unexpected presence was the only thing keeping him from blurting them out.

Zorul had ceased his work, cloth and mugs in hand.

"Noev," Rian said at last, breaking the spell. "What has happened?"

Noev approached with caution. He loomed over them, cast Lusha a tense glance. "You brought a woman here?"

Zorul placed a calming hand on the young man's shoulder. "She likes my fiery drinks," he said with pride, earning a stony stare from Noev.

"Speak," Rian said.

"Who is she?"

"She's—"

"I can answer for myself." Lusha crossed her arms. "My name's Lusha."

Noev dropped his disapproving stare and turned to Rian. "You trust her?"

Lusha stood so she could look the man straight in the eye. "Where I come from, it's rude to talk about someone in their presence as though they're not there."

"And where have you come from? It's the first time I've seen you in Levorotha."

"Hydrus." Lusha felt Rian's warm clasp on her arm, but it was too late.

Noev's eyes twitched. "Silver's daughter?"

Rian raised a warning finger. "She's with us. And she stays. Speak what you have to say."

Shrugging, Noev turned to Lusha. "The tidings I bring concern you. The merchants are here, bringing more news of deaths. Eyedir was last seen leaving Raekandar on a dark night, accompanied by a boy with blond hair. The boy sought refuge at Undeena's Inn after they were attacked by thieves. Eyedir was killed, his body found after the night of the cursed storm."

"Another merchant dead?" Zorul mumbled. "That can't be good …"

"Who was this boy? And how can we be so sure it wasn't he who killed Eyedir?" Rian demanded.

Lusha trembled. She fell back into her chair.

"Perhaps the tidings are far too grave for a lady …" Zorul started.

Noev smirked and motioned at Lusha. "Or perhaps the boy can tell us what really happened that night. For the boy the merchants in Undeena's Inn described looked an awful lot like Silver's daughter, only her hair was cut short to resemble a boy's. But the scar across her face matched."

Lusha reached for words that wouldn't come as the horror of that night invaded her mind. "No," she whispered.

"It can't be her. She has no … oh …" Zorul trailed off. "You have a scar?"

"I didn't kill Eyedir. He helped me escape Raekandar. He was to lead me here." Well, not in truth, but she wasn't eager to reveal the merchant had been planning to exchange her for ransom.

"What do you remember?" Rian said. "Who were these men? What did they want?"

Stones, she thought, but somehow she felt it wrong to mention this. "There was this woman. I didn't see her clearly. She murdered him before my eyes."

"How come they let you go?" Noev said.

Lusha looked at her hands as if they didn't belong to her. "I … fought her. The moon came to my aid, I think."

"How?" Noev challenged.

Blood crept up Lusha's cheeks. "I don't really know …"

"Enough," Rian told Noev. "We shall talk again about this later."

"I'm not done," the young man retorted.

Zorul wiped his forehead with a cloth. "Stones … there's more?"

"Chiefess Crystal is dead."

Lusha gasped. "This can't be true!"

"I'm afraid it is," Noev said, a bit more kindly this time.

Lusha felt tears welling in her eyes. She tried to hold them back—she wouldn't cry in the presence of all these men. Yet they didn't obey her, and they fell from her unblinking eyes.

"You knew her?" Rian asked.

"We grew up together in Hydrus." Lusha wiped her tears away. "I was just with her … I left without even saying farewell."

Zorul sighed. "A sweet chiefess. Unlike our own."

"What happened to her?" Rian said.

Noev's eyes flickered to Lusha for a moment before he spoke. "The chief declared it was a man of Hydrus who killed her. Avalan of the Bloodstone. He ordered his arrest and even set out to find him himself."

"No." Lusha shook her head, trying to drown her disbelief. "Avalan would never do this. The chief is lying. Avalan *loved* her. He wanted …" *Oh, Avalan, where are you now?*

Rian scowled. "I never trusted Ethelnar. But why would he lie about the murder of his beloved wife?"

Lusha chewed on her cheek, afraid to say more. She had to get away from these men, and fast. Her aunt had given her permission to remain in the city, but after these tidings, perhaps her mere presence here would look suspicious. Enough for Shelanna to have her thrown into a dungeon. It seemed wherever Lusha went, death followed. She stood. *I have to find Avalan, learn the truth.* "Where is Avalan? Did the merchants say anything more about him?"

Noev shook his head. "They say he ran away after he murdered the chiefess. He stole her pendant, though, and so Chief Ethelnar set out to track him."

Bhoran. I have to find Bhoran. "Noev," she said, trying to keep the desperation out of her voice. "There was another man of Hydrus in Raekandar. Did the merchants speak of him?"

Noev clenched his jaw. "You speak of the talon? The one wanted for Ronan's murder?"

"Yes." Lusha hated herself for letting them speak about Bhoran so, but there was no time. If Ethelnar thought Avalan had killed Crystal, he wouldn't extend his hospitality to Bhoran for more than a heartbeat.

"Last time they saw him, it was in the city's tavern, drinking with a Nuummite. Some say he's dead, thrown into the sea."

Dead?

"Why would Chief Ethelnar harbor a killer in his city?" Zorul said.

Lusha felt her knees go weak. "I … I need to go."

Rian threw his arms around her. His embrace was so hot she struggled for air.

Below, the familiar chime came again, this time sounding ever more urgent, as if someone had deliberately smacked the rods to announce their arrival. Calla emerged, her eyes stricken with a deep sadness. When she saw Lusha and Rian, she froze, her gaze darting between them.

Swiftly Lusha slipped out of the embrace, but she knew it was too late. Calla strode to them, taking off the bone hair brooch she wore. She flung it at Rian's chest. "You brought her here," she said, her braids falling loose around her shoulders.

Zorul sighed and stared at Rian. "And this is why I'd rather women stayed away. What brings you here, Moonhealer Calla?"

Calla held Lusha's stare for a while before she spoke. Her eyes had lost their sparkle, and gray circles surrounded them. "The man with the Red Weal has died."

CHAPTER SIXTY-TWO

BHORAN SHIVERED. He wasn't certain if the cold that vested him came from the cool touch of the falling night or the freezing of his own soul.

He sat on the wet sand of Olnos's Cove, knees folded to his chest. Water licked his toes. Each time the water touched him, he felt a faint tug. An invisible hand tried to reach for him, take him far across the sea to where he belonged—his tribe.

Behind him, Mheleras was prying the rest of the shells open in search of black pearls. Judging by the silence, he'd found none. The tiny black pearl Bhoran had found made him now think of Lusha's Moonstone. It still lay in his pocket. He took it out, pinched it between his fingers. So small, yet so powerful. *Lusha's grip on my soul.* It gave him some comfort.

He stared at it for some moments, reliving the past days they had shared. He wished they'd lasted forever. Yet no matter how many times Bhoran had given Lusha the Moonstone, it had always found its way back to him. As if it didn't wish to be given. *Or because I'm not worthy of her love.* Bhoran replaced the stone in his pocket.

Mheleras's steady footfalls approached. He nudged Bhoran's shoulder with the tip of his knee. "No more surprises in our supper. I made sure of that."

Bhoran gave him no answer. Instead, he gazed at the orange horizon.

"It will be dark soon," Mheleras said. "Come. A man must see what he is eating to enjoy it."

"I don't care for eating."

"Well, the flesh is only good for this night. If we don't eat it, it'll go to waste."

Waste. Like Bhoran's entire life. He shrugged.

"You are shaken," Mheleras said, his voice firm. "I can promise you, the pain will pass."

"I know nothing else but pain."

"Stand, then, and let us drown it with ale and tales. The sea has enough salt water. It has no need for your tears."

Disgruntled, Bhoran raised his chin and stood. The smiling face of Mheleras angered him all the more. "You mentioned ale."

Mheleras chuckled and led the way.

The mollusks were no longer cool, but they filled Bhoran's belly as he washed them down with ale. Bhoran looked around the table for the Obsidian, but he couldn't see it—Mheleras must have stored it away. "What is our tribe like?"

"Hard skulls. But their spirit is fearless. And some of them have good hearts."

"Yet they didn't aid the tribes in the war."

Mheleras licked some dripping juice off his finger. "Now don't go accusing them of indifference. Those times were different. One side rarely wages a war."

"Say more." The ale wasn't enough to drench Bhoran's desire to call for his serpent. Perhaps a story would.

"It was a custom, a deep-ingrained belief, that tribes should not marry outside their birthstone. In truth, the root behind this was clear: from Onyx always comes Onyx. The tribes were loath to see their numbers swell. The Onyx was known for its vile thoughts of power and domination, but it was their isolation that forced them to move. That and their greed."

Bhoran scowled. From Onyx always came Onyx? It was the first time he had heard this truth, and he now wondered if it had somehow reached Lusha's ears. Perhaps that was the reason behind her taking the mourning …

"You seem surprised. No wonder. The only thing they told you was that the Onyx wished to kill the rest."

Bhoran nodded quietly. That much was true. Whatever little knowledge Bhoran had about the war boiled down to this: the Onyx had tried to slaughter the tribes and conquer the Stone Lands.

"The truth is, the other tribes feared them. And fear brings only hatred. And those who are hated ofttimes lash out."

Bhoran stared at him. He knew Mheleras was talking about the Onyx, but his words came dangerously close to what Bhoran's life had been. "Are you saying the Onyx was innocent?"

A shadow passed over Mheleras's face. He spat out a piece of mollusk flesh. "Far from that. The Onyx was the cruelest tribe that walked these lands. Dangerous folk. Bloodthirsty. And know this: I'm glad we're rid of them." He stabbed the table with his blade. "Push the hilt with your finger," he ordered Bhoran.

Bhoran eyed him and found him to be serious. As he raised his finger to push the hilt, Mheleras did the same. From opposite sides, they both pressed, neither of them yielding.

"All I'm saying is, both sides are needed to keep the balance. Remove one, and ..."

Before Bhoran could say anything, Mheleras retracted his finger, and the knife collapsed under Bhoran's pressure. It landed on the table, spinning. Bhoran eyed the knife with suspicion. "You're saying the Onyx was a necessary evil."

Shrugging, Mheleras grabbed the knife. "Don't take everything I say to heart. My only company is merchants and seabirds. And both of them come to me with something to gain."

Bhoran feigned a smile.

"Now, this is better." Mheleras pointed at him with the tip of his knife. "Would you care for more ale?"

"I would."

Mheleras refilled their mugs to the brim. As he walked back, Bhoran noticed once again the nasty scar that sliced the skin over Mheleras's side. He averted his eyes.

"It's fine," Mheleras said. "I do my fair share of staring as well."

"Does it still hurt?"

"Only when I remember it. So I try not to notice it."

"What happened?"

"The war. What about yours?"

Dhylinea's ink concealed Bhoran's scars. The thought of her burned him deeply. "Ink. For the times ale was too short to drown the pain."

"And the fangs in your face? Do they come out?"

"They're part of me now."

"Do you have your birthstone?"

"They left me as a baby in Hydrus. I never had a family, or my stone."

The murmur of waves reached the shore. The night had fallen now, and a pale moon had risen, bathing the cove in soft silver light. "What if this changed?"

"How?"

Mheleras grabbed the mugs once more and made for the barrel.

"I wouldn't want to finish your stash," Bhoran said. They'd already drunk too much, and with only soft mollusks to line his stomach, the faint shadow of giddiness crept up on him. He hated that feeling, for it threatened to tame his rage.

"Worry not," Mheleras said, returning. The ale inside the mugs swayed and dripped on the sand. "I plan to replenish it soon."

"Expecting a merchant, then?"

"No. I usually save my trips for the middle of the summer, yet your coming here has changed my plans. I am of a mind to leave sooner. Perhaps even with the first light of the morrow."

Bhoran didn't know how to feel about this. He'd only just met Mheleras, a man of his tribe, and yet losing him so fast filled him with worry. "Why?"

"Jorgamur didn't send you to me because you're an Onyx."

Bhoran rubbed his brow. "I'm not sure what—"

"The Nuummite saw who you are. He knows you and I are the same. And that is why he sent you here."

"You're mistaken. Jorgamur gave me an insane speech about the Onyx returning. He says you were the one who foretold Olnos's coming to aid the tribes in the war against the Onyx. And now he's convinced I'm the new Olnos. But you and I know that was all a lie.

You foretold no coming of a hero. You just spread rumors to hide the true nature of Olnos—to keep your … *our* stone protected."

Mheleras's face grew serious, and snowflakes danced in his eyes. "Jorgamur is right—the balance suffers."

Bhoran took the knife from Mheleras's hand and nailed it to the table. Then he gave it a violent push with his finger and sent it down, dislodging a splinter from the wood. "There is no balance. You said so yourself. The tribes pushed too hard, and the Onyx has been defeated." He looked up at Mheleras's face. "Wasn't that what you meant before?"

Mheleras stared at the knife. "What if the Onyx has returned?"

Bhoran groaned. "Not you as well. I thought you were different."

"Who was it that killed your merchant, then?"

"I don't know, but—"

"Only an Onyx can kill with an Onyx-enchanted weapon."

Bhoran clenched his jaw. "What are you saying?"

"I'm saying Jorgamur wouldn't send you here if he hadn't possessed some truth. If he thinks the Onyx is back, we had best listen."

"What would you have me do? I possess no magic. I cannot fight like Olnos did. I know nothing of my stone …" The expression on Mheleras's face made Bhoran realize where this was heading. Bhoran knew nothing of his stone, and Jorgamur had somehow sensed it. And that was why he'd sent him here, to Mheleras of the Obsidian. "You want to take me to our tribe."

Mheleras nodded quietly. "We can teach you. You can learn all the things you didn't know growing up. There is no greater blessing than becoming one with your birthstone. You could be the gift of our tribe to the Stone Lands. We are cowards, but your soul is fierce."

"Leave the Stone Lands?" Bhoran asked this more of himself than Mheleras. His heart danced between the rhythm of hope and fear of the unknown.

"What remains for you here?"

A fight raged in his mind. *I have lost Lusha. Bassalt has sentenced me to death. A shadow leads Avalan to places where I cannot follow …* Bhoran cursed and stood, scattering sand. Mheleras threw his head back and chuckled. "What?" Bhoran snapped.

"Your eyes," Mheleras said. "The snowflakes have returned."

Later that night, Bhoran rolled to his side and stared at the silver froth that licked the sand. The beach beyond the cave glistened under the moonlight. Mheleras had still not returned from his trip to the statue of Olnos. He'd said he wanted to warn their tribe about their coming.

Trying to sleep tonight would be futile, Bhoran knew.

He sat on the shore, dipping his toes into the water. He thought about Mheleras's offer: Go with him to Elasithor, the Obsidian island, meet his tribe, be trained in the ways of their stone. Become a great fighter—like Olnos—and then return to the Stone Lands to help the tribes against the Onyx—like Olnos. But Olnos was a hero. And Bhoran ...

What am I?

He'd spent the last years of his life in pain and waste. Aimlessly roaming the mountain slopes and sneaking into the village to glimpse a piece of Lusha's life, to feel, if only for a moment, that they were close.

But when the time had come to be with her, he'd lost her once again. He reached inside his pocket and took the Moonstone out. It glistened brightly with a blue light, like Lusha's body when she roamed about in the late hours of the night.

Two times he'd given her the stone, and two times it had returned to him.

He strode to the table, grabbed the empty shell of a mollusk. He placed Lusha's Moonstone in its empty belly, then pressed the shell's lips closed. After laying the mollusk on the wet sand, he waited for the sea's reach. Water washed over it soon as the waves came. A few heartbeats later, the shell whirled free, swallowed by the dark sea.

"Farewell, my heart."

Mheleras was leaving in the morning, and Bhoran had now made up his mind to follow.

CHAPTER SIXTY-THREE

AVALAN AWOKE under the blanket of a hopeless darkness. His heart throbbed with an unceasing feeling. *I am trapped.*

He pushed the rough stone beneath him, stumbled to his feet. He was alone. Avalan still remembered the last rays of Dizredek's sphere as both men and the shadow had disappeared behind the twisted wall that marked the entrance. The screech as the wall had twisted back into place had clawed at Avalan's heart.

He wiped clammy palms on his breeches, Vildrith's last words echoing in his mind. *He'll go after my mother.* Avalan touched the darkness. It filled his mind, his mouth, his soul.

How can this wild skeleton of a man be my brother? And yet the seed of doubt had taken root. Vildrith's reaction when he had laid eyes on Avalan had been unfeigned—he'd really believed he'd been standing in the presence of a ghost. The ghost of Avalan's father. Farmera had spoken to him about Azirrad's Onyx son, but Avalan was certain the boy had died in the war.

And then there was that vile dream when he had lain unconscious atop Dhylinea's working bench. For a moment, he had become the skeletal form of Vildrith, had tasted the hatred on his tongue ...

"DIZREDEK!" Avalan yelled into the nothingness. His scream echoed into his prison. Vildrith had spent twenty years in this cave.

The thought sickened Avalan. Even worse, the notion of losing his mother froze his soul. He had to get out, return to Hydrus.

He charged at the blackness before him and crashed against a wall. Scouring the stone, he tried to grab any protruding rocks to scale. If he could find the tunnel, he stood a great chance of stopping them as they descended the mountain. Though his half-brother's magic was strong, his body was mere bones held by parched flesh; it would surely take him a long time to scale the craggy slant.

"He's—not—my—*brother*!" he yelled to himself as he reached up again and again.

It was no good.

His fingers slid against rocks that offered little purchase. He spun, gave some time to his eyes to grow accustomed to the darkness. The air hung heavily around him. *There must be a way out.* Yet he knew this was wishful thinking. Vildrith's filthy look stood as proof of that. *If there were a way out, then in twenty years, the Onyx would have found it,* his mind told him.

"No."

Unwilling to surrender to despair, Avalan returned to the wall. He traced the grainy crystals that powdered the cave. He followed the wall until its curve and then to its next, and to its next, desperately hoping for an opening, a crevice, a boulder, an outcrop—anything that might help him climb up to the tunnel that had led him here.

There were none. Only darkness and more darkness, so heavy it weighed down his very soul.

Avalan brought his mother's face to mind. Farmera's smile had always brightened his foul moods whenever hunting had gone wrong, or when he'd spent a day at the shore, remembering Bhoran. It was a blessing to have her, he knew. As for his father, Avalan hadn't given him much thought until this moment. It seemed that Vildrith fiercely loved him and hated him at the same time for his actions. *Did Azirrad truly leave Vildrith and his mother for Farmera? What father leaves his son behind? My own …*

He shook his head, trying to stop the dire thoughts. He kept on searching, pushing, groping, prodding … All the while, a dreadful truth spun in his mind. *The shadow has been to my home.*

The moments passed, yet his vision wasn't clearing. Dreadful darkness remained. The same emptiness that filled the tunnel now filled the cave.

Avalan had thought the shadow a friend, yet now he understood. It didn't serve only him; it had two masters. Avalan's heart had desired to find Crystal, but after her death, Vildrith's desire for freedom had taken over. And the shadow had led Avalan here to fulfill this bidding. *The blood must run warm.* Avalan's blood ... The shadow had only saved his life in the sword fight and the tower so that the bond wouldn't be severed. Avalan's death meant Vildrith's death.

And Crystal's death? Why did she have to die? Why didn't the shadow protect her? Tears rose in his eyes. His throat tightened. *It was your doing,* a voice in his mind said. *Not everything needs saving.*

Guilt burned inside him like a forest fire. *How can I ever make it right?*

Avalan clutched at the cave wall, forced a throbbing forehead against its roughness. *The bond.* The desperation in Dizredek's voice as he had begged Vildrith not to kill Avalan had been sincere.

If I die, Vildrith dies with me.

It was too late to save Crystal, but perhaps not all hope was lost for his mother. All Avalan had to do was kill himself, and then Farmera would be safe. Vildrith wouldn't have the time to reach her ...

How would I even end my life in a barren cave with no way out? How did Vildrith survive all these years without light, without food, without hope?

Avalan had been here less than a few hours, and he was already losing his mind. All his wounds stung him. His mind turned to sick thoughts. His stomach roiled and churned, gifting him with sour bile.

With a howl, he threw himself to the ground, crushed his shoulder under his weight. Sharp pain shot through his arm. The ground didn't budge; it was as hard as the stone walls around him. He stood, charged at the wall, smashed himself against it. The force threw him back, but he regained his balance and kept charging until he felt the slick hotness of blood trickle down his forehead. "Let me out!" he yelled, throwing his body once more against the rough rocks. "Let me out, or let me *die!*"

His cries echoed through the dark chamber, rose to the ceiling, bounced from the walls, and returned to haunt him. Soon dizziness came over him, and he stumbled to the floor, blood seeping from his wounds. Avalan didn't know how it felt to die; he only hoped it would come soon. He pressed his eyes shut and waited.

Nausea overwhelmed him, and he rolled to his side, retching. As the bile left his body, his mind cleared. The throbbing in his head eased. The beatings he had managed weren't enough, he knew; he'd have to try harder. He made to stand.

A faint groan shook the ground.

Dim light broke the darkness. Avalan shaded his eyes. *The walls.* Crimson symbols were slathered over their rough surfaces now—etchings of blood. *My blood?* It couldn't be. Countless they were, and as Avalan watched, more symbols emerged as if they oozed out of the depths of the mountain.

Avalan rubbed his eyes, smearing blood all over them. The smell of iron filled his nose and made him gag. *What is this?* It felt to him the cave was … *alive.* Avalan wondered if it was his blood that had caused this heartless thing to respond. After all, Dizredek had cut Avalan to turn the entrance wall and gain access. Perhaps it could be his blood that set him free.

Hope rose in his chest, but Avalan quenched it as he stood. *Dizredek possesses stone magic. I, alone, possess nothing.* Weapons had been Avalan's only means, and even these would now have proved useless against the magic of this cave.

His palm hovered over the symbols. *I have seen these before,* he thought, *but where?*

In an instant, he knew. *The game of death.* Dromer had spoken to them about a cave, about Krokador's Stronghold, about Hydrus's monster … Avalan had thought the man deranged, and the game a mere jest, yet now he knew better. In Krokador he had slain Ethelnar, and now this cave claimed his life.

The Cave of Rath, Dromer had called it. *A cave to trap evil souls.*

Avalan pressed fingers slick with blood to his temples, urging his mind to remember what more Dromer had said about this cave. *The symbols. They hold a riddle that leads to freedom.*

But what that could be, Avalan didn't know. Dromer had been so excited to talk to them about the waterdragon of Hydrus that he had moved on quickly from the cave.

The symbols were countless. Some curved into shapes that meant nothing to Avalan, and some looked familiar … *Like this one …* Avalan hovered his palm over a sign of three wavy stripes. *The sea. Hydrus.* It pulled at his hand, daring him to touch it. Avalan brushed his fingers over it. A strong gust thrust him back.

Gathering his wits, Avalan stood and approached another one. Three circles intertwined, and in their midst lay a cube. He touched it, and once again a backward push rewarded him.

Though he had expected it, Avalan's anger flared. He had to get out. This time, he touched two random symbols at once. A fiery blast slapped his face, blinding him.

"What do you want?" Avalan screamed when his vision cleared.

He punched the wall with all the strength he had left, yet it didn't yield. Instead, it rewarded him with a nasty gash across his knuckles. Avalan didn't mind the blood—he'd lost much of it already. *Let the cave have it all.* Perhaps then it would allow him to die in peace.

He touched whatever symbol was closest, the cave blasting him again and again.

Avalan screamed and charged at the wall, but this time, a force like icy wind threw him back before he'd even touched the rock. He fell onto his back. "Now you won't even let me touch you?"

He crouched, approached the wall more slowly this time, but once he found himself a few steps away from the symbols, the force hit him again, smashing his nose. The taste of iron exploded in his mouth. Tears welled in his eyes. He ran his fingers through the slickness of his hair, pressed his head. "I beg of you … just let me die …"

The symbols danced before him, a red sea of the unknown. Despair clawed at his chest. He didn't know how to solve the riddle.

He could just stay there on the ground, inside the belly of the mountain, and wait for hunger and thirst to claim his life. *But it might be days before that happens,* he thought, *and Dizredek knows the way to Hydrus. The shadow has been in my home.*

He longed for his goat dagger. He could just thrust it into his throat, or even cut his wrists and let them bleed. Perhaps in death,

Crystal would wait for him. Perhaps then he would know why she had left him, and he could beg for her forgiveness.

A searing pain tore his heart as he realized no one would ever find him in this place. He'd die alone, and his mother would think he'd abandoned her. He'd never see Sigil again, nor hunt with her through the blackwoods. He'd never have the time to be with Bhoran and make up for all the lost years they'd spent apart. And he'd never again see Lusha's smile and tell her that Bhoran loved her. She had to know that Bhoran loved her.

Curse you, Dizredek, he thought, swaying back and forth. *And curse my soul for believing I could free Hydrus.*

The Heart of the Bloodstone. What a mocking lie. Other stones might hold the greatest magic, but none was in his. The Bloodstone hated him, his scorched hands standing as proof when Stonemaster Delion had summoned it. *Find me,* it had said before it had burned his hands for life. He had expected the stone to aid him, to bless him with its power.

Yet how could it when I never trusted it? Ronan had offered him a dirk to bless with a Bloodstone, and Avalan had refused it. The longsword Ethelnar's blacksmith had forged for him had only proved a burden in fighting. Avalan had been so fast to rid it of the Bloodstone that he had lost. He hadn't used his stone well.

All Avalan could do was fight with bare steel and silver.

Yet now he understood the dire truth: steel and silver were useless in the face of stone magic. These lands were ruled by magic, and they refused to grant it to him. His own stone cursed him for not believing in it.

Avalan.

A faint voice broke through the rambling of his mind. The voice of Crystal.

He raised his face, looked around him. The cavern remained silent, but the illuminated symbols on its walls lingered, challenging him to touch them. After a moment of hesitation, he stood once more.

"My love?" Even as he spoke the words, he felt hopeless. *I'm insane, talking to a cave.* He wondered if that was how Vildrith had felt, staying alone in this place for so many years. *Hopeless and deranged.*

Crystal's whisper came again. *Find me.* A soft command that seeped through the corners of his mind. *Find me.*

Avalan spun. Endless symbols swam before him, confusing him. "Where are you?" he called, his voice a desperate croak from a dry throat. "Tell me how to find you."

Find me.

"Please," Avalan said, turning. His knees were weak, the loss of blood taking its toll. "Help me save Farmera."

Come to me, the voice begged, a saddened plea that now sounded like his mother. *Come to me.*

"I want to …"

Look at your hands. The voice echoed around his mind, but this time, it sounded different. Brittle and warm. Avalan knew that voice. It was the stonemaster, repeating the words he'd told him right after the Bloodstone had dripped caustic blood on his palms.

I'm afraid it will leave a mark.

A mark … Avalan tore Eyedir's gloves from his hands. Under the crimson light of the symbols, his palms remained blackened where the stone had touched him. Avalan stared at the patterned wounds. Back in Hydrus, he'd thought them mere lacerations. Yet now … The lines formed symbols, he realized. *Much like the ones on the cave walls.*

His heart pounded. Two shapes were etched on each palm. "Four shapes," Avalan murmured.

On the outer curve of his left palm, small curves intertwined. *The outline of a small fish,* Avalan thought, his eyes now frantically searching the wall until …

There!

Avalan grazed the symbol on the wall, flinching as he expected another blast, only this time no punishment came. Just a thin noise on the edge of hearing and a faint glow as the symbol turned from scarlet to azure.

Relieved, Avalan smiled at it. He studied the next symbol etched on the innermost part of his palm. A hemisphere it was, its belly facing left, and its downcast part trickled down to a wavy thread that reached his wrist. Up and down he paced, his eyes unblinking. Flowers, tears, towers, seas … *It must be here. It must.*

And yet it wasn't.

He changed direction, paced again, looking, searching. After a while, the lines blurred, the symbols mingled before his eyes. He halted, ran his fingers through his hair … *What am I missing?*

Perhaps there's no such symbol.

A lump rose to his throat, but he swallowed it down forcefully. He couldn't give up, he knew. Not with Vildrith out there, hunting his mother. There must be something he wasn't seeing. Perhaps the loss of blood was weakening his sight. He forced his eyes shut for some moments, hoping that would give them the time they needed to adjust.

With renewed hope, he examined the wall once again, going over the symbols one by one. It was no good.

Hours later, he still could not locate it. The symbols danced before his eyes, mocking, elusive. Avalan arched his fingers back, forcing the skin on his palm to stretch, and yet the symbol remained unchanged.

He looked at his right palm instead. If only he could find the next ones, perhaps he could fight the feeling of despair that crushed his breath. The first sign was again a hemisphere with a jagged lower end that dripped down to his wrist, only this time, the belly of the hemisphere was facing right. Avalan knitted his brows. There were no hemispheres on the wall—of that he was certain. He looked at the next symbol—an upturned trigon. His heart raced and his feet instinctively led him down the wall to the place where he'd last seen this shape.

There.

Without a second thought, he touched it, and the wall thrust him back. Avalan gritted his teeth. The wall was telling him order was important. *Yet why do my palms show me symbols that aren't there? What am I missing?*

This time, he stayed on the floor. The silence of the cave was a heavy veil over his aching body. If he stayed there for much longer, any hope of escape would be crushed, he knew. *Four symbols.* Two of them he had already found among the thousands on the wall, yet the other two remained a mystery. Two hemispheres so similar and yet so different, facing each other, like two crescents in the sky. *Crescents … Could it be?*

These symbols alone held no meaning, but brought together, they would form a circle. Avalan pressed his palms together side by side, connecting the lines. *The moon.* A crescent, whether it looked left or right, always remained one half of the moon.

He leaped to his feet, searched the wall once again, this time for a perfect circle. And there it was, etched at the very top.

And out of his reach.

Avalan stared at it with disbelief. *How can I reach up there?* In his madness, Vildrith had the truth of it: the cave wanted to keep him here forever.

Hopeless though it seemed, Avalan had to try. He touched the fish symbol, backtracked, then raced toward the wall, leaped high, stretched his arm ... Even before his palm had slapped the wall, he knew he'd missed. His fingertips hadn't even come close to the bottom of the symbol. Instead, his hand landed three rows below it, and for his failure, he was rewarded with yet another painful blast.

As soon as his thighs grazed the floor, he shot up. After illuminating the fish symbol, he backtracked even farther, keeping his gaze steadily on the circle, pressing his arms close to his ribs. He sliced the air and leaped. This time, he reached two rows below the moon. He closed his eyes, anticipating the wall's punishment. Harsh, it came, leaving him heaving on the floor.

The fish symbol returned to crimson, a painful reminder of his failure.

Avalan let out a harrowing scream, a howl of his injured soul, and leaped again. With every attempt, he was getting worse. The beatings of the cave became fiercer. His breeches clung to him, soaked in blood and sweat. His chest burned. His eyes stung, the stench of his own fear overbearing. Yet Avalan knew he wouldn't stop; he would either reach the moon or die trying.

The last blow threw him several feet away. As he fell, Avalan thought this time he wouldn't live to even hit the ground. The back of his head hit a jutting rock. Sharp pain exploded in his mind.

He rolled to his side, groaning. "Why?" he yelled. "Why punish me like this? Why show me symbols I cannot hope to reach?" Blood throbbed in his temples. He brought his palms together one last time, forming the perfect moon, his only hope and his demise. A perfect savior, out of reach.

He had failed, he knew. There was no more time, no strength in his body.

He let his hands drop and closed his eyes, begging for the end to come soon.

Avalan, Crystal's voice whispered.

He grunted in pain.

Find me.

"I killed you, Crystal." Hot tears mingled with the blood on his face.

Come to me. Farmera's voice now, soft, comforting, begging.

"I can't reach, Mother ... I'm sorry."

I'm afraid it will leave a mark, the stonemaster's voice resounded.

It had. But it was useless. Avalan had failed.

Look at your hands, the master's voice persisted.

Avalan forced his eyelids to shut tighter. The plan to die was better. It had to work. Death couldn't fail him now.

Look at your hands, the master reiterated.

No.

You must trust your heart, my love. Crystal's voice echoed through him. *Without trust, your Bloodstone cannot guide you.*

I don't have a Bloodstone, Avalan thought bitterly, but then the wrinkled face of Stonemistress Luthea swam before his eyes. The old woman had brushed her heart when he had asked her where he could find the Heart of the Bloodstone. He stroked his bare chest. The Heart, his heart. *I trust you,* he thought with relief.

Despite himself, Avalan opened his eyes. *One last try,* he thought. He brought his left palm close to his nose, the fish and crescent facing him. His gaze followed the lower end of the crescent, where the line trickled down toward his wrist. It seemed to Avalan the crescent was crying. Mourning his untimely demise. And then his heart skipped a beat. *The crescent isn't perfect.*

He looked at his right palm. The other crescent was imperfect as well. He brought his palms together, and even though the crescents formed a circle, the jagged lines at their tips disappeared between the meat of his palms. He had been looking at the wrong symbol all along: it shouldn't be a perfect circle, but an imperfect one. One that remained open at its base, leaking down like the lines that reached his wrists.

With fresh hope in his heart, he staggered to his feet. Every step he took sent searing pain through his mind, yet he had to keep going. He would give himself one last chance, see if a symbol like that even existed.

He pressed the fish first, then scoured the wall, and after a few moments, he saw it. An imperfect crimson circle, exactly like the one his palms formed when placed close together. He reached out a fingertip and caressed it, waiting for a blow that never came. Instead, the circle turned to azure, and Avalan breathed a sigh of relief. He shuffled his feet to the last symbol, the upturned trigon.

With a grunt, he pressed it.

Avalan watched the crimson turn to the merciful shade of a clear blue sky.

The earth beneath his feet shook, the same way it had when Dizredek had opened the twisted wall that revealed a passage.

The symbols suddenly vanished, sinking the cavern into darkness. Avalan fumbled in the dark, frantically searching the wall until he found it: a recess, a blessed opening in the cavern.

He plunged forth. Naked rock scratched his scorched palms. It went on and on. *The gloves.* He spun, but searching for them in the darkness would only slow him down.

He'd leave them behind, he decided. Through the tunnel he staggered, despite his agony. *Mother!* The ground soon changed. He was ascending now. *That can only be good.*

In the distance, a faint light appeared. Avalan's heart pounded. He hurried, afraid the cave would change its mind and swallow him back whole, let him die inside its belly, beaten and alone.

The light got brighter and brighter until at last he emerged. He gulped down the fresh air, forced it into his lungs—life and freedom. Derelict walls rose around him, scorched as if by a great fire.

Krokador's Stronghold.

The dusk air carried voices. Avalan had but a moment to grab a nearby boulder before he collapsed.

CHAPTER SIXTY-FOUR

THE COBBLED PATH simmered under the coppery sky. In silence, Lusha followed Calla and Rian, Noev by her side. She didn't dare look at him, lest she lose her courage and cry. The young man had brought her such dire tidings.

Could my Bhoran be dead? Her heart thumped with her every step. She had long ceased to hear his voice in her mind. That summoning, that irresistible calling tearing into her soul. *I have to be brave.*

To quiet her dire thoughts, she tried to mark the twists and turns of the narrow alleys—a task that proved fruitless, as there wasn't much to help her distinguish one passage from another. The same gray stones, stuck together with white sandy cement, lined all of them.

As soon as the light dimmed, the merchants gathered up their benches. To Lusha, it felt as if the sun here lingered much less than in the rest of the lands. It seemed only a few moments before when she had visited the chiefess in her high tower.

"I'm sorry," Noev told her.

His voice startled her. "For?"

"Chiefess Crystal. It must be hard to lose someone you love."

"I didn't even tell her I was leaving." Lusha lowered her gaze to the cobbles. Hot shame burned her.

"I didn't mean to sadden you."

"It matters not."

"No bad blood, then?"

Lusha lifted her face to him. The light of his Moonstones was dim. "I've had my fair share of that."

Outside the infirmary, Alana still waited for her. Lusha stroked her neck. "We shall be on our way soon, girl," she whispered. Once she had helped Calla with the sick man, Lusha would go. She needed to find Bhoran. In her heart, she hoped he still lingered in Raekandar. Together they could find Avalan, learn the truth. *I beg you, Moonstone. Please let him be alive.*

"Noev and I will bring a crate," Rian told Calla. The two men hurried away.

Inside, the smell of death hung heavy in the air. Lusha followed Calla upstairs to where the man with the Red Weal lay, a swaddled bundle.

"I apologize," Lusha started. "I promised to come back and help you after the audience with my aunt ..."

When they'd reached the shrouded body, Calla shot Lusha a freezing stare. "You didn't waste your time, I see."

"Calla, I—"

"I was mistaken to believe you aren't Shelanna's niece. Apparently, you two share the same precepts."

"Whatever do you mean?"

Calla lifted her chin. "A man isn't worth pursuing unless he's taken."

Blood rushed to Lusha's cheeks. "My aunt refused me. Apparently, I'm not so much like her for her comfort."

"And you found solace in Rian's arms?"

"I'd never—"

"I saw you!"

"Believe me." Lusha took Calla's hand in hers. "I love someone else. And he broke my heart."

Calla twisted free. "Well, you deserved it!"

Lusha bit her lip so hard she tasted the iron tang of blood. "No, Calla, I didn't." Hot tears rolled down her cheeks, and she made no move to wipe them away. "I loved him. And now he might be dead."

The hurried footsteps of the men pounded the staircase. When they appeared, Noev had a confused look on his face, but Rian's gaze was serious, as if he'd been expecting this quarrel.

"Now isn't the time for fights," Rian said in a firm voice. "We need to move the body, or it will fester."

Crossing her arms over her chest, Calla glared at him. "You're a little late to care. If you had been here, as you promised, you could have helped me—"

"He was gone as soon as he caught it," Rian said, a blaze upsetting the Fire Agate in his eyes. "You know he never stood a chance. No one ever does. They all die."

The words echoed in Lusha's head, a dire reminder. *Ronan, Eyedir, Crystal, this man … they all die …* "Everywhere I go," she muttered. The dead eyes of Ronan blended with Eyedir's stony stare. *Wasn't the moon supposed to heal?*

"They would have died anyway," Rian said. "It's not your fault."

"I never should have left Hydrus."

Calla groaned. "You have to make this about you? If death scares you so much, then run back to your father. Why, we could even be the ones to deliver you and earn the reward. Stones know how much we need the coin."

"No one's turning in anyone," Rian said in a strict voice.

"Look at her cower in the face of death. She shames the Moonstone. She has no place among us."

"Calla!" Rian blazed. "That is enough."

Calla stared at him, her lower lip trembling.

"She's right," Lusha said. "I should leave."

"You still love her," Calla told Rian, wiping away a tear that fell despite her efforts. "After all these years … I should have known."

Rian moved to hug her, but Calla twisted away. She stormed down the stairs. Confused, Lusha stared at Rian. How could a man she'd never known love her? From the very start, Lusha had sensed a strange longing in Rian's eyes, but she had thought it to be his kindness. She was new in the city, and he'd seen her struggle. *He is just trying to be nice, isn't he?* She had so many questions, but looking at Rian, she now hesitated. The man looked broken. As if Calla had ripped open a wound he had been carefully guarding.

Rian returned her gaze through haunted eyes. "Lusha, I should explain ..."

Noev cleared his throat. "I'll leave you."

"No," Lusha said. As much as she felt she could trust Rian, staying alone with him was something that would stoke Calla's hatred. And Lusha truly cared about her, she realized. She wanted to fight the Red Weal alongside this brave woman who, even though she knew these men and women held no hope, still brought them here, trying to heal them. It was a thing Farmera would have done. "Please, Noev. Stay."

An awkward silence fell, followed closely by an urgent yell. Lusha rushed to the window as a voice below cried Calla's name. A short man wearing sandy robes had cupped his hands around his mouth. *Nexanthos?* Lusha had seen him only once, but there was no mistaking the man who had saved her life in Raekandar.

"*Rian!*" Nexanthos yelled, panting. "Is Calla here?"

"What happened?"

"We've found a man." Nexanthos motioned to two other men, who staggered behind him. In their arms they carried the half-naked body of a man caked with blood.

"You shouldn't touch him!" Rian warned.

Nexanthos shook his head. "It isn't the sickness. This man has been beaten. Badly."

As he spoke, the carriers hurried within. Rian and Noev were quick to relieve the two exhausted men of their burden and took the senseless man's body to the only empty bed.

"Lusha," Rian said. "Get us some water. We should clean the blood away and examine his wounds."

Lusha rushed down to the small kitchen.

Bowl, water, and cloth in hand, she returned. She knelt next to the man, washed the blood off his belly, while Nexanthos explored the man's wounds. Grazes, blood, bruises, and dust covered the broken body. She rubbed the man's shoulder. *A wound,* she thought, yet once the blood was off, she saw it was an etching. Lusha gulped down fear. The markings reminded her of Bhoran's. She stared at the man's face now. Dry lips, eyelids shut, swollen over his eyes, his long hair an ashen waterfall.

A sickening feeling twisted her stomach.

She dipped her cloth into the water and started cleaning the muck off the man's face. "Where did you find him?" she asked Nexanthos.

"Krokador's Stronghold," the moonhealer said. "Stonemistress Luthea led a group of us there to retrieve Chief Ethelnar's body."

Icy fingers ran down Lusha's spine.

"Ethelnar is dead?" Noev asked.

"By the hands of Avalan of the Bloodstone."

Lusha froze, her heart pounding. *It can't be true. It can't.* "Leave!" she screamed. "Leave, all of you!"

"Lusha—" Rian began.

"Take them all out! This place needs to breathe. We are too many." She fought to keep her voice steady.

"We need to examine the body," Rian warned. "Search for the wounds that could cost him his life. Nexanthos and his men—"

She stood, faced the medic. His eyes were rooted to the man who lay on the bed, his jaw tense. "You once were happy under Chief Othor," Lusha told him. "Until Ethelnar killed him. The chief was full of hatred." She hoped with all her heart the medic would remember his own words.

Nexanthos held her gaze. The light of his Moonstones had now dimmed. He nodded. "Our work is done here," he told his men. "We return to Levorotha with Ethelnar's body."

As soon as the staircase creaked no more, Lusha dipped the cloth in fresh water and started cleaning the beaten man's face again.

"What was that for?" Rian asked her.

Yet Lusha ignored him. She had to see to the man's face. She wiped the dust off the thick ebon eyebrows, then did the same for the man's hair. It glistened black. Next, she cleaned his high cheeks and his lips. And then she trembled.

Noev put a hand on her shoulder. "Do you know this man?"

"Avalan," she whispered. "He's Avalan."

CHAPTER SIXTY-FIVE

A COOL CLOTH wiped his forehead. *I'm not alone.* Avalan tried to open his eyes, but they were leaden. A groan escaped his lips.

"Avalan," a woman's voice called.

Lusha? Another try, and his eyes opened. It was her, he knew at once, only she looked … *different*. Short hair, tucked behind her ears, framed a face free from the nasty scar. The skin over her right eye was now smooth. With great effort, he touched her cheek. "Lusha?"

"You're safe now." Her tears fell.

Avalan made to lift his head. Nausea surged through him, forcing him back. No longer was he in Krokador's Stronghold, he realized. Instead, he lay in a room laden with the smells of sweat, ointments, and blood. So much blood … he could smell it on him. *I should have died,* he thought as memories of the cave returned. If he was alive, that only meant one thing. "Lusha … my mother." Trying to lift his head again earned him blinding pain.

Gently Lusha forced him back. "Try not to move. You've broken some bones, I'm afraid."

"I have to … go."

"The spells need time to take effect," a man behind Lusha said. "You'd better rest."

Avalan twisted his neck to better look at him. Tall he was, with raven and red hair and fire in his eyes. Avalan had a strong feeling he'd seen this man before, but his pain left him no space to think clearly. Beside him another man stood, younger, with cropped blond hair and a Moonstone earring. "What is … this place? Who are you?"

Lusha pointed at the young man. "This is Noev. He saved your life, along with Calla." This time, Lusha pointed to a skulking woman who stood at the corner of the bed, arms crossed, looking exhausted. "And this," Lusha continued, motioning to the older man with fiery eyes, "is Rian. Raekandar's men found you badly injured at the stronghold and brought you here. We're in the city of Levorotha—the island of the Moonstone, the city of healers."

Avalan swallowed hard, his throat dry. Other beds stood around him, some with motionless bundles on them that looked like swaddled men. The place smelled like burning candles and Farmera's home. "Lusha … I have … to get back."

"Back where?"

"He will … kill my mother."

Lusha's eyes darted between his face and his broken body. "Avalan, I do not understand … Where is Bhoran?"

Bhoran, Avalan thought with pain in his heart. They were supposed to meet, escape Raekandar. "Olnos …"

Noev placed a soft hand on Lusha's shoulder. "We must let him rest. His mind is raw, his wounds still open. There will be plenty of time for talk once he's recovered."

Avalan moaned. His body was on fire. His guts, his muscles … the pain cut through to his bones. "Hydrus … the shadow … Dizredek …" He gritted his teeth. A vein throbbed at his temple. "My brother … will kill Farmera." He made to stand again, lifted an elbow this time.

Lost, Lusha just stared at him. "Avalan, you have no brother …"

Rian knelt by the bedside, but instead of pushing Avalan back or scolding him for not letting the healing spells take their course, he placed two strong arms under his armpits and helped him sit up. "You are Farmera's son?"

Even swallowing hurt. "Help me … save her."

"I do not understand," Lusha said. She leaned closer, peering into Avalan's eyes. "Who wants to kill Farmera? What has happened?"

"Must … go …"

Lusha spun, shot a desperate glance at Noev.

The young man shook his head, a solemn expression on his face. "His mind is lost. He only talks because he is in Levorotha. If he leaves, the pain will knock him senseless. He might not make it."

If this man's words are true … Avalan squeezed Lusha's hand harder. "If I leave … I die?"

Noev nodded.

"Kill … me …"

Placing a soft hand on his shoulder, Lusha whispered. "Avalan …"

She thinks I've lost my mind. "I need to … die."

"How could you ask this of me? I cannot let you die. Not you …" More tears fell now. "Crystal is dead."

The way she looked at him, he knew she begged for the truth. His mind was numb. Words came with a great struggle. *There is no time …* "I loved her … Ethelnar. Please …" His eyes betrayed him, slid shut. He fought a strong urge to drift into a painless sleep.

"Can you not give him something for his pain?" he heard Lusha beg.

A firm touch on his knee brought him to his senses. Through blurry eyes, he saw the man of fire.

"Who did this to you?" Rian asked him.

"Cave."

"Which cave do you speak of?"

"Rath …" Avalan drifted, his mind begging him to surrender.

Rian slapped him. "You were inside the Cave of Rath?"

"My brother … escaped …"

Concern was etched on Lusha's face. "He doesn't have a brother," she muttered to Rian, shaking her head.

"Trust me …" *You have to. You must help me save my mother.*

Rian came so close that Avalan could feel the man's skin burning. "Did you release the Onyx?" the man asked him.

A vile snake twisted in Avalan's gut. *No, no, no!* his mind was screaming. But then he remembered the darkness in Vildrith's eyes. His wicked stare, the smirk on his face, the pain from a mere flick of his wrist … "The Onyx."

With disbelief, Lusha shook her head. "It can't be true."

Avalan felt the man's burning hand explore the etching on his shoulder. Round and round his finger went, as if it tried to find the way through the endless maze Dhylinea had drawn. He must have reached the center, Avalan knew, for the man suddenly stopped, sprang to his feet.

"Calla, cast on him the blessing of your Moonstone."

"Look at him!" Calla yelled. "He's lost his mind. Even his dear friend doesn't believe him. Speaking of a brother he doesn't have, talking about the Onyx. You want me to expend my powers for him? Do you not think of the poor souls that need my help?"

"I must return to Hydrus—"

"No!" She buried her fist in Rian's chest. "You promised me … you promised you'd never go back. You *promised*!"

"If what he speaks is truth—"

"But it isn't," Calla protested. "It cannot be. The Onyx is gone. It's gone … Don't look at me like that, Rian. Just don't …"

"You've seen the Red Weal return, Calla."

The woman's angry retorts tore at Avalan. He had to go. He had to. The man seemed to believe him.

Rian spun and grabbed Noev's shoulders. "Cast on him your blessing."

The young man hesitated. "It won't work …"

"I know I'm asking for much, Noev. But you said it yourself. He might not make it."

"Do you really think the Onyx is back?" Noev asked, fumbling with his earlobe.

Rian shot a fiery stare at Avalan. "There's only one way to know the truth."

Nodding solemnly, Noev undid his earring. "You promise to return it?"

"I promise," Rian said.

Avalan struggled to keep his senses as Noev sat beside him. The young healer presented him with the earring: a Moonstone set on a sharp silver hook. "This will hurt," Noev said, pinching Avalan's earlobe. Avalan doubted it could be worse than the storm that tugged at his insides, yet when Noev stretched the skin and pierced it, Avalan groaned.

"I bless you with my Moonstone," Noev whispered. At once the young man looked tired, as if he needed a good night's rest.

Avalan, however, grew stronger. Soon the stinging pain from where the earring had pierced him gave way to a warm sensation that coursed through his body. The Moonstone's blessing found all the painful spots and soothed them. His bones, his heart, his skin … It was as if Noev's stone was hastening his healing. Avalan felt his will return, his mind strengthen. He grabbed Noev's arms. "Thank you."

When he stood, Lusha hugged him tight. Her presence gave him much-needed hope.

Gently he held her at arm's length. "I must return to Hydrus. Farmera's in danger. You say we are in Levorotha?"

Lusha nodded.

Avalan knitted his brows, brought to memory Ronan's maps. If the ink strokes could be trusted, the city of healers lay near Raekandar. Perchance with a horse, he could reach the Craggy Mountains. He had to leave at once.

He turned to Noev. "I thank you for your stone, but I must leave now."

"I will come with you," Lusha said.

"No. It isn't safe …"

"I don't know what has happened, but Farmera's like a mother to me. I *will* come with you."

Rian stepped in. "How will you find your way?"

"I am a tracker."

"It will take you days to reach Hydrus. And crossing the mountain …" Rian slid a finger across his throat.

"We have the shad—" Lusha began, but then she saw Avalan's frown.

Without the shadow's guidance, they were lost, Avalan knew. The mountain paths they'd taken were snaky and treacherous, and most times, there had been no path to speak of. Just the shadow's urging to brave a hostile slope or leap over dark chasms. Avalan stared at Rian.

The fire in his eyes was blazing now, lighting the spark of hope in Avalan's heart. "Is there another way?"

When Rian nodded, Calla stormed down the stairs, sobbing. "Take care of her while I'm gone," Rian told Noev. "And you, children of Hydrus. Follow me."

Outside, the cobbled streets were dark and deserted. As they crossed them, Avalan told Lusha and Rian all: Crystal's death, his fight with the chief, the cave, the bond, the shadow's betrayal, and his half-brother ... "How could he still be alive?" Avalan asked Rian as they turned for the hundredth time. Avalan had lost count now of the alleys, his mind overwhelmed with fear for his mother.

"The Onyx is a nasty thing. Hard to kill, harder even to reconcile with life," Rian said.

The words resounded in Avalan's mind. At one time, he'd also thought Ethelnar hard to kill, and yet Avalan had pushed him to his death. It wouldn't be just the Onyx he'd have to face in Hydrus, though, Avalan knew. He shot a sidelong glance at Lusha. He hadn't told her the truth about Bassalt. The tidings of the Onyx had paled her skin. Avalan wasn't certain he wanted the wound of Ronan's death to reopen. When the time came, he would deal with it, staring into Bassalt's eyes, demanding the truth before ...

"Avalan," Lusha whispered. "Where is Bhoran?"

"I wish I knew. I was to meet him at Olnos with Crystal." The thought saddened him beyond words. With Ethelnar and Crystal dead, Avalan knew there would be little tolerance for Bhoran in Raekandar. He shut his eyes and prayed to the Bloodstone Bhoran was quick enough to hide. *Until I free Hydrus.* "Why did you leave him?"

"I found a woman's dress in his room."

The messenger, Avalan thought, all the pieces falling together now. "Bhoran didn't betray you. Ethelnar sent the girl to lure him to Olnos."

Lusha's Moonstones filled with shame. "Why would the chief do such a thing?"

To kill me, Avalan thought, though why Ethelnar had left the message in Bhoran's room made little sense to Avalan. *Was Ethelnar so certain Bhoran would call for my aid?* He clenched his fists at the memory. He wished to forget the dead chief. "Bhoran saved my life," he told her. Dhylinea's face swam before his eyes. Now that Lusha's scar had cleared, the two women looked eerily alike. "Bhoran loves you, Lusha. I know it in my heart."

The sound of rain broke the silence.

As Rian threaded their way through the alleys, it only got louder. Avalan looked up. The sky was cloudless, clear. *Where is that sound coming from?*

When they emerged into a square, Avalan got his answer. A tall fountain with a bronze disk that shone under the moonlight stood in the middle. Through countless holes, water fell like rain. Stray droplets wetted their faces as they drew closer.

Rian halted. "We're here."

Avalan gazed up at the rainfall. "I don't understand. I thought you were to lead us to Hydrus."

"I know. And as I told you, the road there will only slow you down."

Confused, Avalan tried to suppress the anger that grew inside him. "How is a *fountain* going to aid us?"

Rian's face grew dark. "Someone will take us. I must ask you not to scream. In truth, I am asking you both to hold your tongues. Step back."

Avalan exchanged a worried glance with Lusha. They backed away, holding hands. Rian stepped into the water. The rainfall curtain blurred Rian's words, but Avalan watched him raise his hands in prayer.

With a deafening crack, the water ceased falling. Avalan stared at the disk in disbelief. It was as if the bronze mirror had dried up.

Abruptly the water returned, a massive wave, drenching them. From the gutters of the fountain sprang a creature. Its diaphanous body, covered with opal scales, reflected the blue moonlight. As if having been crammed into a small place for far too long, the beast stretched, its torso measuring at least twenty feet. Sharp talons adorned its four paws, and its snout was longer even than Sigil's, revealing rows of vicious teeth.

What is this?

Beneath the beast, Rian knelt. The creature sniffed the crown of his head. "*Volkan.*" It spoke, its voice deep, rising from the bottom of an endless ocean.

It was only a name, and yet it tugged at Avalan's heart with a great realization. He clasped Lusha's hand. The creature, in turn, bowed before Rian. The Fire Agate rested a hand atop the beast's head, spoke to it gently.

Then Rian turned to them, a solemn expression on his face. "Rise. It is time we returned to Hydrus."

"Who are you?" Avalan asked, though in his heart he already knew. *The game of heroes and stones.* The whole tribe had waited for this man's spirit every summer to appear, to free them, to offer them hope.

"I am Volkan of the Fire Agate," Rian said, and the flames in his eyes blazed. "The rightful chief of Hydrus."

CHAPTER SIXTY-SIX

WITHOUT SILVER by his side on the platform, Bassalt felt exposed. As the night fell, the tribe slowly gathered at the feasting ground of Hydrus. Four great fires had been lit—for food, protection, light, and fear.

Skinned goats turned on spits. Soups boiled in cauldrons, and seeds roasted in copper pots over the fire. The sweet smells made Bassalt's stomach grumble, yet he suspected he was the only one eager to feast that night. The tribesfolk had gathered at his behest, but they had done so unwillingly, their eyes constantly drifting from the platform to the sky.

They still fear Hydrus, Bassalt thought. He couldn't blame them. The waterdragon wasn't a beast of beauty to behold. Bassalt was glad, though. He couldn't have their love, he knew, and so their fear would serve him well. Another uprising would only plunge the village into further despair.

Behind him, Marebore moaned. Bassalt sighed. For a sweet moment, he had forgotten his prisoner's existence. But now it seemed the man had finally awoken.

Marebore was tethered to the same pole that had once held Stonemaster Delion. The fire illuminated the sweat on his forehead. Where the Ruby had once been now lay a gaping hole in his chest. Raw and unwashed, the wound had festered, a foul smell emanating from the dead flesh. Bassalt had wanted Marebore naked and on display.

Let him be a reminder of what happens to those who place their fate on the stones. A bloody fool was the man who didn't break his stone into more pieces but rather fused it as a whole to his body, Bassalt believed.

A knot of men arrived from the seaward gate—fishers, skin drummers, hunters, weavers. To his dismay, Bassalt noted they cradled weapons. Curved knives for gutting fish, small axes for woodcutting, and blowpipes for hunting small animals in the forest. These were the only things left at their disposal after Bassalt's men had unearthed Avalan's hideout. Bassalt didn't feel threatened—the true weapons rested by his side: his stone magic and Silver's men. Though his commander still lay unconscious, his men knew better than to disobey Bassalt's orders. Were a fight to break out, he'd order them to suppress it.

The men took their places behind the drums. With all their power, they slammed the taut skins, their song more a keening than a feasting chant.

Bassalt flicked his wrist, sending vines crawling toward the flames. Once afire, he bade them sway to the rhythm of the drumming. Some gasps came at the pleasing sight, but it was only from the mouths of the children. They were too young to know not to surrender to Bassalt's enchantments, or perhaps too fearless to care.

Ofttimes Bassalt wished his tribe were made of wood and vines and soil. Then he would control their minds, nourish them, lead them in the right direction. But such wishes were made in vain, he knew. How soon the painful memories of war faded from their minds, and thoughts of the stones and betrayal crept back up. *How can I protect you if you won't listen?*

Delion had refused to obey Bassalt's calling. Theran had returned from the grotto earlier that night to inform him of the stonemaster's condition. Ever since he'd destroyed that mysterious stone that resembled an Onyx, the stonemaster had refused to eat or drink. Bassalt had wondered long and hard if that had been the Onyx he sought, but he had swiftly dismissed the thought—the snake ring wouldn't sense the presence of a stone at that distance, and by the looks of Dhylinea's lair, she had been lingering there for more than a mere summer.

He shot a baleful glance at his prisoner. The drumming now drowned out Marebore's moans. *I crushed his stone while he was alive,* Bassalt thought bitterly. He still remembered the dust of the Ruby as it had crunched between his fingers. Of late, his decisions had been made out of fear and without proper judgment.

Over the rim of his cup, he searched for Farmera. There she was, a vision of beauty and anger as she witnessed the torture of a man on display. *They must see,* Bassalt's gaze tried to tell her. *They must know I am not weak. You cannot ask of me anything less.*

Bassalt closed his eyes and took hold of a dozen forest birds. He commanded them to sing, signifying the beginning of the feasting. Platters and cups clattered as the tribesfolk took their shares. They ate and drank, and yet they did so in silence. Bassalt expected nothing more. He munched on soft meat and hard seeds and gobbled up his wine. Its sweetness fueled his stone.

He sent the vines dancing higher, fiery ropes into the sky. He made the birds chirp louder and tuned his Tiger's Eye to the village. The trees became his mind, the mountain his heart, the sand his soul ... He shouldn't waste his powers on such trivial things, he knew. And yet he could not help it. For once, he needed a thing of beauty, a distraction from the dread that tugged at his heart. He needed the feasting ground to be alive and thriving.

Before it was too late.

Beside him, Theran leaned closer, breaking the spell. The manservant had been jumpy all night, barely touching his drink. "My chief," he squeaked. "It's about time you addressed the tribe."

Bassalt stared at the hideous stump on his hand and let the vines fall to the ground, ash and strings. As soon as they touched the soil, the beating ceased, the birds sang no more, and an eerie silence spread over the tribe. Bassalt stood. His long robes fell around him, a gray garment with golden threads.

"The last night of the spirits marked twenty years after the War of the Stones," Bassalt said without preamble. "We do not speak about the war, and yet those of us old enough to remember can hear the cries of death ringing in our ears. Pain, despair, blood ... things I have tried hard to protect you from."

Disgruntled whispers swept the crowd, but Bassalt ignored them.

"I built a fence to guard you. I charmed the land to guard you. I banished the stones to guard you. And this is how you repay me. With *treason.*"

Marebore pleaded for water. The man's lips were pale. Bassalt slid over to him, placed a hand over his head. "You all wish me dead. Gone. Removed from my rightful place. But before you run back to the birthstones, seeking revenge and protection, I wish to remind you what happens to those who put their faith in their stones." He reached a brawny arm beneath Marebore's armpit, set the tribesman on his feet. The festering wound gaped at them. Bassalt withdrew his hand and let him fall. The tribe gasped.

Bassalt laughed, the insanity of it all raking his nerves. *The Onyx has returned, you fools!* he wanted to scream. *Nothing else should matter! Nothing!*

"Stonemaster Delion filled your heads with wonder and awe but failed to teach you that the birthstones claim your body and your very soul. Watch now your leader fade. *This* is what truly happens when you allow a stone to take hold of who you are."

There was the whistling of air, and Bassalt caught a pricker meant for his chest. Between stubby fingers, he snapped it, throwing its pieces to the ground. Theran tugged at his cloak to keep him back, but Bassalt yanked free. Two ... three ... now twenty young men and women stood, blowpipes in their hands, hatred in their eyes. They raised their weapons to their mouths in unison.

A rain of prickers followed, but Bassalt had ample time to sweep them all aside with whipping vines.

"Where is the stonemaster?" a voice demanded.

And then another: "Free Marebore!"

A fresh wave of prickers sliced the sky. Knives spun into the air. Curses flew toward the platform.

"Free Marebore! Free the stonemaster! Free Marebore! Free the stonemaster!" Voices united, echoed, demanded.

Silver's men made to move as Bassalt had instructed them, spears and blades at the ready. Yet Bassalt stretched out a thick root, pushing them against the platform. *No,* he thought. *No more fighting. I shall end it all.*

He grabbed at a flying knife meant for his face, blade first. "I shall *not* release those who harm the peace of our village," he thundered over the commotion.

"You are our chief no longer!"

"Die, Bassalt!"

"The spirits denied you!"

I am the rightful chief of Hydrus, Bassalt thought, the Tiger's Eye in his mind bursting open with rage. *I am … cursed, cursed, cursed …* "NO!" Bassalt spun, tore Marebore from the platform. He bade two vines coil around the now-unconscious man's arms, making him dangle like a lifeless puppet. "I AM"—a vine whipped Marebore's back—"THE RIGHTFUL"—another slashed at his torso—"CHIEF OF HYDRUS!" A final stroke sliced Marebore's throat from ear to ear.

Red blood gushed over Bassalt's face. His back prickled with dozens of bites as prickers found it. Cries echoed from the crowd below, and Bassalt felt the wave of his men as they charged to suppress the anger of the tribe.

Slowly Bassalt turned. Below, another fight had begun.

My tribe, Bassalt thought. *No longer.*

The sound of metal and wood wasn't enough to quench the cries. *"Murderer! Murderer!"* they yelled, cursing Bassalt and his heartless hide. Spears went through flesh. Teeth and nails clawed at faces. Men and women cried, while children ran to hide beneath the tables.

Soon the smell of blood drenched Bassalt's nostrils. A sharp pain tore at his chest where a spinning gutting knife found him. It wasn't enough to deal actual damage, and yet Bassalt felt as though it had slashed his heart along with his pride. *I have lost their fear.*

Bassalt could end it all, he knew. All it would take was the release of all the other spells he had to sustain, and the concentration of his stone power on one thing. An earthquake so strong it would bury the village beneath tons of soil and rolling rocks from the Craggy Mountains. He couldn't stand to watch the village fall into the wrong hands. Not when an Onyx lurked. Not when all his efforts to keep the tribe away from the birthstones had failed. Not when *he* wasn't the chief of Hydrus.

A massive splash resounded through the village, forcing the fight to die. All turned toward the sea.

Confused, Bassalt glanced at his hands. Had he unleashed his power in his despair without realizing? He knew not what to make of this. Screams broke the silence, and faces turned to the sky.

Following their gaze, Bassalt looked up. Hydrus, the waterdragon, circled in the air above the feasting ground. Salty rain dripped from its silver body.

Thrice the monster has renounced me, Bassalt thought. *And yet it doesn't kill me.* More screams broke his wonder, and Bassalt returned his gaze to the tribe below. He watched as the crowd parted, as if someone was making his way through it.

Drenched and dripping, Avalan and Lusha emerged. Behind them walked a man whom Bassalt hadn't seen for near twenty years. A man whom everyone else in Hydrus thought dead, but who Bassalt had hoped would never return to challenge him for the seat. And yet he now walked among the tribe as if he had already restored his place.

Volkan.

CHAPTER SIXTY-SEVEN

THE FEASTING GROUND smelled like death. Avalan knew the stench of a fresh kill all too well.

However, the new-spilled blood wasn't that of a beast. His tribe was injured. All around him they stood, cut, bruised, speared, slashed. And on the mighty platform, Bassalt stood dumbfounded before the corpse of Marebore. A bloodied vine hovered in midair, and in that moment, Avalan knew.

Dizredek had the truth of it—Bassalt had murdered Ronan. And now Avalan even saw how the chief had done it. Marebore's slashed throat was proof enough. *The bloody vines.*

"BASSALT!" he roared, grabbing a small axe lodged in a table. With a yank, he set it free, wood splintering. A fiery palm pressed on his shoulder—Volkan—but Avalan shoved it aside. "No! He *killed* Ronan!" he yelled as he marched forth. "He *sentenced* Bhoran to death! He *killed* Marebore!"

Avalan charged.

A familiar roar tore his eardrums as Sigil fell in beside him, her fur disheveled, her fangs bared and eager to kill. Together they sliced through the night, leaped over cook fires, kicked sand aside, clawed over the platform. Avalan swung the axe at Bassalt's chest, but the chief was quick to dodge the blow. The blessing of Noev's Moonstone surged through Avalan's body, filling him with rage, hope, strength.

Sigil jolted. Her claws found purchase on Bassalt's robe. A tear resounded, and then a cry as Bassalt shoved the tiger aside.

"You must listen to me!" Bassalt warned, raising a hand.

Avalan rolled, swung the axe at the chief's feet.

As Bassalt leaped, the surrounding fires crackled. Flames rose to the sky, spitting twigs, coals, embers. Volkan walked through it all as if fire could not touch him. "Bassalt!" he roared. "Surrender. Your time has ended."

"Stay back!" Avalan yelled, his anger blinding him. "His life is mine."

Sigil plunged forth, securing Bassalt's leg between her fangs. The chief roared, and Avalan swung the axe down. It caught Bassalt in the shoulder, biting into his meaty flesh.

The effort made Avalan trip. He landed face-first on the platform, the blood-slick wood smearing his cheek. *Marebore's blood.* The fires grew larger, hungrier. Hundreds of screams tore the air as more men now charged at the platform.

Then the ground shook.

A deafening earthquake. Avalan covered his ears.

Before his own eyes, a chasm opened. A bottomless crevasse, it cut the feasting ground in half, separating the platform from the rest. The men halted their attack. One of them tripped, slid down.

Avalan glimpsed fiery hair. "Eras!" he yelled.

The rest groped at the boy, hauling him up, all the while screaming for the others to halt their advances.

Volkan stood at the edge, body aflame, eyes terrible fiery sockets. And yet despite his rage, he couldn't cross.

None of them could, Avalan realized. His chest burned afresh with the desire for revenge. He tore his hands from his ears and leaped to his feet as Bassalt plucked the axe from his shoulder. Sweat dripped from the chief's face, and his features were twisted with pain. "Avalan ... you must stop ... I can feel them ..." The axe slipped through the chief's grasp.

Without thinking, Avalan rushed to grab it. He whirled, put all his strength behind the blow. The blade bit flesh again, fresh blood bursting from Bassalt's thigh. "Avalan, you must listen ..."

"Why?" Avalan roared, chest heaving. "Why did you kill Ronan?"

Bassalt raised bloodshot eyes. "He carried birthstones … even an Onyx. No one must know …"

Rage invaded Avalan afresh. He leaped at Bassalt with bare hands.

A furry flank pushed him aside before he'd reached the chief. Avalan moaned as his back scraped against the platform. He wiped away his sweat, bewildered.

Sigil now stood by Bassalt's side. She bristled. Her striped eyes stared at Avalan as if they meant him harm.

"Sigil!"

No! his mind yelled at him as the tiger charged. Her claws found his ribs as Avalan rolled to the side. "Sigil, no!" The tiger slithered on Marebore's blood, roared, spun. Avalan had but a moment to raise his arms above his head before Sigil attacked him. Her claws cut deep, demanding, enraged.

"Release her!" Avalan yelled at Bassalt. "Sigil, no!" He shoved her aside with all his strength, his heart breaking from the betrayal.

Bassalt hurled the axe aside, collapsed to his knees, his face a mask of pain.

He is controlling her.

Avalan reached for the axe, brandished it at the tiger to scare her. He knew it would not do. His mighty companion was fearless. She charged at him again. Her roar drowned out the men's screams from the other side of the chasm. This time the tiger's fangs found Avalan's calf. He groaned in pain. Fresh blood mingled with Marebore's; the axe slipped from Avalan's grip.

Avalan! The maddening voice thudded into his mind.

"No!" Avalan yelled. The last time the voice had come to him during a fight, it had driven him mad. He fell back, putting some distance between him and Sigil. Ethelnar's greatsword blows had now turned into vicious attacks from Sigil's claws and fangs. The tiger charged at him again and again. Around and around they circled, once allies, now enemies under Bassalt's influence.

Careless, Avalan slipped on Marebore's blood. Sigil leaped, thrust him to the ground. He spat, crawled behind Marebore's dead body.

Avalan!

With a mighty leap, Sigil was on him again, her mouth going for his neck. Avalan shoved his arm into the tiger's mouth.

Avalan!

"Stop … calling me …"

Screams tore the burning skies. The heat grew stronger. Avalan's entire body felt as if it were on fire. Sweat stung his eyes. Or perhaps it was tears. He knew not which of the two as they filled his mouth with heartbreaking saltiness. "Sigil …" he begged. Her eyes were blank, unseeing. "It's me. Avalan." She clenched her jaw harder. Avalan gritted his teeth. "Come back to me, girl." Her body was heavy, unbearable against his hold. His arms ached with strain.

Avalan!

Warm blood trickled down onto his face from his arm. His own blood. "Sigil," he begged. "Remember the time we circled that goat? On the mountain …" Her eyes sparked. She bit him harder. "It taunted us. My arrows, your claws, a fast devil that one—*argh!*"

Avalan! the voice screamed as he felt his strength waning. Sigil's snout came closer; her whiskers tickled his forehead.

"We let her go that time. Licked our wounded pride. Do you remember, Sigil?" The tiger snarled through clenched jaws. "Remember, girl. Remember when I found you in the Crystal Lake … our lazy naps among the blackwoods …" He gasped, the pain now lancing from his arm to his shoulder.

Avalan!

He twisted his neck to the side. The axe blade glistened next to Marebore's feet. *If I could reach it …* But no. *I cannot kill her. I cannot even hurt her to save my life.*

Avalan!

"Bloodstone," Avalan said to the voice. "Help me … bring her back."

Reach … claim …

"How?" Avalan lacked Bassalt's stone powers. *She will kill me,* he thought as fear rose in his chest.

Reach! Claim!

Avalan tried to flick his wrists as he had seen countless times now when the stone magic had been inflicted on its victims. Yet one of his wrists was stuck between Sigil's fangs; the other was crushed beneath her belly as he tried to keep her from smothering him. He found her eyes. Striped, dripping with a rage to kill, a rage he knew couldn't be hers. *My Sigil is kind. My Sigil is proud. My Sigil is my friend.* "I love you," he whispered to those eyes before he closed his to surrender.

And then he was himself no more. Instead, he felt a wild beast. Raw anger, fear, confusion surged through him in a flow of emotions. He tasted wet blood. He smelled his own fear. He heard his second heart throb against his chest. He felt the roughness of bone, saw the fear of death in his own eyes. Eyes wide and bloody, the colors of the Bloodstone disappearing to leave behind only a mass of crimson. *I can see through her. I am … she.*

The tiger's jaw opened.

Avalan moaned as he felt the sweet release. He had lost control of her again, he knew. And yet his heart swelled with joy. Sigil licked at his wounds, whimpering. Grabbing at her thick fur, Avalan buried his face in its comfort. "My girl."

"How?" a voice came behind them.

Still kneeling, Bassalt was staring at him in disbelief. His lips, pale as death, trembled. He looked on the verge of exhaustion. "How did you do this?"

Enraged anew, Avalan leaped to his feet. He snatched the axe from the ground. He and Sigil charged, and this time Bassalt didn't resist. Avalan grabbed at the chief's long hair, brought his face close to his, the blade to his neck.

"Where?" Avalan screamed. "Where did you bury Ronan? Speak now before I kill you."

"I promised … to protect you."

Avalan yanked at Bassalt's hair harder. "Protect me from what? You are insane, Bassalt. Charging Bhoran with a murder you committed. Painting an Onyx dagger with Ronan's blood. Turning Sigil against me. I hate you. I hate you *so much.*"

"The Onyx is coming," Bassalt cried. His lips were chapped, his mouth twisted with horror. "Listen to me. I can finally hear them. I can sense their footsteps shaking the earth."

Vildrith … Could his brother be so fast? Disgust shook Avalan's chest.

Avalan … the voice now begged.

He raised his head, watched the terror that consumed the tribe on the other side of the chasm. The young men he had trained were fighting tooth and nail with Bassalt's men. The feasting ground was burning—tables, grass, vines, all now aflame. Over the crackling of the flames, Volkan's voice boomed, "Bassalt! Bassaaaalt!"

"You need me," the chief croaked. "They're coming. I knew I was right. I was right …"

Avalan pressed the axe into Bassalt's neck. A crimson rivulet flowed. *Do it!* his mind screamed at him. *Just kill him. Kill him and free Hydrus!*

"I cannot keep the chasm open for long … I can feel them coming. Seeking revenge …"

Avalan pressed the axe in deeper. Ethelnar's dead stare floated before his eyes.

Avalan … the voice begged.

"You deserve to die!" *Just one more push.*

Bassalt gulped, rolled his eyes. Thick tears fell down his cheeks. "What have you done? You brought the umbra of the Onyx to our village …"

How could they be here so fast?

The stiff fingers of fear trickled down Avalan's spine. His breath caught in his chest. "Mother …" he whispered. In his anger and thirst for revenge, he hadn't gone to her. His rage had blinded him. He searched through the flames for her familiar figure, but the other side of the chasm was a mess of bodies, weapons, screams … "No …"

"What have you done?" Bassalt persisted.

I freed him, Avalan wanted to yell. *I freed the Onyx. I freed my brother* … "No …"

"You cannot protect Hydrus. Spare me … to save yourself."

Avalan kept searching. *Flames, death, steel* …

"What … have you done?"

Despairing, Avalan looked down at the chief. "I freed him," he confessed. "I freed the Onyx." The words were a knife to his heart. He lowered the axe blade from Bassalt's neck. If Bassalt's deranged moans were true and the Onyx was approaching … "Farmera … he wants to kill my mother."

The chief's eyes widened with fear as he searched the chaos across the chasm. He grabbed Avalan's wrist, cascades of blood oozing from his axe wounds. "You must fight the Onyx."

Avalan looked down at him, his throat dry. "I don't know how."

"Destroy his stone—" Bassalt began.

A terrible silence fell over the feasting ground. The fires burned lower, clearing the view over the chasm. Avalan's heart pounded against his chest as he watched Dizredek and Vildrith walk among the crowd. A vision of hatred, Avalan's half-brother was wearing a tunic that fell like an empty sack over his haggard body. He raised a skeletal hand. And then a woman's scream tore the air.

Avalan hurled the axe aside. *"Mother!"*

At once Bassalt staggered to his knees. Vines coiled around the chief's body, flinging him to the other side, where he disappeared among bodies, smoke, and fear. Heart in his mouth, Avalan raced to the edge of the chasm, ready to leap over the dark abyss. Sigil grabbed at his breeches, toppling him to the ground. She growled. Paced the edge.

Too far! Avalan realized. *It is too far … I cannot reach …* "VILDRITH!" he roared over the chasm. His mouth filled with bile.

A figure leaped from the other side. The voluminous presence of Bassalt. In his arms, he cradled Farmera. Avalan thrust out his hand to him, but it was too late. Down into the abyss the chief fell, taking with him Avalan's mother.

"NO!"

A mighty shake drowned out Avalan's cry as the earth trembled.

The chasm closed over his mother and the chief, swallowing both.

CHAPTER SIXTY-EIGHT

A WAIL of anger drowned out Avalan's cries. Across from him, Vildrith had fallen to his knees. His spindly fingers dug into the earth with malice, searching for what had been denied to him. "No! No! NO!"

Dizredek fell beside him at once. "We *must* go!"

A cloud of dust rose. It encircled his half-brother's body. Vildrith merely raised his arm, but Dizredek fell aside as if pushed by a great power.

"You promised me!" Vildrith roared. "You promised me revenge! I am not leaving without her ..." But then his words faded. He raised his face to Avalan. The Onyx in his eyes boiled like black blood. "After all these years ..." He rose, the dark mist a veil of swirling sand around him. "I *will* get what I want!"

Avalan had no time to think before the cloud of mist whipped him. Sand invaded his mouth, stung his eyes, pierced his skin. He felt his body rise before it was slammed into the ground with a force that took his breath away. Avalan rolled, leaped to his feet, flailed his arms about, and yet the cloud still whipped him, blinding, stinging, searing him. A heavy boulder crushed him to the ground, and he felt Sigil's fur on his face, heard her terrible growl as she fought to protect him.

A fiery ball attacked the dust, scattering embers. Avalan rolled to the side, rubbed his eyes. Tears rolled down, and he glimpsed a man holding fire, facing Vildrith.

Volkan!

The old chief stood, another fiery ball at the ready. With a cry, he unleashed it against the Onyx.

"No!" Dizredek roared, conjuring a wall of golden flakes. When Volkan's fire met it, it exploded into a thousand pieces. Dizredek threw his arms into the air, a fervent chanting on his lips. As they fell, the flakes twirled, fused, created the shape of a woman with wavy hair. A song filled the air, a soft woman's voice that made Volkan halt, rooted in place.

Who is she? Avalan thought.

A sharp pain burst in his arm as Vildrith dug his teeth into his flesh, sucking at Avalan's wound. Disgusted, Avalan grabbed the Onyx's tangled hair and tore him away. *He's drinking my blood like Ethelnar!* A wave of dizziness threatened to overtake him, but a rush of power flowed through his body, clearing his senses. *Noev's stone. The blessing.*

"Vildrith!" Dizredek yelled over the sadness of the song. "Remember the bond!"

The Onyx wiped his mouth, smiled a crimson smile of crooked teeth. "How, Diz? How did he escape a cave that held me prisoner for *twenty years*?"

The sorcerer clenched his teeth, the effort of keeping the woman's form together clearly draining his power. "It matters not. We must leave."

Vildrith howled. "Is he stronger than me?"

"He holds no magic! He's nobody!"

Beside him, Avalan felt Sigil tense, ready for a charge. He grabbed at her fur. "No. Down, girl. Down!"

Vildrith crawled closer. "Twenty years, Diz. And he gets out in a day. And you expect me not to kill him?"

"The bond—" Dizredek gritted his teeth.

With a terrible growl, Sigil attacked Vildrith. Avalan grabbed for her, but she slid under his grasp. The tiger tore at his half-brother's chest, sharp claws claiming his life.

The bond! Avalan's mind screamed at him. Without thinking, he charged, toppled Sigil to the ground.

Beside him, Vildrith cackled. Sigil had torn his tunic open. Claw marks scored his skin. The bulge of his vile heart throbbed. Vildrith raised his arms into the air, summoning his dark aura. "Stones take the bond!" He staggered to his feet, spun around and around, forcing a dark veil of mist to encircle him and Avalan.

He's trapping me. Avalan shoved Sigil out just before the dark dust touched the ground. At once the woman's lament ended. Screams rose behind the veil. Still on the ground, Avalan watched fiery golden balls blasting the wall, none of them piercing it.

"Ignore them!" Vildrith yelled. "Just look at me, brother. How did you escape? HOW?"

Lusha's voice broke through the veil, wildly calling Avalan's name. He rose slowly, hands stretched out. "You are insane. The cave took your mind."

"And what of *your* mind, brother? Look at you! Body broken, bruised … arm torn to the bone … and yet you are not howling. Why aren't you crying, brother? How is it you stand before me?"

Avalan jerked his head forward, hoping his hair would hide Noev's Moonstone.

Vildrith cackled, flicked his wrist in a summoning gesture.

A searing pain on the side of his skull told Avalan Vildrith had ripped Noev's earring from him. It shone meekly between them before the earring fell, disappearing into the sand. And with it went Avalan's strength. Pain from a hundred wounds jolted him to his knees. Tears welled in his eyes. Blood throbbed at his temples. He retched. *I am dying …*

Avalan! The voice echoed through his mind. He collapsed.

Through tears, Avalan watched Vildrith loom above him, a silhouette of hatred. He tried to crawl, but pain seared through his body. His vision clouded. *If he leaves Levorotha, he might not make it.* Noev's voice pounded his ears. He gritted his teeth and held Vildrith's scornful gaze.

"Just tell me, brother, and I'll spare you. How did you escape the cave?"

Avalan gasped for breath. "The symbols …"

"Cursed things! Tell me!"

A fiery explosion shook the surrounding wall of dust. Avalan watched hopefully as a small crack formed, only to be restored in an instant as Vildrith spun. *More time … Volkan just needs more time to enter.*

Avalan showed Vildrith his palms. "These …" He felt Vildrith's claws as he grabbed his hands. His beak of a nose touched his skin, sweaty and bony. *I can feel my hands …*

Vildrith crushed Avalan's palm between his skeletal fingers. "You mock me, brother? There's nothing here! Nothing!" He stood, fighting to maintain his hold on the swirling dust wall.

Sigil's growl resounded in Avalan's ears as he glimpsed the clear skin of his palms. The Bloodstone's markings had vanished. His bronze skin had returned, if a bit scored from the fight. *How?* The mere thought gave him a fresh bout of nausea.

The Onyx turned, threw his arms into the air. Invisible strings heaved Avalan's body off the ground. The mere act of standing drained more blood from his body, dipping his mind into a dangerous darkness.

Avalan!

Vildrith's power held him now. A hand slapped his cheek. He threw his eyes open.

"TELL ME! How did you know which symbols to touch? HOW—DID—YOU—KNOW?"

"The Bloodstone …"

"Liar!"

"It showed me …" His pain grew.

Avalan!

"You're lying to me. All of you are. Diz said you possess no magic. But you do, don't you, brother? How is it you escaped the cave and reached Hydrus before me? What are you not telling me?"

Bloodstone, help me …

Against the invisible strings, Avalan writhed. His shoulder ached now with a sickening burning sensation. He leaned his head against Dhylinea's maze. *If only I could escape into it …* One look from Ethelnar's Black Opal stones had been enough to hurl Avalan into the labyrinth. He had been afraid then. Not anymore. The stones knew better. The stones could give pain, but they could also give life.

Avalan!

"The Bloodstone," Avalan whispered. "It guides me …"

A blinding explosion made Vildrith spin. With a swift gesture, he repaired what was broken, letting out a terrible howl of exhaustion.

He's tiring … I need … more time … "Dizredek promised me … the Heart …"

Vildrith staggered. "Hearts … stones … blood … all lies, brother. Tell me the truth now."

Fresh pain tore through him as Vildrith grabbed his wounded arm and drank. The Onyx threw his head back, cackled. "You look pitiful. Like our father just before I *killed* him."

Avalan looked at him. His heart was empty. His mind numb. "Our father …"

"I tore his Bloodstone from him and crushed it before I threw him back to his despairing past. He begged me. He begged for his life. Will you beg, brother? For your life? For *our* life?" Vildrith clenched his fists. "Dizredek says I shouldn't kill you. But I *really* want to. I want to watch you die like our father. Scream. Writhe." He pinched Avalan's skin. "If you won't give me the truth, give me your Bloodstone. I shall not leave here empty-handed. The Onyx must have it all. I must have your heart. Show me your power, brother. Give it to me!"

Avalan flinched. "I have no … stone."

"Lies! Where is it? Where do you keep it?" His hands rushed down Avalan's body, searching, ripping, demanding … "Where?" Finding nothing, Vildrith released Avalan.

He met the ground with a sickening thump. The relief from the invisible shackles was brief; the pain returned with increased ferocity.

"Where?" Vildrith thundered. "Show me. You say the Bloodstone helped you escape the cave. Where is it? Give me your *stone*!"

Keep him talking … until we both die.

"My mind. It comes … there."

"More lies!" Vildrith yelled. "A stone can't be summoned. You really are as ignorant as Diz says. Give it to me. Give me your stone. Take it out!"

Avalan watched Vildrith bang his chest—the strange bulge that jutted beneath his taut skin. *Could it … be?* In Raekandar, Avalan had seen stones adorn swords, rings, bracelets, circlets … but Vildrith fought him bare-handed, his ripped tunic the only thing on his haggard body. *Where is his Onyx stone?* Avalan had seen his brother naked in that wretched cave. *There is no other place left,* his mind told him. *That strange mass in Vildrith's chest …*

"Your stone …" Avalan managed, "inside you?"

"You scorn me?" Vildrith's face twisted in a grotesque grimace. "I am of the mighty Onyx! You thought less of me? You thought we'd keep our stones as jewels?"

It is true, then. That bulge is Vildrith's stone. Twenty years in the cave had been enough to famish him, stretch his skin over his bones. Avalan brought a hand to his naked chest. *Has my stone been living inside me all this time?*

Vildrith's eyes shone. Avalan realized, too late, he shouldn't have done that.

"Diz, Diz," the Onyx said, shaking his head. "You lied to me. My bloody brother has his stone in him. I'll take it out! The stone of our father!"

It cannot be … Avalan knew there was nothing in him. Only flesh and broken bones. *Then … how?*

Before he could think, Vildrith was on him, his fingers slashing his chest, digging as he had dug to reach Farmera and Bassalt.

The end had come, Avalan knew. *Mother. The tribe will be safe now. My death means this monster's death.* Avalan would gladly die if it meant he would kill the last Onyx.

The wall around them crackled with pressure. Avalan turned to see Sigil charge at the dust again and again. Her fur was scorched. *I will miss you, girl.* He closed his eyes.

"THE BOND!" Dizredek's desperate pleas kept coming from beyond, yet Vildrith ignored them. Deeper and deeper he dug, his nails tearing Avalan's skin.

AVALAN! The voice crackled in his mind.

I care no more … he told it.

"Dizredek!" Vildrith yelled, his voice full of fury and impatience. "Curse you for forging that bond! I want to *kill* him. You hear me? How do I sever it? Answer me! WHERE—IS—HIS—STONE?"

The bond, the voice begged. Avalan felt himself drifting into a soothing place, away from all the pain. *If I die, it won't hurt anymore. If I die … the Onyx dies …*

AVALAN!

He opened his eyes. *The bond.*

Vildrith had said stones couldn't be summoned, but if the bond still held between them, perhaps Avalan could summon … *Shadow,* he thought with all his might, a desperate calling. A fiery ball blasted the wall. Something stirred beside him. Avalan twisted his neck. A dark silhouette on the ground, the second shadow pointed at a small mound of sand.

Avalan summoned all the power he had left and dipped his fingers into the sand, searching … As his brother tore at his chest, Avalan's fingers closed around a small bead. *The earring. Noev's Moonstone.* He fumbled, found the sharp end of the hook. He gritted his teeth as he jabbed it into his thumb.

Like a soothing song from his mother's lips, it eased Avalan's pain. His broken body ached less and less. His mind grew stronger. His heart beat with hope afresh. *I need to take his Onyx.*

As if he'd sensed a shift in the balance, Vildrith ceased his digging.

Avalan twined arms and legs around his brother's body, twisted, reversing their positions. Now on top, Avalan grabbed at Vildrith's wrist. Under his grip, it felt bony, unnatural … Avalan cringed. *Mere bones. Bones that haven't seen the light of day for so long. Bones that should be brittle.* Avalan snapped Vildrith's wrist with a sickening crack. Vildrith howled, and Avalan went for the other.

Crack.

His half-brother writhed on the ground, his hands bent at an unnatural angle, dangling from broken bones, held together only by sinew and skin.

Avalan went for Vildrith's chest, trying to get to the stone. Now that his brother had fallen, the attacks from outside came with greater urgency. A glint of light reflected over the darkness of Vildrith's eyes. Filled with hatred and pain they were, yet it seemed they lacked the power to capture Avalan's mind like the Black Opal.

The stone in Vildrith's chest writhed with its master. Avalan pressed harder. With Noev's stone piercing his thumb, pure power surged through him.

Yet all he could do was scratch and score the papery skin. If he was to rip it open, he needed a weapon. Avalan craved his goat dagger. He looked around him like a wild animal, struggling to keep his brother pinned to the ground.

Sand, blood, death …

"Get off … me!" Vildrith struggled, caught between fighting Avalan and keeping the wall raised.

Avalan needed something sharp. *The earring.* He stared at the small bead. His blood was now caked on its surface, taking away its luster. *If I remove it, the pain will return … I might not make it …*

His fingers closed around it, pulled. Pain surged through him, and he bent forth, thrust the hook into Vildrith's chest. It met with the hard surface of the stone.

Vildrith howled like a wounded animal.

Pulling his hand across the skin, Avalan sliced it open. Beneath rivulets of blood, a dark stone the size of a goat's hoof pulsated with fury. Avalan hesitated. *What will happen if I touch the Onyx?*

Take it! his mind screamed at him.

Bhoran had touched the Onyx of the dagger, Avalan remembered. His hand hovered over the stone. *But Bhoran is …*

"No!" Avalan roared. He curled his fingers around the stone and ripped it out of Vildrith's chest.

Vildrith screamed. The surrounding wall collapsed. The mist curled around its master, swirling in endless confusion.

Drenched in blood, the Onyx stone pulsated in Avalan's hand. A beating heart. Through blinding pain, Bassalt's face came to his mind. Bassalt had crushed Eras's stone on this ground between his fingers as if it had been nothing. *Destroy his stone,* Bassalt had warned him as the Onyx had approached the village. Avalan pressed, yet he was weak. *Destroy his stone!*

You will die with him, the voice inside his mind warned.

Beneath him, Vildrith cried. Avalan searched the chest wound for Noev's stone. It wasn't there.

I freed him, Avalan thought, despairing. *I freed the Onyx. I must destroy it.*

You must not die, the voice returned.

I brought him here.

Vildrith's power waned, his writhing easing.

I brought him to our village. I failed them all …

The stones aren't evil. Crystal's voice echoed in his mind, saddened. *You must trust your heart. Ronan told me he wished you could see that.*

Ethelnar's face swam before Avalan's eyes. His first true kill. Bile burned his mouth. *This isn't who I am. I wanted freedom. Not death.* Avalan eased the pressure on the Onyx, let it fall to the sand.

As soon as it touched the ground, the stone flew. Avalan turned to watch the Onyx land in Dizredek's palm. The sorcerer cupped it, a helpless starling in his grasp. The flecks of gold within Dizredek's eyes danced with fury, and gratitude.

Avalan staggered to his feet. Now that no Moonstone blessed his body, his wounds had returned to haunt him. This time he would not make it, he knew. He fell to his knees. Then to the ground. His cheek touched the sand.

A whip of air flew over him. Feet shuffled. The night thickened. The soil of his village burned. His mother … Sigil's tongue against his cheek. His goat dagger. The smirk of Bhoran. Crystal's look of horror. Lusha's healed face …

And then darkness. Silence. He felt and was no more.

Until …

A pain in his ear. The return of power. The Moonstone's blessing flowing through him like liquid love. Lusha. She stood over him now, tear-stricken. Avalan brought a finger to the side of his face. Noev's earring. "Lusha … my mother …" The power of the Moonstone surging through him, Avalan managed to sit on his heels.

Vildrith and Dizredek were gone. The fires burned low, their dim light casting eerie shadows upon the faces of the dead and the living.

Volkan was fast upon them. He knelt. His fire was out. "Stay down. You've lost too much blood. Your mother's safe."

"How …?" Avalan coughed. "How do you know? The ground … swallowed them both."

Volkan frowned. "I'm no stranger to Bassalt's magic. He's taken her somewhere safe. Perhaps an underground cave where his magic is the strongest."

"What if they find her?" Avalan still remembered how Dizredek had lured him into a cave he hadn't known existed.

"They won't. If only you had seen the look on the Nuummite's face. Together we attacked the wall relentlessly. I was trying to save you, but that man's eyes were wild with grief."

Lusha squeezed his arm. "He kept yelling he couldn't lose Vildrith again. He didn't care about revenge. All he wanted was to take this Vildrith out. And Avalan ... he was the one who bade Noev's Moonstone rise from the sand when the dark wall collapsed. He gave it to me, asked me to pierce my ear with it to better aid your healing. Then he cradled Vildrith and left."

Avalan glimpsed Lusha's lobe. Torn it was, and caked with dried blood. Her eyes were filled with worry. One glance at his body was enough to show him why. Having the Moonstone's blessing made him feel stronger on the inside, but his body ... his wounds were a terrible sight to behold, skin torn, bruised, grazed.

A shadow crossed Volkan's face. "Can you rise now?"

He could, Avalan knew. Around them, the feasting ground had been razed. Of the tables, green grass, skin drums, and cooking fires now remained nothing but a pile of ash, scorched wood, and embers. "Where is Sigil?"

Lusha frowned. "When you fell, she scurried off ..."

"Where to?"

"We were trying to save you," Lusha said, ashamed. The scar on her face had returned. "I didn't see ..."

If Sigil was wounded, she would seek a tree in which to lick her wounds and rest. Avalan would search through the blackwood forest later, but now ... "My mother. I need to know she's alive."

Timidly Theran approached them. His robe was torn, its cowl singed. "My chief," he said, bowing deeply before Volkan. Then his voice broke, and he sobbed, ashamed to raise his face. "We didn't know ... Bassalt ... Silver ... they told us you had perished in the great fire of Krokador ..."

Volkan cupped Theran's shoulders, stood him up straight.

The manservant wiped his eyes on the back of his sleeve. Then he threw his head back and yelled for all to hear him. "The stones greet Avalan of the Bloodstone for protecting our village from the Onyx. The stones bless the rightful chief of Hydrus, Volkan of the Fire Agate, for returning to his tribe. The stones bow to Lusha of the Moonstone, the bringer of healing."

Silent surprise gave its place to cheering as the crowd let out cries of joy.

"Theran," Volkan said over the voices. "You must know where Bassalt has taken Farmera."

Theran nodded. "I shall take you there now, my chief."

CHAPTER SIXTY-NINE

THROUGH THE NORTHERN GATE, Theran walked at the front of the procession, cradling a tallow candle.

Avalan, Lusha, and Volkan followed, no words exchanged between them. With every couple of steps, Avalan swallowed, trying to fight the despair that climbed to his throat and stole his breath. Until he'd seen his mother, he knew his heart wouldn't unclench.

Lusha's skin no longer glowed in the night, the moon reduced in power now. She held her head low. *She's thinking of Bhoran.* Avalan reached out a hand to touch her shoulder.

Theran halted. Long ivy tendrils enshrouded a cavern's entrance. Theran pushed them aside and led them through the gaping maw, whispering, "The guarding spell is broken."

Avalan pushed past the servant and rushed into the cave. Before, the darkness would have stopped him, but Avalan had survived the mountain's depths and the murk of the Cave of Rath.

A faint blue light shone from the depths of the cave. Avalan splashed through shallow ponds and trickling rivulets. Once he reached the main chamber, he found his mother lying beside the cavern's wall, Stonemaster Delion at her head and Sigil curled against her legs. Farmera wasn't moving, but Avalan knew deep in his heart she still lived. The others caught up quickly behind him. Lusha let out a faint sob when she saw Farmera.

Delion ceased his chanting and motioned them closer. Eyes sunk in deep hollows, the stonemaster looked worn, wasted. A deep sadness lingered in his eyes, the veil in them more obscure than Avalan had ever seen it.

"How is she?" Avalan whispered.

The stonemaster sighed. "She will recover."

Avalan was relieved to see his tiger. By Farmera's feet, Sigil now lay, her striped eyes closed, as though she slept, only Avalan had watched her sleep many times before, and this time it felt different. "Sigil—"

"Do not disturb her," the master instructed. "The bond between them is sturdy but delicate, like a spider's silky thread."

"What are you doing to her?"

Volkan pressed a warm hand to Avalan's shoulder. "The master is performing a rare spiritual healing. Sigil's soul is one with Farmera's now, soothing it back into life. Stones willing, your mother will safely return to us."

Tears of relief welled in Avalan's eyes.

"Bassalt brought her here?" Volkan asked.

Delion nodded. "Among the great evils that burden Bassalt's heart, his love for Farmera is a blessing granted by the stones."

Avalan flinched at the master's words. *How can the master speak of love in the face of Bassalt's cruelty? He killed Ronan. He killed him just for the stones,* he wanted to yell, but he had to suppress his anger in favor of his mother.

"I know what you're thinking, Avalan," the stonemaster said. "Bassalt is who he is, but you owe him your mother's life. Never forget that."

Volkan cleared his throat. "Where is he?"

"Somewhere far away, I reckon," the master said. "Is your return here a matter of permanence?"

When Volkan nodded, the stonemaster smiled. "Thank the stones and the spirit of Hydrus. You know what you must do."

In answer, Volkan brought a hand to his chest.

"And now, I shall have words with our warrior," Delion said.

Lusha held Avalan's arm, seeming unwilling to let him go.

Timidly Theran stepped forth. "Lusha, your father still lies in danger. Perhaps a visit from you would lift his spirit and urge it to return faster."

Lusha's face hardened, but she stood.

"I will come find you," Avalan promised her. When they all went, he sat next to Delion.

"I see the marks on your hands are gone," the master observed.

Avalan looked at the clear skin of his palms. "When the Bloodstone marked me at the Eagle's Eye, I thought it an act of hatred, disapproval ... I see now the stone knew I'd need its aid. How?"

The stonemaster smiled feebly. "The stones' workings are unfathomable."

Avalan peered into Delion's eyes, trying to dispel the fog that hid the truth from him. "When I was in the Cave of Rath, I heard your voice in my head."

"That was your stone. I was merely a vessel." The master drew closer, his body bearing the excitement of a child ready to be told a tale. "Pray, now tell me all."

Avalan's mind traveled back to the Eagle's Eye when he'd desperately sought help to free Bhoran. "You knew. You sent me to look for Sigil with words about a father seeking his children. Her trail led me to Dizredek. Much as I tried to resist his offer, your voice boomed in my ears. Asked me not to deny that which I fear more than three times." Avalan's chest tightened. "You sent me to him. You made me hunt after the shadow. You *knew* what Dizredek wanted. You knew where the shadow would lead me. You know what I have done ..."

The master steepled his fingers before his long nose. "You released the Onyx. It was about time."

Caught between anger and despair, Avalan tried to restrain his voice from rising. "Why did you make me do this?"

"Son, you must understand. All stones are needed."

Avalan watched Farmera's chest rise and fall in peaceful sleep. "She almost died because of me. Vildrith longed for revenge. I led him to her, to our tribe. How can I live with that?"

"It isn't uncommon for an Onyx to misplace their pain. But you stopped your brother from taking your mother's life, and from harming your people. You trusted the power of the stones and let them guide you, despite all odds. And in so doing, you brought back to us the rightful chief. You freed Hydrus."

"I could have ended it all." Avalan's voice broke. He'd held the Onyx in his hands, yet he had faltered. "Is he … is Vildrith truly my brother?"

"Being related to the Onyx does not make you evil."

How could my father do that? How could he lie with an Onyx? "All these stories, then, about the war … are they not true?"

"They are and they aren't." The stonemaster waved white-fleshed palms. "You can't assign one face to the balance. It needs all of them. Or else it suffers."

Avalan couldn't grasp the meaning of the master's words. The balance … the birthstones. Thinking about the Onyx froze his core.

"Don't let your thoughts darken. You've seen firsthand what fear of the dark stone can do to a person."

Bhoran. Avalan's heart clenched. He wondered where his friend was. *With Ethelnar dead, does Bhoran linger in Raekandar, waiting for Lusha?* His friend had been an outcast for so long; he surely knew how to survive. Despite that, Avalan resolved that once his mother was well, he would find him.

"You mustn't search for him," the master said, as if he'd read his mind.

Avalan looked at him, confused. "I cannot leave Bhoran behind."

"You shall let him fulfill his purpose instead of letting him live in your shadow."

"Bhoran never lived in my shadow. He is my *true* brother."

"He will know his own true family," the master said. "His journey has only just begun."

"You know where he is?"

"No." The master sounded earnest. "But the stones do, and I have learned to trust them, blindly. As should you."

Avalan could see the truth in those words. Great good had come when he had put his trust in his stone: the etchings it had made on his body, its voice in his head, guiding him. The Bloodstone had freed him from a desolate cave that had held his brother a prisoner for all

Avalan's life. "How did Vildrith survive there without food and water?"

The veil in the master's eyes thickened. "The Onyx possesses great power. One that surpasses the physical needs of the body. And your brother had his stone within him. The greatest blessing one can achieve."

Avalan touched his empty chest.

"You are far more than empty," the master told him. "I see the glint of the Moonstone in your ear."

Avalan fiddled with the sharp hook. Noev's Moonstone had saved his life. "It healed me. The cave beat me, tore me, sliced me open … It was in Levorotha that a man"—*how was it that Volkan explained it?* —"blessed me with his Moonstone. It gave me the strength I needed to return to Hydrus. But it isn't mine. I must return it, and its power."

The stonemaster looked at Sigil. "You became one with your tiger."

The words startled Avalan. It had only been for a mere moment, but he *had* become one with Sigil, he knew. He had been able to see through her, taste his blood in her mouth … "How do you know?"

"She told me. Elated she was when Bassalt and I summoned her here to save your mother's life. Before she surrendered to the spell, she said she wasn't afraid to die, because for once she had become you."

Avalan's throat tightened. "How did this happen? Can the Bloodstone also claim animal souls?"

"No. I'm afraid that's an attribute solely of the Tiger's Eye. My stone."

So behind this cloudy veil lies a striped stone. Like Sigil's eyes, Avalan thought. "Then how?"

The master smiled, as if there was something more—a secret knowledge he wasn't sharing. "I see you carry etchings of another stone on your shoulder."

Dhylinea's maze. Avalan looked down at the swirling lines. "I was unconscious. Didn't see what stone etched this onto me."

"The Onyx, most like. If I had my doubts, your taking over of Sigil confirmed my suspicions."

I am marked by an Onyx … Avalan didn't know how to feel.

"In moments of great desperation, the Onyx can draw on the

powers of another stone. It was Bassalt's Tiger's Eye you drew from to gain control of Sigil. Bassalt told me how he felt the pull himself."

Confused, Avalan looked at Sigil. He would gladly give his soul just to be one with her again. Or perhaps stay one with her forever, so no one else could harm her.

"The Bloodstone spoke to you, marked you ... the Moonstone healed you ... the Onyx granted you power beyond your means ... and you could wield the Tiger's Eye ... Do you see now how you're not empty?"

Despite the stonemaster's words, Avalan felt hollow and broken. "I have lost so much. The man I called my father, the woman I loved ... all because I wanted to free Hydrus."

"And yet through pain blossoms great power."

"I have no power."

"You wielded the powers of *four* birthstones."

Avalan halted. The way the stonemaster had said it, it sounded as if a thing like this shouldn't have happened. He frowned. "If I am of the Bloodstone, how did I wield all these stones?"

Delion smiled, placed a feeble hand over Avalan's. "I came to Hydrus to find you. Ronan warned me you were a tough nut to crack, but he and Dizredek saw the truth in you. You would do anything for those you love. If you trust me—"

"How can I trust a word you say when you brought Dizredek here? And now you're telling me Ronan knew?"

"We do not always choose our allies."

"Dizredek is a liar. Tricked me over a snake ring he stole for himself. I saw him wearing it at the cave."

"How can one steal something that was already stolen?" Stonemaster Delion answered. "The ring belongs to the Onyx. Bassalt should never have taken it. Now it has returned to where it belongs."

The air inside the grotto suddenly felt heavy. Avalan fought back confusion and anger. *How much do I not know?* Every thought he'd had, every decision, every word, had been planted in his mind against his will, without his knowing.

"Why me?"

"Because the last time someone could wield more than one stone was thousands of years ago. And now the calling echoes heavily over the Stone Lands. And because Hydrus the waterdragon spoke to me about a boy who swims his sea and walks his sand with a clear heart. The Heart of the Bloodstone. Let me guide you so that you keep your feet on the path of light. Let me show you how to become a stonemaster of all stones."

"Did Hydrus also tell you how I sold my blood for a shadow? How I murdered a man? How I unleashed the evil? I had the Onyx in my hands ..." Avalan said, despairing.

"Tell me, how did you feel when you took the stone?"

A coldness trickled down Avalan's nape. "Elated with power, despairing with hatred, jealousy, fear. And ..." He hesitated, Dizredek's gaze returning to his mind's eye. *Were these other feelings mine or his? That painful warmth in the chest, that cutting longing, that thirst for reuniting ... did I truly feel them, or did I just read them in his eyes?*

"There are more faces of evil than we can see. Some of these remain unknown even to me. But my old bones can feel the tremors of the earth when the balance is changing. And I shall need the best of warriors on my side."

Warrior ... That was what Avalan had always thought of himself as, only he now knew that fighting didn't always end well. Sometimes it was best to just let go ... "Not everybody needs saving," he said, using the words of Bhoran.

"And what of those who do? Will you fight for them?" Stonemaster Delion reached into his robes, pulled out a small stone, shaped like a teardrop, and the dirk Ronan had gifted Avalan when last he'd seen him. He passed them both to Avalan now.

As soon as Avalan touched the stone, the voice boomed in his mind.

Avalan.

He turned the Bloodstone for some moments in his hands. Then he slid it into the stone hollow he had so much despised when Ronan had given him the blade. The stone slipped inside, a perfect match. The Heart of the Bloodstone. Ronan's gift for his twentieth birthnight.

Avalan raised his face to the stonemaster. "I will fight."

CHAPTER SEVENTY

SILVER'S FACE looked so peaceful. The lines that were always etched into his face had smoothed, the frown of disapproval gone.

Lusha sat next to him, gazing at the Heliodor that shone on her father's lap. Lavender and fennel filled the air in Farmera's house, bringing back painful memories. The last time Lusha had been here, she had spoken to Farmera about how much she longed to find her aunt ... to find the motherly love she'd never had. But now Lusha knew it had been wishful thinking. Shelanna wanted nothing to do with her.

It is just as well. She couldn't live alongside someone who hated her mother so. And yet she also couldn't live alongside Silver, though he had adored Amara.

Lusha turned to Volkan, who sat behind her. Theran had excused himself to tend to the needs of the shaken tribesfolk of Hydrus. He had to lay the ground for them to accept Volkan as their new leader, although Lusha suspected that would come naturally to them. Bassalt hadn't exactly been a loving chief to any of them. Powerful, yes, but never endearing.

Volkan had promised to stay by her side, for however long she needed. Lusha had seen the fervor with which he'd fought. His entire body had turned into a blazing fire. His magic had attacked Vildrith's wall relentlessly, even when his face had strained with pain and sweat. Lusha wished she could be more like him. Burn everything that hurt her to the ground. His face was calmer now. His tunic had turned to ashes, leaving his chest bare. A wound coiled around his neck, where the heat had caused his metal necklace to mark his skin.

"Why does Calla hate me so?" she asked him. "Why did she say you'd always love me? I've never laid eyes on you before."

The fire in Volkan's eyes dimmed as if with shame. "She didn't mean you." His sadness echoed in the silent room. "She meant Amara, your mother, and my only true love."

Lusha felt her scar tingling with shame. *But of course …*

"I'm sorry if my bearing caused you pain. When I saw you, I lost my mind. You are the spitting image of your mother. Deep wounds woke in my heart."

She stole a quick glance at her father. He didn't stir. "Did my mother love you back?"

"With all her heart."

That didn't surprise Lusha. She finally understood why her father had always blamed her. Even the reason her aunt had insulted her deceased mother for being of loose morals. Silver had lived all this time knowing the woman he'd married had loved another. Then a thought crept upon her. "Am I your daughter?"

"No." Volkan rose, towering over her. "But I will always see you as one. If you wish."

Lusha untied the chain of her mother's pendant. "This was my mother's." The shine in his eyes told her he already knew. "I hoped I could get it to open. Do you perhaps know how?"

Volkan reached for his necklace. The silver chain held a small pin that looked like a tiny key. He eased it through the hole at the bottom of her pendant. A faint click resounded, and Volkan returned it to her.

Her fingers trembled as Lusha pried it open. There she was—her mother. The smiling face of Amara. It was a simple drawing, made with the sure strokes of a thin instrument. Whoever had drawn Amara had done so with love and adoration. That much Lusha could see.

"Her face … She was the one Dizredek summoned to stop you,"

Lusha said, remembering the shape of the woman the sorcerer had conjured. She let the chief take the pendant.

Tears streamed down Volkan's face.

"Tell me about her," Lusha said.

"She was a kind, brave soul. A star in my dark sky. A true fighter."

"Shelanna said she chased after the Red Weal."

Volkan's expression hardened. "She sacrificed herself to help the wounded. We lost her to the curse of the Onyx. After that, they summoned us to fight the war as it approached the south. I never returned to Hydrus. There was nothing left for me here. All thought me dead, and I was."

"Even after you heard how cruel Bassalt was?"

"I heard he had declared himself a chief and banished the stone-masters, but nothing more. Ronan was the only one who scaled the Craggy Mountains, and he never came to Levorotha, except that one time ..."

Lusha raised curious eyes to him.

"He came to ask Shelanna for a Moonstone. Your true Moonstone."

Deep sadness rose in Lusha's chest. "Bhoran gave it to me, only ... I let it go."

Before Volkan could answer, rain pelted the roof. They both turned their faces upward.

"*Lusha.*" A hearty voice echoed around the hut.

"It's Hydrus," Volkan told her, returning the pendant. "Best you go find him."

Lusha made to replace her mother's necklace around her neck but halted. Her gaze traveled to her father, Heliodor on his lap, death on his lips. Gently she let the pendant fall between Silver's fingers.

You need her more than I do, Father.

As she crossed the village, Lusha was grateful for the darkness. Through the veil of the night, she couldn't see the destruction the fight had left behind, nor the thick-smelling blood that smeared the ground.

With Bassalt no longer here, she passed through the seaward gate with a free heart. Under the waning moonlight, the waterdragon glistened as he floated over the sea. Lusha walked until the shallow waters licked her toes, then sat on the wet sand.

"Child of the Moonstone," the beast began, *"why do you refuse your stone?"*

The words were a knife in her heart. She didn't want to be rid of it, not really. But it was the thing her Moonstone signified that had forced her—the love she shared with Bhoran. It was their secret, their bonding, and their curse. By leaving it behind, she had wanted to hurt him. As much as he had hurt her.

Something rough nudged her toes. Beneath the light reflected by the dragon, Lusha glimpsed a hard shell. Carried by the persistent waves, it nudged her feet over and over until she reached to pick it up. She cupped its slimy surface. An unexplained urge to open it filled her.

The mollusk surrendered with ease to her prying. Where its flesh should have been lay a small bead, gleaming with faint light. She claimed the stone, its surface familiar under her touch, its light shining brighter. Hope filled her. "My true Moonstone."

Hydrus snorted, red steam spouting through his nostrils. *"To receive one's stone is a great honor. To refuse it, a curse."*

"Never again," she promised. "But ... how did my stone end up in the mouth of a mollusk?"

"The stones always find a way."

Lusha gazed at her birthstone with great sorrow. *Did Bhoran throw my Moonstone away in a rage for my leaving him behind without a word?* The thought of him tightened her chest. There were so many things she regretted. "Where is Bhoran?"

"Gone. You must forget him."

"I can't—"

"He loves you no more." The dragon's fangs glistened in the azure light of the sea. *"He spoke his farewells before he let the stone fall into the sea."*

The water cooled her toes. She groped for words that never came. Hydrus snorted one last time before he flew away and plunged into the sea.

Silence lingered for a while. Then Lusha kissed the Moonstone. *Twice you gave it to me, my love, and twice I returned it,* she thought with sadness. And now, though Bhoran had given it as a farewell, Lusha would keep it. He hadn't slept with the girl whose dress she'd found, she knew. Avalan would never lie to her on such a matter. And yet he had given up on the stone.

Perchance it was for the better for them to be apart, she tried to tell herself. They had caused each other so much pain. But in her heart, she hoped that when the stones willed it, their paths would cross again.

And then you might forgive me.

CHAPTER SEVENTY-ONE

THE SHIP of Ravenar sliced through the Nameless Sea. Bhoran swayed gently with the vessel. The less he resisted the stirrings, the more agreeable his stomach found the journey.

On the horizon, the sun sank. Bhoran clenched the handrail, narrowing his eyes. It had been three days since they had left the Stone Lands behind them, and for the past two, he had no longer been able to see the land he called his home.

As the sun fell, a friendly wind rose. It filled their sails and hastened their course.

Mheleras whistled. "The wind is rising," he said with a joyous chuckle. "At this rate, we shall glimpse the land sooner than I thought. You really brought me luck, Bhoran of the Obsidian. The stones wish to hasten your arrival."

Bhoran didn't laugh. A great sadness had grown inside him, but there was no turning back now. A breeze caressed his sweaty forehead, and he welcomed it with gratitude. Being under the sun for days was something Bhoran wasn't used to, and his skin had paid the price. The first day, it had resisted the sun's touch. Bhoran had kept his body wet, scooping up seawater in a bucket and drenching himself in it. Yet by the third day, he knew his skin had lost the fight. It had reddened and flaked under the torturous sun.

Mheleras had told him it was a sign—his skin was changing, as was his soul. And in his words, Bhoran had found some truth about himself.

After long hours under the starry night, the wind left them. The ship now swayed over soft waves. Bhoran made for the ship's belly to grab an oar, but Mheleras shook his head. Bhoran was relieved. After three days of continuous rowing, his swollen muscles were throbbing, and his elbows creaked dangerously loud.

"It won't be long now." Mheleras gazed at the horizon.

Bhoran could see only darkness. "How do you know?"

"I smell it. Ah, the sweet aroma of smoked fish drizzled with honey and love. Sweet, crunchy olives, and figs with cheese. Our women are the best cooks."

Bhoran snorted. "Everyone boasts the same about his home." He bade his mind not to indulge in the vision Mheleras was trying to paint. The seaman had brought with them a barrel full of mollusks, and another one filled with ale, yet Bhoran's stomach could no longer stand the sight and taste of their flesh.

"Rest now," Mheleras told Bhoran with a small smile. "If my nose is right, tomorrow morning we shall arrive."

On the cool planks, Bhoran lay on his back, as he always did—a thing he had picked up during his time as an outcast. He had to be on the ready, should someone attack him in his sleep. There were no stars above them that night, for the sky was bright. Bhoran etched the face of Lusha on it, but sleep took him before he could finish drawing the scar that marred her pretty face.

The next thing he knew, Bhoran awoke to a smiling Mheleras, backlit by the morning sun.

"You should see this," Mheleras said.

Bhoran pushed himself up. His face burned. Yet once he followed the direction of Mheleras's pointing arm, his pain vanished, leaving behind a sense of awe. He grabbed Mheleras's shoulder to steady himself. "Your nose was right."

Across the sea, a land, larger than Bhoran had expected, stretched before them. Tall towers nestled among an endless forest, and snowy mountain crags loomed above the city, casting cool shadows.

Elasithor, Bhoran mused. *My tribe's home.*

"To the oars!" Mheleras urged.

Falling into position, they rowed with renewed strength until their oars met the sandy bottom of the sea.

Mheleras hoisted a heavy rope over his shoulder. They leaped off, waded to the shore. The water was warm. Once they had secured the rope around a tree, Mheleras wiped his forehead. "Welcome, Bhoran of the Obsidian, to your lands."

Bhoran smiled despite himself. Yet it was brief. His heart was anxious. *What will my people think once they have seen me? Will they accept me as their own or cast me aside as an outlander?*

Voices of men traveled through the trees. Bhoran tensed, his hand brushing Avalan's goat dagger he concealed in his breeches, but Mheleras pressed a calming palm over his shoulder. "They come to meet us."

A group of men emerged, four in all. Snakeskin belts hugged their slim waists, holding leather and fur skirts around their thighs. Though the color of their hair was all shades of flax, like Bhoran's, their bare chests were tanned. Bhoran stiffened at the sight of the daggers with bare blades in their hands.

"Don't move," Mheleras told him, but to Bhoran, it sounded more a threat than an instruction in the customs of their tribe.

What tribe greets its members cradling weapons? Bhoran thought.

Beside him, Mheleras moved, and Bhoran plunged to the ground. *He tripped me,* Bhoran realized too late.

The men were fast upon him, dagger tips against his neck, ribs, chest. Through eyes dark like his, they studied him as if he were a foreign beast.

One of them, with rings of steel adorning all his fingers, tossed Mheleras a jingling pouch. "You've done well," he said, his voice deep but young. "Aphnata will be pleased."

Mheleras smiled. "I shall stay awhile to regain my strength."

"Rest now," the man agreed. "Until you're summoned." Turning to Bhoran he said, "Rise, but make no move to trick us."

Bhoran gritted his teeth. "Why?" he growled at Mheleras, earning the hilt of a dagger across his nape.

"You don't speak," the man with the rings ordered. "Just follow."

Mheleras gave Bhoran a last look that betrayed no remorse, and sauntered through the forest, pouch in his grip.

Bhoran stood. He could see no other way. He was surrounded, and his body ached from all those days crossing the sea. He felt light-headed and disoriented. The ring man jerked his head, and two of the men tied a blindfold over Bhoran's eyes.

"Just keep moving," the ring man ordered.

Bhoran allowed himself to be led by these strange men he should call his tribe. Soon the light of the sun was shaded; rough stones pinched at the soles of Bhoran's feet. They were descending, but to where, he could not fathom. The men paused, and soon he felt the warmth of fire close to his face. Sharp stones sliced at his feet now, and the surrounding air turned cooler.

"Hold now." The ring man's voice echoed, and Bhoran knew they were in an enclosed space.

The men relaxed their grip. A clinking noise resounded, metal turning against metal, and then a creaking sound. *Is that a door?* As they thrust him forward, Bhoran lost his footing, falling face-first to the ground.

"We bring you company," said the ring man. "I think you'll find one another quite amusing."

Men laughed. The door clanged shut.

At once Bhoran tore the cloth from his head and rushed to the door. "Let me out!" he yelled after them. Torches burned low in sconces; the shadows of the men disappeared around the corner. "Who are you?" Bhoran screamed after them. "Let me out!"

"They won't." A voice came from behind him.

Bhoran spun. The cell was only faintly lit by guttering torches. In the farthermost dark corner, someone stirred.

"Who are you?" Bhoran said. "Who are these men? Why am I here?"

The shadow of a man stood.

"Come into the light," Bhoran said. Somehow the fact he wasn't alone in this cell made him feel better and at the same time ashamed for his cruel demeanor against a man who shared his fate. "I ..." he began, but then his voice trailed off.

For now the man moved into the low light, and Bhoran saw his face. It was the face of a man he'd seen many a time growing up. A face familiar and comforting. A face that he had only seen carved in stone.

The weary face of Olnos.

ACKNOWLEDGMENTS

First and foremost, I'd like to thank the very first person who believed in me: Randy Rufino. Thank you for letting me gush about my project for hours on end and for listening with a kind heart to all my outrageous plots and twists and characters, who you have brought to life with your amazing drawings. I also want to thank my editors, Jonathan Oliver and Leonora Bulbeck, for their excellent work on my book—without you, nothing would have been the same. James T. C. Prince, thank you for beta reading my book. Your insights helped me make this story stronger. Also, great thanks to Felix Ortiz and Shawn T. King for the cover illustration and design. Working with you guys was a pleasure. My dear husband, I thank you as well for always being there for me on my writing journey, even when you almost had a heart attack when I told you I want to be a full-time author.

Last, but not least, thank you, dear reader. I hope you've enjoyed the journey so far and that you look forward to new adventures within books. Remember to always read what makes you happy.

Philinna
10/18/2021

ABOUT THE AUTHOR

Philinna Wood is an epic fantasy author. She loves telling stories about characters who fight for their beliefs, sacrifice themselves for love, and seek the truths that will liberate the world. *The Heart of the Bloodstone* is her debut novel.

CPSIA information can be obtained
at www.ICGtesting.com
Printed in the USA
LVHW010920190122
708751LV00024B/857/J